PENGUIN BOOKS

WEAPONS OF CHOICE

'an excellent page-turner, laced with black humour . . .'
FHM

'An airport blockbuster and sci-fi war thriller that is definitely one for the boys' *Sunday Mail*

'. . . plenty of grist and humour . . .' *Sunday Times*

'[A] weapons-grade military techno thriller . . . It's like a Clive Cussler novel fell into a transporter beam with a Stephen Ambrose history, and they came out fused together'
Time

'Birmingham's enthralling battleground mixes provocative historical fiction and socially conscious futurism'
Entertainment Weekly

'. . . a hugely readable adventure story that unleashes forces into a world that have the potential for change beyond anything ever seen' *Sunday Age*

'. . . an enjoyable read that stands out because of its relentless pace . . . It's got breakneck tempo and no end of knowing winks at the state of play in contemporary politics'
Melbourne Weekly

'. . . stellar debut novel . . . Unlike many alternate histories, the novel avoids the wish-fulfilment aspect inherent in the genre. This is the first of what should be a hugely (and deservedly) successful series' *Publishers Weekly* (U.S.)

'Smart munitions meet smart writing in a military-grade action-adventure that's impossible to stop reading!'
Garth Nix, author of *Sabriel* and *Mister Monday*

'The clash of cultures is handled with the same verve as the clash of navies, and Birmingham's characters have life and depth; he appreciates that the past is another country, and they do things differently there. I recommend the book, and I'll be looking for new titles by the author'
S. M. Stirling, author of *Dies the Fire*

'This first novel by [John] Birmingham combines solid alternate military history reminiscent of Harry Turtledove with high-tech intrigue and suspense similar to the works of Tom Clancy' *Library Journal*

'[Birmingham] concisely and vividly lays out the historical parameters of the burgeoning World War, and then just as expertly begins to demolish the givens, as the presence of the future-dwellers starts to unhinge the timeline we know. All this while writing stirring, shocking battle scenes'
scfi.com

'If there was a Booker for explosive alternative history techno-thrillers with guts and brains, it would be a cinch. Bring on volume two' *Sydney Morning Herald*

ABOUT THE AUTHOR

John Birmingham is the author of the cult classic, *He Died with a Felafel in His Hand* and the award-winning history *Leviathan*. Between writing books he contributes to a wide range of newspapers and magazines on topics as diverse as biotechnology and national security. Before becoming a writer he began his working life as research officer with the Defence Department's Office of Special Clearances and Records.

Weapons of Choice

World War 2.1

JOHN BIRMINGHAM

PENGUIN BOOKS

PENGUIN BOOKS

Published by the Penguin Group
Penguin Books Ltd, 80 Strand, London WC2R 0RL, England
Penguin Group (USA) Inc., 375 Hudson Street, New York, New York 10014, USA
Penguin Group (Canada), 90 Eglinton Avenue East, Suite 700, Toronto, Ontario, Canada M4P 2Y3
(a division of Pearson Penguin Canada Inc.)
Penguin Ireland, 25 St Stephen's Green, Dublin 2, Ireland (a division of Penguin Books Ltd)
Penguin Group (Australia), 250 Camberwell Road, Camberwell,
Victoria 3124, Australia (a division of Pearson Australia Group Pty Ltd)
Penguin Books India Pvt Ltd, 11 Community Centre,
Panchsheel Park, New Delhi – 110 017, India
Penguin Group (NZ), cnr Airborne and Rosedale Roads, Albany,
Auckland 1310, New Zealand (a division of Pearson New Zealand Ltd)
Penguin Books (South Africa) (Pty) Ltd, 24 Sturdee Avenue,
Rosebank, Johannesburg 2196, South Africa

Penguin Books Ltd, Registered Offices: 80 Strand, London WC2R 0RL, England

www.penguin.com

First published in Australia by Pan Macmillan Australia Pty Limited 2004
Pan edition published by Pan Macmillan Australia Pty Limited 2005
First published in Great Britain in Penguin Books 2006
1

Set in 11.75/14 pt Monotype Garamond
Typeset by Rowland Phototypesetting Ltd, Bury St Edmunds, Suffolk
Printed in England by Clays Ltd, St Ives plc

ISBN-13: 978-0-141-02911-5
ISBN-10: 0-141-02911-0

For Jane, the believer

Acknowledgments

Thanks are due to Garth Nix, who first led me down this long and winding path. To Russ Galen, who filled my beggar's bowl. To Steve Saffel, who suffered as no mortal editor should ever have to suffer. To Cate Paterson, my sword and shield. And Brianne Tunnicliffe, for riding shotgun on this madness. The rock-steady babes at the Queensland Writers Centre are owed my thanks and gratitude. And Pete McAllister, as always, was a dude. There is no way I can repay the loving support of my family, Jane, Anna and Thomas, except maybe by getting away from the keyboard more often.

Dramatis Personae

Multinational Force Commanders

Anderson, Captain Daytona, USN. Commander, USS *Leyte Gulf*.

Francois, Captain Margie, USMC. Combat surgeon and Chief Medical Officer, Multinational Force. (USS *Kandahar*.)

Halabi, Captain Karen, RN. Commander, British contingent; Deputy Commander, Multinational Force; Commander, HMS *Trident*.

Jones, Colonel JL, USMC. Commander, 82nd Marine Expeditionary Unit. (USS *Kandahar*.)

Judge, Commander Mike, USN. Executive Officer, USS *Hillary Clinton*.

Kolhammer, Admiral Phillip, USN. Task Force Commander. (USS *Hillary Clinton*.)

Miyazaki, Sub-Lieutenant Maseo, JMSDF. Acting Commander, JDS *Siranui*.

Moertopo, Lieutenant Ali, TNI-AL. Acting Commander, KRI *Sutanto*.

Willet, Captain Jane, RAN. Commander, HMAS *Havoc.*

Windsor, His Royal Highness Captain Harry, Commander, British SAS contingent.

Multinational Force Personnel

Bukowski, Private Waylon, USMC. 1st Platoon, B Company. (USS *Kandahar.*)

Chen, Second Lieutenant Henry, USMC. 3rd Platoon, C Company. (USS *Kandahar.*)

Damiri, Sub-Lieutenant Usama, TNI-AL. Information Systems Officer, KRI *Sutanto.*

Hannon, Second Lieutenant Biff, USMC. 1st Platoon, B Company. (USS *Kandahar.*)

Harford, Flight Lieutenant Chris, USN. Helicopter pilot. (USS *Hillary Clinton.*)

Hayes, Flight Lieutenant Amanda, USN. Helicopter pilot. (USS *Hillary Clinton.*)

Ivanov, Major Pavel, Russian Federation Spetsnaz. On secondment to US Navy SEALs. (USS *Kandahar.*)

Nguyen, Lieutenant Rachel, RAN. Close-In Weapons System Operator. (HMAS *Moreton Bay.*) Seconded to History Working Group. (USS *Hillary Clinton.*)

Rogas, Chief Petty Officer Vincente, US Navy SEALs. (USS *Kandahar.*)

Thieu, Lieutenant Edgar, USN. Media Relations Officer. (USS *Hillary Clinton.*)

Miscellaneous

Duffy, Julia, *New York Times* feature writer. Embedded 82nd MEU.

Natoli, Rosanna, CNN researcher/producer. Embedded 82nd MEU.

Pope, Professor Manning, Project Director, Defense Advanced Research Projects Agency.

1942 Allied Commanders

Churchill, Winston. Prime Minister, Great Britain.

Curtin, John. Prime Minister, Commonwealth of Australia.

Eisenhower, Brigadier General Dwight D, US Army. Head of War Plans Division. Appointed Commander of US Forces, European Theatre of Operations, June 1942.

King, Admiral Ernest J, USN.
Commander-in-Chief of the US Fleet and Chief of Naval Operations.

MacArthur, General Douglas, US Army.
Commander, Allied Forces, South-West Pacific Area. Headquartered in Brisbane, Australia.

Marshall, General George C, US Army. Chairman, Joint Chiefs of Staff.

Nimitz, Admiral Chester, USN.
Commander-in-Chief, US Pacific Fleet.

Roosevelt, President Franklin D. Thirty-second President of the United States of America.

Spruance, Rear Admiral Raymond A, USN.
Commander, Task Force 16.

1942 Allied Personnel

Black, Lieutenant Commander Daniel, USN.
Assistant Operations and Planning Chief to Admiral Spruance. (USS *Enterprise*.)

Curtis, Ensign Wally, USN. Assistant payroll clerk. (USS *Enterprise*.)

Davidson, Able Seaman James 'Slim Jim'.
(USS *Astoria*.)

Evans, Lieutenant Commander Peter. Acting Commander, USS *Astoria.*

Mohr, Chief Petty Officer Eddie. (USS *Astoria.*)

Molloy, Able Seaman Michael 'Moose'. (USS *Astoria.*)

Ryan, Warrant Officer Peter, New Guinea Volunteer Rifles. Patrol Officer.

Miscellaneous

Cherry, Detective Sergeant Lou 'Buster', Honolulu PD, Homicide.

Einstein, Professor Albert, Nobel laureate.

Axis High Command

Japan

Kakuta, Rear Admiral Kakuji, IJN. Commander, Second Carrier Striking Force. (HIJMS *Ryujo.*)

Yamamoto, Admiral Isoroku, IJN. Commander-in-Chief, Combined Fleet. (HIJMS *Yamato.*)

Germany

Goebbels, Reichsminister Joseph. German Propaganda Minister.

Himmler, Reichsführer Heinrich. SS Chief.

Hitler, Reichschancellor Adolf.

Axis Personnel

Brasch, Major Paul. Engineer.

Hidaka, Lieutenant Commander Jisaku, IJN. Chief of Staff to Rear Admiral Kakuta. (HIJMS *Ryujo*.)

Skorzeny, Colonel Otto. Personal bodyguard to Adolf Hitler.

Steckel, Franz. SS-Obersturmführer of the SD-Ausland, a lieutenant in the Nazi Party's foreign intelligence service.

Ships of the Multinational Force

JDS *Siranui*. *Nemesis*-class stealth cruiser.

USS *Hillary Clinton*. *George Bush*-class supercarrier.

USS *Amanda L Garrett*. *Cobb*-class air warfare destroyer*.

USS *Kandahar*. *Baghdad*-class littoral assault ship.

USS *Kennebunkport*. LPD 12 landing assault ship.

USS *Leyte Gulf*. *Nemesis*-class stealth cruiser*.

USS *Providence*. *Harper's Ferry*-class amphibious landing dockship.

HMS *Fearless*. *Aden*-class helicopter assault ship*.

HMS *Trident*. *Trident*-class stealth destroyer (trimaran).

HMS *Vanguard*. *Trident*-class stealth destroyer (trimaran)*.

HMAS *Havoc*. *Savage*-class attack submarine (conventional).

HMAS *Ipswich*. *Newcastle*-class light littoral assault ship.

HMAS *Moreton Bay*. *Jervis Bay*-class troop-carrying catamaran.

KRI *Nuku*. Reconditioned *Parchim*-class frigate of the Indonesian navy (TNI-AL)*.

KRI *Sutanto*. Reconditioned *Parchim*-class frigate of the Indonesian navy (TNI-AL)*.

Dessaix. *Sartre*-class stealth destroyer of the French navy*.

* Destroyed or lost.

PART I
Transit

I

East Timor, 0942 hours, 15 January 2021

The Caliphate spy, a Javanese carpenter known simply as Adil, resettled himself against a comfortable groove in the sandalwood tree. The small, shaded clearing in the hills overlooking Dili had been his home for three days. He shared it with an aged feral cat, which remained hidden throughout the day, and an irritable monkey, which occasionally tried to shit on his head. He had considered shooting the filthy animal, but his orders were explicit. He was to remain unnoticed as long as the crusaders were anchored off East Timor, observing their fleet and sending reports via micro-burst laser link, but only in the event of a 'significant development'.

He had seen nothing 'significant' in seventy-two hours. The infidel ships were lying so far offshore they were often lost in haze and distance. Only when night fell did he have any real chance of seeing them, and even then they remained little more than a blurred constellation of twinkling, faraway lights. Such was their arrogance they didn't bother to cloak themselves in darkness. Jets roared to and from the flight deck of their carrier twenty-four hours a day.

In deepest night the fire of the launches appeared to Adil as though God Himself had lit a torch on the rim of the world.

Occasionally a helicopter would appear from the direction of the flotilla, beginning as a small, indistinct dot in the hot grey sky, taking on recognisable form only as the muffled drone of its engines clarified into a thudding, growling roar. From his hiding spot Adil could almost make out the faces of the infidels in the cabins of the fat metal birds. American, British, French, they all looked alike, cruel and overfed, a thought that reminded him of his own hunger. He unwrapped the banana leaves from around a small rice cake, thanking Allah for the generosity of his masters. They had included a little dried fish in his rations for today, a rare treat.

Sometimes, when the sun climbed directly overhead and beat down with a slow fury, Adil's thoughts wandered. He cursed his weakness and begged God for the strength to carry out his duty, but it was hard. He had fallen asleep more than once. Nothing ever seemed to *happen*. There was plenty of movement down in Dili, which was infested with crusader forces from all over the Christian world, but Dili wasn't his concern. His sole responsibility was to watch those ships that were hiding in the shimmering haze on the far horizon.

Still, Adil mused, it would be nice to know he had some real purpose here; that he had not been staked out like a goat on the side of a hill. Perhaps he was to be part of some elaborate strike on the infidels in town. Perhaps tonight the darkness would be torn asunder by holy fire as some martyr blew up one of their filthy bars. But then, why leave him here on the side of this stupid hill, covered in monkey shit and tormented by ants?

This wasn't how he had imagined jihad would be when he had graduated from the Madrasa in Bandung.

USS Kandahar, *1014 hours, 15 January 2021*

The marines wouldn't have been at all surprised to discover that someone like Adil was watching over them. In fact, they *assumed* there were more than two hundred million pairs of eyes turned their way as they prepared to deploy into the Indonesian archipelago.

Nobody called it the Caliphate. Officially the United States still recognised it as the sovereign territory of Indonesia, seventeen thousand islands stretching from Banda Aceh, three hundred kilometres off the coast of Thailand, down to Timor, just north of Australia. The sea lanes passing through those islands carried a third of the world's maritime trade, and officially they remained open to all traffic. The Indonesian government-in-exile said so – from the safety of the Grand Hyatt in Geneva where they had fled, three weeks earlier, after losing control of Jakarta.

Unofficially, though, these were the badlands, controlled – just barely – by a revolutionary Islamic government calling itself the Caliphate and laying claim to all seventeen thousand islands, as well as the territory of Malaysia, the Philippines, Brunei, East Timor, Papua New Guinea, Bougainville and, for good measure, northern Australia. Nonbelievers were not welcome. The spiritual leader of the Caliphate, Mullah Ibn Abbas, had proclaimed this as the will of Allah.

The 82nd Marine Expeditionary Unit begged to differ. And on the hangar deck of the USS *Kandahar*, a *Baghdad*-class littoral assault ship, they were preparing a full and frank rebuttal.

The hangar was a vast, echoing space. Two full decks high and running nearly a third the length of the slab-sided vessel, it still seemed crowded, packed tight with most of the 82nd's air wing, a small air force in its own right, consisting of a dozen Ospreys, four ageing Super Stallions, two reconditioned command Hueys, eight Sea Comanche gunships, and half-a-dozen Super Harriers.

The Harriers and Super Stallions had been moved onto the 'roof' – the flight deck – allowing the ground combat element of the 82nd MEU to colonise the space that had been opened up. The GCE was formally known as the 3rd Battalion of the 9th Regiment, 5th Marine Division. It was also known as the Lonesome Dead, after their passably famous CO, Colonel J Lonesome Jones.

Not all of 3 Batt were embarked upon the *Kandahar*. The battalion topped out at more than twelve hundred men and women, and some of their number had to be berthed elsewhere in the three ships that were carrying the 82nd into harm's way. The USS *Providence, a Harper's Ferry* class amphibious landing dockship (LSD), took the battalion's four Abrams tanks, a rifle company and the amphibious assault vehicle platoon. The *Kennebunkport*, a venerable LPD 12, carried the recon platoon, the regiment's Humvees, two more Hueys, the drone platoon and the navy SEAL team that would be providing security to the 82nd during their cruise through the archipelago.

Even as Adil unwrapped his rice cake and squinted into the blue expanse of the Wetar Strait, a six-man detachment from the SEAL team was unpacking their kit on the hangar deck of the *Kandahar*, getting set to train the men of C Company, 3 Batt.

Charlie company doubled as Colonel Jones's cliff assault and small boat raiding squadron, and the SEALs had come to acquaint them with a new toy, the G4, a lightweight assault rifle that fired strips of caseless ceramic ammunition and programmable thirty-millimetre grenades. It was to become standard equipment throughout the US armed forces within twelve months. The marines, however, were always at the bottom of the food chain and would probably have waited two years before they laid hands on these babies. But the battalion logistics officer, Lieutenant Colonel Nancy Viviani, was an inventive and talented

S4. As always, Viviani was determined that the battalion should have the very best equipment other people's money could buy.

Not that long ago she would have been known as a scavenger, a scrounger, and would have done her job under the cover of darkness with a pair of wire cutters and a fast getaway jeep. She would have been a man, too, of course. But Lieutenant Colonel Viviani carried two master's degrees into combat, one of them an MBA from the London School of Economics, and the graduates of that august institution didn't stoop to anything so crude as petty theft. Not when they could play the Pentagon's fantastically complex supply programmes like an antique violin.

Six and a half hours of extracurricular keyboard time had been enough to release a shipment of G4s from prepositioned supply vessels in Darwin. Viviani's genius was in making the process appear entirely legitimate. Had the Senate Armed Forces Committee itself spent a year inspecting her electronic audit trail, it would have found everything in order with absolutely nothing linking the G4 shipment to the loss of a similar supply package scheduled for delivery to an army public relations unit.

'This is the Remington G4,' CPO Vincente Rogas barked at the members of C Company. 'By the end of today's lecture you *will* be familiar with the procedure for maintaining this weapon in the field.' It sounded more like a threat than a promise.

'The G4 is the first solid state infantry weapon,' he bellowed. 'It has very few moving parts.'

A slight murmur passed through the tight knot of marines. They were familiar with the weapon's specs, having intensively trained with them back in the United States. But still, it was a hell of a thing to wrap your head around.

'And this is the standard battle load.' Rogas's audience stared at the long thin strip of ceramic munitions like children at their first magic show. 'The ammo strip is placed in the barrel like this. An electrical charge ignites the propellant casing, driving the slug out with such velocity that, even with a three-round burst, you will feel no kickback – at least not *before* the volley leaves the muzzle.

'Tomorrow, when we move ashore to the range, each of you will be allotted three hundred rounds. I suggest very strongly that before then you take advantage of the full VR tutorial we've loaded into your training sets. The base software package is a standard Asian urban conflict scenario, but we've added modules specifically tailored for operations in Jakarta and Surabaya.'

With deployment less than a fortnight away, similar scenes were being replayed throughout the US-led Multinational Force accompanying the *Kandahar*. Twelve thousand very serious men and women drilled to the point of exhaustion. They were authorised by the UN Security Council to use whatever force was necessary to re-establish control of the capital,

Jakarta, and to put an end to the mass murder of Indonesia's Chinese and Christian minorities. Everybody was preparing for a slaughter.

In the hundred-bed hospital of the *Kandahar*, the 82nd's chief combat surgeon, Captain Margie Francois, supervised her team's reaction to a simulated missile strike on an armoured hovercraft carrying a marine rifle company into a contested estuary.

Two thousand metres away, the French missile frigate *Dessaix* duelled with a pair of Raptors off the supercarrier USS *Hillary Clinton*.

In the other direction, three thousand metres to the west, two British trimaran stealth destroyers practised their response to a successful strike by suicide bombers whose weapon of choice had been a high-speed rubber boat. Indeed, Captain Karen Halabi, who had been on the receiving end of just such an attack as a young ensign, drilled the crew of the HMS *Trident* so fiercely that in the few hours they were allowed to sleep, most dreamed of crazy men in speedboats laden with TNT.

JRV Nagoya, *1046 hours, 15 January 2021*

As diverse as these ships were, one still stood out. The Joint Research Vessel *Nagoya* was a purpose-built leviathan, constructed around the frame of an eighty-thousand-tonne liquid natural gas carrier. Her keel had been laid down in Korea, with the fit-out split between San Francisco and Tokyo, reflecting the multinational nature of her funding. She fit in with the sleek warships of the Multinational Force the way a hippo would with a school of swordfish.

Her presence was a function of the speed with which the crisis in Jakarta had developed. The USS *Leyte Gulf*, a stealth cruiser from the *Clinton*'s battle group, had been riding shotgun over the *Nagoya*'s sea trials in the benign waters off Western Australia. When the orders came down that the carrier and her battle group were to move immediately into the Wetar Strait, the *Nagoya* had been left with no choice but to tag along until an escort could be assigned to shepherd her safely back to Hawaii. It was a situation nobody liked, least of all Professor Manning Pope, the leader of the *Nagoya* team.

Crouched over a console in his private quarters, Pope muttered under his breath as he hammered out yet another enraged email directly to Admiral Tony Kevin, Commander-in-Chief, US Pacific Command. It was the ninth such email he had sent in forty-eight hours. Each had elicited a standardised reply, not from the admiral himself mind you, but from some trained monkey on his personal staff.

Pope typed, stabbing at the keys:

Need I remind you of the support this project elicits at THE VERY HIGHEST LEVELS OF GOVERNMENT? I would not wish to be in your shoes, Admiral Kevin, when I explain to your superiors that we have gone over budget while being dragged into this pointless fiasco. The Nagoya *is a research vessel, not a warship, and we should have been allowed to continue our trials unmolested in the perfectly safe testing range off Perth. As small as it is, the Australian Navy is more than capable of fending off any drunken fishermen who might have strayed too close.*

Therefore I demand *that we be freed from this twopenny opera and be allowed to return to our test schedule as originally planned. I await your earliest reply. And that means* yours, *Admiral Kevin, not some junior baboon's!*

That'll put a rocket under his fat ass, thought Pope. *Bureaucrats hate it when you threaten to go over their heads. It means they might actually have to stagger to their feet and do something for a change.*

Spleen vented for the moment, he keyed into the vidlink that connected him with the project control room. A Japanese man with a shock of unruly thick black hair answered the hail.

'How do we look for a power-up this morning, Yoshi?' Pope asked. 'I'm anxious to get back on schedule.'

Standing at a long, curving bank of flat-screens Professor Yoshi Murayama, an unusually tall cosmic-string theorist from Honshu, blew out his cheeks and shrugged. 'I can't see why not from this end. We're just about finished entering the new data sets. We're good to go, except you know that Kolhammer won't like it.'

'Kolhammer's a chickenshit,' said Pope somewhat mournfully. 'I really don't care what he thinks. He's not qualified to tell us what we can and cannot do. You are.'

'Like I said,' the Japanese Nobel winner responded, 'I don't see a problem. Just a beautiful set of numbers.'

'Of course.' Pope nodded. 'Everyone else feel the same?' he asked, raising his voice so that it projected into the room beyond Murayama. The space was surprisingly small for such a momentous undertaking, no bigger than a suburban living room really. Large glowing monitors shared the area with half-a-dozen senior project researchers, each staffing a work-station.

His question caught them off guard. Their boss enjoyed a hard-won reputation as a thoroughly unpleasant little prick with an amazingly rigid pole up his ass. A couple of them exchanged quick glances, but nobody said anything for a few moments until Barnes, their magnetic ram technician, ventured a reply.

'Well, it's not our fault we fell behind. But you can bet we'll get blamed if we don't hustle to catch up.'

'Exactly!' Pope replied. 'Let's prepare for a test run at .01 efficiency. That should be enough to confirm a stabilised effect with the new figures. Are we all agreed?'

They were.

HMAS Moreton Bay, *1049 hours, 15 January 2021*

Lieutenant Rachel Nguyen had slept six hours out of the last forty-eight. As the defensive systems operator of the troop cat *Moreton Bay*, she felt herself directly responsible for the lives of four hundred soldiers and thirty-two crewmembers. The *Moreton Bay* was a fat, soft, high-value target; so much more tempting for would-be martyrs or renegade Indonesian forces than the *Clinton* or the *Kandahar* or any of the escort vessels. The software for the catamaran's Metal Storm CIWS – Close-In Weapons System – had been twitching and freezing up ever since they'd loaded the update patches during the last refit in Sydney. Nguyen, at the tail end of a marathon hacking session, had just come to the conclusion she'd be better off trashing the updates and reverting to the old programme.

She rubbed her eyes and swivelled her chair around to face Captain Sheehan. The ancient mariner seemed to read her mind.

'You want to dump the new system, Lieutenant?' he asked even before she had a chance to speak.

Damn, she thought. *How does he* do *that?*

'I don't really want to, sir, but it's buggy as hell. The pods are just as likely to target us as any incoming.'

Sheehan rubbed at his chin beneath the thick beard he had sported for as long as Nguyen had known him. 'Okay,' he agreed after a moment's thought.

'Tell the *Clinton* we're going to take them offline for – how long to reload the old software?'

Nguyen shrugged. 'A few minutes to deep-six the garbage code, five and a half to reload the classic. Say ten to be sure.'

'Okay. Tell the *Clinton* we're taking the pods offline for fifteen minutes to change over the programming, so we'll need them to assign us extra cover through CBL. The *Trident*'s closest, she'll do nicely.'

'Thank you, sir,' said Rachel, genuinely grateful to be released from the burden of hacking the software on her own.

Sheehan watched her closely for a moment longer, then turned to peer out through the tinted blast windows of the cat's bridge. The sea surface was nearly mirror still.

Nguyen worried that he might order her to stand down for a few hours. After all, they wouldn't be deploying for another two weeks, and they'd be in port as of this evening. But there was no way she'd be able to sleep until she was sure the problem had been solved.

'How's your thesis going, Lieutenant?' Sheehan asked as Rachel shut down the windows on the screen in front of her.

'I haven't really had time to work on it since we left Darwin, sir,' she confessed. 'But it's not due for three months. I should be right to finish it.'

'Still comparing Haig and Westmoreland?'

'With reference to Philip the Second,' she added.

'You know – sent the Armada, started the Eighty Years War, wrecked the Castilian Empire.'

'*No experience of the failure of his policy could shake his belief in its essential excellence*,' quoted Sheehan.

'You've read Tuchman?' she said.

'Many years ago, for my own dissertation,' he nodded. 'What was it she called Philip?'

'The surpassing woodenhead of all sovereigns,' said Nguyen.

Sheehan smiled in remembrance. 'That's right, she did . . . Anyway, reload the software, then get some sleep.' She started to protest, but the look on his face stopped her. 'I don't want to see you back here for at least six hours.'

JRV Nagoya, *1156 hours, 15 January 2021*

Morley and Dunne were hunkered down in front of the snack machine, trying for a casual look, but everything about them screamed *conspiracy*. They were fixated on a jumbo Snickers bar that had been half dislodged and was threatening to fall into the dispensing bin for free.

'You can rock the machine five degrees off the perpendicular,' said Morley, who was overweight, out of shape, and physically incapable of doing any such thing. This wasn't the first jumbo chocolate bar he had encountered.

'Or we could just buy another Snickers,' protested

Dunne. 'Then we'd get two for the price of one.'

'Jeez, Sharon, you're such a narc. You won't boost a fucking freebie, but one word from Doctor Frankenstein back there and you'd sell out your own grandmother to make him happy. He's evil, I tells ya! *E-e-e-e-e-v-i-l.*'

'Knock it off, dickhead,' she hissed. Sharon Dunne was the youngest of Manning Pope's team, a Caltech graduate with a first-class thesis on quantum foam manipulation. She was also a distant descendant of the poet John Donne and a lesbian goth with a hard-on for the oeuvre of Johnny Depp. As she contemplated the chocolate bar she drummed her fingers on the snack machine. Her nails were painted with black polish, and chunky pewter death's head rings covered her fingers.

'And anyway, *Jonathon*,' she chided, 'I didn't exactly see you stepping forward to make your big speech about how he's Meddling With Powers Beyond His Control.'

At that Morley lost interest in the chocolate bar. He grimaced and whispered theatrically, 'Yeah, well, I didn't fancy getting my head torn off again. Dude went ballistic when I pointed out that hole in his last solution. I thought he was gonna throw me over the side of the fucking boat.'

They both glanced around the small canteen as though Pope might suddenly materialise, like Hannibal Lector with a knife and fork.

'Well, what's the worst that could happen?' Dunne

countered. 'We could brown out the fleet again. That was fun, really, watching Kolhammer tear Pope a new asshole. I'd pay good money to see something like that again.'

'Yeah, or we could rip open the Hellmouth and let out all kinds of orcs and vampires and shit,' said Morley.

'Oh, give it a rest, you geek. You know, the guys on the Manhattan Project thought there was a chance the first A-bomb would blow up the whole world with a blast that would ignite the atmosphere, then just keep getting bigger and bigger. But it didn't, did it? It was never going to.'

'Yeah, well, you ever read that story where they photographed the inside of a nuclear explosion?'

'Yeah, yeah, and they saw the face of Satan. It was cool. But they were looking in the wrong place. I've already seen the real Satan. His name is Pope, and he's going to cut off your dick and use it as a swizzle stick if we're late getting back for the test run.'

'You're right. Of course you're right. Just let me get this Snickers bar.'

Admiral's Quarters, USS Hillary Clinton, *1148 hours, 15 January 2021*

Admiral Kolhammer's cheeks ached from the effort of maintaining the anodyne grin he had fixed in place. *A reasonable man*, he kept repeating to himself. *I am a reasonable man.*

'You would have to agree though, wouldn't you, Admiral . . .'

Kolhammer held up his hand. 'No, I would not, Ms Duffy.'

The reporter smiled as she sucked the end of her pencil. She wore dark, wine-coloured lipstick, and it accentuated the disconcerting gesture. 'You don't even know what I was going to say,' she protested mildly.

'I'm just saving you time by pointing out that I don't have to agree with whatever it is you're about to say,' Kolhammer explained as equably as he could manage. Every time this woman confronted him, he felt as though he were trapped in a resistance-to-torture exercise that never ended.

He was rarely able to enjoy the luxury suite that had been set aside for his quarters on the *Clinton*, and it irked him that this obnoxious woman was ruining the few minutes' break he'd taken today. He should have listened to Lieutenant Thieu, his media relations officer. If he'd given her a few minutes on the flag bridge, Duffy would have been floundering in his natural environment, surrounded by his people and overwhelmed by the pace of activity. In contrast, the admiral's quarters were like a serviced apartment in an expensive hotel. No doubt she felt right at home here.

He resolved to be less generous in the future.

'Well,' she continued, oblivious to his chagrin, 'it doesn't take a master's in international relations to see that sending a "white man's" force to intervene in a religious civil war is a recipe for disaster. Regional governments like Malaysia may be desperate for the US to deal with the Indonesian problem, but you *would* have to agree that they'd be reluctant to contribute their own forces. Especially since this action will be denounced throughout the Muslim world as another Christian crusade.'

Still Kolhammer managed to keep the mask of civility in place. Clearly this woman was no fool. She had obviously done her research, and her line of questioning wasn't far from the hard truth he faced in trying to manage this first-rate clusterfuck of a mission.

'I'm afraid there are a number of holes in that argument, Ms Duffy,' he answered in a pleasant, level tone. 'But most importantly, you seem to have mistaken me for the Secretary of State. No doubt she would be happy to answer your question, but I'm afraid my job isn't to argue, analyse or set our government's foreign policy; I simply do my best to see that it's carried out. Any first-year political science student would understand the distinction.'

He allowed himself a slightly wolfish grin at that. To the reporter's credit, she didn't even blush.

'And *are* you equipped to carry out that policy, Admiral? This Multinational Force is a bit of a kludge, isn't it?'

He actually laughed. Once again she had given voice to his private thoughts, using the very words he would have used – if he had felt like putting a bullet into his career. He turned the moment of bleak amusement back on her.

'Ms Duffy, I have the better part of a carrier battle group here, a Marine Expeditionary Unit and some of the very best assets our friends and allies could pour into the breach at short notice. The Rising Jihad talk a mighty good game, but until now they've been terrorising office workers and unarmed, illiterate peasants. I wish them the best of luck should they try it with us.'

'But you're also facing renegade units of the Indonesian Armed Forces, are you not, and intervention by Beijing if the mass murder of the ethnic Chinese population continues?'

'Once again you're asking me to comment outside my area of responsibility. I can only remind you that the Chinese government fully supported the creation of this force and voted for it in the Security Council. And as for the TNI, yes, a number of units have gone over to the insurgency, but the majority of the Indonesian Armed Forces are standing with the legitimate, elected government. As a matter of fact, we have two Indonesian navy ships sailing with us. They will accompany the Multinational Force at every stage of this operation.'

Duffy smiled as if at some private joke, further irritating Kolhammer. He suspected she was well aware of the *Sutanto* and the *Nuku*, and already knew that they were little better than state-sponsored pirates. But mercifully she chose not to embarrass him over it.

'The *majority* of the Indonesian Armed Forces have simply melted away though, haven't they?' she asked.

'Well, if that proves to be the case, they won't bear worrying about, will they, Ms Duffy?' Kolhammer said as he pointedly looked at his watch.

'Just one last question, sir?'

'You don't have to call me sir, Ms Duffy.'

'Thank you, sir. Now about the civilian vessel you have with you . . .'

'The *Nagoya*.'

'Yes. Can you tell me anything about its role in this operation?'

'It has none,' he answered truthfully. 'It's a research vessel that got caught up in the crisis. The *Leyte Gulf*, one of our Nemesis cruisers, was acting as security during the sea trials of some equipment aboard her – and before you ask, no, I can't discuss those in detail. I can tell you that it has something to do with ocean bed resource mapping. But they do have some very expensive toys on board, and the *Nagoya* had to transit waters infested by pirates to reach the proving grounds off Perth; hence the escort. Now that the *Leyte Gulf* has been assigned to this task force, we'll need to find somebody to chaperone the *Nagoya*. Then she'll be making her way back home. I understand New Zealand is sending a frigate for that very purpose.'

Duffy sucked at her pencil again, affecting a look of deep thought. 'Really? That's not what I hear.'

'Well, why don't you ask the project's venture partners for an interview? I believe they're headquartered in New York. Not too far from your paper in fact. I'm sure their shareholders would love the coverage – if you could convince your editor to run a piece on seabed mapping. I'll ask Lieutenant Thieu to zap you their contact details.'

Kolhammer watched her interest curl up and die.

'No, that's all right, but thanks anyway,' she said.

His smile was lit with genuine warmth for the first time. 'Then we're done here. Now if you'll excuse me, Ms Duffy, I really do have a full schedule.'

The reporter thanked him and walked with him to the cabin door, where Lieutenant Thieu was waiting to escort her back to the media centre. Like many civilians, she was quietly entranced by the military's old-world manners. At the media centre Kolhammer bid her goodbye and carried on up to the flag bridge, where the *Clinton*'s executive officer, Commander Mike Judge, was waiting for him.

'How'd it go, sir?' asked the softly spoken Texan, after the formalities of the admiral's arrival were completed.

'I shall never ignore a suggestion from Lieutenant Thieu again,' Kolhammer said, grinning ruefully. 'Thank God that's over with. Now, is Captain Chandler joining us?'

'Sir, the captain regrets that he'll be delayed

somewhat, though he hopes to be along shortly. The number three catapult is acting up again. Chandler has gone down to the flight deck to personally kick its butt and curse up a storm.'

Kolhammer smiled at the image. The *Clinton*'s CO had a notoriously combustible temper. It was distinctly possible he was doing just what Judge had suggested. But Kolhammer wasn't about to second-guess the carrier's captain. He was already too deeply mired in the political swamp to which Duffy had alluded during their interview. Indeed, a good part of each day was eaten up balancing the competing interests and agendas of the disparate forces under his command.

The Australians and the French, for instance, maintained an icy reserve with each other at best. This was due to the decision of France's new National Front government to renew and expand its nuclear test programme in the Pacific. The relationship between the two governments had deteriorated so far that ambassadors had been recalled and billions of dollars' worth of trade sanctions were being declared. As professional as both navies were, such a climate wasn't conducive to joint operations.

Meanwhile the Malaysian government had flip-flopped on three separate occasions, first committing to the Multinational Force, then withdrawing, then recommitting, and so on. Kolhammer had twice personally flown to Kuala Lumpur to seek, and receive, assurance from the country's defence minister that

Malaysia would meet its treaty obligations, only to land back on the *Clinton* to the news that it would do nothing of the sort.

And of course there were the Indonesians. If Kolhammer's feuding allies and the feckless Malays were a pain in the ass, the Indonesians were a situation screaming out for radical butt surgery. He had them out of sight and out of mind for the moment, running submarine drills to the north. But he was going to have to bring them back into the fold sometime soon. The State Department weenies were insistent.

Kolhammer actually envied Guy Chandler for having gremlins in the number three catapult. If only his problems were that simple.

'Right then, Commander,' he said. 'What do you have for me today?'

Judge consulted his flexipad with an apologetic air. 'How'd you feel about a quick trip to the exotic and mysterious city of Kuala Lumpur, Admiral?'

'Oh, jeez,' Kolhammer sighed.

Rosanna Natoli's eyes lit up as her friend reappeared at the door of the *Clinton*'s media centre.

'How'd it go with the Hammer?' she asked, using their favourite name for the fleet commander. It was not entirely respectful.

The *New York Times* feature writer rolled her eyes and replied in her best Sergeant Schulz, 'I know nuffink! Naaarrffink!'

Natoli snorted. 'And the mystery ship?'

Duffy shrugged. 'Some corporate gig gone wrong. "Seabed mapping," he said. It was strange, though. Even though he made it seem routine, there was something about it that had him more excited than he was letting on. I tell you, boys and their toys. Speaking of which, you wanna go watch the bomb loaders work out? The cute ones are usually down in the gym about now.'

'You fucking nympho.'

JRV Nagoya, *1233 hours, 15 January 2021*

As the two reporters settled themselves onto exercise bikes in the *Clinton*'s main gym, six senior project researchers parked themselves in front of LG flat-screens and engaged the preliminary sequences required for a full-spectrum run on the *Nagoya*'s Quad System. Manning Pope stared into the soft glow of the superthin display panel that lay directly in front of him. The screen was only four millimetres thick, and it seemed as though the data was floating in space. Pope's head tilted slightly to one side as he tried to come at the dense matrix of symbols and numbers from a variety of different angles. After a few minutes of wagging this way and that, he pushed out his lower lip and turned to Murayama.

'At .01, I'm sure we can do this,' he said, almost to himself.

Professor Murayama grunted an affirmation, but

he wore an expression of concern. Still, if he had any doubts, he didn't voice them.

The project was a seventy-nine-billion dollar effort to field-test a number of basic assumptions about the feasibility of combining a heavy-ion collider, a quark-gluon plasma imploder and a rotating photon splitter in order to transfer a nanonic explosive package from an originating point to a target destination without having to travel through the space that lay in between. It was, in essence, a teleporter. Just like in *Star Trek*, except that rather than moving hopelessly complex human beings across thousands of miles of space, it was designed to move a very small, very simple warhead directly into the mass of a selected target, such as the brain stem of Mullah Ibn Abbas.

In Manning Pope, the Defense Advanced Research Projects Agency had retained the world's foremost expert on the engineering of space-time foam, and set him working hard at the second great militarisation of Einstein's theory of relativity. They had also acquired an overweening egotist whose only real interest was in the opportunity the project provided to spend other people's money on his personal obsession – FTL, faster-than-light travel.

Pope's incipient mania and a couple of breathtaking developments in quantum computing had moved the entire schedule onto the fast track. The senators currently overseeing the mission were understandably pleased. Their Japanese, British and Russian counterparts were all likewise thrilled at the prospect of having an exciting new way to kill Chinese infantry and Taliban jihadis. And Pope had never felt the need to burden any of them with the details of his research.

Now on the verge of proving his FTL theories, Pope seemed to hesitate.

A quick, stealthy look passed between Morley and Dunne, but neither said anything. They'd never seen Pope or Murayama look anything other than painfully arrogant, so this sudden change in character set off alarms. But nobody really cared what they thought. And anyway, this might be an opportunity for them to watch Kolhammer beating on the boss again, which was such an appealing thought that Morley had arranged to trap any incoming communications for covert storage on his own flexipad. If they blew circuits all over the fleet like last time, Kolhammer would go postal for sure, and that sort of footage could keep a guy entertained for months on a long voyage.

As the Quad came online, each team member responded with a slightly increased heart rate, slightly shallower breathing and a measurable change in galvanic skin response. They were all excited, no matter what their private qualms.

Wetar Strait, 1234 hours, 15 January 2021

While Pope's colleagues set to their preparations, maybe a dozen pairs of eyes throughout the entire task force were directly fixed on the giant scientific ship. Two sailors on the destroyer trimaran HMS *Vanguard*, enjoying a furtive cigarette to mark the end of their watch, speculated on the contents of the oversized megatanker. Neither guessed correctly.

The pilot of a Marine Corps F-35, climbing through five thousand metres above the task force, happened to glance down at the same moment, but she took in the four strange, bulbous pods on the *Nagoya*'s deck without really registering. The pilot had clocked some serious hours during the last fortnight's exercises, and the sight of the *Nagoya* was entirely routine to her now.

A bored fourth officer on the bridge of the Japanese Nemesis cruiser *Siranui* trained a pair of vintage binoculars on the distant form of their mystery guest, but his thoughts were mostly back home where he was certain his two girlfriends must have discovered each other by now, given his ill-advised decision to start banging a couple of office ladies dorming on the same floor of the same singles complex.

Throughout the rest of the task force a small number of sysops routinely scanning the threat bubble scoped out the 'ghost ship', probing her annoyingly effective electronic defences with low-grade scans, looking to pierce the black hole that enveloped her. The temporary community of task force Electronic Intelligence operators were agreed that a fully amped blast from a Nemesis array would strip her naked. But of course they weren't allowed to do that, so during rare moments of downtime they dicked around with low-power blinkscans, feeling out the *Nagoya*'s electronic perimeter.

After the infamous brownout, Commander Judge had quietly and deniably encouraged such unlicensed shenanigans. Had he known what was coming, though, he would have junked his career and ordered all of the group's Nemesis arrays tuned in and burning bright, twenty-four/seven. But nothing had even remotely suggested that things were about to unravel aboard the Joint Research Vessel.

JRV Nagoya, *1235 hours, 15 January 2021*

Pope seated himself at the command deck of the control room. With little to do while his underlings worked their consoles, he was able to sit back and savour the moment. He almost smiled. If he'd been wearing slippers he might have kicked them off and put his feet up. Instead he sat rather regally in the centre of things on a large leather swivel chair that Morley and Dunne called 'the Kirk'. The lighting was dim. The monitors threw off just enough light to read a book, and anyway, he thought, there was something about the moment that lent itself to a bit of dramatic staging. The only sound, besides Morley's laboured breathing, was the deeply satisfying rapid-fire snapping of keys as the project staffers entered Pope's revolutionary new data.

Having nothing to do at this point, he checked to make certain that the closed-circuit TV was recording the moment for posterity and arranged himself in a suitably commanding pose for the video.

'Ms Dunne,' he said quietly, causing her to jump in her chair.

'Yes, Professor,' she replied, worried that he'd observed some grotesque fuck-up in the settings she'd just entered.

'Relax, Dunne. Nothing to worry about, I merely thought that, as the youngest member of our team and of course, *as a lady*,' he teased, 'we might give you the honour of launching.'

'Me?' She gaped as everyone turned to stare. 'Me?'

'My word.' Pope grinned coldly. 'They really do give away the degrees at Caltech these days, don't they? Yes, *you*. If everyone else is ready?'

Morley spun on his seat, ripped out a brief string of commands in his staccato, two-fingered typing style, then continued the spin and brought himself back around to face the group.

'Done deal!'

Pope just shook his head. 'Young man,' he said, 'when generations yet unborn come to study this day, the greatest mystery won't be how we managed this grand achievement decades ahead of time, but rather how we managed it at all with a moron piloting the accelerator. Ms Dunne?'

Still shocked, Sharon Dunne swivelled to face her large screen. She reached out and stroked it with one long, black-nailed finger. The image display cleared, then another tap brought up one giant icon. It had been a joke, actually, suggested by Morley. The Big Red Button That Doesn't Really Do Anything. Dunne looked over her shoulder at Pope, who nodded. She gave her colleagues a thumbs-up, then pressed the same digit to the screen.

Belying its name, the button went *click*.

The disaster was a few seconds unfolding. A coiled heavy-ion accelerator boosted two baskets of uranium nuclei to fantastic levels of energy before smashing the counter-cyclical beams head on, very briefly recreating the ten-trillion-degree environment that had existed roughly one microsecond after the Big Bang. Protons and neutrons were annihilated, breaking down into a superenergised blob of quark-gluon plasma.

The team watched a schematic representation of the process on their personal view screens, direct exposure being out of the question. Murayama, the creator of the imploder that sucked up the plasma in the next phase, nodded briefly as the amorphous energy cloud was instantly metacompressed by explosive magnetic rams.

The process temperature soared by a factor of

10^{19}, reaching the fabled Planck's constant as the quark-gluon bubble imploded to a sphere with a density of ten trillion trillion trillion trillion trillion trillion trillion trillion trillion kilograms per cubic metre. Indeed, it was so dense that Pope and his crew had just created the first synthetic wormhole, an insanely impressive achievement, worthy of Nobels for all.

But it was only a job half done. Pope felt his heart beginning to race as his own unique contribution came online, a Casimir Inflator that set the wormhole spinning at a speed fractionally slower than light before firing an array of high-powered lasers into its maw to push the throat out before it could collapse inwards.

'Firing up the disco ball!' Morley called out as a ring of perfectly reflective mirrors began to rotate at two million rpm. Two hundred and thirty metres away dozens of beams of coherent light skewered into the mirrors, striking them at a shallow angle that reflected the negative beam pulses half a degree away from their paired positives. The negatives were shunted down a cavity resonator and into the mouth of the wormhole. The nanoscale hole sucked in the lasers, as expected. It inflated, also as expected.

To this point everything had gone as predicted.

And then the process went native, swallowing the chamber that was meant to contain it, sucking in energy like Poe's maelstrom and spaghettifying the very matter that had given it birth, stretching and eating the world all around. Inflation took place instantaneously, the gross tonnage of the *Nagoya* being drawn into the throat like taffy, snuffing out the lives of the only people who possessed any chance of reversing the process, or even explaining it.

Manning Pope died, smiling and unaware.

Pope's wormhole, which should have stabilised at three microns in diameter, instead blew out into a swirling lens of elemental colours fifteen thousand metres across before dissipating just as quickly. In that brief period, however, it punched through the veil separating two universes.

HMAS Moreton Bay, *1235 hours, 15 January 2021*

'Some people,' muttered Rachel Nguyen, 'really get the shit end of the stick.'

She was staring at a flexipad image showing a CNN report out of the Indonesian Exclusion Zone. A woman's yellowed eyes burned back at her from within a sunken, malnourished face, imploring her to do something, anything, to save her children from famine and disease. But she and they were almost certainly two years dead by now.

Rachel thumbed the corner of the screen, shutting down the link and pushing the thin pad across the scarred mess table, out of reach and beyond temptation. The lights in the mess flickered briefly, then returned to normal a few moments later. She couldn't justify putting off her thesis any longer. The boss had ordered her to catch some sleep but she just couldn't, not with a deadline looming. She drained the last of her coffee and considered hassling the cook for one of the muffins she could smell baking in the galley. No, that would probably cost her ten minutes in conversation, and definitely an extra quarter of an hour in the gym. Cooky had a wicked way with a mixing spoon.

Glancing up, she nodded to a lone sergeant who caught her eye as he savaged an impossibly large plate of sausages a few tables away. Rachel quickly ducked her head back to her notes, breaking eye contact, but she needn't have worried. The old soldier only had eyes for his food.

The mess lights guttered again. She had time to wonder why before the world turned black and she disappeared forever.

USS Kandahar, *1235 hours, 15 January 2021*

Colonel J Lonesome Jones willingly gave in to temptation and enjoyed a leftover breakfast muffin with his espresso. At the age of forty-three, the boss hog of the 82nd MEU boasted a middleweight boxer's physique, a shaved head he could forge horseshoes on, and an air of casual menace he had learned to turn on and off at will – a skill he had perfected as a kid in the Chicago projects. Yeah, he could have a goddamn muffin if he felt like one.

As he lingered over the last minutes of a short break in the officers' mess of USS *Kandahar*, Jones watched an immensely satisfying flexipad vid of his beloved Bulls stomping the shit out of the hopelessly outclassed Knicks. These few minutes of real life he allowed himself each day were sacrosanct.

So it was that two young marine officers who entered the mess made their way as quietly as possible to the far side of the room. There they placed an order with the steward for a round of burgers and fries. They filled mugs of standard-issue instant coffee from a quietly bubbling urn lest the hissing of the espresso machine distract the old man and lead to an unwelcome round of ferocious ass-chewage. Second Lieutenants Henry Chen and Biff Hannon were both keenly aware of the colonel's reputation, from first-hand experience.

Consequently both men nibbled at their burgers as though they were communion wafers, all the while maintaining a very low profile.

Jones was aware of them but didn't attend to their presence until he had disposed of the sports downloads, the local Chicago news and the global updates, in that order. When his free time was up he stood, stretched and slipped into character.

'Good morning, gentlemen,' he purred, turning on his two officers and frowning at their fatty meals. 'You're training with the SAS again today?'

They both nodded. 'Sir.'

'Well, I hope you're not going to allow those sneaky bastards to kick your asses quite so badly this time.'

Both men bristled.

'We've worked up a few surprises, Colonel,' Chen quickly assured him.

'Surprises? That's good,' Jones said, deadpan. 'Because I was very disappointed that anyone could get the better of one of *my* units, get close enough, in fact, to light up the farts of the officer in charge.'

The colour drained from their faces under the blast of his fixed, humourless stare. Jones paused for a moment, knowing his silence would be infinitely more effective. Eventually a blushing Lieutenant Hannon stammered something about not letting it happen again. Jones let his stone face rest on the young officer for a moment, then softened it some. Just a touch.

'But it will, son,' he said. 'It'll happen again today. They'll come upon you no matter what snares you lay in their path, and they'll have their evil way with you. Do you know why?'

Neither man spoke. They simply shook their heads.

As Jones leaned in towards his young charges, the lights in the room dipped for a moment. *Damn, almost like I staged it*, he thought.

'They'll make you their bitches because they can,' he said softly. 'I've served with some of those men.

They're older than you in ways you can't even imagine. They've fought their whole lives. They've been making war while you have merely been preparing for war, *pretending* at war.'

The lights surged up to full power again and he leaned back, rolling with the moment. 'I don't really expect you to win today, gentlemen,' he continued, outwardly sombre. 'You'd make your old man very happy if you did, of course. But I do expect you to improve. *Dramatically*. I expect you to *learn* from your training. And I expect that training to be carried out as though you are at war – and not just pretending. Because at war is where we may be, very soon.'

'You think the Chinese will move in, sir?' Chen asked in a paper-thin attempt to deflect the old man's attention.

'I don't know what the Chinese will do, Lieutenant. But I'll prepare for the worst and dare the good Lord to disappoint me.'

A fraction of a second later a pure, obsidian blackness swallowed them whole.

HMAS Havoc, *1235 hours, 15 January 2021*

Captain Harry Windsor was growing used to the relatively spacious surroundings of the submarine. It was a monster, stealthy and huge, kitted out to operate far from home and for months at a time. Indeed, her clean fusion drive meant that were it not for the need to rearm the torpedo bays and refill the galley, the *Havoc* could stay out indefinitely. The Aussies told him there had been even more room before a refit had crammed a bunch of cruise missiles into their video lounge.

Oh well, he thought. *Things have gone pear-shaped all over.*

He was just happy to have enough space to work through an abbreviated series of *kata* before a scrub-down and a feed. He could hear St Clair rustling around behind him, making a God-awful racket, looking for Christ knows what.

Temper, temper. He was beginning to sound like his grandfather, a famously cranky old bugger, as he recalled fondly.

Resettling his thoughts, he worked through a full suite of *atemi waza*, striking techniques from the *Danzan* jujitsu *ryu*. After a quarter of an hour, during which the world contracted to the small circle in which he moved, he forced one last, great breath out from deep within his *hara*, bowed to the memory of his *sensei* and the spirits of the *ryu*, and cast around for Viv, who had disappeared.

Harry squeezed himself into the cramped unisex shower, washed quickly and changed into a T-shirt and sweats. It would be a few more hours before the night's exercise began, and there was no point sitting around in his kit. He made his way through to the mess and found Sergeant St Clair taunting an Australian submariner. They were discussing the chances of the locals rescuing the final cricket test of the 2021 series under the dome in Sydney. *How sweet it is*, thought Harry, *to have yet another chance to humiliate these convict upstarts.* Cricket, rugby, their laughable footy team. They simply couldn't believe they hadn't won a thing for donkey's years. Not a single fucking sausage.

'Guvnor, this idiot is offering two to one against our boys in Sydney,' cried St Clair. 'True, it's only Australian money, but I think we're morally bound to relieve him of it anyway.'

The Australian, an engineer at the end of his watch, grinned at Windsor like a hungry shark. 'If your lordship would care to back his loyal subjects?'

God, but they do take the piss, Harry thought as the lights dipped and the cook began cursing at his microwave oven. A short time later the lights returned to normal.

'Right then,' said Harry Windsor, old boy of Eton, Captain of His Majesty's Special Air Service Regiment and third in line to the British throne. 'Let's see the colour of your money, mate.'

The engineer waved over a female petty officer to hold the bets. As she bore down on the young warrior prince she gave him twenty-five thousand watts of her smile.

But before she could witness the bet, or make a move on His Studliness, the infinite dark consumed them all.

East Timor, 1238 hours, 15 January 2021

'*Allahu akbar! Allahu akbar!*'

Adil hammered out the ancient phrase, part supplication, part plea for the mercy of Almighty God, as he lay prostrate in the dust.

All around him the scrub was alive with screeching, panicking animals desperately attempting to flee the giant, swirling tsunami of light. It had filled the sky, perhaps the whole world, for just a second, but the afterimage would remain with Adil until he was old and wizened. Village children would gather at his feet decades from now, begging to be told the story of how Allah himself had cast the crusaders down into hell.

He fumbled for the canvas pack that held the laser transmitter, still imploring God's mercy. His hands trembled so much he dropped the small device four times before regaining some measure of control over his actions.

As his senses returned to him, he begged God not to punish His unworthy servant for ever doubting the wisdom of pegging him out on the side of a barren hill. What a foolish, pitiable creature he must have seemed, whining to himself about the injustice of his assignment, when all the time he was fated to bear witness to . . . to . . . what?

Adil paused. What *was* that thing? A crusader weapon, perhaps?

His heart lurched and he dropped the transmitter, scrabbling in the bag for his powered binoculars. He brought them up to his face so quickly he nearly broke his own nose. He held his breath for ten, fifteen, twenty seconds as he scoured the horizon. Strange, there was no heat haze now to shroud the fleet. And his German-made field glasses were first class, with excellent G-shock dampeners that quickly compensated for his shaking hands.

The Americans, all of the infidels, were gone. Only one large, burning piece of wreckage remained. The bow of a ship by its appearance. The crusaders had been vanquished by a miracle! And he, a simple carpenter, had seen the very hand of God as it swept them into the seventh level of hell. He let out his pent-up breath in a rush.

He returned to his small pack and had begun searching again for the transmitter to send word of his vision to Jakarta, when his training finally asserted itself. Down in the town of Dili, crusaders were spilling out onto the street like cockroaches. They, too, knew something cataclysmic had happened, and in the next few minutes they would fill the air with their electronic spiders. There was a good chance they would send armed men into the hills and fields as well. They were thorough, the crusaders. He had to concede that about them.

Drawing in a few long, deep breaths to collect his thoughts and further settle his nerves, Adil decided he had best wait for a safer moment. Only a fool would draw a nest of angry wasps upon himself. He had valuable information now, something the Caliph would certainly want to hear in person.

Allah be praised, who would have imagined that he would find himself standing before the liberator of the Caliphate? Adil quickly gathered up the meagre evidence of his stay and buried it all at the foot of the sandalwood tree where he had kept watch these last few days.

There was another cache of equipment hidden near Los Palos. He would make his way there, resuming the demeanour of a starving refugee, walking the land and looking for food, shelter and sanctuary from the Rising Jihad. He smiled at that last thought as he straightened up, stretched, and moved off down the slope, glancing back over his shoulder every now and then to the place of the blessed miracle.

2

USS Enterprise, *Task Force 16, 390 kilometres NNE Midway Island, 2239 hours, 2 June 1942*

At least he didn't have to drink the admiral's terrible coffee. Admittedly, it wasn't much fun stamping back and forth with him along the empty flight deck at night, either. For the first days of June, this was miserable weather in the northwest Pacific. With the fog so cold and dense and rain sleeting in sideways, it was enough to make Lieutenant Commander Daniel Black long for the South Pacific, where temperatures below decks could climb to well over a hundred, and touching the exposed metal topside raised painful burn blisters. But Black could take a little exposure, and the constant questioning, as long as it meant he didn't have to stomach another cup of that goddamn poison green java Admiral Raymond Spruance insisted on grinding for himself.

Black, a big, raw-boned copper miner in his former life, was Spruance's assistant ops chief in this one. He jammed his hands deep into the pockets of his old leather flying coat and turned out of the wind as he and Spruance reached the safety lights surrounding the first aircraft elevator. There had been a freak accident here just a few days ago, when Ensign Willie P West and Lieutenant 'Dusty' Kleiss were strolling the same path. Neither had heard the elevator warning signal and West had stepped abruptly off into empty space. Kleiss found himself teetering on the edge of a gaping hole, and it took him a moment to regain his balance. Having done so, he peered over, expecting to find his friend lying in a crumpled heap. Instead he found West smiling and waving from thirty feet below. He had landed on the elevator just as it started its descent, and said the sensation was like landing on a feather bed.

Commander Black didn't feel like repeating the stunt and gave himself plenty of time to turn around. Admiral Spruance veered away, too, his black leather shoes squeaking on the wet deck. It was a small thing in a way, a pair of black shoes, not really worth noting. Except that they shouldn't have been here on a flat-top. William 'Bull' Halsey, the man who *would* have been in charge of the *Enterprise* if he wasn't confined to his sickbed back at Pearl, would have worn brown shoes, because he was a flyer, not a cruiser jockey. And Halsey wouldn't have needed to constantly pound the flight deck with his officers, picking their brains about flight operations and the basics of naval air power just days before they went into battle. Because Bill Halsey had been flying planes and driving carriers for years.

The men revered him, and with good reason. When Ensign Eversole had got lost in fog on the way to attack Wake Island, Halsey had turned around the entire task force, searched for and found the downed torpedo plane, then resumed the attack a day later. Everyone agreed it was a damn pity the old man was stuck back in Pearl. It meant they were steaming into battle at Midway against a superior foe, under a man with no expertise in carrier operations at all.

During a rare break in Spruance's relentless cross-examination, Black brought up something else that had been nagging at him since they'd set out. 'It's a real shame about losing Don Lovelace.'

The admiral, who was a quiet, self-contained man – so different from the booming, good-natured Halsey – took so long in replying that Commander Black wondered if he'd even heard. The *Enterprise* was making nearly thirty knots, adding its speed to a light blustery cross-wind, and it was possible a gust might have carried away his words. But, true to form, Spruance was just mulling over the statement before fashioning a reply.

'It's a blessing we've even got the *Yorktown* at all,' he said.

That seemed harsh. Don Lovelace was the XO of Fighting 3, the *Yorktown*'s squadron of twenty-five portly but rugged F–4F Wildcats. Or he had been, till another pilot had screwed up his landing and jumped the barrier the first afternoon out of Pearl, crashing into the plane ahead and killing one of the most experienced pilots in the whole task force. The

Yorktown's VF3 was less a squadron than a pick-up team, thrown together at the last moment before the big game. They'd never flown together, and for some this would be their first time on a carrier. Lovelace was supposed to have whipped them into shape.

'It still would have been good having Lovelace.' Black shrugged. 'Zeros are gonna eat those boys up. Chew us all up, given a chance.'

'Jimmy Thach will knock them into shape,' Spruance said. 'Or close enough anyway. We have to cut the cloth to suit our budget, Commander. Pearl performed miracles getting the *Yorktown* ready in three days. I know the pilots are green, and their planes are no match for the Japs, but that doesn't matter. We have to beat them anyway.'

Spruance and Black's return journey had brought them back to the ship's island superstructure, which offered some shelter against the wind that was blowing across the deck. The rise and fall of the swell was also much less evident here. The time was coming up on 2245. They would blow tubes in a few minutes and the working day would end for most of the crew. Black was already dead tired. He had eaten breakfast at 0350.

In a few days, he knew, he'd just be dead. Or so exhausted as made no difference.

He wondered how Spruance did it. How he kept running like a wind-up toy, seemingly capable of absorbing every piece of minutia and fitting it into his grand battle scheme. They'd been discussing the relative merits of the Zero and the Wildcat, massaging the comparisons, the Zero's greater range and manoeuvrability, the Wildcat's higher ceiling, the Zero's lack of armour, the Wildcat's steel plating and self-sealing fuel tanks. The admiral turned to him now, a rare soft smile playing across his severe features.

'Still worried they might sucker-punch us again at Pearl, Commander?'

This time it was Black who was quiet for a few seconds. At a special briefing in Spruance's cabin earlier that day, he had asked the admiral what would happen if the Japs bypassed Midway and made straight for Hawaii, which lay open and defenceless. Spruance had stared at him for a full half-minute before offering his reply – that he hoped they would not. Black had been startled by that – and more than a little disturbed. Unless Spruance knew something his subordinates didn't, he was relying heavily on faith – which Black considered a poor basis for strategic planning.

The admiral seemed on the verge of saying something more now, but a sudden, ear-splitting crack knocked them both to the deck, and left them gasping for breath. Black felt as though he'd been nailed by a jab to the guts.

The gusting wind that had been tugging at their clothes died down. It was curious, though – it didn't just drop off. It stopped dead. It almost seemed to Black as if it was 'different air'. That didn't make sense, he knew, but he couldn't shake the feeling. It smelled and tasted different, too; vaguely familiar in a way, earthier, heavier. Like air in the tropics, which always seemed laden with the weight of rot and genesis.

The night had been very dark, with low cloud cover, no starlight and banks of dense fog. Even so, Black had the distinct impression of being wrapped, however briefly, in a denser, closer form of darkness. A rush of unsettling, half-formed, almost preconscious abstractions clawed at him. He had the sensation of being trapped in a tight, closed space, what he imagined it would feel like to be stuck in a downed plane as it sank in thousands of fathoms of black water.

Then he and Spruance both became aware of a rising clamour of shouts and cries coming from above. Lookouts in the superstructure, up on Vulture's Row, were screaming and gesturing wildly down to the sea on the starboard side.

'I think somebody's gone overboard,' coughed Black, still struggling for breath.

'Come on,' Spruance said with some difficulty.

They hurried forward, around the base of the island and the antiaircraft mounts, only to be confronted by a sight that stopped them cold.

'Holy shit,' said Black.

There, less than a hundred yards away, lay a ship of some sort. A foreign vessel for sure, completely alien, its bow was angled away from the *Enterprise*, opening up a gap as the two vessels ploughed through the foaming breakers. She was lit well enough that they could make out her strange lines. The decks of the vessel were mostly clear. There was an island of sorts, but it was located squarely in the centre of what would have been the runway. It was raked back, like a shark's fin, with no hard edges anywhere on its surface. Only one line of windows was visible, through which Black could make out strange glowing colours and lights, but no people.

As his mind adjusted to the outrage, he began to take in more detail. The forward decks seemed to be pockmarked with the outlines of elevators, but they were ridiculously small, each no more than a few yards across. There was one small gun emplacement, a ludicrous-looking little cannon with the same strange, raked contours as the bridge. As the angle of divergence increased and the warship pulled away, Spruance pointed to the outline of what had to be an aircraft elevator down towards the stern. But it made no sense. Any plane attempting to take off there would crash into the bizarre island on the vessel's centreline.

'Oh, Lord,' muttered Spruance as the ship peeled away at nearly thirty degrees now, revealing her stern. A Japanese ensign flew there. Not a Rising Sun, to be sure, but a red circle on a field of white.

The name printed beneath read *Siranui*, Japanese for 'unknown fires', if Black recalled correctly. He was aware of a *Kagero*-class destroyer just so named, which had been launched in June 1938. This thing, however, which was easily more than half the length of the *Enterprise*, was no *Kagero*-class bucket. It looked like something out of Buck Rogers.

'What the hell is that thing?' asked Black in the tone of voice he might have used if he'd seen a large, two-headed dog.

'I'm not sure what it is,' Spruance replied, regaining his composure, 'but I know *who* it is. Better put on your Sunday best, Commander. I think our guests have arrived early.'

As the mystery ship quietly slipped into the night, a Klaxon aboard the *Enterprise* sounded the alarm.

And then, the horizon exploded.

Suddenly they were beset by madness on all sides. To starboard, the eerie Nipponese ghost ship receded into darkness. To port, there was a volcanic eruption about ten miles away. It was a few seconds before the thunder reached their ears, but they could see clearly enough what was happening as the light of the explosion was trapped between a heaving sea and the thick scudding clouds that pressed down from above.

Black shook his head, determined to remain calm. But as his eyes darted to and fro across the surface of the ocean, his mind was overwhelmed by the monstrous visions he encountered there.

In the flat, guttering light of the distant inferno Black could see more enemy vessels, none that he recognised, most of them freakish cousins to the thing that had just peeled away from the *Enterprise*.

There was one ship – maybe a thousand yards distant – well, he simply refused to believe his own eyes. As it crested a long rolling line of swell he could have sworn the thing had two, maybe even *three* hulls. It was difficult to be sure under these conditions, but he simply could not shake the afterimage. It was either a ship with three hulls, or three ships somehow joined and operating in perfect harmony.

And randomly scattered on the crucible of the seas all around them were more products of the same Stygian foundry. Over there, he was certain, was another double-hulled monstrosity, bursting through a black wall of water. To the north lay more ships like the beast that had sidled up to them before. And there, a way off the port bow, were two flat-tops, both of them large enough to be fleet carriers. One was a real behemoth.

'Commander!'

Black was shocked out of his reverie by the harsh call.

'We've got work to do, Commander,' Spruance barked. 'A hell of a job, too, unless you want your grandchildren eating raw fish and rice balls.'

Bells rang and klaxons blared. Thousands of feet hammered on steel plating as men rushed to their stations on nearly two dozen warships.

The first gun to fire was a twenty-millimetre Oerlikon on the *Portland.* It pumped a snaking line of tracer in exactly the wrong direction. Forty-mil Bofors, pompoms and dozens of five-inch batteries soon joined it, until a whole quadrant of the sky seethed with gunfire.

Spruance and Black raced up to the bridge, tugging on helmets and vests as the big guns of the Midway Task Force began to boom. Huge muzzle flashes from eight-inch batteries lit up the night with a chaotic strobe effect. The bridge was in an uproar with a dozen different voices calling out reports, barking questions and demanding answers where – as yet – there were none.

'Get the bombers away as quickly as possible,' Spruance ordered.

'VB-6 is ready to roll, sir.'

'Coming around to two-two-three.'

The plating beneath their feet began to pitch as the big carrier swung into the wind. Black could only hope that none of their destroyer escorts would be run down by the unexpected course correction. *This is insane*, he thought, *dogfighting with twenty-thousand-ton ships.* He braced himself against a chart table and tried to make sense of the chaos around him. There were hundreds of guns firing without any sort of co-ordination. They were going to start destroying their own ships very quickly if that went on.

As soon as the thought occurred to him, it happened. The cruiser *New Orleans* attempted a ragged broadside at the spectral Japanese ship that had just appeared to starboard a few minutes earlier. The volley completely missed its target, but at least two shells slammed into an American destroyer a few hundred yards beyond. Black cursed as the little ship exploded in flames.

'We're going to need better gunnery control,' he yelled at Spruance. 'I'll get on it.'

The admiral turned away from the sailor he had been addressing and nodded brusquely. Black charged back out of the bridge, heading for the radio room.

USS Hamman*, Task Force 17, 2243 hours, 2 June 1942*

The *Sims*-class destroyer *Hamman* was nearly swamped by the wave that surged out from the giant ship that suddenly appeared eighty yards away as if from nowhere. The men on the bridge, who had all gasped at her arrival, now groaned like passengers on a roller-coaster as their vessel yawed over and threatened to roll down the face of the wave. As the *Hamman* finally swung back through the pendulum to right herself, the officer of the watch, Lieutenant (junior grade) Veni Armanno, was tossed bodily through the air and into the solid casing that housed the ship's compass, dislocating his shoulder. He swore through the tornado of pain that blew through his upper body, and wrestled himself back to his feet with his one good hand.

'You all right, sir?' Someone asked.

'Doesn't matter,' he said. 'Sound to general quarters. Get the captain up here now. Radio the *Yorktown* and find out what's happening.'

'Lieutenant,' called out a petty officer from the radio shack. 'We've just had a message from the *Enterprise*, sir. It's the Japs . . .'

Armanno couldn't make out the next words. They were lost in the volley of curses from the bridge crew.

'Put a sock in it!' he said loudly.

Gesturing insistently, the petty officer announced an order that had come from task force command.

'We're to engage the enemy, sir.'

'Captain True's been injured, sir,' reported another seaman. 'Lieutenant Earls is on his way.'

'Get me the gunnery officer,' Armanno ordered. 'We haven't got much, but let's give her everything we do have. Helm, put another four hundred yards between that thing and us. We'll stick some torpedoes into her, see how she likes that.'

The deck began to tilt again as the destroyer came around on her new heading, plunging into a hectic crosshatched swell. Armanno felt dizzy with the pain in his shoulder. He desperately wanted to crawl outside and prop himself up against a bulkhead until the ship's surgeon could tend to him, but the vast iron mountain of the enemy ship – *Where in hell did it come from?* – nailed him in place.

'Guns ready, sir.'

Armanno didn't hesitate.

'Fire!'

All four of the ship's five-inch mounts roared as

one. Three blooms of dirty fire blossomed on the sheer steel wall of the target.

One dud, thought Armanno as he heard the front and rear twenty-millimetre cannons open up, painting the walls of that towering fortress with whipping lines of tracer. A dazzling shower of sparks fell to the sea like fireflies, marking the impact of the tracers.

The men around him cheered as another brace of five-inch shells screamed across the short distance between them. All four exploded this time. Armanno was certain he could hear the steel rain of shrapnel on the *Hamman*'s plating. He could feel his muscles tensing as he urged the ship's boilers to give them more steam. He needed to get far enough away to use the torpedo tubes. Their target had to be a Jap carrier, probably the *Akagi*, she was so damn big.

How the hell did she get here?

Doesn't matter, he told himself. They'd snuck up on them again. Just like at Pearl. But this time they'd been stupid enough to get into a street brawl with Veni Armanno. He might have grown up on an olive grove outside of Santa Monica, but his blood was still Sicilian, and it boiled as quickly as anyone's from the old country.

'Pour it on, boys!' he yelled into the speaker tube connecting the bridge to gunnery control. 'Give 'em hell. Just a little bit longer and we'll be able to stick a few fish up Tojo's ass.'

Armanno turned back to the fantastic scene that lay outside the blast windows, just as another salvo ripped into the side of the enemy carrier. It was like riding out a hurricane, minus the wind and rain. The whole of the ocean was lit with lightning flashes as hundreds of guns hammered at the Japs. Thunder rolled over them constantly, and the sea was thick with erupting geysers of foam and water, illuminated from within by the explosions that raised them.

'Lookit that fuggin' thing would you,' yelled a voice thickened by years of smoking.

Armanno grabbed a pair of binoculars and followed the seaman's pointing finger. The world was even more confused and unstable when viewed through the glasses. They emphasised every movement of the violently pitching destroyer. Still, he managed to catch a few brief glimpses of a ship that reminded him of a giant manta ray slipping across the surface of the ocean. It was hard to tell, being thrown about so much, but there didn't appear to be any guns on the deck. He wedged in tighter against the corner of the bridge and tried to keep the sleek, alien shape steady within the field of the glasses. The twinned lens circles shuddered as the *Hamman*'s two forward turrets coughed long spears of flame and smoke into the night again.

The Japs weren't firing at all, at least not that he could make out.

'What the hell is this?' Armanno asked, half to himself.

'Lieutenant, we're coming up on range for the torpedo launch.'

'Okay,' he said, dragging his attention back to the mammoth carrier that was still blotting out half the sky. It was weird, the way the Japs just weren't fighting back. Not a single round came from anywhere along its flank.

Maybe they haven't seen us, he told himself. *Just as well.*

'Arm the port-side tubes,' he called.

'Arm the port-side tubes!'

'Torpedoes armed!'

'Torpedoes armed, Lieutenant.'

Armanno waited half a second, expecting the executive officer or even the captain to appear. It seemed like a very long half-second.

'*Fire!*' he called out at last.

3

HMS Trident, *2241 hours, 2 June 1942*

Captain Karen Halabi, commander of HMS *Trident*, had never seen anything like it before. It was like looking into a doll's house. For a few short moments, before the seas rushed in, the vessel's internal spaces were completely exposed, as though a vengeful deity had sliced off the bow with a knife, had made it vanish, like a profane magic trick.

She was certain she was dreaming, and yet sure she couldn't be. She had spilled a mug of hot coffee on her leg and the pain had jolted her to her senses. Her senses, however, had presented her with a nightmare.

She was slumped in her command chair, a giant burn blister already rising on her thigh. Around her the bridge crew were dead or unconscious. The bright light of the tropical day was gone, swallowed by an oily blackness. And four or five hundred metres away, on a collision course off her starboard bow, was the helicopter carrier HMS *Fearless*. It had been, well, 'lopped' seemed the right word. She was paralysed, staring at a cutaway diagram from a children's book.

Except that the 'diagram' was three-dimensional,

and it was moving towards her. And the burn on her leg was real, and the feeling in her body was returning with a painful surge of pins and needles, the worst she had ever known. She realised, in the methodical part of her mind, that if she didn't put pedal to the metal they'd all be dead in less than a minute, when the carrier ran right over them.

Halabi bit down on a gasp and willed her hand towards the touch screen. She drew a deep breath and pushed through the excruciating tingling, a sensation akin to a blast of white noise tearing at raw synapses. Not trusting her fingers, she struck repeatedly at the screen with the heel of her palm. The ship's Combat Intelligence, intuiting that its user had suffered some drastic battle wound, adjusted accordingly. The buttons on the screen grew larger, the choices more restricted, which was fine by her. All she wanted was another twenty knots.

A series of awkward blows to specific points on the screen drew more power from the fusion stacks and dumped it straight into the *Trident*'s three Rolls-Royce aqua jets. The acceleration threw Halabi back into her chair. The ship's CI, alerted to the possibility of disaster, independently powered up a suite of sensors. On the screen before Halabi's eyes, Nemesis arrays began a full power survey of the threat bubble, cataloguing and prioritising a list of potential menaces. It was a long list, but right at the top was the *Fearless*, closing from the north-east quarter.

The CI reviewed Halabi's actions and found them to be appropriate, but decided to fatten the margin for error. It released the codes for the trimaran's supercavitating system.

Below and just above the waterline thousands of pores opened in the radar-absorbent skin of the ship, releasing a bath of small bubbles, a foam of water vapour and air, which surrounded the *Trident*'s three hulls so perfectly that very little *liquid* water remained in contact with the ship. The effect was to reduce the viscous drag on her keels by ninety-seven per cent. The *Trident* leaped forwards again, carving through mist now rather than water. Her speed climbed quickly to one hundred and five knots and three giant fantails of spray sprang up from her stern.

The CI also began monitoring the data stream from the crew members' biochip implants, since it was likely that a percentage of them would have been injured by falls during the unannounced acceleration. It quickly drew the conclusion that the entire ship's complement had been struck down by a malady of unknown origin, and dispatched an instruction via Shipnet. Based on the closest analogue that could be found, the order was given to immediately dump .05 ml of Promatil from the crew members' spinal inserts directly into their bloodstreams.

Captain Halabi felt the soothing warmth of a drug flush as it crawled up her spine. The unpleasant fullbody burning sensation subsided, along with the associated dizziness and nausea.

Her officers and junior ranks began to stir and groan around her, but she was transfixed by the ghastly spectacle just outside her bridge window. It was definitely the *Fearless*. She was simply unable to imagine how it could have been damaged in such a catastrophic fashion.

The metal outline of the ship's cross-section glowed as though white hot. Halabi could see the cavernous hangars high above, with aircraft and equipment already sliding towards the abyss as the ship tilted forward, scooping up water. To either side of the hangars small offices and wardrooms were visible, again reminding her of a doll's house with the front wall removed.

Halabi could clearly see human beings in some of those rooms, moving frantically, trying in vain to escape. She dimly recognised a painful hammering sensation as her heartbeat, but it seemed far away. She had friends on that ship, and any of them could be the anonymous stick figures desperately throwing themselves off the leading edge, plunging to their deaths. The terrible scene recalled images from her childhood of office workers falling through the air in New York, and later in London and Tokyo.

As her own ship passed squarely in front of it, the *Fearless* seemed to lean towards her, as if trying to reach out and take her down too. Her lips worked soundlessly, searching for words, but none came in the face of such horror. She could see a virtual tsunami already rolling down into the belly of the carrier.

At the Naval War College she had studied the sinking of an ocean-going ferry that had inexplicably left its bow doors open on a cross-Channel run. A mountainous wall of water had poured in and surged towards the stern. The weight had actually lifted the bows out of the sea for a brief moment, but fluid dynamics demanded that the wave travel back when it hit the obstruction of the ferry's rear end, and so the pendulum had swung back and dug the bow even deeper into the ocean. Halabi imagined for a split second that the *Fearless* might rear out of the waves and smash down on her in a similar fashion, but she quickly dismissed the idea. The densely packed lower decks of such a ship would not permit the same free flow of water.

Darkness threatened to rush in on her again as the *Trident* cleared the impact zone and passed safely through to the far side, but with a deep breath she fought it off.

'Posh, can you link me to the CI on *Fearless*?' asked Halabi. 'I need damage reports and vision.'

The *Trident*'s Combat Intelligence affirmed the request and four screens in front of Halabi winked into life, displaying video from the carrier. Halabi grimaced at the scenes of screaming casualties and blind panic.

Damage reports scrolled down another screen, too quickly to read, as the *Fearless* plunged on towards her doom, millions of litres of cold seawater roaring in through the gigantic sucking wound, destabilising the vessel and generating a range of forces her engineers had never contemplated. Halabi watched in horror as immense tonnages of water began to back up against the densely filled spaces of the lower decks, putting a brake on the ship's forward impetus.

The Mercedes express boilers, delivering 320,000 horsepower to four shafts, pushed hard against the phenomenal resistance. *Fearless* began to slew around and tilt, causing the water already inside to shift sideways. It burst through aviation and ordnance stores on the third deck and into the air-frame workshop. Under pressure, water even began to rise to the main deck, coursing into officers' quarters and the forward elevator pit. Roaring along both port and starboard passageways on the second deck, the torrent flooded electrical and radio stores, more officers' quarters and washrooms and the crew's mess.

Halabi winced as an ocean of icy-cold brine reached the boiler rooms and sluiced over and into the red-hot furnaces and a cataclysm ensued. The resulting explosion of itself wasn't powerful enough to destroy the ship, or what remained of it, but it triggered an escalating series of secondary blasts, beginning in the armoury on the third deck starboard side, ripping down into a missile store just forward of the drone control room, and from there into the giant avgas tanks.

HMS *Fearless* disintegrated in one titanic blast.

Three-quarters of her mass disappeared in the blinding white flash, which could be seen ten kilometres away.

The *Trident* rode out the shock wave with little more than a rude jolting. She sat very low in the water, resting on three hulls and boasting of no superstructure other than a relatively small teardrop bridge, so the blast swept over the destroyer like a flood surge over a smooth pebble. The ship's CI made some course and speed changes, but mostly the *Trident* relied on her inherent design strengths to ride out the storm.

While her ship may have been little bothered by the spectacle, Halabi was stunned. There couldn't possibly be any survivors. Every man and woman aboard the *Fearless* had surely perished, atomised by the blast. Her mind reeled as it tried to find some semblance of explanation for the disaster. *What could do that to a ship? And who would do it?* She had no immediate answer. But she did have her duty, and that was to fight back.

As her bridge crew began to recover, she repositioned herself in the command chair and reached out to the nearest touch screen. The Promatil dose had eased her illness, or the worst of it anyway, and she tapped out a few orders on the screen, resuming full control of the Royal Navy trimaran. She left the Nemesis arrays collecting data at full power and delegated acute crisis management to the CI.

'Permission to unsafe weapons, Captain Halabi?' the system's voice purred in her ear.

'Permission granted, Posh,' she answered, placing her palm on the DNA reader in the chair's armrest. 'Verification code Osprey Three Niner Lima X-ray Tango Four.'

'Code verified, Captain Halabi. Weapons hot.'

The CI's voice was a flawless imitation of Lady Beckham's, a remnant from the previous ship's captain, who was – in Halabi's opinion – an emotionally arrested Yorkshireman with an unhealthy fixation on pre-millennial pop culture. On taking command she had determined to reset the speech software to RN Standard. However, she had been made aware, subtly but swiftly, that the former pop princess was considered a much-loved member of the crew, and her deletion in favour of the bland, mid-Atlantic voice to which the CI defaulted would be considered akin to a death in the family. So Lady Beckham had stayed on as the voice of the *Trident*, and after eighteen months Halabi had secretly grown quite fond of her.

'Mr McTeale,' she said, addressing her XO, 'are you in any shape to take the conn?'

The ropey Scotsman bit down on the bile that was threatening to rise past his gorge. 'Aye ma'am.'

'Fine, then. I'm on my way to CIC. While in transit, I'll be online via Shipnet. When I've resumed control from down there, shut up shop and join me. All hands below. The *Fearless* is gone. Our holiday cruise is over. Guns are hot and the CI has Level

One autonomy. Any of the ship's crew who remain without Promatil inserts will need to be treated as quickly as possible. Please see to it that the surgeon is informed. Posh has the requisite dosages. IV, not dermal patches. We need everybody vertical ASAP. Sound to general quarters.'

'Aye aye.'

As the ship's alarms began to call her company to battle, Halabi limped out of the bridge through the light-curtain and headed for the stairwell that led down into the *Trident*'s central hull. Beneath her feet she could feel the vessel reach a standard cruising speed of thirty-five knots. The seas were running at one and a half metres on a three-metre swell, enough to impart a significant roll, even with the trimaran's inherent stability and wave-piercing form. It slowed Halabi's progress, but not drastically.

The hexagonal space of the Combat Centre was bathed in a quiet blue light. It was unexpectedly soothing after the neural shock of the last few minutes. McTeale had proven himself as efficient as ever. Medics were shooting up a sysop with Promatil as Halabi entered. One approached her with that disapproving expression physicians have been perfecting for thousands of years.

'Begging your pardon, ma'am,' he said, 'but Commander McTeale informs me you have a serious burn on your leg –'

'I don't have time for gel, Andrews,' she warned.

'Pain relief, then.' The medic tapped the screen

of his flexipad a few times, effectively ignoring the captain's objections. 'Surgeon's orders, ma'am. He's authorised a local-effect anaesthetic pip.'

Before Halabi could speak again, she felt the mild tingle of a spinal syrette spitting its dose, followed by the delicious warmth of an analgesic balm washing over the affected area.

It was only the second time in her career she'd experienced palliative intervention via spinal insert, but it confirmed the wisdom of prohibiting self-administration. Even with the greatest will in the world, if you had the option to hit yourself up with this stuff every morning, the temptation would be to never get out of bed.

'Thank you, Andrews,' she said. 'But that *will* be all. Please proceed with the treatment schedule. We're going to need all hands on station in the next few minutes.'

'Aye, ma'am.'

Halabi quickly surveyed the CIC. Twenty-two specialists were strapped into large, comfortable airline-style seats. Massive touch-screen workstations hovered in front of them. The *Trident*'s commander made her way directly to the supervising officer, Lieutenant Commander Marc Howard, who was examining the holobloc with a fiercely censorious air.

'Well, Commander, what sort of a hellish mess have we got ourselves in now?'

'A right cock-up by the look of it, ma'am. Makes no sense at all. None. Have a gander for yourself. The

Fearless is gone. We've detected just three survivors in the water. And the rest of the task force is scattered to buggery.'

Halabi carefully examined the jet-black, freestanding holobloc. Floating inside was a three-dimensional positional hologram, a scaled-down real-time feed of the battlespace around the destroyer for a sixty-nautical-mile radius. The rest of the task force was represented by eerily realistic but oversized spectral miniatures that cut across a blue sea surface. A few centimetres below the rest floated the submarine HMAS *Havoc*. The Multinational Force, which should have been arrayed in an orderly fashion around the flat-tops *Clinton* and *Kandahar*, was instead scattered to hell and back.

The captain shook her head in frank amazement. Task Force ships were making for all points of the compass. That, in its own way, was more unsettling than the sight of the doomed helicopter carrier had been. More disturbing still were the dozen or more phantom vessels hopelessly mixed in amongst them. None of these registered any ID signal, and Posh hadn't been able to tag them with any designator hack other than Unidentified Vessel 01 through to – Halabi checked the readout on the data cube suspended above the hologram – UIV 24.

'My word, Commander. A cock-up indeed.'

'Aye, Captain. Three carriers of some sort. Four heavy gun platforms. A couple of replenishment ships. And a swarm of little 'uns. Destroyers or frigates, I suppose, but like nothing I've ever seen outside of a museum. *And* we seem to come up short of a few friendlies. Besides *Fearless, Vanguard* is off the 'bloc. *Dessaix* is missing, the nukes and the *Amanda L Garrett*, and those Indonesian tubs.'

'Destroyed?'

'No way to tell. Just missing, ma'am. Without trace.'

'Find them.' Halabi pursed her lips for a second before casting an inquiry over her shoulder to a young lieutenant situated at a nearby station. 'Elint, what are we getting from these unidentified vessels?'

The young sysop, a Jamaican-Welsh woman of unusual beauty, was burning holes in the screen with her intense stare. 'Not a lot of emcon, Captain. But then there's not a lot of emission to control, by the look of it. We've been painted by radar once or twice and it just slipped off the RAM skin, but we collected a sample for analysis. It's primitive stuff. Almost Stone Age. A pirate barge can buy better off the shelf in Bangkok.

'Sigint are gathering a lot of uncoded, unscrambled, basic radio transmissions . . . English language . . . but um . . . pretty weird.'

'Pretty weird is *not* good enough, Lieutenant Waverton. We're dying here. What exactly do you mean?'

The woman hid her chagrin well. 'I mean weird, Captain. Unusual, unexplained. Beyond standard parameters. I can give you a raw sample if you wish.'

'Do so.'

The lieutenant's dark, slender fingers danced over a giant touch screen to her left and the data cube's Bang & Olufsen speakers began to emit a harsh burst of static. It flared and faded as the signal intercept was washed clean of interference. Voices came through. Confused, loud, angry, scared. Most of the CIC crew were too deeply involved in their own stations to bother with the broadcast, but the intel sysops turned to listen, even though they could have taken the sound channel through individual headphones. They heard American voices, educated, military and . . . something else.

Halabi focused on the audio stream, which seemed to have been acquired from the fire control facility of an unidentified vessel. The speaker was demanding to know what the hell he was shooting at, where they had come from. And he wanted to know if they were Japs. Halabi twirled an index finger and the lieutenant flipped into another channel. A ship-to-ship transmission this time. The same burst of static subsided into quantum clear audio.

'*Hamman*, *Hughes* and *Morris* to pick up survivors . . .'

'*Hamman*'s engaged a Jap carrier . . . she's right on top of her. They could put a few fish in . . .'

'*Russel* or *Gwin* then . . .'

Halabi twirled her fingers again. Lieutenant Waverton ripped out a new line of instructions and another channel came up.

‘. . . ayday, mayday. This is the *Astoria*. We have been rammed. We have been rammed . . .’

She snapped a finger now, apologising at the same time. ‘You were right, Lieutenant. *Weird* is the best word for it.’

‘Where’s the hologram feed coming from, Commander?’ she went on, motioning for Waverton to cut the audio and turning back to the holobloc.

‘We’ve lost a few of our task force resources, Captain. This is feeding from three drones at six thousand metres. Deep in the cloud cover. Posh is drawing from memory to project some of the task force assets, and skin sensors for the rest. The audio we’re stealing ourselves through the mast-mounted system and bridge skin.’

Halabi was becoming acutely aware of how quickly things were unravelling around her.

‘Mr Howard, can we raise Task Force command?’

‘No, ma’am. Channels are open and secure. CIs are in contact. But no human operators respond to hail. We’ve tried independent hails to each Task Force ship, all with the same result. We’re on our own for the moment.’

‘They’re out, just like we were,’ Halabi concluded. ‘Have Posh talk to the other CIs, send all the data we have about the illness, the bio-attack, or whatever it was, and details on the Promatil treatment. Boot up the Cooperative Battle Link with any surviving compatible assets.’

She paused, working through the problem in her

mind. Each national component of the Multinational Force was fitted for Cooperative Battle Management. Their CIs could be laser-linked, allowing the entire group to fight as a single entity.

It sounded fine in principle, but politics and human nature couldn't hope to approximate such elegance. Mission programming denied her the ability to take control of any vessels other than the small Australian contingent and her sister ships – HMS *Vanguard*, which was missing in action, possibly sunk, and *Fearless*, which was definitely gone. It was *stupid*, in her view, but the Americans and French in particular were quite touchy about that sort of thing. They didn't like taking directions from anyone but their own. She feared it was going to cost a good number of them their lives in the next few minutes.

On the other hand you could build a snowman in hell the day the Royal Navy agreed to let an Indonesian captain have the run of its warships. So perhaps the Americans and the French had a point. It was just a little insulting to be cast in that sort of company.

While Halabi was racing through her options, Howard relayed a series of orders through his headset, and a row of systems operators who had been relatively quiet suddenly leaned into their stations. Six pairs of hands flew over touch screens and virtual keyboards. Laser nodes embedded in the skin of the *Trident* pulsed, and thousands of metres away smart-skin arrays on two Australian ships, the troop cat *Moreton Bay* and the littoral assault ship *Ipswich*, picked up the photon storm of microburst infrared laser transmissions.

The first data set was an encoded authenticator, which convinced the ship's innately suspicious CIs to accept that their companion vessel was legitimately opening a Cooperative Battle Link. It authorised the CIs to power up all defensive systems and to deploy in protection of task force assets. The next photon shower advised of a possible bio-weapon attack, and gave the recommended response. The last packet of data contained a synopsis of the evolving situation as it was understood by the *Trident*. Unfortunately, this transmission was quite thin.

Half a second later the destroyer repeated the process with a tone link to the Australian submarine HMAS *Havoc*. It returned a surprising acknowledgment from a human operator. *Havoc* was standing to, targets plotted, awaiting authority to release weapons.

'Captain Willet on Fleetnet for you,' Lieutenant Waverton announced.

'At last,' said Halabi.

A screen above the holobloc winked on. The commander of the Australian sub, looking thin-lipped and grim, nodded a curt hello.

'Captain Willet.'

'Captain Halabi. My apologies for the delay in responding. My comms operator was having some sort of seizure, and he wasn't alone. We've got a terrible mess down here. Some sort of neural attack.

The CI took over the initial response. Do we have hostile contact?'

'We have contacts, as you can see, which we have to assume are hostile,' replied Halabi. '*Fearless* has been destroyed, but God only knows by what. I've never seen anything like it. Can you put your intel people onto the data package we just sent? I'm afraid it makes no sense and we have very little time. It's getting quite ugly up here.'

Willet's eyes registered the shock of losing the helicopter carrier, but she said nothing about it, nodding brusquely and signing off. 'Done. We'll get back to you ASAP.'

Relieved to have Willet sharing the burden, Halabi resumed her inspection of the holobloc while the crew took care of business. *One of the first things they teach you in captain school*, she reminded herself, *is never to look like circumstances have the better of you.* But she couldn't help quietly blowing out her cheeks in exasperation. Truly, there was nothing about their situation that made sense. Nothing at all.

The surviving task force ships may have been scattered, but none was making any apparent efforts to rectify that. Each ship, whichever direction it was headed, was maintaining ten knots, as they had been before being struck down.

The three exceptions were the *Trident*, which was circling the flaming hulk of her dying sister ship; Willet's sub, which had dialled back to two knots and was lying stealthed near the centre of the unidentified fleet; and finally, Halabi noted, the American Nemesis cruiser *Leyte Gulf*, which seemed to be in serious trouble.

'Marc, pull in close on the *Leyte Gulf*. One thousand metres virtual.'

The hologram shimmered momentarily, then re-formatted. The image well filled with the shape of the American cruiser and another vessel, which appeared to have rammed . . . *No, that isn't right*, she thought. *It's been . . . what, superimposed?*

'Is this a clean feed?'

The commander consulted the data cube, interrogating a series of screens before nodding the affirmative.

'Systems are five by five, Captain. Boards green. No overlapping, no ghosting or echo effects.'

Halabi felt as if something spiky had lodged in her mind. The two ships were *fused*, presenting an impression of scissor blades opened at nearly forty-five degrees. This would account for the voice intercepts, the panicky radio calls about a ramming. But this was no collision. The blade of the *Leyte Gulf*'s bow projected clean and sharp beyond the flanks of the other ship. There was no crushed or broken metal, no crumpled deck composite. Nothing to indicate that two objects of considerable mass had made any sort of violent, forcible contact.

'Something else, ma'am. The feeds from the drones and skin systems are clean, but that's the *only* intel we're taking. I can't access any satellite links.

They all appear to be down. Military and civilian.'

'Did somebody kill the satellites, or just the links?' she asked, compartmentalising the flicker of real fear that Howard's report sparked. It was far more likely that something had severed the *Trident*'s links, rather than taken out approximately twenty-three thousand separate satellites.

The CIC boss rechecked the *Trident*'s own systems, then had Lieutenant Waverton crosscheck his findings. Marc Howard wasn't prone to histrionics, but when he finally replied, Halabi easily picked up the anxiety in his voice and the set of his features.

'Ship links are fine, Captain. Posh also interrogated the other CIs for the same results. They can't access *any* satellite feeds. Weather birds, comms, media, they're all offline.'

Halabi threw a glance at the two monitors that normally pumped out CNN and BBC World News. The screens were blue, with only two words displayed in plain white type.

NO SIGNAL.

'I suppose GPS is gone, too, then,' she said without emotion.

'That's correct, ma'am.'

'Captain Halabi,' an ensign called out. 'We've acquired significant and increasing volumes of naval gunfire. Some of it incoming. Basic munitions, nothing augmented. It hardly seems directed at all. Laser packs are cycling through the priority targets, but there's a lot of it, ma'am. They just neutralised a very large volley from two platforms. Posh determines that *Siranui* was the target. Metal Storm will be coming online soon.'

As if to punctuate this statement, they heard the first clip from the *Trident*'s secondary Close-In Weapons System tear into the night. Even though the CIC was sheltered deep in the central hull, there was a quick metallic ripping noise as seven hundred and thirty-four projectiles were vomited from two concentric, counter-rotating muzzle rings. This was caseless ammunition, fired electronically rather than by percussion, using a square-shaped combustible propellant wrapped around a fifty-grain bullet. The propellant burned bright yellow so that the effect, when viewed with the naked eye, suggested a small comet leaving the stubby gun mount and streaking away on a thin stream of light, to explode upon contact with its designated target.

After the first clip, further loads were triggered every five to fifteen seconds. Halabi and Howard exchanged a look. Metal Storm was meant to deal with missile swarms, which very rarely consisted of more than twenty or thirty targets. There seemed to be *hundreds* of warheads assaulting their protective cocoon at that moment. If they allowed this to continue, they would quickly deplete their defensive stocks.

Halabi nodded at the holobloc.

'I want you to pull in close on that ship, Commander, the one that seems to have tangled with *Leyte*

Gulf. Best we know what we're dealing with *before* we deal with it.'

Howard quickly adjusted the magnification, zooming in to a virtual height of only sixty metres above the heavily damaged bridge of the vessel, before panning down its length to the stern, where the drones' low-light amplification lenses had no trouble rendering a crisp, clear monochrome view of the Stars and Stripes.

As more than a dozen pairs of eyes focused on the scene, Captain Halabi drew in her breath with a hiss. The *Leyte Gulf* had, indeed, become entangled with a vintage warship of some sort, and as they watched the rear turret of the old-time cruiser tracked around to bear on the stern of the *Gulf*.

'Weapons!' Halabi barked out.

'Aye, Captain,' replied a brusque Glaswegian voice.

'Can we get a laser pod to lock on that rear gun turret?'

The chief weapons sysop, Lieutenant Guy Wodrow, frantically worked his laser station, but the grim set of his mouth gave the answer away.

'Sorry, Captain, but we're directly blocked by the *Leyte Gulf* herself. The *Moreton Bay*, too. *Success* has a clear shot, but her laser packs are fully engaged for the next five to six seconds.'

At that moment, weapons fire erupted in the holobloc image. Halabi spoke in a flat monotone. 'It doesn't matter now.'

She watched without registering any emotion as the smoke cleared from the rear deck of the *Leyte Gulf*. Or what was left of it.

HMAS Havoc, *2245 hours, 2 June 1942*

He found Captain Willet hovering over the holobloc, chewing on her bottom lip, which Harry recognised as a definite warning sign. In fact, the submarine captain looked ill. Her features were gaunt. Dark smudges stood out under her eyes, and her face had an unhealthy malarial tint. He knew he didn't look much better. Nobody he'd passed on his way up from the mess did.

Willet was deeply engaged in a conversation with the boat's Chief Petty Officer, an old navy man with faded tattoos covering most of his forearms and the backs of both hands. The *Havoc*'s CO waved the English warrior prince over to the impromptu O Group. Harry caught the last part of a question Willet had directed to her intel boss, Lieutenant Amanda Lohrey.

'What have we got then, Amanda? Lost Chinese? Javanese pirates?'

But there was only an embarrassed silence to answer her. Nobody seemed able to find the words to explain what the holobloc – and their own eyes – were telling them.

'Well?' pressed the *Havoc*'s captain, who could see

the display as well as anyone. She looked from one person to the next.

Her chief petty officer coughed, almost apologetically, but still said nothing.

'C'mon, Chief,' she coaxed. 'Give it up for your old lady.'

CPO Roy Flemming blew out his cheeks and showed Willet his open palms. 'Well, skipper, I'm only saying what I see, is all, and that doesn't mean anything, it's just what I see, okay? But that? That looks like a *New Orleans* class heavy cruiser, US Navy, vintage 1934. Three eight-inch turrets, two up front, or there would be, and one at the rear, two funnels, eight boilers – very environmentally unfriendly, by the way – Greenpeace would have a fucking cow. Just under six hundred feet in length. Thirteen thousand tonnes in the old scale. Carried a crew of between eleven and twelve hundred . . . I only know because of my models.'

Willet returned the chief's slightly belligerent look with a level gaze. Everybody knew of Flemming's unfortunate obsession with model building. Of the thirty-nine souls on board, only the newest arrivals and the fleetest of foot had avoided becoming trapped in a long and involved lecture on the subject. Even sitting third in line to the throne had provided no protection, as Harry had discovered at great length. Willet, however, could pull rank to avoid such an entanglement, so she smiled, just a little, and nodded at the strange image of the conjoined ships.

'Thanks, Chief. That's what I see too. Right off a history stick. Except for that Nemesis cruiser poking out of it.'

Harry, still tingling from a Promatil flush, kept his own counsel, and the other submariners who had gathered in front of the 'bloc remained silent as well. Willet seemed inordinately calm, poised there in her grey coveralls. Lieutenant Lohrey, her intel chief, was swallowing frequently. And the boat's XO, Commander Conrad Gray, seemed unable to blink, only staring fixedly at the display. Aside from Willet, only Flemming, the oldest, saltiest member of the crew, seemed less than completely bewildered. He just looked pissed off. And he always looked pissed off, in Harry's opinion, so what was to notice?

'Is that the *Leyte Gulf*?' asked Harry, for want of anything better to say.

'Aye,' said Flemming. 'And she's been well mounted.'

A seaman spoke up from a bank of workstations that lay beyond the periscope. 'Flash traffic on Fleetnet, Captain Willet. *Trident*'s CI with another data burst.'

'About fucking time,' muttered Flemming.

'Language, Chief,' Willet scolded gently. 'We have royalty present.'

'Oh, for fuck's sake!' Harry muttered, rolling his eyes.

'Opinions, suggestions?' asked Willet, throwing the floor open to her officers and guest. 'Clock's ticking. Chief Flemming, you care to guess why a museum piece would suddenly sail off a memory stick and do something as perverse as that?' She nodded towards the ethereal copy of the *Leyte Gulf* and the old cruiser.

'No, ma'am,' he answered. 'I would not.'

'You figure it has anything to do with the mace strike, or whatever it was, a few minutes ago?'

'Seems likely.'

'You think the Chinese pulled something tricky?'

'No idea, Captain. Can't think of anyone else to blame, though.'

'You think we're in the shit?'

'There's every chance in the world of that, ma'am.'

'I think so too, Chief.' She sighed.

Everybody stared endlessly at the hologram as though they were trying to decipher a challenging puzzle. While they were thus engaged, Willet pulled her personal flexipad out of a breast pocket in her coveralls and tapped out a command. A panel of the data cube switched from a scrolling text readout to an old black-and-white two-dimensional photograph.

'That looks just like the ship in the 'bloc,' said Harry.

'It *is* the ship in the 'bloc,' replied a sombre Flemming. 'The USS *Astoria*. CA-34. I've got her mounted at home in the billiards room. My Savo Island display. Along with the *Vincennes*, the *Quincy*, *Chicago* and *Canberra*. That last one was ours,' he added, looking straight at Harry. 'HMAS *Canberra*. Sunk in Iron

Bottom Sound at the Battle of Savo Island, 9 August, 1942.'

Nobody said anything in reply. Harry simply stared at the holobloc as though it might be booby-trapped. The naval personnel looked by turns confused, intrigued and sick.

'All right then,' Willet said, sharply enough to snap everyone out of their daze. 'Weapons!'

'Yes, Captain!'

'Give me firing solutions for the forward tubes focused on all non-task-force vessels. Do not, I repeat, do *not* arm the torpedoes. But full countermeasures are authorised.

'Comms?'

'Aye, Captain?'

'Reopen a link to the *Trident*. When they have a spare second, I need to confer with Captain Halabi. Keep hailing our own ships and fleet command. Intel?'

'Yes, ma'am.'

'Assets?'

'We have links intact fleet-wide, Captain,' said Lieutenant Lohrey. 'We're streaming from the drones, mast mounts, and topside Nemesis arrays. We've lost some airborne feed, and all the satellites.'

'Start farming it out, Lieutenant. When you have a clue, get back to me.'

The intel boss raised a finger, just like a child in class. 'Captain? The *Nagoya* is missing as well. There's no floating datum point, no debris of any kind. But fleetwide arrays logged signal deviance similar to the brownout incident just prior to the neural event that seems to have taken out the surface elements.'

Willet clamped down on a flash of anger. 'Well, that's just excellent,' she said quietly. 'Okay, good job, detail somebody down that rabbit hole. Captain Windsor, care to make yourself useful?'

'Yes, ma'am,' said Harry.

'I'd like you to go with Chief Flemming, find yourselves a console somewhere quiet and call up the archives. See if you can figure out what that ship, the *Astoria*, is doing here.'

Flemming nodded at Harry. 'After you, m'lord.'

'Stow it, Salty.'

'Captain!' cried Lieutenant Lohrey. 'We have a situation just off the *Clinton*. Torpedoes in the water.'

The image in the holobloc re-formed. The *Leyte Gulf* and the *Astoria* disappeared, supplanted by the American flagship and one small, antique warship.

'Jeez, what a tin can,' someone said.

'That tin can's about to slice open a fusion-powered supercarrier,' Flemming said.

'Weapons!' cried Captain Willet. 'Can we intercept the torpedoes?'

'No, ma'am. They're too far away.'

'Okay. Lock tubes three and four on the hostile. Arm the warheads. Fire on my mark.'

'Aye, ma'am.'

Harry couldn't stop his mouth from opening, but he stayed an objection to the order. This wasn't his ship. He wasn't even a sailor. He pressed his lips closed.

Willet followed the track of the torpedoes as they moved towards the task force flagship. Harry felt genuine pity for her as she shook her head and made her decision.

'Fire,' she said quietly but firmly.

Harry watched as the weapons sysop tapped two fingers on a touch screen. He wasn't even sure he felt the shots as they left the tube.

'Torpedoes away, ma'am.'

'The *Clinton*'s responding to hail on channel twelve, Captain,' said the communications officer.

'Warn them they have incoming.'

As the submariners around Harry began to move faster and communicate in shorthand technical terms he only vaguely understood, he noticed another element as it entered the tableau of the holobloc.

'Is that a plane?' he asked.

The men and women around the holobloc froze.

'It looks like a suicide bomber,' said Willet.

4

USS Hillary Clinton, *2249 hours, 2 June 1942*

'They're firing at us?' snorted Kolhammer.

Before anyone could answer, the sound of distant sledgehammer blows rang through the bridge.

'Jesus! They *are* shooting at us!' said Kolhammer. He started to shake his head, but a jag of pain stopped him cold. An ugly stain was settling into his shirt where he'd vomited a few moments earlier, but he paid it no heed. Commander Judge was doubled over and dry retching. Half the flag-bridge crew was covered in their own bile, and one or two had lost control of their bowels – if his sense of smell hadn't failed him. So much else had – even daylight, it seemed. A deep void had enveloped the task force, and something had sailed out of it to attack them. Arrhythmic flickers of fire and lightning lit the darkened sea surface in stuttering monochrome.

His bridge was a disaster area. It hadn't taken a hit, but sailors lay everywhere. Some were passed out with their eyes open, putting out REMs like victims of a psywar experiment. Others stood by their stations, their stiff, unnatural stance and glassy stares giving away how much effort that took. One man convulsed repeatedly in front of a large silicon graphics display until Commander Judge, composing himself for a moment, grabbed him by the shoulders and lowered him to the floor.

The zone time readout seemed to have skipped forward ten minutes. Or they'd been unconscious for that amount of time. *And how did night fall? If that's what had happened.* Another far-off hammer blow belled through the giant carrier.

'Suffering Christ, is anyone still alive down in CIC?' Kolhammer shouted. Grey space bloomed in his vision and he pressed both hands to his eyes. He had a terrible migraine, so bad that if he wanted to see someone clearly he had to tilt his head at an uncomfortable angle just to move them into the small part of his sight that wasn't affected. He wanted to curl into a ball, but instead he slowly rubbed his eyes.

'If we can't raise them on Shipnet, would someone who can walk in a reasonably straight line care to go find out what's happening down there?' he asked more calmly. 'And let's get someone in here to police up this mess. Commander, do we have a location on Captain Chandler?'

'Making it happen,' Judge croaked. He'd managed to stop heaving his guts out. 'Last we knew, the captain was still on the flight deck, Admiral, with the catapult crew at number three.'

Judge interrogated a touch screen, his hands still shaking. 'Biosensors place him topside, but unconscious, sir. He's still down there.'

'Send somebody to wake him up. He'll be really pissed off if he sleeps through an attack on his ship. What the hell *is* that anyway?' asked Kolhammer. 'One of those Caliphate tubs. Those pieces of crap the Indonesians bought off the East Germans?'

And Christ, how much do we miss those clowns, he thought to himself. *Great days. Not like this clusterfuck.*

'Can't say yet, Admiral,' said Judge, his head lolling a little as he caressed a touch screen. 'Link's up to CIC, Admiral. And I've got a couple of medics heading for Captain Chandler now. Damage control reports that we're taking hits, but the armour sheath is holding up well. Some penetration on C deck. We have casualties there.'

Kolhammer glanced out the window, worried about Chandler, although he had no chance of seeing the ship's captain several hundred metres aft. The flight deck was littered with crew in different-coloured vests, most of them laid out cold. The task force commander could just make out aircraft directors in blue and yellow, mixed in with handling officers wearing yellow on yellow. Some were completely motionless, others were stirring and a few were even managing to rise to their knees. A landing signals officer in white lay prone in the centre of the main runway.

Through the haze of his migraine he could see a burning vessel some kilometres distant. Searching for a clearer view, he turned to face a big flat-screen that was displaying four feeds, all from low-light

TV mast-cams distributed throughout the fleet. One window was devoted to a frisbee-cam that remained in a static hover six thousand metres above the flag bridge. That screen offered the broadest view of the situation.

By closing one eye and tilting his head, Kolhammer could see that the ships were moving erratically, none of them keeping station, their wakes carving and crossing through the warm tropical waters with no design or purpose that he could discern. The wreckage of a burning ship, a big one, was close to sinking. One of the British trimarans was circling the kill with obvious intent. And there, much closer, was their own would-be executioner. A squat, blocky-looking grey ship. Small, a destroyer, or maybe a frigate. And old, judging by the dark black smoke that was spewing from the funnel amidships. She was steaming erratically, too, but there seemed to be more design behind her movement. As much as a fifteen- or sixteen-hundred-tonne ship could move like a rat in a trap, that's exactly what she looked like. Jinking hard to port for a minute, laying on speed for the *Clinton*, heaving to then veering away. Fire jetted constantly from her three gun turrets, two fore and one aft.

The *Clinton*'s CI was screaming for attention, demanding autonomy and a Cooperative Battle Link with the other fleet intelligences. But despite its insistence, very few human operators were filing damage reports or raising alarms. The ship seemed to be half asleep.

Kolhammer turned to the screen that was carrying video from the Combat Information Centre. Lieutenant Kirsty Brooks was weaving about in front of the cam, looking as though she'd been poleaxed. Feeling a small measure of control returning to his rebellious nerves, Kolhammer stood slowly and looked from Brooks to the scene outside his bridge. Despite his restricted vision he could tell – even without the aid of sophisticated electronics – that a battle was beginning. Guns hammered in the dark, speaking to each other with angry flashes of light. Goose bumps crawled up his forearms and neck.

'What's going on, Lieutenant?' he asked as calmly as possible.

Brooks shook her head, blanched, and vomited discreetly to one side. 'We . . . uh . . . have the hostile on screen now, sir.'

Another window opened up. A hard, clear image of an old fossil-fuel-powered warship filled it. As they watched, the ship's forward gun mount spoke, and a second later the same hammer blow sounded through the hull of the carrier.

'Admiral,' said Lieutenant Brooks from the screen in front of him, 'we have multiple contacts throughout the body of the task force. Presumed hostile. Sensors indicate gunfire and some torpedo launches. Buggy readings, sir, we can't get a fix on weapon types, but these are hostile forces. *Kandahar*, *Providence* and the *Siranui* have all taken fire. *Leyte Gulf* is critical. I'm afraid the *Fearless* is gone, sir. Destroyed. *Trident*'s

CI has sent a data burst which we're breaking down now.' She examined a screen off to her right for a moment. 'Definitely hostile, sir. We're getting a significant volume of fire. Little Bill wants you to release the codes for a mace run and to engage Metal Storm and the laser packs.'

In his peripheral vision Kolhammer noticed a few men and women on the bridge quietly cursing and turning to each other. Some turned to the strip window, although the image on screen was far superior to anything the naked eye could make out. The little grey ship heaved over to present a broadside to the *Clinton.*

'Admiral,' said Brooks, 'we have indications that that ship has torpedo capability. They may be trying to bracket us, sir.'

The fog in Kolhammer's mind began to clear rapidly as a cold wind blew through him.

'Lieutenant Brooks!' he barked. 'Guns free! Autonomy, Level One. Initiate a fleet-wide CBL.'

But it was too late.

HMAS Moreton Bay, 2247 hours, 2 June 1942

Rachel Nguyen was running from hell. She was naked and a breeze slipped over her body – no, over a six-year-old's body – burning the skin. Melting it. Flesh fell from her in long, sloughed-off lumps. The pain was excruciating. Searing and white. She was screaming as the road beneath her blistered feet jumped and rumbled and the air was torn by explosions. She was . . . her great-grandmother . . . in Vietnam during the war. A child fleeing an air strike called in on her village by a desperate platoon commander. Some long-dead boy from Dakota.

She knew, in her dream, exactly what she was running from. It was all behind her, but she could still see burning huts and twisted corpses, some smoking and wrenched out of any shape you could think of as human. She could see all the dead pigs and chickens, soldiers tearing at each other, using their guns as clubs. She ran and screamed, away from a rupture in the thin membrane separating her world from hell, away from the demons who had come through the rip and eaten her friends and family and spewed war all over the world. Demons in the bodies of Americans and Vietcong, the limbs and heads and torsos mixed and matched and sewn together by trolls.

She ran but the road beneath her was moving, back towards the village, accelerating like a moving sidewalk of sand and gravel. She tried to run faster, but her legs were so small and thin. She tripped and the road came rushing at her face.

There were no stones to bite into her cheeks. No sand or grit on which to choke. The road surface was smooth and cool. And sort of . . . wet.

She gasped, pulling in a mouthful of air, as though she hadn't breathed in a very long time. Like when she was a kid and she had those stupid competitions with her brother Michael, to see who could swim the furthest without surfacing. He was such a dick sometimes.

And he was gone now. Lost.

Her thoughts were disordered. Confused. Michael was home in Sydney, not lost.

In a rush it came to her. She had passed out on the table. Probably from exhaustion. Knocked the dregs of her coffee all over her notes. How long had she been out? Not long, or that sergeant, the one with the huge plate of sausages, would have rushed over.

She had a serious headache, though. She'd been out long enough for that. *And God it's bad! Like a migraine. Worse even. Jeez, did I have an embolism or what? A stroke? And where is that guy?* she thought, looking around, a little pissed off. *Why didn't he help?*

She tried to stand, and three things happened. A brutal spike jagged through her head, her legs folded up and a wave of nausea swept over her. She clamped her hand to her mouth as she dropped towards the floor, but it was no use. Everything came out under pressure, squirting through her fingers.

Embarrassment, shock and fear swept over her all at once. *What happened?* Maybe the Chinese, or the Rising Jihad, had hit them with something. A neutron bomb? A transsonic device?

Not the latter, anyway. Not at sea.

Cramps shot up her legs and she began to shiver

uncontrollably, curling into a ball on the deck and dry-heaving for nearly two minutes. 'For fuck's sake!' she whimpered. 'What is this?'

Whatever it was, she tried to haul herself out into a passageway, where somebody might at least trip over her.

Then, all at once, the shivering and the nausea passed. The headache remained – she was sure now it was a migraine – but the other effects, symptoms, whatever, were gone. As though someone had thrown a switch.

Rachel lay, breathing slowly for a minute before climbing to her feet. The migraine had made her dizzy and she had to grab the table to help herself up, but it was just a screaming headache now. Nothing more. She was about to stagger off to sick bay when she heard the first shells detonating close by in the water.

USS Kandahar, *2247 hours, 2 June 1942*

Colonel Jones, sitting astride Hannon's chest, just had the man's arms locked down with his knees when he heard and felt the impact of a shell somewhere on the *Kandahar*. He would have sworn someone had hammered the decking just under his feet. He yelled at Chen to hold the lieutenant's mouth open while he fished in there trying to hook onto the tongue. Hannon had swallowed it during the blackout.

He ignored the shrieking whine in his ears and the chisel banging deep into his frontal lobes. He bit down on the bile that threatened to come bursting up out of his mouth, and he somehow kept up a reassuring conversation with Chen, who was close to bugging out.

Another shell struck the *Kandahar*, more of a wrecking ball this time, throwing them all off balance just as Jones muttered, 'Gotcha,' and snagged Hannon's tongue out with a slick *pop*. The marine stopped bucking beneath him and began to suck in great shuddering draughts of air. Jones flipped him over just before a motherlode of chewed-up burger and fries came out.

'God *damn*!' yelled Chen, who got hosed.

'Make sure he doesn't choke on that mess, son,' Jones said as he staggered to his feet. He knew for sure now that they were under attack. *No idea by whom or with what, though.* You had to figure it was some kind of neural disrupter, given the effects, but those prototypes weren't even out of the labs in the States. And the dinks were still ten years behind in development. Once you eliminated Beijing, however, what then? Ragheads didn't have the delivery platforms, and never would.

The ship seemed to pitch beneath his boots like they'd run into a force-niner. But he knew that was his inner ear, because Chen's coffee rested undisturbed in its mug on the mess table. He fumbled for his flexipad, tried for a link to the bridge, and got nowhere.

Same with the CIC, security detail, and the sick bay. Shipnet was unaffected – so there was no electromagnetic pulse – but nobody was answering. Probably all rolling around in their own puke.

Another dense, metallic boom sounded somewhere nearby. *The hell with this*, thought Jones, gathering his composure and what he could of his balance. Somebody had to get on the stick or their families were all going to be getting a folded flag and a visit from the grief counsellors.

'Chen,' he barked. 'Can Hannon walk yet?'

'I don't think so, Colonel. He's still sort of spasming.'

'Check his air passage for any more crap and leave him. We'll send someone through to look after him, but we have to get to work. Come on now, son. Let's hustle before someone catches us with our nuts in the breeze.'

Again, he added to himself.

Chen arranged his friend to rest as comfortably as possible and pushed himself up towards his CO. The steward who had served them appeared from the galley on his hands and knees, a long string of blood falling from his lips.

'You there!' yelled Jones, cutting through the man's misery and doubling the intensity of his own headache. 'You well enough to attend to the lieutenant there?'

The man groaned but nodded.

'Make sure he doesn't choke, then. And see to

anybody you got back there. Shut everything down. No flames or boiling water. Understand?'

'Yes, sir, Colonel,' the steward croaked as Jones and Chen tottered out of the mess.

There were men and women in various states of collapse all along the corridor. Some were far gone in what looked like the extremes of an epileptic seizure. Others simply appeared to be sleeping. A few were gathering their wits, and none, to Jones's surprise, seemed to have been gripped by the Fear yet.

Probably too fucked up.

As they tried to hurry to the bridge, Jones stopped to encourage those marines and sailors who were rebounding the fastest. He noted that this seemed to be a random process. He saw Aub Harrison, his RSM, a thirty-year man, and just about the toughest son-of-a-bitch Jones had ever met, flaked out, a dark stain spreading down his pants as his bladder emptied itself. Just beyond Harrison, he found his principal combat surgeon, a slight red-headed woman, and she seemed reasonably unaffected. She was moving from one person to the next, jabbing them with one-use syringes. Jones grabbed a trembling Chen by the arm and muscled him over in her direction.

'Hey, Doc, what do we have here?' asked Jones. 'Transsonics? What d'you think?'

Captain Margie Francois left the marine she was tending and moved over to Jones and Chen with remarkable agility. There was just a flicker of dread in her grey eyes. 'Fucked if I know, Colonel,' she said. 'But I got Promatil and Stemazine, antinausea drugs. Seem to help.'

She took up a syringe from a kit at her hip.

Another blast, very close this time. They all turned their heads in that direction.

'Terrific,' said Jones. 'Gimme a shot. And the lieutenant here, too. Can't you do an implant dump? I want a couple of Harriers up as soon as possible. But I'm guessing we got nobody fit to fly them yet.'

'Sir. I've already zapped the implants. That's about forty per cent of our personnel. I'll check on the flyers right away.'

Jones detailed Chen to hustle her up some assistants as another explosion sounded. He was surprised to hear a personal weapon open up on full auto somewhere nearby, and decided to take a detour from his path to the bridge. A few turns later he emerged onto a small weather deck.

A marine had leaned himself against the safety rail and was letting rip at something on the water. Huge fingers of white fire strobed at the muzzle of his weapon and a long line of tracer rounds reached out over the darkened waters.

Jones shook his head in disbelief, first at the trooper and then at the antiquated warship he was shooting at. She revealed herself with the flash of her guns.

'Safe that weapon now, son!' he yelled. And for the first time since he'd come to, raising his voice didn't drive an ice pick straight into his head. That was good. He liked to raise his voice.

The marine, a giant bovine-looking character, seemed genuinely shocked to have been busted by his CO, and actually began to argue.

'But the enemy, they's shooting at us, Colonel.'

Jones stared again at the rogue vessel. A real dinosaur by the look of her. A destroyer maybe? The Indonesians had bought a bunch of them from the East Germans ages ago, back when there were still Indonesians and East Germans. But what the fuck was it doing here, attacking a clearly superior battle group? He was just starting along that chain of thought when his attention ballooned out to the bigger picture. Jones hustled a pair of powered combat goggles from the trooper, Bukowski, and set the light amplifiers to maximum gain.

'Sir. Y'all right?' asked Private Bukowksi.

'Be cool, Private,' Jones said quietly but sternly as he tried to process what he was seeing. A hostile fleet seemed to have materialised in the middle of the task force. Carriers, old battleships or cruisers maybe, a real junkyard collection, but it had snuck in right under their noses, and now that small, angry destroyer was lining up for a broadside on the *Clinton*. Well, she had a castiron pair of nuts on her, you had to give her that.

'Oh, shit,' he spat as his peripheral vision picked up an even greater threat to the aircraft carrier. A small plane, obsolete, incredibly slow, was diving straight for the deck of the Big Hill, pulling out slowly, tortuously at just a hundred or so metres. A small black pearl detached from its belly and followed a fatal, parabolic arc. Jones couldn't tell if the flight path of the bomb would intersect with the deck of the supercarrier, but a heavy, leaden feeling in his guts told him it just might. He reached out and placed a hand on Private Bukowski's shoulder.

'You got the general principle right, son,' he said quietly. 'But you ain't gonna hit jack shit from here.'

The destroyer exploded about five seconds before the bomb tore into the *Clinton*'s deck between the number three and four catapults.

USS Hillary Clinton, *2252 hours, 2 June 1942*

A few people on the *Clinton*'s flag bridge ignored the plasma screens and peered through the armoured glass windows of the bridge to watch the destroyer die in real time. The better view was on screen.

The hostile was eight hundred metres away when something took it amidships. Something big and ugly. A ball of fire and steam erupted and consumed most of the vessel's length. It broke her back, ripped her in half, lifting the separated sections twenty metres out of a boiling cauldron of sea beneath her keel. Kolhammer watched a gun turret pop off like a champagne cork and go skimming across the surface of the ocean. A murmur ran through the crew, those on their feet at least, as the bow knifed into the water and sank instantly. The burning stern remained afloat for just a few seconds before a secondary explosion atomised it.

Metal rain clattered into the carrier's superstructure as shrapnel from the blast whickered through the air to strike them. One twisted iron rivet that must have been travelling at the speed of sound smashed into the armour glass with a giant thud, to leave a delicate star pattern at the point of impact.

Two heartbeats later, a five-hundred-kilogram bomb speared into the flight deck of the USS *Hillary Clinton*, two hundred metres aft of the flag bridge. The dumb iron bomb detonated a few metres from the *Clinton*'s captain, Guy Chandler, and the group of unconscious technicians who had been carrying out routine maintenance checks on the aft catapults when the floor of the universe dropped out beneath them all. They died without ever knowing they had journeyed between worlds.

The deck of the *Clinton* was armoured against mace munitions. The number three catapult, however, was not. Indeed, like all of the ship's catapults it was a vulnerable, high-maintenance bitch of a thing, which demanded constant loving care and attention lest it decide to malfunction with a fully laden Raptor hooked up and ready to roll. It was similar in form to the last generation of steam-driven catapults, consisting of a pair of very long tubes, topped by an open slot and sealed with rubber flanges. But rather than drawing pressurised steam from the ship's propulsion plant, the fuel air explosive, or FAX, catapults used a binary fuel mix that was theoretically easier and safer to handle.

The theory, however, did not account for a bomb strike taking place in the middle of a launch simulation. The technical crew who died at catapult three had been running her through a series of prelaunch tests in preparation for the day's exercises. When the bomb struck, the eighty-metre-long catapult tubes were full of the highly volatile fuel-air mix; enough, when it detonated, to rip a huge furrow out of the angled portside flight deck.

Enough, as well, to trigger a much more powerful and catastrophic explosion in a liquid oxygen tank recessed in a nominally secure area just below the lip of the flight deck, behind the Optical Landing System. It blew with a blinding white light and a head-cracking roar that approximated the effect of a subnuclear plasma-yield warhead. Most of that blast wave travelled up and outwards, raking the flight deck of all human life and obliterating the frail dive-bomber that had launched the attack.

But it did not kill the *Clinton*. The voided double hull and monobonded deck plating absorbed and then shed sixty per cent of the blast. That still left force enough, however, to trash dozens of aircraft chained down out-board of catapults one and two, and to sweep the flight decks clear of any personnel who had not been instantly vapourised.

As large and well built as the supercarrier was, the *Clinton* shook violently through every centimetre of her structure. Men and women tending the fusion stacks thirty metres below the waterline were thrown to the floor.

On the flag bridge, Kolhammer had one brief, idiot moment where his mind whispered that it was just the destroyer going up. Years of training and experience told him the little ship had been taken out by a Type 92 torpedo, probably launched from the *Havoc*, which was packing that sort of heat and loitering with intent, according to the 'bloc.

But even as those thoughts spooled through his mind, his senses betrayed the truth, though he was only dimly aware that something had cleared his impaired vision. In a strange, elongated fragment of time, he watched the screen as a supernova consumed the stern of his own ship. A deep, disordered vibration seized the *Clinton*'s bulk, throwing some of the watch to their knees. He groaned as the blast wave picked up the bodies of every human being on the flight deck and tossed them through the air like leaves before a gust front.

His heart thudded faster in his chest as a deep, unthinkably loud wall of thunder shook the bridge and it seemed to him as though hell's furnace had exploded. He was minutely aware of every detail his bulging eyes took in. The faces of his brother and sister officers, their mouths wide open; a thread dangling from the arm of an ensign as he raised his hand to point at something; the impression his own backside had made in the chair where he'd been sitting. The first flicker of colour in the blast window, all wrong, a burned black and orange blossom amid a field of grey sea and metal at the very edge of his vision. The petal of fire growing, unfurling, expanding. Consuming the space where the *Clinton* had been.

It was wrong. It was impossible. An outrage to the senses. But there it was, before his very eyes.

This confused tumble of thought and emotion seemed to take much longer than was really the case. Admiral Phillip Kolhammer was fifty-three years old. Old enough to have served in the First Gulf War, which made him a figure of mythology to the young men and women in this battle group. He had been at war for most of his adult life. He hadn't been born into conflict, like his young sailors and pilots. But he had grown into it.

A buddy from his first tour of Afghanistan had given him a memento, a piece of shrapnel from the battle-ground at Shah-i-Kot. It had been mounted on a polished cedar base and inscribed with J Robert Oppenheimer's famously mawkish sentiment: *I am become death, the destroyer of worlds.* It was really just a piece of bullshit bravado, the sort of thing young pilots loved and old men indulged with some regret, because they understood the worth and the cost of such things. But Kolhammer had kept the piece in his private quarters where he alone could see it. His friend was long gone, shot down over Indonesia in 2009 and hacked to death by Javanese peasant militia. So it was a keepsake, but also a personal talisman, because he *had* become death. He was a warrior before all else, now, and it was his warrior spirit – a reflex turn towards battle – that saved them all.

'Lieutenant Brooks,' he barked at the flat-screen by his right hand. 'Have you linked the fleet into our Battlenet?'

'We've gained hotlinks to everyone who's available sir, but we seem to have lost contact with *Garrett*, *Vanguard*, *Fearless*, *Dessaix*, *Leyte Gulf*, *Sutanto* and *Nuku*. The *Leyte Gulf* we can locate, but she's not responding. Her systems are fried. She's seven thousand metres away, bearing one-eight-niner. Possibly rammed. The others are missing, possibly sunk. As is the *Nagoya*.'

'Is *Leyte Gulf* burning?'

'Negative, sir. And we can't get a GPS fix on the datum point, either. I've tried interrogating GPS six ways from Sunday, but it seems to be down, Admiral.'

'Down?'

'Nonresponsive, sir. The channels are clear, but it's as though the satellites themselves have been taken out.'

Marvellous, thought Kolhammer, *just marvellous*. Under attack from God knows who, and their position fix goes south for the winter. He stifled an exasperated grunt.

'Thank you, Lieutenant. Find out what happened

to those other ships. I want to know yesterday. Link all surviving task force assets for collective engagement. Unsafe laser packs and Metal Storm. Slave combat maces to the *Clinton*. Hammerheads only, no sunburn. Chapter Seven rules of engagement. Launch on my mark.'

'Aye, sir,' Brooks replied as her fingers blurred over a touch screen. A secondary explosion jolted her and knocked a few flag-bridge crewmembers from their stations. 'Solutions confirmed, Admiral. Locked and tracking.'

'Engage,' said Kolhammer. At the same instant, four torpedoes speared into the *Clinton*.

5

USS Leyte Gulf, *2257 hours, 2 June 1942*

'Say again!' yelled Captain Daytona Anderson. The intercom was working fine, but the voice at the other end was muted by small-arms fire, screams and a brace of explosions, which she felt quite clearly through the soles of her shoes.

'Boarders, ma'am. I say again, we have boarders. Armed and hos–'

A single massive explosion shook the entire ship, cutting off the transmission. A recorded voice boomed out of nearby PA speakers.

'Intruder alert. Intruder alert. Intruder alert.'

Anderson already regretted her decision to direct the fight from the CIC. Ninety-five per cent of her systems were down. Alarms screamed, beeped and pinged all around her. Warning lights flashed and the few screens with any lighted display at all were showing nonsensical data. Examining them closely was like looking into an Escher print. The *Leyte Gulf* appeared to have been rammed.

But it hadn't. The reality was more incomprehensible.

When the two hundred and fifty men and women

aboard the thirty-five-tonne *Nemesis* stealth cruiser had awakened from, well, whatever it was that had hit them, they found themselves occupying the same space as a *New Orleans* class heavy cruiser, the USS *Astoria*. Luckily for the thousand or more men of the *Astoria* and the crew of the *Leyte Gulf*, they hadn't merged hand-in-glove, which would have killed most of the complements of both vessels immediately as their molecular structure was instantly compromised by having to share space with metal, wood, plastic and the bodies of other human beings. Instead, the two ships had transected each other, appearing from above like an open pair of scissors.

Even so, many sailors from both ships had perished; some instantaneously, unknowingly, as they materialised squarely inside structures such as a bulkhead or six-inch gun mount. Others hadn't been so lucky. They had only *partially* merged with various objects or, in the worst cases, people. Their deaths had been slower, more agonising and, for them, totally inexplicable. A pharmacist's mate from the *Astoria* who gasped out his last breaths clawing at a PlayStation console half buried in his chest was typical of their number.

Some even died at each other's hands. Ensign Tommy Hideo from the *Leyte Gulf* and Leading Seaman Milton Coburn of the *Astoria* beat each other to death in a dark, constricted space where the control room for the *Leyte Gulf*'s eight-inch autocannon intersected the three-tiered bunk upon which Seaman

Coburn had been sleeping. The men themselves had been fused at the thigh. The blinding pain and shock of that violation was enough to send them instantly over the edge, past any hope for rational behaviour. Even if they had cooperated and sought out medical attention, the surgery would have needed to be swift and radical. Their blood types did not match, and they were quickly poisoning each other.

For the moment, though, Captain Anderson was unaware of these horrors. The Combat Information Centre was still relatively calm, despite the shrill symphony of alarms. The sailors there looked to her for guidance now. Most of them had nothing to do, since their battle stations had gone offline when the merging of the two ships had severed the kilometres of fibre-optic cables and wiring that formed the *Gulf*'s nervous system.

The CIC was always a dark blue cave, but it seemed more so now, with the dozens of screens blacked out. It was warm too, which was wrong. The centre was supposed to be uncomfortably chilly, allowing the quantum systems to run at white heat.

At least Anderson was in better shape than her ailing vessel; she'd recovered quickly from the transition through the wormhole thanks to a subcutaneous antinausea insert she routinely received every six months.

She had been quick to note that her crewmembers with Promatil inserts or dermal patches were less drastically affected by whatever had happened. When it became obvious that Shipnet was in disarray, she immediately dispatched runners to the nearest casualty stations with instructions to gather supplies of the drug and distribute them as widely and swiftly as possible. That was how she'd learned about the violation of the forward decks. But she didn't have to look at the expanse of dead electronics all around them to know her ship was gravely hurt. She could feel it down in her meat. The *Gulf* was dying.

Anderson straightened herself at the console, squared her shoulders and traversed her gaze over every man and woman in the room. She was twenty-two years in the United States Navy and wore a uniform heavily burdened with decorations won the hard way. In her two decades at sea she had exercised for, and performed, almost every kind of operation it was possible to conceive of in modern naval combat. It had never occurred to her that she would have to issue the orders she now spoke. Keying a button to power up the ship's PA, without really knowing how far the broadcast would carry, she drove any trace of fear or doubt from her voice.

'Attention all hands. Attention all hands. This is the captain. Arm yourselves and prepare to repel boarders.'

If her crew within the cocoon of the CIC were surprised, none dared show it. A few obviously braced themselves for what was coming but only one, Chief Conroy, said anything.

'Captain, if I may? We should get to the gun

lockers, gather crew as we go. They may not have heard the announcement. We'll need to establish a perimeter on all decks and push forward from there.'

Conroy checked the flexipad velcroed to his sleeve. 'Short-range point-to-point links seem workable, at least here, ma'am. We might be able to coordinate through that.'

Anderson agreed but she was haunted, wondering whether she was about to set some calamity in motion. Still, the near-total failure of the ship's quantum systems left her no choice. She couldn't use the weapons systems aboard the *Gulf*, couldn't even scuttle her at the moment. She had crew engaging in close-quarter combat on the forward decks, there were no communications with task force command, and they had absolutely no idea how this mess had come to be. For the moment, then, her choice seemed clear. If the *Leyte Gulf* had been boarded by pirates or commandos or some kind of jihadi suicide squad, she would find the enemy, and destroy them.

Anderson chose a group to accompany her, then ordered six crewmembers to stay and seal the CIC behind her.

Hurrying down the starboard corridor to the armoury, she was immediately struck by how wrong it all felt. Even in the restricted spaces below decks, the geometry of the vessel seemed to have been wrenched or twisted out of shape. And it was obvious that they were no longer making any headway. If anything, the ship was being pushed *sideways*. They began to hear blasts of gunfire and the frequent explosions of handheld artillery. But beneath that, her trained ear could detect the awful screams of metal plate and bulkheads straining against enormous destructive forces, as the structural integrity of the Nemesis cruiser was tested.

Emergency lighting had come on, leaving the corridors dim but navigable. Glowing flexipad screens, activated and secured on each man or woman's preferred arm, bobbed up and down through the gloom, adding their own soft luminescence and throwing off a menagerie of writhing shadows. As they passed ladders and hatchways between decks, Chief Conroy detailed small groups to split off and make their way to A, C and D decks, with instructions to gather other crew and await orders from the captain when she made the B deck armoury.

The *Leyte Gulf* had sailed with a full complement, eighteen officers and two hundred and thirty-five enlisted personnel. The ship's biosensors were offline, so Anderson had no idea of casualties, or of how many were actively engaged with the boarders, trapped forward of the impact point with the hostile vessel, or simply missing or dead. Conservatively, she figured on rounding up seventy or eighty warm bodies for her counterattack. As she and Conroy hurried along B deck, past the berthing spaces, they swelled their numbers with another two dozen sailors, including three specialists trained specifically in hostile boarding ops.

Anderson heard one of her junior officers, Ensign Rebecca Sparrow, mutter that some Navy SEALs would have been nice. The captain dropped her pace marginally to fall in beside Sparrow, delivering a hearty slap on the shoulder. 'Damn right, Ensign. A SEAL team would have been a thing of beauty! But this morning we're going to work with what the good Lord provided. And I have faith in Specialists Clancy, Cobb and Brown here. Don't you?'

Sparrow seemed more unsettled by her commanding officer's unexpected appearance and exuberance than by the King Hell madness of the day. Her eyes widened in surprise but she recovered her composure quickly. 'Hell yes, ma'am.'

'Glad to hear it.' Anderson smiled, her gleaming white teeth shining out of her coal-black face. 'Specialist Clancy!' she called over her shoulder. 'You think you can justify Ensign Sparrow's confidence in you?'

Clancy, nine years in service and a veteran of more than seventy forced vessel entries, smiled at his commanding officer and called back, 'Anything for a lady, Captain.'

They trotted past the brig and came to a halt in front of the armoury. Chief Conroy yelled over the buzz of voices and the harsh, industrial sounds of battle, ordering them to form up in two lines and stand at ease. The boarding specialists hurried forwards into the armoury to suit up and arm themselves, along with two seamen ordered to grab weapons and stand guard back down the passage through which they had just run. The two men took body armour and helmets, a couple of pump-action shotguns, and hustled back past the lines of their shipmates to establish a hasty defence.

While Conroy saw to the arming of the specialists, Anderson tried to raise the other decks on Shipnet via her flexipad. Two windows on screen responded to her page. Lieutenant Matt Reilly on A deck had gathered twenty-three personnel in the chopper bay. They had already armed themselves from the air division's own arsenal and were awaiting orders.

'Good work, Lieutenant. Stand by,' said Anderson. She shifted her gaze to the other functioning pull-down window, where she found CPO Borghino's phlegmatic features. A thin film of static obscured his face, but otherwise the connection seemed fine. The third window, the link to D deck, was a small square of white noise.

'Chief, I can't raise D deck on Shipnet or P2P,' said Anderson. 'How about you?'

Anderson watched as Borghino's eye line shifted within the window. He was obviously manipulating his pad, trying for some sort of alternative link to D. After a few long seconds he turned his eyes back to the microlens mounted in his pad's shockproof rubber casing, rather than looking at Anderson's own image on screen. This created the impression that he was staring directly at her.

'Sorry, ma'am. I'll have to send a runner down.

They'll have formed up in engineering. We can get access from here.'

'Fine, Chief. I'll send down a security team. Lieutenant Carey was in charge on D. Have him secure engineering. He'll be staying put. I don't want anyone fooling around near those fusion stacks.'

Borghino nodded brusquely. 'Eminently sensible, ma'am. With your permission, we'll seal the section as soon as the security team gets down there.'

'Make it happen, Chief.'

Anderson looked up from her pad. The illuminated screen had cast a soft, lambent glow over her features, smoothing out deep-worn stress lines and giving her, just briefly, the appearance of a mother fretting over a sick child. As she turned her gaze to Chief Conroy, the illusion vanished.

'Status, Chief?

'Clancy's team is nearly kitted up, Captain. We got eight suits of full body armour, reactive matrix and tac sets, and twelve sets of standard-issue Kevlar and ballistic plate . . . correction, ten. We just sent two sets forward with Ntini and McAllister. Eight G4s to go with the suits and ten compact shotguns for the rest of the flak jackets. Ten side-arms, standard-issue Glocks. We have a dozen stun rods, too, for what that's worth. And a couple of guys with meat cleavers and boning knives from the officers' mess.' He smiled grimly.

The ship gave a great lurch to port, a dire screeching protest arising from deep within her metal innards. Both the captain and her senior NCO, long accustomed to the sea's arbitrary moods, reacted without conscious thought, adjusting their balance. A few younger sailors were caught off guard and thrown into the men and women standing around them. The emergency lighting flickered for a few seconds and the sounds of battle hung suspended, before ramping up again with seemingly increased ferocity. Anderson glanced at the group in the armoury. 'Recommendations?' she asked.

Conroy pursed his lips for the shortest moment before speaking. 'We're fighting blind. We have no idea where these guys came from, what they're bringing to the game, what sort of reserve they have. Be good to get someone topside to take a look, since the sensors are kaput. Got to figure it's going to be pretty fucking nasty up there, though, probably nonviable without a suit. Even then, I'd send two.

'We got five sets of reactive left. I'd put them on Snellgrove, Palfreyman, Paterson, Sessions and Nix. The first three have completed the basic boarding course, so they've been trained. Nix ran with a pretty rough crew in LA, before the judge made him an offer he couldn't refuse. And Sessions did three years with the Wyoming National Guard, tour of Malaysia, Bronze Star, two Purple Hearts.'

Anderson smiled wearily. 'I remember. I spoke to him when he first came on board. Said he'd had his fill of crazy ragheads getting in his face. Okay. We'll take Clancy's team. Get Sessions and Nix topside for a quick look, then straight back to me with a report. They can link up with Reilly in the chopper bay and take point for them on A deck. Send the other suits down to C with half-a-dozen standard kits, flaks, shotguns, helmets. Chief Borghino will decide on distribution from his available personnel.

'Send two shotguns down to engineering, but load them with jelly bags and pull everyone else out. Seal that section. Everybody outside of engineering packs ceramic rounds, powder puffs. We've got real problems in the missile bays. I don't know why we're not all pleading our case with Saint Peter right now. So let's not push our luck.'

'Aye, Captain,' Conroy said before turning his head slightly to shout into the armoury. 'You heard the woman. Ammo check now. Ceramics only. No penetrator or flechette rounds. We've got sick missiles on the forward decks.'

'One step ahead of you, Chief,' Clancy called in reply. The three specialists made the last adjustments to their body armour, each turning slowly as his buddies tightened a Velcro strap here or snugged down a ballistic pad there. The suits, which looked like padded SWAT coveralls, came out of their lockers a dark charcoal colour, but after a few minutes they began to change, taking on a slightly reddish hue, as they reacted to the ship's emergency lighting. While the three men worked quickly to prepare themselves, the suits drank up the kinetic energy of their sharp body movements, and the adaptive camouflage reaction accelerated.

Within two minutes the superdense intelligent matrix of monobonded carbon nanotubes that gave the coveralls their padded look was fully powered up. The team's Remington G4s were each loaded with sixty rounds of thirty-three-millimetre caseless ceramic, and each man was carrying another three hundred rounds in strip form. Being specialist boarders, they were all neck-chipped and as they strapped into their powered combat goggles and helmet a micronet was activated, biolinking Clancy, Cobb and Brown to their suit systems, and to each other.

They then supervised the 'B team' kit-up, hurrying Sessions, Nix and the others through their preparations.

Captain Anderson, tightening an old Kevlar vest and checking the load on a Glock, struggled against a small spasm of rodent-like panic that had begun twisting inside her chest. Too long. They were taking way too long, and her people were dying because of it. The terrible sound of human combat was drawing closer.

'Okay,' she said forcefully but not too loudly when the last of the weapons had been handed out and each armed sailor had their instructions. On the other decks, in the chopper bay, and down below in the main mess on C deck, men and women peered into flexipads, their own or a shipmate's. Anderson spoke mostly to the crew around her, but occasionally she also looked directly into the mini-cam on her own flexipad.

'I can't tell you exactly what's going on,' she said, 'because I have no goddamn idea. But we're going to find out who's been messing with us, and then there'll be a reckoning. I can promise you that.'

'Damn right,' growled Chief Conroy.

'Something hit us a short time ago. We've lost power to the CIC and most of the sensors and combat systems. We've had no communication with the rest of the task force, but we have to assume they're fighting their own battles. We're calling for assistance. Maybe it gets here, maybe it doesn't. The best we can do to help is to regain control of this ship. We have hostile forces on board. I don't know how they got here or what they have planned, but our plans are simple. We're gonna kill them before they kill us.'

USS Astoria, *2301 hours, 2 June 1942*

You go down to the sea for your living and you'll see some God-awful strange things.

It seemed only weeks ago that Evans had watched the Rising Sun snapping from the staff at the fore of the USS *Astoria* as she steamed into Yokohama Harbour, escorted by the Imperial Japanese Navy destroyers *Sagiri*, *Hibiki* and *Akatsuki*. Those very same ships were now committed to sinking her.

The mission to Japan had been a diplomatic one, the *Astoria* serving as a seaborne hearse, ferrying home the ashes of Japan's former ambassador to the United States, the late Hirosi Saito. She had even exchanged a twenty-one-gun salute with the Japanese light cruiser *Kiso*, the opening movement of an interminable train of ceremony and extravagant hospitality. None of that had had the slightest effect, though, on their hosts' intense preparations for the attack on Pearl Harbor.

Still, he thought, *you don't often see something as strange as that.* The senior officer on the USS *Astoria* – *the surviving senior officer*, he reminded himself – stared through the shattered glass of the bridge and tried to force himself to accept what he found there. His mind, however, was as numb as his left arm, which hung limp and useless, dripping blood, contributing marginally to the killing-floor ambience of the ruined bridge.

Lieutenant Commander Peter Evans, using his good hand to brace himself, stared fixedly forward to where the sinister-looking bow of the enemy ship neatly sliced through his own vessel. Perhaps if he focused more intently, really, *really* bored in, the mirage would vanish and the *Astoria*'s two forward gun mounts would reappear. And the slurry of warm human gore lapping at his ankles would . . .

Fuck it.

Evans had been spared by his legendary clumsiness, tripping and painfully turning his ankle as he leaped from his bunk when the attack began. The delay in reaching the bridge had saved his life. Everyone in there had died, shredded from the waist up by a firestorm from some kind of hellish machine-gun that occasionally popped out of the enemy vessel like an evil jack-in-the-box. Evans had tripped a second time when he charged into the ruined bridge and slipped on the bloody mess. A random stray round had shattered his forearm as he struggled to his feet, gagging in disgust.

As if watching himself from outside, he balled up a fist and drove a short, sharp punch into his wounded arm. Again. And again. By the third blow he had battered through the anaesthesia of shock, replacing it with a terrible shooting pain, which had the utility, if nothing else, of jolting him out of numbness and inaction.

His first response was combative. He raised fire control for the rear gun turrets, and had the barrels depressed as far as possible. Then he gave the order that would unload three shells at point-blank range into the stern of the ship that had attacked his own.

He watched from a lookout platform, which was freckled with thousands of thumb-sized holes. The barrels swung about with excruciating slowness, and he couldn't even be sure they would come to bear, given the angle at which the two ships were locked together. When the turret would turn no further, Evans limped back inside as quickly as he could, snatched up the interphone and snapped out the order to fire.

The roar of the great cannon filled the whole world, the bark of Satan's own hellhound. Gouts of flame leaped out into the churning V-shaped gap between the ships. A shock wave flattened the waters there. In a microsecond the three high-explosive shells covered the distance between the mouth of the guns and their target. A geyser of green flame vented out of a huge fissure in the stern of the enemy ship.

But as Lieutenant Commander Evans yelled into the interphone, demanding a full broadside by everything that could be brought to bear – the eight-inch turrets, a battery of five-inch mounts and all of the port-side machine-guns and AA stations – a curious thing happened. His voice trailed off as he saw two German storm-troopers emerge through a hatch on the small finlike bridge of the enemy ship.

He shook his head to clear it. After all, they weren't the weirdest thing he'd seen tonight.

'*Fire!*' he ordered.

USS Leyte Gulf, *2305 hours, 2 June 1942*

Lieutenant Reilly, the *Leyte Gulf*'s met boss, was not really into violence. He was a weatherman, a really excellent weatherman, if you wanted to know. Captain Anderson had learned that his forecasts often ran two or three days ahead of the bulletins coming out of the fleet, back in Pearl. On occasion, he was seemingly so prescient it was spooky. His small staff on the *Leyte Gulf* used to joke that he could *make* a butterfly flap its wings and start a hurricane on the other side of the world.

But Lieutenant Reilly was lost when it came to small-unit, counterboarding operations. It just wasn't his gig, and he was quietly very relieved when Seamen Sessions and Nix checked in on his flexipad to report that they were going topside for a quick look, after which they would report to him to commence clearing A deck forward of the chopper bay.

Reilly planned to give them very general orders when they arrived, basically reiterating anything the captain had said. After that, the two specialists would have a free hand to deploy the available forces as they saw fit. Reilly had no intention of micromanaging close-quarter combat.

Until Sessions and Nix turned up, however, there was plenty to be done. He'd collected nearly two dozen sailors on his way to the hangar, sorted them into four teams according to specialty. They were gathered in front of the *Gulf*'s pair of Sea Comanche helicopters, spectral figures looming in the faint wine-darkness of emergency lighting. Reilly had ordered the men to switch off their flexipads, lest the glowing screens make them better targets outside the safety of the hangar. Only his still shone, and he had dulled the screen to minimum brightness. Even so, he moved about within a small pearl of dim radiance as he inspected his men and women.

They were all kitted out from the air division arsenal. Most had basic body armour and each team could boast at least one cross-trained medic. Reilly didn't bother trying to whip them into a blood frenzy. It wasn't his style and everyone knew it. Instead he passed quietly from one sailor to the next, checking weapon loads, tightening straps, providing a little encouragement where it seemed needed. It was hard for them, sealed up in the rear of the ship, with no idea what was happening. They could all tell from the *Gulf*'s strange motion that something more than just a firefight was under way.

'We're going to be getting busy soon, aren't we, sir?' a young woman asked him as he handed her another magazine of 5.56 millimetres from the canvas pouch he had slung around his neck.

'Busy enough for government work,' said Reilly. An instant later the world wrenched itself inside out with a cataclysmic eruption of white light and thunder.

The hull of the *Leyte Gulf* was composed of a relatively thin, radar-absorbent, foamed-composite skin. Her designers hadn't engineered her to withstand point-blank volleys of large-bore, high-explosive gunfire. Such things just didn't happen in their world. Unfortunately for the sailors in the hangar of the *Leyte Gulf*, they had left that world behind.

One of the shells fired from the *Astoria* skimmed just over the plasteel safety rail at the very rear of the *Gulf*'s largely flat, featureless deck. Another shell clipped that rail and exploded, most of its destructive force washing harmlessly across armoured carbon plate. But the third struck the trailing edge of the stern itself, detonating squarely against the foam-steel sheeting.

The blast tore through the *Leyte Gulf*'s thin sheath of armour and into the hangar. The helicopter sitting nearest to the impact exploded, setting off fuel and ammunition all over the bay. At least half of Reilly's small command died at that moment. A few, including the meteorologist himself, were saved by the chaotic swirls of the blast wave as it travelled through the complex geometry of the crowded space. But the second volley killed them all.

A savage din deafened the two counterboarding specialists before they had even made the open deck of the *Leyte Gulf*. The roar of the big guns, the detonation on the ship's stern, the eruption of fuel and munitions in the chopper bay all followed so quickly as to form one enormous avalanche of sound. It blocked out, for just a moment, the constant wail and shriek of alarms and sirens, the intermittent crash of small-arms fire, and the confused shouts and screams from the forward decks.

Sessions and Nix braced themselves against the bulkhead on either side of the hatchway that led to the deck. As they were about to push out, a stream of fifty-calibre tracers struck the carbon-composite armour outside, sounding like a jackhammer. The men exchanged a glance, waited for a second, shrugged and dived through the exit.

Another burst of tracer fire slammed into Sessions's chest, throwing him back through the hatch as if he had been punched by a giant fist. Had he not been wearing body armour he would have died instantly. But the three rounds struck ballistic plate and were stopped dead – and beneath that pliable ceramic shield a thick, reactive matrix of nano-tubes and buckyball gel pulsed and shed most of the kinetic energy. Enough remained, however, to throw the seaman through the air, and he thumped into the metal bulkhead inside the hatch before sliding to the ground, unconscious but alive.

Nix crouched instinctively, barely glancing back at his shipmate as the machine-gun fire trailed away over his head. He took in the scene through powered combat goggles, shifting from the cool green of low-light amplification to infrared as he quickly scanned his own ship for damage. Intense heat, streaming in livid waves from the stern of the cruiser, marked the shellfire impact of just a few seconds ago. The mammoth bulk of the enemy ship filled his visual field. The barrels of the big gun turret glowed a dim, satanic red. The battery was tracking for another shot.

Nix quickly stripped out the ceramic rounds he had been issued, substituting a prohibited load of depleted uranium penetrators from a pouch in his black body armour. The sea surface heaved, throwing him to the deck as a twin fifty-cal on the other ship ripped another line of tracers through the space where he had just been standing. Ricochets and small chips of carbon-composite sheeting struck his body armour as he slammed painfully down on his butt. Lines of data from biochip inserts in his neck and torso filled a pop-up window in his combat goggles.

Nix switched off the feed with a tap to a button on the side of the goggles.

As he hefted the G4 to his shoulder and squeezed the grip, another set of schematics and numbers scrolled over his visual field: targeting data. He didn't need it. He fixed his sights on the rear turret of the enemy warship and fired off the entire strip of penetrators. The gun's electronic systems dispatched all eighteen rounds before Nix even felt the recoil. He didn't hear them strike the steel plating a hundred metres away. But bright flares of impact heat and a shower of sparks from the disintegrating propellant casings marked the point of entry. The depleted uranium spikes carved through the angled plating to tear up the innards of the eight-inch mount.

The big gun froze dead for half a second, then Nix's rounds set off the shells that had been ready to fire. The entire stern of the cruiser shuddered and flames erupted from an entry hatch on the side of the turret. Nix rolled back through the hatchway, grabbing his partner and hauling his dead weight away to relative safety. His goggles recorded the whole event, and now he had to get to Captain Anderson. She wasn't going to believe what he had just seen.

Peter Evans cursed and ducked back inside the *Astoria*'s bridge, slipping and falling into an unspeakable pile of offal, bone splinters, and torn cloth. Shuddering and dry heaving with a deep revulsion, he attempted to regain his feet only to slip and fall again and again. He might have given in to despair and just lain there, had he not been grabbed from behind and hauled out of the slaughterhouse.

When he finally could stand by himself, he disentangled himself from the grip of a chief petty officer, a slab-sided former meat worker from New Jersey named Eddie Mohr.

'Thanks, Chief,' he babbled, 'I . . . I . . . I . . .'

Mohr patted him on the shoulder. He'd been wading through entrails all of his adult life, but even he looked a little green around the gills, having caught a glimpse of the bridge.

'That's all right, sir. You done good, Commander, real good, sir. The thing is though. I can't let you sink that ship, sir. You see, we're stuck to it. Christ only knows how, but we are, and if it goes down, so do we. If you understand what I mean.'

Mohr continued in his slow, thick, reassuring 'New Joisey' inflection, leading the ship's surviving senior officer away from the bridge.

'You think you can get down these stairs, Commander? They're pretty steep and all. Would you like a drink, sir? I know it ain't regular, but I always find myself that it's good for what ails you.'

Mohr wiped away a small gobbet of meat and a smear of blood from around the officer's mouth before tilting a cool metal flask to his lips. The contraband liquor, which was quite good, went down smoothly, burning only when it reached Evans's stomach.

'Thanks, Chief,' he gasped. 'You're right. It helps.'

'Aye, sir, it does. My first day on the killing floor, my old man he took me out that night, filled me so fulla beer I figured to burst. Sick as a fuckin' dog I was, sir, if you'll pardon my fuckin' French. But it did the trick.'

A fit of coughing and gagging took Evans and bent him double, until he feared he might lose the bourbon he'd just drunk. But he held on, pulling great shuddering lungfuls of air in through a sucking mess of snot and blood. Finally he regained what he could of his composure.

'Damage control, Chief,' he gurgled. 'I need to know –'

'Well, the thing is, that's a hell of a question, Commander. Some I can tell you, like the rear mount's shot to hell. And some I just gotta show you.'

As Evans limped up the starboard corridor, still supported by CPO Mohr, he became aware of gunfire; small arms, rifles and machine-guns hammering away, the noise muted but reverberating through the confined spaces below decks. The passageways became crowded, too, almost clogging with dozens, maybe hundreds of sailors, many of them carrying side-arms.

'What's going on, Chief?' Evans asked.

'Frankly, sir, I'm fucked if I know. It's like we been rammed, but not, if you know.'

Evans nodded. He knew exactly what Mohr meant.

'But I can tell you we got a way in, sir. We got guys over there, we boarded them bastards and we're giving 'em hell, too. That's also why we can't be firing the big gun on 'em. We'll be killing our own if we don't look out.'

Evans nodded without saying anything. Men were beginning to notice his presence, turning and gawking at the admittedly hellish spectacle he presented. Some looked impressed, others horrified or just scared shitless.

'Make way! Make way!' yelled Eddie Mohr. 'Commander Evans coming through. Move aside, ladies. Some Japs gonna get their asses kicked now!'

Evans tried to live up to the chief's performance. With his good right hand he took a .45 pistol from a sailor who seemed only too glad to give it up. He did his best to ignore the ankle that threatened to collapse under him again. He felt hands slapping him on the shoulder and back. Heard men call out his name. Some even clapped and cheered. He had no idea why. It was mostly a daze. But instinct told him his presence was needed.

So he painfully shouldered his way through the increasingly dense mass of crewmen, not really sure where he was headed, carried along by some current in the seething tide of close-pressed humanity. He caught a confused glimpse of something ahead, an impossible wall blocking the corridor. Then the flux of rank-smelling bodies pushed him left and into a large bunkroom.

It was crowded. And dark. The electrical system must have failed. A few hand-held lamps, hung from the top tier of hammocks, provided the only light. They swayed back and forth, sending macabre pools of shadow spilling over and through the heaving crowd of men in time to the swinging torches. This added to the atmosphere created by the tear in reality that stood across the room.

That's how Evans thought of it, a tear in the fabric of the real world. There was a grey steel wall running through the centre of the bunkroom, in a place where it simply couldn't be. He could see that it was composed of the same material he'd seen so briefly out in the corridor. Perhaps it was even part of the same structure. It divided the room at an odd angle, and the more carefully he inspected the scene, the more unthinkable it became.

Off to one side, three hammocks emerged from the wall like solid ghosts. There was nothing holding them to the blank metal face. It was as if they had been extruded somehow. Nearby, a circle of men was gathered around, pointing at something down at floor level. Evans and Mohr wrestled their way over to discover a boot and most of a leg below the knee, which looked as though it were disappearing into the barrier, like a man who had been frozen while stepping through a stage curtain.

'It was Hogan, sir,' said one of the sailors, poking at the oddity with a screwdriver. 'He was going to the john.'

'Probably to beat off,' somebody added unnecessarily.

Evans heard another burst of gunfire over the clamour of the crowded bunkroom.

'You said we've found a way through, Chief. Where is it?' Evans asked, deciding for the moment to ignore the bizarre tableau.

'Just over here. If you wanna follow me, Commander.'

They left the ghoulish circle of onlookers to ponder the riddle of Hogan's boot. A little further on, just past a hammock containing the lower half of a naked torso projecting from the same steel wall, the smooth regularity of the obstacle failed and gave way to a section of buckled and torn armour plating. A fissure some three to four feet wide had been opened by the titanic stresses generated when two objects of such great mass had fused together and tried to plough on, regardless of their new and decidedly inefficient design.

The steel groaned and screamed in protest. Evans fancied he saw it moving, like the edges of flesh around a sucking chest wound. It was even darker in there, the blackness relieved only by a faint red shift that called forth childlike fears of the Beyond. As Lieutenant Commander Evans stepped towards the rift between two worlds, he shivered like a small boy stepping into the forbidden forest.

6

USS Enterprise, *2255 hours, 2 June 1942*

Lieutenant Commander Black ran from the radio room back past flag plot and hammered up the stairwell onto the bridge. Captain Murray, the *Enterprise* CO, had joined Spruance and was directing air operations – which is to say, he was sending a lot of good men to their deaths.

Bombing 6, under Lieutenant Dick Best, consisted of nineteen Dauntless dive-bombers, none of whom had ever launched from a carrier at night. Nine of the old barges had already gone into the drink at take-off. Six more were destroyed in flight by misdirected friendly fire. And four were awaiting clearance to take off.

Lieutenant Commander Black, two years out of flight ops, could only watch mutely, wondering what those remaining pilots felt as they sat in their cockpits, waiting to open the throttles and accelerate down the darkened flight deck. If, by some miracle, they got away to make a run on the enemy, none of them could realistically expect to survive a return trip and landing under these conditions.

The bridge was preternaturally quiet, in contrast with the scene on the waters around them.

Black moved up beside Spruance. The tension in the small, hard space demanded that he, too, speak in a taut whisper.

'Commander Jolley on the *New Orleans* is trying to establish gunnery control across the task force, sir. I tried to reach Admiral Smith on the *Astoria*, but they're out of action.'

'They've been hit?'

'Rammed, it seems.'

Spruance's jaw tightened.

'Well, they'll have to look after themselves. I need all the firepower I can get turned on the Japs. We can't spare anyone to go help them out.'

Staring out into the night, Black was momentarily transfixed by a bath of flat, white light. Two nearby cruisers had unleashed a coordinated broadside at the spectral figure of the Japanese ship, the *Siranui*. As the thunder of the guns hit them, he felt the detonation inside his chest, profound and imponderable.

Spruance quickly brought a pair of spyglasses up to his eyes to check the results. Black, like most of the others in the room, had to peer unaided into the fractured darkness. The target seemed trapped within a volcanic eruption of white water and fire as dozens of high-explosive shells raked at the waves around her. A coarse, unforgiving cheer rose from a dozen men at the evidence of a single explosion, a distant bud of fire quite different in texture from those shots that had fallen harmlessly into the sea.

'Looks like a hit on the bridge,' Spruance said without feeling.

An ensign reported in. 'Admiral, VB-6 just got their last two away, and the *Hornet* says she has three Devastators up.'

The cruisers fired in tandem again, with the same flashbulb effect, followed by the same tremendous sonic boom. *That must be what it sounds like in front of an avalanche, just before you die*, thought Black.

'Holy shit!' someone shouted.

A fantastic cascade of violent light and fire instantly obliterated a great crescent of the night. It was as though a vast arc of space had ignited and set off every shell fired by the two warships. Eighteen armour-piercing eight-inch shells, and nearly as many high-explosive five-inch rounds, detonated simultaneously just a few hundred yards from the muzzles of the guns that had fired them. To the men looking on from the bridge of the *Enterprise*, it seemed as though the barrage had struck an invisible wall.

'What the hell was that?' Spruance demanded.

'It's like they hit something,' said Black. 'No way could the whole salvo misfire. It just . . . It couldn't happen.'

The staccato flickering of massed naval gunfire was suddenly overwhelmed by a single burst of light. Twin lines of white fire and smoke rose vertically from the source of that flare on the deck of the *Siranui.*

Unknown fires, Black thought to himself.

The strange eruption, which held every man there in its thrall, sent those two slender pyres arcing so high into space that Black wondered for a second if they might just keep going, until they left the atmosphere on their way into the cold vacuum of heaven.

A nervous, insistent voice piped up and broke the spell.

'Admiral Spruance, sir? Please? They're rockets, sir! You have to get those ships moving. They're going to get hit for sure!'

'What's that?' Spruance turned sharply towards the source of the comment, finding there a young, pencil-necked ensign with thick, black-framed reading glasses, the same one who had just run in with the message from the radio room.

'Ensign Curtis, sir. They're rockets. I'm sure of it and they're aimed at the cruisers, Admiral.'

'You seem damn sure of yourself, Ensign,' Spruance said.

Dan Black recognised the dangerous tone in the old man's voice. Another officer, Commander Beanland, stepped around a map table and shouted at Curtis.

'That'll be enough of your nonsense, Ensign. Get the hell off the bridge and back to your post. We're trying to fight a battle up here.'

The boy reacted as though Beanland had jammed

an electric wire into his neck. He went rigid and turned white. 'Sir!' he barked out, snapping a salute and making to turn on his heel. Black thought Spruance was about to stop him, ask him to explain further – the kid had seemed righteous in his certainty. But before the Admiral could properly open his mouth to speak, before Curtis could even complete his about-face, the blinding white light of a newborn sun spilled over them with a roar for the end of the world.

JDS Siranui, *2301 hours, 2 June 1942*

Maseo remembered the agony of stonefish poison, how his arm had burned as though held in a pot of boiling water after he'd brushed against the spines of one on the outer reefs off Cairns. The sense memory punched away at him while he lay unconscious, battering at his submerged mind until something gave way at last and let the real pain flood in. In a confused and sickening split second of vertigo, Sub-Lieutenant Maseo Miyazaki dropped out of his dream and onto the metal stairwell circling up into the *Siranui*'s fin bridge.

He screamed without shame or restraint as burned meat and nerve endings shrieked at him to get moving. Miyazaki had blacked out on the stairwell and had lived while the bridge crew died. But he had been badly burned by the explosion that killed his shipmates, and as he lay in the shallow coma of transition shock, a computer screen melted in the fires above him and dripped molten plastic onto his already scorched flesh.

Shock robbed the young man of his senses for a few long seconds until his training asserted itself and he awkwardly thumbed his flexipad, activating the trauma beacon. Panic flared briefly when he thought the pad may have been ruined in the missile strike, but a warm bath of analgesics and stabilisers soon flushed through his system, spreading out from his spine, up his neck and down into each of his injured limbs.

Thanks to the drugs, Miyazaki was quickly able to consider the small, sharpened spike of bone that was jutting through the torn skin on his right ankle. He wouldn't be able to walk on that, he knew. So he would have to drag himself up into the bridge by the strength of his good arms. He had just gripped the uncomfortably hot metallic gridwork of the step above his head when his flexipad began to vibrate and screech in a way he couldn't ignore.

Pausing and catching his breath, Miyazaki turned to examine the screen, expecting to find a senior officer there, bellowing orders. Instead the screen displayed *kanji* script, identifying the caller as the ship's Combat Intelligence and addressing him as *Acting Commander* Miyazaki. A character voice he recognised from many wasted hours watching anime serials spoke from the pad.

'The ship has been attacked and all senior command elements have been killed, Sub-Lieutenant Miyazaki. You are the surviving senior officer. The ship requests Autonomy Level One in response.'

'Ship,' croaked Miyazaki, before losing his voice for a second. He swallowed with difficulty, tasting for the first time the foul miasma of burning chemicals and human remains coating his mouth and throat. 'Ship, what is the fleet status?'

'All fleet elements are under attack, Sub-Lieutenant Miyazaki. Some are missing, presumed destroyed. The ship requests Autonomy Level One in response.'

'*Siranui* crew status?'

'The crew is incapable of performing any duties, Sub-Lieutenant Miyazaki. The ship requests Autonomy Level One in response.'

The *Siranui*'s CI spoke without urgency. It didn't need any. Given the shrill disharmony of competing alarms, the thick smoke and crackling fire, the thumping impact of shot falling nearby and the evidence of his own wounds, Miyazaki knew something was terribly wrong. It wasn't enough, however. Before he would authorise the release of the ship's weaponry, he had to be completely certain it was necessary.

'Ship,' he said, 'I must inspect the bridge for myself. I authorise Level *Two* Autonomy for response. Please confirm.'

'Ship confirms Level Two Autonomous Defensive Response, Sub-Lieutenant Miyazaki. Arming Metal Storm and laser pods . . . Targets acquired.'

‘On my authority, engage.’

It seemed to Miyazaki that the last word hadn’t even formed in his mind before the entire ship trembled under the awesome tenor of twelve Metal Storm turrets spewing thousands of hypervelocity caseless rounds into the air. The sound was less martial than industrial, the furious crescendo of heavy metal war drums.

The ship heaved to port, steering herself now, and Miyazaki rolled clumsily to one side, catching the bone stub that was protruding from his shattered ankle. Even with the drugs that had been released by his spinal syrettes, he greyed out with pain. When he came to a few seconds later, it was all he could do not to vomit. The *Siranui*’s CI, which was monitoring him like a fretful mother, dumped another blend of anaesthetic and antinausea solution onto his spinal receptors. Miyazaki experienced the flush as a threshold experience, akin to flipping from flat black and white to three-dimensional colour with the twirl of a dial. He drew a quick breath and began again, hauling himself up the metal steps on his hands and knees.

He smelled fire-retardant gas as he hauled himself through the torn blackout curtain and onto the ruined bridge. He gagged on the burned chemical stench and the obscene stink of seared meat. It would have been much worse were it not for the ragged hole that had been punched through the blast windows by the missile impact. Fresh air gusted through, plucking at his blood-stained uniform and matted hair. Smoke obscured the surviving blast windows, but he could see enough through the opening, where growing swarms of primitive, unguided missiles filled the night sky.

Night sky? But how . . .

Miyazaki pushed the thought aside. What mattered now was what lay out there in the punctuated darkness. It looked like something off a history vid, like a battle from the 1940s Pacific War. Dozens of ships weaved through dense and tangled arcs of high-explosive ordnance. Long streaks of tracer fire – barely directed, if at all – twisted about sinuously.

And here on the bridge, all around him, lay further evidence of bloody contention. Outwardly, Miyazaki was still. But inside he reeled from the images, finding it impossible to draw any connection between the first officer and that dismembered torso, between Captain Okada and the charred, severed arm that was still lying on the armrest of the command chair.

A flickering to his left drew Miyazaki's attention. He was grateful for the distraction. The damage seemed less severe over there. A few touch screens still functioned.

Bone-shaking thunder rolled over the bridge and Miyazaki lost his balance as the CI veered the ship away from a cluster of shell impacts. He managed to fall on his good side this time. Sea spray drenched him, spotting the screen with droplets of saltwater, each acting like a small convex lens, magnifying the pixel lattice that shone beneath them. Focusing on the screen, he could see that the *Clinton* was ablaze and the *Kandahar* was listing as though taking on water.

The voice of the *Siranui* spoke through an intact speaker somewhere behind him.

'Sensors indicate that the extreme threats continue, Sub-Lieutenant Miyazaki. The ship requests Autonomy Level One in response.'

Miyazaki did not hesitate this time. He had seen enough.

'On my authority, Level One Autonomy is sanctioned.'

The *Siranui*'s Combat Intelligence cross-matched the speaker's voiceprint with a DNA profile sampled through the smart-skin casing of his flexipad. Verifying that all higher command elements were dead or incapacitated, it confirmed command authority in the person of Sub-Lieutenant Miyazaki, and then instantly assumed operational authority for itself.

The ship's Nemesis arrays had already traced and logged the flight paths of the shells that had struck the bridge, tracing them back to their points of origin. The CI corrected for changes since impact, and identified the enemy vessels. It then activated two Tenix Defense Industries combat maces in retaliation.

Hexagonal silo caps flipped open on the forward deck. The stealth cruiser's Intelligence released the launch codes and attack vectors for an offensive run, and the maces, which on a cursory examination resembled old-fashioned cruise missiles, rose straight up out of the silo on towers of white flame. The boost-phase rockets cut out at two thousand metres, so there was no visual warning of the missiles' approach. Their scramjets burned without a perceptible exhaust.

Miyazaki followed the mace run on the screen in front of him. A time hack counted down to zero in the lower left corner. Two decks below, the same image was reproduced dozens of times on screens distributed around the Combat Information Centre. A small pop-up window on a cracked screen hanging by a thick tangle of wires near Miyazaki's resting place carried a feed from the CIC. It presented an eerie picture of twenty-two men slumped in their seats or sprawled on the nonslip deck, oblivious to the destruction their own vessel had just unleashed.

As the missiles curved downward towards their targets, dipping and swerving to avoid a wandering tracer stream, they maintained a furious laser-linked dialogue with the CI on the *Siranui*, demanding and receiving a constant stream of updated targeting data. Flaps on their stubby wings purred to and fro. On the *Siranui*'s two-dimensional displays Miyazaki watched as the hammerheads lined up on the enemy cruisers, executing course corrections with an economy of movement. Two hundred metres from the stern the leading missile dipped, then levelled off, racing about three hundred metres above the highest point of the vessel.

As the first missile reached a specific point above its target, a very small, controlled fusion reaction superheated two hundred tungsten slugs and spat them out of their containment cells with enough energy in each to destroy a heavily armoured fighting vehicle. The entire load punched through the deck of the cruiser. The kinetic and thermal shock instantly vapourised a significant percentage of the target mass.

The expanding gas, a molecule mix of human tissue, steel, wood, fabric and superheated air, manifested itself as a conventional explosion that blew the rest of the ship to hell and beyond.

Ammunition bunkers exploded. Boilers and the crew who attended them were atomised. Those slugs that drove all the way down into the keel flash-boiled thousands of litres of water that rushed back in through the ruptured hull. Miyazaki watched the death of the enemy ship in two acts. A rippling torrent of white fire raced down the length of the topside decks and superstructure, followed almost instantaneously by a sudden, violent eruption that seemed to detonate beneath the waterline before bursting the thick steel hull like a balloon. In a flash, the ship that had been there suddenly wasn't. A few moments later the second mace destroyed another ship in identical fashion.

Maseo Miyazaki had not wanted to be a warrior. He had dropped out of college to surf in Hawaii, then Indonesia and finally in Australia (where he had met that ugly damn stonefish). He had only returned to Japan and presented himself to the draft board in his home prefecture after a suicide bomber in Malaysia had killed his father, a Sanyo executive. After serving six months in a punishment detail for skipping out on the draft in the first place, he had distinguished himself with his application to duty and his easy familiarity with the ways of their *gaijin* allies.

He had never before felt the thrill and weight of *bushido*. But now, surrounded by dead friends and comrades, he knew the blood-simple joy of vengeance on one's enemy.

One thing bothered him, however.

The ship he had just killed looked nothing like the pirate dhows or *baggala* routinely used by jihadi terrorists within the Indonesian archipelago.

USS Enterprise, *2307 hours, 2 June 1942*

'Sweet Jesus,' breathed Admiral Ray Spruance.

The death of the *Portland* bathed the pilot house in a harsh, flat light. For a few seconds Spruance had an almost perfect view of the cauldron in which the two enemies tore at each other with such blind fury. The Japanese guns poured out eerie needles of light, flash-burning hundreds of shells in midflight, creating a sensational fireworks show. Ribbons of green and gold tracer fire sprayed high into the stars or weaved and twisted low across the waves. It seemed as if every minute brought another apocalyptic blast like that which had silenced the *Portland* forever.

On the flight deck, men still threw their lumbering torpedo planes down the heavy wooden planking, desperate to get aloft and into the enemy. So many of them failed. Those devilish glimmering needles of light struck down most who survived before they could reorient themselves.

It was a slaughter.

In a matter of minutes contemporary American naval power in the Pacific had been crippled. More than half of the destroyers from Task Forces 16 and 17 were destroyed outright. The carriers *Hornet* and *Yorktown* were obliterated by one rocket each.

Just one, God help us, thought Spruance.

The cruisers *New Orleans* and *Minneapolis* joined their sister ship *Portland* on her dive to the floor of the ocean, the latter sunk by the second rocket launched from that damned Japanese ghost ship. The starburst of white light that bloomed amidships and consumed the entire ship still stung his eyes. Dan Black had cursed and said it was 'like looking right into the sun'.

Suddenly the bridge windows blew in with a hollow bang as a long, shark-like blur whipped past the pilot house at phenomenal speed. Two sailors who had been standing close to the glass spun away, crying out and trying too late to shield their faces. A massive *boom* sounded almost simultaneously. Spruance felt it as a quake deep inside his chest, and as knitting needles jammed painfully into his ears. It was two or three seconds before he could hear the profane language of the men around him.

He realised the young ensign, the one who'd warned them about the rockets, was tugging at his arm, pointing out through the nearest shattered pane. He was shouting something but it came through as a faint, far-off murmur.

Spruance frowned and tried to read the boy's lips. But he was certain the ensign was saying something like 'death rays'.

Spruance feared he was losing his mind.

Death rays indeed!

Holy Toledo, yes, they were *death rays*!

Ensign Wally Curtis couldn't understand why nobody else could see it. But then, nobody else on the *Enterprise* – probably nobody else in the fleet – had invested as many hours as he had immersed in the pages of *Astounding and Amazing Stories.*

As soon as he'd seen those brilliant flares lift off out of the Japanese ship, he'd known they were rockets.

And I was right!

And as soon as the blackness of night on the deep ocean became stitched and criss-crossed with those shimmering arrows of light, he'd known they were death rays. Not flak or machine-gun bullets, but honest-to-God beam weapons! And the sky was *full* of them.

Oh, the Japs were gonna win this war for sure.

He knew that really big bang, the one that lit up the giant carrier away on the horizon – the *Akagi*, they reckoned – he knew that was a lucky strike, or maybe just a dive-bomber tumbling into the deck.

Just about every single plane they'd managed to put up had quickly disappeared in a dirty ball of orange flame and oily smoke. He could tell that the enormous volumes of fire they were putting out were trailing off as their sister ships disappeared, one after the other, inside dazzling white-hot dwarf stars. He'd seen the *Phelps* go up just a few yards away like a giant magnesium flare.

He didn't know how they could defend themselves.

But he *did* know that Admiral Spruance had to be told what he was up against.

If he could just tell the admiral, *he'd* know what to do.

When he saw the *New Orleans* go up, Dan Black knew they were all going to die. He watched that long, wingless plane – the thing that looked like a flying hammerhead shark – as it flashed over the flight deck of the *Enterprise*. His thigh muscles bunched and he distinctly felt his ass pucker as he waited for the firestorm to spit out of its belly. He'd seen that happen twice now to other ships. But the *Enterprise* was spared. Christ only knew why. And the rocket – if Curtis was right – passed over them with such speed you could practically *see* the wall of compressed air that attended its passage. It knocked men off their feet down on the flight deck, swept a few of them over the side, and even seemed to flatten the waves beneath it.

In Lieutenant Commander Black's opinion, something travelling that fast, if it was built solid, would punch right through a battleship.

And sure enough, he'd have sworn the *New Orleans* actually rocked on her axis when the thing struck her. All ten thousand tons of her. Just before that globe of silent white light ballooned outwards from the impact point and swallowed up the whole ship.

That was when he knew they were all going to die.

USS Hillary Clinton, *2307 hours, 2 June 1942*

Kolhammer ran his eyes over the screens in front of him and the firestorm lighting the darkness outside. They were in battle. He had no idea with whom and over what. But men and women were dying by the thousands if the flat-screen reports and the evidence of the night outside were to be believed. The deck of the *Clinton* was aflame, reminding him of the oil fires he'd witnessed in all of the Gulf Wars.

'Any word on Captain Chandler?' Kolhammer asked Commander Judge, knowing the answer before the ship's executive officer spoke.

Judge checked both his flexipad and a workstation,

his mouth fixed in a grim line. He confirmed what the admiral had feared.

'He's gone, sir, along with everybody on the flight deck and another six hundred here and there. It's your ship, Admiral.'

None of the men or women on the bridge turned from their stations, but Kolhammer felt the weight of their expectations fall on him. Their lives were now in his hands.

'Lieutenant Brooks.' He addressed the CIC boss, who was looking much less bilious thanks to the Promatil flush. 'Give it to me quick and dirty. Force status and enemy disposition. Mike, give me ship status when the lieutenant's finished.'

Judge began to gather damage reports from the carrier's various departments while Kolhammer watched Brooks's hands flying over her touch screen. The young woman's face was impassive, although Kolhammer guessed her mind and heart would be racing.

'We're still out of contact with our subs, Admiral. Sensors can't find *Chicago* or *Denver* anywhere. *Garrett*, *Vanguard*, *Dessaix*, *Sutanto*, *Nuku* and *Nagoya* are also still missing. There's no available datum point indicating those ships have been sunk. They're just missing. The *Leyte Gulf* isn't responding. Drone surveillance indicates counterboarding operations are under way. *Fearless* has been destroyed.'

Brooks allowed herself a quick, rueful expression at that before continuing.

'The *Kandahar* has taken some fire and reports a torpedo strike. The damage is serious but contained. Eighty-six confirmed KIA. *Moreton Bay* reports multiple hits. The *Siranui* has suffered a major impact on her bridge. Captain Okada is dead, along with his exec and five other officers. Sub-Lieutenant Miyazaki has assumed control and authorised the CI to respond at Level One. The *Havoc* is undetected and has launched one Type 92 heavy torpedo, killing the boat that torpedoed us.'

Kolhammer nodded. He'd been certain the *Havoc* had sunk that ship. At least he'd got that right, he thought dolefully, as Brooks spoke again.

'Begging your pardon, Admiral, but we're running through our defensive stocks at an unsustainable rate. There's just too much incoming. We're taking it out, but if it keeps up at this pace we'll have exhausted Metal Storm within another seven minutes. The laser pods will be okay for another ten, but they'll need to power down pretty shortly after that. All other force elements are reporting the same. The *Moreton Bay* has already run through her stock of MS munitions. *Trident* has taken up a position shepherding her, but they're getting hungry, too.'

'Thank you, Lieutenant. I'll take it under consideration,' he said. 'What can you tell me about who we're fighting?'

Brooks's air of detachment faltered at that.

'I can't with any certainty, sir. They're not returning any signatures from our combatant database. Their signals and electronic profiles don't match anything Chinese or Indian or even Islamic Republic. Weapons suites are . . . well, Stone Age. That was a dumb iron bomb we got hit with topside before.'

'Delivery system?'

'I'm streaming video from topside cams and drones. It's a museum piece.'

Three windows opened up on screen. Each carried low-light amplified footage from various angles showing an old propeller-driven monoplane nosing down a few thousand feet over the *Clinton*'s flight deck. The acid level in Kolhammer's stomach rose painfully, leaving a sour taste at the back of his throat. He understood Brooks's reluctance to make a call on the attacker's ID. But he recognised it immediately.

As a twelve-year-old boy he'd built a plastic model of a Douglas Dauntless SBD dive-bomber. It had taken young Phillip Kolhammer three months to save the money needed to buy that kit. It took him weeks of work, getting every detail right, the flush-riveted stretched-skin wing covering, the Wright R-1820-52 nine-cylinder radial air-cooled engine; painting inside the cut-away aluminium alloy fuel tanks. Two centre-section seventy-five-gallon tanks, as he recalled, and another two fifty-five-gallon outer wing tanks. He'd done such a good job on it, taken such serious, professional care, that his father, a career coastguard man, bought him another model kit as a reward.

He sat, staring at the screen as the vision looped

back on itself. A Douglas Dauntless SBD dive-bomber.

'Admiral?' Commander Judge laid a hand on his shoulder, just lightly. 'Admiral. Captain Halabi's on laser-link. I think you'd better take the call. They've been running analysis a few minutes longer than us.'

'Thanks, Mike,' he croaked, dragging his eyes away from the replay. Outside, the battle continued. As he turned to Karen Halabi's attractive face, which occupied almost all of a single monitor on his left, three violent blooms of light and fire marked the destruction of a volley of incoming shells just a few hundred metres from the carrier's bow. A shower of hot shrapnel pattered onto the flight deck, but it didn't matter. All human life had ended out there a few minutes earlier.

'Captain. Please report.'

'Thank you, Admiral.' The British officer looked unhappy. 'They're Americans, Admiral. We've been killing American sailors. And they've been trying to kill us.'

'How?' he asked, finding himself increasingly exasperated, but not disbelieving her. The plane in the looped video. He couldn't shake the image.

'I don't know how. I really have no idea. But we've had six minutes more than you to get over the neural effect –' Kolhammer noted that she didn't call it an attack. '– We shared data with the *Havoc*, and we can't get past the fact. They're American. Old Americans.'

'What do you mean, Captain?'

Captain Halabi wasn't known for her delicacy. She didn't soften the blow now.

'We've positively identified eight major combatants, cross-matched drone footage with archival data and catalogued enough signals intelligence to confirm the theory. We're firing on Task Forces 16 and 17, out of Pearl Harbor, bound for Midway Atoll, originally under the command of Admiral Frank Fletcher, now led by Admiral Ray Spruance. Fletcher was on the USS *Yorktown*. It's been destroyed.'

Halabi was neither belligerent nor challenging. She could have been war-gaming at staff college for all the emotion she invested in her delivery. Kolhammer couldn't help but sneak a quick peek at the cam coverage of the dive-bomber again.

'Any proof?' he said.

It was as if she had been waiting for the question. The screen carrying her face split into four windows. She occupied the top right corner. The other three cycled through a selection of images, real-time video of World War II vintage cruisers, destroyers and aircraft carriers churning up a maelstrom of foam at their sterns as they manoeuvred frantically – and all too frequently in vain – while attempting to outrun a supercavitating torpedo or combat mace. Kolhammer's nausea returned as he watched a destroyer die inside a small cyclone of ballistic munitions. The image rewound and the ship reintegrated itself as torrents of white fire were sucked back into the decks and superstructure. The vision froze and the other two windows cycled through a series of still photographs of the same vessel.

The pictures, culled from files across Fleetnet, had been taken on a number of different occasions, more than eighty years earlier.

As Kolhammer sat quietly, Halabi repeated the performance with four other ships. Three destroyers and one cruiser. There was no doubt. They were sinking these very ships. *But how?* No, that question would have to wait.

'We have extensive intercepts,' said Halabi. 'Ship-to-ship. Aircraft in-flight. Internal communications.'

'Okay,' said Kolhammer. 'Make it quick.'

A sound channel opened and an avalanche of American voices spilled out. They sounded subtly different from the voices Kolhammer was used to hearing around him, but regardless he listened as men begged for information, for ammunition. For God's help. The raw fear, the crash of gunfire and the animalistic sounds of human beings contending in blood were all intimately familiar to Phillip Kolhammer. The traffic was genuine. He could feel it in his gut. Then, for the first time since the world had gone insane, he had a single, quiet thought.

The *Nagoya*.

'Shit,' he spat quietly.

'Sir?' said Mike Judge.

'Later. Commander, get this out now, fleet-wide. All offensive systems are to go offline immediately.'

'Offline. Acknowledged.'

'CIs to retain autonomy for point defence only. All units to manoeuvre for defensive fire support. Have the CIs work it out, and we'll coordinate through Little Bill,' he said, referring to the *Clinton*'s CI. 'We'll need to put the *Siranui* at our centre.'

'Aye, sir.'

'Captain Halabi, I'll have to get back to you. Please stand by. Lieutenant Brooks, get me the comms boss.'

The freckled face of Lieutenant Stuart Glover filled the window where Karen Halabi had just been resident.

'Lieutenant, open up a line with one of the ships we've encountered. I need to talk to Admiral Ray Spruance on the USS *Enterprise*.'

Before the young man could protest, Kolhammer held up the palm of his hand.

'I know. I know. Lieutenant Brooks will brief you. But later. I need this done yesterday. Just make it happen.'

'Aye, sir,' he answered unsurely.

Mike Judge was staring at him as though he'd lost his mind. Kolhammer reopened his channel to Halabi, and thanked her grimly. She signed off to attend to her own problems.

'Damage reports,' said Kolhammer. 'The lite version.'

'Seven hundred and thirty dead, three hundred wounded, about half of them critically. We've lost *all* the catapults, with heavy damage to the aircraft tied down outboard of number one. Eighteen Raptors totally trashed, and another two can only be salvaged for parts. Four torpedo strikes, but only one detonated. The inner hull retained its integrity but there's a big fucking mess needs cleaning up down there. Little Bill has lost two nodes, but he's reformatted. We've lost two aft laser pods and one Metal Storm mount. We're down to forty per cent of war stocks on the remaining guns.'

'Jesus,' muttered Kolhammer. 'Busy day.'

'They're greedy little boys, sir.'

Kolhammer could see Judge was about to ask him about the instructions he'd given Lieutenant Glover.

'I think something went wrong on the *Nagoya*, Mike,' he said, cutting off the inquiry. 'Were you running any of those sneaky little blinkscans on them before we blacked out?'

Judge nodded briefly, excusing himself to interrogate a nearby workstation.

'Damn,' he said softly a moment later. 'You're right, sir. About twenty minutes ago, just before we passed out, I guess, all the passive sensors monitoring EM shifts on the *Nagoya* went psycho.'

'Christ knows what they were messing with,' said Kolhammer, 'but that briefing from Pearl . . . you were there. What'd you think?'

Judge shrugged and pursed his lips. Two deep lines ran down from the corners of his mouth. 'Honestly, Admiral, I don't know. All that stuff about wormholes and space warps. I figured we were being bullshitted three ways from Sunday.'

'Better check the Fleetnet personnel files, Commander. See who we've got with any postgraduate specialisation in . . . um . . .'

'Warp drives and time travel?' scoffed the Texan.

'Well, let's just start with standard physics grads from the better universities. You and I will have to fill them in.'

The communications officer reappeared on screen, the dark smudges under his eyes standing out even more starkly against a face drained of all colour.

'As requested, sir. I have an Admiral Spruance on audio channel three.'

Kolhammer nodded his thanks as static flared over a loudspeaker. 'Good work, Lieutenant. Push it out over Fleetnet and to all the vessels in Admiral Spruance's group.'

Kolhammer didn't talk into a microphone. A small biochip implanted at the base of his neck, and powered by the electrical charge of his body's own cells, picked up the bone vibrations of his speech and transformed them into a quantum signal, captured by the same sensors that constantly kept Little Bill aware of his exact location and physiological condition.

All of that marvellous technology was no help at all.

Admiral Phillip Kolhammer's mind was blank.

What the hell do I say now?

7

USS Leyte Gulf, *2312 hours, 2 June 1942*

Halon gas and ammonium dihydrogen phosphate dust had smothered the flames in the chopper bay and asphyxiated any lingering survivors of Lieutenant Reilly's temporary command. Specialist Nix scanned the room twice, but failed to get even a phantom return from a single biochip. Everybody was dead. He estimated the gaping maw in the port-side bulkhead at maybe three metres across. The hole gave him a window on the battle outside. As Nix waved his flexipad back and forth one last time, scanning for life signs, a small supernova dawned on the horizon. His combat goggles adjusted to filter out the blinding, incandescent light of a subnuclear warhead. Fanged shadows stretched out across the charnel-house floor of the hangar.

Nix spun out of the hatchway, dragging the waterproof door closed behind him. It wouldn't seal properly. The ship had been wrenched too far out of shape. He abandoned the effort and hurried up the corridor. Sessions was only slowly coming to, still lying propped up where Nix had left him. He ran a quick check on his partner, zapped a message out to send a medic, and hurried on again.

A stairwell outside the mail centre led all the way down to D deck, but Nix descended only as far as B before heading forward. He thought the decks were angled down a fraction. All that extra weight up front, and they were probably breached beneath the waterline, too. Though Shipnet was supposed to track his position, he didn't trust it to be working properly and forewarn the other fire teams, so he yelled out every ten steps or so.

'Nix. Counterboarding. Coming through for Captain Anderson.'

He nearly tripped over a dead sailor outside the main mess. Half her face was missing. A little further on, her attacker – he assumed it was her attacker – had been chewed over by at least half a strip of caseless thirty-three millimetres.

When ceramic ammunition entered an unprotected human body, it unfurled itself inside, expanding from a small, fantastically dense lozenge, into something resembling a miniature thornbush composed of hundreds of semirigid razor tendrils. Ceramic rounds would chew right through Kevlar. Multiple impacts would even significantly degrade monobonded carbon. The effect on human beings, who were engineered nowhere near as well, was dramatic and deeply unpleasant. Above the waistline, most of the attacker had disintegrated into a fine pulp that now painted the corridor.

Nix had seen it before. He checked his pace so as not to slip in the liquid waste, but gave it no heed beyond that. He soon came upon Ntini and McAllister, crouched down behind an upturned desk.

'Specialist Nix, coming through!' he yelled.

They risked a quick glance back, then waved him up.

His body armour afforded more protection than their barricade, but he crouched down to their level anyway. Twenty metres further ahead a wall of wet, grey steel blocked the corridor. Three of his shipmates were sprawled promiscuously over each other just in front of it. Their blood had pooled beneath them, prevented from running down towards McAllister and Ntini by the slight dip of the ship's bow.

A man-sized opening had been blown through the iron curtain.

'How'd they do that?' asked Nix.

McAllister answered in a hoarse whisper. 'A shaped charge.'

'Nice work. The captain in there?'

'You should be able to pick up her locator chip once you're inside. Head right for two minutes. It's a fucking mess like you wouldn't believe in there, but they're trailing tape. You should pick them up. Point-to-point's scratchy once you get in, so let them know you're coming up. They've been hit from behind twice already. Chris Gregory got wasted like that. Clancy blew him away when he popped up without warning.'

'Got it.'

Nix patted the shoulder of McAllister's old Kevlar vest and leaped the overturned table in one bound.

That's five now, she thought.

She'd lost five of her crew since stepping into this twisted nightmare, one of them to friendly fire.

'You okay?' she asked Clancy.

'Fine for now,' he replied. 'Wasn't his fault. Wasn't mine, either.'

'That's right.'

Captain Daytona Anderson knew the tremors and nausea would come later for Clancy. Along with the guilt.

Couldn't be helped.

She repeated that mantra to herself, like a Zen koan meant to exhaust the intellect and prepare the mind for an intuitive response.

Because Christ knows, there's nothing for the rational mind to hold on to in here.

She was wedged into a crawl space created by the intersection of the *Gulf*'s rail gun control room with what looked like an old galley of some sort. Her features creased as she contemplated the sight of two members of her own crew and five strangers who had . . . *What, materialised?* . . . inside each other, *and* within a Gordian knot of metal, plastic and wooden fixtures.

The shooting, which had slackened off for a few minutes, picked up again. A few rounds ricocheted by her head, off a butcher's block that had been fused with a flat-screen workstation, showering Anderson with splinters of wood and plastic. Clancy fired without hesitation. She had no idea what he was shooting at, but somebody screamed. Whoever it was almost cried out loud enough to cover the sick, ripping thud that was the signature note of a ceramic bullet striking unprotected flesh. Then another voice called out, but it was controlled and steady.

'Specialist Nix, coming through, Captain!'

Anderson checked her flexipad. It was working again. The screen displayed icons for the locator chips implanted in the necks of her crew within a twenty-metre radius.

NIX, SPEC 3-010162820 was slowly picking his way forwards.

Three hollow booms crashed painfully close to her ears. Clancy fired again, for the same result: a strangled scream and the sound of something heavy dropping to the floor.

'You might want to hold your fire,' Nix called out. 'We've got a big problem.'

No shit? Anderson thought bitterly.

'Yeah, I know,' said Nix. 'I mean *another* problem.'

USS Astoria, *2314 hours, 2 June 1942*

The niggers and the broads were the least of their problems. And, really, not the most fucked-up thing he'd seen today. But for the life of him, Able Seaman Moose Molloy Jr couldn't figure out what a bunch of niggers and broads were doing on board a Japanese warship.

They'd killed four of them now, two apiece. And lost a lot of their own in return. And yes, it was pretty weird that they'd only got one Jap that he knew of. But his daddy, the senior Moose, who'd walked a beat for thirty years with the Chicago PD, had taught him that your niggers and your wops and your Asiatic races simply couldn't be trusted. There wasn't a damn one of them you'd cross the street to piss on if their heart caught fire. And the broads were most likely sex slaves, he guessed. His buddy Slim Jim Davidson had read him a story from the newspaper about that – how the Japs were capturing white women in the Far East and turning them into camp whores. Made a man's blood boil just to think about those nasty little fuckers poking their weenies into God-fearing white women.

The newspaper, which had specialised in horse-racing tips and murder mysteries before the war, had been red hot on that topic – the so-called Japanese fighting man's anatomical shortcomings. Still, Moose thought, pencil dicks or not, they'd pay a heavy fucking price for sticking them into any woman who spoke English and knew enough to cross herself when she walked into a church.

Hell of a way to fight them, though. Moose Jr was a big man, and these crawl spaces he was forced to squirm through were complicated enough to confuse a bona fide genius, which the Molloy family genes had conspicuously failed to produce so far. It was worse than any carnival maze he'd snuck into as a kid. Things just seemed to grow out of other things all around him. He could recognise pieces of the *Astoria*, but they were all tangled up with the bulkheads and deck plating and fixtures of this weird Jap ship. Not all smashed in together, like you'd get in the car wrecks his daddy had told him about, all crumpled metal and blood and torn-up bits of drivers and passengers. But flowing in and out of each other, smooth and easy as you please. Or not so easy. If you were Hogan or Paddy White, or one of those other poor bastards who had a big piece of armour plating or a chair or something suddenly pop out of their heads or ass.

Oftentimes he'd get himself bruised and half crushed worming his way around some obstacle, only to find he'd come to a dead end, trapped in a cranny created by the intersection of two impassable walls. Sometimes you could see good clear space, but it lay just beyond a gap too narrow for anyone but a stick figure to squeeze through. It was infuriating, was what it was. And dangerous too. Old Chief Kelly got the back of his head blown out lingering too long at one such break in the maze. Moose Jr didn't have no fancy education, but there were some things you picked up quick anyway. With Chief Kelly's brains splattered all over his greying, sweat-stained T-shirt, Moose Jr didn't mess around with no recon at places like that. He just stuck his rifle into the gap and let go a few rounds. It was an old Springfield bolt action, which was a pain. He'd have given a month's pay for one of them new M1 Garands. Semiautomatic, gas operated. Fired a .30-calibre round as quick as a man could pull the trigger, according to Slim Jim. But a Springfield still made an agreeably large hole in a fellow, and Moose Jr was almost certain he'd accounted for at least one of them untrustworthy Jap niggers with his.

A group of shots hammered at the far side of the bulkhead just in front of him. A Jap bulkhead, he was pretty sure. He'd been planning on darting around there in just a second, but the volley forced him back behind cover. He tasted that strange orange dust that floated away from the impact point whenever the nip rounds hit metal instead of flesh. Nips then, for sure. Goddamn if he wouldn't like to get a look at the guns they were using. Had to be some kind of secret weapon, the way they didn't seem to damage anything but human flesh. Apart from the smear of orange dust, they didn't leave no trace at all. Unless they got you in the arm or chest or full in the face like poor old Kelly. God-a-mighty they'd leave a hell of a mess then. Like nothing he'd ever seen – and the old man had let him sneak a peak at some crime scene photos once. Pictures of a freelance boot-legger machine-gunned by some of Al Capone's boys. A terrible sight, but nothing like the unholy meat salad laying where Chief Kelly's bald noggin had once sat.

'Moose! Moose! They Japs up there?'

'What d'you think, you moron?' he spat back at Willie Stolz, who wasn't worth a cup of cold spit in Moose Jr's considered opinion. It was a fair question, though. They'd shot some of their own by mistake in the dark tangle of groaning metal, spark showers and venting steam.

'Moose! Moose!'

'Goddamn, Stolz, I'm trying to kill me some nip niggers up here.'

'It's an officer, Moose!'

'What the fuck? I thought they was all dead.'

'It's okay, sailor,' grunted Lieutenant Commander Evans, who looked about a thousand miles from okay.

The snaking, tortured course through the labyrinth had been hard on Evans's injured ankle and arm. More than once he'd relied on Chief Mohr to push him through a cavity or cleft in the nearly impenetrable snarl of fused flesh and steel. They had made it through to the furthest point of advance, though, a relatively clear space formed by the confluence of an officer's washroom on the *Astoria* and some sort of science lab on the other ship. There was a light source somewhere in there, soft white light coming from within a toilet cubicle, the direct source of illumination blocked by a half-opened door occupying the same space as a desk. Evans didn't see how a desk lamp could still be lit; where would it be drawing power? But there were so many other questions arising out of the last fifteen minutes that he was learning to put the small stuff away in the chickenshit file.

'They through here?' he asked the sailor, a large fellow named Molloy.

He was about to peer through the small slit Molloy was guarding when a giant forearm slammed into his chest and drove him back against a washbasin. His broken arm flared in hot pain and he started to grey out as Eddie Mohr grabbed him.

'Sorry, sir,' said Molloy, 'but those Japs can see in the dark, sir. You put your face up there and you're going to get it shot off, Commander.'

Gunfire crashed in their ears every few seconds. Mostly single-shot rifle and pistol fire, but occasionally someone let rip with a tommy gun on full auto. You could hear the rounds striking dozens of different surfaces as they flew around within the disordered geometry of the combined ship spaces. Brass casings fell to the deck, ringing like a jar full of coins tipped onto a concrete floor. Fire came back at them too. It sounded weird. Really loud, but there was never any ricochet. Just a peculiar sort of thudding *puff* when the bullets struck metal, or a sodden *whack*, like a baseball striking a wet catcher's mitt, if they hit flesh. Seaman Molloy dipped his chin to point out the headless corpse of CPO Kelly, lying where the force of those odd bullets had thrown it.

'He took one with him, though,' said Molloy respectfully. 'You see him coming in, Commander? That Jap got one right through the heart? That was Chief Kelly did that, sir. Woulda put them army sharpshooters to shame, sir.'

'Okay, sailor,' grunted Evans, still reeling from Molloy's heavy blow. 'Better give me a report.'

Molloy gave him a look that said he'd never had to report to anyone more important than Chief Kelly, but then he straightened his shoulders and gathered his thoughts. Clearly there weren't that many of them, but his bovine features grew even more ruminative than usual.

'Well, Commander, we come in through the hole in the bunkroom. We had a lot of trouble finding our way around. We shot a few Japs, turned out to be niggers, and I'm sorry but I think we shot a few ladies they had as sex slaves, too . . . Probably better for them that way, though.'

As Moose was talking, the volume of incoming fire grew alarmingly, forcing him to raise his voice. Evans was going to ask him about the black men and the women, whether anyone had thought to search them for ID, when Seaman Stolz screamed. A very large chunk of his chest disintegrated in a hot red shower that splashed over his shipmates.

He was dead before what was left of him slumped to the deck.

'*Damn.* I told you!' yelled Molloy. 'Didn't I, Commander? They shot him through that little crack there.'

He jammed his rifle into the space, loosed off a round in reply, then wrestled it out with some difficulty just before the response came in. Three rounds passed through and smacked into a solid steel bulkhead just over the spot where Evans had crouched down and curled as tightly as possible. He was totally mystified by what he saw. The bullets impacted the metal surface with dry puffs of powder, leaving no dent and almost no residue. You had to wonder how they'd killed Stolz. Evans resisted the urge to lean over and scrape away some of the dust that clung to the point of impact. But he'd already decided it wouldn't be worth his life.

It was hard enough to hear anyone talk, let alone to think this situation through calmly and rationally, with the harsh thunder of battle going on all around him. Mohr had told him nearly a hundred men were fetched up against dozens of barricades or blockages like Molloy's, pouring as much lead into the enemy as they could, given the Japs' nearly supernatural ability to pick them off with those fucking shotgun blasts. Between the fearful roar of that battle and the agony building from his own wounds, Evans feared the situation was entirely beyond him. He was only Navy Reserve, after all. In civilian life, where he'd been blissfully and ignorantly employed until recently, he was a math teacher at a small school in upstate New York. He'd joined the reserve in the early thirties when work was hard to come by. He'd made some fine friends out of it and the young ladies of Cherrybrooke village did like a man in uniform. But this . . . this was getting out of hand.

He was tempted to give in to the creeping greyness, to fall unconscious and let someone else figure it all out, when the strangest thing happened. The storm of fire coming in at them abruptly ceased.

And then there came a loud crackling sound, like static over a ship's speaker. And an amplified voice boomed out. A female voice, with a clearly recognisable American accent, but unfamiliar in its pitch and tone.

'This is Captain Daytona Anderson of the United States Navy Ship *Leyte Gulf*. Cease fire and identify yourselves immediately.'

Evans looked over at Eddie Mohr, who seemed just as stunned as he was. The chief petty officer shrugged and shook his head.

'It's one of their camp whores,' hissed Molloy. 'You can't trust her, sir. She's been brainwashed.'

'Shut up, Moose,' growled Mohr, before turning back to Evans. 'Well, sir?'

Evans shook his head at this new turn of events.

He drew a deep breath and tried to shout a reply, but his dry, cracked throat failed him. Chief Mohr took out his hip flask again and thrust it at the officer. Evans took a quick swill and tried once more. He was surprised at how weak his voice sounded.

'This is Lieutenant Commander Peter Evans of the USS *Astoria.* Identify yourself properly, and explain what the hell is going on here.' He could hear other members of the *Astoria*'s crew whispering to each other in the brief silence that followed.

Then the woman's angry voice drowned them out. 'I say again, this is Captain Daytona Anderson of the USS *Leyte Gulf.* You have boarded our ship and killed US naval personnel. That enough explanation for you, asshole?'

Evans got Mohr to help him over to the crack through which Willie Stolz had been shot. He yelled into the gap. 'Listen, lady. If the Japs are putting you up to this, just forget it. I'm sorry for your situation, but we're not lying down for anyone.'

Muted cheers drifted into their bunker from somewhere off to starboard. Or what he thought was starboard.

'Listen, you macho jerk, you're going to get yourself and the rest of your crew killed for no good reason. We're not Japanese. We're Americans. You hear me? *Americans.*'

Chief Mohr leaned over and said quietly, 'That sounds like a black woman to me, Commander.'

He was right, Evans realised. That was what threw

him about the voice. It was black, like one of those Harlem jazz singers.

'What're you trying to pull, lady?' he called back. 'There's no such ship as the *Leyte Gulf*, and if there was, the captain wouldn't be a dame. You just put Tojo on the loudspeaker, if he knows any English. I'll take a surrender from him.'

The cheers of his crewmates were punctuated by a good deal of laughter this time. Anderson didn't reply, and he wondered if she'd been hustled away by her captors.

Clancy and Nix crouched on either side of the aperture giving on to Evans and his men. Both men had set their night vision to the soft emerald of low-light amplification. Infrared was useless. There were simply too many heat sources bleeding into the fused mayhem of junk metal. Sparks cascaded from shorted-out wiring. Steam vented from ruptured pipes in brilliant ruby-red geysers, and small spot fires burned all around them, adding a hot smoke haze to the saturated air.

Clancy hand-signed to Anderson. Did she want them to work around through the maze of scrap and attempt to subdue the targets?

The captain shook her head. She cut power to the small bullhorn in her left hand.

'The way you guys look,' she subvocalised, 'they'd take you for a couple of Nazis.'

A chip implanted just below her jawline picked up

the vibrations and converted them into a narrowcast quantum signal. Nix and Clancy heard their commanding officer's words in their helmets as clearly as if she'd spoken at normal volume in a quiet room. Nobody else heard anything.

'Just keep it tight and try not to waste anyone,' she continued. 'I'll try again.'

That amplified voice boomed out again.

'All right, Commander Evans. I'm coming forward with my CPO and Specialist Nix. Are you in the head that intersected our weather station?'

Evans's eyes went wide at that. They were definitely hunkered down in a john and he figured that yes, maybe the science lab stuff could be weather equipment of some sort.

Mohr just looked at him as if to say *What next*?

'Yeah. I guess so,' replied the *Astoria*'s acting CO.

'We're coming armed. You fire on us and Clancy will pop a frag through that crack as easy as the round that killed your other guy a minute ago. Be nice if he didn't have to do that again.'

Crouching low, Moose Molloy tried to muscle into the gap with his Springfield, but Mohr placed a size-twelve boot on his shoulder and stopped him cold. Evans thumbed back the hammer on his pistol, but kept it pointing down at the floor. A moment later he could just make out movement in the gloom and clutter of shadows on the other side of the gap. Three figures slowly resolved out of the darkness. A thin, weak shaft of diffused white light, thrown out by the source somewhere behind the toilet door, barely picked them out.

'That you, Evans?' the woman asked, her voice at normal volume now. She seemed to be speaking directly to him. But how did she know where he was in all this blackness?

'Yeah,' he croaked. 'It's me.'

'I'm going to break a glo-stick,' she said. 'You'll hear a sort of snap and a green tube will appear just in front of you. It'll glow bright enough for you to make us out a little easier.'

Evans, Mohr and Molloy heard a crunch, like someone stepping on glass. A faint green line began to glow on the far side of the gap. Within seconds it threw off enough light to illuminate the figures who had approached them. Evans was aware of Molloy stiffening beside him and adjusting his grip on the old Springfield.

'Sailor,' he said softly, 'I want you to crawl over there, get behind that door, and see if you can get a hold of that lamp or whatever it is. We may need some more light in here.'

Moose seemed about to question the logic of this order, but a cold glare from CPO Mohr cut him off and sent him away, muttering under his breath. Evans was too tired, too befuddled and in way too much pain to bother with the mild insubordination. He let go a long shuddering breath as he regarded the fantastic creatures who stood just a few feet away now.

He figured the older man to be the chief petty officer. He looked the type. Stocky and assured. The woman, sure enough, was a Negro. A big one, by the way she was crouched. She seemed to be wearing a life jacket of some sort and had a pair of goggles pushed up on her head. She and her chief were both toting shotguns, so perhaps it was one of them who had done for Stolz. That was of marginal interest, however, next to the flood of questions raised by the third man.

Nix, was it?

Even in the strange green glow of the light stick, the trooper seemed on the verge of disappearing into the visual clutter. It was almost as though he was drinking up the light, without throwing any of it back. Evans thought he was dressed in black, but he couldn't tell for sure. When Nix moved, he flowed like a ghost from one flickering shadow to the next. His eyes seemed huge and almost insect-like, until Evans realised he, too, was wearing goggles. Unlike the Negro woman, he hadn't removed his, and he seemed to be constantly scanning their surroundings. His weapon, some weird Buck Rogers thing, seemed to float by his side, and Peter Evans had the unnerving sensation that it could swing up and target the small patch of skin between his eyes before he could even blink in surprise. He felt sure it was the same man he'd seen earlier, on the deck of the other ship.

'That's a fucking German storm-trooper!' Mohr hissed in his ears. 'Look at the helmet, Commander.

And dressed in black like that. He's gotta be a Kraut.'

'Seaman Nix hails from Fort Worth, Texas,' said the black woman. 'I'm not sure of his politics.'

'Unreconstructed southern Democrat, ma'am,' said Nix in a broad, recognisably Texan drawl.

'Well, we won't hold that against him. But I can assure you he is not an SS officer.'

'Well, what the hell is he then?' snapped Evans, suddenly finding himself thoroughly exasperated by the conversational tone she maintained in the face of this relentless insanity.

Despite his outburst, the 'captain' – what had she called herself? – replied calmly, 'Nix is one of my boarding/counterboarding specialists, Commander Evans. I'll have him fall back if you'd prefer. Regardless, you and I need to talk. And fast. I don't know how long the structural integrity of our ships can hold out. But at the very least I'd suggest we stop trying to shoot each other and dial back our speed. We're tearing each other apart.'

'What did you say your name was?' asked Evans.

'Anderson. Captain Daytona Anderson of the USS *Leyte Gulf*.'

'And I'm supposed to believe that, am I? You must think I came down in that last shower, lady.'

'Look, Commander. I don't expect you to believe *anything* I say. I don't know how much of what I've seen in the last few minutes I can believe myself, but I'm playing the cards I've been dealt. You said your ship is the *Astoria*? Would you by any chance be sailing on Midway, to confront a Japanese invasion fleet?'

Evans almost laughed.

'You gotta be kidding me. Do you really think I'm going to tell you anything?'

'No,' she sighed, 'not if you're any good at your job. Okay. Let me try this. If you *are* heading for Midway, you're part of Task Group 17.2 with the cruiser *Portland*, under the command of Rear Admiral William Smith, which in turn is part of Task Force 17 under Frank Fletcher on the *Yorktown*. Task Force 16, built around the carriers *Enterprise* and *Hornet*, is steaming with you, and was supposed to be under Bill Halsey, but he's got a case of the hives and is stuck back in Pearl. So Ray Spruance, a cruiser driver like you, has taken over. You think the Japs would know that? The Japanese think *Yorktown* was sunk in the Coral Sea. They have no idea she was repaired in three days at Pearl. They wouldn't believe it possible.

'And do you think, even if they knew any of this, they'd be dumb enough to send me, a black woman, to claim to be a US navy captain and to negotiate with you? You think they'd have the ability to screw around with your ship like this?'

Evans felt as though his stomach was going to do a full forward roll. He and Mohr stared at each other, exhausted, incredulous. His mind seemed to have locked up completely, refusing to process any more information.

'Commander Evans?' she prompted.

Moose Molloy interrupted before he could reply.

'Commander. This is pretty wacky, sir. I think you'd better see this.'

At that a light, even stronger than the green rod in Anderson's hand, pushed back the gloom. Molloy was struggling around the door wedged into the desktop, and he was carrying another glowing object. It was the size of a small book, but it threw out a powerful light, reminding him of the moment in a movie theatre when the dark screen suddenly lit up.

'What the hell is that?' asked Eddie Mohr.

'It's a flexipad,' the Anderson woman answered from the far side of the gap.

A single shot rang out, somewhere in the distance. Before Evans could shout, Mohr had cut him off, yelling at a full roar, 'Knock it off, you blockheads! Cease fire! I'll personally clobber the first man who does that again.'

'Thank you, Chief,' said Captain Anderson.

Mohr said nothing in return, just glared. Moose finally popped out of the constricted space and tumbled to the deck. He carried the flexipad over to Evans like it was a live shell. His CO took the object, smearing sticky half-dried blood over the screen.

The rubberised casing felt odd, like nothing he'd ever touched before. The thing seemed light but solid and kind of dense too. He and Mohr stared at the screen, which showed something that looked like a weather map. But it was in motion, like a short movie, repeating again and again. As strange as it was, Evans could tell that it covered a thousand square miles of the Wetar Strait, off Timor.

It was every bit as baffling as anything else they'd seen so far.

He couldn't shake the idea that he was staring through a small window hundreds of miles high, directly down onto the earth's surface. Overlaying the picture was a mass of thin red lines. The image shifted rapidly, like a movie spooling too quickly through a projector, allowing Evans to watch clouds moving through the strait.

Anderson's voice broke the spell.

'You need medical attention, Commander Evans. I can see that from here. We have a sixteen-bed hospital on the *Leyte Gulf*. It hasn't been compromised. The sort of injuries some of your men are carrying, it'd go a hell of a lot better for them to get treatment from us.'

'You inflicted those injuries, Captain.'

It was the first time Evans had addressed her properly.

'Yes, we did, Commander Evans. We've probably killed more than thirty of your men by direct fire below decks. I don't know how many have died elsewhere. Our defensive systems went offline, but Nix tells me some of them functioned independently anyway. Your casualties will be heavy, I'm afraid.'

'You killed everybody on the bridge,' he said, unwilling to mask his bitterness. 'Shot the hell out of them. They were friends of mine.'

Anderson let it pass. She ripped open a flap holding her vest in place and laid down her shotgun before stepping right up to the thin sliver of clear space through which they were forced to communicate.

'I'm sorry, Commander. But you've killed an unknown number of my people as well.'

'Just fucking niggers and –' Seaman Molloy muttered, before a backhanded slap from Chief Mohr silenced him. Captain Anderson let that one slide too.

'Who are you people?' Evans asked, his voice nearly cracking.

'I told you. We're Americans,' Anderson replied. 'Just like you.'

8

USS Hillary Clinton, *2312 hours, 2 June 1942*

'This is Spruance! Who the hell are you? What's the idea of breaking in on my transmission? By God, you'd better have a good explanation, or you'll hang for this.'

The voice filled the flag bridge of the USS *Hillary Clinton*, the voice of a man long dead when Phillip Kolhammer had finished the last brushstroke on his model dive-bomber. Kolhammer listened in dread and wonder. In a way, that voice was more awful than the firestorm raging down on the flight deck.

He took a long breath before speaking.

'This is Admiral Phillip Kolhammer, United States Navy. Acting Commander of the USS *Hillary Clinton* and Task Force Commander of UNPROFLEET, operating under the mandate of United Nations Security Council Resolution 3312. I request that you cease fire, Admiral Spruance. There's been a terrible mistake. You are engaged with friendly forces. I say again, cease fire. We are American and Allied ships.'

A stream of invective poured out of the bridge speakers. Kolhammer waited until it abated and repeated himself as calmly as he could. The forward laser pods destroyed another five-inch shell as he spoke, emphasising his lack of success in getting through to Spruance. He watched a medic pull someone from the sea of flames that covered almost a third of the flight deck behind the ops tower. A dark, oily smear marked the passage of the body.

'Admiral Spruance,' he repeated, 'you are firing on an American-led force. We have ceased offensive fire. I request you do the same.'

USS Enterprise, *2314 hours, 2 June 1942*

In the cramped, fetid flag radio room of the *Enterprise*, Ray Spruance clamped his hand over the mike and spoke to the operator.

'Have you had any luck raising Pearl yet, sailor?'

'Sorry, sir. This Kolhammer guy is all over us. He's blocked out every frequency. We can't even talk ship to ship. All anyone is getting is this transmission.'

'How is that possible?' Spruance asked angrily. 'No, forget it. That's not important. The fact is, he's doing it.

'Who is he?' he continued, scanning the room. 'Does anyone here know of an Admiral Kolhammer? And that ship, what the *hell* is he talking about? *Hillary Clinton* my ass!'

The four staff officers who had crammed into the shack with Spruance exchanged blank looks and shook their heads.

'Admiral,' said Lieutenant Commander Black, 'these sons-a-bitches have destroyed the *Yorktown* and the *Hornet*. They've sunk our cruisers and most of the destroyer screen. Even making the worst kind of mistake, no American force would do that. It's gotta be a load of horseshit.'

Spruance went quiet for a few seconds, a pause that seemed interminable. Finally, he brought the mike back to his lips.

'This is Spruance. There is no ship or admiral by the names you have given us, not anywhere in the US Navy. Identify yourself truthfully and cease firing on us. I've only got to walk a few paces and stick my head out a hatch to know you're lying about that. I can see your goddamn fire all over the sky.'

Kolhammer's voice crackled out of the speakers. 'That fire is not directed at you. I know it sounds ludicrous to you . . . but it's directed at the shells you've been firing on us.'

Curtis allowed himself a satisfied if fleeting glance at Beanland, whose furious glare wiped any trace of satisfaction from the ensign's face. Spruance and Black exchanged a look that revealed their doubts about this Kolhammer's sanity, but before either could speak, he continued. As the words spilled out, Spruance's expression turned from shock to dark, impacted rage.

'Admiral,' said Kolhammer, 'we know you're heading for Midway to intercept a Japanese fleet under the control of Admiral Yamamoto. We also know that you are ignoring as a diversion a Japanese thrust towards the Aleutians by the Second Carrier Striking Force under Rear Admiral Kakuta. We know that your Pacific Fleet Combat Intelligence Unit, under Commanders Rochefort and Safford, have broken the Japanese naval code JN25, and so you have advance warning of the plan to seize Midway, including the entire Japanese order of battle. I know you won't be happy that I'm announcing all of this over the air, but I can assure you it is irrelevant now.

'I am instructing all the ships under my command to switch on their running lights, and any above deck illumination, in thirty seconds.'

Kolhammer signalled to Judge, who set the order in motion throughout the Multinational Force.

'I know you'll have trouble trusting me,' he continued, 'but I can only ask for that trust. We will not fire on you again. We will reveal our positions. I would request permission to come aboard the *Enterprise* to explain what has happened. I can guarantee both your safety and that of Midway.'

As Kolhammer spoke, trying for the sort of reassuring tone he recalled from interminable post-trauma briefings he'd been forced to undergo as an active fighter pilot, Mike Judge passed him a handwritten note. The exec had taken the initiative and asked the acting commander of the *Siranui* to lower his ensign and park himself behind the *Kandahar*, out of the line of sight for the *Enterprise*. Kolhammer gave him a silent thumbs-up as he continued.

'I understand you've taken heavy casualties, but so have we. It was a terrible mistake. We will do everything we can to make good your losses, and we will stand down any threat to American or Allied interests in this theatre, but I implore you to cease fire immediately, so we can sort out this mess.'

Lights came on all across Kolhammer's fleet. Blazing like carnival rides, their sleek, radical lines occasioned almost as much surprise among the men of Task Forces 16 and 17 as had their initial arrival. A sailor thrust his head into the radio shack.

'Admiral Spruance, sir? I think you'd better come and see this.'

Spruance handed the heavy microphone back to the radio operator without bothering to sign off. He and his staff threaded through to flag plot and out onto a walkway. The sea around them was alight with dying ships, their own, but also with visions of craft from another world. Somebody handed Spruance a large pair of binoculars, which he raised to his eyes with a slight tremor. The carrier's plunging progress made it difficult to get a steady look, but the first ship that came into view stole his breath. The triple-hulled warship was flying her largest ensign from a telescoping staff atop the bridge. The flag was British. No other structure ruined the smooth surface of her deck.

Spruance lowered the glasses, fixed another alien vessel in his sight and raised the binoculars again. It boasted an equally exotic appearance, but this was a monohulled ship. The Stars and Stripes fluttered from a telescopic mast at the top of the raked-back fin, which spoiled her otherwise empty decks.

The admiral shifted his focus again and again, taking in a slab-sided carrier that at least resembled the *Enterprise* in form and size, and then Kolhammer's own ship, the *Clinton*, still burning from the bomb strike. Even at a distance Spruance could tell she was a monster, certainly dwarfing the *Lexington*. The ships were all heading away from him, seemingly towards the burning giant on the horizon. The volume of fire had dropped away, and no more of those garish rocket flares were rising from the decks of any foreign vessel.

It was almost peaceful.

Spruance sighed and turned to Dan Black. He was calmer, but his hands still trembled.

'I think we'd better talk to this Kolhammer again.'

PART 2
Détente

9

USS Enterprise, *2322 hours, 2 June 1942*

'What the hell is that?' muttered Lieutenant Commander Black.

'Search me,' someone replied from behind him.

'You know,' said the chaplain, 'it reminds me of something I saw in Rome, before the war. I was on sabbatical and was lucky enough to be given a tour of the da Vinci archives. I believe he once drew a machine a bit like that, with a propeller on top. He invented the parachute, too, you know.'

'It's a Hiller-Copter,' said Ensign Curtis. Curtis was known as a bit of an aircraft nut. Less-than-perfect eye-sight had barred him from flight school, crimping off a lifelong dream and shunting him into the entirely unglamorous position of assistant bookkeeper in the ship's pay office. His enormous black-rimmed glasses might have been standard issue, so well did they suit him in his job. Most often, however, he had them buried in a copy of *Jane's Fighting Aircraft*, or *Aviator Monthly*.

As Curtis spoke, the strange craft drew closer, riding atop radiant shafts of light.

'A what?' shouted Black over the growing roar.

The ferocious downblast of the rotors forced the spectators to turn away, towards Curtis, who had screwed up his eyes, determined not to miss a moment.

'It's a Hiller-Copter, or something like it,' he shouted, his normally anxious demeanour gone. He sounded completely sure of himself. They were all clustered outside the pilot house for a view of the approaching aircraft. Rumours were already flying around the big ship that these were experimental planes, or maybe motorised blimps, pulled out of the lab and rushed forward to Midway for the showdown with the Japs. Some said it was Yamamoto himself, come to negotiate a surrender. There was even wild talk, coming from the *Astoria*'s radio operators, of space coons and women from Mars.

Ensign Wally Curtis wasn't having any of it. That was a Hiller-Copter, or maybe even a Higgins. As it loomed out of the night and flared for set-down, he decided it looked more like the painting he'd seen of a Higgins in *Aviator Monthly*. The painting was a mock-up, of course, an artist's semi-informed hunch of what the finished aircraft might look like.

But they weren't far off the mark, were they? He marvelled at the contraption. It looked to have a single rotor, instead of the Hiller's two counter-rotating blades. And there at the rear was a vertical torque rotor, which the Hx-44 didn't have.

Gritting his teeth, and squinting against the stinging lash of the rotor wash, he was uncertain whether the pounding in his chest was a response to the controlled violence of the aircraft's descent, or simply excitement at its appearance. He decided it was the latter when his heart skipped even faster at the sight of the second whirlybird. Where the first one had looked sort of fat and heavy, the machine behind it was rapier-like. Unlike its mate, it seemed to have less storage area in the fuselage – for carrying men or cargo, he supposed. Its brutish, hunched, insectile form reminded him of a giant wasp or a hornet.

Wally knew without being told that the stubby little wings weren't designed to provide lift. No, they were made to carry weapons. He could only shake his head in wonder at the thought of what sort of havoc a thing like that could unleash. The long protruding barrel at its nose was obviously some sort of advanced cannon. Perhaps even a machine-gun cannon.

He reeled off all these thoughts as they occurred to him, not really caring whether or not anybody was paying attention. But they were. The hard-bitten copper miner, the well-travelled padre, the professional warriors and draftee sailors who had gathered on the walkway turned to his boyish certainty as a salve for their own fears and doubts. Where they suffered future shock, Ensign Curtis experienced only rapture.

'Where'd they come from, Wally?' shouted Lieutenant Commander Black.

'Well, Higgins is based in New Orleans, sir,' he

cried back. 'And Hiller Industries work out of Berkeley in California. But I don't know, looking at those aircraft, they're just way too advanced. I can't really tell you where they came from, Commander. Maybe off a Hughes programme out in the desert. Maybe a Landgraf or a Piasecki PV plant. I couldn't say, sir.'

The choppers doused their spotlights and set down just aft of the island, atop the main elevator. No landing officer waved them in because nobody knew how. Hundreds of men had crammed onto different vantage points to watch the arrival, either high up along Vulture's Row or scattered throughout the small superstructure, crowding around the AA mounts, crouched down low on the flight deck itself, despite being warned to keep that area clear. Some noted the USN markings and Royal Navy roundel on the strange machines. Others just gaped at their sheer freakishness.

A murmur went up when a woman emerged from the smaller aircraft. No one missed the Negro who hopped down from the other one. Dressed in some sort of camouflage battle dress, he dropped to the wet wooden flight deck with the grace of a panther. The smaller man who alighted behind him wasn't nearly so lithe, but he carried about him the same sense of self-assurance.

It was all an act.

Both Kolhammer and Jones were reeling inside. They had briefly discussed the Transition, as they had begun calling it, during the flight over. Kolhammer had filled his colleague in on what he remembered of the briefing by DARPA. Neither man had any expertise in quantum foam physics but they had agreed that, given their total inability to access any satellite links or detect any kind of digital or quantum signals whatsoever, the odds favoured the theory that they were the strangers here, rather than Spruance's task force.

Still, it was a hell of a thing to ask a man to accept, that he'd been ripped right out of time itself.

As hard as they found it to come to such a preposterous conclusion, however, they at least lived in a world where such things were theoretically possible. Kolhammer clutched a document case containing about two hundred pages of printed material on Multiverse Theory, culled from *Scientific American*, *Popular Quantum Mechanics*, *Esquire*, *GQ* and the broadsheet press. If the locals didn't want to believe him, perhaps the *New York Times* might convince them. He had been surprised to discover that one of the half-dozen *Times* features had been written by Julia Duffy. But it had taken Kolhammer less than half a second to dismiss any thought of bringing her across to do some of the explaining – even if her article had been one of the better ones.

After reading Duffy's piece twice, he now guessed that until an hour ago he'd been riding shotgun over a research team that was developing a military application for Multiverse Theory. But the angry, horror-struck men on whom they were calling knew no such thing. Indeed, there was nothing in their world that might prepare them for such a fantastic concept. For them, the most primitive form of radar was still a marvel. Television was an obscure and probably useless invention; jet engines and helicopters were only found in the pages of adventure magazines. And high-steppin' niggers with uppity dames in tow did *not* waltz aboard the USS *Enterprise* like they owned the joint. Not after admitting they were responsible for the deaths of so many good men in the hour just gone.

Suddenly a squad of armed marines double-timed towards the Seahawk, nearly bringing the truce to a premature end. Jones was forced to scramble forward, waving them down so that they wouldn't be decapitated by an unfortunate dip of the still-turning rotors. Seeing him charge, three men shouldered their arms and drew a bead.

'Crazy black bastard,' spat the sergeant in charge of the detail as he continued forward.

Jones sank to one knee and motioned for them to drop, too, gesturing frantically at the rotors.

'Get down! Get down, you stupid assholes!' he yelled over the diminishing whine.

Finally the sergeant got the message and they halted their advance. Kolhammer emerged and joined Halabi. Both bent nearly double to emphasise Jones's warning. They joined him, and together they hastened out of the danger zone. The helos powered down and their crews exited. Kolhammer had thought it might reduce some of the tension if they were to move away from the controls.

High above them, the group of men clustered outside the pilot house watched the performance.

'Check out the tail on that chicken,' urged a navigator from the torpedo squadron.

'Yeah, but get an eyeful of the jigaboo she's travellin' with, Mack. That guy's gotta be eight foot tall.'

'Hell, I could beat him fair and square –'

'You couldn't beat an egg, you palooza.'

'I'm going down,' said Ensign Curtis, more to himself than anyone else. He was ignored by everyone except Lieutenant Commander Black, who pushed off the rail and followed him back inside.

'What's your feeling about this, Wally?' he asked as they made their way down to the flight deck.

Curtis was so worked up by the rush and excitement that he forgot to be intimidated by the older, more senior man.

'It's something big, sir. Why, I'll bet you it's something we can't even imagine yet, like something out of *Amazing Stories*.'

'You a betting man, Ensign?' teased Black.

'Uh, no, sir. Gambling is a sin, and against regulations, Commander, I just meant –'

'It's all right, son, I wouldn't take your bet anyway. I have a feeling I'd do my dough cold.'

*

Down on the flight deck, surrounded by the hard, unfriendly faces and cocked Springfield '03s of the security detail, Jones wondered how Kolhammer's gamble would play out. They had assumed Spruance would meet them as they disembarked, but only the buzzing ranks of spectators and the anonymous belligerence of their guards awaited them. As they confronted the marine squad, the sergeant in command barked out, 'Identify yourselves.'

All three had grown up in the military and were unfazed by the aggressive command. People had been barking at them professionally all of their adult lives. They replied in kind.

'Admiral Phillip Kolhammer, United States Navy.'

'Colonel JL Jones, United States Marine Corps.'

'Captain Karen Halabi, Royal Navy.'

'We were expected, *Sergeant*,' Jones added, a tightly coiled menace in his delivery that the marine couldn't help but recognise. A twenty-year man, he had been bruted by professionals too.

'Not like this you weren't, *asshole*,' the noncom muttered under his breath.

When Jones stepped one pace forward and spoke, it sounded like the engine of an Abrams turning over. Slowly. 'You don't know me yet, Sergeant. So I'll let your personal disrespect pass. But you know these, don't you, *boy*?' He fingered the silver eagles and Marine Corps insignia on his collar. 'And by God, you'll respect the uniform of the United States Marine

Corps, or I'll beat that respect into you, right here in front of your men.'

Jones's eyes never left the sergeant's as he spoke. The man's jawline bunched and knotted as he struggled to contain himself. Jones could see the guy's entire life in that twisting mask, all of his prejudices and petty resentments, warring against the disciplines of the corps. There were no black marines in 1942, and of all the services the corps would fight hardest against integration. But Jones's command presence was so powerful that it could not be resisted. In the end the sergeant deflated, crushed by a superior will.

'We'll see,' he said, a deep flush of embarrassment discolouring his whole head. He looked as if he'd stepped in something foul.

Kolhammer observed the interchange in silence. He knew Jones well enough, he thought. The 82nd had been attached to the *Clinton*'s battle group for two years. The colonel's reputation had preceded him, but Kolhammer was experienced enough to know that the few minutes of a man's life wherein he earned a Medal of Honour didn't necessarily tell you anything about his soul, or even his character. Awards for uncommon valour are, by definition, won under extreme circumstances, which might call forth behaviour completely *out* of character for the individual concerned. The exchange with the belligerent noncom, however, confirmed what Kolhammer had always suspected.

Nobody fucks with J Lonesome Jones.

Standing next to him, Captain Halabi couldn't help but be affected as well, a wave of goose flesh running up her arms. Curiously, the magic seemed to fade with distance. Over beside the Seahawk pilot Chris Harford, Flight Lieutenant Amanda Hayes affected a faux southern accent, 'Mah word, Jasper, we seem to have stumbled into a teste fest.'

Harford flashed a small but genuine smile for the first time since they'd arrived. It froze on his face when he recognised the man approaching from the carrier's island structure. Admiral Raymond Ames Spruance.

Halabi thought he looked more like a banker than an admiral, perhaps a Rothschild or Rockefeller, with short, straight hair, greying over the ears, a rather Roman nose, and deep lines at the corner of his mouth emphasising the funereal set of his jaw. He fairly stalked over to the commander of the Multinational Force, fixing their CO with a frigid glare.

'You Kolhammer?'

'I am.'

That neither man had made to salute spoke eloquently of their uncertainty. Nobody was sure of what rules applied here, of whose turf they were treading on. Spruance turned to take in the stony visage of Colonel Jones and the bewildering Karen

Halabi. Jones ripped out a parade-ground-perfect salute, to which Spruance merely sketched a return, somewhat grudgingly and after a noticeable pause.

'You people have killed thousands of my men tonight,' he said. 'You've probably lost us this war in the space of less than an hour.'

'And you've killed plenty of mine,' Kolhammer replied equably. 'Tried to kill thousands more. We're both at war, Admiral. People die. Sometimes for the worst of reasons. I'm sorry for your losses, and if you'll allow us, we'll do what we can for the survivors.'

'And what about the Japs?' Spruance said in a cold, level voice. 'What do you intend to do for them, since I notice you seem to be running with them?'

The *Siranui*. Kolhammer knew it had been spotted. It could hardly have been missed, emerging as it did so close to the *Enterprise*. He wondered whether Spruance had laid eyes on her himself. Probably.

'We have a Japanese Self-Defence Force ship operating as part of our task force, that's right. But they're of no threat to you here, or to Midway, or the United States of America.'

'Tell it to the *Portland*,' Spruance forced out through pursed lips. 'I have a destroyer over where she went down and they haven't found a single survivor. Not one! And I watched that rocket fly up off the deck of your Japanese friend myself. So please, spare me. All I want to know is, what the *hell* is going on here? You say you're American, but you're obviously treating with our enemies.'

'Well, if we could just sit down –'

Spruance rode in over Kolhammer. 'Absolutely not. No secret parleys tonight, my friend. You were trying to kill these men a short while ago.'

He took in the hundreds of onlookers with a sweep of the hand.

'You can make your apologies and explanations to them.'

Kolhammer's fuse was beginning a long, slow burn. He'd known this wouldn't be easy, but he had his own casualties, and he'd be damned if they'd be treated as less valuable in some wretched body count. A line of Shakespeare came to him. *We are enough to do our country loss.* If his suspicions held true, every man and woman under his command was going to be counted as lost before too long.

The satchel of printouts and photocopied magazine articles felt heavy and useless in his hands. He could hardly lay them out on the wet flight deck and take a couple of hundred overtly hostile onlookers through a primer on quantum mechanics and Multiverse Theory, even if he knew what the hell he was talking about.

He turned to Jones and Halabi, his eyes asking them if there was any point in sugar-coating it. Both looked back at him, clearly relieved that they weren't the ones in the rumble seat.

'Bad medicine is best swallowed in one gulp, Admiral,' said Jones.

'It can hardly sound more ridiculous than it did to us,' Halabi added.

Spruance clearly didn't feel he had time for double talk. 'Well?'

Kolhammer drew in his breath. He took some time to look around him. Just a second or so to convince himself it was all real: the wet wooden planking beneath his feet; the cumbersome equipment for the antique gun mounts; the unchanging sea of white, male faces peering out from behind the textbook image of Raymond A Spruance. All of this under a lowering sky in the deep of night, with the chilled air tasting of brine beneath the synthetic smells of oil and steel.

They were a long way from the tropics.

'My name is Admiral Phillip Kolhammer,' he said directly to Spruance, but loud enough to carry to the listening crowd. 'I was born in the year 1969. The same year, incidentally, in which you passed away, Admiral. I command a Multinational Force comprising of American and Allied units, which was tasked with forcing a passage through the Indonesian archipelago, what you would know as the Dutch East Indies, and putting an end to the mass murder of ethnic Chinese Indonesian citizens. Until an hour ago we were readying for that deployment in January 2021. In transiting from Pearl Harbor, American elements of the Multinational Force were also providing security for a research vessel, the *Nagoya*, which was undertaking sea trials of a new weapons system.

I can't confirm it yet, but I suspect something has gone wrong with those trials . . . and that we are here as the result of some malfunction of that system.'

With that, he stopped speaking. Spruance stared at him, as he had expected, blinking only once, slowly. The colour had drained from his face, leaving a waxy sheen and two points of high colour on his temples.

'Do you really expect me to believe that?' he asked very quietly.

'No sir, I do not,' Kolhammer replied. 'In your position, I wouldn't either. Extraordinary claims require extraordinary proof, and all I can offer you is our presence. Here we are. Myself. The colonel. Captain Halabi. Our flight crew and helicopters. You ever seen a helicopter before, Admiral? No? I didn't think so. The ships of our task force are some twelve thousand metres – that is, six nautical miles – to the southwest. As alien as the helicopters might appear to you, those ships will be even stranger. You're free to inspect any of them. To ask any questions you might care to ask. But every minute you waste doing that, more of your men die in the water. You can see with your own two eyes, right now, that we don't belong here, this is not our place –'

'You're damn right about that,' Spruance said, then added a little less aggressively, 'Go on.'

'I'd suggest that you come back with us. The Seahawk ride, and a few minutes aboard the *Clinton* and you'll –'

Spruance actually laughed at him, a short flat bark

that left no doubt what he thought of that suggestion.

'All right,' Kolhammer persisted. 'You could send someone in your place. Someone you trust but can afford to lose, to put it bluntly.'

Spruance worked his jaw, staring past the strange interlopers at the even stranger aircraft in which they had arrived. Before he could respond, a deep voice spoke up from behind him.

'We'll go, sir,' said Lieutenant Commander Black.

In fact the man seemed less than happy about the idea, but beside him a much smaller and greener-looking ensign was doing a fair impersonation of a young man who might just shatter into a thousand pieces if denied a chance to fly one of those 'Hiller-Copters'.

'You sure about that, Dan?' asked Spruance.

'Hell, the only thing I'm sure of is that we haven't seen a copper mine worth a damn anywhere around here. So I guess you can do without me, if you have to. And Ensign Curtis here, well, I don't think I'd care to leave him behind, sir. The crying would keep us up nights until the end of the war. Besides, he's the only man on this ship seems to know what those things are.'

Black indicated the two choppers with a tilt of his head.

While Spruance was weighing their offer, Karen Halabi stepped forward.

'If I may, Admiral?'

Both Kolhammer and Spruance answered. 'Yes?'

Halabi smiled, trying to arrange her handsome Eurasian features as innocently as possible. 'My exec has things well in hand back on the *Trident*. I am more than happy to remain here while these two officers cross deck to the *Clinton*. And I've brought some materials that might help us sort all this out.'

She offered Spruance the two books she had carried over. As he examined them like unexploded bombs, she fished a flexipad out of her jacket.

'I also downloaded some files from Fleetnet that the admiral might care to examine. Some history vids. *Victory At Sea* and *The World At War*. And a V3D colourised rendering of *Casablanca*.'

'Excellent,' said Kolhammer. He'd heard that this young woman had advanced quickly through the ranks of her service, and he was beginning to understand why. She was proving herself more adaptable than many other officers he had met over the years. That was the left-handed gift of ceaseless war, he supposed. It was a savagely effective form of natural selection.

'What do you say, Admiral?' asked Kolhammer, turning back to Spruance. 'Time is short.'

'You don't need to remind me!' Spruance snapped. 'We'll have the Japanese navy knocking on the door at Midway any minute now. And when they find out what's happened tonight, I imagine it'll be the Devil's own job keeping them from Pearl too.'

'As I said before,' Kolhammer assured him, 'we understand our responsibilities and will do whatever is necessary. But right now we have a hell of a mess to clean up right here. Men are still dying.'

'And will your *friends* on the *Siranui* do whatever is necessary to defend American soil from their *ancestors*?' Spruance asked frostily.

Well, that was progress of a sort, thought Kolhammer, who chose to ignore the bitterly sarcastic tone. He knew now that Spruance must have caught a close-up view of the Japanese stealth cruiser to know her name.

'The *Siranui*,' he replied in as level a fashion as he could, 'suffered a direct hit on her bridge. The captain and many of his senior officers were killed there, while they lay unconscious, suffering from the effects of the trip here. The cruiser is now under the command of Sub-Lieutenant Maseo Miyazaki, and he has slaved her combat functions to the . . . computing machine that helps run the *Clinton*. That is to say, the *Siranui* is under American control. They can't warm up a coffeepot without my say-so. I didn't ask them to do that. Lieutenant Miyazaki suggested it, and I agreed, in the interests of reducing tensions between our two forces.'

Spruance's thin, haunted face grew even darker while Kolhammer delivered his speech. When he had finished, the hero of Midway stared at him intently. Indeed, Kolhammer had the distinctly unpleasant feeling that Spruance was staring *into* him, decoding him, reading his deepest, pass-protected files and weighing up whether to hold or fold. His jawline flexed as he glowered fixedly and angrily at the invaders who freely admitted to having brought so much ruin with them.

And then suddenly much of the tension ran out of him. His whole frame, which had been so taut, sagged fractionally.

'Right,' he grunted. 'Commander Black, you and the ensign will return to the . . . uh, *Hillary Clinton*. Report back with all dispatch if you think we can gain anything from the assistance offered by these people. But before you go, Commander, a word in private, if you please?'

Black and Spruance walked away from Kolhammer's group until they were far enough removed that they could no longer be heard. Spruance turned his back on the two men and their odd female companion. He and Black both faced out over the bow of the *Enterprise*, which methodically rose and sank on the long ocean swell. It was cold, and they were dressed lightly. They shivered as hundreds of pairs of eyes bored into their backs.

'You'll need a signal. In case you're coerced,' Spruance said. 'Something simple that they won't notice.'

'Well, my sainted mother raised me never to cuss at an admiral, sir. Not even a lousy rear admiral from the Cruiser Division. I could slip in a fucking profanity, begging your pardon, sir. That's not like me at all. Then you'd know we were in trouble.'

'Fine,' Spruance said, smiling weakly in spite of himself. 'That youngster you're taking with you. Keep a close eye on him. His mother would probably like to see him again.'

'I'll do my best, sir. It was his idea, by the way. It's more like Ensign Curtis is taking me. If this comes off, that should be acknowledged. Otherwise, well, I'll take responsibility.'

'Duly noted.'

'Sir?'

'Yes, Commander?'

'Do you believe any of this malarky?'

Stillness came over Ray Spruance. But this time his pause was short.

'I don't know. I really don't. It's just so crazy. But I'll tell you this. I hope they're *not* lying. Because otherwise the Japs are going to roll right over us, maybe even win this war. They'll certainly take Hawaii, and probably Australia and New Zealand if they really feel like stretching themselves. They could even drive through Burma and into India. The Germans could push through Persia to link up with them. That'd be an ungodly mess. But maybe with some of the rockets these bastards turned on us tonight, we might stand a chance.'

'What about the Negro and the half-breed dame? You think they're for real?'

Spruance turned back to Kolhammer's strange little group.

'The wonders never cease,' he said.

10

In flight, 0005 hours, 3 June 1942

Despite his appearance, it didn't pay to underestimate Ensign Wally Curtis. He was no rube. He had grown up in Chicago. Since enlisting he'd met sailors from pissant little backwoods burgs in places like Kentucky and Georgia who could count on one hand the number of times they'd seen a motor vehicle. Assuming they could count, of course. And assuming they had the regulation five fingers per hand. There were times he had his doubts.

Right now, however, Curtis felt like just about the dumbest, most unsophisticated backwoods cracker on God's green earth. Not that he cared. A bright ribbon of joy blew through him. The older men had often teased him about the promise he'd made to his strict Presbyterian parents that he wouldn't lie with a woman until she wore his wedding ring. But he knew as a moral certainty that the thrill of riding in this *helicopter* surpassed anything any of them had ever known while riding some low-rent floozie.

It was all beyond him, gloriously, unreachably beyond his experience and understanding. He'd been right when he'd told Lieutenant Commander Black that the truth of the night would prove to be something they couldn't even imagine. He was young and unscarred, and the raw shock of the future folding back in on itself was enough to set his spirits soaring.

Braced across the cabin from him, Colonel Jones smiled at Curtis's obvious delight. Beside him, Lieutenant Commander Black was doing a fair job of concealing his discomfort, but his white-knuckle grip on the grab bars gave him away. By way of contrast, Jones had to keep pushing the ensign back in his seat as he leaned forward, craning this way and that, to take in as much detail as possible.

The lights and displays of the flight controls kept drawing his attention. He seemed even more fascinated by them than he had been by shaking hands with his first black man – and a full-bird colonel of the marines at that – and only his second lady pilot. His daddy had taken him to see Amelia Earhart once. If it was possible, Flight Lieutenant Hayes seemed even more exotic and beautiful.

'What part of Chicago did you say you were from, Ensign?' asked Jones.

Both Curtis and Black wore astonishingly small headsets, allowing them to communicate over the noise of the Seahawk. But no one else seemed to need them. Jones had tried to explain the devices – he'd called them 'chips' – that enabled each of the other passengers to communicate without the help of an external rig, but he'd been reduced to saying it was like having a radio inside your head. It sounded like something a drunk or a madman might say, and Lieutenant Commander Black had regarded him in just such a fashion. Curtis, on the other hand, simply marvelled at the crystal-clear sound of Jones's soft conversational tones purring in his ear. The man wasn't speaking any louder than you might in your maiden aunt's drawing room, yet they heard every word he said, even over the thundering rotors.

'I'm from Oak Brooke, sir,' said Curtis. 'My father has a hardware store over in North Lake.'

'I know that part of town well,' said Jones.

'Colonel Jones, sir?'

Curtis had no trouble recognising and respecting Jones's authority, something that earned him respect in return – a hard ask, as many junior officers of the 82nd could testify. 'I don't mean any offence, sir, but where you come from, are there a lot of Negroes in the service?'

Airman La Salle smiled to himself as Jones replied.

'No offence taken, Ensign. But we don't use the word *Negro* any more. Most folks consider it offensive. You'll want to bear that in mind when you get aboard the *Clinton*. Both of you,' he added for the benefit of Black. 'I believe the correct term nowadays is *American of colour*.' Jones snorted to show how little regard he had for such things, before continuing. 'But the corps is colourblind, Ensign. All of the armed forces are, and have been for a long time. When Admiral Kolhammer here was fresh out of college he served under a chairman of the Joint Chiefs, a sort of supreme commander of all the services, whose family came out of Jamaica. He'd have been called a Negro, or worse, in your day.'

'That man went on to become the Secretary of State,' Kolhammer added. 'Could have been president, too, if it hadn't been for Ms Clinton.'

'The lady your ship is named after?' asked Curtis.

'The *president* my ship is named after. Best president the navy had, since Ronald Reagan.'

'The cowboy actor!'

'The one and only,' smiled Jones.

'Excuse me,' Black interjected. 'No offence, Colonel. But a coloured president? A lady president? A B-grade cowboy in the White House? What are you, using the funny pages for your history books? You gotta be yanking my chain. I'm looking around your whirligig here and I'll admit I can see a lot of change, a lot of advances. But some things, they just don't change.'

Instead of replying, Jones pulled a satchel out from under his seat and then a pair of powered combat goggles from within the bag.

'Pilot?' he asked over the chopper's comm channel. 'Can you raise Fleetnet for me? I need to access my personal archive.

'Put these on,' he ordered Black.

The former copper miner eyed the goggles suspiciously. He gave Jones a hard, enquiring look, but the marine simply shrugged in reply. After a moment's consideration, Black reached across and took the device. It reminded him a little of antique flying goggles from the Great War. But only a little. These things were lightweight and sleek, with a curious feeling of density to them. Like they were packed tight with impossibly small machinery or wiring.

He needed no help settling them over his eyes. Indeed they seemed to mould themselves to his face. The sensation wasn't entirely pleasant.

The first thing he noticed was the night vision. It was startling.

'Okay,' he said. 'That's a good trick. But what have they got to . . . *whoa*!'

Without warning his entire range of view turned black for a split second, before it was slammed by countless shimmering filaments of light. Sometimes they seemed as delicate as a single thread of a spider's web. In other places energy poured through this strange negative space in torrents. As Jones worked a flexipad, Black rocked in his seat, overwhelmed by the visual effect of flying through this self-contained cosmos of fire and light. He found that he could catch a hint of something every now and then, a glimmer of recognition as something vaguely familiar flashed by: the Globe and Anchor of the USMC, the roaring lion from the beginning of an MGM movie. The images flickered in and out of range so quickly that he could never quite identify any one impression.

In a few seconds Jones seemed to find what he wanted. Lieutenant Commander Black let his head fall back slightly, like a man in the front row of a movie theatre. He was in Washington, hovering above a huge crowd, perhaps a million strong. He could see the Washington Monument and the Lincoln Memorial and then he was right up close to a black man. His rounded cheeks and pencil-thin moustache filled the – *what, the whole screen?* – as he punched out a speech, or perhaps a sermon. It certainly rang with the powerful cadence of the fire-and-brimstone revival meetings Black's daddy had favoured.

'*I have a dream . . .*' roared the Negro. '*That one day this nation will rise up and live out the true meaning of its creed. We hold these truths to be self-evident: that all men are created equal . . .*'

The man's voice rang out and filled the world as the footage segued into film of men and women, black and white, under attack by police dogs and fire hoses.

'*I have a dream that one day on the red hills of Georgia the sons of former slaves and the sons of former slave owners will be able to sit down together at the table of brotherhood . . .*'

Newspaper photographs of a black man who looked as though he'd been shot on a motel patio faded to colour images of a jungle war, of black and white soldiers so befouled with mud and gore that beneath their ruined fatigues all difference had been erased. Lieutenant Commander Black thought he recognised Marine Corps insignia on one Negro whose bandaged, bloody head lay in the lap of a white comrade. The black soldier stared sightlessly into the heavens, his face streaked with tears fallen from the eyes of his friend.

'I have a dream that my four children will one day live in a nation where they will not be judged by the colour of their skin but by the content of their character . . .'

Snatches of colour movies, and strange music, of grinning black basketball and football players cut to images of city workers, black, white, Asian, male and female running blind and fearfully through streets turned grey by clouds of pulverised cement that rushed at them while a stupendously tall building collapsed straight into the ground behind them. And the same preacher still called out his message in Black's ears.

'Let freedom ring from the mighty mountains of New York . . .'

Bright, clear colour film of US Marines, obviously of many races, standing atop the rubble of some palace in a place identified as Damascus faded to a shaky hand-held shot of a beaming Colonel J Lonesome Jones on the lawn of the White House, escorted by his impossibly beautiful and – for Dan Black – improbably blonde and blue-eyed wife.

The woman was teasing Jones, repeatedly stroking the decoration newly hung around his neck, a Medal of Honour. A black woman, beaming fit to burst and identified on the screen as Vice-President Rice, wandered over to shake his hand.

The preacher still roared out. '*Free at last! Free at last! Thank God Almighty, we are free at last!*'

The images froze and Black felt someone tapping on the goggles. He lifted them off. The sudden darkness of the chopper cabin was unsettling.

'You're right, Commander,' said Jones, leaning forward, his face dimly illuminated. 'Some things don't change. But that doesn't mean progress is impossible. My niece made that film you just saw, by the way. She cut it all together for a school project. Even took the footage at the White House herself. It's nicely done, don't you think? She's only eleven years old, and I suspect she's a holy terror to her mother and father.'

Lieutenant Commander Black was at a loss for words. 'Is she . . . uh . . . ?'

'As white as the Grand Cyclops of the Ku Klux Klan. But she loves her Uncle Lonesome and wants to follow in his footsteps, God help her.'

'How did you win the medal?' asked Black, readjusting his headset as he handed the goggles to Ensign Curtis.

'I don't mind you asking, Commander, but I'm not inclined to discuss it with you just yet. That doesn't mean I won't.'

'I think I understand,' Black said with a hint of chagrin.

'No, I don't think you do,' said Jones. 'Have you ever been in combat, Commander?'

'No,' he admitted.

'Well, the admiral, myself, Airman La Salle over there and the pilots of this helicopter, we've all been there. Too many times. If I could wish that away, I would, believe you me. I don't want my niece to live my life, but that's the world she was born into. It's not pleasant, but it has its certainties. One of which is that I know every man and woman in this aircraft would cut their arms off to save me if they had to – and they know I would do the same for them. They're my people, Black, no matter what. You, however, you I don't know.'

'That's pretty goddamn rich, don't you think?' Black protested. 'You blowing in here the way you did and then demanding that we earn *your* trust. That's hardly fair.'

'Fair's got nothing to do with it.' Jones shrugged. 'You'll see that soon enough, if you have any sense.'

'Colonel Jones?'

Ensign Curtis interposed himself between the two men in the unfamiliar role of peacemaker.

'Yes, son?'

'These eyeglasses, sir. Do you actually wear them in combat, so you can see in the dark?'

'We do. But they have other uses too. They'll take a shotgun blast from twenty yards out. Your face'll get shredded, of course. But your baby blues will be A-okay.' He grinned ghoulishly. 'They can display a bunch of tactical information too. Real-time imaging from intel drones, spy-cams and so on. So if you're wondering what's on the other side of a hill, say, you can see without popping your head up to get it shot off.'

Jones could see that neither Curtis nor Black really understood what he was talking about.

'Put them on, Ensign,' he said.

When Curtis had the goggles snug over his eyes, Jones made another series of fingertip adjustments on his flexipad. Wally's head moved from side to side as he was instantly overwhelmed by the mass of data. Inside the goggles he could see five movie screens. Each seemed to contain a different view of the same scene – a squad of soldiers attacking a building. Curtis couldn't tell if it was for real or made up. After a few seconds Jones shut down the goggles and asked him to hand them over to Dan Black.

The second time around Black did better at hiding his surprise, but the look on his face still gave him away. He watched the film through to the end before lifting the goggles.

'I'm no foot soldier,' he said, 'but how in hell is anyone supposed to fight with that five-ring circus to distract them?'

Jones grinned like a hungry wolverine. 'Thousands of hours of training.'

Black nodded. It was just a small movement. 'Admiral Kolhammer?' he said with a slight shift in his voice that indicated he was approaching a personal Rubicon. 'How'd you really get here? Assuming you are here and we're not there, wherever it is you came from.'

Kolhammer sighed. 'Truth be known, I can't tell you that, Commander. Not because it's restricted information, but because I don't really know. When I was last in Pearl, I attended a briefing with the captain and executive officer of the *Clinton*. A bunch of no-name spooks and pinheads gave us a soft sell about this research project we were to ride shotgun on. They said it was for a new weapons system, gave us a lot of bullshit about a gun that wouldn't so much fire a bullet or a missile as take it directly to the target. One of them, a Japanese man actually, talked about "collapsing the distance" to impact. It sounded like a bunch of crap to us, but ours is not to question why.'

'Some things really don't change then,' Black smiled, a small gesture of genuine warmth for the first time.

'No, they don't,' admitted Jones.

'Anyway,' Kolhammer continued, 'I don't expect you to understand the science. Even I only have a *Popular Mechanics* notion of how it all works. But these guys were generating enormous levels of energy, enough I guess to actually warp the structure of space itself. And one of the things we've learned is that, on a certain level, space and time are the same thing. I guess they just got their figures wrong. I promise you, as we know more, we'll fill you in.'

'That's pretty fucking wacky, if you ask me,' said Black.

'Any wackier than this?' said Kolhammer, holding up the goggles and then swinging them around to take in the entire chopper.

'Or me?' said Colonel Jones.

'Yeah, quite a bit, since you ask.'

Lieutenant Commander Black cracked his big broken knuckles. 'You know, I might look like a real palooka, but I have a master's in civil engineering. It's only from West Virginia U, but I had to sit down for five years of book learning like everyone else. Just because I used to break rocks for a living doesn't make me a fuckin' rockhead. I understand progress. The way I worked a mine was a hell of a lot different from the way my granddaddy did.

'I look at this bird and it seems mighty queer to me, but Ensign Curtis, he tells me these things are already on the drawing board. You got a woman flying this thing? Fine. I'll bet Amelia Earhart could fly rings around her. And as for you, Colonel Jones, my great-great-granddaddy on my mama's side was a lieutenant with the 54th Massachusetts, a black regiment with white officers. He died with his men, charging the Confederate guns at Fort Wagner. The grapeshot cut them up so bad, you couldn't tell who was who, or who was what, if you get my drift. So the home I grew up in, you ever spoke the word "nigger", you got your ass whupped good and proper. Maybe *you* want to bear that in mind, Colonel Jones, before *you* go judging the content of a man's character by the colour of his skin.'

Jones gave Dan Black the benefit of his hardest glare, until a sly smile cracked open his granite features.

'Well put, Commander. Touché.'

'Admiral Kolhammer?'

'Yes, Ensign?'

'How can you be sure you went back in time and we didn't come forward?'

Kolhammer shifted his weight as they banked for approach. 'I'm not a hundred per cent sure,' he answered. 'But we can't access any of our satellites. Our radar, which is a hell of a lot more powerful than yours, isn't giving us the returns that it should. We were just off the coast of East Timor, down the bottom of the Dutch East Indies, Indonesia in our day. But it's not coming up. We can't find anything, TV, radio, GPS, nothing. Our equipment is fine. It's just like there's nothing out there.'

The two *Enterprise* officers only understood about half of what he said, but the admiral's demeanour left no doubt as to what he was getting at.

'And what about this ship, the *Nagoya*? Where'd it get to?' asked Black.

'That's one I *really* can't answer.' Kolhammer shrugged. 'We've been looking for it, believe me. I'm hoping to God it hasn't come through and landed in Tokyo Bay. But I doubt it. We're missing a couple of other ships, but they were all some distance from the centre of the group, and the simplest explanation is that they just didn't get sucked up with the rest of us. We lost a couple of nuclear submarines and some Indonesian destroyers like that. Although the destroyers weren't such a great loss. Another ship got cut in half by the event horizon.

'The *Nagoya* was tucked away between the *Clinton* and a couple of cruisers. It would have been at the epicentre of whatever went wrong. It was probably destroyed, but we'll have to invest significant assets confirming that.'

'Because that's your only way home, right?' said Curtis.

'Got it in one, son,' said Kolhammer. 'But for now, if you'd care to look outside, you can see what the *Enterprise* will grow into, given eighty years or so.'

The two visitors leaned over. Black swore softly. Ensign Curtis didn't bother to hide his surprise.

'Good gosh! It's as big as a city.'

USS Enterprise, *0005 hours, 3 June 1942*

Captain Halabi couldn't remember ever being at such an uncomfortable gathering. There were only three of them standing in Spruance's cabin as the admiral methodically leafed through her copy of Fuchida and Okumiya's *Midway*. The other officer present, a Commander Beanland from Spruance's planning staff, had attempted to engage her in polite chitchat, but the conversation had curled up and died on the deck after he had blundered into a morass of nonsensical questions about the hygiene difficulties of 'women's troubles' on board a warship. Halabi had snapped back at him that menstruation proved itself to be much less of a problem than the standard array of sucking chest wounds, compound fractures and deep tissue burns with which one had to deal after a missile strike.

'Fascinating,' Spruance murmured, closing the book with a snap. 'If it's true.'

'Well, it won't be now of course,' Halabi ventured. 'The collision between our two forces has seen to that.'

'Indeed . . . Captain. And so, what now? If you are what you claim to be, what do you do now? Throw the lever on the magic box that brought you here? Leaving us in the lurch? You might very well find when you get home that everyone speaks German and Japanese.'

Halabi rubbed her tired eyes. 'Well, to begin with, we seem to have lost our magic box. And even if we could throw it into reverse, all the currently accepted theories of time distortion posit an infinitely variform multiverse rather than a single linear universe . . .'

She lost them with that and so decided to try a different tack. 'There's a field of physics called quantum mechanics. It's not specific to my own time. A chap called Max Planck kicked it off in 1900 with something he called the quantum theory of light, and Albert Einstein moved it along in 1905 with his work on the photoelectric effect. Basically, he theorised that light can be observed as either particles or waves, but never both at once. It's all about uncertainty, gentlemen, what we call quantum uncertainty. Long story short? It's most likely that there are an infinite number of universes, all existing alongside each other, all of them different, some subtly, some radically. I guess the fact that we're here is the first real proof of that theory.'

'I'm sorry,' said Spruance, 'but that sounds utterly ridiculous. You're saying there's a place where, for instance, America lost the War of Independence, or the South won the Civil War?'

'And infinite variations on that,' she nodded. 'A universe where there was no War of Independence because British colonial policy was more enlightened. An American Civil War after which Lincoln wasn't assassinated. A Second World War in which Hitler won. Or where the whole planet was invaded by, I don't know, space lizards or something. A universe in which Coke tastes like Pepsi. And another in which I'm standing over there drinking tea, rather than here drinking this . . . um . . . coffee. You get the picture?'

'If that's so,' mused Spruance, 'it might seem as if you've dropped into your past, but in truth you haven't.'

'Quite so.' Halabi was encouraged by the man's grasp of the theory. 'This may be a subtly different 1942. Or maybe a radically different one. Perhaps Hitler doesn't make the mistake of invading the Soviet Union . . .'

'He has,' Beanland put in.

'Oh. Well, that's good then. But you're right, Admiral. Maybe things are slightly different here. Maybe nothing we'll ever notice, like the typeface of a small county newspaper being altered, but everything else appears exactly the same. Or maybe our trip here was a straight HG Wells deal. From 2021 to our very own 1942. I don't know. We may never know. Theories are one thing, but actually cracking open the fabric of spacetime and manipulating it without dire consequences, well, that's a whole other sort of something.'

'As you may have discovered to our cost,' said Spruance.

'Yes,' Halabi admitted. 'I am sorry. You were unfortunate enough to tangle with our CIs while there was minimal human supervision.'

'CIs?'

'Combat Intelligences. Computers. Machines that think. They help us run our ships, our whole society actually. And when they detected the threat you posed to the task force with your cannon fire, they responded.'

'Well, that response may have cost us the war,' Spruance observed bitterly.

'It won't,' Halabi insisted. 'The strategic imbalance between the Axis powers and the Allies is so great that it would take a lot more than the destruction of your task force and the loss of Midway, Hawaii or even Australia to tip that balance in their favour.'

'Oh, God, don't let MacArthur hear that,' Spruance muttered, practically to himself.

'With all due respect,' Beanland protested, 'you've done your damnedest to help them on their way.'

'I am well aware of what happened tonight, Commander. I lost a good many friends myself on the *Fearless*. We haven't had a chance to formally discuss it at a command level yet. But I can assure you we won't leave you swinging. If necessary, almost any one of the ships in our task force could sink the Japanese carriers and capital ships closing on Midway at the moment.'

'Yes, but would they?' Spruance asked. 'Do you seriously believe your Japanese comrades would happily send their forefathers to the bottom?'

She answered honestly. 'I don't know. I haven't spoken to them. And since most of the *Siranui*'s senior officers have been killed anyway, their views are no longer entirely relevant.'

'Yeah, but the views of the survivors will be!' Beanland insisted. 'Maybe you got yourself some real tame, friendly Japs where you come from, but we got just about the worst bunch of bastards in the world right here. And I don't fancy them getting their hands on any of those rockets or thinking machines you hammered us with.

'Admiral,' he said, ignoring Halabi now, 'whatever turns out to be the case with these people' – he indicated the British captain with a jerk of his thumb – 'we have to insist on those Japs that came along with them being disarmed and interned. They're just too much of a threat.'

'That may well be, Lieutenant,' Spruance said, nodding, 'but let's just stay calm for the moment, shall we? Captain Halabi, how do you think your boss would take to that suggestion?'

'Frankly, not very well. I don't think any of us would.'

Spruance seemed quite taken aback by the defiant note in the woman's voice.

'And why not, might I ask?'

'Because they're our allies,' she said, as though explaining something to a child. 'This wasn't the *Siranui*'s first tour with Admiral Kolhammer's group . . . Sorry, that means nothing to you. Look, I've served in coalition with that ship before. I know that Admiral Kolhammer has too. They've taken the same risks we have, watched our backs, taken fire when we did. We have no reason to doubt their loyalty or their honour.'

'Yes, but their loyalty and honour might just demand that they lay in a course for the homeland. I take it from the title of this book that Japan didn't have a good time of it by the end of the war.'

'No, granted, they didn't. But the *Siranui*'s crew aren't stupid. They know that what doomed Japan was the hubris of the militarists who ran the country –'

'Who *run* the country, you mean,' said Spruance.

'Okay,' she conceded. 'Who *run* the country. But Japan – *their* Japan – has been a liberal democracy for generations. To suggest that modern Japanese would want to return to the mistakes of their distant past is as fatuous as saying modern Germans would all turn back into Nazis if given the chance.'

‘Oh my God,’ Beanland pleaded, ‘please don’t tell me you’ve got a bunch of German ships out there as well.’

Spruance was genuinely perturbed by the possibility. ‘Well, Captain,’ he demanded, ‘what of it? Any other nasty little surprises you’d care to let us in on? A U-boat, for instance?’

Halabi struggled to control her exasperation at the paranoid mind-set of the two men.

‘No,’ she said firmly. ‘We have no German vessels operating with us. There are undoubtedly a small number of German personnel on secondment to various elements of the task force. There may well be some Italians, too. I know of a couple on the *Fearless*. And we had a couple of Republic of Indonesia boats with us, which might well have complicated things, since you don’t have a Republic of Indonesia . . . but then neither do we nowadays, so I guess it couldn’t be any more complicated. And anyway, they seem to have escaped the Transition here, like the American subs and a New Zealand frigate, which were all some distance away from the event.’

‘So what on earth do you intend to do with all of these Huns and Japs then?’ asked Spruance, who seemed to be growing agitated again. He stood and turned to face her squarely.

‘I don’t intend to do anything with them,’ she replied, ‘until we’ve had a chance to discuss the matter at a fleet-wide command level. A discussion, I can assure you, that will take into account the wishes of all of the men and women concerned.'

'Good Lord,' Spruance cried, 'you can't suggest that you would let them be repatriated to their respective countries, if that's what they desired?'

'Of course not,' she responded. 'Nobody's going to hand Hitler or Tojo the plans to an atom bomb. But they're not going into irons, either, just for being Japanese or German. I have a Russian on my own ship, by the way. I know she'd have no interest whatsoever in returning home. Stalin would have her shot on sight, as soon as he discovered what became of his bloody workers' paradise.'

Spruance slowly began pacing a tight circle around the cabin, rubbing the back of his neck as he turned the whole thing over in his mind. He was surprised to discover that his initial shock and disbelief were fading quickly now. Piled on top of that discovery came the realisation that this annoying woman was mostly responsible. Standing there in her dress uniform, arms folded as arrogantly as you please, tossing off her own opinions while disregarding his as though she considered them largely worthless, she came as a small, intimate herald of change. What sort of a woman was she? The loss of her sister ship and a thousand comrades appeared not to ruffle her at all. She seemed every bit as self-assured of her own godhead as any number of Royal Navy captains he'd met over the years. It was almost as if their blasted empire had never begun to crumble to dust. The jaw-dropping perversity of meeting this odd creature who was so very obviously convinced of her own infallibility, in that recognisably and infuriatingly British way, all helped undermine the scepticism with which he had first responded to Kolhammer's ridiculous story.

Jesus, he thought, *what if it's true?*

He retrieved the book from where he had tossed it on his desk and flicked through it again, leaving Beanland and Halabi to their mutually hostile silence. He scanned a few pages that dealt with the rapid destruction of three Japanese carriers, caught by his dive-bombers while their decks were littered with refuelling planes, high-explosive bombs and thousands of gallons of flammable gas.

'We were lucky, then,' he said, glancing up at Halabi again.

'Yes and no,' she said. 'The heavy bomber flights and the waves of torpedo planes that went in earlier set it up for your dive-bombers. If those pilots hadn't sacrificed themselves – and that's what it was for most of them, a suicide mission – you wouldn't have caught Nagumo with his pants down around his ankles and his cock on the chopping block.'

Spruance smirked at the profane image, even as he cringed at such language coming from a member of the fairer sex.

God help us, are all the women from her day like this?

'Captain Halabi,' he said. 'Can I have your word

as an officer that you have spoken true tonight?'

Halabi straightened herself out of the relaxed posture she had fallen into.

'You have it.'

'Fine,' Spruance said over the rising objections of Commander Beanland. 'We won't delay for word from Black and Curtis. I take it you have some way of contacting your ship and Admiral Kolhammer, and getting them to start their own rescue operations.'

'I do, sir.' She whipped her flexipad out of a breast pocket and opened a link to the *Trident*. A red-haired man with hawkish features appeared on the small screen.

'Captain? We've been missing you.'

'It's nice to be loved, Mr McTeale. We have clearance from Admiral Spruance to begin search and rescue. Get them away in . . . two minutes . . . Will that be long enough for you to get the word out, Admiral?' she asked Spruance.

He was caught off guard by the speed at which she had moved, but waved Beanland out of the cabin with a firm instruction to see that his surviving ships were informed of the order.

'Better give us five minutes, Captain. I know it's frustrating, but we don't have any of those.' He pointed at the flexipad.

Halabi returned her attention to the *Trident*'s exec.

'Five minutes then, McTeale. Get onto Fleetnet.'

'Aye, ma'am.'

'Thank you, Commander. Halabi out.'

Spruance pensively chewed his lip and played with the book Halabi had given him.

'You've made the right call, sir.'

His eyes were haunted as they met hers.

'I really had no choice, Captain. We're finished if I can't trust you. I have no idea how this will turn out. None at all. I don't even know how I'm supposed to explain to Nimitz what happened tonight. And what happens when Nagumo comes over the horizon? It won't be me who stops him, will it?'

'No,' Halabi agreed. 'I guess that'll be down to us.'

11

HIJMS Ryujo, *2331 hours, 2 June 1942*

The thermometer in the pilot house of the carrier *Ryujo* stood at minus seven degrees Centigrade, but to Rear Admiral Kakuji Kakuta it felt even colder. The wind running over the carrier's deck added to the chill, as did the dense banks of fog and damp, clammy air through which the Second Carrier Striking Force had been groping towards the Aleutians. It wasn't the vile conditions that had halted the progress of the Fifth Fleet's Northern Force, however.

Kakuta was a warrior, and as such he expected to fight in fog and darkness, to strike at an enemy whose whereabouts or capabilities he might not know for sure. Nothing was certain in war. But this, this was a mystery beyond the ken of simple warriors. It was as though the gods themselves had intervened in mortal affairs. Such things were not unknown, of course. Huge Mongol invasion fleets had twice been destroyed, in 1274 and 1281, when *kamikaze* – or divine winds, in the form of typhoons – had smashed them to splinters.

But although he was a spiritual man, Kakuta's rational side understood that clumsy wooden boats that tried to cross the Sea of Japan during typhoon season were liable to meet with disaster. Just as he had been dogged across the northern Pacific by these impenetrable fog banks, hundreds of miles deep and so thick that the nearest escorts – just a few hundred yards away – were transformed into murky shadows, even at midday.

The bridge was quiet, except for an occasional directive to the helm to alter the heading slightly, keeping them on station within the body of the strike force.

As bitterly cold as he was, Kakuta was more profoundly disturbed by the turn of events these last few hours. Admiral Yamamoto's fantastically elaborate plan to seize Midway Island and destroy the remnants of America's Pacific naval power depended on exact timing. Yet here they were, behind schedule, creeping through the fog and trying to deal with a ghost ship.

He was anxious for a report from his staff who had boarded the vessel what seemed like an age ago. But he would just have to wait until a motor launch brought Lieutenant Commander Hidaka back with a full account.

KRI Sutanto, *2331 hours, 2 June 1942*

When they had first come aboard they had been grateful for the glorious warmth of this vessel. But that had quickly soured, and Jisaku Hidaka was seriously considering having the men throw open all the hatches and portholes to let in some of the freezing Pacific air. This ship reeked of human filth, of vomit and shit and urine.

The culprits lay everywhere. Not dead, but not quite alive, either. Medics had dragged four men who showed at least some signs of life into a starboard corridor that ran the length of the vessel. There was little to do but monitor them. Nothing brought a response, not smelling salts, kicks and slaps, not even a shallow prod with a dagger.

The casualties weren't Americans. That much was obvious. Hidaka was unsure where they hailed from, but to his eye they resembled the savages of the former Dutch East Indies more than anything else. That couldn't be the case, of course. This warship was simply too advanced. It was small, granted, but it was full of equipment that none of them had ever seen before. The pilot house glowed with ethereal lights, hundreds of them burning and blinking on banks of control panels that made the *Ryujo*'s bridge look stark and simplistic – even though the whole world now knew that Japanese naval technology was unmatched.

Standing on the bridge, he was tempted again to caress the large, magically glowing plate of glass that rose on a sort of stalk from the arm of what must surely be the captain's seat. But the last time he had tried that, shrieking alarms had sounded for a full two minutes. So he stayed his hand, and kicked the man who lay unconscious at the foot of the chair, more out of spite and frustration than from any hope that it might rouse him.

The body absorbed the blow like a sack of rice.

'Keep an eye on things here,' he told a petty officer. 'Don't touch anything, and summon me immediately if one of these baboons decides to raise his head. I shall be in the wardroom.'

He left without waiting for the man to acknowledge his order. Hidaka was becoming annoyed with his own inability to unravel the puzzle of this ship. He had been chosen to lead the boarding party because of his near-faultless grasp of English, but the language displayed on all the signage throughout the vessel meant nothing to him. Once or twice he had found a small plaque written in what seemed to be German, but that only served to deepen the mystery. He proceeded to the wardroom in very poor humour.

The men in there sprang to attention when he arrived. Three of the insensate crew lay on the floor.

'Well?' he asked immediately. 'Anything to report?'

An ensign snapped to attention and indicated a pile of books and papers lying on a table.

'We were just coming to get you, Commander. We have located these, we think some are written in English . . .'

Hidaka cast a wary eye over a tall stack of magazines written in what he assumed was the baboons' language. Most were editions of something called

Detik. A lesser number were of another journal called *Tempo*. He ignored them in favour of the English-language publications.

That was a thin collection, but it was nonetheless astounding. The first item was a pornographic magazine! Hidaka examined the masthead. *Hustler*. He wasn't sure what that meant. The smaller titles, perhaps representing the articles, were no clearer.

We testfuck the latest in V3D pussy.

Inside the Rising Jihad.

Get big and beastly with the latest synth-simian DNA.

Meaningless. Absolutely meaningless. And . . .

'Shit!'

Hidaka wasn't even aware he'd sworn in English, so great was his shock at the image that met him when he flipped open the magazine.

'So the rumours are true,' he mused in Japanese when he'd recovered from the surprise. 'They *are* blonde all over.'

The men sniggered, and he might have spent a few minutes confirming the theory if the ensign hadn't gently handed him a small device.

'And there is this, Commander. It glows like a lantern.'

A strangely lit screen displayed the cover of *Tempo*. Hidaka checked it against the pile of paper magazines. Yes, he was certain they were the same thing. What an oddity. A magazine in an electric box!

It was apparently written in the same damnable tongue as everything else on this ship, but there in the left-hand margin of the screen was a small British flag and underneath it, the word *English*.

Progress at last! Hidaka thought.

He had almost grown used to the magic of these illuminated plates, as they were scattered everywhere aboard the ship. Nonetheless, it was a revelation to find one he could hold in his hand and carry around. But how did it work? What did it do? There were a number of buttons in the base of the thing, but he was disinclined to press them, especially after his experience on the bridge. So he carefully placed the instrument back on the scarred tabletop while he examined the other discoveries.

There was another magazine. Like *Hustler*, it was printed in rich colours on thick glossy paper. The title appeared to be *People*. A strange name for a periodical, he thought. An ethnographic journal perhaps.

Most of the pages were dominated by photographs of idiotically grinning barbarians. American or British, he supposed, for the small amount of text was certainly written in English. But there were an amazing number of Negroes and half-bloods, and people of races he'd never seen before. *A mud race of polyglot people*, he thought, pleased with himself at recalling such an obscure term even though it had been at least five years since he had studied at Princeton University.

Hidaka attempted to glean some wider meaning from the photo captions, but they seemed as vacuous as the *gaijin* about whom they were written. The common themes seemed to be who was fornicating with whom, and who possessed the most riches. There were longer articles, but he threw the magazine aside in a fit of pique because they were just as impenetrable. *People* would have to wait until he had more time.

He picked up the next item, a much thicker magazine, with the title *PC Week*. Opening this to a random page and flicking through, he let go an exclamation.

'Ah! Technical documents!'

The crewmen grunted happily in response. If they had discovered something vital, it would bring them great honour and distinction. As Hidaka flicked through the pages, he nodded his head vigorously, though these articles, written in English, were even more unreadable than those in *People*. At least this time, however, he felt certain his inability to decipher the text was because it so obviously dealt with top-secret technologies.

There were many pictures of those odd floating glass plates, and boxes with wires and boards in them, and even of devices that resembled the gadget with the small British flag on its glass plate. He would dearly love to decipher one of these articles for Admiral Kakuta, but such a task might take weeks – and they had hours at best.

'Good work, Ensign Tomonagi,' he said in a clipped, excited voice. 'Good work to all of you.'

The crewmen drew themselves up, basking in the praise.

'Ensign, detail half your men to search the ship again. Tell them to look for more of these devices.' He held up the portable tablet with the glowing plate. 'Assign someone to drag those monkeys in here. I will run the operation from this room now.'

'*Hai*!'

From a sailor, Hidaka took a chipped mug – a sure sign that he was dealing with barbarians – then picked up the glowing device and walked over to a comfortable-looking armchair. He sat with his legs crossed in a very English manner and sipped the tea while staring at the artefact. The technical magazine referred to this sort of device as a 'flexipad'. The tablet was quite light, given its size, and it was constructed of a material he'd never encountered before. A sort of rubbery leather?

Hidaka sighed deeply as he read the foreign language from top to bottom. He was still no clearer about the content of the tract. There was a picture – of a tank, and another of a venerable bearded gentleman, which he had to assume were associated with the text – but beyond that there was only puzzlement.

For ten minutes he sat and stared at the device, hardly aware of the crewmen's grunting as they dragged the four alien sailors into the wardroom and laid them out on the threadbare carpeting alongside their utterly senseless fellows. Try as he might, he couldn't escape the fact that the only promising clue lay in that little Union Jack and the underlined word *English*. But what on earth did it mean? What did *any* of this mean? And how could he uncover the truth without setting off more alarms and causing possibly irreparable damage? Perhaps it was even booby-trapped.

Hidaka became so lost in his own thoughts that without realising it, he brushed the flexipad screen with his thumb. He flinched slightly, expecting the same blaring alarm that had startled them on the bridge. But nothing happened.

Encouraged, he warily poked the very tip of his little finger at the screen again, touching the picture of the venerable gentleman, and suddenly the fellow filled the whole screen and began to speak. Hidaka was caught by surprise again but managed to smother his reaction this time. The bearded man spoke for nearly half a minute in some diabolical language that sounded to Hidaka like a choking animal attempting to clear its throat. At the end of the little movie, which amazed him with its colours and clarity, the picture shrank back to its former size and location.

Well, that was something. It took the emboldened Hidaka less than a second to tap the screen where the tiny British flag was displayed. In the blink of an eye the display transformed itself into English. A wide grin broke out on the commander's face. *Excellent! Most excellent.*

But his good mood turned grey again as he read the text. It seemed to relate to a struggle – a civil or maybe a religious war of some kind, he thought – being raged on a group of islands. As he read on, the bearded man was identified as the Emir of the Caliphate, Mullah Ibn Abbas, and the island of Java was mentioned three times as the location of the most violent clashes.

That simply could not be. There was no 'Caliphate', and Java itself had been wrested from Dutch control more than two months ago. It was now part of the Empire. Chagrined, Hidaka squeezed his eyes shut, then returned to the article.

There were detailed accounts of bitter street fighting between Indonesian marines and elements of the Indonesian army that had defected to Caliphate forces. Something called suicide bombers were reported to have breached the marines' command centre and killed many senior officers, gravely disrupting the secularist defences.

Hidaka felt as if he had picked up some sort of trashy American novel – this had to be fiction. What were Indonesians? Or secularists? Or Caliphates? Or suicide bombers? What sort of crazy man, given the alternative, would fly his plane into the enemy rather than just bombing them? *A desperate one perhaps*, he conjectured. *But crazy nonetheless.*

At the bottom of the absurd story, beneath the words *Related Links*, sat four lines of blue text, underlined as he had seen before. Perhaps touching them might reveal more? Unfortunately he doubted his fingers were small enough to pick out an individual line. So he took a pencil out of his shirt pocket and tried that.

It worked! The spirits of his ancestors were smiling on him now.

He touched the line that had intrigued him as soon as he read it. *America warns China.*

The screen changed instantly, just as before. And just as before, the result was absurdly perplexing.

The US Secretary of State, a *woman* calling herself Jamie Garcia, had warned Chinese Premier Hu Dazhao that the gravest consequences would flow from any Chinese incursion into the exclusion zone around Java. She pledged that something called a 'UN-mandated Multinational Force' would ensure the safety of ethnic Chinese refugees from something else called a 'jihad'. And she warned China that any further expansionist moves on its part anywhere in South-East Asia would be severely challenged.

Hidaka rubbed his face, irritated beyond measure. There were so many things wrong with what he had just read, he wouldn't know where to begin. Certainly, Chiang Kai-shek would like to consider himself some sort of 'premier', but in truth he was little better than a scabrous dog being hunted down by the Imperial Japanese Army. And this *woman*! Garcia? The American Secretary of State was Cordell Hull. A vile creature known to all as an uncultivated savage who had attempted to humiliate the Emperor with his outrageous schemes and demands. Even if that had somehow changed since they had sailed from Ominato, only a maniac would imagine that a woman – a Mexican or an Indian one at that, by the sound of her name – could ever attain such an important office.

Hidaka sipped the nearly forgotten tea and grimaced to discover that it had gone cold.

There were more 'Related Links' at the bottom of this story – or perhaps fairy tale might have been a better name. He 'linked' to a story about 'Free Indonesian' warships that had joined this so-called Multinational Force. An Indonesian government-in-exile had insisted that two of its ships, the *Sutanto* and the *Nuku*, participate in the enforcement of any exclusion zone over the contested archipelago.

Something in that nagged at Hidaka. It was all as preposterous as the rest, but . . .

The *Sutanto*!

He leaped from the armchair, upsetting the cup of cold tea, which spilled onto the floor. Heedless of the accident, he rushed over to the unconscious sailors. One who had collapsed in the wardroom still sported a baseball cap on which was stitched a silhouette of a ship. And the caption *377 KRI Sutanto*.

He had been seeing that word all over the ship, and now he knew why. This *was* the *Sutanto*, presumably of the Free Indonesian Navy.

Without a doubt this had to be some sort of American trick, perhaps even a trap. But what could be the point? And why bait the trap so oddly? And where did the fantastic machines such as this glowing tablet come from anyway?

A thousand questions spilled from his one small success. He was nearly overcome by a wave of hopelessness, when a crewman called urgently.

'Commander! One of the men is waking. *Look!*'

'At last,' Hidaka muttered. He moved to stand by the man's head. The barbarian was blinking rapidly. A storm of twitches and tics ran across his features, briefly seizing his whole body at one point. Without warning he vomited prodigiously, a yellow-green geyser that erupted vertically from his mouth only to fall back and drench him. With distaste branded into every line of his face, Hidaka used the toe of his boot to turn the man's head to one side, lest he choke to death.

Hidaka unshipped his revolver from its holster as the foreigner began to cough out a series of unintelligible words. The man tried to lever himself up off the floor, but Hidaka placed a foot on his chest and pressed him firmly back down. Incomprehension and a touch of fear crossed the man's face.

Good, thought Hidaka.

'Name!' he barked out, first in Japanese, then in English.

The man coughed and gagged on his own bile. He appeared to be trying to answer, so Hidaka only gave him a slight nudge with his boot.

'Name. And rank. And position aboard this vessel.'

The man, who was dressed in soiled tropical whites and sandals, of all things, squinted at Hidaka as if trying to focus properly.

‘Moertopo,’ he answered. ‘Lieutenant Ali Moertopo, Executive Officer.’

He spoke English then. Hidaka was quietly relieved.

The man, Lieutenant Moertopo, finally focused on Hidaka’s pistol. He seemed genuinely surprised, and somehow *affronted.*

‘What is going on?’ he demanded with more authority in his voice than Hidaka cared for. ‘Who are you, and what are you doing aboard this ship?’

The demands were delivered in a weak, faltering voice, but there was no mistaking the challenge inherent in their tone. Hidaka flushed with anger that someone so obviously low-caste could think to presume upon him in such a fashion, but Admiral Kakuta had chosen him well for this mission. He swallowed his own indignation, carefully holstered the pistol and dropped a handkerchief onto the man’s chest.

‘Clean yourself up, Lieutenant,’ he said.

Moertopo thanked him somewhat doubtfully, and wiped the vomit from his face and neck. His movements indicated to Hidaka that he was in considerable pain. It did not register on his face, however, granting him some esteem in the eyes of the Japanese officer.

Moertopo looked around slowly, taking in the bodies of his shipmates laid out on either side of him. They were breathing and twitching, but would clearly offer no assistance.

'You have not answered my question,' he said in English.

'My name is Hidaka. I boarded your ship with a rescue party three hours ago. Your shipmates are alive, but appear to have been incapacitated. You would have to tell me how that might be, Lieutenant. I am afraid I have no idea.'

'You are Japanese, yes?'

Hidaka nodded, noting that the information neither alarmed nor upset his prisoner.

'We were on station, just north of the main task force, carrying out antisubmarine drills,' Moertopo said.

'Why?' asked Hidaka. 'And which task force?'

Moertopo gave him an odd look, as if the question had been meant to mock him.

'Why indeed?' he said, bitterness evident in his voice. 'The Caliphate has no submarines. And the Americans certainly wouldn't trust us to protect them from the Chinese. It was laughable. They just wanted to get us out of the way.'

'The Americans?'

'Sorry, the Multinational Force. But yes, basically the Americans. They said it was because we couldn't link properly to their CI network, but the truth is they simply don't trust us.'

Hidaka wished he had some idea what the man was talking about, but he didn't let his confusion show. This Moertopo seemed quite happy to discuss state secrets with him, despite the fact that he seemed to be allied in some way with the United States. Notwithstanding the pressures of time, Hidaka would need to play this very carefully indeed.

'Can you stand?' he asked. 'Would you like some tea?'

The man nodded gratefully. Hidaka clicked his fingers at a sailor, who hurried over to help Moertopo into the armchair. After some hasty instructions the crewman set about drawing another two mugs of tea. Hidaka took a plain chair from the wardroom table and spun it around to face Moertopo. He sat to bring himself down to eye level with his subject.

'Lieutenant Moertopo,' he said, forming the name carefully, 'this task force, was it heading for Java?'

'Of course,' the lieutenant replied, gratefully sipping his tea. 'The president himself insisted that we play our part in any operations taking place in our home waters.' As he spoke, a measure of pride worked its way through the layers of illness and discomfort.

'And you were sailing from?'

'Dili,' he said and then, 'East Timor,' as it became obvious Hidaka was confused by the answer. 'We were training in preparation for deployment.'

'Lieutenant Moertopo, you will have to excuse my ignorance, I have been at sea for many months. But I must say, your ship has me baffled. I have never seen its like before.'

Moertopo snorted in a thin imitation of good humour. Obviously the effort taxed him severely.

'That is not surprising . . . I am sorry . . . Mr Hidaka.'

'Lieutenant Commander.'

'Lieutenant Commander. We're the last of the old *Parchim*-class missile corvettes, purchased in bulk from the East German navy in the 1990s. They've been refit –'

'Excuse me,' Hidaka interrupted. 'Did you say the 1990s?'

'Yes. I forget the exact year. It was before I was born. But President Habibie bought thirty-nine of them. Most rusted away for want of funds to maintain them. Saboteurs destroyed some early in the war, but the *Sutanto* and the *Nuku* escaped. Did you know we carried the president himself and his family away from Tanjungpinang to Singapore?' Moertopo asked proudly.

But Hidaka wasn't attending to the question. He was staring at the young naval officer in sheer disbelief.

'No, I did not know that, Lieutenant,' he said distractedly. 'Do you know your current location, roughly?'

Moertopo shrugged. 'You would know better than I, Commander. Clearly you haven't been unconscious for Allah knows how long.'

'Yes, yes, but roughly.'

'Somewhere in the Wetar Strait, I would hazard. Near the rest of the task force. Tell me, have you all been affected? Is the *Nuku* okay?'

Hidaka was truly flummoxed. He shook his head in a distracted fashion. 'The Wetar Strait, you say?'

'Yes. But enough of this pointless questioning – we're just wasting time,' Moertopo said as he struggled to get to his feet. 'I should see to my shipmates. We may need to consult your surgeon, or the Americans, if they haven't been attacked too. Do you know if they have? Or what sort of weapon it was? A neural attack maybe.'

'I am sorry, Lieutenant. What sort of attack?'

'That would mean that it was the Chinese, not the Caliphate,' he said, not really helping Hidaka at all.

The Commander's heart was racing now. He had often wondered how he might fare in combat, and now he had reason to doubt his own courage. He was becoming increasingly unnerved by this encounter. Goose flesh was crawling up his arms, and he shivered involuntarily.

'Do you know the date today, Lieutenant?'

Moertopo glanced at his watch. 'It is the fifteenth today.'

'Of?'

Lieutenant Moertopo gave Hidaka a quizzical look.

'Of January.'

'And the year? Please . . . humour me.'

Moertopo shrugged and, without being sure why, glanced at his watch again.

'2021.'

'Shit,' said Lieutenant Commander Hidaka.

But he said it in Japanese.

12

HIJMS Ryujo, *2358 hours, 2 June 1942*

Admirals don't normally answer summons from Lieutenant Commanders. But Hidaka had been so inured to censure, so insistent that Admiral Kakuta make the trip to this *Sutanto*, that the commander of the Second Carrier Striking Force had relented.

So it was that he found himself on the bitterly cold flight deck, cloaked in fog, when the strange lights appeared.

All of his doubts about Hidaka's mental stability evaporated when the giant mechanical dragonfly materialised out of the gloom. Instead, Admiral Kakuta had reason to doubt his own sanity. A monstrous insect was the only image he could conjure up in the face of the abomination. It approached with a sort of thudding buzz, and *hovered* over the deck. A great gale blew away the fog. An icy, knifing wind painfully lashed at his exposed skin. Grit, spray and even oil from the deck stung his eyes, forcing him to turn away.

As he huddled, shamefully, against the polar blast, he tried to sort his impressions into some comprehensible form. It had to be an aircraft of sorts. Not a dragonfly or a demon. But it had no wings, and the blurring of the air above the blinding lights suggested a propeller of some type.

Kakuta felt it settle with a slight *thump* on the deck, and immediately the frightful sound tapered off to a dull roar and an odd, mushy thudding. He thought he heard a high-pitched whine and the sounds of hydraulic equipment. The shouts and curses of the *Ryujo*'s crew were blessedly familiar, even if they betrayed astonishment and distress. When the admiral felt it was safe to straighten up, he turned to face the thing squarely. There were two men in the . . .

Cockpit?

He assumed it had to be.

A man in an oversized white helmet, his face obscured by a dark lens, occupied one berth. Ensign Tomonagi sat beside him. The junior officer scrambled out quickly as the massive propeller . . .

Yes, most certainly a propeller!

. . . ceased its rotation altogether. The ensign was shaking, no doubt with excitement and more than a little fright, at having been strapped into a plane without wings.

Kakuta had been enraged that a simple recon task had put them hours behind schedule, but his fury was crimped off by the appearance of the craft. Something very unusual had happened out there.

'Ensign. Explain this!' he barked at Tomonagi.

'I cannot, sir,' the ensign replied. 'Commander Hidaka has all the information. He sent me to assure you that your presence on the captured destroyer is vital.'

'But what *is* this thing? And who is that pilot?' Kakuta demanded.

'It is called a helicopter,' Tomonagi said, having some trouble pronouncing the word. 'And the pilot is a Flight Lieutenant Hardoyo. He will take you back to the *Sutanto*.'

Kakuta examined the machine with a very wary eye. The fog and darkness gave its queer lines a sinister appearance. Dozens of men were gathered around it, though at a safe distance, their breath pluming in front of them as they swapped wild theories about its origin. The pilot waved to one or two, who pointed at him.

'Lieutenant Commander Hidaka is juggling with hot coals,' said Kakuta. 'He should be back here reporting to me, so we can continue towards Dutch Harbour with all speed. The operation has no margin for delays like this.'

Tomonagi drew a breath. He was shivering visibly. 'Commander Hidaka says you will not believe his report unless you are there to see with your own eyes what he has found. He asked me to tell you that he does not believe the attack on Dutch Harbor, or even on Midway, will proceed once you have had the chance to inspect the vessel yourself.'

Kakuta's anger, subdued by the arrival of the 'helicopter', was bubbling over again.

'And you, Ensign? What do you believe to be

our correct course of action? To follow Admiral Yamamoto's direction, or that of Lieutenant Commander Hidaka?'

Tomonagi didn't answer immediately. Despite the lethal cold on the exposed flight deck, a single trickle of sweat still ran down his face.

'Admiral, I have seen inexplicable things on that ship. Certainly *I* am not able to explain them. But Commander Hidaka is convinced the course of the war will be changed by what we do here in the next few hours, not by what happens at Midway. And I am sorry, but he also wishes you to know that the Americans have broken our codes and have known about Operation MI for weeks. They are lying in wait.

'But he says that is now irrelevant too.'

Tomonagi flinched as he spoke those last words.

'What!' exploded Kakuta. 'Why did you not tell me this *immediately*?'

The young man apologised profusely, bowing as deeply as he could without actually banging his forehead to the flight deck.

'If that is true, we must inform Nagumo and Yamamoto at once,' cried the Admiral.

Captain Tadao Kato, the skipper of the *Ryujo*, stepped up from behind. 'Begging your pardon, Admiral, but we have the strictest orders, already breached once, to maintain radio silence. And we have no confirmation of this wild tale. We could imperil the entire plan with one transmission.'

Kakuta felt trapped. The evidence of that outlandish aircraft, sitting just a few yards away, confirmed that Hidaka had discovered something of great import. But Kakuta's mission was of paramount consequence too. The attack on Dutch Harbor was necessary to draw the remnants of the American fleet away from the centre of the Pacific, leaving Midway open to attack. Without that feint, the entire gambit might simply collapse. He was already behind schedule, and now Hidaka wanted to drag them further into the mire.

Yet he trusted the man's judgment as he did his own. That was why he had assigned the investigation to him in the first place. And this *thing* in which Tomonagi had arrived! It was obviously an aircraft of great power and sophistication. Its very form threatened violence, and he had seen with his own eyes how it hovered in the air like a gigantic hummingbird.

'I will go then!' he snapped, exasperated beyond measure. 'But Captain, if you have not heard from me within one hour, forge on with the original plan. It will mean I have fallen into a trap and must be abandoned along with Hidaka.'

'One hour,' confirmed Kato.

Twenty-five minutes later a small, book-like electric gadget Ensign Tomonagi had brought across from the *Sutanto* flared into life. It had been resting against a window of the *Ryujo*'s bridge, continously scrutinised by Tomonagi, who had remained with the *Ryujo* on Commander Hidaka's direct orders.

'Captain! Captain Kato!' cried Tomonagi. 'It is Admiral Kakuta.'

Kato looked over his shoulder at first, thinking his superior had somehow snuck back aboard the ship. But then his eye caught the glow of Tomonagi's electric book, and the captain found it difficult to suppress a gasp of surprise. Kakuta himself seemed to be floating within.

'Captain Kato. It is I, Kakuta.' He sounded tired now. 'Please contact the fleet and bring them around. You may use the low-frequency radio. The attack on Dutch Harbor is not to proceed. I repeat, the attack on Dutch Harbor is *not* to proceed. I shall inform Admiral Hosogaya myself . . . Just obey!' he added firmly, when he saw that Kato was preparing to argue.

KRI Sutanto, *0024 hours, 3 June 1942*

'Amazing . . . simply amazing,' muttered Kakuta as Lieutenant Moertopo cut the link that connected them with the flexipad on the *Ryujo*'s bridge.

'The admiral expresses his heartfelt amazement at this most sophisticated machine,' Hidaka translated.

'I suppose it must be a shock,' said Moertopo, who had been confronted by a surprise much more profound than one's first exposure to a simple flexipad. The dermal patch on his neck held back the physical sensation of nausea, but he still felt sick in his mind.

'Admiral, I suggest that we have some of the men go up on deck to ensure that Captain Kato has followed your orders,' Hidaka said, translating again for the benefit of the Indonesian.

'That won't be necessary, Admiral,' Moertopo interjected. 'I can do that from here.' In a few seconds he linked to the *Sutanto*'s sensors and handed the pad back to Kakuta, who was then able to watch a radar image of the entire fleet, slowing and turning for home. Hidaka explained the meaning of the image that filled the flexipad screen. At this point in history, Japan had not invested deeply in radar technology. Moertopo noted with a degree of satisfaction that neither man was able to hide his admiration.

'I can get you an image of any individual vessel you'd care to observe from the mast-mounted cameras,' said Moertopo. 'It doesn't matter that it's dark and foggy outside. The cameras can pick out your ships anyway.'

He took the pad back, entered a few instructions and, just as he had promised, the screen filled with a black-and-white image of the *Ryujo* herself, coming around on the new heading, leaning into the swell, throwing up a prodigious bow wave.

'Again, I am astounded, Lieutenant,' said Hidaka with real reverence in his tone.

'I doubt you could be more astonished than I.'

They sat at the wardroom table, sipping fresh tea

from the ship's finest china, last used when the *Sutanto* had spirited the Indonesian president and his family away from the Caliphate rebellion. In deference to the Indonesians, who were dressed for the tropics, the ship's climate control had been set to approximate a warm spring day in Bali. The Japanese had stripped off the outer layers of their arctic-weather gear, but were still sweating in the heavy uniforms they wore underneath.

The small room was much busier now, with nearly two dozen Indonesian sailors revived and attending to those comrades who were still unconscious, or cleaning up the unpleasant aftermath of their illness. The Japanese and Indonesian sailors remained wary of one another, but their officers had turned to the task of coping with the unprecedented situation.

Lieutenant Ali Moertopo was trying hard to keep relations with the Japanese as friendly as possible. The bulk of his countrymen, including his own captain, were still unconscious and showing little sign of responding to stimulants, so he was well aware that the initiative lay with Kakuta. If circumstances had been more conducive, they might have just sunk the Japanese fleet and sailed off to Pearl Harbor, there to offer their services to the eventual winners of this war.

Assuming, of course, that this insanity played out, and they actually *had* travelled back in time.

He found he still couldn't accept that as a real possibility.

For the moment, though, he was content to

present a mask of civility and cooperation to his captors, for that's what they were, no matter how much buffalo shit they fed him about 'rescue' parties. He'd got a good long look at the mouth of Hidaka's pistol when he came to, and he remembered only too well that conceited sneer. He noted that the Japanese sailors – or perhaps they were marines – hadn't put down their arms.

Moertopo had offered Kakuta the chance to observe his fleet on the *Sutanto*'s radar only because he needed to know what sort of enemy he was up against. There appeared to be four capital ships, probably consisting of two carriers and two cruisers – or maybe battleships – and another group of smaller escorts, probably destroyers and maybe a tender. He would endeavour to interest them in a lengthy demonstration of the mast-mounted cameras, and in doing so confirm that conclusion. Captain Djuanda would need every possible scrap of information when he recovered and took command.

If he recovered.

Moertopo willed the captain to revive, so that he might be relieved of the mind-bending responsibilities presented by this situation.

'Lieutenant, are you ill again? You look quite distressed.'

The *Sutanto*'s exec pulled out of his reverie with a shake of his head. In fact, he still felt awful, and the physical effects of their arrival were compounded by the stress of confronting the impossible.

'I am sorry, Commander,' he lied. 'I was overcome by this sickness again. It's much worse than any nausea I have felt before, even in heavy weather.'

'Perhaps you have other treatments for it?' Hidaka suggested. 'Medicines as powerful as your machines?'

His captor was playing with him, he knew. Fishing for more information about their technology. Moertopo was convinced that if he didn't handle this exactly right, neither he nor any of his men would live to see the next dawn.

'Perhaps,' he agreed. 'I shall have an orderly bring some syringes.' With that, he dispatched a junior rating to the sick bay with instruction to bring back a supply of Promatil fixes.

'While we are waiting,' Kakuta purred in his native tongue, 'you might enlighten us with some historical information. Commander Hidaka informs me that the *Yorktown* was not sunk in the Coral Sea engagement, and in fact it lies in wait for Nagumo, just off Midway?'

Moertopo, who managed to catch the drift of the Japanese officer's question, waited for Hidaka's translation anyway. It gave him a few vital seconds to construct his reply. And when he spoke, it was slowly and carefully, as if he were concerned not to rush the fluent, English-speaking commander.

'I am afraid,' he said, 'that in the time from which I came, your efforts at Midway were undone by a stroke of bad luck. As I recall, Admiral Nagumo beat off numerous attacks by American flyers in heavy bombers and torpedo planes, only to be caught by a flight of dive-bombers when his decks were cluttered with refuelling and rearming planes. I think three carriers were destroyed in just a few minutes. But I am sorry, I cannot remember which ones. I would have to consult our library.'

Hidaka looked around the wardroom, searching for the bookshelves. Moertopo easily divined his intention and smiled, holding up the flexipad.

'Our library is in here,' he explained.

The two Japanese conferred rapidly in their own language. Lieutenant Moertopo used the opportunity to casually check the radar images again, confirming his earlier, rushed observation. He desperately wanted to see the familiar image of their sister ship out there. But he was completely surrounded by Kakuta's battle group. The *Nuku* was probably back with the Americans.

He dropped the pad back on the table, as if it were of no concern at all to him. Then Hidaka spoke up again. 'Thank you, Lieutenant. As you can imagine, we are most interested in anything that might help us avert this catastrophe. I am sure that you, too, would be happy to see the European powers driven from their colonies, your homeland.'

Ali Moertopo nearly laughed out loud, but that would have been fatal. Instead he restricted himself to a small, disingenuous smile. He knew only too well that, were these animals to take dominion over his homeland, they would construct a slave state rivalling the Caliphate's ugliest tyranny. Now was not the time, however, to deliver a critique of fascist Japan's risibly named 'co-prosperity sphere'.

Now was the time for lying through his teeth. The long run would have to take care of itself.

'Do not imagine,' Moertopo said, 'that just because my government found it convenient to enter into an alliance with the United States we did so happily. The policies of the Americans reduced my country to ashes and bone, picked over by madmen and ignorant savages. Clearly any patriot would leap at the opportunity to avoid that outcome.'

Moertopo was surprised at how easily this rubbish spilled from his lips. Still, he had to convince Kakuta and Hidaka that they had found a powerful and trustworthy ally. One who wouldn't need to be kept under close and constant guard.

Curiously, he had the impression that Hidaka was the one to convince. The older man seemed so overwhelmed by events that he was ready to dance with any devil. Behind his smile, however, Lieutenant Commander Hidaka regarded Moertopo with all the benevolence of a hungry shark.

'If I understand you then, Lieutenant, you would propose an alliance?' Hidaka inquired.

Ali arranged his features as credibly as possible. *I would offer you my firstborn on a plate*, he thought, *if that's what it took to get your boot off my throat. Whether I deliver is another matter.*

When he spoke, however, it was to say, 'I can offer

nothing until I have consulted with Captain Djuanda. But I cannot imagine he would forgo such a unique opportunity to set history right.' He grinned wolfishly. Or what he hoped was wolfishly.

The admiral seemed satisfied. Hidaka, too, was appeased, but seemed to retain a certain reserve.

Working the archipelago under an old pirate like Djuanda, Moertopo had developed a smuggler's sense for risk and opportunity. Both lay in front of him, but the risk seemed much greater. Best to give an impression of avarice, coloured by a longing for vengeance and not a little stupidity. Nobody feared an idiot.

The midshipman reappeared with a box of one-use Promatil syringes. Moertopo jabbed himself, then ordered the middie to distribute them among members of his crew.

Kakuta spoke again, holding the flexipad as if it were a Ming vase.

'Your library, Lieutenant? You implied you have information in here' – the idea of a library in a box evidently bewildered him – 'that would help us avert a disaster. Time is of the essence. We need to know what to do.'

'I cannot tell you what to do,' Moertopo replied through Hidaka. 'That is not my place. I can only tell you what we know of the battle, through our archival files. Any decisions are yours to make.'

He didn't feel up to the task of explaining a distributed information system like the web to a couple of rubes whose idea of a computer had stalled at the abacus. And he certainly didn't want to give them the keys to the kingdom. His knowledge of history was patchy. What details he knew of the battle at Midway came mostly from the Tom Cruise mini-series he'd watched on a pirated media stick. But he *did* understand the enormous power of the United States, even in this era. And he flattered himself that he understood their culture too. Better than these two, at any rate.

America could lose Midway, and even Pearl Harbor, and it would prolong the war, but not change the outcome. As a people the Americans were a strange mix of sophistication and barbarism. They wouldn't feel avenged until Japan had been burned to the ground. Within a few years they would detonate atomic bombs over Hiroshima and Nagasaki. It was inevitable that the Japanese would learn about that from the ship's files, or more likely from one of the crew.

They might react by suing for peace. More likely they would engage in a race for the weapon themselves. And they would lose. Everybody lost when they fought the Americans, didn't they?

He sighed and reached for the flexipad. But before he could bring up the data his hand was stayed by the sounds of a struggle just outside the wardroom.

Besides Moertopo, only two men capable of working the Combat Information Centre were conscious. One of them was a systems engineer named Damiri. Ten minutes after coming to, he opened a file containing stored radio intercepts picked up by the *Sutanto*'s passive arrays while he'd been unconscious. The CIC was immediately flooded with a graphic audio tableau of the hostilities near Midway.

He lunged for the control panel. A Japanese marine took the sudden movement as a threat, shouting and pulling Damiri back by the hair. The guard threw one arm around the Indonesian sailor's neck, attempting to drag him away from the console while still holding his rifle in the other hand.

Damiri, with some basic training in the Indonesian martial art of *Silat*, reacted instantly, clamping one hand over the wrist and jerking it down, away from his windpipe. At the same time he gouged at a nerve bundle in the man's forearm. The guard grunted in pain and surprise, then slammed his rifle into the side of the engineer's head. White flares exploded behind Damiri's eyes, compounding the low-grade misery he'd suffered since awakening. He slumped, and the guard heaved him away from the console.

A couple more Japanese guards quickly appeared and butt-swiped the Indonesian with their rifles. His screams brought Moertopo and the others running.

Now, heavily bandaged, Damiri was back at the workstation, finessing the ship's antennae for maximum gain without alerting the Americans to his presence.

*

Moertopo wasn't happy with the way things were shaping up. He briefly considered telling the young engineer to secretly ping the Multinational Force with an ID pulse and 'duress' signal, but decided to hold off. For one thing, Hidaka had made it clear to the Indonesians that any extended conversation in their native tongue of Bahasa would not be tolerated.

When Damiri had located a block of intercepts suggesting that the *Clinton* had exploded, Moertopo had suppressed a horrified grimace. He could have wrung Kolhammer's neck at that point. How could he allow himself to be knocked over by these pygmies? If these stupid Americans all killed each other down there, where on earth was he supposed to run to when he had the chance?

For the first time since awakening with Hidaka's gun jammed in his face, he actually contemplated throwing his lot in with the Japanese. Trying to plot a course through the contrary waters of fate was turning out to be more difficult than he had imagined. Hidaka certainly gave no indication that he was ready to pay out the leash even a fraction. Furtively scoping out the armed Japanese guards ringing his CIC, watching his every move, Moertopo began to doubt they would *ever* wriggle out of the yoke that now restrained them.

'*It's a Jap ship, a nip bastard for sure*,' cried an American flyer over his radio. '*I'm going in. I'm going to . . .*'

The speakers crackled for a second with the

recorded sound of a dive-bomber disintegrating under the impact of a barrage.

'What was that?' Hidaka demanded to know.

'At a guess, Commander,' Moertopo replied, 'a defensive Close-In Weapons System known as Metal Storm. I doubt a bolt of lightning could sneak through. That pilot had no chance.'

'Fascinating,' snapped Hidaka. 'but that's not what I meant. He said he saw a Japanese ship. You told us that Nagumo's force would be nowhere near the Americans yet.'

The speakers continued to crackle with snatches of dialogue, some of it still referring to a Japanese ship. Admiral Kakuta gave him a frozen look that made clear the consequences of betrayal. Moertopo held up his hands, palms out, begging for a chance to explain.

'We had a ship with us, a Japanese stealth cruiser, the *Siranui*. That's what they're talking about. It probably shot down that plane.'

'A Japanese ship attached to an American fleet?' scoffed Hidaka.

Moertopo shrugged. 'You lost the war, Commander. I have already told you that. You were annihilated. The defeated do not get to dictate terms. In my time Japan is a baseball-playing democracy and a staunch American ally.'

He was taking a risk, speaking so bluntly, with the Japanese officer already incensed. But Moertopo judged that the truth was his best defence. Kakuta murmured softly and quickly to Hidaka, the older man's hand restraining the younger one's temper. When he spoke again, it was clear that Hidaka nearly choked on the words.

'I apologise for my outburst, Lieutenant Moertopo. An understandable reaction, I'm sure you would agree.'

'Yes. Of course.'

'The admiral asks you to explain the nature of this ship. The *Siranui*, I believe you called it.'

Ali Moertopo patted his systems engineer on the shoulder and motioned for him to turn down the volume of the recordings. Desperate voices still filled the CIC, but in the background now.

'We can review the intercepts later,' said Moertopo. 'You will need to know what sort of damage the Americans have inflicted on each other . . .' He carefully neglected to add that he, too, would need to know exactly what had happened. And whether the *Nuku* was down there with them.

'The *Siranui*,' he continued, 'is a Japanese adaptation of a standard US Nemesis cruiser. Its arrays are perhaps even a little better than the originals, but it doesn't have as much firepower. In this context, however, it has more than enough. That one ship could sink your entire force, Admiral.'

While Hidaka relayed his comments, Moertopo instructed another sysop to bring up some images and cutaways of a Nemesis cruiser on one of the centre's flat-screens. Hidaka finished speaking with the admiral and turned back to Moertopo.

'The admiral wants to know about the captain of this Japanese ship. What sort of a man is he? Will he recognise his duty to the Emperor?'

'Will he join you, you mean? I have no idea. I've never met him. Captain Djuanda has had occasion to deal with him, but he is still unconscious.'

'What is your *feeling* though, Lieutenant?' Hidaka asked, his eyes on the big screen, greedily drinking in the stored vision of the Nemesis cruiser.

'I may be wrong, but my feeling is that he would be unlikely to see the benefit of aligning himself with you.'

Hidaka rolled the words around in his mouth like a handful of poison pebbles. Admiral Kakuta accepted the answer without any visible reaction. He said only one word in reply.

'Why?'

'You are asking me to explain the mind of a man I have never met,' protested Moertopo. 'I am really just guessing, but I imagine that he – not me, but he – would hold your government responsible for taking Japan into a war it could not win. I don't know what he might do under such circumstances, but he is not of your time. His view of the world is different.'

'But his duty as a warrior is eternal,' Hidaka protested. 'His duty is to the Emperor. Not to the Emperor's enemies.'

'He may see his duty as belonging to Japan.'

'But we *are* Japan!'

'Not his idea of it.'

'Ideas! Damn your ideas! The Emperor is descended from gods! It is our *destiny* to serve him.'

Moertopo could feel the ground shifting dangerously. Hidaka was becoming overheated. Kakuta, who could not follow the discussion fully, was growing similarly agitated. And Moertopo was playing devil's advocate on behalf of a man he had never met and probably never would. If he pressed this case too far, they might leap to the assumption that he agreed with the unknown captain's treasonous behaviour. Time to pour oil on troubled waters.

'Admiral Kakuta,' he said as soothingly as possible, 'I am not responsible for the world I came from, nor for the men who came with me. I will assist you because I understand that it will assist my own countrymen in this time and in the future. If the officers aboard the *Siranui* prove traitorous and unreliable, there may be other ways of dealing with them – luring them into a trap, for instance, where they might be directly confronted by their treachery. They may then see reason and choose the correct path. Or not. But the *Siranui* itself, which is undeniably the property of Japan, might then be turned over to her rightful owners.'

He knew he was talking a lot of crap, but his situation was precarious, and it was crucial to convince these two to trust him before they went off on some hysterical banzai charge of indignation, lopping off heads and arms with gay abandon to salve their wounded pride.

Kakuta, he was relieved to see, calmed visibly and nodded as Hidaka translated for him. Moertopo put the few seconds' grace to good use, and asked for an update from Damiri. In fact, there had been a development, but Moertopo was unsure of how it might play with the Japanese.

They noticed the perplexed look on his face.

'You have something to tell us?' Hidaka demanded.

'Yes. Our discussion appears to have been premature. Sub-Lieutenant Damiri informs me that the *Siranui* has been hit. A shell strike on the bridge has killed the captain and a number of officers.'

Hidaka informed his superior, who had by this time regained his equilibrium. He digested the information without any visible sign of distress.

'The admiral asks if the ship itself was badly damaged.'

'I don't know, but probably not,' said Moertopo. 'The bridge of a modern warship is more for sightseeing than for fighting. There will be peripheral damage, and we know of casualties, but her combat capability should be relatively unaffected.'

Kakuta smiled when this was relayed to him. He searched for a suitable reply, and when he spoke at last, it was in English.

'Good,' he said.

His contented grin didn't leave Moertopo feeling cheery at all.

13

SAR 02, 0024 hours, 3 June 1942

Flight Lieutenant Chris Harford took the Seahawk out fast and low. Conditions were midlevel challenging. Search and Rescue control had vectored them onto a point some six thousand metres to the southwest of the *Clinton*, where drone-cams had located men in the water. The sea state remained choppy, the weather difficult. Daylight was still hours away, but their night vision systems were coping. Fourteen other SAR missions were in flight, and two choppers had taken fire from nervous AA crews on one of Spruance's surviving destroyers.

At least the Promatil dump had cleared his seasickness, or whatever the hell it was. Harford was something of a connoisseur when it came to seasickness, never having found his sea legs. It was kind of strange, considering he'd never once suffered from airsickness. But without fail he spent the first half hour of any foray beyond sheltered waters rolled into a ball of misery in his bunk, waiting for a dermal patch to kick in. It was a source of unending frustration to Harford that most people just assumed sailors and marines were immune to seasickness. His misery was, of course, a source of unending mirth to his shipmates.

There wasn't much chatter as they ate up the distance. Everybody seemed caught in a weird headspace, not so much frightened as unbalanced by the morning's events.

'Nintendo piece of shit!' cursed his SO, Flight Lieutenant Hayes, as she gave the dead GPS unit another swat. Chris sometimes suspected that, despite five years in service as a systems operator, Amanda still thought that any piece of equipment could be fixed with a solid whack upside the head, like an old TV set.

He brought the big grey helicopter to a hover above the rough centre of the debris field. Amanda peered down into the flotsam that was dispersing under the fantastic downblast from the Seahawk. Scraps of cloth floated everywhere. Body parts. Broken, smashed-up pieces of wood floating on an oil slick that was burning here and there, degrading their infrared NVS. Amanda thumbed her ear bud to open a channel to the crewman in the back of the chopper. 'Tobes, you see anything worth bagging?'

Airman Toby La Salle came back at her, all growling South Bronx, but quantum smooth, as though he were right there in her ear. 'Not much, Lieutenant. Burning oil's messing with my vision. Somebody knew what they were doing really opened a big can of whupp-ass down there . . . Wait, hang on, think I see a coupla dudes. Two o'clock, two hundred out.

Swimming away from us, so they're in one piece . . . prob'ly.'

Harford tilted the stick a fraction and sent them roaring towards the survivors.

'Dudes're swimming faster!' La Salle cried out. 'Like they're trying to get away from us.'

'Maybe they think we're gonna be mad at 'em,' said Hayes. 'Think we flew all the way over here to finish the job.'

Harford cut in over the top of them. 'Drop the line.' He held the Seahawk directly over the men, who were desperately thrashing away in the rotor wash. La Salle winched down a padded rescue collar, which flapped around madly, but the men only whirled their arms faster.

'Time for a swim, Tobes,' said Hayes. She heard La Salle's 'Gotcha' in her ear bud. Harford eased the chopper away from their reluctant targets while La Salle, who was wearing a thin spring wetsuit, wrestled into a pair of flippers and goggles. A few seconds later he jumped.

La Salle covered the short distance to the first sailor in less than a minute, carving through a mat of wreckage as he went. The sailor, a much smaller man and a comparatively poor swimmer, had no chance of escaping. But he tried. As La Salle pulled level with him the man turned about, hooking burned fingers into claws and swiping at the rescue jumper's face while letting go a series of terrified, guttural cries.

Both men bobbed on the chaotic swell and cross-chop, flattened some by the rotor wash, but not completely. Stinging spray lashed their faces and made it very difficult to breathe. La Salle had a little trouble keeping his head above water and the burned sailor went under a few times, vomiting as he resurfaced. La Salle finally abandoned the soft approach, wrestled him into the harness and signalled for a winch up. He rode with him for a moment, then dropped straight back down to search for the second survivor.

But it was too late. The sailor's companion was floating face down, dead in the water.

USS Hillary Clinton, *0029 hours, 3 June 1942*

The *Clinton*'s media centre was a mess, in a very civilian way. Jackets lay over computer screens. Food sat atop flexipads. Discarded coffee cups had multiplied like rabbits. And most days, there was more hubbub than Lieutenant Thieu could bear.

For once, however, it was quiet. As a group the reporters were older, fatter, whiter and infinitely more prone to whining and mischief than the military personnel on whom they reported. None of them had mil-grade spinal inserts, and the illness that had come with the wormhole transition had hit them hard. Most were still unconscious, laid out on canvas cots hastily set up in the corner of the centre, where a single orderly watched over them. Most, but not all.

Lieutenant Edgar 'The Egg' Thieu, the *Clinton*'s media supervisor, tried putting on his best stone face for the only two journalists who remained awake. But stone faces only work on those who have something to fear from the person behind them, and neither Julia Duffy nor Rosanna Natoli had any reason to fear the worst that The Egg might dish up.

A lapsed Buddhist, he considered their furious glares and wondered what crime he had committed in a past life. This was a karmic backlash of bin Laden proportions. *What a pair of fuckin' raptors*, he thought. They were working him into a corner and blindsiding him, all razor teeth and slashing claws. He'd nearly wet himself watching *Jurassic Park* as a little kid and he had the same feeling of free-floating horror now, eighteen years later, facing this pair of shrews.

'Ladies . . .' he said, offering them his open palms.

'Jesus, Nat!' cried Duffy. 'Now it's not just patronising bullshit, it's patronising *sexist* bullshit!'

'Uh . . . I'm sorry ladi –, uh . . .'

'Look, Edgar,' said Natoli, a petite brunette with axes in her impossibly deep brown eyes. 'You got caught with your pants down. You lied to us, which means you lied to the American people. But now you can make it up to them.'

'Yeah, just let us out of here to do our job,' Duffy finished for her.

'No,' he said firmly. 'Under no circumstances. It's too dangerous.'

'Oh, come on, Edgar!' Natoli protested. 'Why not? This is the fucking story of the century. You can't Roswell it. It's just too *big*. You got ten thousand witnesses, two dozen or more of them journalists. You probably got your satellite links being hacked by CNN right now.'

'Excuse me, Ms Natoli, but CNN won't be hacking any of our communications for a very long time. I can assure you of that.'

Both women snorted in amusement.

'You think so?' asked Natoli, who worked for the Atlanta-based broadcaster.

The Egg smiled kindly, which put both reporters on alert. 'Oh, no. Your sources seem to have misled you. You see, the *Enterprise* is exactly where it's supposed to be. They're not the ones who've gone missing.'

He let the implications of that hang in the air.

'Holy shit,' Duffy said after a brief pause.

'Yep,' nodded The Egg sympathetically. 'So you see. You could interview those guys we brought over, lock them down for an exclusive if you want. But who you gonna call? I don't think they've even invented the television here yet.'

'Oh,' said Rosanna Natoli. Then, 'Oh shit.'

She slumped into a chair. Her eyes seemed to lose focus.

Duffy rummaged around in a pocket and came up with a small bottle of pills. She dry-swallowed one and handed the rest to her friend. Thieu wondered what the medication was. It might explain why they were still conscious.

Whatever. At least I shut 'em up, he thought.

And for a few seconds at least, Lieutenant Edgar Thieu got to enjoy the feeling of being in control.

Dan Black was out of his depth. A few seconds after they had jumped out of the Seahawk, he'd received word that his mission was redundant. Spruance had authorised the Multinational Force to carry out search and rescue. The helicopter had lifted off almost immediately, taking Colonel Jones and leaving the two *Enterprise* men stranded on the *Clinton*. Kolhammer apologised to the pair, shouting over the sound of the rotor blades. He said it was critical they get SAR away as fast as possible.

A Negro woman appeared, wearing camouflage pants, a heavy, blue, long-sleeved T-shirt, and a bulky yellow crash helmet. She hustled them all off the flight deck, which was swarming with emergency and damage control teams. Fires burned everywhere amid the wreckage of smashed aircraft and equipment.

Black noticed that there seemed to be two island structures on the deck, separated by hundreds of yards. They hurried into the first one, and the change of atmosphere struck him immediately. The smell of burning chemicals was completely masked.

'Overpressure,' said Curtis. 'Wow.'

The corridors, which were much wider, well lit and better ventilated than the narrow passages of their own ship, were nonetheless crowded with personnel charging from one crisis to another. Corpsmen carrying stretchers busted past every few minutes. Firefighters in silver space suits straight out of *Flash Gordon* came and went. Sirens sounded, the PA blared. Ensign Curtis snapped his head left and right, trying to take it all in at once. Black was more controlled, but the mayhem conspired to knock his feet out from under him nonetheless.

Kolhammer put a hand on his arm and tugged gently.

'You might as well come with me, Commander. I'm heading back to the bridge.'

Black shrugged and fell into step with the admiral. They passed rooms that seemed to be full of nothing but movie screens, and a mess hall that looked more like a swish restaurant and smelled of things he vaguely recalled from port visits in the Far East and the Mediterranean. It was impossible to ignore the cosmopolitan nature of the carrier's crew. Men and women of all races seemed to work in close proximity without any apparent difficulty. He saw white men take orders from what looked to be a Mexican woman, and watched as the men obeyed without question.

The same Tower of Babel effect was repeated on the flag bridge when they arrived. Black was as bemused by the way different sexes and races were all mixed in among the bridge crew, as he was by the staggering display of technology. The cockpit of the helicopter had looked like something on a space rocket. This room, with its banks of glowing movie screens and flashing lights, was even more bewildering. How on earth did anyone know how to operate this stuff? And what sort of a world was it where women barked orders at men, and coloured folk were placed in charge of whites? Dan Black preferred not to think of himself as a prejudiced man, but his mind locked up. This was simply beyond his comprehension.

He missed Kolhammer's introduction of some officer named Judge.

'Got the butcher's bill, sir,' the man said. 'Damage and casualties across both forces.'

He's from Texas, thought Black.

'Thanks, Mike,' said Kolhammer.

A Seahawk flew past the blast window. They shuttled constantly between those ships with working flight decks and an ever-widening search and rescue zone. Kolhammer waited as Judge consulted his flexipad, unvarnished distaste creasing the exec's features in the light of the screen. He noted that while Curtis had his face glued to the armour glass, watching the flight operations, Lieutenant Commander Black had settled into a quiet corner to watch the *Clinton*'s executive officer.

'Every one of our ships has taken significant damage,' said Judge. 'The close-in systems harvested a shitload of incoming, but another two shitloads arrived right behind the first. So far we have six hundred and thirty-seven confirmed dead on the *Clinton*. One thousand and fifty-three KIA on the *Fearless*. Another eight hundred and ninety-two throughout the task force. We have more than fifteen hundred injured. Half of them from the *Clinton* again. We've definitely lost contact with our two boomers, and with the *Vanguard*, the *Dessaix*, the *Garrett*, and the Indonesians. We're not leaping to conclusions, but it could be they just didn't come through.'

'That's not the case with the *Nagoya* though,' said Kolhammer.

'No, sir, it's not. We're pretty sure now the *Nagoya* was the source of the event and was destroyed by it. Makes sense, given what they were messing with. We've got some video on screen three.'

The flat-screen came to life, quartering into four windows displaying mast-mounted cam coverage of the *Nagoya*. The video ran at normal speed for a few seconds then seemed to stop. Both Black and Curtis moved around to watch the video. The ensign whistled softly, but the older man scowled at the screen as if he didn't trust it.

'We had to dial back the replay speed,' said Judge. 'Even then it's hard to say what happened, it was so quick.'

Kolhammer watched as the giant research vessel suddenly seemed to contract to a single point before a lens of swirling light bloomed out from the same spot. 'What the hell was that?' he asked. 'It looked like they got sucked down a drain or something.'

'Yeah, it did, didn't it? Lieutenant Dietz from the working group trying to nut this out called it *spaghettification*. He says it's what happens when matter is drawn down into a singularity. Like a black hole. He doesn't rate it as an enjoyable trip.'

'Fatal?'

'And then some.'

Curtis leaned over to his superior officer and whispered, 'What's a black hole, sir?'

'Dunno,' said Black.

'We'll explain later,' said Kolhammer as an idea struck him.

'Excuse me, Commander Black. Mike, that reporter we have on board from the *Times*, Duffy, she wrote a piece about this stuff a few years back. It was in the briefing pack I took across to the *Enterprise*. We should get her to write us up a briefing note. Something clear and concise we can use for our own people and for the locals. Lord knows, we're going to need something. She still with us?'

'I believe Lieutenant Thieu is rattling her cage even as we speak, sir.'

'Make a note, I'll want to speak to her later. She can start earning her room and board. Okay.' He nodded, drawing a mental line under the topic. 'Our missing ships, we sure they didn't come through and get turned into noodles?'

'No, we're not sure,' said Judge as a Seahawk lifted off from the heavily damaged deck of the carrier. 'But it's unlikely. The event had an edge. We know that because Captain Halabi saw it cut the *Fearless* in two. That took place eight thousand metres from the *Nagoya*. The subs were a long way beyond that, assuming there was a uniform shape to the phenomenon.'

'Do we have any reason to assume that?' asked Kolhammer, a note of incredulity creeping into his voice. 'This thing did throw everyone out of position, after all. It moved the *Havoc* about seven thousand metres closer to us.'

Judge looked worried, but he could only shrug in agreement. 'Admiral, we can't assume anything about a process we don't understand. The phenomenon seems to have been . . . anomalous. Our relative positions got mixed up. For instance, the *Havoc* was closer, but the *Siranui* was ten thousand metres further from us than she should have been when we emerged. It's possible the missing ships got scattered all over the globe. Or out into space. Or a hundred kilometres beneath the earth's crust. We simply don't know.'

'Okay then, we don't assume anything. What about Spruance's group? How badly are they hurting?'

Mike Judge flicked a glance at Dan Black and sucked in through his teeth with a hiss. 'We fucked them three ways from Sunday, Admiral, if you'll pardon my French. Two cruisers are gone, the *Yorktown* and the *Hornet*. That's more than seven, eight *thousand* dead, right there. They got maybe another thousand dead on the destroyers, five sunk, two going down right now. We can't rightly say anything about final casualty figures yet. They don't have any implants here.'

Judge sounded morose. There was nothing Kolhammer could say in mitigation. He felt as awful as the executive officer looked and sounded. Curtis and Black were even more subdued. Although they stood near the centre of the room, nobody looked directly at them.

'Okay, Mike,' said Kolhammer. 'For now we can only take the first steps. Search and rescue. Care for the wounded. How's that going?'

Judge stared out the blast windows as he answered. 'Doc Francois over on the *Kandahar* is in charge of that, Admiral. We lost Preston when the liquid oxygen went up. Francois is the senior surgeon now. She's organised triage for both forces. We're taking the worst on our ships because we have the best facilities. The locals are doing what they can. They've got some of our medics on their ships now.'

'And how's that working out?'

'No problems yet, but it's early. There is one other issue, of course.'

Kolhammer rubbed his neck. 'Midway,' he sighed.

Black and Curtis stiffened.

'You told us you'd stand down any threat,' Black reminded him.

'Admiral Spruance *does* want to know what we're going to do about it,' said Judge, 'since we pretty much crippled his ability to act.'

'Do we know where the Japanese should be at this point?' asked Kolhammer.

Judge leaned over a touch screen and danced his fingers across the surface. The lines and creases in his weathered face seemed unnaturally deep in the dim red light of the flag bridge. Ensign Curtis shook his head in wonder as dozens of icons moved around the screen under the officer's fingers, sometimes opening out into windows full of scrolling text and numbers, sometimes expanding into pictures of men and women in various uniforms.

'I scanned the crew records,' said Judge as he pulled the files. 'I took a couple of history majors off other duties, set them to work on the archives tracking the progress of the Japanese according to the books.'

A screen next to Judge filled up with a map of the Pacific. The relative positions of the Japanese and American fleets were recorded from 1 June to 7 June, 1942.

'The Nemesis arrays already have a good lock on a large body closing from the west, exactly where Admiral Nagumo should be at this time.'

'When's the first strike due?'

Judge checked the flexipad. 'At 0800 on 3 June – that's today – the Second Carrier Striking Group under Admiral Kakuta will launch a diversionary attack on Dutch Harbor in the Aleutians. At 0553 on 4 June, the radar station at Midway will pick up the first wave of attacking planes, which will be over the island from 0630 to 0643.'

Kolhammer nodded, satisfied with small mercies. 'Okay then. We have a day and a half until the main attack. Let's work up a plan for a strike on the carriers heading for Midway. If we can't get any planes off, we'll take them out with missiles.

'We'll need to discuss all this at fleet command level first. Schedule a conference for the soonest possible time, invite Spruance and whoever he needs to bring along. We can chopper them over here. But let's get the SAR finished first. And I'd best have a talk with the acting CO of the *Siranui* well before the general conference.'

'That'd be Sub-Lieutenant Miyazaki. You want to laser-link to him or talk face to face?'

'I think we'd best meet in my quarters, man to man. Show some respect.'

'I think he'd appreciate that, Admiral,' said Mike Judge. 'He's likely to find it scarce around these parts for a long time.'

Lieutenant Commander Black said nothing.

USS Kandahar, *0029 hours, 3 June 1942*

Captain Margie Francois paused for the first time in two and a half hours. It was just a moment's break.

As chief combat surgeon of the 82nd MEU, her first priority had been to get her own medical staff back online, then the *Kandahar's* defensive sysops, then the ship's most critical naval personnel and the 3 Battalion staff officers.

Then the casualties began to arrive, some caused by the Transition, like the kitchen hand suffering third-degree burns from collapsing onto a gas oven, and a marine who'd gone head first down a hatch between decks, breaking his spine. Shortly after that, the first shells had hit the ship, and her real work had begun.

There was no lull between that and the arrival of the first survivors from Spruance's task force. The newcomers had filled all one hundred beds in the *Kandahar*'s hospital and still they came: burns, amputations, compound fractures, split skulls, crushed limbs, ripped torsos. Hundreds of men had swallowed oil, some had lungs half full of contaminated seawater. Many screamed, some moaned quietly. The hospital smelled of charred flesh, blood, shit and fear. When an orderly handed Francois a tube of chilled fruit pulp, the contrast between the sweet, fresh taste and the charnel-house atmosphere of the ward came as a smack in the face.

A brief sense of dislocation took hold, and she stopped for a few seconds to observe the scene.

So, she thought without allowing herself any real feeling, *this is what it looks like for the other guy*.

'Captain? Captain Francois, ma'am?'

The voice dragged her back into the world.

'We're starting to run low on burn gel, ma'am. It's not critical yet. But it will be soon enough, if we keep running through it at this rate.'

Francois looked at the intern. 'Thanks for the snack. It helped.'

'Ma'am?'

'Yeah, I know, the goddamned burn gel. Can't be helped, Ensign. It's there to be used. You know the principles of triage. That's all you need to worry about for now.'

'Yes, ma'am.'

The young man saluted and hurried away.

'Captain?'

Francois turned towards the deep bass of Colonel Jones's voice, acknowledging him with a tired salute.

'You need anything down here, Doc?' he asked.

'Some answers would be good,' she said a touch bitterly. 'Failing that, more burn gel and vat tissue. We're going to need plenty of both.'

Jones rubbed his shaved head in frustration. 'How many of *our* people are down?' he asked, meaning the battalion.

'Sixty-two dead,' she replied without hesitating. 'Another fifty-three wounded. Mostly from blast effects, but a few were just unlucky. Happened to be in the wrong place at the wrong time.'

'At the Transition point?'

'If that's what we're calling it, yeah.'

A man lying in a bed nearby suddenly howled like a wounded animal. Francois hurried over, reaching him before anyone else. His uniform had been stripped so there was no way of telling to whom he belonged by just looking at him. A quick scan with a sensor wand told her he had no inserts, which meant he almost certainly came off an old ship. A transmitter node on the bed beamed his data to her flexipad: Leading Seaman Murray Belknap, one broken hip, seven broken ribs, a ruptured spleen and second-degree burns to fifteen per cent of his body. A trauma team arrived as she finished reading his slate.

'We got him, Captain,' one of them shouted.

Jones took Francois by the arm and steered her away.

'Let them work, Margie. You've trained them well. Give them some room. You can't lay hands on everybody who comes in. You got the bigger picture to keep you up nights.'

'I know,' she admitted. 'You just get into the groove, that's all.'

'I understand. How many of the locals do you have with you here?'

'Nearly three hundred here, just a shade under two thousand spread out through the rest of the fleet. We're at capacity now. We've started taking over the sleeping quarters.'

Jones nodded. 'And how many are we going to lose? For certain?'

Francois took a few seconds to think it over. She consulted her flexipad for a minute after that before answering. 'My best guess at this stage, we'll lose about eight per cent.'

'Okay, better than I'd expected.'

Jones didn't insult her with any platitudes about trying harder. He knew her well. She'd give it everything she had.

Francois just hoped it would be enough.

14

HIJMS Yamato, *0146 hours, 3 June 1942*

Admiral Isoroku Yamamoto was incandescent with rage. A lesser man might have howled like a dog and hammered at the bare bulkhead until his fists were mashed into a bloody pulp. He had not wanted this war! He had not wanted the glorious baubles and empty honours that had poured on his head after the victory at Pearl Harbor. He had not wanted them, because he suspected they would lead to utter ruin.

The United States of America was a colossus that he had little chance of besting in a fair fight. He knew in his heart that the only hope was one decisive engagement, the *Kessen Kantai*, which would leave the Americans so stunned, naked and bleeding that they would have to sue for peace.

But it was a tremendous gamble. The life of a nation bet on the turn of a card. And now this oaf, this *fool*, this butcher's bastard son Kakuta had lost his mind and upturned the entire card table.

He examined the lengthy radio transcript. *The radio!* He cursed volubly and at great length. Eavesdroppers be damned! How many times had he stressed the importance of maintaining absolute radio silence lest the Americans unravel his plot before it ensnared them? His thick, calloused hands, the left one missing two fingers, were shaking with fury as he reread the message.

Kakuta had turned the entire Second Carrier Striking Force around and was heading back towards the home islands. Admiral Hosogaya's Northern Force was following, in great confusion. Kakuta was demanding – *demanding!* – that Yamamoto order his own main force and Nagumo's First Carrier Striking Force to turn tail and make for Hashirajima with all dispatch. And he was flying – *flying!* – back to the battleship *Yamato* to personally brief the commander of the Combined Fleet on some supposedly momentous development that had necessitated all of this.

The only momentous development Yamamoto could see in Admiral Kakuta's future was his inescapable beheading when they fished him from the sea beside the *Yamato*. Or had he forgotten, in his derangement, that the *Yamato* was a battleship, *not* an aircraft carrier?

Yamamoto crushed the paper in his good right hand. He had read it so many times now that he could probably recite its litany of delirium from memory. Kakuta said the Americans had broken the JN 25 code and were waiting in ambush for Nagumo's flattops. An unsettling development, if true, but then the whole reason for their being out here in this hellish weather was to engage the Americans in decisive battle and sweep away the last remnants of their fleet.

So what did it matter if they were waiting? He had assembled the greatest naval force since Jutland. Its sheer mass would crush them, even without the benefit of surprise.

Perhaps the answer lay there. The US Navy would surely know they were coming, now that Kakuta had blurted his plans to the heavens. But he had gained the *Ryujo* and the *Junyo* to augment Nagumo's force. How could they hope to resist six fleet carriers and dozens of heavy battleships and cruisers with the few tin toys they had left? Perhaps another gamble might bring even greater rewards, against greater odds.

He drew a deep, cleansing breath, and focused on finding his centre, his *hara*. He would need to move quickly. Plans would have to be remade on the run. There was so little time that he might not even be able to spare a minute to watch Kakuta's execution.

In flight, 0212 hours, 3 June 1942

The Eurocopter Panther 2E hammered through the fog about two hundred metres above the surface of the ocean. Kakuta and Hidaka were strapped into seats in the bay, where they could look forward to the cockpit. The old admiral found himself continually craning around to gawk at the multiplicity of illuminated displays, wondering how the pilots managed to keep control of them all. The Indonesian, Moertopo, who seemed more and more subdued as the distance from his own ship grew, repeatedly assured him that they would not lose themselves in the vastness of the northern Pacific. He conceded that the 'GPS' was gone, whatever that meant, but said that he had faith in something called 'SINS' to bring them within a short distance of Yamamoto's main force.

Moertopo also assured them that the helicopter's 'radar' would have no trouble finding a body of iron as substantial as that, even though it lay many kilometres away. Furthermore, he said, they were far enough from their erstwhile colleagues at Midway that any 'radar leakage' would not be detected.

Kakuta's heart lurched every time he imagined having to explain all this to Admiral Yamamoto. He felt like a bug that had nipped the toe of a giant. There was a chance that the admiral would be so incensed by his actions that he would shoot them out of the sky. For his part, he had assured the Indonesians that he could forestall such precipitate action, but privately he had his doubts.

Hidaka seemed more sanguine. He had the heart of a true samurai, and Kakuta hoped that whatever came of this, no dishonour would attach itself to his favoured protégé.

Lieutenant Moertopo pressed a hand to one ear.

'The pilot reports that we are one hundred and fifty kilometres out, Admiral. We should be able to establish a secure tightbeam contact at this distance.'

The sound of Hidaka's translation came through beautifully clear on the lightweight headset they had provided him. Another small piece of evidence in favour of this whole crazed scenario.

'And so I am just to speak into this little twig?' he asked, tapping the slim metal rod that reached around to the corner of his mouth.

Moertopo held up his hand until the copilot gave him the sign that they had broken into the *Yamato*'s frequency. He pointed a finger at Kakuta and nodded.

'*Yamato. Yamato*. This is Admiral Kakuta. Commander of the Second Carrier Striking Fleet. This is Admiral Kakuta of the Second Carrier Striking Fleet. We are flying inbound on a heading of two-four-three relative to your position. Please acknowledge this transmission.'

'This is Chief Signals Officer Wada,' came the startlingly clear reply. 'Stand by.'

The men in the helicopter waited as a full minute dragged by. They were all tense, even though they still sat well outside the range of the fleet's antiair defences. Moertopo had explained that they might not have sufficient fuel for a round trip to the *Yamato* and back. The Panther bucked violently on turbulence, adding to the stress. Admiral Kakuta was about to repeat his message when a cold, angry voice filled his headset. It was like having the commander-in-chief growl into his face from just a few inches away.

'So, Kakuta,' rumbled Isoroku Yamamoto, 'you have broken radio silence again.'

'Yes, Admiral . . .'

At this point, Kakuta's nerve failed him. He groped

for the right words to carry them through the next few minutes, and nothing came. The roar of the Panther's engine filled the warm, close space. He was acutely aware of the vibration of the airframe and the eyes of the men around him, boring in, urging him to speak. But what could he say that would not mark him as a lunatic? The right *form* of words. That was all he needed. Their refusal to take shape in his mind was absolutely maddening. He might never . . .

'Admiral Yamamoto.'

It was Hidaka.

'Who is this?' Yamamoto demanded.

'Lieutenant Commander Jisaku Hidaka, of the *Ryujo*, sir. I am accompanying Admiral Kakuta on this mission. It was on my initiative that we undertook it.'

'*No!*' mouthed Kakuta as his subordinate bared his neck to the blade. The dishonour of allowing one's inferior to accept blame for such a perilous scheme – he might never live it down.

'So,' snarled Yamamoto, 'another mutineer. Or are you just a maniac, Commander?'

'You will think us both maniacs, initially, Admiral. But we have come as saviours. If we speak falsely, let the spirits of our ancestors bear the shame.'

'Oh, they shall bear a heavy burden of shame, believe me, Hidaka.'

'I believe not, Admiral. You were steaming towards defeat and catastrophe. We can avert that, if you will just hear us out.'

'I am listening. No doubt the Americans are listening, as well. The whole world is waiting on you, Lieutenant Commander Hidaka.'

'*Here we are now, entertain us*,' Moertopo sung under his breath.

Hidaka shot him a withering look. The reference meant nothing to him, but the potentially disastrous effect of that one line of English did not bear thinking about.

'Admiral Yamamoto, begging your pardon, but we shall not even attempt to explain ourselves over the radio. It would be futile. We shall be over your position in approximately twenty minutes. We shall manoeuvre to land in front of your forward eighteen-inch turrets. I am informed it will be a very dangerous approach. The pilot requests that you adjust your heading in order to place the wind across your decks.'

'It will be more than dangerous,' exclaimed Yamamoto. 'It will be fatal. You cannot land a seaplane on a battleship. I am warning you. I will have you shot down if you approach the *Yamato*.'

'We are not in a seaplane, and we can land without damaging the *Yamato*. Please do not shoot us down. You will soon understand. Hidaka out.'

He drew his fingers across his throat, motioning Moertopo to sever the link.

The commander-in-chief was cut off mid-rant.

Admiral Kakuta stared at him as though he had just lost his mind. Nobody spoke to Admiral Isoroku Yamamoto like that.

Hidaka gestured helplessly.

'From what I have heard, the admiral is a gambler. So am I.'

Yamamoto's mouth opened and closed. Opened and closed. But no sound emerged.

Perhaps they could land on the *Yamato* after all. That *thing*, that giant insect in which Kakuta had so quickly navigated nearly two thousand kilometres of fogshrouded sea – and at night! – seemed to hang in the air as if suspended from a thread. No. No it didn't *seem* to hang in the air. It simply *did* hang there.

The seas were running at two metres. The bulk of the *Yamato* would pass through a single wave as though it were composed of nothing more than smoke. But over the long haul from Hashirajima the ceaseless roll of the northern Pacific had imparted a long and rhythmic plunging motion to the sixty-five-thousand-ton battleship. Yamamoto, who had quietly ordered the ship brought around when he had finally laid eyes on Kakuta's mysterious 'seaplane', stood transfixed in the freezing night air as the pilot hovered over the forecastle. The aircraft dipped when the bow dipped. Rose when it rose. It was almost as though the pilot were dancing with the hulking behemoth beneath his wheels.

Admiral Yamamoto, Captain Takayanagi, all of the officers who had assembled on the high walkway, were mesmerised, watching to see if the strange wingless plane would falter, to be slapped from the sky by a rogue surge of the deck. How the pilot could see through the darkness and the typhoon of spray thrown up by that huge propeller was anyone's guess.

But clearly he could. With one last skilful dip, the craft settled onto the deck and the roar died away as the pilot cut power to the engine. As if by sorcery, giant propeller blades materialised above the cockpit, revealing how this miraculous device stayed aloft. A dozen sailors ran forward with ropes to lash the thing to the deck.

KRI Sutanto, *0237 hours, 3 June 1942*

'Ensign Tomonagi, come quickly, the captain is stirring.'

Tomonagi followed the crewman back into the wardroom of the *Sutanto*, where the man whom Moertopo had identified as the ship's commanding officer was indeed throwing off his coma-like unconsciousness.

Tomonagi's stomach heaved, and a thin, greasy film of sweat quickly lacquered his forehead. But Commander Hidaka's instruction had been quite explicit.

'You two, quickly!' he barked at a couple of his own sailors. 'Grab him and follow me.'

A handful of Indonesian ratings who tried to help their skipper were roughly forced back by armed guards.

'We shall take care of him,' Tomonagi declared. 'Go back to your duties.'

None of them understood a word he said, but the tone was unmistakable. Reluctantly they stood by as their captain was carried from the room, his body convulsing in the arms of the sailors who bore him away.

Tomonagi led the small party out into the fresh air and over to the plasteel safety rail. He looked around for witnesses, but apart from another Japanese sentry, there were none. He nodded at the sailors, who heaved Captain Djuanda over the side. They heard the impact very clearly as his body hit the icy waters. There was no scream.

HIJMS Yamato, *0328 hours, 3 June 1942*

Lieutenant Ali Moertopo didn't know enough about Admiral Yamamoto to be awed. His flagship, the battleship *Yamato* – now *that* was awesome. But the man himself just looked like another pissed-off sushi chef. He'd come to recognise the type. It appeared as if they were all over this ocean.

Moertopo stood beside and slightly behind Commander Hidaka in the planning room of the *Yamato*, a huge space to the eyes of somebody who had been confined to a comparatively tiny ship like the *Sutanto*. Before them lay a large table with a map of the Pacific covered in little wooden boats and flags, symbolising the disposition of hundreds of Japanese naval vessels surging across the empty wastes of the northern Pacific. Now, apparently, they were in disarray, and the men responsible were facing a solid wall of dark uniforms and darker faces.

Lights glinted off Yamamoto's shaven head as he listened to Kakuta and Hidaka attempt to explain themselves. The grand admiral's face remained utterly impassive, but the men around him glowered with increasing degrees of incredulity and umbrage. When Kakuta finally fell silent, a terrible ticking stillness blanketed the gathering.

'And you, Lieutenant Moertopo. What say you of all this?' asked Yamamoto at last in thickly accented but otherwise flawless English.

Moertopo, who had quickly downloaded everything he could find on Yamamoto and Midway from the *Sutanto*'s Fleetnet storage banks, wasn't surprised by the man's grasp of the language. He now knew that Yamamoto had studied at Harvard, and later worked in Washington. But he was nevertheless shocked at being spoken to directly by the supreme commander of the Combined Fleet. He had been rather looking forward to keeping his opinions to himself. Hidaka prodded him forwards.

'What do you want me to say . . . sir?'

'Do you really expect me to believe that you are from the future?'

'No.'

'Then why waste my time with this fiddle-faddle?'

Moertopo thought he understood the slant of the

question, even though it had been phrased so oddly.

'I do not expect you to believe it. But it is true. I was born in 1997.'

'I see.'

The room again fell into uncomfortable silence.

'And how did you come to be here?' asked Yamamoto after a short interlude.

'I do not know,' Moertopo answered truthfully. 'But here I am.'

'And here your friends are, too – the Americans,' Yamamoto stated flatly.

'You believe that?'

'Our radio intelligence has detected a very large volume of traffic from the Midway area. A battle has been fought there. But not by us.'

Moertopo quickly scanned the faces behind Yamamoto, hoping for some sign of how to play this. All he found, however, was a wall of anger and suspicion.

'We picked up those signals ourselves,' said Moertopo. 'It appears that the Americans have hurt each other very badly.'

Again, his answers brought no measurable response from Yamamoto or his staff. Moertopo had been hoping that they might tip a couple of flexipads onto the table, maybe a history book or two and a couple of pirate video sticks – he'd even managed to locate a copy of *Tora Tora Tora* – after which the locals would offer him a nice warm sake and a couple of horny geisha girls to welcome their new best friend to the original axis of evil.

Yamamoto purred in a deceptively friendly tone, 'Tell me, Lieutenant, what was supposed to happen, before the interference of you and your friends?'

'The . . . they're not my friends,' Moertopo stammered. 'I copied files to these flexipads if you want to read them, or watch them,' he hurried on. 'I have documentaries. There are some good ones there. *The World at War. Victory at Sea.* I have the Tom Cruise miniseries. I could –'

'I am not interested in your toys, Moertopo,' growled the admiral. 'I want you to tell me what was supposed to happen next.'

Hidaka leaned over to whisper something, but Yamamoto cut him dead with a glare.

Moertopo had studied the archival material on the flight down. He was well enough acquainted with a scratch history of the Pacific War to deliver the briefing that had been asked of him. But he was certain these arrogant dogs would tear him apart as soon as he spoke. The way he understood it, they wouldn't – *didn't* – believe they could lose until well after their butts had been well and truly kicked. It was hopeless. He was trapped. Until a thought occurred to him.

'You were right,' he said.

Yamamoto's wide, Buddha-like face regarded him dispassionately. 'What do you mean?'

Moertopo picked up the flexipad that sat on the table in front of him and quickly brought up a bookmarked page. 'When you spoke to Prime Minister

Konoye in 1940,' he explained, 'just after he had signed the treaty with Hitler and Mussolini, you said, *If I am told to fight, regardless of consequences, I shall run wild for the first six months or a year. But for the second and third years I have utterly no confidence.* You always thought that war against the United States was national suicide.

'And you were right. It was. Three years from now the Americans will drop a bomb on Hiroshima, where you attended the naval institute, if I remember correctly.'

Yamamoto nodded.

'This was, or will be, a special bomb. There was only one dropped that day, but it exploded with a force of more than fifteen thousand *tonnes* of TNT. Not pounds, Admiral. Tonnes. It killed seventy thousand people instantly and destroyed most of the city. It was called an atomic bomb. They dropped another on Nagasaki two days later, and Japan surrendered unconditionally. You didn't live to see it, though. The Americans shot down a plane carrying you on . . .'

He checked the flexipad again, gaining confidence from the stunned silence.

'On Sunday, 18 April 1943. Over Bougainville.'

'Lies!' someone cried. But Yamamoto raised his hand and stilled the protest.

There. The cat was out of the bag now. Moertopo wasn't sure what the long-term results would be, but at least it appeared he'd saved himself from being weighted down and tipped over the side of the ship. He had read more than once of how captured

American flyers had suffered just that fate at the hands of these primitive oafs. And they considered themselves the pinnacle of martial civilisation!

'It appears,' Yamamoto said, 'that a heavy blow has landed on the Americans tonight. What is to stop us continuing east to finish the job?'

Moertopo was physically and emotionally worn out. He couldn't contain a small, wan, shadow of a smile. 'The power of the bomb that destroyed Hiroshima,' he answered, 'is *nothing* compared to the weapons they have brought with them. With your permission I *shall* speak my mind now, Admiral Yamamoto. You were right to oppose this war. You would have lost it. You will still lose it, no matter how badly damaged the Americans are by the events of tonight. If just one warship from Kolhammer's force remains afloat, it would be enough to sink every carrier you have. You can avoid the disaster that would have befallen you. You have that opportunity. You should grasp it with both hands.'

This time Yamamoto said nothing. His eyes glinted like two small opals.

Moertopo drew deeply but furtively on the clove cigarette. The embers at the tip burned brightly for a few seconds, casting a dim red glow on the base of the empty bunk above him. He was unsure whether the Imperial Japanese Navy enforced a nonsmoking policy, but he was reasonably certain they had not yet invented smoke detectors, so fuck them.

He and Flight Lieutenant Hardoyo were being accommodated – or detained, to be perfectly accurate – in separate cabins far apart from each other. They hadn't been badly treated or abused. Indeed, the reception for Kakuta and Hidaka had been much sharper. For the moment, the Indonesians were regarded as curiosities and potential assets. When that changed, he knew, he'd better have an exit strategy locked down. Or something of great value to trade for his skin.

The sweet notes of the cigarette induced a lonesome melancholy in the *Sutanto*'s executive officer. An intensely childlike desire to run away from home overwhelmed his confusion and anxiety, while compounding deeper feelings of desolation and irrecoverable loss. He was surprised to find his throat tightening as hot tears welled in his eyes. Moertopo quickly jammed a knuckle into his mouth, lest the guard outside his room hear him. The grief built in intensity until there was nothing to be done but to give himself over to it, curling into a tight fetal ball on his bunk and fighting to draw breath between the great racking sobs that overpowered him. It was as though he were being pummelled underneath a tsunami of sorrow.

In time, a few minutes at most, the seizure passed, leaving in its wake a bleak despair. Moertopo lit another cigarette and raised it between shaking fingers. He drew in a sharp, shuddering breath. As stupidly soothing as this clove cigarette was,

Moertopo turned it in his fingers, examining it with a frown. It was emblematic of all his problems. The company that produced this before the war had been a monopoly. In the year before he was born, it had been handed over to an idiot son of the president, who had added the profits from that corrupt transaction to his already formidable business holdings. Both the son and the old man were gone within three years, swept away by the blast wave of the 1990s' financial meltdown. The cigarette company reverted to its original and natural owners, the armed forces, which generated seventy per cent of its budget from commercial enterprises, most often monopolies.

Little wonder, then, that as Indonesia had begun to disintegrate under the onslaught of radical Islamists, the generals and admirals had reacted less like professional military men than as the ham-fisted, profiteering mafia they actually were. Moertopo cursed the fools and robbers who had delivered his country into slavery beneath the heel of the Caliphate. But mostly he cursed them for so mismanaging their affairs that he should end up here, in the belly of an iron behemoth, decades before he was born, when he could have been safely tucked up beneath the wings of the Americans.

If only they had trusted him.

But then again, he admitted, why should they?

The *Sutanto* was little better than a pirate ship. And in a dismal insight, Lieutenant Ali Moertopo realised his only hope lay in embracing that.

15

USS Astoria/Leyte Gulf, *0331 hours, 3 June 1942*

Slim Jim Davidson hadn't ever seen anything like it. Not even at the World's Fair in New York, before the war. The future was here, and it was a fucking treasure trove. If it weren't for Chief Mohr riding his ass like a chariot driver he'd have stowed away enough loot to set himself up for life.

He'd already grabbed and stashed away two of them electrical books, three electrical watches, one pair of goggles – also electrical – and a pistol that looked like it'd stop a bull elephant. The hand cannon he understood. The watches, sort of. They had to be like something out of Dick Tracy, radio watches or something. But the other stuff, that was a mystery. He just took them because he recognised a first-class score. There was just something about those gadgets that cried out, *Take me, Slim Jim. I'm yours.* At some point he was going to have to drop the loot off and start again. Or else Mohr was certain to get wise.

But it was worth the risk. That's why he'd allowed himself to be 'volunteered' by the chief for the gruesome business of cleaning up the body parts that lay throughout the dense labyrinth created by the intersection of the two cruisers. The confusion and darkness created endless opportunities for profit. One of the watches, for instance, had just 'slipped off' a severed arm and into Slim Jim's pocket as he cleared out a niche where the *Astoria*'s electrical storeroom met a small crew cabin on the *Leyte Gulf*.

It was hotter than hell down here, maybe even hotter than Alabama in high summer, which Slim Jim knew from personal experience was worse than being trapped in the Devil's own butt hole. In July of '36 he'd done three months on a road gang just outside Montgomery. At the time he'd sworn never to get himself into that sort of trouble again, but here he was, picking up dead meat, Chief Mohr kicking his ass, Moose Molloy stepping on his toes, the Imperial Japanese Navy hell-bent on killing him, and now this crazy bullshit thrown in for good measure. He'd be a damn fool if he didn't take what little chance he had to profit from these unpleasant circumstances.

And Slim Jim's mama didn't raise no fools. Sharpies, grifters and one crooked jockey, for sure. But no fools.

Slim Jim's normal approach to a job like this would have been to affect an impression of grim industry while goofing off at every turn. But now he hurried to fill his burlap bag with its obscene cargo and the occasional item of plunder, trying to look like the world's busiest little beaver. Moose Molloy, who was working beside him, droned on without let-up, his tiny pea brain grappling with the night's events. Slim Jim upheld his side of the conversation only when necessary. His mind worked furiously behind a mask of barely contained disgust.

Oxy cutters blazed around them, burning narrow passageways through the tangled mass of iron. The air stunk of ozone and corruption. Slim Jim's back hurt from the dead weight collected in his sack. His throat was parched dry, his tongue furry, and he was covered in cuts and bruises from banging against twisted metal in the dark. It was, he thought, worse than that fucking road gang. At least *they'd* had fresh air. But he stuck at the joyless task long after he'd normally have found an excuse to escape.

'I can't wait to see the mess on this ship,' grunted Moose as he pulled at something wedged between two imperfectly fused bulkheads. 'They got so many mess men on this ship they must have a mess as big as the *Enterprise*. You remember when we snuck on board for their Christmas party that time, Slim Jim? How big that mess was, with all of them niggers? I never seen so many of them before.'

'They're not mess men,' Davidson answered as he pocketed what looked like an electric fountain pen. 'Look at their uniforms, you lunkhead. They're officers, some of them. The dames too. And the captain's a broad *and* a Negro.'

'Oh, a *Neeegro*, excuse me, Professor. Anyhow, I *know* that,' Moose protested. 'I was there, remember?'

'Goddamn! This thing weighs a ton,' cursed

Davidson as he hauled the bag through another tight crawlspace. The effort left him breathless and shaking. He leaned against a bulkhead by Molloy to rest.

'Hey, Moose,' he said quietly when he'd caught his breath. 'Listen. I wouldn't go calling 'em niggers to their face if I was you. Or nips or broads or nothing.'

'But that's what they are!' Molloy protested.

'Maybe,' Davidson conceded, 'but they're officers, too, a lot of them. And officers stick together. I been around. I seen a few things. Just 'cause the black man's been set lower than us doesn't mean he likes it. These guys coming here? It's trouble for everyone. For the Japs if they get a taste of those guns and rockets like we did. But for us, too, I reckon. And when trouble blows in, a smart guy keeps his head down, waits for it to pass. When it's gone you can see how things lie.'

Around them the noise of rescue and salvage created a din that covered their conversation. Davidson didn't exactly think of Moose as a friend. He didn't exactly have any friends. But Moose stood six-foot four in his bare feet and could probably kill an ox with his right hook. He made a good ally for someone like Slim Jim, who'd always relied on ratbastard cunning to make up for his less-than-intimidating physique. If he was going to work an angle on this, he didn't need to have the big ape messing things up for him by mouthing off to the new guys.

'You think about it, Moose,' he said in a conspiratorial tone. 'You ever meet an officer didn't think the sun shone out of his ass? It's because in their world it does. And there's nothing you or I can do about it. I don't know how that bitch got to be captain of a ship like this, but you can bet she thinks she deserves it.'

'But that just can't be,' Moose argued.

'It doesn't matter!' Davidson said, cutting him off sharply. 'What should be and what *is* almost never turn out the same. I *should* be lying back in a big feather bed at the Waldorf getting my dick sucked by Rita Hayworth. But I'm stuck here covered in blood and shit wondering what the hell happened to the laws of fucking nature this morning. You take my advice, Moose, one of these bastards says boo to you, you just tell 'em *Yes sir no sir three bags full sir.* Even if it's some broad looks like she should be cleaning the toilets in a fucking speakeasy.'

Moose was silenced by the vehemence of his best friend's delivery. And everything Slim Jim Davidson had just said ran one hundred per cent contrary to what his daddy, Moose Sr, had raised him to believe. But of course, Moose Sr wasn't here, up to his ass in dead meat and craziness. And Slim Jim had looked after him ever since they'd fetched up in the same quarters. He reluctantly agreed to heed the advice.

'That's all right then.' Davidson nodded. 'Now I gotta take this shit topside and get rid of it. I'll see you soon.'

And with that he hauled the big, oozing bag away,

all the time thinking of where he might stash the treasure he had hidden inside it.

Captain Anderson ran her fingers along the join between the two ships. The nanotube sheath armour of the *Leyte Gulf* met the rivets and iron plating of the *Astoria* perfectly. She supposed they had bonded at the molecular level.

'How long, Chief?' she asked.

'They've got the pumps running full bore in the *Astoria*, Captain. We've sent over what help we can, but unless we get her to a dry dock in the next eight to twelve hours, we're both going down.'

'There's not a dry dock in the world could fit them in,' Anderson pointed out.

'That's true,' conceded Chief Conroy.

'And we'd tear both ships apart making any kind of speed to get there.'

'Reckon so.'

They had gathered in a small group on C deck of the *Leyte Gulf*, where the port-side corridor was entirely blocked by a section of the *Astoria*. The deck tilted forward perceptibly beneath their feet, as the stealth cruiser's bow was dragged down by the growing weight of the other ship. The structural integrity of the *Astoria* was failing. A large fissure had opened up just aft of the nexus with Anderson's ship and the sea was flooding in, gradually overwhelming the pumps and the efforts of a three-hundred-man bucket brigade.

There were other problems.

'The children aren't playing well together,' said Conroy.

'I've got Mohr and my other chiefs working on it,' said Lieutenant Commander Peter Evans, 'but . . .'

He trailed off.

Anderson gathered that Evans was an educated, well-travelled man, but even he was obviously having trouble coming to terms with Anderson's ship and crew. The *Leyte Gulf* 's captain stood with her arms folded in the flickering, failing light of the corridor.

'Commander, I'm aware that we've all had a lot of trauma to deal with this afternoon, or morning, or whatever. You can't throw people from different worlds together under such extreme pressure and expect them to work smoothly. Not when they've just been trying to kill each other. But we're going to have to work together, because our fates are fused.'

She punched the armour plating of the *Astoria* for emphasis.

'I can't have Eddie Mohr running around punching every guy who looks sideways at one of your ladies,' said Evans. Frustration was beginning to get the better of him.

'Commander, they're not ladies,' Conroy said before Anderson could reply. 'They're officers and sailors of the US Navy. They can take almost anything you'll throw at them. But they *don't* have to take sexual harassment.'

'But nobody's been having sex with them!'

protested Evans, who couldn't believe they were even discussing the matter.

'Jesus, you really don't get it, do you?'

'No, apparently I don't . . .'

'Look, this isn't the time or place,' Anderson interrupted. 'Either we save these ships together, or they go down together. Chief, get hold of Borghino and Reilly . . .'

'I'm sorry, Reilly's dead, ma'am.'

Anderson had known that, but the memory had slipped away in the turmoil. She cursed herself for the slip.

'Damn, sorry. Right, get Hillary Beaton instead. Get around to the crew and chill them out. I need engineering to give me an answer. Are we going to save the ships or not? I suspect not, so we need to work up a plan to evacuate the crews and salvage everything we can. If it turns out we're stuck here, even the smallest things could make a difference. We need to strip this ship down to bare bones, take off every piece of technology we possibly can. We'll need to coordinate that with Kolhammer.

'Commander Evans, no offence, but I suggest that there's nothing worth saving on your ship. Nothing that can't be replaced, at least. You should have all your men either pumping out the flooded decks, or throwing as much weight as possible overboard to lighten the load. If you have any spare bodies, we can use them over here for our salvage work.'

Evans had deep, grey bruises under his bloodshot

eyes. Every line in his face looked as though it had been gouged there. Anderson saw she'd offended him when those lines stretched and his eyes flared with anger. She instantly regretted her blunt Sagittarian ways. Evans was only just holding it together, and she needed him to stay the course.

Evans listened to the Negro woman's speech with mounting distress. He couldn't believe she was just writing off the *Astoria* like that. After all, there were some decent holes punched in her own ship, courtesy of the old girl's eight-inch batteries. He could feel his anger building, but it never came to a head. He suspected the drugs they'd given him for his injuries might have been damping down his temper as well. He had a strange feeling, like a fine head of fury was trying to build somewhere inside him, but every time it threatened to break, the anger slipped away.

He rubbed at his eyes with his good hand. They felt gritty and hot. The bruises on his face ached painfully, in spite of the drugs.

'I'll have to confer with Admiral Spruance,' he said flatly. 'He's already lost a few cruisers tonight. He won't be happy about scratching another one.'

Anderson opened her mouth, ready to argue, but she held her peace.

'I'm sorry, Commander. Please excuse my poor manners. I don't mean to make it sound as if your ship or her crew are unimportant. I'm just playing the numbers. The equipment on the *Leyte Gulf* will be of tremendous value to your war effort. I don't want to give up on her either. She's my baby. But she's been run through the heart. We can't make any headway without tearing each other apart, and we're already sinking. I'll have to confer with Admiral Kolhammer and the engineers, but I think they'll agree. The *Leyte Gulf* is finished, and so is the *Astoria*.'

Chief Mohr had been suspicious when Davidson put himself forward for the clean-up crew in the confused snarl at the intersection of the two ships. Davidson was one of the laziest, shiftiest sons of bitches you'd never hope to meet. Mohr knew he'd only joined the navy to avoid a prison term for passing bad cheques in Baltimore. The judge had given him the option of military service or the big house, and Davidson, true to form, had joined the navy because he heard it had the best chow and the least exercise. He was also scared of flying.

It was almost reassuring, in a way, when Mohr crawled back into the *Astoria* to discover that Slim Jim was inexplicably absent. Moose Molloy had done his best to cover for the lazy bum, but that didn't necessarily work in Davidson's favour. Mohr waved away Molloy's excuses and determined to deal with the slacker later. For now he had other problems. He'd just bruised his knuckles on the thick skull of some moron who'd grabbed a piece of ass over on the other ship. Personally, Mohr couldn't see the problem. If you put a bunch of broads on a ship, they're gonna get their fucking asses grabbed. That was only natural.

But that Captain Anderson, who didn't look like anyone had grabbed her ass in a long while, had gone bitching to Commander Evans, who was over on the *Leyte Gulf* having his injuries tended to by their super-medics. Evans had gone to Mohr, and Mohr had gone to the source of the trouble, some dumb-ass gunner by the name of Finch.

'You grab her ass, Finch?' he had demanded to know.

Finch had sort of smirked and shrugged, so Mohr had slugged him one, right between the eyes. At that point Captain Anderson had gasped. But what the hell had she expected him to do? A guy grabs some ass ain't his to grab, you put Chief Eddie Mohr on the job, the guy gets knuckled good and proper. Case closed. You woulda thought from her reaction that the knuckling was nearly as bad as the original ass grabbing.

'The fucking saints preserve me,' Mohr grumbled as he hauled himself back into clear space aboard the *Astoria*. He was gonna get himself a corned beef sandwich and a coffee, and then he was gonna find that lazy fucking Slim Jim asshole and maybe he was gonna knuckle him some too.

Lieutenant Commander Helen Wassman taped off the IV line and stood up to stretch her back. She'd been crouched over for nearly four hours, attending casualties from both ships. Her back ached and the muscles in her legs burned with fatigue. It had been nearly thirty hours since she'd rolled out of her bunk, and she wondered whether the time might be coming when she'd have to dial up a little stim flush from her implants.

'Doctor! Doctor, over here!'

The *Leyte Gulf*'s medical officer had trouble focusing on the direction of the voice. The mess hall was full of wounded men and women. The worst cases had first call on the *Gulf*'s relatively small hospital, where they were stabilised before being choppered across to the *Clinton* or the *Kandahar* – a process that had been complicated by the destruction of the helicopter bays. The patients had to be carried up onto the deck through the bridge structure, a long and winding route.

'Doctor! Please!'

Wassman urgently cast around for the source of the cries. There had to be sixty people laid up in the mess. Most of them were in pretty bad shape. The walking wounded were all helping with salvage operations. The room presented a tableau from one of Goya's nightmares – bloodied bandages, burned limbs, chaos and horror. She'd treated deep-tissue lacerations, compound fractures, crushed vertebrae, shrapnel and bullet wounds and, of course, some terrible injuries caused by ceramic flechette rounds.

'*Doctor*!'

Wassman sourced the cries to a reedy-looking officer, off the *Astoria* judging by his uniform. He didn't look too badly hurt. He had a good long scrape on his forearm and a bruise on his forehead. But that was it.

This better be good, she thought.

The lieutenant fidgeted impatiently as she approached him. As she did so, his eyes roamed up and down. She was running into that a lot, and she was struggling not to react badly to it.

'Yes . . . Lieutenant?' she said, drawing up in front of him. 'Is one of your men in need of treatment?'

'No, Commander . . . uhm, Wassman. But *I've* been waiting here for a blood transfusion for nearly an hour.'

Wassman was genuinely confused. Her eyes flicked from the small bandage on his forehead to the one around his arm.

'I'm sorry, a transfusion?'

'I've lost some blood,' he explained. 'I may need a transfusion, but nobody has spoken to me about the type of blood I would need.'

She shook her head, wrestling with her irritation. Then she leaned over and somewhat peremptorily plucked his dog tags out to examine them.

'O positive,' she read out. 'There you go, Lieutenant . . . Charles, is it? Done deal.'

A strange look flickered across the lieutenant's face. Levering himself up, delicately he motioned for her to follow him a few feet away, into the corridor.

Wassman was disinclined to follow at first, but was forced to comply when Charles carried on regardless, stepping over a black woman who was leaned up against a bulkhead, nursing a hand with some nasty-looking burns.

'Lieutenant!' barked Wassman. 'I really don't have time for this.'

Charles stopped, sighed heavily and rolled his eyes before turning to face her.

'What *is* your problem?' Wassman demanded.

People were beginning to stare. Most of the men and women in the room were too lost in their private struggles to notice the scene by the door, but those who were nearby, such as the woman with the burned hand, were turning to watch.

Lieutenant Charles sighed with exasperation. He tried to lean in as if to talk discreetly.

'You misunderstand me, Doctor. I didn't mean blood type. I meant *type* of blood.'

Wassman scrunched her eyes shut, then blinked twice, rapidly.

'You're right. I'm sorry, I don't understand. Type of blood?' She gestured with her hands – which were sticky with gore – to emphasise her lack of comprehension.

He grimaced with distaste and rolled his eyes towards the black woman on the floor.

'*Type* of blood,' he murmured. 'Don't you see?'

What little concern Helen Wassman had felt for the man abruptly evaporated, and she gave him a cold stare. Before he could say anything else, she turned away.

Charles reached out to grab her elbow and was stunned when she spun around and slapped him across the face. It was a hard, stinging blow. He gasped and, without thinking, slapped her back. His blow wasn't particularly firm, but the slap galvanised everyone who saw it. Someone grabbed a handful of his shirt. It was a Chinese–American sailor.

'Get your hands off me, you damn coolie!' Charles shouted. He made a fist and drove a fierce uppercut into the man's chin, angling the blow to drive the jaw sideways.

Before the man had even hit the deck, though, another of Wassman's shipmates came at him. A white man this time, with a padded sleeve covering one arm. His other arm was fine, though. Wassman watched as it drew back and the hand formed a fist. Charles flinched as the blow came in.

The office housed the ship's training department. It was packed with VR gear, computers, screens and office equipment. They had to break it down and get it all off the ship in less than forty minutes.

Seaman Davidson wasn't really helping with his endless stream of questions.

What's that?

What does it do?

How's it work?

But the ensign from the *Leyte Gulf* who was

supervising the salvage detail in this part of the ship tried to answer as many questions as he could because Davidson was one of the few men off the *Astoria* who'd shown any inclination to be friendly. And his buddy, Molloy, he could carry a goddamn Xerox all on his own. Ensign Carver was glad to have them. They'd been no trouble at all, really, and had mixed in well with the rest of the work detail. He'd just made a mental note to talk to their Chief Mohr and tell him what a good job they'd done, when shouting and the sound of something like a brawl reached him.

'What the hell is that?' said Carver.

'Sounds like a brawl,' said Davidson.

The officer swore and told his team to keep working. Then he headed for the door.

Slim Jim resisted the urge to pocket another handful of the small, pencil-like objects they called data sticks. He was here to learn, and to establish his bona fides as a stand-up guy.

'Come on,' he said, swatting Moose on the back. 'He's gonna need some help.'

'But he told us to stay here,' a young female sailor protested. Quite a cutie, too, thought Davidson. These guys really knew how to fit out a ship.

'Yeah, well he won't be telling nobody nothing when he gets his fucking teeth kicked in. Listen up, would you? That's a real fucking fight out there, toots. Come on, Moose.'

The sound of bedlam seemed to swell. There could

be no doubt that a pitched brawl was under way. Slim Jim grabbed a small crowbar and dived out through the door, with Moose close on his heels. The three remaining sailors, all of them from the *Leyte Gulf*, hesitated for just a moment before following.

Slim Jim and Moose joined a general rush towards the mess where the fight had broken out.

'Watch my back,' said Davidson. 'But keep an eye out for that officer, too. We don't want him getting hurt.'

'Why not?' Moose asked.

'Just fucking do it, okay?'

They had to step on it. The melee had spilled into the passageway, and Carver was already at the edge of the fighting. Davidson could see that he didn't have the first idea about mixing it up in a real brawl. He was actually trying to haul a couple of guys off someone.

'Oh, for fuck's sake,' muttered Slim Jim.

The confined space roared with a tribal savagery. Men and women from both ships were mixed in together, punching, biting, kicking, swinging wildly. Slim Jim saw a guy he recognised from the *Astoria*, one of the apes from the boiler room, turn and swing at Ensign Carver. The much smaller officer was knocked right off his feet and slammed into a bulkhead. His attacker, a brute with arms like tree trunks, grinned and pushed him back into the wall.

Tortorella, that's his name, thought Slim Jim. *Stupid fucking wop.*

Stoker Tortorella grabbed hold of Carver's throat and pinned the ensign down. He cocked one giant fist back behind his ear, ready to drive it right through the man's head, just as Slim Jim reached him.

'Hey, asshole,' Davidson called out.

Tortorella smiled at Slim Jim, who raised the crowbar and whipped it down on the arm that restrained Carver. The smile disappeared as the man's bones broke with a sick, wet crack. His dark features turned grey, then white. A look of terrible confusion came into his eyes just before Slim Jim lashed him across the forehead with the heavy iron bar. Then his eyes rolled back in his head and he started to slump to the floor. Moose grabbed hold of him and heaved the deadweight down the corridor. The three sailors who'd followed Davidson and Molloy out of the office nearly tripped over the body.

'You all right, sir?' asked Slim Jim.

Carver coughed twice and struggled to draw breath, finally settling on a quick nod.

'Let's break 'em down, Moose,' Davidson yelled as he swung the crowbar at yet another of his own shipmates.

Moose commenced laying into the heaving mob with great looping swings of his fists.

'*What the hell is going on here?*'

Slim Jim flinched and turned quickly at the sound of Chief Eddie Mohr's bellow.

'I might have fucking known,' he growled as Slim Jim caught his eye.

Mohr had arrived with Captain Anderson, her own chief – Conroy or Condon, or something – and a couple of those scary-looking bastards in SS outfits. They weren't toting those weird guns of theirs, but they had something just as worrying – long black sticks with a small metal prong at the end. Slim Jim's eyes bulged a little when he realised that there were sparks jumping between the prongs.

Anderson's CPO calmly touched his baton to a tall, muscular sailor off the *Astoria*. He jerked rigidly, as though he'd been electrocuted, then dropped to the deck, unconscious. Or maybe even dead.

The two black-clad storm-troopers started zapping people at the edge of the fray. The result was the same every time. They'd go stiff as a board and then fall in a heap.

'No, don't!' Slim Jim cried in genuine fear as Mohr advanced on him. Some idiot had given him one of those things. Jim was getting ready to cave in the chief's skull with the crowbar when Ensign Carver laid a restraining hand on Mohr's shoulder.

'It's okay, Chief. He was helping me break up the fight.'

Mohr appeared to have real trouble overcoming his momentum. He *really* wanted to jab Slim Jim with that electric prod. But Captain Anderson laid another hand on his arm.

'Knock it off, you jerks!' she yelled. 'You ought to be ashamed of yourselves!'

The combination of her voice and another two or

three prods with the stun rods collapsed the brawl, which had been largely confined to an area around the doorway. Anderson pushed her way in among the rowdy combatants, roughly elbowing aside anyone who didn't give her space. She had her own sparking baton, but she didn't use it on anyone. The unruly squall tapered off into a bruised and sullen stillness.

Slim Jim backed away from Mohr, who still had murder in his eyes, and stepped on tiptoes so he could see Anderson.

'Well, I'm waiting,' said the captain.

Lieutenant Commander Helen Wassman stepped forward over a number of fallen sailors. She was bleeding from the nose and had a real shiner rising on her left eye.

'I'm afraid it was my fault, Captain,' she said.

'The hell it was!' cried a white man to her rear.

'This racist asshole bitch-slapped the doc,' somebody else called out.

Chief Mohr forced his way past Slim Jim, drawing up beside Anderson and looking down at the prostrate form of Lieutenant Charles.

'Oh, that'd be fuckin' right,' he said darkly.

16

USS Enterprise, *0409 hours, 3 June 1942*

Karen Halabi was only too aware of the outlandish presence she introduced to the small space. The men around her had so far paid due deference to the respect Spruance seemed to accord her, but she could tell from the prickling of her skin and the occasional hostile glance that she was there under his sufferance.

Spruance stared morosely out at the burning wreckage of his task force.

Dawn was coming, and the extent of the carnage was no longer hidden by full darkness. A few hours from now, they all knew, Japanese planes would be over Dutch Harbor on a diversionary strike. The American commander was fast approaching the point where he would have to contact Admiral Nimitz in Pearl and try to explain what had happened. Halabi didn't fancy changing places with him. Down below on the flight deck, a landing signals officer from the *Clinton* waved in a Seahawk with four survivors just plucked from the water.

'Michaels,' said Spruance, 'have the *Gwin* and the *Benham* stand by the *Leyte Gulf* for salvage and evacuation. They are to place their men under the direction of Captain Anderson on the *Leyte Gulf*. She'll command the operation.'

There wasn't so much as a murmur of dissent, but Halabi could feel the men bristle. Spruance remained silent, watching the lights of the helicopters as they hovered and swooped against the black curtain of the Pacific night. Karen would swear that her neck was burning with the intensity of the glares being directed at her by some of the bridge crew. But she clasped her hands behind her back and tried to take what small measure of consolation she could from the experience of riding atop one of history's greatest warships.

She was startled out of her reverie when Spruance next spoke.

'Your people are very professional, Captain. They've saved a lot of men tonight.'

He didn't add what a few men around him no doubt thought, that Halabi's people had killed even more.

'Standards haven't slipped, Admiral.'

'How long have you been at war, Captain?' Spruance asked in a distracted voice.

'Myself? Twelve years, sir. But it's a different kind of war. More complicated, I suppose.'

'I don't see how that could be,' Spruance said.

'Politics, religion, history.' She shrugged. 'It gets very complicated, believe me. Often we're not even fighting other states, just a state of mind. Ideas.'

Spruance turned completely around. Silhouetted

against the glass, it was nearly impossible to see his face. 'You can't fight ideas with rockets and jyguns.'

'On the contrary, that's exactly what you were doing out here, Admiral. You came here to kill men and sink ships. But it was ideas that sent you and the Japanese to war. And it's ideas about how men and women should live that sent England to war with Germany. I know that all sounds far too abstract, what with so much blood being spilled. But even after Pearl Harbor you don't understand the nature of the thing you're fighting.'

Karen watched as Spruance folded his arms in the dark space of the bridge.

'You sound like you're running for Congress – sorry, Parliament.'

'It's just my MA showing. Conflict Studies at Cambridge. You'll have to excuse my academic interest in your war. It happened a long time before I was born. But we studied it closely. Because of the immense scale of violence and cruelty this conflict unleashed, there persists in our culture a horror of war, a belief that it is an unmitigated evil, even though this is also recognised as a just war. One that could not be morally avoided.'

'Because of Pearl Harbor?' said Spruance.

'No. Because of Auschwitz.'

Spruance shook his head. 'Sounds like a Kraut name, but I've never heard of it.'

'You will.'

USS Hillary Clinton, *0409 hours, 3 June 1942*

A large wall-mounted flat-screen in the media centre displayed a stored high-res satellite image of the southern reaches of the Indonesian archipelago. Dan Black knew that because Lieutenant Thieu had explained it when they arrived. He wasn't quite sure what the hell that all meant, though.

Lieutenant Thieu looked a lot like a Jap to Lieutenant Commander Black's way of thinking. But he sounded as though he'd spent his whole life on the beaches of California.

'Santa Monica,' Thieu said when Black asked. 'My parents were deep green, Earth First types. I surfed a lot to get out of the house. Then when they tried to get me to paddle my board out to hassle some long-line tuna boats, I ran away and joined the navy. I don't think they'll ever forgive me.'

Black had no idea what he was talking about, but the mystery of Thieu was nothing compared to the two civilian women who were straining at the leash just behind him. Black figured them for civvies because of the complete lack of respect they brought to their dealings with the lieutenant.

'And what's your job, Lieutenant?' asked Black.

'Right now, I'm just looking after you until you can get back to the *Enterprise*. But officially, media relations.'

'And we're the media he's trying to have a relationship with,' said one of the women.

Thieu exhaled slowly. 'Lieutenant Commander Black, Ensign Curtis, this is Julia Duffy, a feature writer for the *New York Times*, and Rosanna Natoli, a producer for CNN. You don't have it yet. It's a bit like the *Movietone* newsreels, I guess.'

'So, we're supposed to talk to the press now?' asked Black, who was openly confused.

He'd felt about as useful as tits on a bull up on the flag bridge and had been happy enough to get out from under Kolhammer's feet as the search and rescue effort accelerated. With Curtis eager to try out a 'computer', they'd been escorted down to this 'media centre' – although it looked like an aid station to Black, with maybe two dozen civilians laid out on cots.

Thieu explained that they were reporters who'd been 'embedded' with various elements of the Multinational Force, but that didn't make Black feel any more comfortable.

'You don't have to talk to anyone if you don't want to,' Thieu added quickly.

'Oh, come now,' said Natoli. 'I'm sure these boys wouldn't be scared of talking to a couple of lady reporters. They were on their way to kick Yamamoto's butt. They'll be safe with us, Edgar.'

'And who are you going to file for?' asked Thieu. 'Ms Duffy still might be able to score a gig with the *Times*, but I don't know if Ted Turner's even been born yet. And if he has, he ain't hiring.'

'Well, first off,' Natoli argued, 'you don't know for

sure that we're stuck here. We could all be back home selling our stories by this time tomorrow. None of us knows *anything* yet. Meanwhile, you have your job. We have ours.'

Black watched the exchange with growing curiosity. These women didn't defer to the officer at all. Their demeanour was challenging, bordering on ill mannered. He dismissed the idea that it was a function of Thieu's race. It was possible, he realised, that they just didn't like each other. If so, it might be useful to get to know them. They might have a different angle on what was happening. He wasn't sure he trusted Kolhammer's people yet.

Behind the women a whole wall was taken up with what Black thought of as movie screens, displaying scenes from all over both fleets. He could even see his own ship, the *Enterprise*, with two helicopters just setting down on her deck.

The view seemed to be coming from on high, directly above the flight deck, and Black assumed another helicopter was taking the photos. When he asked, though, Thieu explained that the feed was actually coming from a small saucer-shaped 'dronecam' keeping station about three thousand five hundred metres – that meant twelve thousand feet, apparently – above the deck of the carrier. That almost made sense. Other panels on the big wall screen showed vision of a few surviving destroyers from his own group alongside sleek, flowing ships from the future, with a constant transfer of men between both.

Men *and women*, he corrected himself.

Nodding slowly to the Italian doll he said, 'I can't speak for Ensign Curtis, but I don't mind chatting with you while things get cleared up outside, miss. I can't do any interviews, though. You can't put me in your story, right?'

Lieutenant Thieu closed his eyes and muttered something beneath his breath. But the two reporters smiled radiantly.

'Fabbo,' said Duffy.

'What about you, Ensign Curtis?' Natoli asked. 'You up for a little deep background?'

Curtis blushed down to the roots of his hair.

Captain Jurgen Müller arrived directly from a SAR mission and was still wearing his flight suit. Commander Enrico Prodi made his way up from the *Clinton*'s hangar deck. And Major Pavel Ivanov of the Russian army had crossed from the *Kandahar*, where he had been taking part in the SEALs' tutorial on the G4 assault rifle when Pope's wormhole had swallowed them all.

The men picked at a tray of sandwiches in Kolhammer's private quarters while the admiral handed out mugs of coffee.

'Where is Colonel Gogol?' asked Ivanov.

'I'm afraid he didn't make it,' said Mike Judge.

The Spetsnaz officer took in the answer, processed it and grunted.

'Too bad.'

Ivanov didn't look like he needed commiserations. Judge restricted himself to replying, 'Yeah, too bad.'

A knock sounded at the door and Kolhammer called out, 'Enter.'

The three visitors all turned to see Sub-Lieutenant Maseo Miyazaki, acting commander of the *Siranui*. One arm was encased in a bright green gel tube, and he stood with the aid of a stick.

In spite of his injuries, Miyazaki bowed deeply, every line in his body rigid. It was as if he had fibre-steel cable instead of muscle and bone. Kolhammer took his cue from the young officer and, rather than staring directly into his eyes, he averted his gaze, just slightly. He discreetly studied the stoic mask Miyazaki had drawn across his feelings. Grief and pain were obvious, but survivor guilt was there, as well, a gnawing sense of shame and remorse that one should live when better men had died.

'I'm sorry, Lieutenant,' he said, bowing his head. 'I served with Captain Okada on a number of occassions. He was a fine warrior. A man of *giri*. I would appreciate it if you let your men know how deeply we feel his loss and the death of his comrades.'

The young officer carefully straightened his back. 'Thank you, sir. I understand two of Admiral Spruance's ships were destroyed by the *Siranui*,' he said. 'As the officer responsible, I now forward our most abject apologies to the admiral and place myself under arrest pending court-martial for the unauthorised killing of Allied naval personnel.'

Kolhammer was stunned. Nobody moved. The other three foreigners were obviously as taken aback as he was. They looked like props placed by a director. His stateroom, panelled in oak and furnished with a leather lounge and deep blue carpets, suddenly seemed strangely artificial to him, like a stage setting. As he recovered his wits, he put down his coffee mug and searched for a reassuring but authoritative tone.

'Please stand at ease, Lieutenant. In fact, sit down and take the weight off. Please, I mean it. The release of your combat mace was not unauthorised. I sanctioned an overriding autonomy for the fleet CIs and the consequences of that decision are mine to bear, not yours. I'll be certain to forward your apologies to Admiral Spruance but I won't allow you to take the blame.

'Unfortunately, I fear that won't satisfy the demands of the situation.'

Miyazaki entered the room with a small degree of difficulty. But he carefully lowered himself into a chair next to Ivanov and gratefully accepted a cup of green tea from Commander Judge.

'*Domo arigato*.'

'You're welcome,' smiled Judge.

Ivanov gave the young Japanese sailor a slap on the knee.

'Good shooting,' he deadpanned.

Kolhammer grimaced inwardly. He had served with a lot of Russians. He was used to their gallows humour. 'Gentlemen, I won't bullshit you. We have a problem,' he said. 'I doubt we're going home any time soon. Maybe never. That leaves you men up faecal creek. We have twenty-one German, eighteen Italian and fifteen Russian personnel serving on attachment throughout the task force. And, of course, we have the *Siranui*. You're the senior surviving officers of your national contingents. If we are indeed trapped here, your homelands are dictatorships, and in the case of Germany, Italy and Japan, they're enemy states.'

Ivanov let out a short, humourless laugh. 'I suspect that for me and my comrades, Admiral, the Soviet Union is an enemy state.'

'That's why you're here as well, Major.'

'And us?' bristled Müller. 'Are we to provide you with some sort of loyalty pledge?'

The Italian, Prodi, threw up his hands. '*Alora!* You have no reason to be concerned with my feelings, Admiral. Have you visited Rome and seen the fascist architecture? It's an abomination! Profoundly anti-human and a total misreading of imperial design. That pig Mussolini deserved to hang by his heels!'

Two seconds of confused silence greeted the Italian's outburst.

'Right, then,' Kolhammer said when he recovered. 'Thank you, Commander Prodi. To answer your question, Captain Müller, no, I'm not looking for loyalty pledges. But there are people here who will. And even if they get them, they'll still want to lock you up.'

'I expect Stalin shall try to put an icepick in my brain,' said Ivanov without much emotion. 'But we shall see how that works for him, *da*?'

'Stalin isn't my concern,' said Kolhammer. 'J Edgar Hoover might be.'

The blank looks he received told him they hadn't boned up on their American history before accepting their postings.

'Look, I harbour no doubts about your dependability, but you can expect a lot of shit from the locals. Not so much you and your guys, Ivanov. But then, like you say, you'll have your own problems. We can sort this out properly when we have more time, but I want you to personally get around to your people and tell them to keep their heads down. Especially when we get to Pearl Harbor, or Brisbane, or the West Coast.'

'We don't know where we're going yet?' asked Ivanov.

'We don't know much about anything,' Kolhammer conceded. 'Commander Judge has pulled together a list of the personnel you'll need to contact. Forget about your other duties until you've done this.'

Sub-Lieutenant Miyazaki coughed, and spoke in a halting voice. 'And what am I to do, Admiral? How do we hide a Nemesis cruiser?'

Kolhammer propped himself against his desk. The Europeans seemed almost as interested in his answer as the Japanese officer. He worked a kink out of his neck and sighed.

'The next few days won't be easy, but as long as my command remains intact I am responsible for your welfare and security. I won't allow it to be compromised. Is there anything you need, by the way?' asked Kolhammer. 'Medical supplies or personnel?'

'I'm afraid our casualties were mostly killed in action,' said Miyazaki. 'Indeed, I have organised for our surplus medical supplies to be taken off for distribution to those vessels more in need. I understand the *Kandahar* is running low on burn gel and vat skin.'

'Thank you, Lieutenant. That's much appreciated. I'll see to it that your generosity is acknowledged.'

Miyazaki seemed truly affronted by the proposition, becoming animated for the first time in their encounter.

'That will not be necessary,' he insisted. 'It is not a gesture!'

'I understand that, Maseo,' said Kolhammer, gently and deliberately choosing the informal, intimate form of address. 'I also asked you about personnel. Being blunt about it, I had a reason. You've lost all of your senior officers. I've had significant casualties on the *Leyte Gulf*. We're going to lose that ship in the next few hours. It would help smooth things over with the locals if you accepted Captain Anderson and a small cadre of American officers as replacements for your casualties.'

Miyazaki was silent. Kolhammer could see the

effort play out on the young man's face, as he wrestled with conflicting demands and desires.

'I don't mean to be insulting, Lieutenant. But we don't have a lot of time. On the other hand we do have a shitload of resentment and fear and outright loathing to contend with. I'm going to have my hands full keeping your crew out of a prison camp.'

He could see that Miyazaki was about to leap to the defence of his men. Holding up one hand, he ploughed on. 'I know. It's not fair, but that's just tough shit. I know that you've slaved your CI to the *Clinton*. I've told Spruance that, but it means nothing to him. He won't rest easy until he sees an American in charge of that ship.'

'A black woman?' scoffed Miyazaki. 'You think that will please him?'

Kolhammer smiled weakly. 'Well, he can't have everything his own way, can he?'

He felt real sympathy for the youngster. His behaviour during the battle had been entirely proper and courageous. Under different circumstances it would have earned him a medal. Instead, he stood implicitly accused of being untrustworthy and dishonourable. Of lacking *giri*. There weren't many worse insults you could hand a Japanese fighting man, but Kolhammer had no choice. He remained motionless, perched on the edge of the desk, frantically searching for a way that Miyazaki might save face. He was thus a little startled that it was Captain Müller who was provoked into an outburst.

The German, who looked as though he was chewing on something sour, barked out, 'This is a lot of bullshit for nothing, Herr Admiral.'

Miyazaki appeared grateful for the distraction. Kolhammer chose to ignore the lack of deference.

'No, it is not bullshit, *Captain*. We've killed a lot of men tonight. Widowed thousands of women. Taken fathers and sons and brothers from Christ only knows how many people. And we've done Yamamoto's work for him, destroying the American Pacific Fleet. We arrived in company with a Japanese warship, and we have dozens of *enemy aliens* serving on our own ships. It won't matter a damn that we lost a lot of good men and women too. There are going to be some very powerful people demanding that we *all* be locked up. And you men are the first ones they'll come for.'

Ivanov smiled frostily. 'And what will you do about this Hoover, some kind of secret policeman, yes? Will you turn him away when he comes?'

Kolhammer regarded all three of them with a level gaze. 'You're part of my command and I won't have you treated with anything but respect. I do need to know, however, what sort of role you'll be comfortable with, should we have to stay here and fight.'

Captain Müller's lips were compressed into a thin white line. When he spoke, it was to spit each word like a bullet.

'Admiral Kolhammer, my great-grandfather commanded a company in the *Gross Deutschland* Division.

He was killed in Russia – but not by the Red Army or partisans,' he said, nodding towards Ivanov. 'He died after holding a river crossing for three days against waves of tanks and infantry. He held fast with the remnants of his company, about seventy men, while two thousand comrades escaped across the water. When he reached the other side, the last German to do so, he was arrested and shot for desertion in the face of the enemy.

'His wife, my great-grandmother, was interned in a camp with her children, six of them. Only one survived – my grandfather. He carried the scars of the beatings by the camp guards all his life. He told me many times of his brothers and sisters. He retained a perfect memory of each and he wanted me to remember them to my children. His oldest brother Hans was beaten to death while protecting his younger brother Erwin from a homosexual rapist. Erwin was later shot for no apparent reason by a visiting SS officer. Their sister Lotti froze to death. Sister Ingrid, twelve years old, died of syphilis. And baby sister Greta was murdered by a guard, who crushed her head with the heel of his boot when she refused to suck his penis.

'You ask me how I feel, Admiral?' he said softly. 'I feel sick with the possibilities.'

Nobody spoke when Müller had finished. Kolhammer himself felt ill. Miyazaki, he noted, was nodding quietly. The restrained violence of the German's delivery had done more to shake his incredulity in the face of the impossible than had the battle on arrival or the visit to Spruance. He was about to reply when Judge's flexipad beeped. The *Clinton*'s XO checked the message he'd just received.

'Admiral,' he said with surprise in his voice. 'Something's happened.'

Kolhammer was annoyed at himself. He should have been concentrating on the main screen in the CIC, but he couldn't shake his dissatisfaction at the way his meeting with Miyazaki and the others had gone. He didn't really feel as if they had resolved anything. More to the point, he was pissed off at himself for not clearly understanding his own motivations. Was he really afraid the *Siranui*'s crew might *mutiny*? That was preposterous. He had worked with that ship on a number of occasions. Okada was, if not a friend, then at least a trusted colleague. But of course, Okada was dead. And any fears he had that the surviving men might – *what, steal the technology, and give it to Yamamoto*? Well, it was ridiculous and insulting to the survivors. After all, he didn't expect the Germans to run back to the Führer.

'Admiral Kolhammer? Sir?'

Lieutenant Brooks had caught him with his mind wandering.

'I'm sorry, Lieutenant. Fatigue. Give it to me again.'

Kirsty Brooks gave no hint that she'd been put off by his reverie. She repeated her last statement a little louder, as though he merely hadn't heard over the buzz in the room.

'You can see for yourself, Admiral. Nagumo's battle group has definitely turned tail. And although Yamamoto and the other fleet elements are at the edge of our sensor range, they all appear to have altered course, as well. They're bugging out.'

The *Clinton*'s CIC was a hive of activity, with all of the departments fully staffed and working hard to compensate for the vast inflows of national source intelligence that they had left behind in the twenty-first century. Antiair, antisubmarine, antisurface warfare centres all hummed ceaselessly. Only the antiorbital centre seemed to be running at a moderately relaxed pace.

'And this trace contact,' said Kolhammmer, 'how long ago was that?'

'Twelve minutes ago, sir,' Brooks replied. 'Could have been an echo effect, but it didn't read that way. Little Bill picked up the silhouette. He figured an eighty-four per cent probability that it was the *Garrett*.'

'In the Antarctic?' said Kolhammer doubtfully.

'Near enough, Admiral.'

The CIC was bitingly cold. Kolhammer shivered.

'ETA for Spruance?' he asked.

Brooks checked on her main screen.

'Should be touching down now, sir.'

USS Amanda L Garrett, *Southern Ocean, 0434 hours, 3 June 1942*

Extreme low-pressure weather systems, whether they're called hurricanes or typhoons or cyclones, are memorable events for those caught up in them; so memorable, they're often given names whenever they cross paths with civilisation. In the deep, circumpolar belt of ocean between fifty and sixty degrees south, however, dozens of giant storm cells are generated every year without being named, because there's nobody to witness them in the vast, empty swathes of the Southern Ocean.

Very little landmass occupies that belt of water. With almost nothing to impede them, the great storms can pile up incredible amounts of water at their leading edge. The surges gather power as they travel around the world. Sailors who have witnessed such things say that nothing bears comparison with them: fast-moving, hundred-metre-high walls of black water. Even larger rogue waves can be caused by a combination of factors – a storm surge, a pressure convergence line, a sub-surface feature such as the edge of a continental shelf, or the meshing of two or three single waves into one behemoth. Such monster waves rarely survive for long, and are even more rarely reported.

Almost nobody who encounters them lives to tell the tale.

So it was with the air-warfare destroyer USS *Amanda L Garrett.*

Thanks to the unstable, anomalous field generated by Pope's experiment, she emerged a great distance from the originating event.

The crew of the *Garrett* was only one hundred and twenty strong. None awoke immediately from the temporary coma of Transition sickness. A small number, however, did perish quickly. Nine men and four women, who had been on deck when the wormhole inflated, were swept away by the enormous seas into which they emerged. A few more broke their necks and backs as their bodies were flung about below decks. Many suffered broken limbs and concussion.

Eventually, after three hours, a handful of sailors did regain consciousness, but they were in no condition to control the ship. One, a petty officer, managed to crawl into the bridge, hoping to cede autonomy to the CI. But a twenty-metre wave had smashed the blast windows and poured in, shorting out the equipment. Before the petty officer could exit the ruined post, the destroyer slipped over the ridge of a colossal wave and speared down the reverse side. The wave behind it rolled over the vessel. Thousands of litres of freezing seawater poured in and sucked the screaming woman out.

The *Garrett* succumbed at 0435 hours when she ran headfirst into one of those massive, unstable mountain ranges of water that stalk the wastes of the

Southern Ocean. The warship climbed gamely up the face of the cliff, but it was simply too big to surmount. In her final moments she slewed around on the nearly vertical surface and rolled.

The flickering echo of a distress call from her CI, which bounced off the troposphere and spattered weakly against the Nemesis arrays of the *Siranui* a few minutes later, was the last anyone heard of her.

USS Hillary Clinton, *0448 hours, 3 June 1942*

Spruance couldn't help but be impressed. The size of the *Hillary Clinton* was imposing to begin with. He imagined you could fit the *Enterprise* into her three times over.

The flight deck was a wreck, littered with piles of scrap and ripped open like an old tin can down aft of the second fin-like structure, which he assumed had to play the same role as the island on the Big E. Even wounded as badly as she was, however, the ship hummed with power. The admiral found himself deeply conflicted: proud that his men could dish out so much punishment to a vastly superior adversary, and deeply sorry that they had done so. He might have been able to win the war in a day with this floating brute.

He'd heard his name whispered repeatedly as Commander Judge led him through the vessel. It was so very strange that these men and women, many of them looking like foreigners but speaking in accents he recognised from the corridors of his own ship, seemed to look upon him as if he were some sort of movie star. As some pointed and others stared, he saw real awe and respect in their eyes. It wasn't altogether pleasing. He must have returned over a hundred salutes, all of them ripped out with parade-ground perfection as he made his way through the vessel. Dan Black had rejoined him, with that young ensign trailing along in their rear beside half-a-dozen officers from the *Enterprise*.

They turned into a room dominated by the biggest movie screen Spruance had ever seen outside a theatre. Kolhammer and a number of his officers, looking like a delegation from the League of Nations, were waiting. Spruance didn't waste any time.

'So, the Japs are running, are they? How do you know? They might be making a flanking manoeuvre for Pearl. They could pull it off if they wanted to.'

Kolhammer pointed a smooth black stick at the big movie screen. It filled up with some kind of radar image. But it looked like . . . Spruance searched for a metaphor, but all that came to mind were the cartoons you sometimes saw before a Saturday matinee. The images looked *drawn*. They most certainly weren't the fuzzy lights and blurred, sweeping arcs he associated with radar. He could see Nagumo's force neatly illustrated with little boats and name tags. Dozens of vessels surrounded four carriers. Most of them were identified too.

'What the hell is that?' asked Spruance, unsure whether to be impressed or pissed off.

'It's a computerised representation of our intelligence take,' said Kolhammer. 'Just think of it as an illustration of what our radars can pick up. It's easier to show you this way.'

'Don't patronise me, Admiral. Just tell us what's happening.'

The briefing room wasn't large for the number of men and women it contained. They had clustered around their respective leaders, and the dozen or so gathered behind Kolhammer tensed at Spruance's outburst. In turn, the men off the *Enterprise* stiffened and jutted their jaws out that little bit further. Most of their aggression flowed towards three officers of Asian appearance who stood near Kolhammer.

'They're running. I can't put it any more simply,' said the *Clinton*'s CO.

'That's all well and good,' said Spruance, 'but do you have any idea *why* the Japs are running? If it's true.'

Kolhammer motioned to some seats. Spruance thought they looked very odd. They were misshapen and composed of some hard, unknown material. He indicated that he preferred to remain standing. Kolhammer shrugged.

'It's true,' he said. 'But I don't know why they've turned tail. They almost certainly picked up the radio broadcast I made to you last night, followed of course by the traffic between your own ships and pilots during the battle. Nagumo was, or is, incredibly conservative. The exposure of his plan and your trap may have been enough to cause him to abort the operation.'

Neither Spruance nor his men looked at all convinced.

'Are we supposed to just accept that?'

'You'll have to accept that they're running,' said Kolhammer, indicating the image behind his back. 'Our radar confirms it.'

'With all due respect,' Spruance said, leaving no doubt he had very little respect for his new, unwanted allies, 'you only know these bastards from your books. We know them first-hand. They don't turn and run like that without a very good reason. And I don't see one. You wouldn't have had any other ships with you off the East Indies, would you? Something else that might have spooked Nagumo?'

Spruance could tell he'd hit a raw nerve with that question. Kolhammer seemed to be chewing over a very tough piece of gristle as he pondered his answer.

'Well, there has been another development,' he conceded. 'We may have located a missing ship from our task force. A destroyer, the *Garrett.* She appears to have emerged in the Southern Ocean. We had a very faint distress signal from her. We've heard nothing since. Weather down there is pretty wretched at this time of year. If the crew were unconscious, she may have foundered.'

Spruance felt a tingle run up his spine. It wasn't at all pleasant.

'And how many other ships have you misplaced, Admiral?' he muttered, barely able to contain his growing rage.

'First,' said Kolhammer in a clipped tone indicating that he did not appreciate Spruance's insinuation, 'we didn't misplace them. We're as much victims of the accident that brought us here as you are. Second, I can't tell you with any certainty which ships are missing because I don't know which came through. But it's possible that others may have arrived. We're following up a ghost return from the southwest that might be a British destroyer, the *Vanguard*.'

'And you've sat on this for how long?' asked Spruance, incredulity struggling with fury in his voice.

'We haven't suppressed it at all. These signal traces are less than fifteen minutes old. I was informed on my way here to meet you. We're still analysing them.'

Spruance exploded.

'*Goddamn* it! Have you got any of your precious analysts evaluating what sort of a mess we'll be in if Japan or the Nazis get hold of one of your ships? You've got no goddamn idea where all this shit of yours has landed, do you? They could be raining those missiles of yours down on Hawaii or Washington, even as we stand here.'

The confrontation between the two men was mirrored in the stance of their officers. The scene in the briefing room looked like the moments just before a gang fight. Kolhammer's jawline knotted in anger as he struggled with a response.

'Admiral Spruance,' he said slowly and evenly, 'you have suffered grievously at our hands tonight. But we have our own casualties. *We* are not laying blame or seeking to avoid our responsibilities. We are not going to let your enemy profit from this. But you are going to have to accept that, if we have a duty to fight here, we also have rights due to any free man or woman who accepts the burden of their responsibilities.'

'And what the hell does that mean?' asked Spruance.

'I think it means that this thing between you and me, this is a fight for another day, Admiral. We've got thousands of sailors who need urgent medical treatment. The immediate threat to Midway has receded. I can station assets there to ward off any further attempt to take the island. Your task force is in no shape to fight. I suggest we withdraw to Pearl, establish exactly what other vessels, *if any*, have arrived here, and what has become of them. We repair the damage to my task force as best we can. And *then* we deal with the consequences of the night.'

The task force leaders locked eyes across the short space separating them. Spruance appeared coiled and furious. Kolhammer was uncompromising. The only sign that the confrontation was not going to escalate was the excruciating silence.

And then Spruance breathed out. He nodded, a movement so slight it could easily have been missed.

'This is going to be a hell of a thing to sort out,' he said quietly.

Kolhammer put out his hand.

'It'll go a lot easier if we work together.'

They shook on it. Warily.

17

USS Hillary Clinton, *0612 hours, 3 June 1942*

Later, as the survivors of the combined task forces steamed back towards Hawaii, Kolhammer sat alone, in silence, staring at the flat-screen on his stateroom wall. It displayed an image of his home in Santa Monica, with his wife, Marie, in gardening gloves, attacking a dense wall of agapanthus. Lucy, their black Labrador, lay under a eucalyptus, sheltering from the sun.

As Kolhammer gazed at the scene his throat grew tight and two tears squeezed out like hard little bullets of grief, tracking down his freckled face.

'I'm sorry, Marie,' he whispered to her. 'I promised to come home and now . . . I just don't know.'

He stared a while longer, then reached for the control stick and thumbed through a series of flawlessly reproduced images. More garden shots. A picture of Marie and Lucy on the old couch in the sunroom. A few pictures of their son, Jed, killed off Taiwan. No grandchildren, sadly. But a few much-loved great-nephews and -nieces. And other family portraits, becoming stiffer and more formal as they moved back through the years, tracing the

Kolhammer family journey from the German city of Magdeburg in 1934 to the New World, and then west across the continent. Following a trail laid down by generations of the damned.

Kolhammer froze the slide show on a sepia-toned studio image of his Great-Uncle Hans and Great-Aunt Hilda. The photograph had been torn before being digitised long ago, and Kolhammer had asked the image bureau to leave the imperfection as it was. He liked it that way. Family photographs, he firmly believed, should be weathered and a little damaged by age and handling. It was proof of one generation handing on history to the next.

He stared at the portrait of Hans and Hilda, peering into the hollow space around their eyes. Knowing and yet not really understanding what misery and horror danced slowly in there. The photo had been taken in New York in 1952, but both were still draped in heavy European clothes. Kolhammer accepted that the long sleeves weren't simply an expression of émigré formality. He remembered spending many hours with his great-uncle as a boy. And he knew that under the heavy serge suit was a tattoo of which Hans was unspeakably ashamed. It had been burned there by a minor functionary of Heinrich Himmler's SS and it marked him as a survivor of the Final Solution.

Hans had kept it hidden for many years, but late in his life – just after a young Phillip Kolhammer had taken his commission in the US Navy – a trembling, wasted Uncle Hans had left his nursing home and travelled across the continent to visit his great-nephew. The trip was unannounced. Hans simply up and left one day and there was hell and high interest to pay when he got back. He was struggling with the latter stages of Parkinson's by then, a foe that would claim him where the Führer's minions had failed.

Young Phillip was surprised, enchanted and a little concerned when the old guy turned up without warning. He hadn't taken his medication with any sort of regularity and the cross-country road trip in a Greyhound bus had been awfully tough on his old bones. But Hans had waved that aside, seized his favourite great-nephew in a weak, shaky bear hug and told him how proud he was to see a Kolhammer in the uniform of his liberators. After a few hours of drinking and bullshitting, and of Marie fretting endlessly, Uncle Hans took Phillip aside. They had men's business to discuss, he told Marie as he led her husband into a bedroom.

They stood in there, alone, and a terrible stillness came over Hans's twitching face as he stripped his sleeves and bared his arm, pointing at the tattoo.

'You promise me now, nephew,' he said. 'Promise me that for as long as there is breath in your body and you wear the uniform of a free country, you promise me that you will never allow this evil a place in the world again.'

Phillip Kolhammer had promised.

PART 3
Alliances

18

The Saruwaged Ranges, New Guinea, 0445 hours, 7 June 1942

The last village lay a thousand feet below them – Amyen, a small, tight cluster of bark huts set among the limestone lakes and gardens of sweet potato, which gradually gave onto forest at the foot of the ranges. It was unmarked on any maps, unknown to the colonial authorities in Port Moresby.

Warrant Officer Peter Ryan huddled in the mouth of the cave and peered out into the freezing mists. He knew that seven thousand feet below them lay the Wain and Naba country, and the flatlands of the Markham River. Were it not for the accursed mountain weather he'd probably be able to see Lae and Salamaua, where the Japs were already busy digging in.

It was another world down there, oppressively hot and humid, with thick, primordial jungle clinging to the edge of fast-flowing rivers. For Ryan, the dense, superheated air of the lowlands was reminiscent of a big Chinese laundry, or some other confined place where you'd find large quantities of boiling water. Up here, though, the conditions were practically arctic as they clumped together in the cramped limestone cave.

A thick, foul-smelling fug of body odours, smoke and human grease reached out for him from the dark recesses of the cave. The last of his native carriers were huddled together in there on sheets of beaten bark. He'd set out from Amyen with fifteen stout boys. The last four had gone down with a fever in the cave the previous night. Ryan knew he'd get no more work from them. His native sergeant, Kari, had offered to try to get the bearers to their feet, but Ryan told him not to bother. They were best left there, under the watch of Constable Dinkila, while the two of them made the last push up to the ridge.

'We'll move faster without them or the baggage,' said Ryan.

'They won't be here when we get back, boss,' Kari argued. 'Then we won't need baggage. Just coffins.'

Ryan essayed a weak smile at his friend.

'Needs must when the devil drives, Sergeant. There's something quite odd going on up this mountain. And I'm Johnny-on-the-spot.'

Just before dawn a freezing gale howled down from between the jagged, broken teeth of the Saruwageds, blowing away the mist and their last excuse for staying tucked up in the relative warmth and comfort of the cave. Ryan and Kari ate three tins of bully beef and a packet of biscuits, washed down with a canteen of water collected from the many trickles of condensation running down the smooth black rock face outside their shelter. They put on their last dry socks and best boots, gave Constable Dinkila strict instructions about caring for and guarding the carriers, and then they set off, carrying their Owen guns and long lengths of vine rope.

They traversed a sickeningly steep, razor-thin ridge line on their hands and knees before plunging back into the forest. Ryan thought it akin to stepping into a darkened basement from a bright-lit garden. A soft dark-green, evil-looking moss covered everything, sometimes to a thickness of a foot. Trees took on the appearance of fleshy, bloated green monsters from one of Grimm's fairy tales. Walking was a matter of sinking their feet into a spongy, moss-covered sludge of rotting vegetable matter. Sometimes they sank in up to their thighs. At one point, curious about the true depth of the strange, clotted mulch, Ryan pushed in a sharpened stick. It was eight feet long and met no resistance. They trod more carefully after that.

The complete absence of hard edges or solid surfaces served to dampen any sound. Their voices sounded flat and alien, and they found that after a while they had fallen into the habit of talking only in harsh whispers. Ryan thought the silence unearthly. Their footfalls made no noise apart from a sort of muffled squelch as they withdrew their boots from the sucking green ooze. Occasionally a small rat would dart out and run off. But no skittering or rustling attended its flight.

Eventually, the eerie forest gave way to sparse, stunted upland of twisted, dead, iron-grey tree trunks. Many exhausting hours were spent threading their way through the tangle. Ryan wondered whether the carriers would have been able to come this far anyway. Rain began to fall, and Kari pulled on a curious tent-like cowl of laced pandanus leaves, giving Ryan the impression he was walking behind a native hut on legs.

It was one of the few light moments of the trek. A sharp, stabbing pain had settled into his chest, just below the heart. His nose bled and he was thirsty all the time, no matter how much he drank. When they passed out of the rain band, Kari stopped and built a small fire from a supply of kindling he had tied to his belt. They warmed themselves and heated a pot of water for tea. Ryan produced some sugar from a small cloth bag and tipped it in. They revived their spirits with the strong, black brew and a couple of Constable Dinkila's yam pancakes, eaten cold with a smear of Vegemite.

'Getting close now, boss,' said Kari. 'You want to finish it today or tomorrow?'

Ryan really wanted to be home in Melbourne, curled up with a good book in front of a warm fire. But he said, 'Today. It's important. The orders came directly from MacArthur's HQ.'

'Maybe the big fellah should be here himself,' Kari said, grinning. 'If he's so keen to know what's up there.'

'Maybe,' Ryan agreed. 'But he's not. And unfortunately we are. So it's onwards and upwards.'

They cleaned up the makeshift rest site, kicked out the small fire with deep regret and set their course for the next ridge. It was early afternoon, but darkness was gathering as the daily shroud of mist appeared and the sun passed over the top of the range. Light and heat leaked out of the day. Ryan checked their map.

'The possum hunter's hut should be just over that saddle,' he whispered, pointing ahead about five hundred yards. 'And then the crash site, another hour beyond that.'

'If the village head man wasn't lying,' said Kari.

'Yes,' agreed Ryan, 'there's always that.'

They hauled themselves through an increasingly dense field of the limestone outcrops. Sometimes the slabs were so large they presented the blank facade of a great wall. Ryan felt giddy and nauseous from the thinness of the air. He stopped at one point and made the nearly fatal error of sitting down. At once, deliciously warm waves of lassitude stole through every muscle in his body. Sinking down against the hard wet rock felt as luxurious and decadent as crawling into bed in some opulent hotel suite. He recalled in almost Proustian detail the soft pillows and thick blankets of his childhood bed. How nice it would be to tuck himself in under the covers for just a few . . .

Sergeant Kari manhandled him to his feet.

'Sorry, boss. No good to be sleeping up here. Never wake up again.'

Ryan apologised for his weakness. They'd been on patrol for weeks when the new orders came through for them at Kirkland's, down near the river crossing. He was really in no fit state for this Lord Jim jungle wallah nonsense.

He put one foot in front of the other and painfully got himself moving again.

When they crested the saddle, there was no possum hunter's hut, and thus no shelter for the night.

'Damn them,' cursed Ryan.

'Listen boss. Shush now.'

Kari cocked an ear to the higher ground.

Ryan couldn't hear anything at first, but after a short time he noticed a faint, metallic banging, and perhaps the sounds of human voices.

'Japs,' said Kari.

'Good Lord, so they *are* here. We'd best push on for a look-see then,' said Ryan, a small surge of adrenaline flushing the fatigue from his bones.

From that point on, they slipped around through crevices and over nearly vertical naked rock faces like a bead of water running over a fat pandanus leaf.

There were more banging noises and voices – definitely Japanese – as they neared the lip of the plateau. Ryan was quietly impressed that they had made it up here before him.

A stiff breeze quickly strengthened into a hard, cold wind and, within a few minutes, into a howling pitiless gale. That was good. It was blowing from their direction. Down from the peaks. The Japs wouldn't hear them approach now. They would have to take care not to run into a sentry, but Ryan didn't think that likely. This mountain was evil. Men huddled together on its face. None would stray too far.

On hands and knees they slithered forward until they'd reached the lip of the little plateau. Crab-walking sideways until he made the cover of a small bush, Ryan chanced a peek over the edge.

About three hundred yards away, clearly visible through the thickening gloom, was a ship. A giant grey warship, sinking into the mountain, its bow pointed to the heavens.

The ship was posed as though she were about to go down, slicing through the rocky spine of the Saruwageds as she would pass through the waters of the Coral Sea on a death plunge to the ocean floor. And yet she remained poised, knifing into the mist and the sky, as though she had always been there.

While Ryan's mind adjusted to the discovery, he began to take in other features of the tableau. The platform into which the ship was forever sinking was covered by a field of giant toadstools, thousands of them, with caps a foot or more across. The moss had colonised them too, and presented the onlooker with the bizarre vision of a dense mat of knobbled green felt, high in the sky. An occasional granite spike thrust up out of the blanket of moss and fungi. And sheltering in the lee formed by the warship, a dozen tents strained at their ropes as the roaring wind tried to carry them away. He wondered idly how they'd been tied down.

He already knew who had raised them in this strange place. Japanese soldiers had beaten them to the scene.

19

Oahu, 0548 hours, 9 June 1942

The bodies lay undisturbed for hours. They had been seen during that time but were ignored. Three sailors on a small motor launch puttering through the bay noticed the forms entwined on the beach and assumed a partying couple had fetched up there after a night on the booze. An hour and a half later an army air force officer riding a motorcycle through the dunes briefly caught sight of them, but he actually had been drinking all night and was far too inebriated to bother with the sight of a couple necking down on the sand. He had to sober up, get back to barracks and get rid of the stolen bike.

Eventually a squad of marines from the 82nd MEU, pounding the soft sand on an early morning run, discovered the corpses. Sergeant Clifford Hardy, jogging a few metres in front of his men, was the first to notice the dark shapes at the water's edge a couple of hundred metres down the beach. Like the others who'd seen the bodies from a distance he immediately assumed them to be a couple flaked out after a long night. They were entwined closely enough to be lovers. Bouncing along five kilometres into an eight-kilometre run, with sweat in his eyes, he caught just a glimpse at first, a watery blur, and was inclined to ignore the sight. If anything, he was slightly pissed at the prospect of having to detour around them, but when a stronger line of shore break closed out just a few feet from the couple and washed right over the top of them, he knew straightaway they were corpses. The bodies rolled with the white water. One of them, a much darker one, he realised then, flipped right over with the lifeless heft of the dead.

Sergeant Hardy was a twenty-year man. He was well acquainted with the dead.

'Yo! Hold up!' he yelled.

The line of marines, deep in the trance of a long-distance run, stumbled over each other at the unexpected halt.

'S'up, Sarge?' cried Warlow. 'Your ticker giving out? You need your pills?'

'Shut up, Warlow,' Hardy said quietly, his stillness silencing the men.

They all switched instantly to a watchful alertness. They were dressed for PT, not combat. None carried weapons. One man rubbed the tips of his fingers together. Another cracked knuckles within a closed fist. All of them shifted on the balls of their feet, turning outwards, scanning for threats.

The morning was warm and fresh. A small half-metre swell broke on the soft crescent of sand in regular sets. A light onshore breeze ruffled the men's hair and cooled the sweat that slicked their bodies.

'Warlow, run up that big dune there and have a look around,' said Hardy. 'See if we got any company.'

The marine took off with a stealthy lope. All the backchat and sass were gone from him.

'They dead, Sarge?' asked a giant rifleman.

'What do you think, butthead?' said Hardy, his eyes traversing like gun barrels.

'Looks like,' said Private Bukowski.

'They ours?' another man asked.

Hardy turned around. It was Snellgrove.

'What makes you think that, Smelly?'

The marine, a raven-haired boy from Kansas, inclined his head towards the bodies. Another wave washed over them.

'Looks like a mixed couple. And you can see their implant scars, I figure.'

Warlow yelled down from the heights of the dune. 'All clear, Sarge!'

Hardy took in a deep draught of clean air. It was so much cleaner here. You simply couldn't deny it. Made a man wonder about the shit he'd been breathing all his life. He took another look at the empty beach. It was a pity to fuck up such a nice place. The sea would be just about perfect for bodysurfing. The glassy green rollers crunched in with a nice hollow boom, and the sand was so white you just knew it'd blind you when the sun got higher. There wasn't a single piece of trash to be seen anywhere. No condoms. No broken glass. No discarded syringes.

'Okay,' he sighed. 'Y'all know the drill. We'll take

it like any other atrocity site. Just pretend you're back in Yemen or Syria. Form a box, two hundred metres out. Bukowski, you come with me. We'll have to drag 'em up or else they'll get washed away. We'll walk over there through the surf. But keep your eyes peeled anyway. We might get lucky. Lazy fuckers might've tossed a weapon into the water.

'Okri, you get your ass back to town. Call *our* guys first. When they got their shit together, let *them* call the local yokels.'

Private Okri, who could run the legs off the rest of the squad, nodded and took off, being careful not to intrude into the invisible box Sergeant Hardy had drawn around the scene.

USS Kandahar, *Pearl Harbor, 0812 hours, 9 June 1942*

Captain Francois and Colonel Jones regarded the body with a mix of sadness and disgusted anger. Second Lieutenant Myron Byers had killed himself with a single shot through the temple. The wall behind his body was still sticky with blood and matted hair. A letter, a photograph and a wedding ring lay together in a Ziploc bag on a fold-down bedside shelf. The lieutenant and his wife of eight months smiled out of the photo. It had been taken on their honeymoon.

The brief note apologised for the mess in the cabin

and asked that his wife's family on her maternal grandmother's side be given the ring, the photograph and all of his personal items. They were to keep his belongings in trust for her until her eighteenth birthday, many decades away. His savings were to be invested and held in trust for her until that time as well.

'Jesus, what a fucking mess,' Jones said despondently.

Francois knew he was talking about the request, not the clean-up job.

'You gonna do it?' she asked.

'It's a man's dying wish,' he said. He fell quiet for a few seconds. 'I should have been paying more attention, seen this coming.'

Captain Francois rubbed her burning eyes with the heel of one palm.

'Don't beat yourself up, Colonel,' she said. 'He won't be the last one we lose this way.'

Jones had already accepted as much. He hadn't had time to think much of his own wife and family. There was just so much to do, although, if truth were known, he was probably avoiding the issue. There had been one or two quiet moments since Midway, but he hadn't sat down by himself to think through the personal implications of the Transition. If they were stuck here, he'd never see Monique or his niece again. It neatly inverted the burden of separation they always felt when he was away on active duty. Now he got to share in their sense of loss and dread.

'Colonel?'

He returned from the unhappy line of thought. 'I'm sorry, Captain. You were saying?'

'I said we might want to think about screening our personnel for acute depression. People are going to respond differently, but some will want to check out, like the lieutenant here. He's not the first, you know.'

That surprised Jones. He leaned over, plucked the Ziploc bag up between the tips of his fingers and motioned Francois out of the cabin. She shut the door behind them.

'You've had more suicides?' he asked in a low voice.

'Four,' said the combat surgeon. 'This is the first on the *Kandahar*. Oddly enough, they've all been male so far, even though we've got about five hundred mothers serving on ships throughout the task force. You'd think this would have hit them the hardest.'

'What, you're saying women miss their kids more? That sounds awfully old-fashioned, Doctor.'

'Fucking A, that's what I'm saying, Colonel. And it's true.'

Jones was mildly surprised by her fervour, but he chose not to argue with her, even though just that morning he'd found a young marine sobbing on the shoulder of a female petty officer. Jones learned that the man's wife had given birth to a son just a few weeks before the ship had left for East Timor.

On the other hand, he knew, not everybody was upset by their circumstances. He was aware of a pilot on the *Clinton* who'd broken out in a huge wolfish grin when he realised he'd escaped three ex-wives and one fat, famously unsympathetic Chechen bookie named Anxious Stan, to whom he owed about forty grand.

And some lucky individuals, he guessed, were probably too stupid to comprehend the situation at all. They'd react as they did to all the important events in their lives, by continuing to find undiluted enjoyment in eating, sleeping and evacuating their bowels whenever the opportunity presented itself.

'So, how serious do you think it could be?' he asked. 'We're living in a heavily armed village here, Doc. Wouldn't do to have the natives go weird on us.'

Francois took her time with the question, and he knew why. Under normal circumstances, most of the twelve thousand men and women in the task force understood that they might be injured, disfigured or even killed while on duty. They knew, too, that there was always a fair chance they'd never see or hold their loved ones again. But even the combat veterans, always the most fatalistic types, knew that war spares many more than it takes. And the cherries naively thought it would all happen to somebody else.

Jones doubted anyone really knew what the circumstances in which they now found themselves meant.

'Depression's not something a biochip will pick up,' she said finally. 'But we've got to figure it'll be there. Everyone's going to fit somewhere along the spectrum, from mildly ticked off to thoroughly suicidal. But how that will manifest, I can't tell you, Colonel. I'd say there'll be a few incidents over the next week or two, as everyone adjusts. But I'd be hopeful that most would adjust, and pretty well, too. These aren't normal people. They accepted the prospect of their own deaths when they signed up. I guess we'll see.'

Jones weighed the plastic bag in his hands. It felt very light to be the sum trace of a man's life.

'It's not death, though, is it?' he muttered. 'More like exile.'

A couple of exhausted seamen arrived from the mortuary to clean out the cabin. Francois gave them their instructions before pushing off back to the hospital. She was due to fit an artificial heart in eight hours and wanted to check on the patient's preparation. Jones fell in beside her.

'Here's a question, Colonel,' she said. 'How are you going to get the money to his family?'

'Dunno, Doc. Hadn't really thought that one through. Now you mention it, I can't exactly authorise a net transfer.'

'No net.'

'Right.'

'Another question, seeing as how you got so much time on your hands. Even if you find a bank to deposit the money in, how much do you actually put in? One of your platoon leaders probably pulls down as much a year as President Roosevelt did in 1942. Did you think of that?'

Jones felt a little peeved. 'No, Doc. But thank you so *very* much for pointing it out.'

'Well, it raises more than a few questions, don't you think? If we're trapped here. Like, who pays our bills and wages? You've got marines going ashore in Honolulu for a few hours' liberty tomorrow. How are they going to buy a beer? Amex credit stick?'

'Damn. I've got no idea.'

Before Francois could entangle him any further, his flexipad began to beep. So did hers. They excused each other and took the calls.

Both swore at exactly the same moment.

Their eyes locked and they knew they were dealing with the same issue.

'Secure the site,' said Jones in a flat voice. 'I'll be there ASAP.'

Francois signed off and gave Jones a challenging look.

'I'm going too. I worked Srebrenica and Denpasar for the UN. I'm crime scene qualified.'

Jones held up his open palms.

'I'm not standing in your way, Doc.'

The admiral's stateroom was so much larger than her cabin back on the *Trident* that Halabi felt lost in it. She'd tried to convince Kolhammer she could just as easily act as task force commander from her own ship, but he'd insisted she work from the *Clinton* during his absence. He wanted the locals to give her the respect she was due, and nothing demanded respect like a hundred and thirty thousand tonnes of fusion-powered supercarrier. Even if it was a little scratched and dented.

She'd enjoyed the luxurious surrounds for about thirty seconds, until she realised how close she was to the flight deck and how poorly insulated were Kolhammer's quarters; not that she was going to get a lot of sleep while he was away. The giant flat-screen on his desk was completely blocked out with files flagged for her immediate attention. Until she muted the speakers, a tone announced the arrival of a new 'highest priority' email every few seconds, and her schedule apparently contained more meetings than the day had minutes. Her paternal grandmother had a saying that seemed appropriate.

'Let's not try to eat the elephant in one whole bite,' Halabi muttered to herself.

She was about to open a report detailing distribution of the fleet's remaining war stocks when a window opened on the screen, displaying the rather drawn features of Captain Margie Francois.

Halabi was on site, grimly shaking hands with the combat surgeon twenty-five minutes later.

The scene looked chaotic from the air, with helicopters, Humvees, Honolulu PD cars, old-fashioned jeeps and at least a hundred or more individuals all buzzing around the victims. When she'd touched down and exited the chopper, Halabi had got an even stronger sense of barely controlled mayhem. A small group of Colonel Jones's marines was butting heads with the local police and MPs, trying to keep them from stomping all over the crime scene. Jones himself stood as still and silent as a black granite obelisk while a heavy-set white man in a bad suit turned beet red while screaming and gesticulating at him.

'What the hell is going on?' the acting task force commander asked.

'Nothing good,' said Francois. She took Halabi by the arm and walked her away a little. 'One of our platoons was out on a run this morning when they found the bodies, and they called us before the locals. Well, of course, Honolulu PD's tear-assing around with an atomic wedgie over that and . . .'

Halabi's puzzlement must have been written all over her face, because Francois backed and filled for the Englishwoman.

'They've got their knickers in a twist,' she explained.

'Oh right. Thanks.'

It was going to be a scorching hot day. Halabi noticed that even at so early an hour she didn't cast much of a shadow. She could hear another siren approaching, possibly two, as the marine went on. Francois didn't seem to care who overheard her.

'We can't have these dumb-ass crackers all over our crime scene,' she complained, sweeping a hand in the general direction of the local authorities. 'Granted we're not a homicide squad, but we've got a lot of expertise in war crimes investigation and we sure as hell got better procedures and equipment. These guys don't even know what DNA is. You gotta get them to step back, Captain. Let us take care of our own people.'

Halabi ran her eyes over the beach again. A hundred metres away Jones was still doing his stone face. The suit was still screeching at him and flapping his arms like a giant flightless bird. The marines and the cops and military police were getting even more muscular with each other.

And the corpses of Captain Daytona Anderson and Sub-Lieutenant Maseo Miyazaki had begun to stiffen with rigor mortis.

'What were they doing out here?' the British officer asked.

Francois squinted at the bodies. She shrugged. 'We don't even know they got whacked out here. Could have been hit in town and dumped. There's a team from the War Crimes Unit coming over to work the grid.'

'Was it working out, having Anderson and her people on the *Siranui*?'

Francois shrugged again. It seemed to be a compulsive gesture with her this morning.

'Far as I know, but I couldn't tell you for sure. I wasn't there. But I didn't hear anything. Why? Did you?'

Halabi shook her head. 'No. Just wondering.'

'Well, they had good reason to be together,' said

Francois. 'It can't have been easy, integrating the two crews. Language difficulties and so on. If I had to take a guess, I'd say they were having a drink at the Moana, probably just sorting some shit that was better handled through back channels. Maybe they went for a walk. I doubt they'd have strayed too far, though. We're not encouraging any of our people to mix it up with the locals yet.'

'Looks like they did,' said Halabi.

'Maybe,' the marine surgeon agreed. 'But it's all guesswork and that's all it's ever going to be if we don't quarantine this site and let the CSI team go to work.'

Halabi nodded. She checked her watch.

'Okay. I'll call Nimitz. I'm sure he can sort out the turf war. And then I'd better see if I can raise Kolhammer, but I'll be buggered if we can contact him so far. I'll tell you what, Captain, I'd sell my arse for just one little satellite.'

20

Gormon Field, Los Angeles County,
0408 hours, 9 June 1942

A cold, unseasonable wind blew down off the California mountains, across the howling wastes of the saltbush and hardscrabble. Outside the corrugated-iron arch of the Quonset hut, grit hissed through the air and dead leaves spattered against windows covered with heavy blackout curtains. Dust devils swirled across the new concrete tarmac. A single oil lamp lit the knot of men gathered in the spartan setting.

A rifle squad stood at ease at the rear of the room, separated from two loose knots of men in uniform and civilian clothes at the other end. The two groups coalesced around a frail figure in a wheelchair. He had a blanket draped over his legs and was forced to shoo off a young officer who unwisely attempted to wrap another around his shoulders. An older man, one of the civilians, detached himself from the conversation he'd been caught up in and wandered over to the wheelchair. He sported a shock of white hair and his deeply lined face had worn a perpetually harassed and haunted expression for years. His wife had died not long ago, but that wasn't what lay behind his melancholy. He hadn't laughed freely since fleeing from Germany in 1933.

He affected a cheeky smile now, however, and offered up a book of matches.

'Mr President. Do you need a light?'

'Why, thank you, Professor. I wouldn't have thought it would take a genius to work that out,' said Franklin Delano Roosevelt, throwing a severe glance at his disapproving aide, the one with the blanket.

As Albert Einstein struck a match and leaned in to light the Camel at the end of FDR's long black holder, a distant roar reached them, like a single bass note from a thunderstorm, drawn out for an impossible length of time.

'They're here,' said Einstein, as the tobacco caught alight and the President took in a deep draught of smoke.

'I want to see this,' FDR declared.

His aide hurried forward.

'Mr President, I don't think –'

'Just push me to the door,' snapped Roosevelt. 'I want to see these rocket planes.'

He stubbed out his cigarette with a show of annoyance.

'There! You can wrap me up like a granny, if that makes you feel better. But I'm going to see these things with my own two eyes.'

He clamped the cigarette holder back between his teeth. The broken, stubbed-out butt, still stuck in the end, lent him a slightly crazed air as he gripped the wheels of his chair and began to push himself towards the flimsy wooden door of the hut. Half-a-dozen military men moved to help, but Einstein was closer than any of them. He took the handles of the chair and leaned into it.

'Let's go see what the future brings, Mr President.'

A few of the civilians, scientific advisers for the most part, managed to scramble out into the biting wind before Einstein parked the President's chair in the doorway, effectively bottling up everyone behind them. An undignified scramble for position took place, with Brigadier General Eisenhower and Admiral King grabbing the best spots on either side of Einstein. The rest either gathered at two small windows or tried to see over the shoulders of the men jammed in the entryway.

Shivering slightly under his blankets, but determined not to show it, the President leaned forward until he could make out the end of the runway. An army air force colonel had briefed him about the rush job to prepare the landing strip. It was three times longer than the main runway at Edwards, he'd said. It seemed a hell of a wasteful thing to Roosevelt, all that extra cement and hard work for a couple of planes. But it surely wasn't the craziest thing he'd heard in the last week.

No, that had to have been the moment when an ashen-faced navy commander had appeared to tell him what had happened at Midway. Roosevelt shook his head at the memory as he spotted flashing red and white lights descending from the northwest.

'Hell's bells, Turtletaub,' he'd yelled out at the unfortunate officer just a week earlier. 'What madness is this? Next you'll be telling me space lizards have landed.'

Well, he'd had to apologise to the young man later, hadn't he? It turned out the world *had* flipped completely off balance, and now here he was, stuck out in the California desert, waiting to meet men from the future.

Damn it all but he needed a cigarette.

'Interesting,' said Einstein as twin spikes of blue-white flame speared from the tail of the dart-like craft as it roared down out of the night sky and past the hut at a seemingly breakneck speed. 'Those are the jets they told us of, Mr President.'

The aircraft seemed like death incarnate to Roosevelt. Every line seemed to threaten violence. More than a few of the onlookers gasped like children at a fireworks display, awed by the screaming passage of the sleek, lethal craft.

As the President wondered whether they'd built a long enough runway, parachutes unfurled behind the monster.

Another plane just like the first descended from the night sky. Its very appearance suggested something deadly, like a flashing blade or a bullet. Blinking lights gave away the position of yet another two aircraft banked up behind them. A familiar drone gradually emerged from beneath the monstrous thunder of the rocket planes.

'Prop driven,' said Admiral King. 'I guess they don't –'

He never finished the sentence, stunned as he was by the appearance of the third aircraft. It looked a lot more conventional than the first two, a bit like a Grumman Goose, or even a Catalina, at a stretch. But in contrast with the windswept lines of the rocket planes, this lumbering barge sat underneath something that looked like a giant cigar welded to a couple of struts sticking out of the fuselage. It droned past without deploying chutes, and then the last plane touched down. It was the least prepossessing of the three.

'Looks like a transporter,' said someone behind Roosevelt. He didn't recognise the voice.

One of the civilians huddled in the small group out in front of the hut turned around with his hands jammed deep in his duffel coat.

'That'd be their tanker, I bet. They can refuel while they're in the air. You'd have to figure those rocket planes burn gas like a bastard . . . Um, sorry, Mr President.'

Roosevelt waved away the apology.

For the first time since he'd been told of the disaster at Midway he didn't feel as if he was falling helplessly down a bottomless well. No, now he was intrigued.

*

Kolhammer hit a switch to crack the seal on the Raptor's bubble canopy. It opened with a slight hiss as he stripped off his mask and flipped up the helmet visor. He lost night vision, but his eyes soon adjusted from the artificial jade green of low-light amplification to the soft silver tones of moon and starlight. Any initial pleasure he'd felt at the chance to fly a fast-mover again had been lost in the sickening whirl of emotions stirred up at crossing the West Coast. They'd come in well to the north of Los Angeles, not wanting to start a panic. He'd still seen the heat dome of the city on infrared, however. It seemed impossibly small and feeble, but of course LA was nearly twelve times bigger in his day.

It was a jarring episode. He was used to looking down on that coastline, whether in daylight or darkness, and searching for his own home; not the exact house of course, but the general area, in the centre of the bay, at the edge of the city's apparently unbounded sprawl. It was one of the few safe mooring points of his life, the knowledge that Marie was down there, waiting for him. Except that she hadn't even been born yet, and if he couldn't get back to her, he'd most likely die before she was. Then their son, Jed, would never be, which seemed even more upsetting than having lost him off Taiwan. The sorrows and consequences of this fucking insanity twisted in on themselves like a snake devouring its tail.

'Admiral Kolhammer? Sir? They're coming.'

Kolhammer shook his head and consciously pulled out of the dark well of self-absorption. He reminded himself that the woman in the rear seat had left behind two daughters, aged three and five. The Raptor was named for her firstborn, Condi.

'Sorry, Lieutenant,' he said. 'I think I'm getting too old for this.'

'We all are, sir. Little kids and make-believe, that's what this reminds me of.'

The drumming of boots across the tarmac wasn't make-believe. A six-man squad was double-timing in their direction with rifles at the ready. They pounded to a halt about twenty metres away. A sergeant called out, 'Which one of you is Kolhammer?'

'Over here,' he yelled back, waving a small torch.

The sergeant spoke to a couple of his men who trotted away into the darkness at the edge of the tarmac. Kolhammer heard the sound of an iron door swinging open and being dropped with a clang. He peered into the gloom and saw the soldiers haul a stepladder out of a pit in the ground beneath the trapdoor.

'Five-star service,' he muttered to Lieutenant Torres.

The noncom waved the men with the wooden ladder over to a spot just below the fighter's cockpit. It bumped against the fuselage with a dull thud. For some reason the noise sealed the deal for Kolhammer. They were lost forever – of that he was certain.

'Age before beauty, sir,' said Flight Lieutenant Anna Torres with a tired smile in her voice.

Kolhammer swung himself out and over the side. He could see men and women dropping to the ground from the AWAC bird and the refueller.

He took the ladder in three steps and landed back on the US of A.

It didn't feel like home.

Nevertheless, Kolhammer was surprised to feel his heart beating faster as they approached the hut. A small cluster of men in dark coats and hats stood in the malarial glow of a yellow lamp at the foot of a set of steps leading up to . . .

President Franklin Delano Roosevelt.

His heart gave a *real* lurch.

And there, standing behind Roosevelt, was the unmistakable figure of Albert Einstein. The unruly explosion of grey-white hair was as recognisable as Elvis in a jumpsuit or Marilyn Monroe standing over a grate with hot air blowing up her white dress. Kolhammer stiffened his back, an impulse that seemed to run through the other flyers at the exact same moment. They finished the last few metres in lockstep and snapped out in perfect unison a salute to the thirty-second President of the United States of America.

Roosevelt found himself in an electric moment. He could feel the charge running through the men around him. Even Einstein seemed to flinch, or shiver. The President sensed powerful currents of antipathy and fear from some of the military officers gathered around his chair. Admiral Ernest J King, in particular, appeared to be struggling with his volcanic temperament. The man's knuckles were white, he'd clenched his fists so tightly. Even Eisenhower seemed incredibly tense.

Roosevelt returned the salute, fumbling with his cigarette holder as he did so.

He saw their commander, Kolhammer, hesitate momentarily as he took in the sight of Eisenhower. He saluted uncertainly. The brigadier returned the gesture after a very obvious pause.

A few seconds of uncomfortable silence enveloped the small tableau, during which the only sound was the faint moan of the desert winds.

Roosevelt realised that he was utterly absorbed by the sight of these men and women, generations removed from his own. They all wore flight suits of some kind and carried rocketeer helmets, probably because they flew so high. About half of them looked to be cut from the same cloth as his own officers – educated, middle-class white men. But there was no avoiding or denying the stone-cold fact that the rest were a lucky dip of sorts. Men and women. Some white. Some black. Some Mexican and even Asiatic. And some? He honestly had no idea. The awe and amazement he'd felt at the sight of their arrival remained. But he was a politician, and in his gut, political instincts were also engaged.

Whatever the military consequences of these people's arrival, the politics were going to be diabolical.

'Well, Admiral Kolhammer,' he said as pleasantly as he could, 'you'd best come in out of the cold.'

The room wasn't set up for a meeting. Kolhammer had been told that Roosevelt and his advisers would be at the Ambassador Hotel in LA. Curiosity must have got the better of them. There were only a handful of chairs and two desks, one of which was missing a leg. A stack of books propped up one corner. There didn't even appear to be a reliable power supply. Three naked bulbs hung from wires, but a single gas lamp was the sole source of light inside the hut.

Actually, that was untrue, he thought as he stepped through the door. At least half of those present, including the President, seemed to be smoking cigarettes. Clouds of smoke drifted from their glowing tips, burning his eyes and throat.

The locals backed away towards the rear of the room as Kolhammer's people surged in quietly, nodding and smiling uncertainly. They took up positions, standing at ease, in the corner to the admiral's left.

'I'm sorry we can't offer more in the way of hospitality, Admiral Kolhammer,' said Roosevelt, 'but I'm afraid that's my fault. I insisted on coming out here to meet you. Couldn't stand to wait in that hotel.'

'It's really not a problem, Mr President.'

Kolhammer wasn't sure what to say next. He'd

expected to have another hour or two to compose something appropriate. He'd also been thrown by the presence of Eisenhower, and had to fight an impulse to address him as *Mr President.* He really hoped he wouldn't have to deal with a young John Kennedy, Richard Nixon or George Bush any time soon.

Before he could blunder into a morass of fatuous small talk, Roosevelt surprised him by saying, 'Please accept my condolences for your losses at Midway, Admiral. I know they weren't as serious as ours, but we don't measure out our grief in teaspoons for the purposes of comparison. I'm sure you don't either.'

'No sir, we do not. And thank you. We lost some fine men and women. As did you . . . or, um . . .'

He was about to clarify that inaccuracy, but Roosevelt waved it away.

'We know what you mean, Admiral. Since you're here, you'd best meet everyone now. General Eisenhower, could you do the introductions? I'm afraid I'm not as familiar with everybody, particularly the scientists, besides Professor Einstein.'

Eisenhower looked stumped for an instant.

Roosevelt grinned wickedly. 'You're not president yet, young man. You still have to work for a living.'

A small but genuine wash of laughter ran through the room.

They must know about Ike, Kolhammer realised. *Word travels fast.*

*

Eisenhower had put together the shortlist of scientists, with the help of Professor Einstein. But he suspected the President had asked him to do the introductions because Roosevelt and one of the scientists, Professor Millikan, loathed each other. Eisenhower had joked to King they needed the rifle squad inside the building to keep the two men apart.

Millikan, the director of the California Polytechnic Institute's physics lab, merely grunted at Kolhammer. He appeared actively hostile to most of the other flyers. Eisenhower knew him to be a bit of a nut on racial issues, so perhaps that had something to do with it. By way of contrast, Theodore von Karman, the top man at Guggenheim Aeronautical Laboratory, and Leo Szilard from Columbia University, had to be dragged away from the flyers. Robert Oppenheimer, Linus Pauling and a relatively young man called Robert Dicke from the Massachusetts Institute of Technology restricted themselves to nods and perfunctory smiles.

'And this is Professor Albert Einstein,' said Eisenhower. 'He's probably done more than anyone here to help us adjust to your arrival.'

All the time travellers reacted as Einstein shuffled forward to shake hands with Kolhammer. They treated him like some kind of big-league-ballplayer or radio star, suddenly crowding around to take his hand or just touch him on the arm or the shoulder. It was odd. One of the flyers produced a thin black briefcase and handed it to Kolhammer.

'We thought you might appreciate this, Professor,' said the admiral. 'It's a computer. It'll help you in your work.'

The physicist thanked him and carefully unzipped the bag. Eisenhower had been told about their electrical books, the flexipads, as they called them. This would have fit the description, except that it seemed to be too large. Perhaps it was a more powerful flexipad.

'It's called a data slate,' said Kolhammer as Einstein turned it over in his hands. 'The sort of calculations that'd take months to do by hand, you can do in a split second on this baby.'

Eisenhower suppressed a smirk. He could see the other scientists eyeing it covetously.

'Does it play movies and music?' asked Einstein. 'I've heard that it does.'

'Do you mind?' Kolhammer asked, taking the slate back and looking enquiringly at both Einstein and Roosevelt. Neither objected.

The admiral brushed a corner of the slate's glass screen and it lit up, throwing out considerably more light than the single gas lamp in the room. Eisenhower could see that most of the illuminated page appeared to be a blank blue rectangle. Half a dozen or so small objects, about the size of postage stamps, were clustered down the right-hand side of the – *what would you call it, the screen? The page*?

Kolhammer brushed one with the tip of his finger and it suddenly whooshed outwards to fill the entire space with a moving picture of people in evening dress. Violinists, he realised as the first sweet notes of a Paganini concerto stole into the room. A murmur arose from the scientists and even from some of the military officers. The recording sounded as real as if they were in the front row of a concert hall.

Kolhammer handed the slate back to Einstein, who was clearly entranced. He nodded and grinned and stroked the glowing glass plate like a blind man, attempting to 'see' through his fingertips. He turned and bent over so that Roosevelt could see the display more clearly. The President took the machine gingerly, handling it like a precious crystal vase.

'It's pretty tough, sir,' said Kolhammer. 'Military-grade construction. You could kick it across the room and it'd be fine.'

Einstein straightened up. He was smiling as though very pleased.

'It is good, *ja*? Not everything in your world is about war making and destructive potential?'

Eisenhower thought he detected something in Kolhammer's response – a fleeting moment of indecision, as though he wasn't quite sure of how to respond. In the end, the man shrugged and smiled with a mixture of warmth and possibly regret.

'No,' said Kolhammer. 'Not everything.'

21

The Eastern Front, May 1942

Eternity was so cold they had piled up the dead to shield themselves.

The wind cut deeply into Brasch's bones on the short run from the trench to the forward observation post, until he wondered whether he would ever stop shivering, although 'shiver' was too mild a word for the spasms that shook him to his core. He shuddered so violently, and with such little hope the convulsions would ever cease, that he began to wonder if he might die from exhaustion.

There was no source of warmth in the filthy dug-out. The three men he found there were wrapped in so many layers of clothing scavenged from fallen comrades and Russian prisoners that they no longer resembled men. They looked like swollen, fuzzy ticks. Brasch tried to speak to them, but his voice stuttered so much he gave up. He had only platitudes to offer anyway. When the next wave came it would sweep them from the face of the earth.

From eternity, as he now thought of it.

Certainly this wretched country stretched out end-lessly. Russia was a hell of frozen, never-ending space and enemies without number. Thousands of them lay in the darkness just beyond this hole.

They had stacked up a dozen or more of the most pliable bodies in the vain hope that they would offer protection against the howling wind that roared across the plain and knifed through every layer of rotting, fetid cloth. One of the Russian corpses with which they had constructed their windbreak had frozen with an arm protruding. Somebody had hacked it off with a spade, and the sharp bone stump dug into Brasch's neck, forcing him to shift into a more exposed position.

He couldn't see the faces of the men who huddled there with him and he didn't know their names. This wasn't his unit. He'd been separated from the Engineers for three weeks. They were eight hundred miles away, but it hardly mattered. He now fought with a battalion of Panzergrenadiers and didn't think he would ever see his comrades again. He had come forward to encourage these men in their vigilance, but was reduced instead to curling in a small ball and trying not to moan.

Brasch knew that far in the rear, across an impenetrable sea of snap-frozen mud, lay mountains of provisions and arctic weather gear that would never reach them. He knew because he had helped build the great depots himself and seen them fill up with thousands of hooded lamb's-wool jackets and mountains of thick blankets, with exquisitely warm insulated boots and soft cat-skin gloves. He knew there were half a million sturdy kerosene heaters still packed away in boxes – just one of which might have made habitable this dismal sinkhole in which they suffered.

Instead they were forced to piss on their cracked and blistered hands, the only way they had of even briefly warming and cauterising fissures and scabs filled with infected, frozen pus. Their wounds made it almost impossible to hold a Mauser, let alone fire one.

One of the men in the hole – Brasch thought somebody had called him Franz – began to sob. Nobody moved to comfort him. Every breath produced a rattling sound from deep within his chest, and sometimes an explosive burst of coughing that sprayed them with mucus.

The boy's wailing and coughing increased. '*Mutti, Mutti* . . .' he cried incessantly.

Brasch painfully levered himself up to peer over the rim of hardened bodies.

'Look alive, my friends,' he croaked. 'Ivan will be joining us for breakfast soon. Check your communications lines.'

A white-haired sergeant picked up the handset and raised it near his ear. The Feldwebel did not press the instrument there, though, lest it stick to his flesh in the cold.

'Lines are fine,' he grunted.

The dawn was near enough now that Brasch could see steam pluming from his mouth. The dense forest of arms and legs once more resolved itself into an open field littered with innumerable corpses. The shell holes were now visible too. Thousands of them, curiously delicate if viewed with some detachment, against the vast canvas of the snow-covered steppe. Somebody had once pointed out to him how much they resembled flowers – the dark brown centres of scorched earth, a sallow tinge around the mouth of the oldest holes, red blooms of bloody snow marking the newest. Having been alerted to such a perverse notion, he was never able to shake it.

Brasch was gathering his strength, trying to shake off the lassitude that threatened to overwhelm him, when the vague horizon that blurred between white ground and grey sky was unexpectedly thrown into sharp definition. A solid black line appeared, extending as far as he could see. His balls had just started to climb into his body when the Soviet war cry reached him.

Ooooouuuuurrraaaahhhhh . . .

Brasch wrenched the phone from the claws of the white-haired sergeant and began cranking the handle to generate a charge. When a small, impossibly distant voice answered, he screamed into the mouthpiece, demanding artillery support. The connection was poor, and the line crackled and hissed with static so that he began to suspect they could not even hear him on the other end. That faraway, tinny, nearly nonhuman voice repeated the same senseless mantra, again and again.

'*Wo sind Sie? Wo sind Sie? Was ist los? Wo sind Sie?*'

Brasch called out his identity and demanded an artillery barrage.

'*Wo sind Sie? Wo sind Sie?*'

The boy screamed for his mother, reminding Brasch for one insane moment of his own son Manfred, just turned four years old. The soldier's grief and rage sounded just like Manny when, as a toddler, he ran into the sharp corner of a table, splitting open his head.

'*MUTTI! MUTTI! NEIN NEIN NEIN!*'

The sergeant and the last man, a displaced driver from a transport company, wrestled frantically with the Spandau, attempting to thread a new belt of cartridges with stiff, shaking hands. The black line on the horizon grew thicker as more and more communists poured over the gentle rise.

'God, there are millions of them,' cried the Feldwebel, his voice cracking with terror. 'We must go, Major, we have to run *now*, before they get here.'

Ooooouuuuurrraaaahhhhh . . .

'We need artillery,' Brasch shouted stubbornly as he leaned over to place a firm hand on the shoulder of the truck driver, who was quite obviously seconds from fleeing the post. The man's trembling hands still fumbled with the ammunition belt. He bounced up and down at the knees, and his head snapped back and forth between the awful spectacle of the approaching human wave and the beckoning safety of the tree line, some three hundred yards behind them. A low keening sound, like an animal that knows it is being led to slaughter, emanated from deep within him.

'Fire!' ordered Brasch, pointing at the Soviets, who rushed on like a surging black tide. The machine-gun crew began to fire, the harsh industrial hammering coming in short bursts that did nothing to halt the advancing horde. They must have killed a hundred men in less than ten seconds, but Brasch would swear another hundred thousand simply trampled down the corpses.

'*Where is the artillery?*' he roared into the phone.

'*Was ist los? Wo sind Sie?*'

Ooooouuuuurrraaaahhhhh . . .

'*M-m-m-m-mutti* . . .'

A single shot rang out, sounding flat and insignificant beneath the rising din of the Soviet charge and the snarl of the heavy machine-gun. It was so close that Brasch jumped, not realising for an instant that a warm shower of gore had just sprayed him. Then the boy soldier was dead, his body twitching spastically as the nervous system fired its last mad messages. One side of his head was missing, blown off by the pistol he had placed within his mouth and triggered when his mother had been unable to chase away the monsters rushing at him, as she had once shooed off the gremlins that hid beneath his bed.

OOOOOOOOOOOOOOUUUUURRRAAAA-AAAHHHHH . . .

The Spandau lashed at the black tide. The boy

stopped twitching. Brasch spoke calmly into the phone again, like a man enquiring at the butcher shop after his weekly bratwurst order.

'Where is my artillery?'

'*Was ist los?*'

He replaced the receiver.

The flood of berserkers began to slow, impeded by fresh snow, the thickness of their clothes, stiff muscles and the littered corpses of their countrymen – but the advance remained unstoppable. Half the eternal steppe seemed filled with them and still they poured over the horizon.

Brasch was so far beyond terror that he placidly took out his Luger, stood up in the dugout, placed one boot on the rock-hard cadaver of a Russian corporal and commenced firing, slowly and meticulously, even though the Soviets were still well beyond the effective range of any side-arm. He wished he had a cigarette to smoke. The white-haired sergeant begged him piteously for permission to retreat, but Brasch ignored him. *What's the point?* he asked himself. *You can die here, or a few yards from here.*

The thunder of the charge hid the first rumble of the German guns so that Brasch didn't realise an artillery barrage was on its way until the first shells shrieked overhead, to explode in the centre of the Russian mass half a second later. Enormous fountains of fire and ice and hateful Russian soil erupted just behind the leading edge of the attack, silhouetting the front ranks against a curtain of flames. They rushed on regardless, as smaller detonations started to thin out their ranks.

'Mortars,' said Brasch with a detached air.

The machine-gunners weren't listening. They screamed at the Soviets, pouring a constant stream of fire into the maelstrom.

'You'll melt the barrel,' said Brasch, whose wits were returning. He hopped down from his exposed perch and holstered his pistol. A frightful din, the thunder of a world riven in two, shook the frozen mud beneath their feet, as the big guns walked their barrage back through the densely packed Russians. He could no longer see any of the attackers inside the wild conflagration. He wondered how many had just died. Fifty thousand? A quarter of a million?

Then it was time to leave. The attack had been broken, but a few hundred crazed survivors might yet emerge from the killing field and overrun their little outpost.

'Let's go,' he said to the old sergeant, turning back to the carnage.

But some new horror paralysed the man. His jaw hung slack and his eyes bulged. The lorry driver simply howled and ran like a dog, stumbling over the corpse of the dead boy.

Twisting slowly back towards the open steppe, so slowly that it seemed as if he were forever turning, Brasch stared into the abyss. A million Russians appeared from within the boiling shroud of black smoke and blasts of flashing light.

OOOOOOOOOOooooouuuuurrraAAAaaahhhhh . . .

'Manfred,' whispered Brasch as the barbarian horde came upon them.

A single man, a Siberian or a Mongol by his features, accelerated from the foremost rank, heading straight for their dugout. He launched himself into the air, clearing the windbreak of dead communists, slamming into Brasch, his hands closing around the engineer's neck, his teeth finding purchase in the unshaven bristles of his throat.

KRI Sutanto, *Hashirajima Anchorage, 0438 Hours, 6 June 1942*

'Herr Major, Herr Major, wake up sir, wake up. You are disturbing the others.'

The Siberian's rough, choking grasp became a lighter, more considerate touch, shaking his shoulders, dragging him up out of the nightmare that had haunted him for weeks.

'Willie?' Brasch was disoriented. His heart still raced, almost as it had that day outside Belgorod. 'Willie, is that you?'

'No, sir. It is I, Herr Steckel. From the embassy.'

Brasch came upright and instantly a sharp, nearly blinding pain bit into his scalp. He cursed.

'Careful, sir, there's not much headroom in here.'

Brasch rubbed his head and blinked the crust of sleep from his eyes. The first thing he noticed, as always, was the warmth. He'd never expected to be warm again. Then he became conscious of his freedom of movement. He wore only a light vest and undershorts. Finally, he remembered. He was no longer at the Eastern Front. He was in the Far East, on the ship of wonders. A rush of half-formed thoughts and feelings blew through his sleep-disordered mind. Dominating them all, however, was a profound blankness and disbelief in the simple fact that he was still alive. He had numbered himself among the dead for so long, he felt ill at ease to be amongst the living once more.

'I am sorry, Herr Steckel. Please excuse me,' he rasped. 'My throat is dry. Some water, if you have it.'

Steckel passed across a glass of chilled water. They had been through this ritual every night since the engineer's arrival. At first the diplomat had been awed and humbled just to draw breath in the same room as the legend of Belgorod. But two weeks of tending to this shattered husk of a man had drained him of any such respect.

Brasch finished the drink in one long pull and eased himself out of the bunk. His vision was too blurred to read his watch, so he asked Steckel for the time.

'0438, Herr Major, as usual.'

Is that a hint of peevishness I detect in his voice? Brasch wondered idly. *Well, damn him anyway.* Brasch pointed to the chair where his pants and yesterday's shirt hung. The attaché fetched them without uttering a word.

'Find me some breakfast, Steckel. Some real breakfast, with sausages, and none of their damned rice. I'm sick of it. We might as well get working on this puzzle box again, eh?'

'Yes, Herr Major, right away, I have already seen to it.'

'And coffee?'

'Right here, sir.'

Brasch gratefully accepted the mug. Perhaps Steckel wasn't such an odious fellow after all.

'Is Captain Kruger with us yet, Steckel?'

'Still asleep, Herr Major. He turned in only three hours ago.'

Brasch thought he detected a trace of censure in the man's voice. He seemed to think Brasch should be working twenty-five hours a day. He had no idea what it cost the engineer to get out of bed at all.

'What about Commander Hidaka?' he asked. 'I'll bet he's awake.'

'Yes, sir. I don't believe I have seen him off duty yet. But then, I'm not here as much as you.'

'That's right,' said Brasch. 'You're not. Come on. Let us join the other master race, shall we?'

Steckel, who was uncomfortable with Brasch's less than reverent tone when discussing matters of genetic purity, covered his disquiet by retreating into form.

'But you have not shaved, Herr Major!'

Brasch stopped exactly where he stood, with

one foot half in his boot. He stared at Steckel for some time before breaking out in a loud, raucous laugh.

'Herr Major?'

Brasch shook his head.

'It does not matter, Herr Steckel. Believe me.'

The *Sutanto* lay at anchor in a secluded section of the moorage off Hashirajima Island, blocked from view by a screen of light cruisers and surrounded by three lines of torpedo nets. A squadron of Zero fighters circled perpetually high above. Admiral Yamamoto had decreed there was never to be a second when the precious ship lacked air cover. There would be no Doolittle raids over Hashirajima.

No deck lights burned on the Indonesian vessel, and blackout curtains had been draped across all her openings, allowing work to continue twenty-four hours a day. Contrary to rumour, Lieutenant Commander Jisaku Hidaka was not awake for every one of those hours, but he did drive himself for as long as humanly possible each day. Like Steckel, he made it clear he found Brasch's apparent lack of commitment perplexing, and occasionally disturbing.

'Good morning, Commander,' Brasch said in nearly flawless Japanese.

Hidaka looked up from the computer screen and returned Brasch's greeting in his own faltering German. 'Guten Morgen,' was about all he could muster. Brasch's English was also better than

Hidaka's, but there were occasions when they used it to confer, nonetheless. Neither man really trusted Steckel. When he was within earshot, they spoke in the enemy's tongue, of which he had no knowledge.

'And what do you have for us today, Commander Hidaka?'

The Japanese, he found, tended towards a scattergun approach, skipping from one fantastic discovery to the next as they swarmed over the ship. Brasch, on the other hand, had spent most of his time patiently arguing in favour of a more systematic method: choose a category of investigation – such as the offensive missile system – draw up a template to guide the research, and move methodically through each stage of the study.

He had also prevailed upon them to exploit the Indonesians, Lieutenant Moertopo and his men. Yamamoto had been detaining them in heavily guarded luxury on the island. But the admiral was disinclined to let them anywhere near their controls again – especially since the vessel now lay at the very heart of Japan's naval power. Word was that Yamamoto lay awake at night, fearful lest half his fleet be disintegrated beneath a brace of doomsday rockets. Even the cavalier Hidaka had to agree with that.

Still Brasch had argued, finally appealing directly to the admiral himself.

'Those men are cowed,' he insisted. 'They are as pliable as sheep. They feel abandoned by the

Americans, and remain unbalanced by their presence here.'

'So you would have unbalanced men sit in the midst of my fleet, controlling weapons of a power we can hardly imagine?' asked Yamamoto.

'Yes,' asserted Brasch, 'if you would have me come to understand those weapons. We could stumble along for years trying to figure out how even the simplest devices work. Or we could just *ask* them. If they cooperate, we reward them. If not, we force them.'

Yamamoto finally relented when Brasch explained that the sensors on the *Sutanto* gave him reason to suspect they could not keep the Indonesian vessel a secret for much longer. Moertopo had already explained that the other ships in this Kolhammer's task force were larger and even more capable. Their devices would surely sniff out the truth before long.

'And then, Admiral Yamamoto, you can expect to lose a great many ships just outside your window, to *their* doomsday rockets.'

Yamamoto had surrendered to the argument.

For his part, Brasch alternated between sincere fascination at the wonder of the ships and the blank flatness that had come upon him in Russia. In his most lucid moments he understood that he was sick, afflicted by a paralysis of both mind and soul. Depending on his mood, he might be reduced to tears by a letter from his wife and son, or so unmoved that he couldn't be bothered opening the envelope.

He occasionally wondered why the army had sent him here. A mix of reasons, he presumed. His Japanese was fluent, thanks to many childhood years spent travelling the Orient with his parents. Father was a diplomat, just like Steckel. Or maybe not so much like Steckel. His father's career had eventually stalled under the Nazis.

And Brasch's engineering skills, as even Hidaka acknowledged, were exceptional. But he knew there was more to it. They had tried to make him a hero after Belgorod. His insanity in standing atop the pile of Russian dead, to calmly empty his pistol into a Soviet horde, was an exact fit with the Führer's 'stand fast' principle. He had even met Goebbels when they brought him home to show off this fine example of Aryan manhood.

Unfortunately his shattered nerves hadn't equipped him for the public role of superman, and after two instances of ill temper and a breakdown in a radio recording studio, his schedule of appearances had been cancelled.

A small article in the *Völkischer Beobachter* announced that he had been dispatched overseas on an important mission for the Führer, but that was before the mystery ships had even arrived. The bizarre communiqués from Tokyo had simply provided an excuse to be rid of him for even longer. He suspected the high command thought this whole adventure was an absurdity dreamed up by the Japanese to explain the abortive end to their Midway invasion.

The reality had reduced him to helpless laughter more than once, further convincing Herr Steckel of his mental frailty.

He rarely worried about the report he would have to make, and soon. He knew Steckel had already been sending inflammatory messages. For Brasch, who had walked in the land of the dead for so long, the *Sutanto* presented an intriguing puzzle that diverted him from the unbearable burden of living.

HIJMS Yamato, *Hashirajima anchorage, 0824 hours, 6 June 1942*

Admiral Isoroku Yamamoto flexed his injured left hand. He had lost two fingers many years ago in battle at Tsushima, and he was troubled every now and then by phantom pain in the missing digits. The discomfort was so much a part of him that he did not attend to it with his conscious mind. *That* was beset by a multitude of problems arising from the events of 3 June.

A cursed miracle was the only way to describe it, an inexplicable event that smashed the American fleet at the same time as it delivered untold power into their hands. It still felt to him as though the whole world had been tipped off its axis and now wobbled precariously, threatening to spin completely out of control.

As for the Indonesian vessel, the technical aspects

of their amazing find were in some ways the least challenging. Given enough time, engineers like Brasch would unlock every secret contained within that ship. No, it was the *historical* ramifications that would prove the most challenging, the most dangerous. Who was to tell the Emperor how this conflict was destined to end? And who would tell Hitler of his ordained fate, dead by his own hand three years from now, his body burned beyond recognition to keep it from the communists who would enslave half the Reich?

Well, Brasch would have *that* unhappy task, he supposed. Yamamoto did not envy him. It was undoubtedly a death sentence.

Yamamoto peered out the porthole at the farms that climbed the sides of nearly every hilly little island dotted throughout this part of the Inland Sea. Atop each hill sat batteries of antiaircraft guns hidden beneath thick camouflage netting. Anchored all about lay nearly one hundred and fifty ships of the Imperial fleet.

The admiral quickly abandoned the small glimpse of the outside world, returning to his desk, which was buried under thousands of pages of paper: reports from the team examining the *Sutanto*. Most were technical updates, the latest explanations of some astounding new technology. Set to one side, however, was a pile of documents Yamamoto found even more disturbing than the report about the superbombs. This smaller set of papers represented the findings of his intelligence officers who had been assigned to trawl the ship's so-called 'electronic files' for historical information.

Therein lay a description of his own death, shot down by American fighter planes over New Guinea. That was a macabre curiosity, but in fact of no great concern to the admiral. Not when measured against the larger picture that had emerged of the course this conflict was supposed to take, and still would, in his opinion. Every misgiving he had ever expressed – about the folly of warring with both the United States and the British Empire – had come to pass.

Or would come to pass.

From the top of the pile he plucked the time line he had ordered drawn up. He could see that in less than a fortnight Tobruk would fall to Rommel, but his advance would peter out at Alamein within a month, and vast tonnages of American firepower would begin to crush the life out of the Afrika Korps. On the Fourth of July, the very first US Army Air Force operations over Europe would commence with attacks on Dutch airfields being used by the Luftwaffe. Soon enough the skies over Europe would be full of Yankee bombers and fighters.

At the end of July, Japan was supposed to advance on Port Moresby in New Guinea. He had seen the plans himself. But that would mark the furthest expansion of the empire. Australian troops would soon hand the army their first defeat on land.

On 9 August, Vice Admiral Mikawa was to destroy an Allied cruiser squadron at Savo Island. But that could not happen now, because the Allies must surely know of it. And, of course, some of the American ships fated to perish there had already been destroyed.

It was confounding in the extreme to try to untangle these knotted threads of fate and circumstance. But one thing was becoming clear: the trend of events could not be allowed to proceed on their appointed course. Unless he was able to conceive of some master stroke, unless the Axis high command could be convinced to abandon their strategic follies, all was lost.

Yamamoto's stomach burned with acid as he reread the most unsettling dossier of all: an incomplete but deeply troubling account of China's rise to power under a communist regime, and the long, dark shadow that cast over a declining Nippon in the next century. Even if they laid down their arms and begged the Allies for mercy this morning, annihilation at the hands of the Mongols seemed inevitable.

No. Yamamoto could not let that come to pass.

He picked up his stateroom phone.

'Get Hidaka and Brasch, and that Moertopo creature. Bring them over here at once.'

Lieutenant Moertopo was rather put out at being hauled off the geisha girl and forced into his pants. Apart from the few hours a day when Hidaka demanded his presence to explain some worthless piece of equipment, Moertopo had spent most of his de facto captivity luxuriating atop a series of pliant Japanese whores.

At first his new friends had sent him a lot of painted ice maidens who seemed interested in little more than calligraphy and flower arrangement. It wasn't long before the Japanese realised that Moertopo's appetites ran to a less refined sort of female company. Since then he'd hardly had his pants on, which went a great way towards reconciling him to the entire situation. Most of his men felt the same way. Given a choice between fighting homicidal jihadis, being imprisoned by the Japs, or plunging into some giggling trollop, who wouldn't choose the latter?

The pleasant haze of sex and sake abruptly deserted him when his 'bodyguard' reported that a personal appointment with Yamamoto was in the offing. Moertopo possessed enough rat cunning to know that any variation in routine was threatening. And no matter what angle you came at it, swapping a happy prostitute for an irritated admiral was never going to rate as the first step up the happy staircase to paradise.

So fear rendered him quite sober as he waited outside Yamamoto's stateroom.

Hidaka soon arrived with the German, Major Brasch, in tow. Brasch didn't look like a Hollywood Nazi at all. To Moertopo he looked more like a farmer with a drinking problem. They exchanged a greeting in English, their one common language, after which an aide led them into Yamamoto's presence.

Inside Hidaka bowed deeply and Moertopo saluted as crisply as he could. Brasch saluted but without much vigour or sincerity. Yamamoto seemed to ignore the insult.

The Japanese admiral also spoke in English.

'Lieutenant Moertopo, I hope our hospitality has not strained you greatly.'

Moertopo was never quite sure where he stood with these fascists, but he took the ribald grins of Yamamoto and Hidaka as a sign of good humour.

'I fear Miss Okuni's hospitality will soon put me in hospital,' he replied.

'Excellent, excellent. Now, please sit down, gentlemen. If only we had more time for such affairs, yes? But time itself weighs on my thinking. Major, how goes your work? Will you soon be finished?'

'No,' said Brasch. 'Even with the help of Lieutenant Moertopo's men, there is an impossible amount of information to synthesise. It's not just the workings of a particular technology I am confounded by, but the principles that gave rise to it, and the context in which it should be employed. And the production methods used to fabricate its components, and imagining the industrial base that employs those methods, and the precursor technology that evolved into that base. I'm trying to make intuitive leaps backwards, if you will. It's like an archaeologist excavating the future.'

If Brasch expected Yamamoto to be angered by the response, the great bull-necked warrior disappointed him by merely nodding. 'And you, Hidaka, what say you?'

Hidaka glanced at Brasch, frustration written across his face. It was always like this with the German. He seemed more taken with the puzzle than the answers.

'Moertopo has been of some use in helping us understand the rocket technology,' he said. 'He tells me the missile batteries of his ship are not nearly so powerful as those of the Americans he came with, but still they offer great advantage if used wisely. And radar, which we had dismissed as an irrelevance, is found here developed to an unbelievable degree. Radar-controlled gunfire potentially guarantees a direct hit with every shell fired. You can imagine the implications for the side possessing supremacy in this area alone.'

'But can *we* build radar like this?'

'No,' answered Brasch before Hidaka could reply. He held up a flexipad that he had taken as his own. 'These machines they all carry, we know of their capabilities now. But even the casing on such a machine is beyond the current limits of our production facilities. You are looking at eighty years' worth of developments in materials science, just for the shell that contains this device.

'Correct me if I am wrong, Moertopo, but the strange rubbery material of this electrical information block –'

'A flexipad, Major.'

'A flexipad, yes. The casing itself is integral to the unit, because it helps power the machine, correct?'

'Exactly,' he said. 'It's made of solarskin plastic, which draws power from the light in this room. The warmth of your hands provides a power source too.'

'Right,' said Brasch, a hint of actual enthusiasm creeping into his voice. 'But to fabricate such a thing, you'd have to factor in advances across a whole range of areas.' He turned back to Yamamoto. 'The thinking machines used in the design of this pad, and which control most of the machinery on the *Sutanto*, use what Moertopo calls "quantum processors", and they rest upon multiple generations of antecedent technology. Would I be right in assuming, Lieutenant, that using an abacus to design a quantum processor would prove impossible?'

'You would.'

'With twenty years' work, I suppose we might just leapfrog our current industrial base up to speed, but –'

'But there are many more pressing problems,' Yamamoto agreed. 'These processors, Moertopo,' mused the admiral, 'they're like electrical calculating machines?'

'Much more than that, sir,' interrupted Hidaka. 'They are almost like brains. In fact, the Americans who arrived with Moertopo call their computing machines Combat Intelligences, and allow them to make significant decisions.'

'And it was they who decided to annihilate Spruance's fleet?' Yamamoto asked.

'I imagine they detected a threat and reacted, because their human controllers could not,' Moertopo said before hurrying on to add, 'The *Sutanto* is not equipped with a CI system.'

'Luckily for Kakuta,' said the admiral.

'And we were not fired on,' said Moertopo. 'Unlike Kolhammer's force.'

'Tell me, Lieutenant, what sort of a man allows a machine to make his decisions for him, especially such a fundamental choice as when to flee and when to strike?'

Moertopo struggled to answer. He didn't know whether Yamamoto was speaking philosophically or demanding a hard answer. When it became evident he was out of his depth, Brasch grasped the opportunity to interpose himself.

'If I may, Admiral Yamamoto, this is the crux of our dilemma. *What sort of men could do such a thing?* you ask. Whereas I say, what sort of world produced them? What paths led them to their destiny? Moertopo tells us, and the library files on the *Sutanto* confirm, that the Allied force that arrived here represents a pinnacle of military technology. What we must ask and answer quickly is – how did this come about?

'I would say the question is even more important

than determining how they arrived. That they are here is an established fact. How they will change events is not.'

'I think I understand your point, Major. You are less concerned with artefacts such as rockets than with historical potential. Does the Axis have the potential to prevail in this conflict?'

'Until now, I would have said no.'

'And I would have agreed with you,' said Yamamoto, raising his hand to forestall any protest from Hidaka.

'Even now,' continued Brasch, 'with everything in flux, the advantage lies with the Allies because of the manpower and vast productive potential of the English-speaking world. True, we have both benefited from a windfall, but they – like us – have received a finite gift. Missiles, once fired, can never be fired again. On the other hand, the *knowledge* of those missiles cannot now be withdrawn.'

'Which means *what*?' Hidaka demanded. 'That we are to be destroyed more efficiently by American factory workers? You contradict yourself, Major Brasch. You just said that we couldn't hope to produce these super-weapons for many years. If we cannot, neither can they.'

'Indeed,' said Yamamoto, 'but the issue may not have been decided. Moertopo, from your understanding, did this Kolhammer command a force capable of deciding a war against the combined resources of the entire Axis?'

Ali Moertopo felt the full weight of expectation fall on him. His first instinct was to dissemble, but a finely honed sense of self-preservation suggested that honesty was in fact called for. None of these men was a fool. With time to study the files on his vessel they could find their own answers. But if Yamamoto came to value his opinion, he could trade on it.

Nevertheless, the gilded cage didn't fool him. His life still hung in the balance.

'If his battle group had survived the journey here intact, they would sweep you from the oceans in a day,' he said. 'Without satellite coverage, it might take a short while to fix the position of your fleets, but once found they would be sunk to the last ship without the loss of a single American life. However, as I understand it, his carrier has been crippled and grave damage was inflicted on the rest of the task force.'

He didn't add, *Or I wouldn't be here.*

Yamamoto leaned back in his chair and regarded the Indonesian like a cat considering a feathered breakfast. 'You base this on the signals you intercepted when Kolhammer arrived?'

'There was a lot of traffic.'

Yamamoto barely moved his head as he grunted noncommittally.

'How long before they are repaired?'

The query was directed at Moertopo, but Brasch smiled. 'If I may,' he said. 'Here we find the Allies entrapped by the same problems that face us. Am I right to assume, Lieutenant, that a ship as large and complex as the *Clinton* – is that her name? – will spend a good deal of her life in a very specialised docking facility undergoing maintenance and refit?'

'I think about one year out of three would be right,' guessed Moertopo.

'But of course, those facilities did not come with you, did they?'

'No, of course not.'

'So you see, Admiral, already the spectre of this supership begins to recede. They will be able to manage some repairs from the stocks they carry with them, but I suspect they will be severely restricted in what they can achieve. Moertopo, quickly, those fighter-bombers they carried, what did you call them?'

'Raptors.'

'Yes, thank you. Can you build a Raptor from scrap metal in the hold of a ship like the *Clinton*? No. I thought not. So the planes they lost in the flight deck explosion, they are gone forever.'

Yamamoto appreciated Brasch's line of reasoning. It paralleled his own. However, he didn't want to rush headlong into any decision. That sort of precipitate action would lead to annihilation – as history would confirm. So he gave Brasch no sign of encouragement, choosing instead to play devil's advocate.

'But with the missiles these ships carry, they could still cripple us before we even knew we had been targeted.'

'Indeed they could,' said Brasch. 'We must ascertain how many they retain, in order to fashion a worst-case scenario.'

Hidaka had held his patience while the discussion circled around, but now he jumped at an opening.

'If these ships are such a mortal threat, we have no choice but to strike at them as we struck at the American carriers in Pearl Harbor.'

'And look how well that worked out,' smirked Brasch.

Moertopo thought Hidaka's head might pop right off, so deeply did he colour at the remark.

'You insult the man who devised that master stroke!' he spat.

Yamamoto lifted his shoulders and grimaced slightly. 'Do not draw your blade on my account, Commander. I am more than capable of defending my honour. The major has a point. If that operation had been successful, we would not have troubled ourselves over a battle at Midway. We failed to achieve the killing blow at Hawaii. We should have pressed the issue on the day and driven the Americans from the islands entirely. Just as the Führer, Major Brasch, should not have turned his back on the United Kingdom in order to pursue a political crusade in Russia. Right there, in the opening moments of this war, we both lost our way.'

Brasch simply nodded, crossed his arms and said, 'It was madness.'

Hidaka sneered, 'You would not be so free with your opinions if Herr Steckel were present.'

Brasch favoured the Japanese naval officer with his most frigid stare.

'You may have judged Steckel well,' he said softly, 'but you do not know me at all.'

Moertopo, who sat between the men and had been trying to render himself invisible, tensed, expecting to be caught between two flailing madmen. The thought made him long for home and the joys of pirated satellite TV, fast food and freedom of a sort.

'Gentlemen,' said Yamamoto, 'do not waste your considerable energies on each other. We have common foes, perhaps closer than we realise. Commander Hidaka, Major Brasch, I need the technical analysis to continue. Your Captain Kruger can oversee that process, Major. I want you two, however, to concentrate on historical material pertaining to this war. Lieutenant Moertopo, I am led to believe that a wealth of such material remains within your electronic library.'

'Yes, yes of course.'

'Good, then,' Yamamoto declared. 'Waste no more time. I will see you in four days, when you will explain to me and me alone exactly what would have gone wrong for us in this war, and how you think we might avoid those mistakes. I may or may not heed your advice, but nevertheless, I expect you to give a full report. Spare nobody in your censure. Not me, not the cabinet, and not even the Führer himself, Herr Major. That is why you shall report to nobody but me. I expect that if you perform this task properly, it could cost you your lives. I shall try to see to it that doesn't happen.'

Yamamoto grinned wickedly at that. Brasch seemed to appreciate the joke more than Hidaka. Moertopo didn't find it funny in the least.

'Yet, there is the matter of my shadow,' said Brasch. 'Herr Steckel is a true believer, convinced of the Führer's infallibility. He will not appreciate this new line of inquiry.'

'We shall see,' replied Yamamoto.

22

USS Hillary Clinton, *Pearl Harbor, 1021 hours, 9 June 1942*

Ensign Curtis had a new job. He was no longer just the assistant bookkeeper on the *Enterprise*; he and Lieutenant Commander Black had been assigned to the *Clinton* to undergo 'familiarisation', learning the basics of operating with the Multinational Force. Having done so, they would train their colleagues on the *Enterprise*. The idea of Wally Curtis having anything to teach some of those old salts back on the Big E was enough to keep him awake at night. They were going to eat him alive. He was just sure of it.

But then, Admiral Spruance had personally told him that his quick thinking at Midway had singled him out as a young man who could adapt to change under pressure, and that was something they were all going to have to work on. And he did have Commander Black along to look after him.

Curtis had nearly choked on his pride when he wrote to his mom and dad to tell them. Of course, he couldn't send the letter yet. The censors weren't letting anything out about the arrival of the Multinational Force. They were the talk of Hawaii. Every bar, every shop, every warehouse and factory, every home and office was abuzz with excited – and occasionally hysterical – talk, rumour and argument about the people from the future. But not a single story had been printed in the local press. It was an invisible sensation. And Curtis was right in the middle of it.

He spent most of his time here, in the media centre – except that it wasn't called that any more. The journalists had mostly been confined to their quarters. It was the research centre now, and Ensign Wally Curtis was one of the first researchers. He was currently learning about helicopters.

It was a dream posting, like being sent on a spaceship, only better. Buck Rogers didn't have a fraction of the stuff these guys took for granted.

Unfortunately Curtis wasn't allowed to use the computers without supervision, not yet, and Lieutenant Thieu was nowhere to be found, so he occupied his time reading conventional books and journals. Some of it was great, but some . . .

'Would you like to have a go on my computer, Ensign Curtis?' Rosanna Natoli asked.

She'd appeared from nowhere.

Curtis was used to that. The reporter and her friend, Miss Duffy, were frequent visitors to the research centre. Unlike some of the other journalists, they'd agreed to help out. They told him they were writing a paper to explain the Transition.

Here and there around the room other sailors

and one or two civilians sat quietly at workstations, tapping keys, scribbling notes. Curtis would have liked to ask them for some help, but truth be known, he was a little frightened of approaching them. They all seemed sort of fierce to him. Even more so than the old salts.

'I'd love a turn on your computer, Miss Natoli!' he said with real relief.

'C'mon then, Ensign. Let's take her out for a spin.'

Curtis fairly leaped out of his chair to follow Rosanna over to her workstation. As they went, she handed him her personal flexipad.

'The big computer is more powerful, but of course I can't carry it around with me,' she said. 'When I insert the flexipad into the drive slot, however, this baby reformats itself into my personal workstation. So now I've got the nice big screen, the keyboard and faster access to the net. Or I would have, if we had the net. We're making do with whatever the *Clinton* had cached. Still with me?'

'Not really,' Wally said, pulling up a chair.

'Don't sweat it. You're a smart kid. You'll pick it up quickly. Where'd you say you were from? Chicago, right? Okay. Type that in.'

Wally was actually quite an accomplished typist. He'd taken lessons at his mother's insistence. But the combination of the very busy screen in front of him and the strangely shaped keyboard beneath his wrists proved so unsettling that he retreated into a slow, two-fingered hunt-and-peck style.

'Jesus, kid, you're gonna have to speed it up if you want a job at the *Trib.* Okay, click the mouse . . . this thing here.'

The picture on the big screen changed instantly. While Wally squinted at the flood of information, Natoli explained that Fleetnet had more than four thousand CNN references to Chicago stored in its lattice memory. Beginning to get the picture, Curtis stared in awe.

'All right,' Natoli said. 'A big cheer for the Windy City. Now, let's refine the search. Whereabouts you from in Chicago?'

While Rosanna played nursemaid to the ensign, at the other end of the room Julia Duffy was just beginning to feel the need for another chill pill. She'd been chewing through her supply of Prozac like fucking M&Ms ever since they'd arrived. As she listened to Lieutenant Commander Black describe the raid on Pearl Harbor, she began to feel again as if the floor of the world was dropping out from beneath her feet. *Like, here's this guy, completely sane, kinda cute even, and he's talking about something happened way back in the last century – as though it was just yesterday*, she mused, hoping it didn't show on her face.

'You all right, Miss Duffy?' Black asked.

Julia placed her coffee cup on the table and saw that her hand was shaking.

She didn't know whether it had been such a good idea after all, agreeing to help Kolhammer out by writing this layman's account of the Transition. The more she looked into it, the more obvious it became that they were trapped here. Without the *Nagoya*, which everyone agreed had been destroyed, they were fucked. You just don't build a time machine out of box tops and vacuum tubes, which was roughly the level of technology available in 1940s America.

Then again, she didn't feel like being confined to quarters like the other reporters – about half of them – who hadn't signed up for the programme.

'I'm sorry,' she said. 'It just hits me sometimes. That we're really here. Our whole world has gone.'

Dan Black cracked his knuckles, a sound like small rocks breaking. He could see that the reporter was growing gloomy. He didn't know what to say, but felt as if he had to try to cheer her up.

Truth to tell, he liked her. She was odd but intriguing. And pretty as all get-out, of course. She was interested in him as well. He knew that much. Black had been with a few women in his time, but it had never worked out for the long run. He wasn't sure why, but he had a feeling, half formed and little understood, that he lost interest in them when they began to lose themselves in the courtship. He shook his head. That sounded screwy. He went back to copping a look at the reporter's legs. She'd caught him once, but didn't seem to mind.

'Anyhow,' he said, 'Ensign Curtis doesn't think it works that way.'

'What way?'

'That your coming here affects what happens in your own time. It's still there, where you left it. He's been reading things on those computers, reckons you might have made a whole new world of time by coming here, or something like that. I don't know. I'm just a copper miner, and, lady, I'm all at sea.'

She brightened a little at the weak joke.

'I think you've got more to you than that, Dan. You're not just the sum of what you've done, you know. There's what you can be, as well. That's just as important.'

'Guess I won't argue with that,' he said, taking a pull at his cold coffee. 'Fact is, I haven't worked a mine in nearly twelve years. The Depression killed my daddy's business. Damn near killed him, too. I had to hit the road, look for work. My parents, they couldn't afford to have me in the house. I eat too much.'

'But you still call yourself a copper miner, even though you've been in the navy how long?'

'Eight years,' he confessed. 'I only got in because of my pilot's training. I did some crop-dusting in '31. Then that dried up. I scratched around, did some roadwork under the Roosevelt programme. That dried up too. I was picking fruit in California when I heard the navy was looking for flyers. Seemed kind of screwy but I was getting real tired of eating figs three times a day.'

'And you don't think you're in denial, just a little

bit, putting yourself out as a miner, when most of your working life has been spent in uniform?'

'Tell me, are all the dames from your time so damn thinky and sure of themselves?'

'Dan Black,' she smiled, all slow and warm, 'the dames from my time, they'd eat you up.'

He wasn't sure why, but he liked the sound of that.

Before he could enjoy the idea any further, a beep sounded from within his shirt pocket.

'You've got mail, future boy.' Duffy smiled.

He carefully pulled out the flexipad they'd given him and pressed a fingertip to the envelope that had appeared on screen.

'I've gotta go, Julia,' he said after reading the message. 'The boss wants to see me.'

'Don't be a stranger,' she called out to him as he left.

Black had grown accustomed to the quality coffee on the *Clinton*. It was a rude shock, then, having to force down Ray Spruance's unpleasant green brew again.

They sat in an office a short walk from the docks where the surviving destroyers had tied up and a few minutes' ride from the hospital where the less serious casualties had been taken. They couldn't see Kolhammer's task force. It had dropped anchor on the other side of Ford Island, where it kept watch over the skies out to a distance of eight hundred miles. The British ship, *Trident*, remained on station near Midway, watching for surface threats.

Spruance sipped at his coffee as though it tasted just fine.

'It's a bad business, this killing, Dan. Kolhammer is going to go nuts when he finds out.'

Black stared out the window. Three nurses walked by, one of them with her arm in a sling.

'They haven't told him yet, sir?'

'Haven't been able to raise him. Their communications aren't so good without those space satellites. They're trying to get him, but we're not sending anything about them by radio or cablegram for the moment. It's all hand-to-hand courier, for security.'

'Were they an item?' he asked.

'The Jap and Anderson? They tell me not. It looks like a pretty vicious murder. There's some, uh, sexual matters associated with it. But more in the line of, you know, rape.'

The word hung between them for an eternity. This was going to make things even more difficult.

'Has word got around yet?' asked Black.

'There's been no official statement,' Spruance said. 'Won't be for a while. Officially, they're not even here yet. But I'd say everyone in that task force of theirs will know by the end of the day. And everyone will have an opinion about the likely culprits too.'

'One of ours, you mean.'

'It's human nature to blame the other guy.' Spruance shrugged.

Black forced down a last mouthful of cold, foul-tasting coffee. He wondered whether Julia had heard of the deaths yet. As soon as she did, he guessed that she'd be straining at the leash to get off the ship and do some digging herself.

Spruance obviously found the topic of the murders upsetting and certainly distasteful. He pushed himself up out of his squeaky swivel chair and paced over to the window. Hot sunshine fell on him through the glass. In his white uniform it made him quite uncomfortable to look at.

'So what do you think, Dan?' he asked. 'Do you think it's going to work out between us all?'

Black mulled it over.

'They're not like us, sir, but they're okay. I guess they're what we become.'

'And you're comfortable with that?' asked Spruance.

'Not entirely. I've learned a lot about them that scares me, frankly. But on the whole, they mean well.'

'They killed a lot of our men, Dan.'

'They saved a lot, too. And don't forget we killed our fair share of them in return. Far as I can tell, they're not holding that against us.'

A look of fleeting irritation passed across the admiral's face. 'They wouldn't want to go comparing scars,' was all he said in reply.

Neither man said anything for a while. Black was still pondering Spruance's question. Like Curtis, he'd been told to stay on the *Clinton*, to get acquainted with their procedures and technology. Like Curtis, he spent a lot of time reading. He wasn't a great reader and it frustrated him, but the guided tours he'd taken hadn't gone well. His guides assumed a level of knowledge about their ship and its technology that he just didn't possess.

'And this woman you've met?' said Spruance, breaking into his thoughts.

'Julia Duffy.'

'She's a reporter, am I correct?'

'For the *New York Times.* I believe she wants to keep working for them,' said Black, who had little doubt she'd get what she wanted.

'I'd like you to spend some more time with her while she's here, Dan. Get *her* reading on Kolhammer's people. She was writing about them. She must have her own opinions.'

'She certainly does,' he agreed. 'As a matter of fact, she's kind of ticked off at Kolhammer. I think she blames him for bringing her here. I think she'd much rather be home.'

'Wouldn't we all. You get on well with her then?'

'I like her, sir. Quite a bit.'

Spruance started to say something, then he seemed to think better of it. 'That's good. Spend as much time as you want with her over the next week or so. I'd like to get an independent opinion about what might happen if these characters are forced to stay. They certainly don't seem very hopeful of getting back.'

Dan Black shifted uncomfortably on his hard wooden chair. He'd already grown used to the vacumoulded seating on the *Clinton*. If he understood Spruance right, he was being asked to snoop on a girl he might have some feelings for. It didn't sit well, and he saw no alternative but to say so.

The admiral must have read his expression.

'Oh, I don't want you to betray any confidences, Commander,' he said. 'Frankly, you're not nearly pretty enough to play Mata Hari. I think we just need to know what sort of people we're dealing with. How they're likely to react to these killings, for instance. If you feel uncomfortable with that, why don't you invite her to dinner with the both of us? You can tell her up front that I want to pick her brain.'

Black's mood lightened considerably at that. 'She has a friend, another reporter, sir. She's a loudmouth too. I think we should take both of them along.'

Spruance seemed alarmed by the prospect of anything that might look like a double date. 'My wife would kill me!' he objected.

'Then we could invite Ensign Curtis along. I think he has eyes for Ms Natoli.'

'*Mzz?*' said Spruance.

'Oh, believe me, sir,' sighed Black, 'you're going to hear *all* about it.'

23

Ambassador Hotel, Room 522, Los Angeles, 1100 hours, 9 June 1942

The room felt like a museum piece, or perhaps a bedroom display in a department store that hadn't seen a paying customer in eighty years. Kolhammer's nose wrinkled at the smell of stale cigarette smoke. It was everywhere, blending with the body odour of a thousand previous guests, and the diffuse reek of old socks, sour perfume and greasy, broiled meat. He found it hard to believe that the past stank so badly. It was a sick joke, really. He'd never thought he could be nostalgic for blank glass towers and thousands of miles of ribboning freeway. But he was.

Gazing out of the window, across Wilshire Boulevard to a diner shaped like a derby hat, and beyond that to blocks of low-rise, brown brick Art Deco apartments and office buildings, Phillip Kolhammer felt his mind drifting again towards disintegration.

He'd arrived before dawn in a DeSoto, been driven into the basement car park and shepherded up to his room by a secret service agent. The drive in had been like a carnival ride at first. The DeSoto was the real thing, a great cavernous chunk of heavy metal with leather seats that looked as though they could have been taken right out of the hotel lobby. But he quickly tired of his fellow passengers, who smoked the entire time, and of the steel springs that dug into his back. Not to mention the lack of anything he'd recognise as a decent suspension system.

He'd tried to grab a few hours' sleep on the bed, but the uncomfortably dense and inflexible mattress felt wrong, and the air in the room tasted dead in his mouth.

A wardrobe full of civilian clothes awaited him, but Kolhammer had found them too heavy and prickly. He'd feel like he was in costume, wearing the dark, double-breasted woollen suits. Instead he'd showered and changed into a clean uniform that he'd brought in a travel case, stored in the small luggage bay on the in-flight refueller. LA was full of uniforms. And not just Americans. Contingents of Canadian, British, Australian, New Zealand, Free French, and even Dutch officers were quartered on the west coast. He wouldn't stand out.

Kolhammer thought of his own people stuck at Edwards AFB. He hoped they were being treated well. You had to figure that facilities were pretty primitive out there.

He checked his watch. Two hours until he was to meet with Roosevelt again. He was supposed to rest, but instead he picked up the heavy handset of the phone on his bedside table. It wasn't even an old dial phone. The face was completely blank.

A male voice answered. 'Yes, sir.'

'I'd like to go for a walk, clear my head.'

'We'll be right there.'

He waited. The door wasn't locked, and he could have left any time he wanted to, but he accepted the need to maintain strict security. The papers were already full of rumours out of Hawaii. A copy of the *Examiner* that had been pushed under his door had a lead story about the Japanese being driven away from Midway by a secret navy superweapon.

The real story was going to break soon. Everybody could feel it. The embedded journalists back in Pearl were screeching like caged baboons, demanding to be let loose. Personally, he would have let them go well before now. He was used to working with the embeds. They'd generally do the story you wanted, as long as you spoon-fed it to them. But the locals were still trying to get their heads around the reality of the Transition and the destruction of the Pacific Fleet. They wanted to keep the lid on a little longer. And Kolhammer could feel the pressure building.

Somebody rapped on the door, twice, softly. 'Admiral?'

'Come in.'

The special agent who'd led him up to the room entered with another man. From the generic cut of their clothes, and a common air of high-tone thuggery, Kolhammer took the new guy to be another special agent.

'Agent Stirling will secure your room and equipment, Admiral,' said the first man, confirming the assumption.

'You mind if we call on Professor Einstein?' Kolhammer asked. 'I'd like to talk to him before the meeting.'

The agent shrugged. Clearly it mattered nothing to him.

They padded along the thickly carpeted corridor to a room six doors down. The whole place put Kolhammer in mind of an expensive bordello. The thin squeal of a violin behind the door told him that Einstein was up and about.

'I'm sorry, Agent,' Kolhammer said quietly. 'I've forgotten your name.'

'Agent Flint, sir,' the secret service officer replied as he rapped on the door, twice, firmly, to be heard over the violin.

The sound of the instrument ceased with an abrupt, atonal note.

The door opened and the sight of that famous shock of hair greeted them. Standing there in his boxer shorts, Einstein looked a little ticked off, until he saw Kolhammer.

'Ah! Come in, come in. Good morning to you, Admiral.'

'Actually, I was wondering if you'd like to come out for a short stroll, Professor. Maybe we could grab a coffee.'

Einstein laughed, a short sharp bark.

'Not much *caffe* to be had in Los Angeles, I'm afraid, Admiral. Not that you'd want to drink what they do have, anyway. But, yes, a stroll would be nice. And I'm a little hungry too. Just let me get my pants on. With pants comes dignity, yes?'

The old man shuffled back into the room, which Kolhammer could see was fogged up with smoke from his pipe. He and Agent Flint stared at the walls while Einstein wrestled himself into a pair of brown corduroy trousers and pulled on a pair of slippers before joining them in the hallway. 'I have been using your superb electric book, Admiral. Amazing. Simply amazing.'

'We thought you'd like it. Did you see yourself in the movie we saved on there, *Insignificance*?'

Einstein roared with laughter. 'I did! I did! Who would have imagined, me with Joe DiMaggio's wife? An actress, yes, this Marilyn?'

'She will be, I suppose.'

Einstein's mood sobered as they reached the elevators.

'But with such a long face, that's not what you want to talk about, is it?'

'No, sir. It's not. You saw the other movies?'

'From the concentration camps,' said Einstein as all the happiness washed out of him.

'We call them death camps,' said Kolhammer.

The scientist sighed heavily. A chime sounded, and the elevator door opened. Agent Flint's eyes, which never stopped moving, swept over the man seated at the controls. Otherwise the lift was empty. He ushered in his two charges.

'Yes, I saw them,' said Einstein as they stepped in. 'That's why I was playing when you knocked. I play to relax, to forget about the world.'

Flint told the operator to take them to the ground floor.

'Sometimes,' said Kolhammer, 'it's best not to forget.'

They walked in silence for a while, each man lost in his own thoughts, until the dead neon signs out on Wilshire Boulevard gave Kolhammer a split second of dizzying dislocation. In his day, the city had funded the restoration of nearly a hundred and fifty neon signs along this strip in mid-Wilshire. The very same hoardings, unplugged now because of the wartime blackout, greeted him under a hot blue sky as they stepped out through the Ambassador's grand gated entrance. Jarring the moment of déjà vu, however, a yellow street-car went rattling by, full of Angelenos on their way downtown. Gone were the Koreans and Taiwanese. Replacing them was a homogenous population of middle-class whites. Gone, too, he noticed, was the brown sky and the close, sticky feel of heavily polluted air on his face.

'Are you okay, sir?' asked Agent Flint, taking Kolhammer lightly by the elbow.

'I'm sorry,' he apologised. 'It's just a shock, that's all.'

The three men came to a halt on the side of

the road. Einstein managed to appear simultaneously amused and moved by Kolhammer's plight.

'You know, Admiral, your world is still here,' said the scientist. He rubbed the tips of his fingers together. 'It is this close, right here and now. You came here. You can get back. You have family, yes?'

Another streetcar clattered past. Old car horns blared. Wilshire looked like the venue for a vintage auto festival.

'My wife lives over in Santa Monica. Or she . . . well, you know.'

'Are you going to be okay, sir?' asked Flint. 'Would you like to go back to the lobby and sit down?'

Kolhammer drew in a long, deep breath. He could smell petrol and exhaust fumes, but they stood out against a clear background. To his twenty-first-century sinuses, the air was mountain fresh. He gathered himself together and nodded across the street to the bizarre dome of the Brown Derby Restaurant.

'Is that the original Brown Derby?' he asked.

Neither Flint nor Einstein knew.

'Is it supposed to be a hat?' asked Einstein.

'Well, the sign says "Eat in the Hat". If you're hungry, Professor, we could get a light lunch over there. They might've invented the Cobb salad by now. They're the guys who came up with it in the first place.'

As they crossed the street, Kolhammer could have sworn he caught sight of a young Ronald Reagan taking a seat in the restaurant's tree-shaded courtyard fronting on the street. He suddenly worried that this was going to be a Hollywood place, where they stood no chance of gaining entry. Einstein might even suffer from some egregious episode of discrimination – being Jewish, and wearing slippers as he was.

He needn't have bothered himself over it. Agent Flint pushed through a small group of young women hanging around the front steps, clutching autograph books and occasionally standing on tiptoe as they tried to peer in through the swinging doors. The girls ignored Kolhammer, but a couple of them gave Einstein a quizzical look as he followed the admiral inside.

Kolhammer watched as Special Agent Flint badged the first dish monkey in a white tux he came across. He couldn't hear the exchange, but the waiter's palpable reluctance – to admit a strange old man into such refined company – ran headlong into Agent Flint's hard-boiled refusal to take no for an answer. The maître d came over to buy into the scene. Flint flashed him the badge, then gripped the man's bicep so strongly his knuckles turned white. He leaned over to mutter something into the man's ear, jerking his head back at Kolhammer and Einstein. The head-waiter began nodding vigorously, then shaking his head, then nodding again.

'I wish I knew how to do that,' whispered Einstein.

'Confidence is half the battle,' said Kolhammer. 'This is my treat, by the way.'

Flint returned, the ghost of a smile playing across his features.

'They found a nice table for you out on the terrace,' he said. 'Right next to Mr Crosby's party.'

Einstein didn't visibly react to the news. Perhaps he wasn't a Bing fan. Kolhammer nodded once, briefly, trying to conceal a sensation of free fall. He'd already checked out the Reagan lookalike. It wasn't the future president. But there were a couple of familiar faces out on the sun-dappled balcony. He couldn't place them, but he was certain that he knew three or four of them from somewhere. It had to be from old movies. Marie loved them. She had about a thousand on video sticks back home.

They threaded through the nearly empty dining room, with its walls completely covered by hundreds of framed sketches of movie stars, and out into the fierce radiance of high summer in LA. The patio was already buzzing with lunchtime trade. Kolhammer squinted into the sun to hide a mild grin at the sight of the food. A goodly number of the guests were tucking into hot dogs and cheeseburgers. He wondered how he'd go ordering a truffle-infused salad of wild porcini mushroom on arugula and witlof, or a bowl of hokkien noodles and wilted bok choy with flash-fried tofu croutons – two of the menu options in his stateroom back on the *Clinton.*

Agent Flint showed them to a table, blocking the waiter with his body until both men had sat down.

'Are you not joining us?' asked Einstein.

'I'll be around,' he said, before giving the waiter a glare and disappearing back inside. Kolhammer tried not to stare. But it was true. At the table next to them sat Bing Crosby and a party of three. The crooner, who looked impossibly young to Kolhammer, had split his lip recently. His guests, two men and a woman, gaped openly at the military man and the badly dressed odd-ball. They had been discussing something quite intently, but now they just stared. An uncomfortable silence began to spread to other nearby tables. The waiter started to shift from one foot to another, glancing back inside the main dining room.

Kolhammer stood up, gave Crosby the benefit of a scornful look, informed by his awareness of the actor's violent, drunken home life, then smiled and said, 'Mr Crosby, you seem to recognise my colleague here. It's Professor Albert Einstein, winner of the Nobel Prize for Physics. He's helping us with the war effort.'

Crosby flushed a deep shade of red and stammered a greeting.

'Professor. Pleased to make your acquaintance.'

Einstein grinned hugely, nodded hello, and said to the waiter, 'I'll have what he's having. If that is the famous Corncob salad.'

The waiter coughed nervously. 'It's a Cobb salad, sir. Named after Mr Cobb, the owner. There's no corn in it.'

'The professor will have the salad. Just bring me a coffee,' said Kolhammer in his unmistakable command voice.

Crosby's table went back to discussing some new record or film deal.

Kolhammer sat down and cocked an eyebrow at Einstein. He leaned across the table and rumbled in a voice loud enough to be heard by the nearest tables: 'The guy earns more money than God, everyone *thinks* he's a saint, but he gets loaded and beats on his wife and kids. Go figure.'

Crosby gawked at them, open-mouthed, for a long, long time. Then he angrily waved over the maître d.

'We'll be leaving,' he said curtly. Don't bother to make up the check.'

His companions all stood as one, and beat a confused retreat.

Kolhammer grinned at Einstein. 'I never did have time for assholes like that . . . Anyway, screw them. We're not here to gape at the movie stars. I needed to talk over a few things, Professor. Did you get through all of the README file on your data slate?'

Presidential Suite, Ambassador Hotel,
Los Angeles, 1210 hours, 9 June 1942

The heavy brocade curtains of the suite had been drawn against the fierce California sunshine. Each lens of President Roosevelt's glasses picked up the glow of the data slate screen, so that his eyes were lost behind the reflected oblongs. General George C Marshall, perched on an imitation Louis XIV footstool just across from the commander-in-chief, fought down a childish urge to jump up and look over Roosevelt's shoulder.

'It's quite amazing,' the President said. 'Do you know they've sent nearly a hundred motion pictures, and thousands of books, all inside this box?'

Marshall, who'd just arrived from Washington, shook his head a fraction. He was still spinning from the cables he'd read on the flight over. He wasn't sure what had most upset him – the loss of the fleet or the arrival of the time travellers.

Goddamn! Time travellers. Every time he used that cockamamie phrase he wanted to slap some sense into himself. But Roosevelt, King and Eisenhower had all been out at the airfield when the rocket planes had come in. Eisenhower was still out at Edwards with Kolhammer's people and a dozen staff officers who'd flown across the continent overnight. King and the President, alone in the luxury suite except for the ubiquitous secret service detail, were still talking excitedly about the planes when Marshall arrived. And they weren't the only ones.

Down in Australia, MacArthur was already on the warpath, beating the drum so loudly you could hear him across the Pacific. He wanted Kolhammer's marines, the tanks, the planes. Everything. He wanted to take them to Tokyo next week. Marshall felt as though he was a long way behind in the game of catch-up.

He snuck a glance at Admiral King. The navy chief

and MacArthur openly despised each other, but there was an issue on which they were of one mind. Japan first. Marshall, who knew the real threat lay in Nazi Germany, was expecting to get caught in a pincer movement between them.

Despite the terrible losses at Midway, King seemed to have reconciled himself to the changed circumstances. He'd already presented the Joint Chiefs with his broad recommendations for deployment of the new assets. Not surprisingly, under King's proposal none of them, not even the British forces that arrived with Kolhammer, would find their way back to the Atlantic. The old dog had even suggested allowing Kolhammer to retain control of his task force as an integrated unit, just to keep the ships together and concentrated in King's personal fiefdom, the Pacific.

If Marshall wasn't careful *and* quick, Roosevelt would probably back the shift in strategy, just to regain some control over the runaway course of events.

The President certainly was taken with that electrical book, or whatever in hell it was.

'Will you look at this, General Marshall?' Roosevelt said with real wonder. 'A space rocket to Mars.'

24

USS Hillary Clinton, *1055 hours, 9 June 1942*

For just a second or two after that first moment of clarity, Lieutenant Rachel Nguyen had actually been relieved that, for the time being at least, she wouldn't have to write a doctoral thesis. The *moment of clarity* – also known as the *'Oh no' moment* – was the term Margie Francois had coined for those few seconds of dizzying intellectual free fall that came on when somebody realised deep down in their bones that they had fallen through a hole in the universe. If you were going to check out for good, they said, you were mostly likely to do so within thirty minutes of your own moment of clarity.

After her momentary spurt of guilty glee, Rachel's reaction had shifted back towards the average – a mix of bewilderment and grief. Her first rational thought had been for her mother and father, who'd alternated between pride and alarm when confronted by their daughter's choice of a career in the navy. She was the only Nguyen daughter, and they'd been aghast at the possibility of losing her. *Well*, she thought ruefully, *they've lost me now*. She wasn't dead, but she felt so utterly lost it seemed as if she might as well be.

Such was her mood when the two reporters knocked on the door of her temporary office aboard the *Clinton* where she'd been transferred to work with a small group of history graduates. There was no escaping her damn degree.

'Hey, are you Rachel?' asked one of them. 'I'm Julia Duffy, and this is Rosanna Natoli. The Hammer said we should come down and help you out.'

'Cool,' Nguyen said, though without much enthusiasm.

'Hey,' Natoli said, 'you an Aussie?'

Nguyen glanced down at the shoulder patch displaying her national flag.

'Apparently.'

'My cousin Stella married an Aussie. They moved to Melbourne. You from there? You might know them.'

'Yeah, Stella from Melbourne. Everyone knows her.'

'Jeez,' said Duffy, 'you're a bright beam of sunshine, aren't you, Lieutenant.'

'I'm sorry,' said Rachel. 'I was just thinking about my oldies. You know, my parents.'

Natoli pulled a chair out, patted Rachel on the arm, and launched into a therapeutic routine that consisted of endless, labyrinthine tales of her five sisters' weddings and her own plans to get to New York as soon as possible to find her grandparents and tell them to invest in IBM. Julia Duffy drifted about the small office, which was fitted out with half-a-dozen workstations and a large whiteboard Nguyen had been filling up with a local time line of the last month and the next two.

'Are you the only one working on this, Rachel? Do you mind us calling you Rachel?' Duffy asked during a lull in the Natoli family saga.

'No. It's my name. And there are another three of us on this project. I'm just the only one who's here right now. There are two Yanks and a Brit. We've all got doctoral qualifications in history, or were going for them when this shit went down.'

'You don't look old enough,' said Duffy.

'I was still going for mine. Had a thesis due in a few months. It was killing me.'

'There you go!' said Natoli. 'A silver lining.'

'And look,' said Duffy, jerking her thumb at the board as she sat down, 'you can do field research for your PhD. Talk about winning the lottery.'

'You guys don't seem overly upset,' said Nguyen, intrigued by their chirpiness.

'Antidepressants,' said Duffy, smiling sweetly. 'Come and see us when they run out. That'll be a dark fucking day.'

'So why are you guys here?' asked Nguyen. 'Kolhammer promised us more hands, but nobody said anything about civilians.'

Duffy shrugged. 'They won't let us talk to our offices. Well, I guess most of us don't have offices now . . .'

Natoli rolled her eyes.

'So we volunteered to help. It's that or stay locked in our cabins. I guess they figured this is where we'd do the least amount of damage. We're supposed to be writing some puff piece for the local yokels, explaining how the hell we got here. That took all of two hours. So now we've got nothing to do, and I really don't want to go back to watching Rosanna's knickers dry in our cabin.'

'Okay,' said Nguyen. 'You guys do any history at uni . . . sorry, in college?'

'Not a scrap,' said Duffy.

'I majored in Old Icelandic legends.' Natoli grinned.

'Super,' said Rachel. She cleared a pile of paper from the keyboard in front of her and brought up the Fleetnet search window.

'What we're doing,' she explained, 'is looking at things that are supposed to happen during the next few weeks in all the theatres of this war. We'll start with the web cache first, because it's much quicker and we have a lot of full-text stuff stored anyway . . .'

'Like war histories and so on?' asked Natoli.

'Yeah, occupational hazard. When we've exhausted that, we'll get into the hard copy.' She indicated a pile of cardboard boxes pushed into the far corner of the office. They were packed tightly with books. 'But the net's keeping us busy for now. You get ten thousand people, they're going to build up a lot of data over time.'

'You know any of the guys in the physics group?'

asked Duffy. 'Maybe we could speak to them to pad out our story.'

Lieutenant Nguyen nodded. 'A friend of mine got seconded to that. They got no hope. The basics are easy. The simultaneous existence of all possible times has been accepted, at least theoretically, since Einstein. And quantum foam engineering is mundane enough to have been written up in *Popular Science*. Even I've read some stuff about it.'

'I wrote a weekend feature about it once,' said Duffy. 'But I thought all the lab work was really unsophisticated, a bit like nanotech during the 1980s. I wouldn't have thought we had enough quantum muscle to push a cold fucking taco back through eight decades, let alone a carrier battle group.'

'Guess you were wrong,' said Natoli.

'That'll be *another* correction for the *Times* then,' Duffy joked.

'But you don't think we can find or rebuild whatever sent us here?' Natoli asked. Her voice said she was searching for a glimmer of hope.

'Not a chance. Not for fifty, sixty years at best,' said Nguyen.

'You know what this means, don't you?' said Duffy. 'We're living in the Dark Ages, ladies. They haven't even *heard* of feminism here, let alone the female orgasm.'

'You don't think we'll ever get back?' asked Natoli.

'I'd like to hope so,' said Rachel. 'My parents, they really worry about me.'

'So you joined the navy to put their fears at ease?' Duffy asked.

'I like to surf.' Rachel shrugged. 'I figured if I had to join up, I might as well get some tube time in. I guess I was kind of an idiot.'

'So, what you got for us, Lieutenant?' said Natoli, clapping her hands to dispel the maudlin atmosphere.

Rachel gathered herself together, stood up and moved over to the whiteboard.

'Okay. Today is 9 June. A Czechoslovakian village by the name of Lidice will be destroyed today, in reprisal for the assassination of an SS guy called Heydrich, by a couple of Czech soldiers flown out of Britain. The occupants will be massacred and thousands of other Czechs will be shipped off to concentration camps over the next few weeks.'

'Jesus,' breathed Natoli. 'Can't we do anything about it?'

'Like what? Broadcast a warning on CNN? Fly a bunch of marines in from Germany? It's a different world here.'

'Couldn't we warn off the Nazis?' asked Duffy. 'Tell them we know what they're up to?'

'They'd laugh in our faces,' said Nguyen. 'Just forget about it. We already told the local guys. They're like, "Too bad, it's war, get over it." Nobody really cares about the small stuff.'

'The small stuff!' cried Natoli.

'That's right. Fifty million people are going to die

in this war. They couldn't care less about a little village full of peasants with alphabet soup for names. Too bad, it's war, get over it.'

Nguyen turned back to the board. 'Tomorrow the Pacific Fleet gets reinforced by the carrier USS *Wasp* and some cruisers and destroyers. It would have made up for some of the losses they suffered to the Japs at Midway. Now it'll make up for their losses to us instead. Also, tomorrow, Field Marshal Rommel of the Afrika Korps is going to break out of the Cauldron in the Battle of Gazala, destroying three hundred and twenty British tanks in a two-day battle. You won't be surprised to know the locals were very keen to get as much detail about that as they could. The Brits have a bunch of guys stationed here for liaison. They've been hammering us for days about it. That's where the others have gone,' she said, indicating the empty chairs. 'They're briefing the Brits about where and when to hit Rommel. Maybe they'll take the advice. Maybe Rommel will just kick their butts anyway. We'll see.

'At some point our presence here is going to start fundamentally changing the course of events, and this type of research will become moot.'

'That's happened already,' said Natoli.

'Around these parts, for sure. But the ripples haven't spread very far yet. The Japs are probably still trying to figure out what the hell's going on. Unlike Nimitz and Spruance, they don't have us to walk them through it.'

'And I guess they don't have ships like these to make them believe,' Duffy ventured.

'Let's hope not,' said Nguyen. 'Now, back to the board. On 11 June, the Germans are going to start mining the eastern seaboard of the US –'

'Is anybody else having a Twilight Zone moment?' asked Natoli.

'Every minute of the day.' Nguyen sighed. 'Again, the locals want to know as much as possible about that. They'd like to be able to pinpoint the German subs, but we can only give them general indications right now. The archives aren't a crystal ball.'

'How about we try to help out with that?' suggested Natoli.

'Admiral King would be your new best friend if you could deliver,' said Nguyen.

'Who's that?'

'The current US Navy boss, and apparently a very, *very* unpleasant man to deal with. I'd love to be in the room when he and Kolhammer finally meet up. Apparently Nimitz was on the line to him for three hours after we arrived, mostly getting his arse kicked black and blue.'

'How do you think he'd take to advice from a couple of civilian girlies in Prada skirts and high heels?'

'I think we owe it to history to find out,' Nguyen said, smiling at last. 'Why don't you crack open those boxes of books? Somewhere near the bottom of that big sucker there's a whole stack of memoirs and biographies. You find some guys who did time in the coastguard or the destroyers, you might just get lucky.'

The two reporters fell to the task for the next couple of hours, skimming through dozens of old volumes, mostly without luck. At lunchtime the three of them shared a couple of sandwiches in the *Clinton*'s main mess. It seated nearly one thousand personnel and most of the places were taken. Rachel and the reporters squeezed in next to a couple of sailors who were minding half a dozen visitors from the *Enterprise*. The contemporary personnel – or 'temps' as they'd been christened – looked like kids on their first day in school, lost and scared and trying not to show it; except for one, an Italian kid, who was forking down a mammoth serving of sand crab lasagne like it might be his last meal.

'You got any plans, for when you get some leave?' asked Natoli as she sprinkled fresh parmesan over a dish of spinach and ricotta ravioli. The parmesan was only *grana*, not *reggiano*, but it was a well-cooked dish. 'I am so going to find Great-Auntie Tula and tell her not to marry Great-Uncle Al,' she added.

'But what about your cousins? They wouldn't be born then,' said Nguyen as she wrestled with a giant hamburger.

'Oh yeah, that's right. Damn.'

'I wouldn't know where to find my family at this point,' Nguyen said. 'They'd be in some paddy field near the Delta. But that's Japanese territory now anyway.'

'Well, I'm going to write something like *Sexual*

Politics or maybe *The Female Eunuch*,' Duffy declared. 'I don't suppose anybody will be interested during the war, but just imagine if we could save all of those women from being chained to the kitchen all through the 1950s.'

'Maybe they wanted to be chained there,' said Rosanna.

'I'm sure they did,' said Duffy. 'For about two minutes.'

'That sounds like a version of Marxist false consciousness,' said Nguyen, before adding with a grin, 'I always knew the *Times* was full of superannuated commies.'

'I'm serious,' said Duffy. 'Right now, we're all together. We make our own rules, or we live by the ones we already have, I suppose. But what do you think will happen when I arrive at the *Times* and ask for my desk back? They're gonna take one look at my tits –'

'Two looks,' said Natoli. 'You got such nice boobs, Julia.'

'– and then they're probably going to pat my head –'

'Your butt, you mean.'

'– *Okay*, my butt. And then they're going to show me the door.'

The half-dozen local boys sitting at their table were beginning to notice the small group of loud women. Another woman in Marine Corps fatigues, walking by with her tray, pulled up beside them.

'You mind? I couldn't help hearing. You guys reporters?' she said.

They nodded.

'Thought so. Listen, did you hear what happened?'

The marine leaned forward as if to impart a state secret, but spoke loudly enough that anybody within ten metres could hear.

'They told Kolhammer he had to get rid of all the women and nonwhites if we were going to be staying and fighting. Can you believe it? You should do a story on it.'

Rumour deposited, the woman walked off without waiting for a response.

'Well, did they?' asked Natoli, turning to Nguyen.

'How would I know? I wasn't there, neither was she, I'll bet. But the locals are going to come up against a hard truth if they try to pull something like that. Thirty per cent of the personnel in this task force are women, and only sixty per cent of the guys are white. And they're not going to side with a bunch of bigots against their own friends, anyway.'

'You think they really are bigots?' asked Duffy, dropping her voice.

'Nah, they're just ignorant. They haven't read your book yet, Julia.'

'Hey, Jules,' said Natoli. 'Here's your favourite primitive, just back from the tundra.'

Lieutenant Commander Black, in a newly pressed uniform, threaded through the mess tables towards them. He smiled at Natoli and shook hands with

Lieutenant Nguyen. He was past being surprised at finding little Asian women in military uniform. He turned towards Julia Duffy.

'I've got a few days' liberty,' he told her. 'And they gave me a room over at the Moana. I thought you might like to come into town for a swim. You can sneak through the barbed wire on the beach, if you know the way.'

'My word, Commander, that's awfully forward of you,' she mocked gently.

Black wasn't sure what to say next. He looked uncomfortable, like a man trapped in an exchange with somebody whose mind worked much faster than his own.

Julia Duffy turned the full wattage of her smile on him. 'Lieutenant Commander Black, I do believe you will die of embarrassment right where you stand if this goes on. Relax. I'd love to come over, as long as you can get Rosanna a room as well. But right now, we're helping Rachel with something. You want to go strutting through Honolulu with your trophy bitches, you'll have to lend us a hand first.'

Now Black really was embarrassed. He actually blushed, down to the roots of his thick, slicked-back hair. The six sailors from the *Enterprise* all froze, as though poleaxed. They openly gawked at the two civilians now.

'Oh my God, Julia,' Natoli squealed happily. 'You're killing this poor guy. Just put him out of his fucking misery, would you? Listen, Daniel, my friend here, she's toying with you like a cat plays with a mouse. My advice is, if you want her, don't let her get away with it. Hit her with a club and drag her back to your cave. She'll chain herself to your kitchen stove and start popping out bambinos before you know what's happened.'

Black gave the impression he didn't know whether to laugh or curse or tuck his tail between his legs and run like a dog. The three women were obviously enjoying themselves enormously at his expense.

'Maybe we should just parachute-drop you witches straight into Tokyo,' he said in the end. 'A few days of your company and the Japs would be begging us for mercy.'

'Not if they know how to treat a girl,' said Duffy.

'Perhaps they could give me a few tips,' Black muttered, before addressing Rosanna. 'Miss Natoli,' he said, 'you were always invited, by the way. Admiral Spruance wants to talk to you both. It's nothing heavy, a dinner and a talk. He's just curious about the future, I guess.'

25

Hickam Field, Hawaii, 0610 hours, 8 June 1942

Slim Jim Davidson couldn't believe how his luck had run hot and cold since the future had turned up to wreck the *Astoria*. First and most importantly, there was a chance he might live now. He'd been stunned to discover that he was supposed to die in a few weeks at the Battle of Savo Island. One of the crew on the *Leyte Gulf* had searched Fleetnet for him – Slim Jim was assiduous about learning the lingo – and had pulled his name out of a database of American war dead.

That was some powerfully spooky shit there.

'Guess you should be glad we turned up to kick your ass instead,' the guy had joked.

But Slim Jim hadn't thought it was funny at all. It had landed him in a blue funk for two days. He'd only surfaced when Mohr had told him everyone off the *Astoria* would be moving ashore as soon as they hit Pearl. There was nowhere to berth them on the surviving ships. That got him to thinking on how he might fence the stuff he'd lifted from the *Leyte Gulf*, which got him to thinking about how much money he stood to make. Which, in turn, led him to the conclusion that if he made enough of the folding stuff he might be able to grease the right wheels and roll right on out of the firing line. Then he could land himself a position more befitting a man of his talents.

Once ashore, they had set up tents for temporary quarters. That had dampened his spirits again. Pitched in a burned-out expanse of sugarcane stubble a mile or so from Hickam Field, they reminded him of his time on the road gang. But there was no work to be done, which suited him fine.

All he had to do was figure out how to get down to Hotel Street in Honolulu. Given a few hours down there, he was sure he'd be able to move this loot. Unfortunately they were all confined to camp indefinitely. Somebody told him it was because a couple of Japs from the future had got themselves whacked, but Slim Jim took that for bullshit. The navy had stuck him in this shithole with a moron for a roomy because the navy had nothing better to do than make his sorry life even more miserable than it might be.

Surprisingly enough, it was the moron, Moose Molloy Jr, who came to the rescue. Mohr had asked him to volunteer for a work detail, helping shift a bunch of gear that had belonged to some dead officers out of the Moana Hotel. There was certain to be heavy lifting involved, a Moose Jr specialty.

'You gotta be fucking kidding me, Davidson,' the chief had said when Slim Jim had confronted him, eager to pitch in. 'What, did you take a round in the head or something? You forget what a lazy asshole you are?'

'Come on, Chief,' he'd pleaded. 'I'm going outta my fucking nut in this cane field. We been here three days with nothing to do but scratch our balls. I just about scratched mine right off. It's Montgomery all over again, Chief. You gotta let me outta this joint. Even working is better than this!'

No doubt Mohr knew he was being played, but he must've decided to let the bum have a bit of rope, see if he looped it around his scrawny neck and hanged himself.

'Okay, Davidson, get on the bus with Moose and Barnes. And don't let me find you pocketing the effects of any of them fine, dead officers and gentlemen.'

Slim Jim managed to sound reasonably offended. 'Stealing from the dead? That's not my thing, Chief,' he said as he hurried onto an old school bus repainted in dun green for war service.

'No, bouncing checks off old ladies is more your style, dickwad,' Mohr grumbled.

The ride into Honolulu was brief, and Slim Jim couldn't help but laugh at all the dumb jerks they left behind, running along, begging for a chance to get out of that hell-hole of a field. They raised a cloud of black ash and dust as they trotted beside the bus. Mohr kept a close eye on his least favourite charge as they bounced and squeaked their way into town. But cops had been eyeballing Slim Jim a lot longer than Eddie Mohr. He knew to keep himself clean, which meant staying in character. He regaled the men in the seats around him with the exploits from his previous visits to the body shops along River and Barretania Streets. Mohr eventually tired of his bull-shit and tuned him out. Slim Jim kept it going all the way to the Moana.

'Would you look at this joint,' said Moose Jr with real awe in his voice as they piled out in front of the hotel. Forty years old and fronting directly onto Waikiki Beach, the Moana had serviced some of the wealthiest tourists in the world before the war. Along with the Royal, it was one of the few grand structures in Honolulu. The coral reef that covered the floor of the bay had been smothered in sand dumped from barges in front of the Moana, so that the dainty feet of wealthy tourists wouldn't be too badly cut up.

Ever since the Japanese raid in December, naval personnel had replaced the tourists, and barbed wire now ran along the beach, blocking access to the brilliant green water.

Slim Jim nudged Moose in the ribs. 'What'd I tell you about officers, Moose?'

'To love, honour and obey them,' said Mohr, punching Slim Jim in the back. 'C'mon Vladimir, the workers' revolution can wait. We got barges to lift and bales to tote.'

The duty wasn't excessively heavy. Mostly they had to ferry a lot of sea trunks and personal luggage out of the hotel and into a truck for transfer to graves registration. A couple of the former occupants did have some curious and inconvenient items, like the pilot who'd acquired an antique mahogany dining table on a tour of China and had somehow managed to carry it through two other postings. Moose, Slim Jim and four other guys were needed to shift that baby.

As tempting as it would have been to pocket a curio here or there, Davidson knew not to tempt fate. Mohr had eyes in the back of his box-shaped head and he was a lay-down certainty to be watching like a hawk. No, Slim Jim was a patient crook, content to pretend he wanted nothing more than to escape the prison camp of the cane field. If he behaved himself and didn't give the chief reason to get on his case, he might just get enough wiggle room to do some real business before long.

So he lifted and grunted and sweated with the others, grumbling occasionally, as was his style, complaining about officers who lived like royalty and bullshitting about how he'd stayed in plenty of joints that'd make this place look like a flophouse. They finished up at 1730 with a few more hours of work to go. A strict curfew was in place from 1800, however, so Mohr herded them back onto the bus for the trip back to the cane field.

The bullshitting wasn't nearly as loud or energetic on the way home. Talk turned to Midway, to curiosity and speculation.

'I heard they put a new heart in Smithy,' said a

voice from the rear of the bus. 'Like a fucking wind-up clock it is, I heard. All gears and wires.'

'Crap,' said someone else. 'It'd rust in there.'

'No,' said Chief Mohr, 'that one's true. I visited Smithy myself on that big Marine Corps flat-top they got. They split him right open, took out his old heart and put in this new one, made of some kind of miracle plastic or something. Reckon it'll be beating a hundred years after he's gone.'

'I heard they all got machines inside them, that they can talk to each other without even speaking out loud.'

'No way.'

'Yep, and they can grow you new skin and muscles and stuff, if you get a piece shot out of you –'

'– or burned off.'

'That's right. And they got that jelly they put on the burns. You seen that shit? It smells something terrible but I tell you what, guys got that stuff on them, it's like they can't feel a damn thing from those burns, and when it comes off they just patch you up with some of that skin they grow in a bucket. It's like you never got burned.'

'What if they fucked it up, though? Gave you some nigger skin when you're meant to get white. You'd be a sorry-looking piece of shit then, wouldn't you? Like a zebra.'

'It wouldn't take,' said Moose, quite earnestly, over the laughter. 'You couldn't put black on white. They's two different types. Wouldn't work – just like if you got the blood types wrong and mixed 'em. It'd kill you.'

Moose was particularly pleased with himself for that analogy. And for Moose, it was a decidedly sophisticated piece of reasoning.

'We coming back in tomorrow?' Slim Jim asked Mohr. 'To finish the job?'

'I don't know, Davidson. Could be that some of the others need a break too.'

'Screw them,' someone called out, saving Slim Jim the trouble. 'Those lazy bums didn't put their hands up today. Why should they get a reward tomorrow?'

Mohr said he'd think about it.

'Hey,' said Slim Jim, 'did anyone hear about the pill they got that gives you a boner for three days straight?'

The next day the same sun that beat down with such malice in the burned-out cane field felt dappled and wonderful downtown in Honolulu. Slim Jim was so happy he had unknowingly slipped into his Downtown Strut. Davidson hadn't had cause to break out the Strut since getting busted and press-ganged into the navy. But this morning he felt like he was walking with the King.

They had finished work at the Moana by 1030 and Chief Mohr, in an unprecedented show of slack, had given them liberty for the rest of the day. They were free as birds until 1700 hours. Slim Jim had quickly shaken off Moose Molloy and headed straight for

Hotel Street. It was said of this quarter of Old Honolulu that you were as much at risk here as storming a Japanese pillbox. If the cops didn't get you, the crooks surely would. Dozens of booze barns and cathouses lined the narrow pavement. Bouncers and con men, vicious Kanaks, the shore patrol, syphilitic hookers, drunken sailors – there were a thousand ways to get into trouble down on Hotel Street.

Slim Jim Davidson felt right at home.

He joined a long line outside one of the cheaper bordellos and remained there until he was certain Chief Mohr had disappeared into Wo Fats bar and grill. Then, pointedly mumbling about how a man could die of horniness in such a slow line, he stepped off, apparently determined to seek a quicker release.

Instead he walked down by the canal and into an old warehouse once run by the Dole Pineapple Company but abandoned after a fire about a year ago. Picking his way through the charred debris, he stepped out onto a narrow and quiet back lane. Dog shit lay everywhere among broken glass and hundreds of discarded cigarette butts. Slim Jim stood and waited.

It took less than a minute. A dark calloused hand appeared at the edge of a sheet of corrugated iron a few yards down the alley. The thin metal sheet scraped on the ground as someone pulled it to one side. A giant slab-shouldered Maori with elaborate tattoos covering his whole face squeezed out of the gap. A long white scar ran from his right ear down across his throat, marring the intricate tattoo before disappearing into a filthy white T-shirt. The expression on his mangled face was murderous, until he straightened up and got a look at Slim Jim. At once he broke out in a wide grin, displaying at least three missing teeth.

'Hello, Tui,' said Slim Jim. 'Is Big Itchy 'round?'

'He's so round we can't hardly fit him through the door no more,' laughed Tui. 'He's still eating like a condemned man.'

'Still got a thirst that'd cast a shadow?'

'You bet.'

Slim Jim came forward, gingerly stepping around dozens of dog turds. He plucked a fifth of bourbon from his pocket.

'My compliments to the big guy,' he said. 'Sorry it ain't more.'

'Things are tight all over, Slim Jim,' said Tui as he beamed and slapped a huge meaty paw on the white man's shoulder.

They climbed through the gap in the ramshackle wall, entering a small wrecker's yard on the other side. Tui slid the iron sheet back into place and picked up the shotgun he'd placed by the entrance.

'You see any of the action at Midway?' asked Tui as they walked through the yard to the office.

'My friend, I was up to here in it,' said Davidson, tapping his chin with the back of his hand. 'That's why I'm here.'

'Is it true what they're saying about these visitors?'

'Depends what they're saying, brother.'

Tui's glance was almost furtive, like he thought they were under surveillance.

'That they're from the future, and they've got death rays and super-rockets and they take their women with them when they fight.'

Slim Jim laughed. 'That's closer than I thought you'd get. Yeah. I've met them, been on one of their ships. I'll tell you about it when we meet Big Itchy, but you ain't gonna believe a word of it.'

'And the women. I heard they got women of all colours with them.'

'Damn, boy, you *are* well informed. Yeah, they do, but here's the hell of it. The dames aren't just travelling pieces of ass. The ship I was on? The *captain* was a nigger woman. And the officers were black dames and Asians. Mexicans, too. I tell you, it turns a man's head. God only knows how they keep out of the sack when they're supposed to be working.'

'You're shitting me.'

'Not a word of it, brother. I brought some stuff. You'll see.'

'The captain was a nigger you say,' mused Tui. 'She the one got plugged on the beach, d'you think, with the Jap guy? Maybe the Klan did it. There's a lot of southern boys on the island at the moment.'

Slim Jim shrugged. He'd heard about forty-three different versions of what had happened to Captain Anderson. It wasn't his problem, so he didn't care. They arrived at the office, a creaking timber cabin with threadbare towels hung for curtains in the broken windows. Tui pulled up to a full stop.

In contrast to the state of the yard, the interior of the cabin was uncluttered, clean and comfortable. It was spacious, seeming larger on the inside than it should be. In fact the cabin jutted a few yards into the adjoining property, a lumberyard, which also formed part of Big Itchy's fiefdom.

On balance, as long as the Japs didn't invade, Big Itchy figured the war was a bonus. It brought a flood of money into the islands and a huge amount of passing trade from the millions of servicemen in transit to Australia and the Solomons. They tended to be much better customers for Big Itchy's operation than the toffee-nosed swells who'd arrived on the China Clipper before the war. On the other hand, the town was now full of guys who'd been trained to kill and who weren't at all interested in being stood over by Big Itchy's muscle men. After Tui and the boys had got the shit kicked out of them for the third or fourth time down on Hotel Street, Itchy had decided to beat a tactical retreat from the mugging business, concentrating instead on sly booze, broads and a modest numbers racket. Turned out these palookas would just give you all their money if you asked them nice and got them laid or drunk in return.

Big Itchy's office was neatly stacked with the raw material of his operation: crates of stolen booze, cigarettes and food. The girls never came here. They hardly ever got out of the flophouses. Slim Jim knew there was a safe buried in the floor beneath Itchy's desk, and it was a sign of the trust he'd earned that the knowledge hadn't cost him his life. Big Itchy kept every dollar he earned in that safe. He didn't trust the banks. They were full of Jews.

'Aloha, Jimmy,' the two-hundred-and-forty-pound criminal rumbled from the chair that sat astride his fortune. 'You're alive. That's good. The war over yet?'

'No, the war's got a way to run yet.'

'Fat times then.'

'Getting fatter by the day.'

Slim Jim undid the top button of his shirt. There were six men in the room watching him – Itchy, Tui and four silent toughs. Big Itchy was unusual for his times, being an equal opportunity employer. As the bastard son of a white plantation owner and a lei girl, he had no truck with discrimination. As long as a man could throw a punch or shoot a gun, and keep his mouth shut, he had a future with Big Itchy Enterprises. The men who stood, without speaking, as Slim Jim stripped off his shirt, were a mix of Kanaks, one local Japanese and two white men. As Davidson's shirt came off they all saw the bandages he had strapped around his torso.

'Somebody's husband catch you?' asked Tui.

Slim Jim just smiled. The wrapping bulged under his left armpit. He gritted his teeth and ripped off the plaster. A flexipad came away, stuck to it.

'That's a lot of effort for a cigar box, Jimmy,' said

Big Itchy. 'What's it made of, gold or something?'

'Nope,' said the sailor as he removed the last of the bandages. 'Worth its weight in gold, though. Watch this.'

He was familiar enough with the device to power up and load a vid of *Casablanca* in just a few seconds. Handing the device to a quizzical Big Itchy, he put his shirt back on as the film's soundtrack filled the room. It was surprisingly loud and rich. A few of the men jumped slightly, but all quickly gathered around Big Itchy.

'Damn! I heard of this,' one of the white men said. 'It's a Bogart movie, supposed to be great.'

'Yeah, but we won't see it here for ten fucking years,' said the Japanese.

The screen was relatively small, but the picture was crisp, drawing a few childlike noises of appreciation from the huddled gangsters.

'You got any Edward G Robinson?' asked one. 'I love his stuff. *You dirty rats.*' The hoodlum did his best Robinson, with a tommy gun, cutting down a room full of rivals.

'So it's true,' said Tui. 'They came back in time.'

'Sideways, they tell me,' said Slim Jim.

'I don't understand,' said Tui.

'I don't think anyone does,' Slim Jim said. 'And what the fuck does it matter anyway? They're here. They brought a shitload of dough with them, and all of this stuff too. Stuff you can't even imagine, that people are going to pay a fortune for. And information too. Goddamn, the things these guys know.' Slim Jim smiled, breaking into a laugh when it all got too much. 'The possibilities, Itchy. Just think of them.'

Reluctantly, the corpulent gangster dragged his eyes away from the screen. The others, except for Tui, kept watching.

'What do you mean?'

'That machine there, they call it a flexipad. It's not just a little movie screen. It's a telephone, although it doesn't work so well now they don't have their *satellite* cover' – he was careful to say the word properly – 'and it's like an automatic bookkeeper. You could do your taxes for the whole year in two minutes.' He grinned, eliciting a chuckle from both men. 'Their doctors, they've got flexipads they just wave over your body and they can tell all sorts of shit about you, whether you're sick or not. They've got these games on them, I'd have to show you them, you just wouldn't believe me otherwise. But most of all, they got information.'

'Again with the information, Jimmy. What the fuck are you talking about? You think I want to know how to build a death ray? My old shotgun works just fine for now.'

'No,' said Davidson, 'that's not what I mean at all. Although that stuff you can get too, and I'm thinking that maybe some of the syndicate boys would like to know. But no, I'm talking about the real inside dope, Itchy. Like, would you want to know every winner of the Kentucky Derby for the next fifty years?'

Everyone stopped still. A few stopped breathing.

Slim Jim held out his hand for the pad. He shut down the Bogart vid and brought up a webpage he'd downloaded from Fleetnet himself. He'd never been so proud as the moment he successfully called up that site. It had taken every one of his sneaky, underhanded tricks to get unsupervised access to a workstation. And then it had required real intelligence to work the search interface to find something like this. Originally, he'd been looking for scores of football games, but had found nothing. Betting there had to be at least one fan of the track among ten or twelve thousand sailors and marines, he went looking for the Derby instead. And bingo! Here he was with the inside running.

'The thing is, Itchy, we gotta move quickly. Some other smart guy's gonna figure this out real quick, probably in the next couple of days. I grabbed as many results as I could and stored them in here. You'll find them in the folder called "Winners". I can't get to a bookie, but I figure you can. We got to get as much dough down as quick as we can. Because pretty soon the future's gonna start changing.'

Big Itchy nodded slowly. 'Right. Who's gonna run a race where everyone knows the result?'

'The mob,' said Slim Jim. 'But of course, they don't mean *everyone* everyone.'

'You want to take down the mob?' said Big Itchy.

'I'm incredulous, Jimmy. Flabbergasted even. I never took you for no suicide case. As soon as they found out what you'd done, they'd come back for their money, and take your nuts as interest.'

'They would, they really would,' Davidson admitted. 'And there's no cutting them in, because they're not going to believe you. Not yet. So no, I was just joking about the mob. But if you can lay off twenty, thirty big bets around the whole country, we can clean up. Get a nice float for some other things I got in mind.'

'Like what?' asked Big Itchy, sounding more interested with every passing minute.

'Big man, I'd have to sit down and split that fifth with you while I filled you in on these characters and what they're like. Things are going to change, Itchy. Even more than because of the war, I can feel it in my guts, man. And every time things change, there's always some guy smart enough to cash in. I want to be that guy. You should, too. You all should,' he said, broadening out his appeal to the other men in the room.

'Okay,' said Itchy, 'we'll talk. Talking's for smart guys and I like to think I'm smarter than the average guy.' He paused for a moment, then said, 'You tell me these guys got a lot of money.'

Slim Jim leaned forward, looking at each of the men before he said quietly, 'A Marine Corps private starts out on a salary of thirty-five grand a year. That's more than ten times what I make.'

A chorus of soft hoots and wolf whistles paid homage to such an impressive figure. Even Big Itchy had to respect a wad of dough like that.

'So how do we get our hands on it? These guys, they like a drink, all guys like a fucking drink, don't they? And getting laid, too, everyone loves to get laid.'

For the first time, Slim Jim looked a little less sure of himself.

'You know, Itchy, they're kind of uptight, if you want to know. A lot of them, they don't seem the type to be lining up outside some skanky whorehouse for two hours just to stick their thing into a dame's been getting things stuck in her all day.'

'What, are they queer or something?'

'I don't know, man. Maybe it's all the dames they got on the ships. Maybe they don't need to. I haven't been around them long enough to know. But I'm guessing you'll make more of a buck getting them hammered than laid.'

Slim Jim could almost see the gears and wheels cranking over slowly in Big Itchy's mind. It made him wish he had a classier connection out here in the islands, but this wasn't his home turf. He'd have to make do with the shoddy materials he had at hand.

'What about I clean out one of the bars, really clean it out, you know, and put some of my best girls in there. Real clean and pretty ones. Let them make up their own minds.'

Slim Jim made a show of thinking it over.

'Only problem I can see with that,' he said, 'you can guarantee it'll end in a brawl.'

'So what? We got brawls every day.'

'Yeah, but they don't like brawling much, either.'

'Holy shit, Jimmy, they *are* a bunch of queers. Still, you know, it's gotta save me some dough on repair bills. It's killing me, replacing the bar stools these fucking idiot marines are always breaking over each other's heads.'

'Up to you, Itchy. You want to open a new bar? That's your business. But it's a risk. And it's a risk in a way that this ain't.'

He held up the flexipad.

'So, are we going to do some business?'

'Tui,' said Big Itchy to his right-hand man, 'you get to work on my new bar. Take a few of the boys, shut down the Black Dog, throw out the trash, get it cleaned up and ready for a more refined sort of clientele, the sort that gets out of the bath to take a piss.'

'Right, boss.'

'And you, Jimmy, you take this pencil and paper and get to work on your crystal ball there. Fucking navy's got this place sealed tight since you guys came back, but I'll make sure we can get a line to the west coast later today. That good enough for you?'

'Sweet as a nut, my man.'

26

USS Hillary Clinton, *Pearl Harbor,* *1143 hours, 9 June 1942*

A Mexican pimp in a zoot suit had put a .38 slug into Detective Sergeant Lou 'Buster' Cherry's thighbone. Buster had returned the favour, of course, putting a clean six into the greaser's head, turning it into a pile of bone splinters, teeth and blood pudding. But he'd never really been the same afterwards. His leg healed up after six months but he limped if he had to run for more than a few yards, and occasionally a small shard of bone or a fragment of the pimp's bullet would work its way up out of his skin.

He'd tried to enlist after Pearl Harbor, but they'd stamped him unfit for active duty and sent him back to the force.

Like the fucking force wasn't active duty!

At least they'd been glad to have him back. A lot of the younger guys, they'd been accepted by the army and marines straightaway, and now he was left holding the fort with a bunch of old geezers and a couple of asthmatic queers with flat feet. God help him.

His leg was aching. His haemorrhoids were playing

up. He had a dull headache from the fifth of Old Grandpa he'd polished off last night, and now he had to drag himself up what looked like about five hundred steps to get onto this fucking big boat to watch some lippy dyke chop up a dead nigger and her Jap boyfriend. He shoulda been down the mortuary doing this, not all the fucking way out at Pearl, tooling up for a turf war with these asshole time bandits.

He badged the greaseball at the foot of the gangplank, who checked him off against a list on one of them flexi-things and waved him on up. It was a hot bitch of a day and his shirt was already stuck to his back. The limp started up. The headache got worse. He stopped to catch his breath and when he looked up, it was like standing at the foot of a steel fucking mountain range.

A marine met him at the top – which is to say, a coloured broad of some sort, not even a regular nigger. She was dressed in fatigues and sporting a USMC patch. She snapped to and told him to follow her. At least she looked like she had a good ass under those fatigues. Buster was an enlightened guy when it came to ass-related issues. He'd take it wherever he could find it.

As they moved past work details and piles of strange-looking machinery and burned-out wreckage, he could see that the deck of the carrier had taken a beating.

Good. Serves 'em right.

From what he'd heard, these assholes had deep-sixed a lot of good boys out there. Some said it was robots did most of the killing. But from all the greasers and rock apes he could see running about, Buster had his doubts. Those bastards were always hot shit on a trigger.

He really had to drag his bad leg along to keep up with the broad, but he'd be damned if he was gonna call on her to slow down. She was probably doing it on purpose, just to show him up. Christ only knows what'd become of the country if the marines were going to be taking on crossbreed trash like her in the future.

Nobody paid him any attention, he noticed. But he guessed they'd be used to sightseers picking their way through the scrap metal by now.

'Are you all right, Detective?' the woman asked. 'Do you require assistance, sir?'

The black dame – she looked part Apache, or maybe even Chinese, now that he thought about it – had pulled up and was checking him out as he hauled his injured leg over the baking hot, rubbery surface of the flight deck.

'Don't you worry about me, doll,' he wheezed. 'I'm just saving my energy.'

Buster winked at her, but the woman just gave him a flat, level stare that betrayed nothing of her feelings.

Well, fuck you.

He made himself walk without favouring one leg over the other, and they didn't speak again. She led him into the first of the two smooth, sort of swept-back cones that dominated the deck. It must have been like the island on the *Enterprise*, he figured. He could see the other carrier a mile away. It looked like a tin can next to this monster.

It was mercifully cooler inside, and the harsh brightness of the midday sun gave way to the soft light coming from who-knew-where. Now that he was out of the heat and glare he noticed even more how his suit clung uncomfortably to the sweat-soaked shirt, and he could feel his pants grabbing and riding up at the crotch. He was really going to have to get a bag to the Chinese laundry. He'd been putting it off for weeks. But even he had to admit that he probably smelled bad. He hadn't had a clean change of clothes in an age.

Things just got away from him after the shooting.

Although, when you thought about it, things had been slipping since Lauren had left him three years before that.

Well, fuck her, too.

They seemed to walk for miles along a single corridor, forcing him to high-step over dozens of knee knockers as they passed through watertight doors. Then they had to climb down a series of switchback metal staircases. That was a private kind of hell with his leg, but damned if he was gonna give this bitch the satisfaction of seeing him fall behind or hearing him whine about his troubles.

Just when he thought it was going to be too much,

they stepped off the lower level of the main passage and into a smaller walkway that seemed to run right across the ship. Another turn took them through a pair of heavy swinging doors that looked as though they were made of clear rubber or something.

The letters WCIU were stencilled on the doors, but Cherry recognised the smell immediately. They were in some kind of morgue.

The forensic laboratory of the War Crimes Investigation Unit was familiar turf to Captain Margie Francois. She'd been attached to two such units during the previous fifteen years, earning a medal from the United Nations Human Rights Commission for her work in identifying the members of a 'special purposes' battalion of the Iranian Army, which was active during the second Iran–Iraq war. The purpose of the battalion had been to spread terror among subject Iraqis through a programme of systematic rape.

Francois was first and foremost a Marine Corps combat surgeon, but she was also cross-trained as a special victims investigator. She had the graduation certificate from Quantico and a mass of emotional scar tissue to show for it.

As the wait for Detective Cherry dragged on, she worked hard at damping down the first sparks of her temper. There were five people in the morgue with her: Doctor Brumm, from the coroner's office in Honolulu; Assistant District Attorney Crew, standing in for the DA; Lieutenant Commander Helen

Wassman, formerly the medical officer on the *Leyte Gulf*; Ensign Mitsuka, surviving senior officer on the *Siranui*; and Commander Hugh Lunn, from the *Clinton*'s Legal Affairs Division, who doubled as the head of the War Crimes Unit when it was operational – it wasn't at this point, but Lunn was there as the senior legal affairs officer in the task force.

They were all waiting on Cherry.

The morgue wasn't meant to hold so many observers, so the space was cramped. They all wore masks but only the doctors, Francois and Wassman, were gloved and gowned. The 'temps', Brumm and Crew, had arrived together, but seemed uncomfortable talking in front of the Multinational Force personnel. They were obviously ill at ease in Mitsuka's presence, and Francois suspected they weren't too happy riding in the back seat while a couple of chicks drove the post-mortem process, either. But the look of dismay on Dr Brumm's face – at the array of unusual lab equipment – was reason enough to disqualify him from a hands-on role in the post-mortem.

The naked bodies of Anderson and Miyazaki lay on stainless-steel benches in the middle of the room. The Japanese officer rested stiffly on the table nearest to Francois. His toes were pointed straight at the laboratory door, as if he were diving into a pool. Gravity had pooled his blood, giving the underside of his corpse a bruised appearance that contrasted with the waxy yellow colour, turning noticeably to green, elsewhere on his body.

Anderson was posed more dramatically. One fist was clenched and her right leg was drawn up towards her stomach. Her left leg was bent backwards at the knee. It had obviously been broken with great force. Her dark skin meant that the green tinge of putrefaction wasn't as immediately evident, but she still looked unreal, like a posed wax model. Everybody in the room avoided staring at her private parts. Something terrible had been done there.

Francois checked the clock again. Fifteen minutes late. She could feel her face colouring with anger. She didn't know either victim personally, but she always took this shitty sort of business personally. It was why she'd turned down so many requests to participate in other war crimes investigations over the years. It dredged up memories.

'Detective Cherry was shot in the leg last year,' said ADA Crew. 'He finds it hard to get around.'

'And they couldn't send anybody else?' asked Francois, barely controlling her irritation.

Crew shrugged. 'They're shorthanded. A lot of cops joined up the day after Pearl. Cherry caught the case. It was his turf the stiff . . . the bodies washed up on.'

Francois was about to snap a comment at Crew's indelicate choice of language when Detective Cherry came through the swing doors.

Jesus Christ, what a bag of shit, she thought.

'Sorry I'm so early,' the cop said with a lopsided grin.

Francois had never seen a man so obviously teetering on the edge of a massive coronary, and a stroke, and liver failure, and God only knew what else, all at the same time.

His limp was pronounced, but that was the least of his problems. The man's fingers were yellowed with nicotine. He had a paunch that fell about twenty-five centimetres over his belt. His breathing sounded like something a dying animal might squeeze out when crushed to death by a boa constrictor. His face was livid, the colour of bad blood and meat sickness. And he stank. She wasn't sure which was worse – the sour sweat or the stale haze of cigarette smoke and alcohol fumes that followed him into the room.

'So,' grunted Cherry, nodding at the bodies. 'The happy couple.'

'Buster, please,' Crew said quietly.

Wassman and Mitsuka both stared at him, appalled.

Francois could feel the moment turning into a circus. Then she thought, *Buster Cherry? Oh, for fuck's sake.* She was going to find it real hard warming up to this asshole.

'If you're all right, Detective, we'll start. You can prop yourself up on that stool if you need to.'

Cherry bristled at the suggestion. He folded his massive arms and shook his head.

'Don't you worry about me, Doc. I mighta slipped over my fighting weight, but I'm not about to feed the worms just yet.'

'What the hell do you mean by that crack?' snapped Wassman.

Cherry shrugged, a slow movement that shifted a hell of a lot of shoulder meat around under his crumpled suit. 'It's just an expression, sister.'

Francois took a deep breath before speaking. 'Lieutenant Commander Wassman is a US Navy combat surgeon, Detective. Not your sister.'

Cherry smiled. His teeth were nearly as nicotine-stained as his fingers.

'Like I said, Doc. Just an expression. You ladies might want to lighten up, if you're gonna make a habit of this kinda work. Send you to the fucking nuthouse otherwise.'

The atmosphere in the small theatre was growing palpably worse. Commander Lunn pushed off the bench where he'd been leaning and said, 'Why don't we get to work?'

Dr Brumm and ADA Crew nodded and mumbled their agreement. Francois held Cherry's gaze for a second, her eyes cold and level, before turning her back on him and flicking a control switch to power up the morgue's video cameras.

'This is Captain Margaret Francois, United States Marine Corps. I am about to begin the autopsy on Captain Daytona Anderson, formerly the commander of the USS *Leyte Gulf*.'

Francois named everybody else present for the benefit of the recording before going on.

'I'll commence with a visual examination of the

subject. Anderson was a forty-two-year-old female of African descent. DNA-matching with US Navy data has confirmed that she is the subject of this post-mortem examination. For the benefit of local authorities, this information has been matched with dental and fingerprint records. The body has also been positively identified as that of Captain Anderson, by Lieutenant Commander Wassman, Medical Officer of the USS *Leyte Gulf*.'

Francois paused. Brumm and Crew had been briefed on the role of DNA in forensic investigations. They were willing to take it on trust. Cherry had insisted on the dental work and prints. She couldn't quibble with his belt-and-braces approach, but it smacked to her of game playing.

The cop had leaned himself up against a bulkhead and was watching her intently. Francois bent back to Anderson's body.

'The head of the subject shows signs of trauma inflicted with a blunt weapon. The left eye has swollen closed, the skin is broken, and a small dent is visible in the forehead. The subject's jaw appears on initial examination to have been broken by a separate blow, delivered from the opposite direction, that is, from the right-hand side. Ligature marks are clearly visible on the neck. Two entry wounds from large-calibre bullets sit over the subject's heart. Her right hand shows signs of cadaveric spasm. The fist is clenched tightly and knuckles of the first two fingers appear to be displaced, possibly as the result of a defensive blow she delivered while extant. The subject is wearing a ring on the third finger of the right hand.'

Francois reached up and pulled down a large, fluorescently lit magnifying lens on a jointed metal arm. She waved Brumm and Crew over to examine the ring, which loomed as large as a baseball in the looking glass.

'If you gentlemen would care to study the ring, you'll see that small shreds of flesh have been trapped within the irregular facets. It's possible that she struck her attacker. If so, we can retrieve DNA from the sample.'

Detective Cherry suddenly heaved himself upright.

'Whoa! How do we know she hit the guy who necked her? I hear they had a pretty willing fucking brawl on that ship of hers. She might have clocked half a dozen guys. Maybe your fucking crime labs are better than ours, but you still gotta get beyond reasonable doubt, don'tcha?'

Francois nodded. 'That's right. I said *it's possible that she struck her attacker*. That's all, Detective.'

Cherry subsided. 'Okay,' he said. 'Because, you know, she could have gone upside the head of her boyfriend over there.' He waved a meaty paw at Sub-Lieutenant Miyazaki's corpse. 'The whole damn thing's probably a lovers' tiff.'

'Hey, just a minute –' said Wassman.

Francois ground her teeth and placed a restraining arm on her colleague.

'Detective, I can assure you that Captain Anderson

was not having a relationship with Lieutenant Miyazaki.'

Cherry rolled his eyes. 'Please don't tell me she had a little man waiting for her at home.'

Francois gave him a poisonous look. She paused the recording, waited for just a beat and then spoke again.

'Captain Anderson was gay.'

The three locals were visibly perplexed.

'Are you saying that she was a happy individual?' ventured Dr Brumm.

Commander Lunn rubbed his eyes and shook his head. Wassman swore under her breath.

Francois prayed for the patience to get her through this. 'Captain Anderson was a lesbian,' she said.

She expected astonishment, even embarrassment, but in fact she herself was surprised when Detective Cherry actually laughed.

'Three strikes, hey? A nigger, a broad *and* a rug muncher. Christ, what the fuck happened to America?'

27

Honolulu, 1534 hours, 9 June 1942

Down at Wo Fats, the bar and grill favoured by the chiefs and warrant officers, Eddie Mohr nursed the second of the two beers he was allowed to purchase on any given day, and held court. Half-a-dozen Old Navy men had gathered around him to hear him tell of the *Astoria*'s bizarre fate.

'It was like crawling through a fucking Chinese puzzle box in there, I'm telling you,' he assured the doubters. 'You never seen anything like it in your whole goddamned life. And these guns they got, tear a man to pieces like a fucking grizzly bear, they would, but they hit steel or wood and it's like getting dusted by some dame's powder puff. That's what they call the bullets, powder puffs. A fucking obscenity, if you ask me. They got Bud Kelly with one of them. Turned his fucking head into something looked like chopped liver.'

'Fuckers,' somebody muttered. Mohr wasn't sure who.

'Well,' said Pete Craven, 'he was never that pretty a sight to begin with.'

A few sad smiles acknowledged the point. Craven,

a heavily tattooed former longshoreman, now serving on the *Enterprise*, raised his glass.

'To Chief Kelly.'

Half-a-dozen thick voices responded, '*To Chief Kelly.*'

Around them the familiar chaos of Wo Fats roared on, as eternal and reassuring as the sea itself. Men cursed and bellowed. Beer steins clinked and sometimes crashed. The turntable spun and speakers crackled and blared with the hits of the day, 'Goodbye Mama I'm off to Yokohama' and 'Let's Put the Axe to the Axis'. A handwritten poster announced a special showing of *Andy Hardy's Double Life* throughout August at the marine canteen.

Mohr tapped himself another Camel out of the pack resting amid the confusion of empty glasses, cigar and cigarette butts, and spilled beer.

'Did I tell you about the well-deserved knuckling of Seaman Finch?' he asked nobody in particular.

Pete Craven blew a thick blue stream of smoke down at the table.

'Only about four times so far,' he said. 'You heard she got topped, didn't you, Eddie? That Anderson broad. The nigger. And someone interfered with her, too, they reckon.'

Mohr's beer stopped halfway to his lips. 'You're shitting me! That was her? Fuck! I heard one of their dames washed up on the beach with a Jap, but I never woulda thought it was her.'

He took a meditative pull on the stein.

'Jeez, that's a fucking pity, you know. She wasn't so bad, that Anderson. For a black dame.'

The other men at the table didn't visibly react to the statement, but their silence spoke for them. The fact that such a thing as a black female captain even existed was a source of amazement and not a little disbelief to those who hadn't been there. That she'd then turned up dead, and 'interfered with', was kind of interesting. But Eddie Mohr sitting in Wo Fats, looking upset and glum, and saying that he thought she was all right, well that was downright disturbing.

The silence at their table seemed to balloon outwards as the background roar suddenly fell right away. All around them, heads began to turn towards the front door. Soon the only sound Mohr could hear was the crackling of the speakers as Sammy Kaye crooned 'Remember Pearl Harbor'.

Mohr stood up, craning to see over dozens of ugly, shaven boxheads in front of him. He could just make out the silhouettes of three figures near the front of the bar. He guessed from the cut of their uniforms that they were off one of Kolhammer's ships. He was surprised. They were supposed to keep to themselves at the Moana and the Royal. As he pushed his way through the crush of thick, sweaty bodies, a hunch began forming. A few seconds later he'd confirmed it.

Two white guys and a nigger – sorry, Negro – sorry, African American serviceman – were standing at the entrance. He could see that the confusion on their faces was quickly congealing into anger, and there, a few feet away, was the cause. A Marine Corps sergeant and half-a-dozen of his buds were barring their way.

'Shit,' Mohr said to himself as he started to hustle forward. Unfortunately he wasn't the only one with the same idea. The crowd heaved towards the scene of the confrontation and the resulting crush actually slowed his progress. He could see the marine sergeant blocking the entrance with one arm as a phalanx of men packed in behind him.

Mohr caught a movement out of the corner of his eye. The barman had placed a well-used Louisville Slugger on the bar.

Mohr could feel it coming. He'd been in enough of these things to know.

He struggled to push forward through the crush and got himself close enough to hear the exchange. One of the visitors, a white marine, was arguing with the sergeant, explaining that his great-granddaddy drank in this very bar before shipping out to get himself killed on Iwo Jima. It didn't impress the sarge much.

'Yeah, but your fucking granddaddy's not here now, asshole,' the noncom declared. 'And if he was, he wouldn't let you in neither, not with no fucking nigger in tow. This is a whites-only establishment.'

The three things Mohr remembered later were that he was sure the guy had said 'heshstabishment', and it wasn't the black marine who threw the first punch. It was the guy whose great-granddaddy had just been insulted. The other thing was that the big, dumb oaf trying to keep them away from the bar was fucked from the get-go.

He was definitely drunk, but Mohr would swear for the rest of his life that even stone-cold sober and waiting on that punch, he'd never had a chance. This other guy's arms just sort of *blurred.* The sergeant's head snapped back, teeth flying in a long high arc halfway down the back of the bar and one long gobbet of blood landing – *splat!* – right on the poster announcing the Andy Hardy movie.

The room surged forwards. It felt like being sucked into a big wave on a surf beach. A hundred voices roared and Mohr distinctly heard the scratch of the record player's needle as someone dragged or knocked it across the grooves of 'Remember Pearl Harbor'. Then the crowd surged right back, unbalancing a lot of them and upending those men whose footing wasn't certain. Sailors, marines and army noncoms all piled into one another, spilling precious drinks, tripping and stomping on each other's feet, swinging left and right with elbows and fists to clear some room.

The original cause of the melee at the front of the bar was forgotten or ignored by most of those present as personal insults and service rivalries sparked an all-out brawl. Mohr ducked instinctively as a bar stool flew past his head and smashed into the mirror behind the bar, adding the crash of broken glass to the patchwork of shouts, curses, exploding bottles, collapsing furniture and a roiling pandemonium of slamming fists and thudding boots.

About two dozen men decided to back the sergeant in his feud with the newcomers. Mohr wasn't surprised. He figured some would be genuinely pissed at the idea of a black man having the gall to show his face in their bar. Others were hurting from the battle at Midway and looking for payback. Some were just plain ornery, and some of these guys genuinely enjoyed the prospect of a good clean fight.

If anyone was worthy of sympathy, it was these last, poor, stupid chumps. They sailed into the fray with ham-fisted gusto, only to find themselves targeted by a focused and unforgiving type of violence with which the average American was unacquainted, even in the early days of 1942. The three men who braced themselves in the door of the bar didn't seem to place much store in dramatic flourishes. They quickly and somewhat mechanically crippled anyone foolish enough to attack them.

The thing that stayed with Eddie Mohr was the look on all their faces. They weren't snarling defiance or obscenities. They weren't scared. They just looked *blank*. Like they were somewhere else. They fought like machines. It was fucking Midway all over again.

A Seabee went at the intruders on their own terms. He flipped the bottle of Royal Beer he'd been drinking, smashed it on the edge of the bar and advanced on the trio with murder in his eyes. The ground in front of his intended victims was strewn with the fallen bodies of men who screamed and thrashed while clutching at broken elbow joints and kneecaps. They impeded the engineer's progress sufficiently that he changed his target to the black marine, who parried the strike with a compact hand block. Using the momentum of the weapon's thrust, he turned his hip slightly and swept the engineer's hand up level with his chin. He took control of the bottle and jerked, breaking the man's wrist. As the unnerved attacker cried out in pain, the marine shifted minimally at the hip again, driving his elbow into the engineer's own. The pressure shattered the joint and the man blacked out before he could scream again.

It appeared to Mohr as if the three of them were constructing a berm of their victims. They were obviously much fitter than anyone else in the bar and they expended a minimum of energy in the way they fought. Mohr thought they looked like they could wipe out the entire joint, but they weren't there for the entertainment value. They were methodically edging towards the exit as though they wanted nothing more than to get safely away. The fury of their attackers made that difficult.

Dan Black was out running with Julia when they noticed smoke pouring into the sky over Honolulu – or rather, he was getting his ass kicked by Julia after foolishly taking her up on the challenge of a race. Rosanna had tried to warn him. Duffy had made the top one thousand finishers of three New York

Marathons, she said. But Dan simply hadn't believed a woman could get the better of him, and so they agreed on a race and a swim afterwards. The loser was to buy drinks that night for all four of them at the Moana. Dan hadn't felt bad about the prospect of taking Julia's dough. She said she was carrying about four hundred bucks around in her wallet and the local businesses had been ordered to honour the strange plastic banknotes at their face value.

He knew he was in trouble after the first mile, however, as she maintained a steady flow of chitchat while he laboured to draw breath and match her pace. After three miles she'd even spurted ahead a few yards, spun around and run backwards, all while lecturing him on the necessity for universal birth control and an Equal Rights Amendment. He was set to give in and admit defeat when he noticed that the expression on her face had changed.

She slowed down, came to a full stop, and as he drew level with her she pointed back towards Honolulu.

'Come on,' she said.

He saw the smoke as soon as he turned around. His first thought was of an air raid, but surely they would have heard that.

'Must be trouble,' he panted as they started back into town at an even quicker pace.

'No shit, Sherlock.'

By the time they made the edge of town Dan was in serious pain. A deep, burning stitch ran down the left side of his body and he could feel the muscles in his legs starting to cramp. Julia was sweating, but otherwise looked comfortable.

The thunder of a riot was only slightly muted by distance. They had entered town away from the worst of the disturbance. Flickers of madness had drifted over, however, like the embers of a forest fire carried far ahead of the main blaze. As they swung onto the main strip a crazy man came at them with a club. Dan barely had time to notice that the club seemed to be a chair leg and that the guy was white and dressed in torn civilian clothes, when Julia suddenly pivoted on one foot and drove her other leg out like a steam piston.

Their would-be attacker jackknifed over as she rammed the heel of her running shoe into his groin with an elegant, sweeping back kick. She continued the pivot to bring her other leg to bear, grabbing the man's lank, sweaty hair in her bunched fists and using it to guide his head down towards her knee, which she smashed into his face three times. She turned ninety degrees, imparting a sharp twist to the guy's head that spun him to the ground. When he fell she seemed to step back, only to sail in and snap two more kicks into his ribs.

She bent at one knee, plucked the club from his hand and placed one running shoe on his throat.

'We'll be going now,' she said. 'Don't bother to get up. I'd just have to split your fucking skull open. Okay?'

The man groaned and coughed blood before nodding weakly.

Dan was stunned. He could tell she was about to head *into* the trouble.

'Julia! Wait on!'

'No. Come on!' she snapped. 'We've got to get down there.'

Dan shook his head.

'No we don't.'

In the opinion of Detective Sergeant Cherry it wasn't an entirely bad thing, that nigger and her toy Jap getting themselves killed. From what he'd seen and heard of these time travellers, they needed putting in their place.

Buster had been on the job for twenty-three years, eighteen of them in Chicago, and if he'd learned anything it was that once you had your boot on somebody's throat, you didn't take it off. They were liable to come at you with a knife or a gun. Your niggers and your spics and dagos and so on, they needed keeping down. They bred quicker than white folk. They had no respect. And if they got wind of the idea that a bunch of superniggers had somehow grabbed the keys to the kingdom, there'd be no stopping them. They'd come roaring out of the ghetto demanding a piece of the action for themselves.

Buster was certain of it, even if his thinking was a little slowed down by the three bourbons he'd taken after the autopsy. Not that he was squeamish, mind you. He'd eaten his lunch during post-mortems in the past.

No, he was just shook up by that ship full of freaks.

He was so shook up that, rather than heading back to the station, he drove down to Hotel Street and walked into the Black Dog, where he ran a tab that was probably larger than his annual wage. He'd never bothered to keep track and the owners were never going to ask him about it.

As soon as the barkeep saw Cherry force his way through the crush of humanity, a shot glass and bottle of Old Fitzgerald appeared on the bar. Buster knocked down the first two shots without much of a gap between them. But he took his time over the third. He was used to the jostle and chaos of places like the Black Dog. It felt more like home than his own miserable apartment. He nursed the drink and tried to calm down. Two or three times he'd been tempted to pop that Francois bitch right on the hooter. She was a goddamn ball breaker, and she looked at him like he was something nasty she'd found on her shoe.

Old Doc Brumm and ADA Crew, they weren't much help. Not that he could blame them. There was a ton of pressure coming down from above on this case. The chief himself had called Buster and told him to break as many arms as it took to wrap the fucking thing up as quickly as possible. He was taking heat from the military, no doubt about it. And that heat was being applied directly to Buster, like a blowtorch to the belly.

Well, fuck them.

If they couldn't see how dangerous these fuckers were, they were gonna get swept under. Buster recognised power when he saw it. And those half-breeds and dykes out on that ship thought they had it. You could see they were used to getting their own way at home, and he'd pay a thousand to one that they were already trying it on here. Otherwise, why would the chief be on his ass about a couple of dead coloured fuckers? That sort of shit was what his old ma used to call 'an everyday happy-stance'. You didn't waste time breaking arms over it.

Buster hunched his giant shoulders against the seething press of the crowd. Hundreds of men were crammed into the Dog. They were mostly drunk and stupid. They stank. They roared. They shoved and pushed and elbowed each other. But they were mostly good guys when you got down to it. They were going off to die, a lot of them. And for what? A country that was gonna turn itself into a fucking ghetto.

Buster threw down the last of his drink and was just about to pour another when the roaring bedlam of the crowd dipped unexpectedly. He turned away from the bar as a general push towards the doors began. There must be a fight outside. He would have ignored it. After all, it was none of his goddamn business, and he'd seen enough ignorant fucking drunks beating on each other over the years that the prospect held no interest for him now.

But the tidal flow surging out of the door, and the increasingly furious sounds coming back in from the street, told him this was no ordinary brawl. It sounded more like a riot.

Buster checked his gun and the heavy leather blackjack he carried in a back pocket, and then he headed out.

He was right.

It seemed to him that the dusty, sun-baked street was choked with thousands of brawling men, most of them in uniform, but not all. The sound was deafening, like the blast of a huge crowd at a sports stadium when you emerged into the open, having gone to get a beer and a hot dog. Smoke and fire poured from the upper windows of two buildings across the street. A thick mass of struggling men surged around two jeeps in the middle of the street. Buster saw a flash of white helmets in the centre of the melee. Normally he would have walked away. A man can get himself killed very easily in a shit fight like that. But the bourbon and the resentment he felt towards that snooty fucking lady doctor lit his fuse, which was admittedly short at the best of times.

Somebody cannoned into him from the left. But Buster stood six-foot four in his socks and weighed a hundred and ninety-eight pounds. Even a little drunk and hung over, his street smarts were more finely tuned than most men's, and he sensed the impact before he felt it. Buster braced himself and drove an elbow into the guy's head. It wasn't a clean hit. His elbow caught a cheekbone, which gave under the impact, but most of the force of the blow was misdirected, unbalancing him a little.

He didn't bother to check on the man he'd just knocked out. Buster was vaguely aware of the body falling away into the threshing machine of arms and legs that now surrounded him. But he was locked into his own narrow world. He slipped the blackjack out of his pocket: eight inches of stitched leather with a solid lead weight sewn into one end. It felt like an extension of his hand. He didn't have a lot of space in the violent, heaving mass of brawlers, but he didn't need much. He began to lay into the crowd around him.

Eddie Mohr could hardly see through the blood and sweat running into his eyes. Somebody had knifed him just outside the bar. It wasn't a deep cut. The blade had glanced off a rib. But between that and the open gash on his forehead he was starting to lose more blood than he ought to. He knew, from working on the floor with his old man, how that sort of thing could sneak up on a guy. One of the boners at the stockyard had shivved himself with a knife so sharp he didn't feel the cut. He bled to death, standing in a lake of his own blood, boning a yearling calf.

The riot wasn't breaking up, but it was spreading out. Eddie didn't like the way every breath felt like he was sucking in fire. He'd broken a knuckle on somebody's head and was limping from a kick to the back of his knee. It was time to get going. The MPs would be here in force soon, breaking heads with their nightsticks. And if they brought any reinforcements from the Multinationals with them, they'd be carrying those electric batons. He didn't fancy getting one of them stuck in his ass.

He'd lost contact with the other guys. Last he'd seen of Pete Craven the dumb bastard was pounding on a corporal from the Engineers. Hundreds of men still fought like that, piled atop each other, gouging, biting and knocking heads. Nothing like the fights you saw in the movies. He'd fought his way clear by using a trick his old man had taught him. Swinging a bar stool like a club, he'd made as though he was going to brain any bastard who challenged him. When they instinctively threw up their hands, Mohr swung the stool low and fast into their knees, knocking them down like cornstalks. The stool had broken after the fourth time, but by then he was outside.

Smoke and dust, hot ash and the sounds of the riot filled the air.

He felt dizzy and tired.

He started to move off, closing up like a prizefighter and taking a couple of poorly aimed hits on his shoulders and arms. A section of burning wooden sunshade crashed down in front of him. Men jumped away from it, cursing and shouting. Mohr altered his course, heading for a side street that seemed a little quieter.

He turned the corner at a bar called the Black Dog and recognised one of the chiefs from the *Leyte Gulf*. The guy's face was badly banged up, but he was pretty sure it was Jose Borghino, or Borgu, or something. He was leaned up against a car, obviously in trouble. Mohr started to move towards him when a man in a torn, bloodied suit crashed into him and knocked him to the ground.

He heard somebody call out, 'Get away from the car, asshole.'

And then a big gun, a .38 or .45, boomed twice, so loud it deafened him.

Half blinded by blood and grit, Mohr looked up as Borghino fell away from the car. His mouth full of dirt, his ears ringing, he was about to scramble up and confront the suit. That guy had to be the shooter. But a white-hot bomb went off inside his head and he tumbled down into darkness.

Restricted to camp after the riot, Slim Jim Davidson was anxious to hear from Big Itchy. The confinement was driving him nuts. He feared the dumb gangster would be so preoccupied by the destruction of his clubs on Hotel Street that he wouldn't have followed through on the plan to clean out the stateside bookies. Slim Jim was stretched out in his rack, cursing his luck and the suckass pattern of his so-called life, when the cry of 'Mail call' went up.

Moose Molloy Jr, who was resting on his cot, leaped to his feet.

‘C’mon, Slim Jim. Mail’s here,’ he enthused.

‘Big fucking deal,’ said Slim Jim flatly.

‘Oh, don’t be like that. We’ll be out of here soon. I even heard they’re gonna kick the niggers – sorry, the *African Americans* – off those ships and let us crew ’em. Wouldn’t that be great, Slim Jim? Can you imagine fighting the Japs in one of them babies? They’d never lay a glove on you.’

‘Yeah?’ said Davidson. ‘They gonna leave the pussy in place? Did you happen to hear that?’

Moose didn’t pick up on the sarcasm.

‘No,’ he answered ingenuously, ‘I didn’t hear nothing about the lady sailors. I don’t reckon they’d let us keep them, though. There’d be another riot if everyone thought we was getting girlfriends *and* a new ship.’

‘Oh God,’ groaned Davidson as he pulled a threadbare pillow out from under his head and attempted to smother himself with it.

Moose waited patiently for another minute before asking whether Slim Jim was planning on getting up. They could already hear the mail being handed out in the distance.

‘C’mon, Slim Jim, maybe some Girl Guide sent you some cookies.’

‘Unless she sent me a picture of her fanny, I couldn’t care less,’ he moped.

‘Slim Jim!’

Moose seemed genuinely offended that anyone could sully the image of the Girl Guides of America. As far as he was concerned, protecting them from the ravages of the Japs was one of the main reasons they were here, camping out in this godforsaken burned-out cane field.

'I'll tell you what, Moose,' Davidson said finally, 'if I get any Girl Guide cookies, you bring 'em back for me and we'll share them.'

'Is that a promise?'

'You can bank on it. Just let me get some rest.'

Moose hurried off in pursuit of free cookies. Davidson thought about whipping his shank out for a quick pull, but he couldn't even work up the enthusiasm for that. He lay on his cot, scratching his balls until a thought occurred to him. Checking that Moose really was gone, he rolled to his feet and dragged his duffel bag out. The flexipad was at the bottom and it took some digging to retrieve it. When at last he had the stolen pad in his hands, it felt heavy with possibilities.

A quick check out the tent flap again. No sign of Moose. Davidson smiled as he powered up the unit. He'd become quite adept at controlling it and quickly found the file he'd been meaning to check out. A few taps on the touch screen and suddenly he nearly wet himself at the sound of a nigger band – called Death Row of all fucking things – punching out a weird number called 'Rape The Bitch Now'. The title had intrigued him since he'd first seen it a day earlier. The jigaboos sounded like they were doing some really angry, fucked-up poems to a jungle beat and it was hard to understand everything they said.

He dropped the volume and shook his head in disbelief throughout the two-minute performance. It took him three repeats to fully understand the lyrics, and when he did, he struggled with a tangled mass of feelings. He found that for the first time in his life, he was genuinely affronted. His morality – *Could you believe it? His fucking morality!* – was actually outraged by those fucking hoods. But contending with that outrage was excitement at the images that accompanied the 'music'. He'd never seen women dance like that, not even in the skankiest fucking New Orleans whorehouse. Those hussies were like damn dogs in heat, the way they were throwing their fannies around.

'Goddamn,' Slim Jim hooted softly. 'The future looks rosy!'

He cycled through another performance by Death Row. It sounded so similar that he couldn't be certain, if he closed his eyes, that he was listening to a different song – if you could even call it a song. But the new clip featured an entirely different bunch of 'bitches', as he quickly and effortlessly came to think of them; and Slim Jim had no trouble at all telling one bitch from another. He was about to revisit his decision not to haul his shank out for a quick one, when he heard the heavy tread of Moose approaching. Davidson hastily shut down the pad and jammed it under a blanket.

'Hey Slim Jim, you're up.'

'And at 'em.'

The big oaf had a package for him. If it was cookies, it was the biggest pack he'd ever seen. Davidson pushed himself up on one elbow. He was slick and sticky with sweat. The tent felt like the inside of an oven.

'You got laundry,' Moose said as he tossed over the package.

'Laundry? I didn't send no fucking laundry out,' said Davidson.

'You must have left some with the Chinese place before we shipped out for Midway,' said Moose.

'Chinese?' said Davidson, suddenly coming wide awake. 'Yeah, now that I think of it, I did leave some pants behind.'

'You're always losing your pants, Slim Jim.'

'Ain't it the truth? What'd you get, buddy?'

'Just a letter from my old man. He says they're having real trouble keeping the greasers in line now that a lot of the younger fellows have left the police force for the army. But he reckons the old boys on the force, they still got a few tricks in them.'

'I'll bet,' said Davidson.

'And I spoke to Chief Craven, he said Chief Mohr's gonna be out of the hospital tomorrow and there's no way we're shipping out with the other guys. We're staying here.'

'Well, you gotta take the good with the bad,' shrugged Slim Jim, who'd die a happy man if he never set foot on another goddamn boat.

'You gonna open your package?'

'For a pair of pants? No. I thought I'd save the excitement for this evening. Give me something to look forward to in the cocktail hour.'

And it was early evening before Moose left the tent again, giving Davidson a chance to tear open the brown paper parcel. He found a couple of shirts inside and two pairs of socks. Wrapped up in one pair was an IOU from Big Itchy for six thousand dollars, payable when next they met.

A grin as big as the Grand Canyon broke out on Slim Jim's face. He could almost feel that money in the tips of his fingers. A lot of guys would have wanted it right there with them in the cot, thinking they could keep it safe that way. But Slim Jim Davidson knew his dough was more secure locked up in the strongbox beneath Big Itchy's desk. Any sticky fingers straying near the combination lock were liable to get themselves hacked off with a machete.

There was a note with the IOU.

Got any more ideas?

The two men sat in the shaded portico that ran around the hospital, sipping at iced water and squinting into the glare of the midday sun. Eddie Mohr was in far better shape than Lieutenant Commander Evans. The funny little gizmo they'd stuck on the back of his neck seemed to block all the pain he should have been feeling from his cracked skull and stitched-up wounds. But he found that he still got dizzy if he had to walk very far. Evans had it tougher.

His ruined arm was encased in one of those fat, blow-up sausages and he told Mohr that most of his arm wasn't even his any more. It had been in a test tube.

'Musta been a big fucking tube, sir,' said Mohr.

'More of a vat, they told me,' said Evans.

The *Astoria*'s senior enlisted man shook his head at the idea. Eddie Mohr had spent a good part of his life on the floor of a slaughterhouse. He wasn't a squeamish guy, but the idea of growing your own meat in a glass bowl made him feel distinctly giddy. Still, there were friends of his alive because of it, and because they'd been cracked open and fitted with mechanical hearts and plastic bones and Christ only knew what else.

Rumour had it that one guy off the *Hornet* was sporting a brand-new dick. Two inches longer than his old one!

Mohr wondered if you could put a request in for that sort of thing.

Other casualties meandered slowly about the grounds under their own power, or were pushed about in wheelchairs by nurses. The sun was so fierce it hurt to look at their white uniforms, unless you were wearing sunglasses. It seemed that almost everyone from the future did just that, even indoors. It was just another of the many things about them that made Eddie Mohr's head spin.

He felt himself dozing off, nodding forward in his cane chair, until Evans's voice cut through his torpor.

'You hear anything about Captain Anderson?' he asked.

The topic had hung between them like an unspoken curse and Mohr found himself looking for eavesdroppers before he replied. He'd learned that not everyone appreciated or understood his respect for the late commander of the *Leyte Gulf*. In fact, there'd been some ugliness over it.

He leaned over to Evans and lowered his voice. 'The way I hear it, they collected enough evidence at the scene to nail whoever done it, if they can figure out whoever done it.'

Evans crinkled his brow with the effort of trying to understand as Mohr continued.

'Doc Wassman, remember her? She tells me they can collect a sample of a guy's . . . uh, stuff. His come. And they can test it to show exactly who left it behind.'

'She was raped, then?'

Mohr's features contorted with distaste. 'Oh yeah. There's a lot of bullshit talk about this Miyazaki guy. How he might have fucked her before they got waxed. But Wassman says that's just crap. They can tell, because of the come. It ain't his. In fact,' he muttered, drawing even closer, 'it was a coupla guys.'

Evans nodded slowly. 'But they don't know who?'

Mohr waited while a man who was seemingly wrapped from head to toe in white gauze bandages was wheeled past. When they were alone again he said, 'They know it wasn't one of their guys. They can tell from the DMA.'

'DMA?'

'It's like a fingerprint for the come,' whispered Mohr.

Evans took that in without much reaction. He stared at the bright green tube around his arm for a few seconds.

'So what happened?' he said at last.

Mohr shrugged. 'Dunno. Anderson and the Jap were on shore. She'd taken over his ship with a bunch of other officers from the *Gulf*. Americans. The Japs lost a lot of their top guys when a shell hit the bridge. Captain Anderson and this Miyazaki were probably just walking along talking things through, you know, admin stuff, when they got hit.'

Evans sighed. He suddenly seemed very tired. 'What a mess.'

'Yeah, it's a fucking pity,' said Mohr. 'I thought that dame was all right, you know. A good captain.'

He said it tentatively, as if expecting an argument. But Evans simply bobbed his head up and down.

'Yeah. She was okay.'

28

Brisbane, Australia, 1411 hours, 9 June 1942

Commander Judge, Captain Windsor and the Australian submariner, Captain Willet, fell into step as they left the hotel and turned down Queen Street, heading for MacArthur's HQ. Trams that managed to look both antique and brand new rumbled past in both directions. They'd been in town for two days but it was still disorienting in the extreme. None of them had trouble recognising their surroundings. And yet they were so *different.*

Willet shook her head. She'd grown up in Brisbane and kept turning around as if trying to catch her bearings. The absence of skyscrapers didn't mean she was lost. The street layout was the same and some of the buildings were even familiar. A few pubs. A couple of old commercial stores and warehouses from the nineteenth century that had been listed as national heritage items in the late twentieth. The cottages on the ridges around the small, undeveloped business district. They'd been snapped up and renovated by yuppies in her childhood and were fetching millions of dollars apiece, last she'd heard. Here they were slums. Dark, wretched and stinking in a way she recognised from postings in Asia.

'Bit of a head spin, isn't it?' said Harry, who walked next to her, taking it all in. The English prince knew Brisbane reasonably well. Twenty-first-century Brisbane, anyway. He'd had some mad times during the Rugby World Cup in '03 and had been back to watch the cricket a couple of times after that.

'It's a hell of a thing,' said Willet. 'You can see the sky all over. You couldn't do that before . . . or . . . you know, in the future.'

'I do know,' Harry agreed. 'It's really rather upsetting, isn't it?'

'Not as upsetting as it's going to be for the locals,' said Judge. For the moment, full knowledge of their arrival was restricted to a relatively few American and Australian officers on MacArthur's staff, the British High Commissioner and Prime Minister Curtin down in the national capital, Canberra. They'd flown in under the tightest security on an old Douglas C-47 Skytrain, or rather a brand-new one. The metal finish inside the plane still gleamed from the factory floor. AWACS and refuelling aircraft were precious commodities now, and there was no sense in stripping the *Clinton* of any further capability for what was essentially a courtesy call.

So the C-47 it was. Slow, uncomfortable and with such a limited range that they were twice forced to land to top up their tanks. At least it meant there was no need for special arrangements to deal with their arrival, and the Skytrain's comparatively 'roomy' interior allowed them to carry nearly one hundred kilograms of kit, most of which was now secured under guard at MacArthur's HQ.

The trio walked past an alley where half-wild dogs and giant rats picked at an enormous mound of trash. It stank to high heaven. Even in the southern hemisphere's winter the subtropical city was still warm. They could smell open drains and raw sewage nearby. The commercial heart of the town didn't really run to more than two or three blocks on either side of the main strip down which they now walked in the warm mid-afternoon sun. The buildings here were generally no more than three or four storeys tall. After a while the streets tended to peter out into unpaved tracks. Jungle and mangrove swamp still penetrated the inner city at outlying points, and all of them had been perplexed by the sound of big cats roaring in the night.

The concierge had explained that the zoo was nearby.

The walk from Lennons Hotel took them along a streetscape that bore occasional reminders of their own time. A bookshop now would become a nightclub later; a teahouse here was sushi bar at home. Willet recognised the outline of a boyfriend's apartment block in the facade of a department store.

Crude brick pillboxes had been run up at seemingly random locations, often blocking busy footpaths and forcing shoppers to detour into the gutters. They passed a vacant lot, criss-crossed by slit trenches, some covered in thin sheets of corrugated iron, one with a single log thrown across it. And newsboys on every second corner shouted out the headline of the hour. Not news from Midway, but a scare involving tins of imported Japanese fish. It was feared they'd been laced with ground-up glass.

Many shop windows had already been boarded over, with only thin slits for potential customers to peer through. More than once, the three officers were forced to step around lines of people patiently waiting their turn to do just that. Horse-drawn carriages vied with trams, old trucks and US Army jeeps on the narrow roads. The headlights of the motor vehicles were all hooded for blackout conditions.

Without the Manhattanised skyline that had begun to eat up the heavens in the 1960s, you could still see the town hall clock from most streets. Indeed, it completely dominated the skyline. Captain Willet tried not to stare at the faces of the passers-by, but she found herself unable to drag her gaze away from the children, often dressed in what looked like hand-me-downs from the Great Depression: ill-fitting sweaters, poorly cut short pants, odd socks, shapeless dresses, and cloth caps. She couldn't help but wonder if any of them were her relatives.

For Judge and Prince Harry, who weren't natives of the city, fascination lay in the dowdy fashions, the grand vintage cars, and even the doughy, old-world faces, unaffected by intermarriage with generations of postwar migrants from the Mediterranean and South-East Asia. But for Jane Willet, who'd grown up in Brisbane, it was as though . . . well . . . there was no appropriate metaphor. She simply came to a halt outside the Tattersalls Club – a VR porn club in her day – stared at her companions and croaked, 'We're fucked.'

A passing woman, dressed in a heavy, black fur coat that was entirely inappropriate for the increasingly hot day, almost tripped over as she threw on the brakes.

'No! I'll not have it,' she protested, spinning on her heel and pointing at them with her parasol. 'What bad language and poor manners! How dare you! And we'll beat those heathen monkeys yet, I say. But not if young people like you give in to despair. You should be ashamed. My Charlie would turn in his grave!'

And with that she spun again and waddled off up the street. They watched her go, too surprised to say anything. After a moment, Willet apologised.

'Nothing to be sorry for,' Harry assured her. 'I'm sure if it was London or – was it Dallas, did you say, Commander? – we'd be just as buggered. I could run into my grandmother for God's sake . . . except she'd be younger than me.'

They walked on the few hundred yards to the sandstone chambers that housed the headquarters of all Allied forces in the South-West Pacific Area. Judge was actually familiar with the building. In his time it had been converted into luxury apartments and an entertainment centre with one of the best sports bars on the Pacific Rim. He'd visited it more than once while on shore leave. In comparison, it seemed somewhat crude in its original form.

They'd seen increasing numbers of military personnel as they approached. The town's civilian population tended not to notice them in the throng of uniforms, but they'd drawn some stares from the contemporary soldiers. The cut and style of their uniforms set them apart.

A surprising number of African American soldiers were on the streets. An engineering battalion, they'd learned. Judge found them to be deferential to a fault. He didn't dwell on it. There were some older branches of his family tree that had laid claim to the sort of good old boys who'd thought regular lynchings and cross burnings were a pretty good idea. He wasn't proud of it.

A double beep on the flexipad in his briefcase warned of an incoming transmission. Normally, live video from the far side of the world could have been instantly relayed via satellite, but of course the sky was empty, so he had to wait a few minutes while the single, highly compressed data burst bounced off the troposphere and down onto a 'footprint' that covered more than one hundred square kilometres. His pad was currently located in the centre of that area. It was considerably bulkier than a standard flexipad, packed tight with boosted comms circuitry and quantum processors, developed when military planners correctly surmised that their satellites might be among the first targets in any high-level military conflict. Even so, it was grossly inadequate and seemed to be nonfunctional most of the time. Judge really missed instant and reliable comms.

'News from fleet,' he told the others.

They hurried up the stairs of the headquarters building, flashing newly printed passes at the guards. Once off the street Judge hauled the pad out of the old leather bag.

He brought up the short, encrypted message. The pad decoded the burst and displayed the text.

'It's from Flag Ops,' he told the others. 'Operational concepts for the Pacific theatre.'

'That should please MacArthur,' said Willet.

'Am I to be usurped?' roared General Douglas MacArthur.

Commander Judge had racked up a lot of practice being roared at by the late captain of the USS *Hillary Clinton*. Guy Chandler had spoken in a dull roar even during normal conversations. When something *really* ticked him off, you could hear him over the din of an F-22 spooling up on the flight deck. Still, being roared at by Douglas MacArthur was a unique and even worthwhile experience – if you could stand back and appreciate the historical incongruity of getting hammered down by the volcanic temper of the Supreme Commander of the South-West Pacific Area.

'I already *have* an operation planned to hit back at the Japanese,' MacArthur thundered. He stalked over to the large paper map hanging on the wall of his office.

'I've studied the electrical files and information you brought with you, Commander Judge. And even with your forces degraded by the incident at Midway, I still believe you have the power to smash the Japanese advance and drive them from their base at Rabaul. And your very own history books bear me out. We can dig those little yellow fiends out of there now, or kill thousands of marines getting them out of Guadalcanal in August.'

Prince Harry opened his mouth to speak, but MacArthur ignored him and ploughed on.

'The Japs are stretched thin throughout the southwest theatre,' he said, tapping the map with a wooden pointer. 'If only I'd had the resources, I would have defeated Homma back in Bataan. However, I place my trust in God, who has by some miracle placed you here at my convenience and given me the power to drive these devils all the way back to the home islands.'

Judge winced imperceptibly at the attempted hijacking of the Multinational Force. But he spoke as soothingly as he could.

'General, as I said, we are more than willing to commit to any future operations. But you must understand that our forces are not –' He paused for just a heartbeat, wondering how to handle this massive but fragile ego. 'Well, they're not conventional forces as you would construe the term. They're not equipped or trained to fight in the same way as the forces you command.'

'*And just what do you mean by that*?' demanded MacArthur in an explosive discharge that made them all flinch. 'Am I to be undermined? Am I not the supreme commander in this theatre? I would have thought that operational judgments were my prerogative. But it sounds like that prerogative is to be usurped. Correct me if I'm wrong, but you *are* sitting there telling me I don't know what I'm doing.'

'No, General,' said Judge soothingly. 'Please. Just hear me out. As you well know, military doctrine advanced a great deal between the end of the Great War and the start of this one. You yourself were instrumental in recognising the importance of armoured mobile warfare, long before many in the German high command.'

That point was arguable at best, but Lieutenant Nguyen had advised him before he left Pearl that he should take every possible opportunity to stroke MacArthur's ego. True to form, the general nodded at the compliment as if it were his due. It seemed to calm him down a little.

Judge continued. 'Doctrine and war have likewise advanced in the decades between the end of this war and our time.'

Judge then made a fist, unfurling his fingers as he ticked off each of his next points. 'Stealth platforms, directed energy weapons, quantum processors, comm nets and bio implants, intelligent munitions, hypersonic flight, high-earth-orbit kinetic-impact devices, remote sensing, night vision. You may well be the finest general on the face of the planet at this time –'

MacArthur grunted and nodded his agreement again.

'– But the greenest marine in our task force has an innate understanding of our war-making capacity, which it will take you some time to fully comprehend. And, as I have explained, we do *not* have much time.'

Judge paused, and waited on MacArthur's response. He was surprised by the man's gaunt appearance, but reminded himself that MacArthur had only recently escaped Corregidor, where he'd shared the same privations as his men during the siege. Deep fissures raked his hollow face and the skin hung slack beneath his chin. He was thinking openly, the play of his thoughts so apparent on his face that no one spoke.

He looked up at the three visitors and sighed. 'You know, millions died pointlessly in the last war because those charged with its prosecution hadn't learned the lessons of our own Civil War,' he said.

'We don't have many lessons to teach you, General,' Judge offered to smooth over the difficult moment.

'No, but I hope you have a few for those bastards in Tokyo.'

The flexipad emitted another double beep and a long chirrup. Flash traffic.

'Excuse me, General. Do you mind?' asked Judge. 'This will be urgent.'

MacArthur nodded his assent. A knock sounded at the door as Judge consulted the pad. An adjutant handed MacArthur a slip of paper and a black-and-white photograph. The general's eyebrows shot up when he read the note.

He handed it to Prince Harry, who was sitting closest to him. The prince mouthed an obscenity when he read the document.

Mike Judge didn't mouth or whisper anything.

He said quite clearly, 'Motherfucker!'

His colleagues turned sharply towards him and MacArthur was jolted out of his own reverie by the outburst.

Judge shut down the pad, a sour look creasing his tanned features.

'Anderson and Miyazaki, two of our commanders back in Hawaii, General, they're both dead,' he announced. 'Murdered.'

Jane Willet was obviously shocked by the news, but Judge noticed that neither MacArthur nor Prince Harry reacted as sharply as he might have expected. Then he noticed the look on MacArthur's face. His heart already thudding from the news out of Pearl, lurched again. Something else must have happened.

'It's the *Nuku*,' said Harry. 'She's turned up, and the Japs have got her.'

29

Parliament House, Canberra, Australia, 2132 hours, 9 June 1942

There were few wartime friendships more unusual than that between General Douglas MacArthur and the Australian Prime Minister, John Curtin. Watching the two men together, Paul Robertson could never quite shake himself of the feeling that theirs was a partnership doomed to succeed.

MacArthur was an imperial figure, an overweening egotist, a favourite of the far right in America and a demonic character in the imagination of the left for his role in using troops to smash a demonstration by unemployed veterans and their families in Washington during the Great Depression.

Curtin was a labour organiser and left-wing politician who'd been jailed for opposing conscription during the Great War. Much less a firebrand than a man of unassuming stillness and modesty, he provided MacArthur with the one thing the general could never hope for at home – unconditional support.

Robertson, a well-travelled banker who'd given up a lucrative career to serve as Curtin's principal private adviser, shook hands with MacArthur in the PM's cramped parliamentary office before taking one of the two seats in front of Curtin's desk. MacArthur, carrying one of those fantastic machines they called a 'slate', dropped into the other.

Prime Minister Curtin looked to be as intrigued by the device as Robertson. It was the first time either of them had encountered direct evidence of the 'Arrivals'.

'It's a shame those officers couldn't have come with you, General,' said Curtin. 'I would have liked to have met them, particularly the local lass.'

MacArthur, holding the data slate like a royal flush in the last round of a poker tournament, brushed the grey casing and said, 'Couldn't be helped, Prime Minister. As I said in the cable, there've been developments. They've had to get back to Pearl.'

'But we can expect them back soon, can't we?' said Curtin. 'Yamamoto is still on the loose, and there's no American fleet to stand between him and us now. I'd feel a lot better with one of those rocket ships here. Especially an Australian one.'

His voice betrayed a deep anxiety. He'd been catching hell from Churchill over his decision to bring home two battle-proven Australian divisions as insurance against the threat of a Japanese invasion. The British wanted to send them to Burma, of all places!

Robertson knew the PM had suffered terribly for the decision, harangued by London and prodded by

Washington to do as *they* wanted, not as he thought best. And when he'd faced down the demands from Churchill, there was the even greater stress of actually waiting for thousands of Australian troops to make it home across waters infested with U-boats and raiders and Japanese carriers. Robertson had more than once found the PM alone in this office, doubled over in pain. It was as if the responsibility of leading the country through its darkest hour were eating him from the inside out.

MacArthur leaned forward and rapped the desk with his fist.

'I'm going to move heaven and earth to get those forces sent here as quickly as possible, Prime Minister. It would help if you could cable the President in support. After all, there are some Australian units attached to this Kolhammer's force. They should be here in this theatre, placed under my command.'

Robertson suppressed a smile at MacArthur's choice of words. He composed his face into a suitably neutral expression before interrupting.

'These developments you mentioned, General MacArthur, I take it you mean the report out of New Guinea?'

The American's features clouded over momentarily. He fidgeted with the device. After a few tries he got the screen to light up, and handed the slate across to Curtin. Robertson could see there was some sort of picture displayed on the glowing face of the machine. It was a dark, midwinter's day outside, and when lit the slate was bright enough to throw the PM's shadow up the wall.

'That's a photograph taken by a long-range patrol, operating in the Saruwaged Ranges of New Guinea,' explained the general. 'Commander Judge was kind enough to transfer it to this machine for me before he left. We would have dismissed it as a fake a month ago. But given what's happened, I think we have to take it seriously.'

Robertson watched the Prime Minister's face as he examined the picture. He frowned like a man confronted by an intricate puzzle. After a few seconds his eyes opened wider and he sat bolt upright.

'Is that a . . . ?'

But words failed him.

'Yes, Prime Minister,' said MacArthur, 'it's a warship. Sticking out of a mountain, thousands of feet above sea level.'

Curtin handed the slate to Robertson. It felt dense but light. The casing was made of something that gave under the fingers, like rubber. The PM's adviser was careful to avoid touching any of the buttons arrayed across the bottom of the case. Holding it gently by the sides, he saw a photograph of what looked like a destroyer or a frigate, with her stern buried in the ground. A few tents were clustered around the base of the vessel and he could make out human figures here and there.

'The men in the photograph are Japs,' said MacArthur. 'They found her first and they've been working on her for nearly a week as best we can tell. The patrol report says they appear to be salvaging what they can.'

'Good God,' said Curtin. 'So they've got access to this sort of machinery too.'

'I'm afraid so,' MacArthur answered. 'That's why Judge and the others returned to Pearl. And that's why it's imperative we strike as quickly as possible. Kolhammer's people are going to attack this ship in the next hour or so. But we have to assume the horse has bolted.'

'Could they have found any more of these ships?' asked Robertson.

MacArthur didn't answer immediately, giving the question some thought. Sleet blew against the windows and a minor gale howled outside, whipping through the branches of the eucalyptus trees and stripping long ribbons of wet bark from their trunks.

'Judge tells me they're missing a number of ships. The scientific vessel, which they suspect to be the cause of their arrival here, was almost certainly destroyed in the process. So they doubt they're ever going home. An American warship seems to have foundered in the polar waters to our south. One British and one French vessel apiece are unaccounted for. And there are doubts now about the location of another small frigate from a country called Indonesia. It grew out of the Dutch colony in the East Indies. That's their boat on the mountain.'

Curtin visibly blanched. 'So these things could be anywhere. Under anyone's control.'

MacArthur took the suggestion sombrely. To Robertson he looked like a man considering an important move in a game of chess. The day was growing even darker outside, and Curtin turned on a green-shaded desk lamp to give them some more light.

The American rubbed at his West Point ring as he spoke.

'It's possible,' he conceded. 'Judge was less concerned about the British and French vessels than the Indonesian one. He said those ships could look after themselves. But he said that the Indonesian ship, the *Sutanto*, didn't have, um, Combat Intelligence, I believe he called it. It's like a machine that can fight the enemy even when the crew is incapacitated. So the Japs could conceivably capture them. On the other hand, the Indonesian boats are much less capable.'

There was something profoundly disturbing in that line of argument. It sounded to Robertson like a sales pitch. 'But surely the danger of the Japanese getting their hands on these ships lies as much in the knowledge they contain,' he said.

Holding up the data slate, he went on. 'I understand these machines are a bit like having a whole university at your fingertips. What's to stop them or the Germans from learning how to build superweapons like the ones that destroyed the American fleet at Midway? Granted, they couldn't leap right into the next century. But they could give their scientists and manufacturers a hell of a boost.'

Prime Minister Curtin slowly rubbed his face with both hands. He was a picture of despair. MacArthur took in the questions without visible anguish, but neither did he exhibit any of his usual confidence.

In the end he could only shrug.

'We have to strike first.'

London, 2301 hours, 9 June 1942

The dispatch from Her Majesty's man in Hawaii arrived at Admiral Sir Dudley Pound's club late in the evening. The First Sea Lord received the long typewritten note from his man in Pearl Harbor, Rear Admiral Sir Leslie Murray, just before midnight. Pound had suffered from quite terrible headaches for some time, and an absolute blinder was keeping him awake when the Royal Navy courier arrived with a brown leather briefcase hand-cuffed to his wrist.

Pound took delivery in the club's library. He wasn't the only member who was padding about at that time. Many of the older members found their repose had been so badly disturbed by the war, and especially by the bombing of London, that they slept in fits and starts at all hours of the night and day. A few of them dozed in soft leather armchairs. One had nodded off over a copy of *The Times*, which had spilled onto the rich Turkish carpet where it lay until spied by a passing servant. Another had propped open Livingstone's original African journal on his lap, but had fallen asleep halfway down the Zambezi River. A couple of retired brigadiers, one of whom had been quite handsomely shot up with the New Zealanders at Gallipoli, pushed chess pieces around a board in the far corner.

Sir Dudley was deep into his third brandy of the evening when a footman showed through a young man from Naval Intelligence. Quietly grateful for some work to distract him through the graveyard hours, Pound thanked the officer and broke the seal on the dispatch from Sir Leslie.

Three paragraphs into the report he snorted a mouthful of brandy through his nose. With remarkable understatement the Royal Navy's liaison to the US Pacific Fleet had given a detailed account of the arrival of Kolhammer's task force.

I must report a most unusual event: in the Pacific theatre, the message began, before describing in quite spare prose the destruction of the American fleet and a British carrier, HMS *Fearless*. Murray relayed the astounding capabilities of the arrivals in equally detached terms, but it was clear to Sir Dudley that his stiff upper lip failed him when it came time to report on the individuals who had arrived in the ships.

A most remarkable bunch, he wrote. *A more confronting collection of half-caste upstarts and hysterical women you would not find outside a whorehouse in Cairo!*

Murray recommended in closing that the British ship, HMS *Trident*, which had arrived with Kolhammer, be reassigned immediately to the Home Fleet and staffed by reliable men drawn from the present-day Royal Navy. Some of the twenty-first-century personnel could, of course, be kept on to provide whatever training and familiarisation was needed. The CO, Captain Halabi, was a curiosity at best, and a disaster-in-waiting at worst. Murray's opinion was that she and her crew would be of little use in a high-intensity theatre of war such as the Atlantic. Allowing himself what seemed to be a moment of wit, he wrote that their major utility seemed to be to act as a warning concerning England's future immigration policy. He suggested that perhaps a position might be found for them in the coastal patrols of the various West Indian colonies. After all, so many of them seemed to hail from there.

Pound read the two-thousand-word communiqué twice, shaking his head and grunting in disbelief each time. It was nearly one in the morning when he finished, too late to check on the credibility of the story through independent sources. So he summoned another brandy and decided to send a cable directly to Honolulu in the morning. Sir Leslie Murray had obviously gone insane and would need to be replaced.

He hauled himself upright and laid in a course for his sleeping quarters.

Strangely enough, he slept like a baby for the first

time in months. Not even a large raid over the East End could wake him.

Thirty-six hours later Sir Dudley stood outside the Prime Minister's office, deep within the rubble-choked streets of London. Though well rested, he was still reeling from his meeting with the American ambassador, Mr Kennedy. The former bootlegger had confirmed that yes, he'd received much the same information as Pound. No, he didn't really believe it either, but what the hell was he gonna do? Roosevelt himself had sent a handwritten note, confirming many of the basic facts. And Roosevelt always tried to keep his personal communications with Kennedy to a minimum. They didn't get on.

Pound waited in the cramped anteroom, watching the concrete walls sweat, while he wondered how on earth to explain all this to the PM. A young woman in a dark blue Royal Air Force uniform ignored him while she hammered away at a typewriter, producing a sound not entirely unlike a machine-gun. He was developing a headache, and each clack speared into his head like a sharpened knitting needle.

A slight tremor in his hands betrayed his anxiety.

Churchill, still dressed in his gown and slippers, suddenly appeared at the door and took in Pound's presence through rheumy eyes and a slight haze of gin fumes.

'Come in, Admiral,' he said. 'I hope you've brought glad tidings for a change.'

Pound clutched his briefcase tightly and followed the Prime Minister through the door. The sound of rapid-fire typing ceased as the secretary jumped up to follow them.

'Would you like your breakfast now, sir?' she asked Churchill.

'Kippers and toast,' he barked back.

'And would you like some tea, Sir Dudley?'

Pound said he would, and they seated themselves as she hurried off.

'So, Admiral, what's this business in the Pacific? I've heard some wild rumours so far. I hope you're not here to add to them.'

Pound took a breath and jumped in at the deep end. 'I'm afraid you're not going to believe me, Prime Minister, but I have to do this anyway.'

He pulled out the dispatch from Rear Admiral Murray, and a copy of Ambassador Kennedy's report, which the American had helpfully given him, along with Roosevelt's handwritten cover note.

As quickly and with as little drama as possible, he informed Churchill of the events at Midway, as he had been told of them. The Prime Minister's expression grew more thunderous with each fantastic revelation. Finally, he exploded.

'Enough! Is this your idea of a joke, Admiral?'

Pound's voice showed not the slightest hint of amusement. 'No, Prime Minister, it is my idea of a bad dream.'

Churchill's head seemed to wobble on his bulbous,

unshaven neck as though he were seeing the room in front of him for the first time. He pushed a piece of paper to one side, dragged it back, opened a drawer, presumably to put the paper away, and then simply crumpled it up and dropped it into a waste-paper basket. Pound half expected him to haul it out and start over again.

'Well, how on earth did this happen? If it did happen.'

The First Sea Lord was at a loss. Neither Murray's report nor Ambassador Kennedy could provide him with any information that made sense of the situation.

'It appears that even these chaps who've turned up don't know how it happened,' said Pound.

'And they have Japanese ships and German soldiers sailing with them?' Churchill mused.

'And Russians and Italians and a couple of chaps from places I've never even heard of,' Pound added.

'I see. And they've got them under guard?'

'Apparently not.' Sir Dudley was just as perplexed by that as the PM.

Churchill sighed deeply. He rubbed his eyes and then his entire face. The rasping sound of his hand on unshaven bristles was the only noise in the room.

'I'm supposed to meet Roosevelt in Washington in a few weeks,' he said. 'I suppose we'd better bring forward the schedule.'

'Yes, Prime Minister.'

30

USS Hillary Clinton, *1939 hours, 9 June 1942*

It was quiet as Lieutenant Nguyen sat outside the *Clinton*'s conference room, nervously holding the plastic folder that contained her briefing notes. Though the supercarrier never truly slept, it did slow down every now and then.

She was the last briefing officer of the day, and she had a tough act to follow: the poor bastards from Physics, who were still riffing on old *Star Trek* episodes. She patted her breast pocket for maybe the tenth time to make sure the data stick was still there and tried to focus on her breathing in an effort to calm down. She wished she could take Julia and Rosanna into the meeting with her. Nothing seemed to freak them out. But they were ashore, having written her a three-page summary of US antisubmarine operations in June 1942.

It was a left-handed gift. She was discovering that when you gave a bunch of admirals a golden egg, they invariably came back at you wanting a dozen more.

She could hear a man speaking with an English accent. He seemed to be saying that they should reprogramme Metal Storm to prioritise kamikaze attacks and traditional iron bombs, rather than hypersonic, wave-skimming antiship missiles. It was off topic, but he had a point, she thought. Resentfully aware that her bloody PhD had come back to haunt her, she quietly cursed her decision to enrol in postgraduate history. Just then an ensign called her in.

Her fatigue fell away as she entered the meeting room. She recognised most of the senior commanders from the Multinational Force, but it was the immediate familiarity of men like Nimitz and Spruance that gave her a start. She'd seen those faces countless times in books and on screen, but here they were, alive and looking to her for . . . what? Salvation? To their minds they were still in the first days of a war they could very well lose. A couple of the men who sat with them shook their heads at her arrival.

She took her place at the lectern and fumbled in her pocket for the data stick, nearly dropping it as she tried to slot it home. She exhaled audibly to settle her nerves as the stick clicked into place and the massive wall-screen behind her winked from neutral blue to a map of the world.

'Good evening. This is a summary of the relevant disposition of forces across the global theatres as of 9 June, 1942.'

She paused briefly to glance up at her audience. Most of the faces were neutral; some, such as her own captain's, were even encouraging. For the first time, however, she noticed that two men were openly scowling at her; contemporary Royal Navy types, to judge by their uniforms. They sat next to Captain Halabi from HMS *Trident*, who was acting on Kolhammer's behalf while he was away in Los Angeles and Commander Judge was briefing MacArthur. Their body language betrayed the insurmountable gulf that she would be asked to somehow cross. Unfortunately, her presentation wasn't likely to cheer up the Brits.

'A massive series of battles around Kharkov and Sevastopol, under way at the present time, will eventually see nearly one million Soviet troops killed or taken prisoner. Sevastopol will fall to the Germans on 1 July, two days into the German summer offensive, Operation Blue.'

As she spoke, a PowerPoint show filled the giant wall-screens. Two-metre windows displaying archival footage of combat on the Eastern Front played in one corner, directly over a panel listing the various German and Soviet formations that would be involved and their losses over the period of the campaign. Rachel snuck a quick peek at the two sour-faced Royal Navy men. No, they weren't looking any happier.

Oh well, she thought, *here goes . . .*

'British attempts to support the Soviet war effort through shipment of matériel via convoy will be severely hampered by the poor judgment of the First Sea Lord, Admiral Sir Dudley Pound, who is suffering from a brain tumour that will kill him within a few years –'

She got no further, flinching in surprise as somebody smashed an open hand down on the table.

'How dare you! I've had just about enough of this!' barked the Englishman seated next to Captain Halabi. 'We've sat here all evening listening to a bunch of darkies and shrews tell us what we've been doing wrong and now this . . . this . . . bloody coolie child has the nerve to come in here and insult Sir Dudley, a man who –'

'Admiral Murray,' Halabi said through gritted teeth, 'I would appreciate it if you would shut the fuck up and listen to the lieutenant who, I can assure you, is *infinitely* better informed about these matters than you are.'

Ah, that'd be Rear Admiral Sir Leslie Murray, CBE, thought Nguyen.

'I don't have to listen to this!' Murray declared.

'No, you don't,' agreed Halabi. 'You can leave any time you want.'

Rachel could see that Halabi was only just containing her desire to strangle the man. She won the battle of wills, however, and Murray returned to his silent glaring.

The acting commander of the Multinational Force spoke to Nguyen in a much calmer tone. 'Please go on, Lieutenant. I believe you were about to discuss the destruction of Naval Convoy PQ 17.'

'I was, ma'am, thank you.'

She composed herself again and returned to her notes, determined not to lift her head again until she was finished. 'PQ 17 is scheduled to depart Iceland for Archangel on 27 June. It consisted of fifty-six freighters, an oiler, six destroyers and thirteen other vessels. Admiral Pound, wrongly assuming the German battleship *Tirpitz* was loose, ordered the convoy to scatter and the escorts to withdraw. Aircraft and submarine attacks then sank twenty-four unprotected ships, carrying nearly three and a half thousand motor vehicles, four hundred and thirty tanks, more than two hundred aircraft and nearly one hundred thousand tonnes of supplies. The losses, coming at the most critical juncture just before the summer blitzkrieg, and the subsequent refusal of the Western Allies to force the convoy route again for many months, led to a severe strain on the relationship between the Allies and the Soviet government.'

Rachel drew a breath and peeked up. Admiral Murray still looked furious, but he was keeping his own counsel for the moment. About two dozen strong, her audience was a study in parallel but contrary natures. Nobody looked comfortable or remotely assured. She'd nearly majored in psych before switching to postgrad history, and would have loved to watch a video of the whole meeting, to tease out the personal clashes, to watch alliances take shape as the various interests manoeuvred for dominance.

What a pity the outcome was so far from academic with thousands – if not millions – of lives dependent on the decisions that would be made in this room. She was glad the burden of decision-making did not fall on her.

'In North Africa,' she continued, 'the Afrika Korps under Rommel are due to press an offensive to El Alamein . . .'

She delivered the rest of her brief speech with growing confidence now that she knew Halabi would act as her shield. She reminded the senior commanders that the SS was carrying out an atrocity in Lidice at that very moment. She warned of attacks on convoys bound for Malta on 14 and 15 June, detailing the individual losses to air attack, torpedo boats and surface raiders. She pointedly advised the British liaison officers to attend to the inadequate state of Tobruk's defences – advice she could tell they were going to ignore. She told Nimitz that General MacArthur should know that significant Japanese forces were supposed to land in New Guinea on 22 July, and as things stood they would be opposed only by a limited number of Australian militia.

She concluded by pointing out that tens of thousands of Allied POWs were, for the moment, being held in large central camps in the Philippines and Singapore, and that many of them would die quite wretchedly over the next few years of their captivity. At each stage of her talk a panel of the wall-screen switched from displaying the world map to running images of the relevant topic. There was no escaping the human consequences of Lidice, or the Bataan Death March.

'Is there a point to that, miss?' asked Admiral Bill Halsey. 'Or are you just rubbing our noses in it?'

Rachel was familiar with Halsey's reputation as a blunt speaker. She struggled not to take it personally.

'I'm just doing my job, Admiral. You have the information I was asked to provide. Making decisions on the basis of that information is not my responsibility.'

'Thank you, Lieutenant,' said Captain Halabi, forestalling any reply from Halsey. 'Does anybody have any questions relating to the presentation?'

Rachel handed over the data stick that held the briefing information and extended background notes. Halabi inserted the stick into her flexipad and broadcast the files around the room. Rachel could see that each of the contemporary officers had been provided with a flexipad, and she wondered how many would actually use them.

'Lieutenant, how long will it be before those POWs are dispersed to labour camps?' asked Colonel Jones.

'The first group of about three thousand have already left from Changi in Singapore for the Burma–Thailand railway. Another fifteen hundred will go on 8 July. All of the officers will be moved on 16 August. Casualties among Allied POWs in Japanese camps will run between thirty to forty per cent, depending on the conditions in each individual camp. I'm afraid that hundreds of Americans have already perished on the forced march from Bataan to prison in central Luzon.'

Nimitz, who clearly was tired and grappling with an infinitely more tangled web of problems than he'd ever imagined might arise in this war, rubbed at his eyes and spoke quite irritably, which Rachel knew was unusual for him.

'I don't see where this advances the discussion of our strategic options, Colonel Jones. Nobody has to tell us what a bunch of bastards the Japs are. There'll come a heavy reckoning for their crimes in the future, but the best we can do for those men who've been captured is to defeat the enemy that is torturing them.'

'In fact, Admiral,' Colonel Jones said carefully, 'that may not be true.'

Nimitz was beyond understanding. He gave the marine commander a blank look and indicated with a weary gesture that he should explain.

'If they were our men,' Jones said, 'we'd go and get them.'

Two hours later, Rachel couldn't keep her eyes open. She'd been sent back to her office after her presentation to further research the POW issue. She had been awake for all but four hours of the last forty-eight, and was nearing the time when she would have to sleep or get a stimulant patch. Those things always gave her hideous nausea, so she was hoping to grab a little shut-eye; however, she was called into Halabi's temporary quarters aboard the *Clinton* to present her supplementary data.

'Here it is, ma'am,' she said, stifling a yawn as she handed Halabi the data stick. 'It's only preliminary. If we all go at it tomorrow, we can get a lot more for you.'

The British officer wasn't alone. Colonel Jones was perched on the edge of a desk, and another marine – a doctor to judge by her insignia – was nursing a glass of something on the couch, resting her eyes. Rachel knew that American ships were supposed to be dry, but she was certain she could smell bourbon. The doctor sat up and smiled at her. It was too late for formalities.

Halabi gestured for Rachel to sit down.

'Would you like some coffee, Lieutenant?'

'No, thank you, ma'am. I plan to sleep soon, if that's all right.'

'Good luck to you,' Halabi said sympathetically. But first I'd like you to fill Colonel Jones and Doctor Francois in on that note you sent me after your briefing.'

Rachel felt more than a little uncomfortable with the request. She'd beamed Halabi the message as an afterthought.

'All I said,' she began, 'was that we'd have little trouble defeating the Axis navies if we engaged them ourselves. Even with the damage we took at Midway.

Their weapons and doctrine are generations behind our own. But just as they're generations behind us, so are the Allies, not just technically, but culturally as well. We can help here. We could probably rescue those guys in the prison camps, for instance, and they'd be insanely grateful. At least at first.

'But if we're here permanently, we pose a significant threat to their way of life just as surely as would defeat by the Axis powers. Not as dire a threat, of course. But a threat nonetheless.'

'How so, Lieutenant?' came the deep bass rumble of Colonel J Lonesome Jones. She suspected he already knew the answer.

'This is 1942,' she said. 'Begging your pardon, Colonel, but by the standards of this time, you are not an African American –'

She was going to continue, but she didn't have to. Jones finished the thought for her.

'No. I'm a nigger.'

'And I'm a little coolie girl,' said Rachel. 'And Captain Halabi is a half-breed, and some of us are wogs and kikes and dagos. These guys aren't Nazis, but they're not going to understand us. And my guess is that what they don't understand and cannot control, they'll eventually treat as threatening.'

'There's nothing eventual about it,' said Francois from the couch. She rubbed her eyes. They looked very red and watery.

'It's already begun,' the doctor went on. 'The riot down in Honolulu today, Borghino getting shot,

Anderson and Miyazaki getting whacked. I tell you . . . what they did to that woman . . .'

Halabi looked as though she was about to ask the doctor to shut up, but the surgeon ploughed on anyway. She was bitter and furious, and she spat her words out like poison darts.

'They stuck a piece of barbed wire inside her, and used it like a fucking pipe cleaner. I tell you, Lonesome, if we catch these assholes and they still get away with it, I am going to personally draw down and cap 'em myself.'

Halabi folded her arms uncomfortably. 'Now, Doctor, I don't think it's come to that –'

'But it's coming, Captain, believe me. You didn't meet that asshole detective today. I'll lay money on the barrelhead that he soft-pedals the whole thing, and when it turns out to be some good ol' local boy, the fix will go in. You can fuckin' bank on it. They plucked two slugs out of that chief petty officer this afternoon. Damn near killed him. But do you think they kept the fucking things? Even though we specifically told them to hold on to them, so we could test them? No. They're "missing". Lost in the confusion at the hospital. It's already begun.'

Rachel thought Halabi was going to argue the point.

But she didn't.

31

Berlin, 0721 hours, 8 June 1942

The sealed case travelled from Japan to Europe in the diplomatic pouch of the Spanish embassy's military attaché. He took a Portuguese flying boat to Ankara and thence to Athens and Berlin, where the package was turned over to a colonel of Reichsführer Heinrich Himmler's personal guard. From there it went directly to the SS head himself.

Himmler was a quiet man. His hands were dainty and lined with blue veins. He always looked short of sleep, and he wasn't given to histrionics as many of his colleagues were. He licked his lips, took a sip of the herbal tea in the cup on his desk and read the instructions for operating the device that Steckel had sent.

He wondered, briefly, whether he should have it checked. It might be a bomb.

He read the instructions again, and then summoned his secretary.

'Wait until I am out of the room, then press this button,' said Himmler. 'I will return momentarily.'

The young man clicked his heels together and barked, 'Immediately, Reichsführer.'

'No,' sighed Himmler. 'When I am safely out of the room. Not until then.'

The flint-eyed young man nodded.

Three minutes later Himmler was back. The device, a 'flexipad', according to Steckel, glowed serenely atop his desk. His secretary was impressed.

'It is made by the Braun company,' he said helpfully. 'German technology is a wonder, mein Reichsführer.'

Himmler nodded and dismissed him from the room. He perused Steckel's notes again and followed the first set of instructions.

The handsome, perhaps too-pretty face of the SD man filled the glass plate on the front of the pad.

'Heil Hitler!' he shouted.

Himmler jumped in fright and his secretary came rushing back in.

'It's all right,' the SS chief said shakily. 'It is just a recording on this unit.'

'Remarkable,' said the young man as he retreated again.

Steckel continued to speak on the screen.

'Reichsführer, I have taken the liberty of sending you this device because the wonders we have discovered out here must be seen to be believed. With the help of Major Brasch and our Japanese comrades, I have prepared a short presentation for you, outlining some of the major developments.'

Himmler propped the pad up against a framed picture of his mistress. It threatened to fall under its own weight. He carefully picked up his tea and sipped as a series of movies played over Steckel's voice.

It was both amazing and infuriating. He felt certain there was a great deal he wasn't being told. The colour movies, which were astoundingly sophisticated, detailed weapons systems and technology that boggled the mind. Missiles that could fly into space and spit dozens of insanely powerful warheads onto different cities, killing millions of people, and destroying whole nations in the blink of an eye. Infantry uniforms with *padded* armour that could stop a round from a Mauser. Machines in the sky that could listen in on every telephone conversation or radio broadcast in the world, *and* sort them into the relevant and immaterial. Oh, what the Gestapo could do with that!

But nowhere in this litany of magic tricks was there an explanation of how an inferior race, from a country no one had ever heard of, could possibly develop such things. How could a mud race such as these Javanese peasants prosper in the very first century of the thousand-year Reich? Where did the Führer appear in this fairy tale? This astounding contraption and Steckel's tales of *Untermenschen* from the future raised the obvious question.

What was the future for the Fatherland?

Even with such thoughts swirling in his mind, Himmler gave no outward indication of reacting at all. When the movie finished, he sat and thought for a few minutes before pulling half-a-dozen sheets of parchment from his desk drawer and inking a fountain pen.

In all of the Reich there were only two men the Führer trusted completely. Heinrich Himmler and Otto Skorzeny.

It was time to send Skorzeny to the East.

But first Himmler would need to talk to the Japanese ambassador.

Three hours later Reichsführer Himmler and Lieutenant General Oshima Hiroshi met in the grand compound at the spiritual heart of the Waffen-SS. Lichterfelde had once been a school for military cadets, but the old butcher Sepp Dietrich had convinced Hitler that his personal army should have a headquarters befitting their elite status as supermen and praetorian guard to the Führer himself.

Himmler, who was unusual among the higher-caste Nazis in having no taste for extravagance, nevertheless appreciated Dietrich's achievement as his Mercedes swept in through the front gates guarded by two giant, iconic statues of German soldiers in modern battle dress. Gravel crunched under the limousine's wheels as it motored quietly towards the four grand, stone barracks designated 'Adolf Hitler', 'Horst Wessel', 'Hermann Göring' and 'Hindenburg'.

Squads of tall, blond Nordic warriors jogged to and fro with machine-like precision. The crunch of their hob-nailed boots spoke of perfect regimentation. A magnificent black stallion from the barracks stables, the finest in Europe, clopped past, led by an old farrier, a veteran of the Führer's own unit from the Great War. A comrade who had proven himself at the Führer's side in single combat, he smiled and nodded as Himmler emerged from the car. Himmler indulged the man's familiarity. He suffered from mild shell shock and was a favourite of Hitler's. The Führer had asked Himmler to find him a suitable sinecure, and there could be no more prestigious and comfortable surroundings in all of Germany for the old soldier to see out his remaining days.

Hitler had been pleased, which meant that Himmler was even more so.

'*Guten Morgen*, Herr Meyer. A beautiful day for a ride, *ja*?' said Himmler.

'It would be,' said Meyer. His voice was a harsh whisper, the result of a French shell fragment that tore into his throat in 1917. 'But my friend here needs new shoes first.'

Horse and man turned and ambled away to the stables.

Himmler took a moment to enjoy the bucolic scene under a warm summer sky before heading to the barracks' reception area. He did not smile once.

Inside the great hall huge oil paintings of the Führer hung from the stone walls. Candles and burning torches threw back the gloom, which was considerable after the brightness of the day outside. Nordic runes, inlaid in silver, ran around the room, which was magnificently furnished with carved oaken benches and tables. A receptionist glanced up from her desk and blanched at the sight of Himmler in his black uniform.

'Reichsführer,' she stammered. 'We were not expecting you until after lunch.'

'I am early,' he announced. 'Has General Hiroshi arrived yet?'

'Yes, sir. He is in the guesthouse. I shall take you right to him.'

'Don't bother,' he said. 'I know the way.'

Lieutenant General Oshima Hiroshi knew the SS commandant to be a man who was more than a little infatuated with the supernatural. The Japanese ambassador privately thought that the Reichsführer's mental state was somewhat tenuous. He certainly suffered from runaway paranoia, and a mild form of madness that caused him to believe in the spirits and Teutonic gods as if they were a real force in the world and not just a useful myth. He supposed it explained Himmler's remarkably phlegmatic response to the incident at Midway.

In a way, the ambassador conceded, he was very well adapted to deal with the shock of the *Sutanto*. Himmler saw plots everywhere, perceived the most bizarre meanings in the most mundane of circumstances, and had long ago lost his connection to the world of real things. A demonic individual, who himself saw demons in every shadow, he needed little encouragement to believe in deliverance via their agency.

Looking at the slight, stunted figure of the man who sat before him, Hiroshi wondered what would happen if and when the Axis was triumphant. Given the racial philosophies of Nazi Germany and the Japanese empire, conflict between them must be inevitable. He shrugged the thought off as he poured a cup of tea. At least when he dealt with the Reichsführer he could drink tea instead of the Germans' abominable national beverage, coffee.

'I would very much appreciate the opportunity of examining the material you have been sent from Hashirajima, Ambassador Hiroshi,' said Himmler. 'And of course you must feel free to study the information and equipment I have received.'

The guesthouse at Lichterfelde was sumptuously appointed, although Hiroshi personally found it cluttered and busy, the furniture overstuffed and the decorations gauche in the extreme. It had the advantage, however, of being one of the most secure sites in the world for a sensitive discussion.

'Do you feel as if you have been misinformed by your researchers?' he asked Himmler.

The German's ridiculous little moustache twitched, reminding Hiroshi of a small rodent sniffing for danger.

'No, not as such,' said Himmler. 'But I feel there is much I have yet to learn. Perhaps things young Steckel would rather I didn't have to hear.'

'Like how you will die?' asked Hiroshi, barely suppressing a mischievous smirk.

'You know this?' Himmler asked, suddenly all ears.

'I know that in the world the *Sutanto* arrived from, our victorious enemies hunted you down like a dog. You took poison when captured. Cyanide, I believe. A most painful and prolonged death.'

What little colour there was in Himmler's face drained away completely.

'I see,' he whispered. 'And the Reich?'

'Reduced to rubble and slavery under the Bolsheviks.'

Himmler's hand shook so badly he spilled his tea on the coffee table. Small beads of perspiration stood out on his forehead. He dabbed at them with a handkerchief.

'You seem remarkably composed, Herr General. Surely Japan does not escape unscathed.'

'Burned to ashes and bones,' said Hiroshi. 'Literally.'

Himmler looked as if he might actually be sick. Hiroshi had to clamp down on his distaste for the man's weakness.

'But of course, that was in their world,' he said. 'This is ours, and things have changed now. We can avoid the fate that awaited us. If we are bold.'

Himmler nodded uncertainly. He licked his thin, bloodless lips.

'Yes. If we are bold . . . Perhaps, if you would come with me when I tell the Führer of all this?'

Hiroshi indulged himself by sipping at his tea for a moment, letting the German wait on his answer.

'Of course,' he said at last. 'We are in this together.'

Rastenburg, 1247 hours, 10 June 1942

The Führer was taking lunch with Martin Bormann and Dr Goebbels at his East Prussian headquarters, the Wolfschanze in Rastenburg, when Himmler and Hiroshi arrived. The three men had finished their vegetarian strudel and potato salad and were tucking into Black Forest cake and coffee as Hitler explained his role in the development of the Volkswagen, a technological triumph of Aryan engineering of which he was inordinately proud.

'The Volkswagen,' he said, 'is the car of the future. One has only to see the way in which they roar up the Obersalzberg, skipping like mountain goats around my great Mercedes, to be tremendously impressed. After the war, it will become the car *par excellence* for the whole of Europe . . .'

Bormann and Goebbels nodded enthusiastically, neither man game to draw attention to the bright blob of cream that clung to the Führer's moustache. Hitler ploughed on, as he so often did after dining, expounding on topics as varied as the fictitious value of gold, the lure of paperwork and the ugliness of Berlin.

A black-uniformed SS-Obersturmbannführer knocked at the door. Only a member of Hitler's personal bodyguard could gain admission to his private dining room, where talk of military campaigns was banned and officers of the Wehrmacht were not generally welcome. If the SS colonel was so bold as to interrupt lunch, there must indeed be something wrong.

'Yes?' he asked peremptorily.

'I am sorry, mein Führer, but Reichsführer Himmler is here with Lieutenant General Hiroshi.'

'What a curious couple,' mused Hitler. 'Perhaps they have something to confess. Admit them and we shall see.'

The bodyguard clicked the heels of his jackboots, saluted and left. He did not mention the cream in Hitler's moustache either.

As soon as Himmler entered he saluted, rubbed a finger under his nose and whispered, 'Mein Führer.'

Hitler licked his moustache, finding the dollop there.

'Oh, thank you, Heinrich. Martin, Joseph, you should have said something earlier.'

Both men looked suitably abashed.

'Sit down, sit down, gentlemen. Ambassador Hiroshi, such a pleasant surprise to find you out here. I do hope nothing is wrong. Or is something right? Has Churchill died of brain syphilis, perhaps?'

Bormann roared with laughter and Goebbels smiled, but no light touched his dark, sunken eyes.

Hiroshi bowed formally and pulled out a chair. The table was large and there was plenty of room for the newcomers, although the ornate silver service had only been set for three. Glancing at the sickly sweet German cakes and the big pot of coffee, Hiroshi was secretly relieved.

'We bring news of an unusual nature, Reichschancellor,' he said. 'Most unusual. In fact, you must promise not to have us chased from the building like madmen when we tell you. For that is exactly what we shall sound like.'

Goebbels was instantly alert. He wore the look of a wolf sniffing at some new predator on its hunting ground. Bormann simply looked overstuffed from his lunch. Hitler tilted his head, supporting it on his fingertips as he considered the fearful expression on Himmler's sallow face, which compared unfavourably with Hiroshi's bemused smile.

'What is the matter, Reichsführer?' he asked, speaking directly to Himmler.

Himmler eased himself into a chair like a man nursing a painful wound.

'Do you remember that fellow Brasch? The one we sent to Japan?' he said. 'The medal winner.'

'I do,' Goebbels replied, rolling his eyes. 'Shell shock, a head case. He broke after the fighting on the Eastern Front. I understood his mission to Japan was simply a cover to get him out of the news.'

'It was,' said Himmler. 'But something has happened out there. Something terrible. Brasch has been giving technical assistance with some engineering issues. It sounded like madness when I first heard of it, but I'm afraid that I am now convinced. As are the ambassador and Grand Admiral Yamamoto.'

Hitler reached over and plucked a glacé cherry from the chocolate icing atop a half-eaten piece of torte in front of him. He popped it in his mouth and licked his fingers.

'Well, don't keep us in suspense,' he said.

'No,' muttered Himmler. 'No, of course not.'

His face flushed bright red and he fumbled about inside his briefcase.

'An SD agent in Tokyo sent this,' he said. 'It is called a flexipad.'

Tokyo, 2121 hours, 9 June 1942

Franz Steckel was far more than a mere civil servant. He served as an SS-Obersturmführer of the SD-Ausland, a lieutenant in the Nazi Party's foreign intelligence service. He had been assigned to Tokyo station three months earlier, on the direct orders of Reinhard Heydrich, who suspected that the Reich's embassy harboured a small clique of homosexuals.

Lieutenant Steckel, an attractive young man, had resigned himself to the most bestial depravities in the service of National Socialism. The world was full of perverts, and it was his unpleasant duty to hunt them down and ensure the purity of the Aryan race.

At first he had been annoyed that so important an investigation should be compromised by the lunacy of

Commander Hidaka. But one visit to the Indonesian vessel changed all that. After nervously sending the initial details back to Berlin by safe hand-courier, he now found himself reporting directly to Reichsführer Himmler on the miracles in the East.

The Grand Inquisitor surprised Steckel by accepting the extraordinary tale of time-travelling *Untermenschen*, apparently without demur. So Steckel was ordered to finalise the embassy investigation, personally sanction the deviants, and concentrate all his efforts on the mystery ship. Like Yamamoto, Himmler was less immediately interested in the technology than in the information contained within the *Sutanto*'s electric archives.

Steckel had nearly fainted away when confronted with the first webpages relating to the Jewish state known as Israel. Shock and nausea – imagine the very notion of a Jewish state in a world without the Reich! – quickly segued into mortal terror at the prospect of informing Berlin of his findings. He expected that his next message from home would be a recall to the Fatherland where he was certain to face a People's Court, before his execution.

He'd panicked and foolishly attempted to remove the offensive files. But of course, he soon realised there was no point. The Americans and British – the ones the Indonesians had come with – all knew of the Jewish eradication programme. It was part of their own history. There would be no suppressing it. Dr Goebbels would certainly try, and any number of sacrificial goats would die during his attempts. But it would come out, and probably soon. The Allies would doubtless make a great play on it for propaganda purposes. The fucking hypocrites. They all hated the Jews just as much, but they had not the will to rid the world of the problem forever.

Still, it wouldn't do to be caught in the crossfire over the next few weeks. No doubt that liberal idiot Brasch would be sending his own communiqués back to the army. *Good.* Let him take the heat.

Steckel resolved to take some time away from Hashirajima to settle the matter of the two queers. Time enough to get well clear of the shit storm he knew was coming.

Admiral Yamamoto was very understanding. He'd even been kind enough to spare a seaplane to take him back to Tokyo. Steckel did not elaborate on the reasons for his unexpected leave of absence, and Yamamoto did not ask.

So Steckel had returned to Tokyo and settled back into the routine work of the embassy, liaising with his opposite number in the Japanese Kempeitai about the exchange of medical data between the Reich and the Empire. Both had invested significant resources in experiments carried out on captive human subjects, but they'd concentrated on different areas. The limits of physical endurance for the Nazi camp doctors; the study of chemical and biological warfare agents for the Japanese.

His work gave him the opportunity to reacquaint

himself with the queers, Schenk and Oster, who worked in a related section, exchanging information with Japan on Allied weapons systems and codes. He intended to gain their trust, then lure them to a small bar a few miles from the embassy. They'd met there once before, retiring after too much rice wine to a nearby bathhouse, where the diplomats had openly incriminated themselves. But the *Sutanto* had arrived before Steckel was able to personally organise their arrest and, quite frankly, he'd let the matter slip after that. It seemed less important than accompanying Brasch to Hashirajima.

This time, however, Steckel had alerted the mission's security chief, who would be waiting for the right moment to seize the perverts in flagrante. They could be executed on the spot. Nonetheless he intended to keep them alive for a while. Their interrogation would give him an excuse to stay away from the *Sutanto* while this ugly business over the Jewish question and the Reich's ultimate failure worked itself out. It surely wouldn't take long.

As the SD man picked his way through a narrow alley that stank of fish guts and human waste, he couldn't throw off his nagging concerns. A world without the Reich? Without the Führer! It didn't seem possible. And a Jewish state? That was an abomination. He huddled deeper inside his black trench coat as a light rain fell. The evidence he'd seen and touched with his own hands was undeniable. But what to do? Reichsführer Himmler was surprisingly open to the mystical and otherworldly. The fact of the ships' emergence may have stunned and troubled him, but he hadn't rejected the idea out of hand, as Steckel had expected him to. Indeed, he had leaped on the first reports, demanding more information and asking for clarification on dozens of points.

The Indonesians, for instance. Where did they fit on the human evolutionary scale? From Steckel's preliminary notes, Himmler thought they seemed almost subhuman. What did the Nipponese think? Were they an Asian subrace? And if that were so, how did they acquire their technological sophistication? Himmler had pressed him for evidence of the triumphs of the Aryan race, as well.

Steckel had replied that it seemed as if some vast Jewish conspiracy *may* have thwarted the inevitable march of the German people to their destiny. He'd placed a flexipad, containing some very carefully chosen files, in a diplomatic pouch and sent it back via a Spanish airplane.

An ominous silence had been his only answer from Berlin, until another flurry of demands and questions had suddenly arrived, along with news that Himmler was sending even more men out to help with the investigation.

Perhaps, thought Steckel as he picked his way through the ancient wooden city, Himmler could be persuaded to protect him, if it appeared to be in his interests to do so. The SS-Obersturmführer decided that, when he returned to the *Sutanto*, he would devote his energies to researching the future of the Reichsführer himself. Things would not have gone well for him if the Allies had won and the Soviets had overrun the country. Surely he would want to know how to avoid such a fate.

The Soviets. His stomach turned at the thought. Steckel was well informed of SS policy on the Eastern Front. To have Bolshevik savagery visited upon the soil of the Fatherland itself – it did not bear pursuing.

Steckel was so absorbed in thought that he tripped on a cobblestone and lost his footing on the wet ground. Twisting as he fell, he jarred his arm quite badly, sending a burst of pins and needles shooting up from his elbow. He cursed as he felt the filthy groundwater leaching into his pants. It was dark, with only wooden lanterns to light the way, and he realised, as he looked up from his ignominious perch next to a mound of rotting garbage, that he had wandered off his path.

He was lost.

Steckel had only a superficial familiarity with this part of the old city. He knew how to navigate to the bar and bathhouse, and that was it. He would have to ask directions. That realisation led quickly to another. There was nobody about. The alleyway, framed by facades of ancient stone and wooden cottages, curved into blackness some sixty feet on. Steckel turned on his heel, but it was the same behind him, too. He stood in a small, isolated pool of flickering lantern light.

For some reason goose flesh crawled over his arms

and legs, and he shuddered as the hair on his scalp stood up on end. It was ridiculous. What was there to be . . .

Two shadows detached themselves from the inky void of a small side passage just behind the German spy and flowed like jet-black quicksilver around the edge of his peripheral vision. A stifled cry caught in his throat and his heart lurched in response to a warning from the deepest, most reptilian part of his hindbrain. His hands fumbled at the buttons of his leather coat, frantically seeking access to the Luger he carried in a deep breast pocket.

The faint swish of a descending *Bokken* was the last sound he heard before his arm shattered with a blast of blinding white-hot pain. The scream building in his throat had no time to emerge. He sensed, rather than saw, the briefest glimmer of a shadow, or a silhouette, or just a flicker of negative space, as the hiss of a wooden sword, swung with inhuman speed, presaged the end of his life. The leading edge of the hard wooden blade crushed his larynx, choking off the cry and the last breath he would ever draw.

As he twitched and shuddered on the wet cobblestones, clutching at his throat, desperately trying to drag air in through the crumpled windpipe, his eyes, bulging and bloodshot, darted everywhere for a sign of his assailants. But he died without ever truly seeing them.

32

HIJMS Yamato, *Hashirajima Anchorage, 1324 hours, 10 June 1942*

Isoroku Yamamoto did not look up when he had finished studying the paper. Brasch and Hidaka sat as quietly as they had during the hour and a half it had taken the admiral to read the document. Yamamoto did not speak. He exhaled a long, slow breath, as though he had been holding it all along. He closed his heavy-lidded eyes, and they remained closed for many minutes.

Brasch ventured an enquiring look at Hidaka, who shook his head wordlessly.

'You have exceeded my expectations, gentlemen,' Yamamoto said at last.

The two officers, near exhaustion after a marathon work session, thanked him quietly.

Yamamoto held the ninety-page laser-printed document aloft. 'As I predicted, this is worth more than your lives.'

Hidaka remained motionless. Brasch sketched a sardonic lift of the eyebrows.

'Our lives aren't worth that much anyway, Admiral.'

'Well put, Major. You would not like more time for research?'

'No point,' Brasch said without embellishment. 'We might flesh out the details and the argument, but the line of reasoning that lies at the core would remain unchanged. We weren't really undertaking original research. One of the ship's systems operators was able to direct us to a wealth of material prepared by scholars who had been picking over the rubble of this war for three generations. They wrote with the value of hindsight; we merely harvested their labour.'

Hidaka leaned forwards. 'If I might, Admiral. This systems operator, a junior lieutenant named Damiri, has proved much more cooperative and useful than Moertopo. He seems to have a genuine hatred of the Americans. I suspect he may prove a more willing collaborator. Moertopo is trying to play us for fools.'

Yamamoto held the paper with his deformed hand and flicked through it again, stopping here and there to re-examine a particular point or argument.

'I agree with you about Moertopo,' he said without looking up. 'But we need his skills for now. If you wish to cultivate this other barbarian, go ahead. You have done great service to the Emperor so far, Hidaka.'

The Japanese officer looked as if he might burst with pride.

As Yamamoto reread another section of their paper, he murmured, 'I was sorry to hear about Herr Steckel, Major Brasch.'

'I sent my condolences.'

'Sometimes they are all we have,' Yamamoto said, letting the paper fall to his desktop. 'And I agree with your recommendations, Commander Hidaka. I might have written them myself. They are bold and will meet much resistance, but I do not see any other way out of the trap we have constructed for ourselves.'

Hidaka nearly levitated at the praise, but Brasch punctured his brief cheer.

'You could surrender.'

'It is lucky for you that Herr Steckel is no longer with us,' Hidaka sputtered. 'I understand that defeatism is a capital crime in the Reich.'

Brasch, as was his way, refused to rise to the provocation. He smiled in his slow, dreamy fashion, folding his arms as if discussing a football match in a beer garden.

'There are so many ways to die in the Reich, my friend. What does it matter how one departs this life?'

Hidaka, who had grown even more exasperated with the German's morose fatalism these last days, could stand it no longer. His temper launched him to his feet.

'The manner of one's death is the most important thing in life,' he gasped. 'I would not expect an ordinary *gaijin* to understand, but you are supposed to be the vaunted warrior of a warrior race. Instead you speak like the most ignorant barbarian. It is as if you do not care who wins this war.'

'I care very much,' said Brasch.

'Then you should behave as if that were true.'

Yamamoto watched the exchange without any visible sign of concern, but he intervened as Hidaka's irritation threatened to get the better of him.

'You forget yourself, Commander,' he said sharply. 'Resume your seat. A true samurai does not succumb to rage like some wild dog. Even in the heat of battle he is tranquil. His own death means *nothing* to him. Perhaps it is you who has something to learn from Major Brasch.'

Brasch had the luxury of snorting at the proposition, while Hidaka was forced to choke on his own pride. Stiffly lowering his head, he first apologised to Yamamoto and then to the engineer for his outburst.

The admiral stretched and stood, motioning for the others to remain in their seats. He stepped out from behind his desk and paced the room with his hands clasped behind his back, his chin resting on his chest. Shaking his head and pursing his lips, he was the very picture of a man caught in an unbearable dilemma.

'This is how it will be from this moment forward,' he conceded unhappily, stopping to stare out of a porthole. 'We will need to throw our shoulders against the axis of history and tip it over. But the very people we are trying to save will be the ones who most violently oppose us. I have no doubt my counterparts at Pearl Harbor are having this same discussion, perhaps even right this minute. And I fear they will seize the opportunity of this miracle – or mishap or whatever it may turn out to be – to reinforce their strategic advantages, no matter what their current tactical weaknesses may be.'

Yamamoto turned from the porthole.

'Major Brasch, what chance is there that you will receive a fair hearing in Berlin?'

'They already think I am a madman,' he confessed. 'And they may be right.'

The admiral rolled on the balls of his feet, examining the carpet as though the answer lay there.

'It is not a matter of belief alone,' he mused. 'They *will* come to believe. At some point, one of these new ships will appear in the Atlantic and sink every battle cruiser Admiral Raeder sends against it. From what Moertopo tells us, the captain may even be a woman.'

All three shook their head at that absurd notion.

'So it becomes necessary to advance the moment of their belief,' the admiral continued. 'I think you will need to return to your history lesson, gentlemen. Scour the electric library and learn all you can of events set to transpire over the next few weeks in the European theatre. We will need to intervene decisively in some issue, making use of the bounty that has come our way.'

'Do you mean to take this ship into battle?' asked Hidaka with growing excitement.

'Perhaps Lieutenant Moertopo and his men do deserve an opportunity to prove their loyalties,' Yamamoto mused.

'But what if they are found wanting?' Hidaka asked.

'We shall not let them fail us.' Then he noticed the expression on the German's face. 'You disagree, Major?'

Brasch was lost in deep thought. He responded slowly to Yamamoto's query.

'Oh, no. You are right of course. I was simply wondering whether it was such a good idea, to risk such a valuable resource. And one that cannot be replaced.'

Yamamoto considered the question a fair one.

'The *Sutanto* is a card to be played,' he said. 'But there is something to what you say. The value of this ship goes beyond the guns and rockets she carries. The information in her archives is potentially more valuable.'

Hidaka leaned forward eagerly. 'And not just that, sir, but a thousand little pieces of equipment we wouldn't need on a basic mission. We should strip her down to the bones, leaving only what we require to make our point.'

He dragged out the flexipad that he now carried with him everywhere and held it up.

'There are nearly a hundred and fifty of these on the *Sutanto*,' he said. 'Just one would be of untold value to our scientists and engineers. As Major Brasch has pointed out, we cannot hope to build one. But they are such powerful machines in their own right that they can help us develop – what did you call it, Major? – precursive technologies.'

'Precursor,' Brasch said in a monotone.

'Yes. Moertopo tells me the number calculator in these machines can perform a trillion mathematical operations in the blink of an eye. Then there are the even larger computers and the signalling devices and the automatic rifles and –'

Yamamoto held up his hands. 'I take your point, Commander. And on that point I have some good news for a change.'

The other two men reacted in their own way. Hidaka sat up ramrod straight, while Brasch reclined in his lounge seat and raised an eyebrow.

'I have been keeping something from you. We have found another ship,' said Yamamoto. 'The *Sutanto*'s sister ship, in fact.'

'But where?' gasped Hidaka.

Yamamoto smiled. The small lines at the corners of his eyes crinkled with honest delight. 'On top of a mountain in New Guinea,' he said, shaking his head at the outlandish notion.

'My God,' breathed Brasch.

'Indeed, Major. Her stern is buried in the mountainside. I'm told she looks like she's sinking right into the earth. There is unfortunately no chance of digging her out. The metal has somehow fused with the rock. As did many of the crew. However, a unit of the Kempeitai is stripping her down.'

'Were there survivors?' asked Brasch.

'Initially.' Yamamoto nodded. 'Oh, it's not what you think, Major,' he hastened to add. 'The conditions up there were quite inhospitable. Most of the crew died from exposure while still comatose. I understand we have saved five or six men. They are on their way here now.'

Hidaka was fairly bounding from his seat. 'This is excellent news,' he said. 'We have doubled our gains!'

The Grand Admiral of the Combined Fleet sighed. 'But we will soon lose the advantage of surprise,' he said. 'Australian militia scurry about that country like ants. They will soon get word back to MacArthur or Nimitz. And then, my friends, the game will be on in earnest.

'So, Hidaka, by all means, strip the *Sutanto*. You can start now if you wish. But I want an operational recommendation within two days. If we are to bring off a *Kessen Kantai*, we must strike before Nimitz.'

Both men left the office to return to their research. Hidaka, with action in the offing, could hardly contain his natural restlessness. Brasch found it irritating, but said nothing.

After they had left, Yamamoto had a pot of tea brought in. He felt the loneliness of command more than ever in these strange days. There would come a juncture very soon where he would have to confide in the members of the general staff and the cabinet. For now, though, they were as paralysed by shock as anyone. They trusted the commander-in-chief of the Combined Fleet to fashion their immediate response to the sensational events of the past two weeks. But would they agree to his grand strategy? Would the Germans? He had no idea.

And what was worse, he had almost no confidence in the decisions he was making. He picked up the research report that had been prepared by Brasch and Hidaka. There, on the very first page, they had produced a comprehensive list of faults with both the Pearl Harbor and Midway operations. He detected the hand of Brasch in that. Hidaka would not have been so bold.

And much of the criticism he agreed with emphatically. He had raised all the same objections to war with America. He had foreseen with remarkable prescience the inevitable consequences of waking a giant. But he had *not* foreseen the result of Midway. He had been so confident of his choices in that matter.

His hands shook as he read the summary of what would have happened, had Kakuta not turned tail and run for home. The breaking of their naval codes meant Nimitz had known exactly what was heading his way. The repair of the *Yorktown*, which they had thought sunk or at least damaged beyond salvage, had added a crucial platform to the American order of battle.

The incredible sacrifice of wave after wave of American pilots – all of them knowingly flying to their deaths – touched him in a way he had not thought possible. They had died with great spirit, just to give their dive-bombers a shot at Nagumo's carriers. In five minutes three of those carriers had been destroyed, and the war lost. The fourth soon followed. All because of a stupidly complex and wasteful plan for which he bore sole responsibility.

Yamamoto had to lean against his desk as waves of dizziness and nausea swept over him. He, and he alone, had brought unutterable shame upon the Emperor and devastation on the homeland. He did not need to reread the brief account of the atomic blasts that would have devastated Hiroshima and Nagasaki. Nor did he need to examine the photographs again. The images would stay with him for the rest of his life.

He wondered bleakly how long that might now be.

Would his new grand strategic design change anything? Or were they all trapped in a cycle of predestination? Was Japan doomed to lose this war and face subservience to a communist China in the next century?

Yamamoto put down his tea. Such things could not be known until they had come to pass. Resolution took hold of him, driving out his doubts and fears. His choice was clear. He must do everything he could to safeguard the Emperor and the home islands. If he should fail, such were the fortunes of war.

A convoy of twenty-seven trucks arrived in the early evening to carry away the equipment that had been stripped from the *Sutanto*. At least three of the vehicles were filled with an eclectic assortment of twenty-first century artefacts that had little or nothing to do with the ship's military role. All of the printed matter was boxed up and carried away along with video game consoles, televisions, DVD players, camcorders, coffeemakers, waffle irons, rice cookers, digital watches, most of the ship's pharmaceutical supplies, a hundred and twenty-five personal flexipads and thousands of data sticks containing games, books, movies, music and pornography. The seemingly endless list of exotic devices threatened to make Yamamoto's head swim.

'Don't be so glum, Lieutenant,' he said to Moertopo. 'You're not being robbed. Far from it, you're probably being saved. That ship will be the Americans' first target when they discover we have it. You must realise that yourself.'

They stood on the dock watching the operation with Major Brasch. Hidaka was down in the vessel, overseeing the removal process. Moertopo remained defiantly sullen.

'Nevertheless, it is my ship, Admiral. Surely you must understand that.'

'Of course,' said Yamamoto.

Brasch snorted in mild derision. 'Sailors. You are like old women.'

Hidaka had grown expert in the use of his flexipad. He carried it around the ship, checking manifests and loading schedules against the actual progress. They were doing well. The Indonesians were brisk and enthusiastic as they went about the business of emptying the vessel. No doubt this was because they had been given more liberty, better conditions and more frequent visits by the comfort women in the last few days.

It had worked wonders for their morale, especially the whores. Many of them were Englishwomen from Hong Kong and Singapore. The sailors seemed particularly appreciative of the chance to have their way with them.

Hidaka smiled as he paused outside the CIC, but his good mood quickly dissolved when he saw Sub-Lieutenant Usama Damiri advancing on him. Damiri, the *Sutanto*'s information systems officer, had proven to be much more supportive and competent than Moertopo, who preferred to spend his time in bed, smoking hashish and fucking blondes. But Hidaka found Damiri's lack of deference irritating, and his constant demand to be consulted was dangerously impertinent. He'd cultivated the man as an alternative to Moertopo, and though it had borne results, they had come at a cost.

Damiri marched up to him. 'We need to speak,' he said.

'You mean you feel the need to bother me,' Hidaka corrected him. 'I don't see that we have any need to do anything other than finish our work here.'

'You cannot denude the ship of all its defences,' said Damiri.

'Oh, really?'

'But you do not understand –'

'I understand that you are irritating me, Damiri, and slowing down progress.'

The Indonesian planted his hands on his hips. Men swirled around them, carrying boxes and computer screens and chairs on wheels. There was very little elbow room in the confined space, and Hidaka was jostled a couple of times. This added to his ill temper.

'Have you not read the email I sent you?' Damiri asked.

Hidaka sighed volubly. 'I swear, Damiri. You and your emails. You are trying to bury me alive in them. What is it this time? If you're still insisting on five breaks a day to worship your ridiculous god, you can forget it. Once is enough. He's all-seeing. He'll understand that you're busy.'

Hidaka was a little startled when Damiri poked a finger in his face and spat out furiously, 'If you had *read* my email, you would understand that, far from complicating your struggle against the Americans, Allah – praise be His name – could deliver you your victory.'

Hidaka was tired and growing impatient. He was aware of the sly grins that appeared on the faces of the Indonesian sailors around him. Sub-Lieutenant Damiri's sudden religiosity was widely thought to be a sign of his difficulty in coping with the events of the past week. He'd also suffered a nasty blow on the head, and the other Indonesians seemed to think it had left him testy and irrational.

Hidaka looked at his watch. If he wasted much more time with this loon, it would disrupt the schedule. He made to brush him off, but Damiri grabbed his wrist and held tight.

'Just hear me out,' he said. 'I know how you can use this ship to destroy Kolhammer's fleet. But you'll have to stop stripping her down like this.'

Hidaka had been about to draw his revolver and shoot the insolent dog in the face, but he stayed his hand.

Damiri inclined his head towards the door of the small CIC.

'Not here,' he said. 'In private.'

Pleased with the rate at which the trucks were leaving the dock, Yamamoto was about to make his excuses and catch a few hours of much-needed sleep. More Germans were coming tomorrow. Personal emissaries from Hitler, this time. He still had to put the final touches on the message he wanted to send back with them.

He'd been anxious all day and most of the night. His neck was stiff from craning around to search the sky for American missiles, even though Moertopo had said there was no chance he'd ever see them coming.

The Combined Fleet remained at anchor in the darkness around them. Apart from the stars, the only lights visible were the hooded headlamps of the trucks. Yamamoto had borrowed a night-vision headset to examine the other ships around Hashirajima. The carriers and great battleships slept behind their torpedo nets. They looked invincible, but he knew their armour plate would prove no better than a silk veil if Nimitz came upon them with his new weapons.

Surely that day must be drawing close.

Just a few more hours cooped up like chickens for the slaughter, he thought, *and then they'll be away*.

They sailed on the morrow. He could hardly contain his desire to be gone from the anchorage. As familiar and homely as it was, Hashirajima was such an obvious target. Moertopo had told him it was sure to be struck. And soon.

The admiral bade Brasch and Moertopo farewell and was just turning to leave when he heard Lieutenant Commander Hidaka calling up to them from the *Sutanto*. Yamamoto peered into the night but couldn't make him out.

'I think he wants to talk to you,' said Brasch.

Perplexed and more than a little irritated at the prospect of losing more sleep, Yamamoto frowned and waited. The young officer came running up to him with an Indonesian in tow.

'Admiral, Admiral! You have to hear this. Damiri here has an idea that might just rid us of these new Americans.'

'Really,' said Yamamoto, not bothering to hide his surprise or doubt.

Moertopo, he noticed, had gone rigid, as though he had been electrocuted. The Indonesian commander turned to him and hissed as the others approached at a trot.

'Do not trust this man, Admiral. The journey here has addled his mind. And it was no good to begin with. He is a fanatic, or has come to imagine himself so.'

Yamamoto heard Brasch laugh. 'When will you understand, Moertopo? You have fallen in among fanatics.'

Hidaka drew up a few feet away and bowed. He was puffing. The other man was younger and thinner. It was difficult to make out his features in the dead of night, but it looked like he sported a wispy beard, and he had a wiry muscularity about him. Before anyone else could speak, Moertopo stepped forward and slapped the man.

The other Indonesian laughed, and spoke in his native language. 'You are a dog, Moertopo. You were a dog for Djuanda, for the Americans, and now for these infidels. If you lay your hand on me again, I shall cut it off.'

'That's enough,' barked Yamamoto. 'What's going on here? If you're about to drag me into some squalid mess-room quarrel, I'd advise you to think again.'

'My apologies, sir. I am Sub-Lieutenant Usama Damiri,' the thin man said in English. 'And I have held my tongue long enough while this fool' – he pointed at Moertopo – 'has lain about like a scabrous dog in heat.'

Hidaka was forced to block Moertopo's path as he lunged forward.

'Do that again and I will cut you down where you

stand,' said the Japanese officer. 'Your comrade here has been of more help in the last three minutes than you have managed since you woke up.'

Work continued down at the ship, but some of the sailors had begun to notice the confrontation.

Moertopo turned to Yamamoto. 'Don't listen to this man, I beg you, Admiral. He doesn't have your best interests at heart. He is unbalanced. He thinks God has sent us here to smite the unbelievers, which, I might add, includes you. He is mad, or very quickly getting that way.'

Yamamoto turned to Hidaka for help. The commander nodded. 'It's true. He thinks his God has sent him here to atone for his sins. And he thinks we're all heathen dogs who are doomed to perish in a – what did you call it, Damiri? Yes, a jihad. A religious war. He doesn't deny that at all. But he says he has a way to destroy, or at least cripple, the Americans. And I believe him.'

Moertopo cursed and stalked away a few feet.

'I cannot believe this insanity has followed me here,' he muttered, but nobody was listening.

Yamamoto regarded Damiri with a new measure of interest, if not respect.

'Tell me your plan, Lieutenant. I hope it's good, or you should prepare yourself to meet this God of yours.'

Damiri smiled contemptuously. 'You have no idea what you're talking about.'

Yamamoto could make out his face quite well now.

He was intrigued to see that the young man was not at all frightened of him.

When Damiri explained what he wanted to do, Yamamoto understood why.

33

KRI Sutanto, *Hashirajima Anchorage, 2043 hours, 11 June 1942*

Lieutenant Moertopo lay in his bunk, smoking a clove cigarette laced with a small amount of hashish. It was his only comfort now. The luxury quarters and flexible geisha babes had been withdrawn since that madman Damiri had replaced him in the Japs' affections. Allah only knew what they'd do with him when the *Sutanto* put to sea under Damiri's command.

For now, he spent most of his time in here, his old cabin. He was still the senior officer. He should have been placed in Captain Djuanda's small but comfortable stateroom, but Hidaka was in there. That wasn't surprising. It'd been fitted out at great expense for the rescue of the president and his family from Tanjungpinang – an adventure that was literally a world away now.

Moertopo smiled at his memories of that near disaster. It had seemed like a wild ride at the time, maybe the wildest, with the autocannon hammering at a huge Caliphate mob and every available member of the crew firing in support with side-arms and grenade launchers and even a flare gun as the president raced up the gangway. He well remembered Djuanda, the old pirate, smoking a ridiculously oversized cigar, bellowing orders at the wheelhouse crew and laughing like a maniac as he fired an antique, silver-plated Colt .45 into the murderous rabble surging up the dock. 'Say hello to the virgins of paradise,' he'd yelled at the jihadi hordes. 'Tell them to save some pussy for me.'

Moertopo really missed the old goat. They'd had many great days. And Djuanda would have known what to do about Hidaka. Probably would have drilled him with that damn Colt as soon as he'd opened his eyes. Djuanda was a good judge of a man, and never slow to use his guns when the situation demanded. He hadn't trusted Usama Damiri, either. How could you trust someone named Usama?

Moertopo felt ashamed at his own failure to live up to the buccaneering spirit of the *Sutanto*'s former commander, just as he was shamed by his reluctance to confront Hidaka over the old man's death. An accident, the Japanese had called it. Said he'd woken up while nobody was looking and fallen overboard. He was groggy, disoriented, and the sea was heavy, with a lot of reflected waves and cross-chop making the deck quite treacherous underfoot. '*A tragedy*,' said Hidaka, '*a real tragedy*.' Moertopo had mutely agreed, even though he'd seen Djuanda keep his feet in a typhoon while drunk on a whole bottle of *arak*.

A knock at the cabin door interrupted Moertopo's

litany of woe. He sighed and carefully stubbed out the cigarette. He had a buzz from the hashish and had hoped to quietly drift off into a drugged sleep. Stripped of all but the most basic components, the ship seemed hollow to him, and he preferred to spend his time drugged and insensible to her violation by the Japanese. Grumbling, he dropped his feet to the deck and peered at the figure in the doorway. It was Damiri.

'I have come to offer you one last chance to join us,' he said.

'Oh fuck off,' Moertopo said wearily.

The other man sneered at him with a mixture of contempt and pity. 'Look at you, Moertopo. You're a disgrace. They will bury you with a pig's carcass one day.'

'Not for a long time, though,' Moertopo said, relighting his reefer. 'And they won't bury you at all, Damiri. There won't be enough of you left. And the Japanese wouldn't bother anyway. To them, you're just a dog with a trick.'

Damiri's eyes shone with an unnatural intensity, but to Moertopo they looked utterly vacant. The maniac was already in paradise.

'You should seize this opportunity to atone, Moertopo. Others have.'

Moertopo sniggered. It was only partly the hashish.

'So you've found a few converts, have you? Let me guess, they'd be the poorest, dumbest, sorriest sacks of shit in the whole crew. Who'd you turn?

Those Surabayan peasants from the engine room, haven't got enough sense to wash their hands after wiping their asses? Or that rock ape from Kalimantan, the one who still thinks the CIA blew up his grandfather in New York?'

Damiri's strained, almost constipated look caused Moertopo to burst out laughing. He rolled in his bunk, clutching his sides and howling. 'Go on, Damiri. Go off and martyr yourself,' he managed to gasp.

The born-again jihadi stalked out of his cabin as Moertopo subsided into a fit of giggles.

With his role in Japan drawing to an end, and a return to the Fatherland looming, Brasch knew he should be looking forward to seeing his wife and son, but a terrible wasting of the soul had taken hold of him again. It was even worse than the depression he'd suffered on returning from the front. He felt as if it would never lift. There was no mystery to the condition. The explanation lay in his hands, in a file called *Belsen*.

Brasch had once believed he was fighting for Germany. Then, in Russia, he was simply fighting for his life. Now, after two weeks' exposure to the *Sutanto*'s files, he was beginning to understand that he was fighting a losing battle for a monstrous cause that had nothing to do with the salvation of Germany at all. Germany, it transpired, would do very well without the Nazi Party. Under Hitler, however, it had become a charnel-house and a byword for evil.

His back ached and his head pounded. As he lay in his bunk, propped against the gentle motion of the ship, he came to the desolate conclusion that while he could fight for Germany, he could not fight for Belsen or Auschwitz or Treblinka. He had no real feeling for Jews, and was as happy to be rid of their presence as not. But this Final Solution, no civilised man could support such a bestial policy. Especially not a man whose own family might one day be touched by the *Einsatzgruppen*.

As a little deaf boy with a cleft palate, Brasch's son Manfred was eminently suitable for disposal under something called the T4 programme – the elimination of the physically and mentally undesirable.

The engineer's stomach burned at the very idea. He didn't bother to delude himself that his own status as a hero of the Reich would protect Manny forever. He had come to understand that Germany under the Nazis would inevitably eat its own young.

He had no idea what he could do to save his family.

At some point he dozed off and slept fitfully for a few hours. He no longer suffered regular nightmares from the Eastern Front. Now his sleep was tormented by visions of Manny dying in an SS camp.

An Indonesian shook him awake sometime well before dawn. He'd been sobbing into his pillow.

He came to with a start and waved the concerned sailor away.

There was a bottle of pills by his bed. Happy pills, Moertopo called them.

He dry-swallowed three and hauled himself up.

'At last,' said Hidaka.

He took a pair of Starlite night-vision binoculars and moved from the bridge onto a gangway. The flying boat leaped into bright, emerald-green clarity as he put them to his eyes. The toys these little monkeys had to play with were forever amazing him. While he waited for the plane to pull alongside the *Sutanto* he occupied himself with the binoculars. Moertopo had told him that such things were standard issue to the marines in Kolhammer's fleet. Indeed, he claimed their kit was much better than this. Some people in his own time, the Indonesian said, had even been 'gene clipped' to see in the dark, like cats. Hidaka thought that patently ridiculous, but he would withhold judgment for now.

He was learning that it didn't pay to be too sceptical of Moertopo's fairy tales.

On the deck below, a party of Indonesians wore bulky night-vision devices on their heads. The awkward-looking instruments didn't seem to hamper them, though, as they scurried about in the dark. Their visitors climbed out of the plane and into a small motor launch that had puttered over from the docks.

'A fine night for it, Captain.'

Hidaka recognised Brasch's voice. The German

had come out of his cocoon again. He was a moody character. Hidaka had given up tracking the man's intemperate emotional shifts. He hoped this positive frame of mind would last, but he held no great expectations. Major Brasch would probably swing through a few more highs and lows before they were done. At least his work ethic had improved.

'A beautiful night, Major,' said Hidaka. 'And an important one, yes?'

'We'll see,' said Brasch. 'These SS types are prone to tunnel vision. They'll love a lot of what they'll see here –'

'But they'll hate the message we've brought,' the Japanese finished for him. 'I don't envy you, Brasch. Your Führer has never struck me as a reasonable man. He may have you shot, just on general principles.'

The prospect did not seem to bother him.

'I'm just the messenger. It's Yamamoto he'll curse. And the admiral is beyond even the Führer's reach.'

Himmler's men, an Oberführer and Standartenführer – Brigadier General Hoth and Colonel Skorzeny, respectively – scrambled over the deck rail. Brasch knew nothing of Hoth, but Skorzeny was already a legend among veterans of the Eastern Front. A former bodyguard to the Führer, he stood six-foot four and was one of those very rare individuals who led a life of mortal danger without ever knowing fear. Brasch had never met him, but he could recite half-a-dozen stories of his exploits against the Soviets. Some of them may even have been true.

The giant storm-trooper slapped a deckhand on the back, and the sound of the blow against the sailor's leather jacket cracked in Brasch's ear.

'Who is that giant oaf?' asked Hidaka.

'His name is Otto Skorzeny. And a piece of advice, my friend – do not let him hear you say that. His concept of honour is even more outlandish than yours. He'll kill you where you stand, and damn the consequences.'

'Really?' said Hidaka, intrigued. 'Where do you know him from?'

Brasch laughed. 'Everyone knows him. In America they have Superman comics. In Germany we just have Superman. And there he is, stomping all over your precious ship. He'll probably dent it.'

They left the walkway, entering the bridge and making their way down to where the two guests waited. Hoth's greeting was perfunctory. He was distracted by the surroundings. Skorzeny, by way of contrast, roared a welcome to Brasch as though they were the oldest of chums.

'I have wanted to meet you since I heard about your fucking madness at Belgorod. To pile up their dead and rain fire down on them like a Viking god. Take my hand, Brasch, but do not crush it, you are obviously not a mortal man.'

Unable to match Skorzeny's ferocious hail-fellow-well-met routine, Brasch didn't even try. He sketched a smile that was half grimace. 'I was merely taking a piss when the Soviets interrupted with their damned charge. How could I sit down again? I had not finished shaking off.'

Skorzeny's laughter roared out so loud that Brasch thought he must surely damage a lung. 'That's the spirit that wins the Iron Cross. Shoot them or piss on them – it doesn't matter as long as you kill them. Come along, Herr Major, introduce us to your comrades and show us around your magic boat.'

Brasch did as he was asked. Hidaka was so taken aback by the giant Nazi's theatrical presence that he restricted himself to the briefest formalities. For that alone, Brasch was happy to have the Standartenführer on board. Moertopo looked like he would give his right arm to be anywhere in the world but there.

They moved through to the officers' mess, where a light supper and a presentation of the previous week's research awaited them.

'I *like* it. I like it *a lot*,' bellowed Skorzeny a short time later. 'And the Führer will *love* it. The best bits anyway.'

It seemed to Brasch as if the man never spoke at less than half a bellow. It must have driven the seaplane crew to distraction. 'What about you, Herr Oberführer?' the SS man boomed. 'It should give those pansies in London something to cry about, don't you think?'

Hoth's sour face hadn't changed since he'd stalked

into the room an hour earlier. Uncomfortable in the presence of the mud races, he was affronted by the idea of subhumans like these Indonesians possessing such advanced weaponry. The sooner they were off these ships and into a shallow grave, the better.

'I am not a naval expert,' he said, making it sound like some form of perversion, 'but I will report to Admiral Raeder, and we shall see. The technical ministries will no doubt be interested. There is some potential here, if we can neutralise the threat of the other ships, the aircraft carrier and her escorts.'

'Ha!' cried Skorzeny. 'We'll give those dogs a flogging they'll never forget!'

He took Sub-Lieutenant Damiri in a fierce but playful headlock. 'Our holy warrior here shall see to them,' he boomed. 'You're a credit to your race, Damiri, a credit.'

The Indonesian grinned uncertainly and attempted to wriggle out of the giant Nazi's grip.

Oberführer Hoth regarded Damiri with the sort of expression you might reserve for a dog that has just lost control of its bowels on your new carpet.

'As for this, I do not see why the admiral's communiqué could not have been written on paper.' He held aloft a data slate that carried an encoded personal message for the Führer, sent by Yamamoto and Prime Minister Tojo.

Brasch answered on behalf of the Japanese.

'The slate contains briefing material that the Führer needs to see with all dispatch. It cannot be presented on paper. It consists of many sound and motion picture files. I would recommend highly that you do not delay in getting it to the Wolfschanze, Herr Oberführer. I suspect it would not be worth your life.'

'It has apparently cost Steckel his,' said Hoth in a flat, almost accusing tone.

'Then I'd guard it carefully,' replied Brasch.

There was no threat implicit in Brasch's voice. He spoke as if he was delivering the weather forecast on an unremarkable day. The SS brigadier coloured vividly at being addressed so dismissively, but the total lack of emotion in Brasch's demeanour gave him pause.

'I shall see he gets it, Herr Major,' he hissed. 'And if he is not happy with the contents, I shall make certain he knows of your eagerness for him to see it.'

Brasch wasn't intimidated by Hoth's poisonous expression. 'I doubt he will derive much joy from the material,' he said. 'But all the same, in the opinion of the Japanese high command, he *needs* to see it.'

Hoth might have exploded at the notion of Adolf Hitler needing anything sent by an Asian race, but with Hidaka and a handful of other Japanese close by, he restrained himself, snatching the slate away.

'That's better. All fighting on the same side again,' cheered Skorzeny. 'I, for one, cannot wait to see what you can do with this odd little ship, Hidaka.'

'I think even you will be surprised,' Hidaka said.

'You hear that, Brasch! Even me, the fellow says.

I like him already. He knows me well. Come, let's send poor Hoth on his way quickly. He doesn't like messing about in boats. And we shall have some fun while he is gone. You, Hidaka, tell me all about the fun you had at Pearl Harbor. I am looking forward to killing some cowboys before we are done with this war. But for now, I'll have to content myself with stories from our comrades in the East . . .'

Skorzeny's bear-like voice filled the room so completely there was no escape.

34

Ala Moana Hotel, Honolulu, 0815 hours, 10 June 1942

Some habits die hard. Julia's first instinct on waking was to check her flexipad for messages. She had been mildly obsessive about staying in contact back in the twenty-first, and it would take her a while to shake off the pattern of her first few minutes each day.

There was only one message this morning, which was one more than she'd had most mornings since the Transition. Rosanna had beamed her a quick note in the Moana Hotel's cocktail lounge last night. Just text: *I WANT ALL THE DETAILS, YOU SLUT.*

That cut through the Mai Tai hangover as the memories came crashing in on her. She spun around in the old feather bed and – yes – there he was. He was lying on his stomach, not snoring, God bless him. Julia's heart gave a small lurch and she slid over to his side of the mattress, slipping one of her legs in between his as she slowly mounted him from behind and began to nip at his ears. Bristles scratched her chin as he shifted beneath her, coming awake.

'What the hell?' he muttered into the pillow.

'Liberated women,' she purred into his ear. 'I'm afraid you'll find us very demanding.'

Two hours later, at a table in the Moana's courtyard under the banyan tree, Rosanna Natoli leaned forwards, her eyes twinkling like those of a squirrel with its mouth full of nuts.

'Quickly, while he's inside – *tell me tell me tell me.*'

Julia shot a quick look at the retreating figure of Dan Black, dispatched to the dining room to fetch them some fruit salad.

'Three little words,' she said. 'Oh. My. God.'

Rosanna simply could not contain her squeal. It pealed out over the courtyard, attracting bemused and irritated looks from the other tables.

'I knew it!' she cried. 'Didn't I know it? I could tell from the moment that guy laid eyes on you, baby. He was gagging for it! How'd you bag him?'

'I think it was the riot yesterday. That dude I had to fuck up. I think it kind of excited him. Or maybe he was just too scared to say no.'

'Was he, you know, equipped for the job?'

Julia blew out her cheeks, as though she'd been stuffed as full as a Christmas goose. Another shriek pealed off into the brilliant blue sky. Rosanna seemed to be enjoying herself almost as much as her friend had.

An elderly couple at the adjoining table allowed their cutlery to clatter noisily to their plates, but if they thought the two women were about to pay them any heed, they were wrong.

‘Time check?’ giggled Rosanna.

Julia held up one finger, then two, then three, then four and then all of the fingers on one hand. She paused for dramatic effect, before holding up two more.

Natoli’s mouth dropped open as wide as it possibly could. No screams emerged, but a series of short, high-pitched squeaks, before her lips slammed shut again.

‘Seven fucking hours. Literally. I think you might be dating Superman,’ she said.

‘No,’ said Julia, shaking her head. ‘Superman’s a fag compared with this guy.’

‘Was he, like, old-fashioned?’

‘For a while.’ She smirked. ‘He’s over that now.’

‘Bragworthy?’

‘Bragworthy.’

‘Goddamn,’ said Rosanna in wonder.

The civilian couple stood up with as much dignity as they could muster and huffily left their table. The woman, whose hair was tinted a confrontational shade of blue, hissed as she passed by the journalists. Julia simply smiled at her.

‘Exit’s that way, you old crone. And while you’re there, why don’t you get a fucking life?’

The woman’s mouth dropped open like a ventriloquist doll’s. She snapped it shut before anything could fly in.

‘Well I never!’

‘Damn,’ said Natoli. ‘Did she just say what I thought she said?’

'Yeah,' said Julia. 'It's like we're living in two-D black and white.'

The far-off drone of a hovercraft coming ashore about a kilometre up the beach drifted into the courtyard. Rosanna peered off into the bright morning light. About twenty task force personnel, mainly officers from the *Leyte Gulf*, had overnighted at the hotel. A few of them had partnered up with 'temps'. Rosanna made a show of checking out a chopper pilot who'd bagged herself a rather dashing destroyer captain from Spruance's task force.

Dan Black returned and set down a tray of fruit salad, which was very heavy on pineapple, and a plate of bacon and eggs.

'Sorry, ladies,' said Black, 'but I haven't seen real cackleberries for a while.'

'Don't sweat it, sweetie,' said Julia. 'You need to keep up your strength . . .'

The comment dropped into one of those unfortunate, unforeseen holes that sometimes develop in conversations and background noise.

Duffy, completely unfazed, simply deadpanned, '. . . For the war effort.'

Blushing lightly, Dan settled himself as the background buzz cycled up to a normal level again.

Music started up from somewhere behind them. The Stones. 'Sympathy for the Devil'. The bongos that opened the track were a perfect fit with the tropical setting. Julia and Rosanna hardly noticed. They lived in a world where no item of pop culture was allowed to die. Every song, every movie, every cartoon or TV show ever made was important to somebody, which meant that it had to be instantly available, twenty-four/seven, virtually anywhere in the world.

Dan Black had not.

Both women noticed the perplexed expression across the table before they noticed the music.

'Is he really singing about the Devil?' asked Dan. 'I think he just sang something about the Devil being a German tank driver. Did you hear that? Where's it coming from?'

'A ghetto-blaster,' said Julia. 'Why? You don't like it? That's very disappointing, Dan. You're not supposed to come over all Archie Bunker for another twenty years yet.'

'It just sounds strange, is all.'

'It's the Stones, baby,' said Julia. 'It's great to fuck to.'

Dan nearly choked on a mouthful of egg.

Julia was about to tease him some more when she felt a tap on her shoulder. A long, thin streak of misery in the form of the hotel's assistant manager, Mr Windshuttle, loomed over her. He wore a tired expression, which perfectly matched the wilted flower in his jacket lapel. Ignoring the two women, he spoke directly to Black.

'I'm afraid we've had complaints, sir. About the *ladies*' language and deportment.'

Before Black could speak, Julia opened fire.

'Hey, cabana boy, if those old fossils who just shuffled out of here on their way to extinction have a problem, you can send them back in to talk to us.'

'I do not imagine that will be happening, *Miss* Duffy. *They* are senior State Department officers and valued guests of the hotel.'

Somebody turned up the volume on the Stones. It was like they'd pushed a hot wire up Windshuttle's butt. He winced noticeably.

Black took a swig from his coffee, wiped his mouth with a napkin, and addressed the manager over the music. 'I don't think we want another riot, do we, Mr Windshuttle? And believe me, sir, these ladies are more than capable of it. They're quite mad. I believe *Ms* Duffy here is probably packing heat. You can tell by just looking at her that she'd be the sort. Now, if you just back off a little bit, I'll see what I can do about bringing her down from the fine head of psychotic rage I can see building behind her eyes.'

Mr Windshuttle's mouth pursed to form a reasonable facsimile of a cat's anus, and he spun away, storming off in high dudgeon.

The three of them burst out laughing before he was out of earshot.

Dan returned to the *Clinton* for the rest of the day, leaving the women to lounge around the hotel. He thought it would put Julia in a relaxed frame of mind for the dinner with Spruance, but he was wrong. When he returned to the hotel he found her pacing their room like a caged wolf. She was beginning to chafe at the restrictions on her movements.

'This story is going to break, Dan,' she said, 'and if I want to have any chance at getting my job on the *Times*, I need to be there on day one.'

Dan slipped an arm into the jacket of his dress whites.

'I think you're getting all worked up over nothing, baby. You're the man on the spot, so to speak. They're going to want as much as you can write for them.'

'They're going to want to know why I didn't get on the blower to call them right away. That's what they do here. They get on the blower. Right away.'

Dan finished buttoning his jacket and leaned over to kiss her on the forehead.

'Nobody is getting on the blower at the moment, baby. So what is it you say? "Chill out"? You're going to dinner with Admiral Spruance, and there's a story for you right there.'

'He's not going to tell me squat about what you guys are cooking up. First thing I'll know, there'll be newsreel footage of a mushroom cloud over Tokyo and some asshole who sounds like he's got a pole up his butt doing a voice-over like, *That'll put the Nips in the stir-fry*.'

Dan sat at the end of the bed to enjoy the sight while she pulled on her stockings. Julia rarely wore dresses, and he wondered why, given how good she looked in this one.

'You brought that frock with you, I'll bet,' he said.

'Nice shuffle, Dan. I did. I got it in Milan a couple of years ago. It's great for travel because it crumples to nothing in your bag but never creases. See?'

She held the dress against herself, not a crinkle or fold to be seen, even though she'd just pulled it out of her suitcase in a tightly rolled ball.

'How do they do that?' asked Dan, who was almost as interested in the answer as he was in copping another look at Julia in her stockings and underwear.

'Nanonic manipulation of the silk fibres,' she said. 'It's the same sort of process they use to make body armour, except with a few twists you get a cocktail dress that feels like air on your skin.'

'Well, you look a hell of a lot better than some jarhead.'

'Better than Lieutenant De Marco?' she asked with an arch of one eyebrow.

'Hey, I wasn't . . . I didn't . . .'

Julia burst out laughing.

'Chill out yourself, Daniel. Word gets around. I hear all of you primitives get one look at Gina De Marco and the blood rushes right to your pants.'

Julia drew the dress over her head and let it slide down into place. It seemed to flow down her like black oil. Dan thought that was almost as good as watching it come off.

'Don't panic, Commander,' she said. 'That Marine Corps chicky-babe is a hotty. I'd probably fuck her myself after a couple of drinks.'

Dan didn't know whether to be excited or horrified by that revelation. In his embarrassment, he opted to change the subject again.

'Julia, why is it okay for you to call her a chicky-babe, but it's a federal crime for me to?'

'Well, for one thing, I *am* a chicky-babe, so it's cool.' She smiled. 'And also, I say it with a sense of irony. Work on your irony, Dan. If you want to hang around with my gang, you're going to need it. You want to know a secret about us modern chicky-babes?'

Dan handed her a clutch purse as they headed for the door.

'Sure,' he said.

She stopped by the door, leaned over and kissed his ear while whispering, 'A boyish grin and a sense of irony will carry you through almost anything.'

With that, she bit him, ducking quickly out of the door as he yelped in surprise.

Captain Karen Halabi had nobody to joke with as she buttoned up her dress whites. She was in no mood to dine with Admiral Spruance. Acting in Kolhammer's position had drained her of any desire to do anything other than drive a missile boat. The politics of the situation were starting to get to her. She'd spent the entire day hosing down brush fires, dealing with the aftermath of the riot, sorting through the double homicide, and juggling what felt like a thousand other competing problems.

But Spruance had insisted that she join him and his party for a late supper. So she padded quietly into the cocktail lounge of the Moana, her temper improving when she discovered that the two female reporters were to be part of the evening.

'I'm glad to have your company,' she said quietly as they all shook hands. 'At least that's one flank secure tonight. Where's your date, Julia? All I hear about from my spies is this Cro-Magnon character you snagged for yourself.'

Julia smiled. 'He's patching himself up in the bathroom, Captain. A bit of rough-house in the boudoir, I'm afraid.'

Ensign Curtis arrived, tricked out in his dress whites and looking incredibly nervous. He saluted, then shook Captain Halabi's hand and stammered a greeting.

'Wally, just calm down,' said Rosanna. 'What's up, you never been surrounded by so many beautiful women before?'

'Uh, no,' Curtis confessed sincerely. 'Never. Oh, sorry, Captain, I didn't mean that you were beautiful, I just, oh darn . . .'

Against her better judgment Halabi found him endearing. He was a geek, just like she'd been, a long time ago.

'Be cool, Ensign,' she said, patting him on the arm. 'Take a few slow deep breaths, and don't worry about what you're going to say to Admiral Spruance. Trust me, you'll hardly get a word in edgeways with these two at the table.'

Curtis looked only vaguely relieved. 'I'm sorry, ma'am. It's just that nobody back in Oak Brooke would ever believe that Wally Curtis would find himself having dinner with a real admiral. And I can't write my mom and dad about it, the censors would just cut it out, and anyway they'd never believe me, and –'

'Ensign, calm down,' Halabi said firmly. 'You're babbling. I imagine there's plenty that folks won't believe about what's happened to you the last few weeks. But it has, and you'll always have that. Admiral Spruance told me you were the first man on the *Enterprise* to have any idea of what was happening. That makes you just about one of the most interesting people in the world right now. Imagine that.'

'I can't,' he confessed.

'It's pre-Warhol syndrome,' said Natoli. 'Nobody here realises they have a constitutional right to fifteen minutes of fame and their own cable talk show.'

'It's kind of sweet, don't you think?' said Julia.

'Heads up, the boys are here.'

Dan Black and Ray Spruance appeared at the same time. '*Ms* Duffy,' said the admiral, 'Commander Black here has been telling me all about your adventures after the riot. I'm glad you're giving him back to me in one piece.'

'I'm not quite finished with him, Admiral,' she teased. 'I might just break him yet.'

'Well, please don't kick him around like you did that fellow in town. I need him to run a few errands for me. And you, Curtis, how are you finding the *Clinton*?'

'It's amazing, sir! They let me sit in a Raptor today. One of the jets that flew all the way to New Guinea and back. And Ms Natoli has been teaching me to use the computer net. It's got *everything* on it.'

'Would you like to know who played you in the movie of Midway, Admiral?' asked Rosanna. 'I bet we could get that off the net.'

'I'd hope it was Errol Flynn,' quipped Spruance.

'Sorry,' said Rosanna. 'But it could have been Clint Eastwood.'

'No way,' said Julia. 'Harrison Ford.'

'That's the remake of *Tora Tora Tora*,' Halabi said, correcting them both.

'I thought *Pearl Harbor* was the remake of that,' said Rosanna.

'*Pearl Harbor* was full of Ben Affleck making kissy face,' said Julia. 'There's no kissy face in *Tora Tora Tora*, just lots of ass-whupping.'

'*Pearl Harbor* was a cautionary tale about the impossibility of making a chick flick that guys would go see,' said Rosanna.

'But *Pearl Harbor II* was all right,' said Julia. 'It had that great butt shot of Dylan McDermott.'

'Highlight of the sorriest damn movie ever made,' said Rosanna.

As they reached their table, Spruance made to pull out a chair for Rosanna but found his arm stayed by a light touch from Dan Black. The junior officer shook his head sadly as if to say *Don't bother*, and sure enough, the young woman simply plucked the seat out by herself and plopped down on it without any ceremony, never once interrupting a lively monologue on the best comparative butt shot from her favourite Oscar nominees.

'I'm beginning to regret broaching this topic,' Ray Spruance confessed to Black.

'Don't worry, sir, the night's still young. There'll be plenty of other things to regret.'

After that, the table quickly divided in two. Spruance talked business with Halabi and Black for the first hour, while the reporters engaged in a champagne-fuelled quest to tease out of Ensign Curtis the meagre and possibly nonexistent details of his dating history.

Spruance was struck by the contrast between the two civilian women, who were obviously intelligent but seemed wantonly dizzy, and Captain Halabi, who was unnaturally grave. She wouldn't allow herself to be drawn into polite chitchat until she had worked through the riot, the ongoing murder investigation, and arrangements for moving more casualties off the *Clinton* and *Kandahar* and into shore-based facilities.

The reporters, who promised not to divulge

anything they heard at the table, hung on Halabi's every word while she hammered Spruance about applying more pressure to the local police, but otherwise they seemed content to tease poor Ensign Curtis.

Spruance wasn't so naive as to think them rude. He assumed they weren't behaving out of the ordinary at all, and he was fascinated by their lack of . . . what? Refinement? They both seemed well travelled and sophisticated. Manners? Both obviously knew how to deal with a silver service place setting and had a relaxed way of relating to the dining room staff that he associated with the idle rich. Was it their lack of *gravity* perhaps?

At one point he listened while the two women discussed another outrage yet to pass, some sort of germ bomb attack on LA, which he gathered they'd both covered as journalists. They seemed inured to the horrors they described, as though it was all passé.

Spruance stirred his coffee. *What sort of a world have they come from*? he wondered.

'You look pensive, Admiral.'

It was the British officer. She'd caught him gathering wool.

'I'm sorry, Captain. I was just wondering about your world. About how different it is from ours.'

Halabi leaned back to give the question its due.

'I guess you look at us,' she said, 'you look at me and people like Julia and Rosanna and Colonel Jones, and you can see some hard changes coming. All I can do is remind you that change was inevitable, whether we came or not.'

Spruance and Black said nothing. The conversation at the other end of the table fell away, too, as the reporters picked up on the sound of their names. Spruance was aware of how quickly the other two women shifted gear, from flighty to sober.

'In some ways, no matter what your views, or how broad-minded you might consider yourself,' Halabi continued, directing her remarks at Black now as well, 'you would look on our world and shudder. But if time has taught us anything, it's that you can't pick and choose your freedoms. You take freedom's curses along with its blessings.'

Halabi stared into the middle distance as though examining her own world from a new vantage point. 'In some ways, our world is no different from yours,' she said. 'It's violent. I'd hesitate to say it's more violent, seeing as you're engaged in a world war. But so are we, of a sort. And ours has gone on for years longer than yours.'

'Why haven't you won?' asked Curtis. 'You're so powerful.'

'Weapons are one thing, Ensign. You can kill a man; reduce him to nothing, literally. But the ideas that made him your enemy, those survive. Ideas are much harder to kill than men. They outlive us all.'

'Could you avoid it, your war, knowing what you do now?' asked Spruance.

'I don't know,' she replied honestly. 'Why do you

ask? It's a way off yet. It won't be yours to worry about.'

'It just seems to me,' said Spruance, 'that you'd want to avoid it by all means. The things I've heard, a whole city destroyed by a bomb in a bag, millions killed by germ war, planes flying into high-rise buildings and football stadiums. It makes me wonder what we're doing here if that's the only future.'

'It's not the only future,' said Halabi. 'Little girls still go to ballet practice. Little boys still want to be firemen. Families get together at Christmas and Thanksgiving. Life goes on. Just like here. If you have children or grandkids, you're willing to die for them. And to kill for them, too. Well, *we* are your children. We appreciate what you did. It's just too bad that our turn came around, too.'

'You agree with that?' Black asked Duffy and Natoli.

'Pretty much.' Duffy shrugged.

'It's so bleak,' said Dan Black.

'It's fine. We'd still all rather be there. It's home.'

'You'd rather live in a place where your whole city could be blown up by one madman?'

'It's home,' she repeated. 'It's really no worse than here.'

'It's better, in some ways,' said Natoli.

Spruance looked across the table to Karen Halabi. She just held his gaze and nodded.

35

Ambassador Hotel, Los Angeles,
1320 hours, 11 June 1942

The Ambassador Hotel was set within nearly twenty-five acres of manicured lawns. After lunch, Kolhammer and Einstein sat on a bench under a palm tree in the gardens while Agent Flint lurked nearby. Kolhammer was impressed. He'd experienced more than his fair share of close personal protection, having served once as the deputy UN military commander in Chechnya. Flint's technique could use some updating, but he was still pretty good.

'I suppose such things are routine in your world, Admiral,' Einstein mused.

Kolhammer was intrigued by the insight. 'That's true. But why do you say so, Professor?'

Einstein crossed his legs and leaned back to feel the sun on his face.

'You seem to come from a militarised society, Admiral. The ease with which your men and women in uniform mix together, the way you don't appear to heed the race or creed of your comrades – some might see that as enlightened, and I suppose it is. But you could also see it as the defensive response of a society that has been fighting for so long it has shed itself of all trappings save those needed to wage war. You can see the same thing happening here, to a lesser extent.'

The reasoning was sound, even though the particulars weren't exactly as Einstein put them. Kolhammer took a moment to study their surroundings, the affluence and luxury, the monocultural certainty of 1940s America. LA was starting to fill up with minorities, drawn to the war industries, but you wouldn't know it here in the grounds of the Ambassador Hotel.

'You're partly right,' he told Einstein. 'Things have changed a lot in the last twenty years, my last twenty years, I mean. But the things you noticed, they were well on the way before the jihad.'

'Your holy war?'

'I wouldn't call it that.'

'Do you mind?' asked Einstein as he fetched his pipe and pouch from a trouser pocket. 'None of you seems to smoke much, either.'

'Not really.' Kolhammer smiled. 'But go ahead. It reminds me of my Great-Uncle Hans.'

'From the death camps?'

'From the death camps,' said Kolhammer.

They sat in silence for another minute. It wasn't a companionable stillness. The sun beat down out of an azure sky just as before. The hint of a sea breeze ruffled Einstein's wild hair and took the edge off the day's heat. But a shadow that brought no comfort had fallen over them.

'You find yourself at a loss, Admiral. Faced with evil on so vast a scale, do you think it beyond your capacity to effect change for the good?'

Kolhammer frowned and wiped at his damp brow. 'I made a promise once, that I would never let that sort of thing happen again if I could do anything to avoid it. I just wonder what I'm supposed to do now, what would be best.'

Tendrils of blue smoke began to curl away from the bowl of Einstein's pipe. The smell did remind Kolhammer of his Great-Uncle Hans. The old guy would be in the camp pretty soon. Although he wouldn't be old, of course.

'Have you spoken with Roosevelt?' asked Einstein.

'Yes. They're all aware of the Nazis' programmes. They were horrified at the extent of the Holocaust. But I got the impression they'd rather I hadn't brought it up. They said the best way to help the victims was to beat the Germans.'

Einstein took that in like a professor considering a gifted student's thesis.

'And you do not agree.'

'No, I do not.'

'So what *are* you going to do?'

Before they could say anything more, Agent Flint appeared at a run.

'Excuse me, Admiral. Professor. But you have to come right away, sir. Your people are calling from

Pearl. On your communications device. They've been trying to get you for some time.'

'Dead? But how?'

The connection was flimsy. The boosted comm circuits and a large portable dish antenna, presently pointing skywards from the roof of the hotel, provided a real-time vid link, but Captain Karen Halabi appeared on the screen of Kolhammer's flexipad through a shower of static. They'd been trying for a secure link for over a day. He cursed their lack of satellite cover for about the hundredth time. Admiral King and General Eisenhower, however, standing behind him in the hotel room, exchanged whispers about the marvel of secure global communications by 'movie phone'.

'We're going to have to get on the ball with this stuff,' murmured King.

Kolhammer pointedly ignored the chatter behind him and concentrated on the acting Multinational Force commander.

'It's very obvious . . . oubl . . . urder,' said Halabi, her voice and image jumping as the signal bounced erratically off the troposphere.

'Any suspects yet?' Kolhammer asked loudly.

'Oh yes, thousands of them,' Halabi said.

Great, thought Kolhammer. Halabi continued before he could reply.

'There's more, Admiral. The *Nuku* has been found. It materialised on top of a mountain in New

Guinea. About half of it was fused into the rock, but the rest was sticking out, and I'm afraid the Japanese have got their hands on it.'

King and Eisenhower suddenly appeared at Kolhammer's shoulder.

'What the hell is this about?' King demanded to know.

Kolhammer held up a hand to fend him off. 'Just a minute, Admiral. Captain Halabi, do we know the status of the ship? What weapons and sensor systems were intact?'

Halabi disappeared inside in a small blizzard of static, which lasted for a few seconds. Kolhammer asked her to repeat herself.

'From the picture we . . . our intelligence analysts don't . . . they could . . . retrieved the choppers or most . . . mast-mounted arrays. They were buried . . . ooks like the ship's CIC would have been cut in half by the edge of the mountain. But that . . . the forward missile mounts and a lot of incidental technology they . . . unbolted and walked off with.'

'Suffering Christ,' spat Admiral King. 'Is she saying the Japs have their own missile boats now? I *knew* this would happen. I knew those little bastards would get hold of this shit.'

'Settle down,' said Kolhammer. Turning back to the small screen, he collected his thoughts before going on.

'All right, Captain. You're on the spot. I'll leave the micromanagement of the *Nuku* to you. But I suggest we lay a world of hurt on that mountain ASAP.'

'Already in hand, Admiral. We're just working our way around the lack of GPS now. We've got one catapult patched up and we should have a strike in-bound within four hours.'

'Good work. What about Anderson and Miyazaki? What's the situation there?'

Kolhammer ignored King's muttered resentment at the distraction.

'We had a real pissing match with the locals at the crime scene,' said Halabi. 'Nimitz intervened on our behalf. We got carriage of the forensics – Captain Francois off the *Kandahar* is handling that. And your Commander Lunn is working with the local DA's office on the investigations.'

Sitting on a footstool, hunched over the mini-cam sending his image back to Pearl, Kolhammer clenched and unclenched his fists.

'Local cops doing the footwork?' he asked.

'I'm afraid so,' said Halabi, unconscious of the effect her words had on Admiral King.

'Arrogant fucking limeys,' he muttered.

Kolhammer leaned forward and tried to focus on the stuttering video image.

'We got any hand at all in the detective work?'

'Nimitz is leaning on the local PD, but they're . . . difficult in all . . . orts of ways. Also, it's no . . . related, but we've had trouble on shore, a brawl in . . . tween some of our people and their . . . It's not connec . . .

to the murders as far as . . . but it's not helping relations.'

Kolhammer chewed his lip as he thought it over. 'What sort of damage are we looking at?'

The link to Halabi suddenly cleared.

'A lot of burned buildings and broken heads in town. No deaths that we know of, although one of our guys did get shot. He'll pull through. Funny thing is, the local commanders aren't all that worked up. I get the impression they have to put up with a lot of this stuff.'

Kolhammer didn't doubt it. He'd been worried that a confrontation between his sailors and the locals would only be a matter of time. But if Nimitz wasn't raising hell about it, he'd be content to let the matter lie, for the moment. There was no ignoring the killings of two of his officers, however.

'Okay, Captain,' he said. 'Tread softly on the brawl. If it doesn't bother them, we shouldn't let it bother us. But I'll want a full report for my own benefit, to see if any of our guys are at fault. As for the local cops, lean on the fuckers. If you have to, send a SEAL team through their garbage cans. Maybe they'll dig something up we can use to heavy them. We're not taking any shit over this. Not with two of our own in the morgue.'

Halabi nodded once. 'Got it.'

Kolhammer was aware that the two men behind him had heard everything he'd just said, but he couldn't have cared less what they thought of his tactics.

'Pass on my thanks to Admiral Nimitz for his help,' he said. 'And contact the other fleet commanders – ours, I mean. I want to convene on O Group tomorrow. 0800 hours your time. We'll be back in Pearl by then. Keep me updated on the *Nuku* by compressed data burst in the meantime. I'll handle the fallout at this end.'

Halabi said she'd get on it and they signed off. Kolhammer stood and faced the others.

'I'm sorry about your men, Admiral,' said Eisenhower.

'It was a man and a woman,' said Kolhammer. 'Captain Anderson off the *Leyte Gulf*, the ship that materialised inside your cruiser. And Miyazaki, the senior Japanese officer. We'd put Anderson and some of her people onto the *Siranui*.'

King took that news without visibly reacting.

'Uh-huh,' he said. 'Now, what about these fucking Japs in New Guinea? Are we gonna have these bastards all over us with one of those rocket swarms that wiped out Spruance?'

'No,' said Kolhammer. 'It's a complication, a real one. But that ship's not going anywhere. It'll be taken care of in a few hours. They'll salvage some useful gear off her, but whether they have the capacity to exploit it quickly enough is another matter.'

'Well, you better fucking hope they don't,' said King.

Kolhammer ignored the challenge.

Something was puzzling him, though. He couldn't

understand why it had taken so long for the news of Anderson's death to reach him. King and Eisenhower probably didn't think of a day's delay as being significant, but coming from a world of instantaneous communication, he did. He accepted the fact that without satellite cover, his own encrypted links were tenuous at best. But surely Pearl could have sent a cable?

'What's on your mind, Admiral?' asked Eisenhower.

'I just wonder, Admiral King, why I didn't get the news about the murders of my people from you?'

King seemed nonplussed by the question. 'Well, I only just heard it myself.'

As far as Kolhammer could tell, he didn't seem to be lying. 'You heard nothing from Pearl at all before now?'

King pressed his lips together and his eyes crinkled slightly. 'Admiral, I'd remind you that you were the one who insisted that no information be sent via radio or cable. Not when it has anything to do with you or your arrival. We've been communicating about your task force by written memo, delivered by safe hand-courier. It's been a hell of an inconvenience, if you want to know. Your goddamn notification is probably making its way here the same way everything else concerning you people does. Very . . . fucking . . . slowly.'

His point made, King stalked out of the room without further comment.

A long message from Nimitz, detailing the murders

and the follow-up, did arrive at the hotel the next day. It had taken nearly two days to travel from Hawaii.

All things considered, Flight Lieutenant Carol Llewelen was happy to be in the cockpit of her F-22 with a full weapons load, no SAMs to speak of, and an agreeable dumb-ass cracker like 'Stiffy' McClintock as her wingman.

The Raptors screamed along the coastline at Mach 2. For the moment their heading was slaved to an AWAC flight, but a touch of the stick would bring the craft back under pilot command. For now, both flyers were content to hitch a ride, while a navigational programme down-loaded from the *Clinton*'s Combat Intelligence did the thinking for them.

A voice in Llewelen's ear, almost as though it was inside her head, said, 'We have you ten minutes out. No threats. You have the stick.'

'Acknowledged,' she replied. 'Stiffy. You're upstairs.'

McClintock acknowledged her order and his jet climbed away on a precipitous curve. He was normally a talker. A terrible bullshitter actually, in her experience. But he'd stayed well within mission parameters today. Llewelen hadn't heard a peep out of him. He took up a slot five thousand metres above her.

Her heart beat faster and her breathing deepened as she swept along the southern coast of New Guinea. No radar facilities painted the fighter. No air traffic controllers challenged her. The island rushed past her at twice the speed of sound. She switched on her bellycams to capture the mission on video.

A ping in her ear and the sudden appearance of targeting data on the HUD confirmed the fact that her Terrain Following Radar had matched the mission-specific holomap copied from the *Clinton*'s database to the topography of the coastal ranges beneath her. Eighty years might be a hell of a jump to make in human terms, but mountains don't change at all in that sort of time. The Raptor's navigational processors recognised the landscape and suggested a course for the pilot to follow. A series of blue circles appeared on her HUD, curving up and away over the shoreline and over towards the soaring spine of the island. Llewelen eased the joystick over until the small arrowhead icon representing her F-22 floated into the centre of the nearest blue circle. She punched a series of buttons to lock in the new course.

Mangrove swamps, primordial jungle, river plains and razor grass swept beneath her wings in a frenzied blur. Foothills approached at an insane velocity. She steered the Raptor into the vivid green slash of a long valley that snaked up into the sky. Photon streams poured down from multiple nodes along the belly of the jet fighter, feeding data about the terrain to her processors. The Raptor felt its way up the range like a blind man running his fingers over a face.

A chime sounded in Llewelen's ear and her HUD lit up with targeting data. The most important was a red box hovering in virtual space a few miles in front of her. She was only vaguely aware of the world outside her cockpit. She knew that sheer mountain walls ripped by out there at twice the speed of sound, but she stayed fixated on the targeting data.

The box suddenly inflated and filled the HUD. A loud pinging filled her head and two two-hundred-kilogram land-attack penetrators dropped away from the hard points under her wings as she peeled off. Seeker heads on the missiles strobed wildly, painting the mountain with a rudimentary form of laser radar. They recognised the terrain features that had been loaded into their chips. They roared away, up and over the edge of the plateau, before spearing directly into the *Nuku.* The penetrators sliced through the skin of the ship and drilled down two metres into the Saruwaged Ranges before detonating.

A pair of titanic blast waves rippled out from the mist-shrouded plateau, atomising the Indonesian warship and every Japanese soldier working on her.

'Jeez, Stiffy,' Llewelen said to her wingman, 'you really don't see that sort of thing every day.'

They watched the recorded footage from the Raptor's belly-cam for the third time. A Sony digital projector threw the image up onto a screen in Roosevelt's suite at the Ambassador Hotel. After the first run-through, Kolhammer watched the others rather than the video, which had arrived as a compressed, encrypted burst from Hawaii. Like the audience in a V3D theatre they swayed from one side to the other as the Raptor weaved through the winding valley on its way to take out the *Nuku*.

He wondered if any of the Indonesians were alive when the missiles hit home. If so, it was a pity, but Halabi had made the right call. The target had to be hit.

At least nobody in this room would disagree with that. Marshall, Eisenhower, King, and the British ambassador, Lord Halifax, had all joined Roosevelt for a private briefing on the raid and the implications of the ship's discovery by Japan. Kolhammer shut off the projection as the attack ended for the third time.

A moment's silence descended before Lord Halifax spoke up.

'I wish we'd had some of those Raptor thingies last year when Hitler was bombing us silly.'

'That was very impressive, Admiral,' said Roosevelt. 'Destroying that ship so quickly.'

'And it was the British captain who ran the show, was that right?' asked Halifax. 'The PM will want to know about that.'

Kolhammer nodded. 'Captain Halabi is acting force commander in my absence. She did good. But if we'd had satellite cover we could have killed that target inside twenty minutes. And the Japanese have probably made off with a good haul anyway. I'm sorry, Mr President. It's a complication for you.'

King spoke up from the couch across the room.

'And for you, Kolhammer. Even if you could get back home before, you couldn't go now. Not with the Japs having grabbed Christ-only-knows-what sort of weapons off that ship.'

'You don't need to explain my responsibilities to me, *Admiral* King,' Kolhammer said pointedly. 'I'm going back to Pearl to confer with my task force commanders on that very issue. And we know exactly what sort of weapons may have been salvaged – primitive ones, by our standards. The Indonesians weren't running the world's best navy.'

Eisenhower interposed himself between the two volatile tempers. 'We're going to have a hell of a time making this work, gentlemen. I suggest we stop beating up on each other and think about how we deal with the Japs. And with the Nazis, God help us, if they can lay their hands on any of this.'

Roosevelt gripped the wheels of his chair and spun himself around with some difficulty on the thick carpet. General Marshall helped him with the last part of the turn, until he finished up facing King and Kolhammer directly.

'Ike's right. It looks like you're here for good, Admiral Kolhammer. I don't imagine for a second that it's going to be easy. I can already think of dozens of problems, and those are just the ones on the political side. The military implications of scattering your technology all over the globe . . . well, I don't even want to think about that right now. But I suggest you and Admiral King quit sniping at each other and come up with some plan to smooth your transition here, and get us back on the front foot.'

Kolhammer gave King the benefit of a very long stare, before slowly turning away.

'I've been thinking about that, Mr President,' he said. 'I need to get back to Pearl right away. There's an idea I'd like to discuss with my people.'

PART 4
Impact

36

USS Hillary Clinton, *0815 hours, 12 June 1942*

Apart from the grey metal bulkheads and exposed piping overhead, the main conference room in the USS *Hillary Clinton* looked like the meeting space at a business convention centre. A semicircle of Ikea workbenches curved around in front of a video wall. When Kolhammer walked in, all his surviving commanders were present; the captains and executive officers of the Multinational Force had gathered in person, a rare occurrence, to discuss their options and settle on a course of action.

No '42 personnel were present.

Kolhammer thanked Captain Halabi for filling his seat while he'd been gone, and then launched straight into the meeting.

'Right. You've all read the condensed report from the physics research group. Anybody still think there's a chance we can get home?'

He waited for somebody to put up their hand, but this was a room full of professional realists. They'd all studied the video of the *Nagoya* crumpling down into a singularity. They'd read the classified material about the sort of research Manning Pope's team was supposed to be carrying out. And they'd read the physics group's conjecture as to why that experiment had gone wrong. Having adjusted to the miracle of their arrival in 1942, nobody was holding out any hope for a second miracle to carry them home.

Kolhammer gave it ten seconds. He could see individuals searching within themselves, counting up their personal tally of loss and pondering the consequence of their bizarre fate. But no one seemed as if they were about to jump up and demand that a new time machine be constructed.

It just wasn't possible, and they knew it.

Finally Kolhammer broke the spell.

'Okay,' he said. 'Options. We fight or we don't.'

He waited for a return but none came. A couple of officers threw quick glances at the Japanese representative, Lieutenant Commander Mitsuka. The young man stared fixedly back at Kolhammer. The Multinational Force commander had commissioned him 'in the field' – over Mitsuka's own objection – arguing that it simply wasn't practical to have an ensign in charge of the *Siranui*. What active role the ship and her crew might play, however, was another matter.

'Well, then, I guess that means we fight,' Kolhammer said. 'I don't see much of an alternative either, given the damage we did to the Pacific fleet and the fact that the Japanese found the *Nuku* on top of that mountain. We have to assume they'll have salvaged material and information from the ship. It won't make an immediate difference, but if they share it with the Nazis, and we have to assume they will, we could be looking at a greatly accelerated German rocket programme, followed by a viable nuclear threat.'

There was, at last, some reaction; an uncomfortable murmur and a noticeable number of men and women shifting about in their seats, almost as though they were trying to squirm away from the implications of such a nightmare.

'I'm not here to impose my will on anybody today. There is an option I want to discuss. But it's only an option. I'm going to throw the floor open to anybody who feels the need to speak first.'

He leaned up against the edge of a desk and swept his eyes over the room. There were no assigned places, but almost everybody had grouped together by nationality. Americans, making up three-quarters of the group, sat along one side of the room and around the curve of the desks. Next to the last of them was Lieutenant Commander Mitsuka. On the other side of him sat the Australian commanders, Willet, Sheehan, Captain Tranter off the *Ipswich*, and an army officer, Brigadier Barnes. Captain Halabi and her XO, Commander McTeale, were ensconced with Prince Harry, the senior SAS officer.

Halabi raised an eyebrow at Kolhammer. He nodded at her and resumed his seat next to Mike Judge.

'Captain.'

'Thank you, sir.'

The Royal Navy officer pulled an envelope out of her jacket and dropped it onto the table.

'I have an order from the First Sea Lord in London, via Rear Admiral Murray here in Hawaii, directing me to detach the *Trident* from this force and return with all dispatch to Portsmouth. My crew and I will be "evaluated" and reassigned to training duties pending the outcome of those evaluations. Sir Leslie phoned me this morning to make sure I'd received the orders. He helpfully pointed out that disobeying them could be construed as mutiny, a capital offence.'

A few people snorted and laughed. Some swore. Prince Harry rolled his eyes.

'I see,' said Kolhammer. 'What about you, Captain Willet? Have you had anything similar?'

The Australian submariner shook her head. 'No, but Commander Judge tells me that Canberra is very keen to see us back in home waters. They're not putting pressure on yet, but you can bet they will if there's any concerted Japanese push south. At this time, mid-1942, they very likely think of themselves as facing a full-scale invasion.'

Commander Judge spoke up from beside Kolhammer. 'That's about right, Admiral. They'll take their lead from Washington for now. But MacArthur is down there banging the drums, desperately trying to get his hands on the whole force. If he thinks he can get in Prime Minister Curtin's ear to recall the Australian national contingent, I'm certain that's exactly what he'll do. He wants Brigadier Barnes's battalion and the SAS under his wing as soon as possible. If he can get the 82nd as well, he'll be in seventh heaven.'

'He only thinks so,' said Colonel Jones.

Kolhammer nodded as he digested the information.

'This isn't an immediate issue – at least not yet,' he said. 'For now, unless anyone has any drastic objection, I don't intend to split our forces. Captain Halabi, you leave London to me.'

He looked at the foreign commanders. None of them said a word. Kolhammer stood up again and walked around in front of the wall-screen.

'We agree we're stuck here, for the moment,' he said. 'Effectively forever. Even winning this war and accelerating the rate of technological development in this time line, the best guess says we won't be able to build anything like the *Nagoya* for thirty or forty years. I'm not just quoting from our own amateurs in the physics group. I spoke to Professor Einstein and a whole bunch of other eggheads back in LA, and they agree. They're poring over the information we took with us as I speak, but even leapfrogging their theoretical understanding forward by three or four generations, we have to wait for the industrial base to catch up.'

He began to pace back and forward as he built his argument.

'Bottom line, we've got to make this work, and

we've already got problems. Some people will never forgive us for Midway. Then there's Anderson and Miyazaki, that's a bad business. Maybe it was an opportunistic homicide, maybe it wasn't. The riot in Honolulu, that chief petty officer getting shot, none of it bodes well. We don't fit in here. I don't know that we ever will with any great ease. But I think we have to try. We've got to bring something more than disruption and chaos with us. That's why I'm thinking of hitting those Japanese prison camps. We can save more lives than we took when we came here. I think we need to do it. Not just politically, but morally. We owe them.'

Silence and a sense of expectancy greeted his statement. Nobody rushed to contradict him, but neither did they rush to endorse the idea. Halabi chewed her pencil, obviously deep in thought. Willet seemed to nod once. Colonel Jones leaned forward and clasped his hands together.

'It's a hell of a task, Admiral. Even for us.'

Kolhammer smiled. 'I believe you were the first to raise the idea, Colonel.'

'I was, but my people will be the ones getting shot at. Are you talking about hitting both Singapore and Luzon? Because you have to split your forces to do that. And what about the Japanese carriers that survived Midway? They don't impress us much, but they scare the shit out of the locals.'

'They do,' Kolhammer agreed. 'And I think we do need to deal with them. We know they've hightailed it back to the home islands. Captain Willet, you can get the *Havoc* to Japan in, what, three and a half days?'

'Yes, sir.'

'Well then, in four days, those ships are scrap metal.'

'If they're still there,' said Jones.

'That's right,' Kolhammer nodded. 'If they're still there. And if they're not we will have to find them and destroy them, but nobody here doubts our ability to do that. And yes, Luzon and Singapore are a hell of a way away from each other. But if we do this we have to get them all out.'

Captain Halabi stopped chewing her pencil. 'While you were away, I had a chat with one of the young officers in the working party we put together to do some historical research. We talked about this. She thinks the locals will be grateful to get their men back. But she doesn't think it'll make all that much difference to their attitude in the long run. She said we're just too alien.'

Kolhammer thought about it for a moment.

'She might be right, Captain. But we're here and have to make these choices. I guess the consequences will take care of themselves.'

Washington, The Oval Office, 2210 hours, 12 June 1942

Admiral King preferred good old-fashioned paper to those infernal data slates and flexi-whats-its. You could roll a bunch of papers up and bang them like a gavel. You could fold, spindle and mutilate them. You could tear them and crumple them and throw them into the waste-paper basket.

And that's what he felt like doing with the papers he was holding in his hands, a summary of Kolhammer's plan to intervene in the Pacific. King had no trouble with the idea of turning those rocket ships and planes on the Japs, but this maniac was talking about wasting precious resources on some ridiculous prison breakout in Luzon and Singapore.

Granted, he was also proposing to attack Hashirajima and give the Japs a taste of their own Pearl Harbor. But to King's studied eye, the whole thing looked like fantasy. They were sending one lousy Australian submarine to hit the Combined Fleet in the home islands, while the rest of their force would be split up between an attack on a couple of POW camps. It made no sense at all.

Singapore was deep in the heart of the empire now. You didn't just sail in and tie up at the yacht club before popping into Raffles for drinks. And this POW camp at Cabanatuan on Luzon – it was miles inland. They were talking about evacuating thousands of prisoners. King would dearly love to get those boys back, but this wasn't the way. This was fucking madness.

He could barely control his urge to slap the data slate from Roosevelt's hands. The President was engrossed in one of their goddamned movie presentations. A neat little cartoon pitch about how they planned to win the war. It was enough to make you retch, after what they'd done at Midway.

'Are you going to let them go ahead with their plan, Mr President?' asked King. The tone of his voice told Roosevelt that his navy chief didn't think that was even remotely a good idea.

Roosevelt fell back in the chair and struggled to find a comfortable position.

'I take it, Admiral, that you would not.'

'No, sir. If I had my way, I wouldn't be letting them out of my sight.'

Roosevelt peered out into the darkness of the White House lawn. Even with the lights down it was difficult to see past his reflection in the windowpanes.

'They're talking about destroying Yamamoto's fleet before it puts to sea again. Do you think they can do it?' he asked. 'Your honest appraisal.'

'I have no idea, sir. We couldn't, and I don't know that I'd be happy letting these bastards off the leash to try. You know about the sort of personnel they're carrying. That's a hideous can of worms, right there.'

Roosevelt levered himself around to face King

more directly, pushing his elbows into the armrest and lifting his crippled body a few inches. He grunted as he settled again.

'Admiral, that's an argument for another day. My good lady wife is already in my ear, carrying on about integration, and I fear she won't rest until I sign an executive order turning half your navy over to her suffragette friends.'

Seeing the expression that contorted the admiral's face, Roosevelt had his first good laugh in weeks.

'Relax, Admiral. I'm joking. Eleanor doesn't get everything her way.'

Though the tension ran out of King's shoulders as he slumped back into his own chair, he still looked worried. 'So this plan,' he said, 'I have a feeling you're going to approve it.'

'Your intuition is correct. If we can destroy the Combined Fleet, we go a long way towards winning this war. And they say they can do it without losing a single man. I'd deserve to be impeached if I said no to that.

'As for this rescue mission, I admit, it looks shaky on paper. But having seen what happened to those men, the pictures of them in those prison camps, I couldn't live with myself if I turned down a chance to save them. *And* I'd have their families coming over the fence to get me.'

'That's why Kolhammer sent you those pictures, sir,' King said, unable to keep the disgust out of his voice. 'To force your hand.'

Roosevelt smiled like an old wolf. 'I know. He'd make a good politician.'

The admiral tried another tack. 'They're asking us to divert a hell of a lot of shipping capacity to their little adventure,' he pointed out. 'MacArthur, for one, is going to have to wait for reinforcements in Australia. He'll howl like a stuck pig.'

'He always does,' Roosevelt countered, waving away the point. MacArthur's good opinions counted for little with him. 'And anyway, he's already assented. Not that he had any real say in the matter.'

King was unable to contain his surprise, and in turn his annoyance.

'I hadn't been told that MacArthur knew anything of this,' he said.

'I only found out myself two hours ago, when he cabled me his approval of the operation.' Roosevelt shook his head in wonder at the man's gall, dealing himself into the hand when he wasn't even at the table.

King looked as though he'd stepped in something nasty whenever the subject of MacArthur came up. 'I suppose he got one look at those marines and their equipment and decided to put them in his back pocket,' he sneered.

'Possession is nine-tenths of the law, Admiral. They're in his theatre. And I'm surprised at you. You're always trumpeting the case of Japan over Germany. If they can catch the Japs at Hashirajima, they'll cripple Tojo. After that, well, I thought you'd want to get your own hands on Kolhammer's ships for the Pacific, too.'

King tried to look insulted but failed. Roosevelt smiled again.

'I'm approving the operation, Admiral. Let Kolhammer run it his way. We'll worry about the niceties afterwards. This business in Honolulu with the murder and the riot, I fear it's a taste of more to come. If these characters can pull this off, it will create a reservoir of goodwill, and I suspect we're going to need every drop of it.'

37

USS Kandahar, *1238 hours, 13 June 1942*

The planning room of the USS *Kandahar* was only a third the size of the *Clinton*'s main conference centre, but marines are a hardy bunch, quite capable of working up a major op without the benefit of buffet service or an espresso machine. For many of the 1942 personnel, a mix of Marine Corps and navy officers, this briefing was their first real exposure to a twenty-first-century environment. A few of them struggled to maintain their focus in the face of numerous distractions, both technological and human. Lieutenant Commander Black felt fortunate to be one of the few who'd already begun to adapt to the situation.

The officer who delivered a short history lesson on the original liberation of the POW camp at Cabanatuan on Luzon was Lieutenant Gina De Marco, a strikingly pretty blonde woman who already had a reputation among Black's contemporaries as a ball breaker.

Sure enough, a wolf whistle greeted her when she took the podium. If she was supposed to giggle and blush at that provocation, somebody was in for a shock. Lieutenant De Marco fixed the offender with a frigid stare.

'Do you have a particularly small penis, sir? Is that why you feel the need to compensate for your inadequacies with this behaviour? If so, let me assure you, it didn't work. You still have a very small penis, and now you look like an idiot too.'

De Marco's shipmates exploded into hoots of laughter. The whistler and his buddies didn't really know where to look, and settled on a range of more or less shit-eating grins as their response. The lieutenant's micro-celebrity grew just that little bit more potent.

She continued without further interruption, silencing the room with her grave delivery.

'The death toll for American personnel at Cabanatuan in June of this year will be five hundred. In July it will reach eight hundred. There are also civilian prisoners being held, many of them women who have been or will be forced into sex slavery by the Japanese.'

The uniformly white male audience of '42 personnel squirmed quietly as the flat-screen behind the Lieutenant segued through dozens of archival images of the death camp, including some of white 'comfort women'. Sitting in the second row, Lieutenant Commander Black found the images disturbing, as he was meant to, but he was also unsettled by the methodical, dispassionate way in which the beautiful young woman went about her briefing. He didn't need to ask whether all the young women of the future were so confounding. He already knew from personal experience.

Black shook his head at the memory of Julia crippling that guy in Honolulu.

He still didn't know how he felt about it. She was the most challenging and vibrant woman he'd ever met. But sometimes he found himself wondering what planet she came from. She shared with De Marco an ability to deal dispassionately with the most gruesome of subjects. It was kind of off-putting.

The pretty lieutenant was still talking, and he dragged his attention back to the briefing.

'In 1944 the Rangers who rescued the POWs from the camps had extensive help from local guerrilla forces, which we can't expect because of the confused situation on the ground in Luzon. However –'

Dan found himself wondering whether this woman had ever kicked a man half to death. If you got past her beauty, she certainly looked competent enough in her camouflage fatigues.

'– the rescue was accomplished with the loss of only two Rangers, Corporal Roy Sweezy and Captain James C Fisher. One of the prisoners died of a heart attack during the extraction.'

The screen behind the lieutenant filled with still photographs taken by combat photographers from the 832nd Signal Service Battalion, who had accompanied – or would have accompanied – the Rangers on the rescue mission to Cabanatuan. The images drove all thoughts of Julia from Dan Black's mind. Like his fellow officers he gaped in horror at the skeletal, nearly inhuman creatures who stared out at them.

'These are the defenders of Corregidor, gentlemen,' said Colonel Jones, taking over from De Marco. 'Your comrades and our forebears. Thousands of others did not make it. Some were killed during the siege of the island, but most died on the forced march into captivity and during years of internment in the death camps. There is nothing we can do for the men who are gone, but there are thousands of our people we can still save.'

Black wondered whether he was the only one in the room who noted the lieutenant's use of the phrase 'our people'. More than a few of his contemporaries had been mouthing off on the way over about having to work with Negroes and Mexicans and uppity women, completely oblivious to the hovercraft crew that contained examples of all three. Black was surprised at how tiring he found the endless gripes on the subject, and wondered how Kolhammer's people managed to keep a lid on their temper.

The briefings by Kolhammer's people continued for hours, finishing late in the day with an address by a female combat surgeon.

'We'll need more transport,' said Captain Francois, 'enough for thousands of men. And most of them will be in very poor shape, so we can't just toss them into the hold of a troopship. They'll need something more sophisticated than that if they're going to survive the return trip.'

She stood in the briefing room of the *Kandahar*, five hours after Lieutenant De Marco had opened the session. The air in the room felt close and stale to Black, even with the air-conditioning running. Papers and coffee cups littered the floor, and normally crisp uniforms were becoming dishevelled. The planning session was taking so long because of the need to constantly explain basic issues such as in-flight refuelling to the 'temps. Black wasn't sure how he felt about being called 'temp. It didn't sound very dignified.

'The good news,' Francois continued, 'is that the sort of care they'll require is intense but very basic. There's not much apart from some drugs and mega-vitamin and mineral supplements that we'd need to add to the amenities you already have for treating the sort of malnutrition and illness we're likely to see. What we need from you are medics and lots of berths on big comfortable ships.'

Nimitz raised his hand to speak. 'Excuse me, Doctor. I can deal with that right away. We have a lot of converted liners that have just finished ferrying troops to New Caledonia and Australia. They moved about fifty thousand men and their equipment. They might fit the bill. They're not as luxurious as they once were, but they'd be more agreeable than a hammock in the hold of a Liberty ship.'

'That sounds just fine, Admiral. What about medics?'

'We'll round them up,' Nimitz promised.

Rachel Nguyen was growing accustomed to these strange conferences that were as much history tutorials as intelligence briefings. This group was smaller than many she'd spoken to over the last few days and was composed entirely of twenty-first-century special forces – SEALs, SAS, Marine Recon. They should have been a more intimidating audience, but unlike some others they accepted her right to be here. Whatever she had to say, they wanted to hear.

She keyed a control stick and the wall-screen split into four sections.

'These are the best contemporary overheads we have at the moment, gentlemen. As we draw nearer, we'll have drone coverage to verify their accuracy, but the 'temps who've just been there vouch for the Singapore maps, and the images of Cabanatuan are drawn from official DoD archives, so we'll take them on faith until we have real-time vision.'

She clicked the controller again, filling the entire screen with the prison camp in the Philippines.

'This camp is a former army base,' she explained. 'It's surrounded by flat, open ground and lies eight kilometres from the village of Cabanatuan, which we can assume contains a heavy concentration of Japanese army units. It sits astride a major transport axis from Manila and the camp itself is often used as a transit base for Japanese army units.

'You can expect a strong garrison in the town, between three and five thousand strong with armour and artillery support. The Ranger unit that originally liberated the camp in 1944 moved from American-held territory on Luzon through the Japanese lines and deep into their rear areas. They had extensive help from local guerrilla forces, which we cannot assume even exist yet. And I guess I don't need to point out that there is no American-held territory in Luzon at the moment.'

HMAS Havoc, *1435 hours, 13 June 1942*

Nimitz and an aide climbed down the well of the submarine *Havoc* to accept a somewhat casual salute from the Australian captain. Unlike some of the Multinational Force commanders, she hadn't bothered to change out of her grey combat coveralls.

'Welcome aboard, Admiral,' she said. 'And Lieutenant Fraser, right?'

The aide was unable to stop his eyes from drifting south to the captain's breasts. He made an effort to tear his gaze away, but it was all too obvious. Nimitz had no trouble hiding his thoughts behind a mask of restrained civility.

The admiral stepped forwards to shake her hand. Were she of his own time, etiquette would have demanded that he kiss it. But Jane Willet didn't have an inviting demeanour. Her grip was cool and firm.

Nimitz was taken aback by the size of the vessel. There was so much more room than he'd expected. And it was clean, too. The rank smell of confined humanity, a feature of every submarine in their own fleet, was noticeable mostly because of its absence. It added to the spacious effect. Even with the banks of instruments curving up the walls, there seemed to be enough room to dance a waltz in here.

'We'll do a quick tour of the *Havoc*, gentlemen,' Willet said, 'and then my divisional heads will join us in the wardroom, where they can answer any questions. You're standing in the belly of the beast now. This is my combat, communications and nav centre.'

She guided them towards a freestanding block with a glowing glass top. They had expected to find maps and charts there. The positional hologram was a shock. A scaled-down representation of Pearl Harbor floated within the 'bloc. The rest of the task force and every contemporary naval vessel were also represented in there. As spectral miniatures, they floated on a blue sea surface a few inches above the *Havoc*.

'It's a wonder,' breathed Fraser. 'Like a movie I suppose, Captain, but in three dimensions.'

'Effectively,' she agreed. 'The nav 'blocs have stored holomaps of every important ocean and littoral environment in the world. Our sensors simply place us into context on those maps. Of course, some of the most interesting holomaps are useless now because the harbours and ports in our records haven't been built yet – a pity really, since we may be visiting a few of them. We've already edited Pearl's map to correspond to local conditions.'

The *Havoc*'s captain brought up a cutaway hologram of the submarine itself. 'This class of submarine replaced the old *Collins*-class boats, which came into service in the 1990s,' explained Willet. 'They utilise the same teardrop hull shape and X rudder arrangement. They're much bigger, though. Eight and a half thousand tonnes. Ninety-five metres in length, with a twelve-metre diameter – that's about three hundred feet by forty feet to you.'

As she spoke, the ghostlike submarine underwent a rapid series of inversions and optical modifications, its grey shark-like skin melting away from one end of the cigar-shaped hull to the other. Various decks and sections detached themselves and grew larger in a separate quadrant of the hologram field. Nimitz and Fraser watched, enthralled, as a chunk of the foredeck disengaged itself and twisted in space to reveal a forest of rockets.

Willet continued. 'All the extra real estate accommodates a vertical launch missile system on the forward deck and eight torpedo tubes in the bow. The tubes can launch torpedoes, of course, antiship missiles, mines or miniature submersible vehicles for special operations work. The vertical tubes carry a full suite of much heavier sea surface and land-attack munitions, all delivered by extended range cruise missile. All sensors and weapons are totally integrated via a Nemesis 2 quantum array battlespace management system, so that each of those delivery options, eight tubes and a dozen missile silos, can independently engage a separate enemy in separate theatres.'

'Do I understand you correctly, Captain Willet,' he asked quietly, 'your submarine can attack multiple targets at sea and on land at the same time, over great distances?'

'It could, if we had satellite coverage. But we don't. Still, even with our reduced capacity, in this antique environment, we could sink every capital ship in the Japanese navy before they even realised their cocks were on the chopping block.'

Nimitz frowned at the obscenity, but he let it pass without comment. His gaze drifted over the bridge crew and their equipment. Each crewmember was stationed at a glowing screen, which they occasionally brushed with their fingertips, sometimes to no discernible effect and sometimes with obvious consequences. Nimitz watched as one young seaman danced his fingers over a screen that pulsed and flowed with different colours and shapes under the caress.

'At least I recognise that,' he smiled, indicating the periscope.

'We still use it,' said Willet, 'but not much. We do most of our business via the 'bloc.'

'And your business will be in Hashirajima,' said Nimitz.

'If they're at home. We won't be going right in, so

we won't be able to use the torpedoes. But we'll deploy a drone to light up the targets for us, then we'll slam them with hypersonic cruise missiles. They drive themselves into the body of the target vessel and then go supernova. It's quite a sight. Like a tiny sun has materialised inside the hull. Makes a hell of a mess. My weapons chief can brief you fully, if you wish. But all you really need to know is that one missile will kill a battleship or an aircraft carrier, or you get your money back. The Japanese won't have a clue what hit them. If they're real quick thinkers, they might just realise something's wrong, and then they'll be dead.'

'And I take it you have this stealth business too,' said Fraser.

'We have a full range of stealth protocols and countermeasures. But most of them are redundant in this environment. The material coating our skin will simply absorb the primitive sonar available in this period. We could be sitting directly under a contemporary subhunter, having a keg party, and they wouldn't have a clue. It's not fair, but then, you know, tough shit.'

Nimitz was beginning to suspect that Bill Halsey would warm to this blunt female.

'You seem very motivated, Captain.'

Willet's face didn't soften, but her posture did, just marginally.

'My great-grandfather was captured in Malaya, sir. He died on the Burma railway in 1943. The Japs caught him trying to escape, killed nine of his mates right there in front of him. Then they tied him to a tree and used him for bayonet practice. But right now he's in Changi. I never knew him, of course. But I loved my granddad, and I remember him crying when he'd talk about his father. I'd like to give him back his old man.'

Captain Francois mashed the palms of her hands into the balls of her eyes, trying to rub out the feeling of hot sand. She hadn't slept in twenty-six hours, and it was beginning to affect her judgment. She would need to get some time in the rack very soon. But first she had one more cut to make.

She leaned forward, her lower back aching, and scanned the list again. The screen showed a register of every patient she might – just might, mind you – be able to transfer from the fleet's ship-borne hospitals to Pearl's more primitive shore-based facilities. She needed to free up another hundred and fifty beds to accommodate the critical cases they would likely pick up in Singapore and Luzon.

She just didn't see how she could do it without killing at least seventy or eighty patients.

'What a fucked-up way to earn a dollar,' she grumbled.

Perhaps the burn case off the Astoria? *They're used to dealing with burns here. Perhaps he could go ashore.*

She reached out to click the mouse and consign the man to Dark Ages medicine.

'No,' she sighed, stopping herself. 'He'd die for sure.'

She spat a quiet curse at the ceiling of her office and went back to the start of the list.

At her elbow lay another file, one she pored over compulsively when she wasn't working on the patient lists. It was the results of her post-mortem examination of Anderson and Miyazaki. It included the DNA profiles of the men who'd raped the *Leyte Gulf*'s Captain. She felt sick every time she read it. But she was convinced that if Anderson and Miyazaki were to have justice, it would come from their own people. Not from someone like Buster Cherry.

There was something else about the case that she hadn't discussed with anyone. It brought back memories. Not just of the war crimes she'd investigated for the UN in Srebrenica and Denpasar, but also of her own rape at the age of seventeen.

Margie Francois had been a college freshman in pre-med when a bunch of drunken jocks had jumped her as she walked back to her dorm from the library late at night. She'd never told anyone about it. There were times when she still felt ashamed.

Kolhammer stood in the bridge of the *Clinton*, watching the activity down on the flight deck. Hundreds of men and women toiled around the clock to prepare the ship for war. The feeling recalled the days before the Transition, when they were still preparing to deploy into the Indonesian Archipelago.

He was still getting by on only four or five hours' sleep. There was so much to do. The Multinational Force was battered and much reduced, but it was still the most powerful fleet of ships on the face of the earth at this time. He had the *Kandahar* and the two ships of her MEU intact. The torpedo strike on the marine flat-top had been patched up well enough to put her back to sea. The *Kennebunkport* and the *Providence* had come through relatively unscathed. HMS *Trident* lay at anchor just abaft of them, and the *Siranui* beyond her. She was now crewed by Japanese and American sailors, the latter mostly coming from the *Leyte Gulf*. Those Japanese who did not feel they could fight against their forebears, about eighty per cent of the crew, would await her return on shore.

He couldn't see the submarine *Havoc*. She was prowling the approaches to Midway.

The Australian troop-carrier *Moreton Bay* had been patched up and quickly fitted out as a hospital ship. The four hundred members of the 2nd Cavalry Regiment who had been on their way to Timor in her were now squeezed with their armour into the monohulled assault ship HMAS *Ipswich*.

And of course there was the *Clinton*.

Only one of her catapults had been repaired. She had only four jet fighters in one piece. Nearly three-quarters of her combat power was gone, wiped out at Midway, and her corridors were much less crowded. They'd buried so many of her complement at sea. But like her murdered namesake, the most uncompromising wartime president in the history of the United States, she was a hard-charging, life-taking bitch who'd crush anyone or anything that got in her way.

He trained his binoculars on the old *Enterprise*. She was as much a scene of activity as the *Clinton*. He wasn't sure that he agreed with Nimitz's decision that she accompany them, but he didn't feel he could argue against it. If nothing else it gave them more carrying capacity, and they'd need it. They were looking to bring home nearly twenty thousand prisoners.

'Penny for your thoughts, sir?' asked Commander Judge.

Kolhammer lowered the glasses.

'I just hope we can pull it off, Mike,' he said. 'We're doing the right thing. I'm sure of that. But there are any number of things that can go wrong.'

'That's right,' said Judge. 'Can and probably will when the shooting starts. But it's like you said, Admiral. It's the right thing.'

Dan Black came awake to the smell of freshly brewed coffee. For one terrible moment he thought Ray Spruance was about to subject him to another mug of his terrible java. Then his head cleared and he remembered he was in bed at the Moana, not in his bunk on the *Enterprise*. The room was still, but a figure was coming towards him.

'Here, get this into you, Daniel. We've got to get back to Pearl in an hour.'

Julia pushed the coffee towards him before opening the curtains. The reporter was already dressed in the jeans and hiking boots she seemed to prefer. He had been hoping for a little roll before heading off, but she was all business.

'I don't understand,' he said. 'What's wrong?'

'Nothing, Dan, but we're both shipping out today, and my call is a little earlier than yours. I figured you'd want a brew to wake up.'

'There are better ways to wake up, darling.'

She ruffled his hair affectionately, but without a hint of sexual playfulness.

'There are,' she agreed, 'but we've got to get to work.'

His heart tripped over in his chest. 'You're going to work? You got your job back in New York? I was hoping we'd be able to see more of each other.'

Julia was halfway through a big mouthful of coffee, which Dan's slightly panicky outburst forced her to cut short.

'Just be cool,' she gulped. 'I'm not going to New York yet. They still haven't let us contact our offices, those of us who actually have them. No, I'm going out with the *Clinton*.'

Dan fumbled in the dark to set his cup down on the bedside table. His eyes were adjusting to the dark and he could see the defiant set to her arms.

'You're going into combat?'

'I have no idea where we're going. They'll tell

us just before we need to know. But Kolhammer decided he wants us there. Keep your friends close and your enemies closer, I guess.'

'But –'

Julia cut him off. 'Let's not do this scene, okay, the one where you tell me it's no place for a woman, I could get hurt, you're only trying to protect me.'

'But all those things are true.'

'They're not. Not all of them.'

'But –'

'But nothing. Dan, I've seen more combat than you. End of story. I'm touched that you feel strongly enough to be an asshole about it, but if you and I are to have any sort of future, you'll have to accept that it's *me* you're with. Not your idea of me, and what I should be. I don't know what's coming, but I know my job. Ninety minutes from now I clock on again, so drink up. We'll split a ride back to Pearl. They're sending a couple of Humvees. They'll be downstairs in half an hour.'

Dan Black was in free fall. He had never been spoken to like that, had never even heard of a woman speaking like that. Julia stood there in the dawn, an intruder, raking at the secret places in his heart.

'Will you marry me?' he asked.

She didn't even give him the benefit of a slight hesitation.

'No, Dan. Not yet anyway. I'd like us to live together for a while first. See how we go with the daily grind when we don't have all this bullshit to keep us entertained. If we're still fucking like rabbits at the end of that, ask me again.'

'You want to live in sin?'

'Yeah. It sounds really sexy when you put it like that, doesn't it?'

He was completely unbalanced by her. Women weren't supposed to bat away a proposal of marriage. That's not how it worked in the movies. They were supposed to collapse into your chest and burst into tears. Julia was stuffing her running shoes into a gym bag and Dan wondered if *he* might actually get teary. Up till now he'd always suspected there was nobody special for him – and then she'd stepped through a rupture in space and time.

'I think I'm falling in love with you, Julia.'

She stopped stuffing the bag and came over to sit down next to him, placing a hand on his thigh.

'Dan, you think that because we've shared an intense period of excitement, where we found ourselves physically attracted, and then intrigued by the strangeness that sits just under our similarities. We're sexually compatible. I suspect we're emotionally and intellectually well matched as well. And before your face gets any longer, it's a two-way street – I think I'm falling in love with you too.'

They nearly missed the ride back to Pearl.

38

HMAS Havoc, *2003 hours, 20 June 1942*

The control room of the *Havoc* was unnaturally quiet as the navigator, Lieutenant Malcolm Knox, manipulated a dozen icons on the wide touch screen at his workstation. Without GPS satellites the task of position-fixing was much more difficult. The sub's inertial navigation processors could place them with reasonable accuracy about three hundred nautical miles south of the Japanese home island of Shikoku, but Captain Willet wasn't a reasonable woman. She'd often said that without GPS coverage the modern military couldn't find its own arse with both hands in a small well-lit room. The joke had come back to bite her.

'How's that fix coming?' she asked the navigator.

'Just scanning for the last beacon, ma'am.'

They'd placed three position transmitters on the way over, on small rocky islets for which they knew the exact holomap reference points. Willet practised a breathing exercise while she waited for the *Havoc*'s quantum arrays to calibrate and align the incoming signals. She watched a small blue bar crawl across a window in the navigator's flat-screen. When the bar was filled, a series of faint chimes sounded and Knox gave her the thumbs-up.

'We have a firm position fix, ma'am. CI is plotting firing solutions for the drone launch.'

'Thank you, Mr Knox. Weapons?'

'VLS 3 is armed, Captain. Boards green. And we have the solution.'

A soft, familiar tone sounded once as the submarine's Combat Intelligence downloaded flight data to a Tenix Defense Industries surveillance mace.

'Take her down to one hundred metres and launch,' Willet ordered.

The voice of the CI, a factory default mid-Pacific accent, warned the crew to prepare for a dive. The conning tower was sealed. Nobody had gone topside when they surfaced, so there were no hatches to shut. Procedure had to be followed, however, and the officer of the watch cycled through all the CCTV cams, calling each one clear as he checked for personnel who couldn't possibly be on deck.

Captain Willet felt the nonslip flooring tilt beneath her feet and reached for a grab bar with practised grace. Strapped into their chairs, the combat centre sysops continued to work at their stations, leaning against the angle of the sub's descent.

'One hundred metres, ma'am.'

'Launch the Big Eye,' said Willet.

'VLS 3 launching, Captain, in five, four, three, two, one, *launch*.'

She heard and felt the discarding sabot spit out of

the vertical launch tube in the forward missile bay. Her intel controller, Lieutenant Lohrey, counted off the seconds until the cruise missile discarded its casing.

'Big Eye has fired, Captain,' she announced. 'Tracking for Hashirajima. On station in seventeen minutes.'

A quarter of an hour later and hundreds of kilometres away the nose of the surveillance mace split open and ejected an object that looked very much like a frisbee. Its mission done, the missile continued on across the home island of Honshu before diving down into the Sea of Japan and destroying itself.

The small whirring drone, a doughnut of superlight plasteel wrapped around a high-speed turbofan, deployed a series of antennae. Tiny doors swung open on the underside and long spools of micro-light fibre dropped down from the ring.

One thousand kilometres to the south, the command centre of the *Havoc* was quiet as the submarine lurked just below the waves, its high-gain antenna deployed. The boat's active and passive arrays were all operating at maximum return. The men and women on board were still and tense as the *Havoc* waited, like a predator. Signals from her telescoping mast pulsed across the sky, unheeded until they brushed past the tendrils of monobonded filament dangling beneath the drone.

The feed from Hashirajima came online at 2021.

'We have contact and control,' said Lohrey as two

screens lit up in front of her with a live feed from the Big Eye surveillance module. One screen carried multiple windows, showing a cascading series of numbers and letters. The other displayed three video windows. Infrared, low-light and a blank rectangle for full colour.

Willet immediately recognised the outline of Hiroshima Bay and the Kure Naval District, but she waited while the CI cross-matched the incoming vision with its holomap banks.

'Target confirmed,' said Lohrey. 'I'm moving Big Eye south, Captain. We're about eighteen thousand metres north of the anchorage. We have a tailwind of 115 knots. Should be there inside six minutes.'

The scene relayed back from the drone was eerily beautiful. Six separate drone-cams panned wide to take in as much of the world below as possible. Willet could see the old castle city of Iwakuni sitting astride the Nishiki River with its back to the Renka and Rakan mountain ranges. Iwakuni was a major industrial centre, but the wide-angle infrared cams transformed it into something ghostly and medieval, reminding Lohrey of the fantasy novels she'd read as a teenager.

The *Seto-naikai*, as the Japanese called the five water basins lying between Honshu, Shikoku and Kyushu, were home to hundreds of islands. Willet silently wondered how many of them were populated at this time. Quite a few, she guessed, if only by antiaircraft gun crews, watching the skies over the home waters of the Japanese fleet. Dozens of islands drifted across a large window displaying light-amplified video. They looked like small, irregular emeralds.

Small boats were clustered around some, probably belonging to fishing communities or one of the many villages devoted to harvesting salt from the shores of the *Seto-naikai.* As the drone moved away from the twisting, corrugated channels and inlets of Edajima Island and towards Hashirajima itself, larger vessels began to appear. Destroyers and corvettes. Oilers, seaplane tenders and torpedo boats. Mine-layers and depot ships, submarines and sub chasers. She smiled at the thought of being pursued by the latter.

The first capital ship appeared on screen and the *Havoc*'s commander whistled softly.

'You sexy, sexy bitch. What d'you say, Chief?'

Her senior enlisted man, CPO Flemming, leaned forward to peer at the screen.

'Looks like a second-class cruiser, ma'am. Maybe the *Kumano* or *Mogami.*'

Willet smiled at her chief petty officer. 'You should really get out more, Roy.'

'Tried to pop outside for a quick smoke before, Cap'n. Got wet.'

Big Eye was relaying footage of more and more capital ships. But not as many as Willet had expected.

'Have we got a full house, Ms Lohrey?' she asked.

'Afraid not, ma'am. Looks like some of them shot through. Only two carriers visible so far.'

Willet took up a position behind the intel boss.

Lieutenant Lohrey danced her fingertips across a touch screen so quickly that they covered the brightly glowing surface in afterimages. Extra windows opened up, putting on view more cruisers and battleships, but refusing to display any carriers beyond the two flat-tops they'd already tagged.

At least two-thirds of the Combined Fleet was missing.

'Bugger,' muttered Willet. 'Okay. Comms. Burst transmission to Kolhammer, maximum compression. The fleet has either scattered or sortied. *Havoc* to engage remaining targets on schedule. Be advised there is a risk of encountering significant enemy surface units.'

The warning sent, Willet returned to her tasking.

Hashirajima still presented an attractive target. At least a dozen very large warships and twice as many destroyers lay at anchor beneath the unblinking eyes of the drone.

'Weapons, designate the flat-tops.'

'Targets assigned, ma'am,' replied the dour Scot, Lieutenant Yates.

A signal pulsed out and seven thousand metres above Hashirajima a multifaceted laser node winked on beneath the Big Eye drone. Two thin beams of coherent light from outside the visible spectrum locked onto the flight decks of the two carriers.

Back in the *Havoc*'s CIC, Willet chewed her lip and quietly contemplated the flat-screen that was carrying real-time video from the target area. Picking up a light-wand, she drew boxes around the four largest gunships.

'That looks like Kakuta's Aleutian force,' she said. 'That'd make those big bastards the *Hyuga*, *Ise*, *Fuso* and *Yamashiro*. Weapons, put a White Dwarf into each of them.'

Yates acknowledged her order as she drew another box around a slightly smaller vessel. It looked like a heavy cruiser rather than a battleship. She magnified the image on screen, closing to a virtual distance of six hundred metres. Wisps of smoke drifted from the stacks in the low-light display. Blooms of rose-coloured radiance leaked from the funnels on the infrared view. Willet compared the image with archival shots running on an adjacent screen.

'And that looks like the *Kitikami*,' she said. 'Mr Yates, you'll probably kill yourself a couple of admirals if you take her out.'

'Nice work if you can get it, ma'am.'

The captain leaned over and touched the screen with her wand, confirming her targets as crew-members seated up and down the command centre began to report.

'Targets acquired. Strobing and designated.'

'Payload online, Captain. No countermeasures. Nothing on the threat boards.'

'All links feeding, Captain. Clean vision to weapons.'

'VLS ready and missiles hot, ma'am.'

Willet checked the time. Three minutes to go.

Silence settled on the small group of men and women. Those members of the crew not directly concerned with the attack or with attending to the boat's own defensive systems watched on screens throughout the vessel. In the corner of each monitor a red time hack counted down.

Willet felt a presence beside her. It was the *Havoc*'s exec, Commander Gray.

'Do you mind, Captain?' he asked quietly.

'No, of course not,' she answered, her own voice just as subdued.

Gray spoke softly, almost to himself. '*Vengeance, deep brooding over the slain, had blocked the source of softer woe; And burning pride and high disdain, Forbade the rising tear to flow.*'

Chief Flemming threw the young officer a glance; his own rough-hewn features giving nothing away as the time hack counted down to zero.

00.03

00.02

00.01

00.00

Nobody pressed any buttons. The sequence was already programmed. The boat shuddered as it absorbed the energy of the missile salvo lifting off.

The defensive sysops redoubled their watchfulness, lest the launch give them away. But the radar screens remained empty and the threat boards glowed green.

Captain Willet worked the screen, pointing, clicking and defining a small box that took in the bridge of the largest battleship. The green-tinted image expanded to fill the whole display, resolving itself quickly from pixelated ambiguity into a picture as sharp as the original image. She repeated the process. The control centre remained still and silent as the screen filled with a slightly fuzzier but still-detailed image of two men on a gantry outside the bridge itself. The figures were smoking and chatting. Willet wondered if she would see their reactions as the missiles approached. She'd had that experience before, but after two minutes they disappeared into a hatchway. When they failed to show themselves again, she returned to a standard top-down perspective from six hundred metres virtual.

Hashirajima anchorage, 2038 hours, 20 June 1942

Lieutenant Moertopo gazed out over the oily, black waters of the Seto Island Sea from his vantage point in a small cabin on Hashirajima Island. He couldn't see the famous city of Hiroshima. It was nearly thirty-two kilometres away, hidden behind Edajima Island, but he still didn't like being so close to the site of the first atomic strike in history. It made him nervous. Irrationally so. He knew it would be years before the Americans dropped the bomb, but still. He was very, very keen to get away from here.

He wondered where the *Sutanto* was now. The dock

where she had tied up was empty and had been for three days. He was certain he would never see his ship again.

'I would have thought a man like you could sleep on a hot night.'

Moertopo recognised the German's voice and smiled. He'd warmed to Brasch. The engineer was level-headed and even a little cynical. It was actually refreshing when fanatics like Hidaka surrounded you every day.

'Does the heat bother you, Major?' he asked.

Brasch had walked up the narrow cobblestone path to the wooden lookout platform in nothing more than shorts and an undershirt. Moertopo could see by the moonlight that he was sweating.

'No,' said Brasch. 'The heat doesn't bother me. Not after Russia. But it does keep me awake at night.'

'The heat, and other things,' said Moertopo.

The German didn't reply, but his silence was heavy. Moertopo lit a clove cigarette and offered it to him.

'No thank you, Lieutenant. Those things smell like fragrant dog turds.'

A half-moon hung over the Inland Sea. From their vantage point they could see the flotilla of ships that remained at anchor off the island. Ripples and wavelets caught the moon's reflection and turned it into a net of spun silver on the surface of the *Seto-naikai*. The hint of a breeze carried the perfume of half-a-dozen local wild flowers to mask the salt-laced sea air. It was an arcadian scene, but they would not be staying much longer to enjoy it.

Brasch was scheduled to return to the Fatherland with Skorzeny before long, there to personally address the Führer. Moertopo would be joining his men in the city of Hakodate, far to the north in Hokkaido, where the research effort had been transferred. He was surprised to realise he would miss the jasmine-scented gardens and the old stone cottage that had been his gilded cage since they'd arrived.

'You know they'll kill you one day.'

The Indonesian officer nearly choked on an inhale, coughing violently and painfully as the *kretek* smoke burned his air passages.

'I'm sorry?' he gasped.

Brasch clapped him on the back a few times. Starlight softened the severe lines of his face and he seemed to be smiling. Something approaching warmth lit his eyes.

'They'll kill you, Moertopo. Your value to them declines each day as they become more familiar with your technology. One day you will be of no use to them at all. And then . . .' The German shrugged.

A cold ball of acid seemed to burn at the Indonesian's gut.

'Why are you saying these things?' he asked, his voice nearly squeaking with indignation and fright.

'Because they're true,' smiled Brasch.

Moertopo's hand shook as he tried to take another puff on the cigarette. Twice he opened his mouth to argue, but nothing came. He knew that what Brasch had said was true. There were days he wondered why he was even alive now. The night, which had seemed so pleasant and tranquil, now seemed darker and more malevolent. Shadows pooled under bushes, hiding assassins. He shuddered.

'Don't worry,' Brasch said. 'We're all dead men anyway.'

His face seemed to freeze in the flash of a photographer's globe, but the blaze of white light did not fade. It grew stronger. And the thunder of the apocalypse shook the ground underfoot. Moertopo threw himself at Brasch.

'*Hiroshima*,' he screamed.

'Wha–'

They crashed to the wooden deck and Moertopo flinched, expecting to see his skin blacken and begin to smoke, just before a blast wave pulverised them against the rock wall to their rear. Giant explosions hammered at the island again and again. And when Moertopo found that he was still alive after a few seconds, he realised how foolish he'd been.

'Are you all right?' he shouted at Brasch.

The engineer was already climbing to his feet. His eyes bulged as he took in the sight before them. The idyllic panorama had been utterly transformed. The sleeping fleet, the silver moonlight, were gone. The anchorage was now a cauldron in which half-a-dozen ships blazed like Roman torches.

'It's started,' said Moertopo.

Shouts and cries reached them as the Japanese soldiers guarding their quarters realised they were under attack. A siren began its mournful wail and the first lines of tracer fire weaved up from the deck of a destroyer about three kilometres away.

A sergeant of the guard appeared at a run, panting and gesturing for them to follow him to a shelter.

'There's no need,' said Moertopo.

Brasch regarded him with a strange expression. It took the Indonesian a second or two to recognise the look. It was respect.

He smiled. 'There's no need to run or hide because they don't miss, Major. If we were meant to die, it already would be so.'

USS Hillary Clinton, *2141 hours, 20 June 1942*

Admiral Spruance watched, mesmerised, as the missiles dived down on their prey like steel hawks. The rate of descent was so great, it actually made him feel a little giddy seeing the Japanese carrier rise up to fill the entire wall-screen so quickly. He marvelled at the idea of putting a movie camera inside the nose of a bomb, and just had time to make out the aircraft spotted on the flight deck before they filled all three panels and the image cut back to recorded footage from the *Havoc*'s spy drone. The switch, managed by a young woman in the *Clinton*'s CIC, was so slick that the admiral was able to see how the mass of the

Japanese carrier actually shuddered under the impact, just before a brilliant white starburst blossomed from deep within the body of the vessel.

It seemed almost peaceful, if that were possible. The brilliant globe of silent white light bloomed out to consume most of the ship, then disappeared just as quickly. For half a second he was left with a ghostly vision of what appeared to be the *Ryujo*, or what remained of her, resting serenely at anchor – an astounding sight, because three-quarters of the ship was gone, everything vaporised between the first forward gun mount and the rear elevator. For that brief moment it appeared as though the two sections, fore and aft, might just sit there indefinitely – and then they toppled into the waves and were ripped apart by secondary explosions.

'Holy shit,' said Lieutenant Commander Black.

They were standing in the otherwise empty section of the supercarrier's Combat Information Centre that had once been devoted to antisatellite warfare. It afforded Spruance and his men a ringside view of the way Kolhammer's people made war. What they saw was chilling.

The big screen that dominated one whole wall of the centre briefly divided again, presenting coverage of the other Jap ships dying in exactly the same fashion as the *Ryujo*. Then a single-field view pulled back to show the entire anchorage. Small bursts of light suddenly twinkled along the flanks of one vessel, a cruiser. The effect spread throughout the body of the fleet.

'Flak,' explained Judge.

Looking at the faces of the men and women sitting quietly at their banks of little movie screens and instruments in front of the giant wall-screen, Spruance felt the power gathered in this room in a new way. At Midway he'd been hammered into a near state of shock by their weapons. Now, afforded the luxury of watching the onslaught from a distance, he was struck forcefully by the singular and passionless way they went about their killing. Their damned thinking machines had taken it upon themselves to slaughter his men while they slept. But seeing the indifferent response to the deaths they had just witnessed – deaths they had *caused* – he wondered whether these people were any more capable of feeling genuine emotion than their machines.

He could see they were satisfied with the result, but only his men seemed to have responded like true combatants.

Even young Curtis, who'd probably never seen blood spilled outside a shaving nick, reacted with greater emotion than the woman whose submarine had just unleashed such destruction. The ensign was babbling on to Dan Black, pointing at the screen and asking the same question over and over. 'Did you see that, Commander? Did you?'

Captain Willet, by way of contrast, appeared at the start of her little war movie to explain the events that had transpired. Spruance saw no sense of triumph or vindication, or even mild regret at having cut so many lives short on her say-so. For the second time in a week he found himself wondering what sort of a world produced women like that.

And then – how long before they'd try to remake this one in their own image?

He shook his head. This was ridiculous. These people had been at war for nearly two decades. It was only natural that they would be completely inured to its savageries by now, just as his countrymen would surely grow coarse and insensitive to the horrors that lay before them. And he couldn't forget that this wasn't their war. It belonged to their history, and the men who had died since they arrived were to them already long dead anyway. Perhaps that explained it.

Spruance heard somebody behind him, a woman. 'Well, that's the end of that.'

But he understood it was just the beginning.

'Singapore strike is inbound,' another voice announced.

He turned back to the big screen. He wanted to see what happened next.

39

HMAS Moreton Bay, *2132 hours, 20 June 1942*

A long swell, generated by a storm in the Bay of Bengal, rolled under the twin hulls of the *Moreton Bay* as Lieutenant Nguyen methodically checked and rechecked Metal Storm and her laser pods. She was glad to be back in her old seat on the fast troop-carrier, converted now to an evacuation ship for the raid on Singapore. They'd drawn supplies for the Close-In Weapons System from stocks salvaged off the *Leyte Gulf*.

She calibrated her sensor arrays and tested the Cooperative Battle Link to HMS *Trident*, five and a half kilometres off the port bow. The *Bay* didn't run to a full CIC, and her workstation was tucked away in a corner of the bridge. Most of the 2 Cav troopers who'd sailed for Timor with them had moved across to the littoral assault ship HMAS *Ipswich*, which was trailing two nautical miles to stern, although one company remained to provide security for the medical staff on board.

Sixty medics, three-quarters of them 'temps, had embarked at New Caledonia, when they'd rendez-voused with the convoy of troop transports and converted passenger liners for the long run to the South China Sea. They ploughed along between two antique Royal Navy destroyers and the three modern ships, of which only the *Trident* was really a fighter. Their course took them through some of the same waters they'd crossed on their way to Timor in the twenty-first century. Like many of her colleagues she was past being bothered by a fractured sense of déjà vu. It was there all the time now, like your heartbeat.

Nobody had spoken on the bridge for a while. The tension was building as they rounded the northern tip of Sumatra and laid on steam for the objective. Even so, they were restricted to the speed of the slowest ship in their group, a Dutch liner, the *Princess Beatrix*. She made twenty-one knots, which wasn't bad, Nguyen supposed. But even the *Ipswich* could break thirty at a gallop, and she was a sea pig, loaded down with 2 Cav's armour and attack choppers.

A half-moon illuminated the ships and their phosphorescent wakes.

'Won't be long now,' said Captain Sheehan.

Nguyen checked her threat boards out of habit. She needn't have bothered. They weren't about to be swarmed by Chinese sea skimmers. A screen at her station, one of three, displayed the threat bubble out to one thousand kilometres, courtesy of the CBL with the Nemesis arrays of HMS *Trident*. Seven aircraft were being tracked and three surface contacts, further down the Strait of Malacca towards

Singapore. The stealth destroyer's sensor and weapons suites were infinitely more powerful than anything she had to play with. When the shit hit the fan, there'd actually be very little for her to do. The *Trident*'s Combat Intelligence would take control of all of Nguyen's defensive systems and wield them as one with its own.

She wondered what the crews on the old ships made of it all. She didn't even know what they'd been told of the mission. Perhaps nothing. No sane man from this time would willingly steam into the heart of the Japanese empire. Rachel used a trackball to train a mast-mounted cam on the nearest vessel, a New Zealand hospital ship, HMNZS *Christchurch*. She smiled at the image of three sailors lined up against a railing on the forecastle. She could see them quite clearly through her night-vision lens. They were swapping a single pair of binoculars, pointed first to the *Trident*, then to the Australian catamaran. They seemed less interested in HMAS *Ipswich*. It was a more conventional-looking ship.

Captain Sheehan appeared at her shoulder.

'You have to wonder what they make of this.'

A tone in Nguyen's earpiece told her that *Trident* had locked onto a possible hostile aircraft.

'Message from Captain Halabi, sir,' the communications officer announced. 'Two potentially hostile aircraft have changed course and are moving in our direction.'

'Acknowledged,' said Sheehan.

Lieutenant Nguyen stretched her neck and back muscles. Her seat was comfortable, but she'd been sitting in it for hours.

She watched her main screen as the two contemporary destroyers piled on speed and hove to. The ships were visible in four separate windows.

'They're placing themselves between the threat and the convoy,' said Sheehan.

'What's the point?' asked Nguyen.

Sheehan patted her on the shoulder. 'You really don't have salt water in your veins, do you, Lieutenant?'

HMS Trident, *2143 hours, 20 June 1942*

'What are those ships doing?' Halabi demanded.

She was in the CIC, below the waterline, but she could see the destroyers on any number of screens through the centre.

'Their job, Captain,' said Rear Admiral Sir Leslie Murray.

'No, they're not. Tell them to resume position. I can't have your bloody ships tearing all over the ocean. Everybody holds position and everybody gets to go home in one piece.'

The mood in the CIC was thoroughly unpleasant. Sir Leslie was entirely to blame for that. He'd insisted on coming, even produced a cable from Winston Churchill ordering him aboard the *Trident*. Halabi had relented, against her better judgment, and had been regretting it every day since.

A Welsh voice rang out. 'Contacts will be within visual range of the convoy within five minutes, ma'am.'

'Targets acquired and missiles on the rack, Captain.'

Halabi was disinclined to waste two perfectly good antiair missiles to bring down a couple of canvas and balsa-wood kites. She ignored Murray's irritating presence to her left and thought it through. They were deep in Japanese-controlled waters. The aircraft had probably been vectored onto them after coast watchers had spotted the convoy. They were passing through one of the most populated archipelagos in the world. This wasn't really a stealth operation.

Halabi checked the mission clock on the main screen.

The advance teams were already on the ground in Singapore. They'd been there for nearly a day.

'What's going on, Halabi?' said Rear Admiral Murray. 'Are you going to see off these Japs or what?'

'Tell your ships to resume their position and please sit down where I told you, Sir Leslie. We're about to get busy.'

She returned to her command seat and took one last look at the disposition of her forces. Sir Leslie was, with much bad grace, speaking into a microphone, telling the captains of the *Rockingham* and the *Sherwood* to resume their previous stations.

'Four minutes until they see us, Captain.'

'Weapons,' she called out.

'Aye, ma'am!'

'Power up the autocannon, high-explosive anti-aircraft ordnance, and slave to the Nemesis arrays. Sensors!'

'Aye, ma'am!'

'Try to get a lock with the long-range mast-cams. Let's get a peek at them.'

The young technical officer leaned to his task, which wasn't all that easy in the steep swell. He linked the gyroscopically mounted cameras to the *Trident*'s radar in order to establish an initial contact, but with that achieved it was down to his dexterity with a trackball to achieve a laser lock that captured the aircraft for the camera.

A window on the centre's main screen, which had been filled with static, suddenly cleared. Grainy video of two big, four-engine, prop-driven planes filled it.

'That's a couple of Emily flying boats, Captain,' said Rear Admiral Murray. 'Recon planes.'

The clicking of fingers across keyboards became faster and a touch louder. The buzz of voices picked up a little.

'Weapons,' said Halabi. 'Estimated time to fire mission?'

'Twenty-three seconds, ma'am.'

'Guns hot.'

'Guns hot, Captain.'

Halabi ignored the video, concentrating instead on

the screen at her side that rendered the battle space into animated form. Blinking icons that represented the two aircraft kept moving towards them and flashed blue for another twenty seconds. Then they turned red with a *ping*.

'Fire,' said Halabi.

The weapons boss punched two buttons. Halabi felt and heard the autocannon cycle through a brief burst of shellfire. It sounded like a very short, frenzied drumbeat, less than a second.

'That's it?' asked Murray, somewhat incredulous. 'You're sure you got them?'

The *Trident*'s commander pointed to the flat-screen in front of them. 'Quickly, Sir Leslie, or you'll miss it.'

The Royal Navy liaison officer turned back to the video coverage. At that instant both planes disintegrated in a sudden and silent eruption of fire and light. The long, heavy-looking hulls detonated into a dozen pieces before dropping away as the wings folded up like a book snapping shut, and the last of the debris dropped out of shot on the screen.

'You were asking if I was certain,' said Halabi.

'My mistake,' said Murray, who was subdued by the spectacle.

'Signals, what did they get off?' Halabi called across the CIC.

'Just a brief transmission, Captain. Less than two seconds.'

She gestured to the technician to play it on the

CIC speaker system. A hiss of static flared and dropped away as a Japanese voice said a few calm words before being cut off in midsentence.

Air Station 23, Sumatra, 2155 hours, 20 June 1942

The Japanese squadron had trained exclusively for night fighting since 1937. Ironically, and much to the men's disgust, their special skills had kept them out of the most important battles of the war so far. There had been no call for them because the American and British flyers couldn't take their pathetic ox carts into the air at night, so there was no enemy to oppose. Squadron Leader Murata had insisted on training at the same fever pitch, however, even after it had become obvious to them that they would most likely never fire a shot in combat.

As he sat in the cockpit of his Zero, the engine growling, a line of firepots stretching out in front of him down the crude runway of pressed dirt, Captain Murata's heart raced. Not with fear, but with the fierce joy of a samurai who has spent his life preparing for combat. None of his men was quite sure what was steaming down the strait, and their airplanes were not, strictly speaking, designed for attacking surface ships. But he was sure they'd still give a good account of themselves with their twenty-millimetre cannons.

He'd ordered the ammunition changed, to include a heavier load of incendiary tracers. If you pumped enough of them into a tanker it would go up like a giant bomb. At least so they hoped. This, too, was a theory that had never been tested.

His ground crew chief banged on the canopy, and Murata pulled it shut over his head, only slightly muting the engine's howl. He examined his instruments with the aid of a small flashlight fitted with a red bulb that wouldn't degrade his night vision. Everything was as it should be. He pushed the throttle forwards. The chocks came out from under his wheels and he immediately began to bump up and down in the padded seat as he rolled along the slightly corrugated runway.

He gripped the stick, increased his speed and dropped the flaps as the firepots blurred into one long yellow streak in the darkness outside the cockpit. Acceleration pushed him back into the seat.

He flicked a switch to turn on the blinking red lights at his wingtips. The rest of the squadron would follow these lights up into the sky. The tiny strip of light that was their airfield fell away below. The other planes strung out behind him, small snorts of blue flame coughing occasionally from the engine cowlings. Only moments after take-off Murata spotted the three Imperial Japanese Navy destroyers far ahead of them in the strait. If he could spot three relatively small vessels like that so quickly, there was little doubt he would find this mystery convoy before long.

Murata hoped the air controllers had done their job. It wouldn't do to be shot down by his own navy as he flew over them. But he needn't have worried. His Majesty's Imperial Japanese Navy was the finest in the world. Murata's squadron roared over them without incident.

He took a moment to appreciate the scenery in this, his last few minutes as an unblooded warrior. The world was a patchwork of shadows and deeper darkness. The island of Sumatra was a black void to his left, a line of mountains discernible only where the stars disappeared, cut off by the highest ridges. The waters of the strait unfurled below like a great, wide ribbon of lesser blackness, shot through with small diamonds as small waves threw back shards of light from the half-moon, hanging like an ancient blade in the night sky.

It took them less than an hour to reach their objective.

Murata waggled his wings, signalling to the other Zero pilots that they should form up on him and prepare for a strafing run. Below them, in the strait, the spreading wakes of the big, slow-moving ships taunted him. They weren't taking evasive action. They weren't firing at him. They must be asleep, he decided.

He smiled.

They simply could not be allowed to proceed as if they cared nothing for the might of imperial Japan. Murata took a deep breath, centring himself in his *hara.* The Zero became more than just a machine. It was a divine blade, an embodiment of the Emperor's will. Descended from gods, destined to take dominion over the lesser peoples of the world, the spirit of the blessed Emperor Hirohito rode with him in this plane. Murata could actually feel the presence of divinity as he plunged down on the prey.

Then an explosion rocked him.

Ah, awake at last, white man.

For one brief shining moment he knew the rapture of the samurai. Nothing could deflect him, the Emperor's sword, from slashing into the enemy. Not high-explosive shells, nor twisting lines of tracer. Not twenty-mil Oerlikon cannons, or Bofors mounts, or even the bark and cough of five-inch guns on the enemy destroyers.

He almost laughed with glee, and then . . .

Murata gasped.

The explosions weren't flak bursts. They were the planes of his comrades, disintegrating in dirty orange balls of flame. Within seconds the sky was empty, save for the burning wreckage tumbling towards the sea. Murata's eyes bulged at the sight. Wings sheathed in flame fluttered downwards like cherry blossoms. Strangely beautiful cascades of fire rained down as aviation gas ignited. He was certain he saw the nose of a Zero, the propeller still turning. It flew past him like a blazing comet.

He had time to wonder why his own plane was suddenly so hot.

And then he was consumed in a fiery maelstrom.

*

The focus of activity in the *Trident*'s CIC shifted from the antiair division to antisurface. Halabi brushed past Sir Leslie, jostling him slightly on her way over to the small group of workstations. The Royal Navy's representative to Hawaii said nothing. He'd been silenced by the brutal efficiency with which Halabi and her crew had wiped out the Japanese squadron. The Zero had achieved a mythical status every bit as powerful as the RAF's own Spitfire. To see them swatted away like flies was a rather confronting experience for the rear admiral.

'Excuse me,' Halabi said as she brushed past him again.

'Yes, of course, Captain,' he muttered in a distracted fashion. He watched, fascinated, as Halabi clasped her hands behind her back and considered the feed from the drone they had hovering above the three Japanese ships a few hundred kilometres ahead. The screen was split into two panels displaying low-light and infrared. The enemy ships were steaming towards her at what must be their top speed. White water boiled at their sterns in the pale opalescent green of the low-light video, while hot smoke poured from the glowing stacks amidships of each vessel on the infrared window. Murray had trouble believing the God's-eye view of battle on the huge screen in front of him.

The destroyers were tagged as Hostile 01 to 03. Flashing icons marked the spot where the Zeros had died. A time hack over the island of Singapore read

2321, indicating the amount of time the SAS had been on the ground.

Halabi could kill the destroyers now, but she said that she wanted to close with them, placing her own ships closer to their objective before alerting the Japanese to the fact that a major force had entered their waters.

'Designate them, Mr McTeale, and launch on my mark.'

The *Trident*'s commander turned briefly in Murray's direction. 'You can watch the missile launch on the display, Admiral. Just there in front of you.'

Rear Admiral Murray stared at the monitor, where a movie showing the activity on the upper decks was running in black and white. It seemed rather pointless to him – the *Trident* was mostly featureless. As he was about to turn away, however, a hexagonal cap flipped open. An Indian-looking chap at a bank of nearby controls spoke up with a flawless Surrey accent.

'Hard target lock confirmed. Firing in three, two, one . . .'

Murray watched the screen again. White smoke and flame jetted from the silo and a dark bolt shot out with extraordinary speed. He heard the rocket's take-off as dull thunder that echoed through the hull.

The image switched instantly and he found himself viewing the *Trident* as if from another ship. The screen filled with a panoramic view that clearly showed a long, curving finger of smoke climbing away into the night sky.

The image switched again to another wide-angle shot. Six more grey spears erupted from the deck. He felt this launch through the soles of his feet, as a small shudder. He had no real idea what was going on, and the men and women around him gave little indication. There seemed to be a slightly increased level of activity at the dense banks of computer stations, but . . .

Murray felt a tap on his arm. One of Halabi's young men, an ensign, directed his attention to the giant video wall that dominated the darkened battle room.

'That's a full-spectrum Nemesis battle-space display, sir,' the man said quietly. 'You've got radar, drone coverage, and over there, in the corner, a feed from the camera in the nose of the missiles.'

To Murray, the monochrome image also seemed very unstable.

He cast his eyes around the combat centre. Every screen was attended by an operator. All of them seemed to be talking at once, and somewhat to Murray's surprise, the captain stood in the centre of this ferment, calmly providing instructions without a hint of panic. She seemed almost graceful.

'Weapons, bring the hammerheads around to one-oh-four.'

'One-oh-four, ma'am.'

Murray stared into a large screen carrying a black-and-white movie radioed back from the camera in the nose of the lead missile.

'Weapons, I want simultaneous hits on those

destroyers. Quickly now. We don't want any intel leakage, if possible.'

A young black woman near Murray click-clacked at the plastic keys of her computing machine with a speed and confidence that astonished the admiral. Surely one false keystroke would doom the mission.

Halabi appeared in front of him.

'All done.'

'But they're –'

'Watch the screen, Admiral.'

Murray saw then that the centre's main screen had split into a confusing grid of tiled windows. Some carried jumpy black-and-white footage of the Japanese ships. In the space of a few seconds the outline of each target swelled to fill the screen. Then all of the displays turned black.

'What's wrong?' asked Murray. 'Where did the pictures go? Were all the rockets shot down?'

'No, Sir Leslie. Think, what would happen to the camera when the missile struck armour plating?'

'Oh,' he said. 'I see.'

HIJMS Akatsuki, *2348 hours, 20 June 1942*

Commander Osamu Takasuka surveyed the heaving ocean from his eyrie's nest. It was only mildly turbulent tonight, with the bows knifing through two-metre waves. Still, each plunge of the ship threw plumes of water high into the air.

Takasuka wondered what awaited them ahead. The fleet had been alive with rumour ever since the cancelled mission to Midway. Some said the Russians had declared war. Others claimed with righteous certainty that the Americans were about to capitulate. One wild tale originating with an old salt on their sister ship, the destroyer *Hokaze*, spoke of a gigantic whirlpool that had sucked two American carriers down to the very bottom of the Coral Sea. By the time that rumour had reached Takasuka's ears, it had twisted itself into a perverse story that as you dropped down the funnel you could see old Viking raiders and the bones of Roman galleys on the grey floor of the seabed.

He never failed to be amazed at the bullshit sailors were able to dream up.

As he stood into the freshening breeze, waiting for a radio message relating what the Zeros had discovered up the strait, he thought perhaps a falling star had dropped from the heavens in front of them. He gazed at the sight, captivated by its simple beauty, until it became apparent that the bright comet trail wasn't moving from the heavens towards the waves, but *across* them, towards him.

More lights appeared, and he tried to get a fix on them through his binoculars, but the heaving motion of the ship and the shaking of his hands made it impossible. The fantastic speed of the lights struck him next, and the sense of intent that seemed to lurk behind their progress. At that point he raised the alarm.

Bells rang and klaxons blared but it was too late.

Commander Takasuka's existence came to an end inside an expanding globe of hellfire.

Another four missiles shrieked over the scene on their way to Singapore.

40

Singapore, 2351 hours, 20 June 1942

The heel of a Japanese sentry's boot pressed into the earth eighteen centimetres from the tip of Captain Harry Windsor's royal nose. The prince's night-vision goggles were switched to low-light amplification and small-unit narrowcasting. The other members of his section, including Sergeant St Clair and two Australian SAS troops, captured the video feed in lime green on the small pop-up window in the corner of their own goggles.

Harry lay as still and quiet as the warm soil beneath him. He breathed as little as possible. Even so, the smell of Singapore was overpowering, a heady brew of open drains and dried fish, of swamp gas and Chinese spices.

In his own pop-up he could see that both St Clair and Captain Pearce Mitchell, the ranking Aussie, had drawn a bead on the Japanese soldier. A microlight targeting dot, invisible to the sentry, had settled on the side of his head just above the ear, while another dot, emanating from Mitchell's silenced HK nine-millimetre submachine-gun, had glued itself to the centre of his body mass.

Harry was trying to centre himself in a mental exercise, releasing his ego and allowing the world to flood in through all of his senses without interruption. Unfortunately the steady stream of piss gushing from the Jap into the bushes beside his head was proving to be a hellish distraction. His heart refused to stop hammering and a smirk was threatening to break out all over his face. This would no doubt give rise to a fit of fear-inspired, hysterical laughter if he let it.

The fellow must have been bursting with tea, judging from the time it took him to empty his bladder. At last, however, the stream began to gutter and die and then, with a few shakes, which splashed a drop or two on Harry's goggles, he was done. The special ops teams listened to the rustle of his fly being fastened and the crunch of his boots through the undergrowth as he continued his patrol. They waited five minutes before moving or even resuming normal breathing patterns. When Harry judged it safe he subvocalised, 'Fuck me, that was unpleasant.'

The small biochip implanted at the base of his neck, and powered by the electrical charge of his body's cells, picked up the bone vibrations caused by the comment, transforming them into a quantum signal that was captured by the processors in his ear bud and narrowcast to the rest of the soldiers. They heard his voice in their helmets as clearly as if he had pressed his lips there and whispered to them.

'And I thought those pricks were supposed to revere royalty,' whispered Mitchell.

They lay on a small ridge that rose twenty metres above a Japanese barracks complex at the edge of the town. Familiar with Singapore in his own time, Harry found himself amazed at every turn by the primitive, colonial outpost through which they'd crept. There were no high-rise buildings, no architecture he thought of as modern in any way. You could see the water from almost every vantage point. Shrieks and chirps and a thousand other noises of the jungle never ceased. Monkeys still roamed everywhere.

A strict curfew kept the captive population of Malays and Indians inside after dark, and most of the Europeans were locked up in the Changi prison camp. Even so, he could tell when they passed near one ethnic neighbourhood or another. The Indian quarter smelled of peppers, curry powder and exotic fruits; the Chinese of fried meat and jasmine rice. The odours must have settled into the skin of the place, he thought. There was very little food in Singapore at the moment.

Since this was far from the war front, security had been allowed to slacken off. Singapore was a garrison town. Only three men made a regular desultory sweep of the jungle around the barracks, sticking strictly to schedule and a well-beaten walking track. Harry's squad members were lurking just off this path, waiting for a signal from three other SAS units that were moving into position closer to the buildings. They'd traversed the city via the dense tunnels of verdant growth that ran all over her. Only the very centre had been too built up to provide safe passage. A grid of wide avenues ran there, fringed with flame trees and frangipani. The grass verges, untrimmed in the wet heat, were already overgrown, but the white government buildings were all occupied by Japanese troops and administrators now.

They were somebody else's problem. Harry's team was assigned to take out the main barracks on the road to Changi, temporary home to more than two thousand Japanese soldiers.

His tac display went active.

'Payload inbound,' he said. 'Thirty seconds. Sergeant, fire up the laser strobe.'

'Strobe active, targets acquired,' said St Clair as six thin lines of invisible laser light stabbed out from a small, tripod-mounted device in repeater bursts modulated to the microsecond. The photon stream pulsed across the night before silently painting the centre of four long huts in which slept hundreds of Japanese. The laser strobe looked a little like a video camera, and indeed it would record what happened in the next few minutes.

'Teams two, three and four report strobes active and targets acquired,' said Mitchell.

The other SAS teams, stationed at the base points of a triangle surrounding the barracks complex, had locked strobes onto the remaining buildings and facilities including a small guard tower, three machine-gun and mortar pits, and a line of light tanks. With fifteen seconds till showtime one man peeled away from each team, moving silently into the scrub, stalking the sentries who had last passed by.

There was no visual warning that preceded the approach of the cruise missile. Its turbojets burned without visible flame. Its imminent arrival registered as a time hack in the lower left corner of the goggle displays. The team leaders, had they chosen to, could have watched the missile's progress as a receiver embedded within their goggles picked up a signal from the seeker warhead, which translated into a series of red arrowheads tracking across their heads-up displays. But being pragmatic, they all chose to plant their faces in the dirt and breathe out against the wave of overpressure that would soon hit them.

Harry imagined that he just might have caught a rumble of distant thunder as the missile popped up and chose the closest of the targets designated by the laser strobes, all in a sliver of time too infinitesimal to be comprehended by any human mind. Flaps on its stubby wings purred into position. Gated doors swung open down the length of its belly. A very small, controlled fusion reaction cooked up deep inside the missile for just over two microseconds, enough to superheat its two hundred tungsten slugs and spit them out of their containment cells with enough kinetic energy in each to destroy a heavily armoured fighting vehicle.

The huts, first on the target list, were only constructed of plywood and corrugated iron.

Sixty per cent of the missile's submunitions load,

one hundred and twenty white-hot slugs travelling at hypersonic speed, slammed into those frail structures and literally vaporised them. The expanding gas, a molecular mix of human tissue, building materials and superheated air, manifested itself as a conventional explosion, which blew the rest of the target mass to hell and beyond.

The Japanese crews manning the weapons pits didn't even have time to turn around before the slugs shrieked in on top of their positions. The guard tower bought just two per cent of the load. A toilet block got three. And the light tanks took what was left.

The explosions sounded like the birth of a volcano.

The missile then swung through one hundred and eighty degrees to head north for a secondary target, which had been programmed into its seeker head: the naval base, where high-altitude drone flights confirmed a large amount of Japanese shipping was tied up.

'Right, gentlemen,' said Captain Windsor. 'Let's have them.'

HMAS Ipswich, *2359 hours, 20 June 1942*

From the moment they'd helped him into this weird padded armour, Captain Tom Shapcott had done everything he could to stop worrying about the bulky feel of the 'ballistic plate', or the awkward weight of his 'powered helmet', and the confusing array of little movies, message boxes and floating screens full of numbers and meaningless letter codes that appeared in front of his eyes when he turned on his 'combat goggles'. He knew he would need to focus on the job at hand.

He stood within the giant steel cocoon of the Australian ship's vehicle deck, awed into silence. The four Abrams tanks waiting there were generations beyond the Shermans he knew. They were still obviously tanks, but the size of them, the brute promise of destruction that lay within their hulking mass, robbed Shapcott of words. Behind them squatted ten so-called light armoured vehicles, LAVs, each seeming larger and more formidable than a German tiger tank, each bristling with an individual missile suite and a twin-barrelled fifty-millimetre chain gun that they'd told him could reduce a concrete bunker to dust and rubble within minutes – perhaps even seconds.

Beyond those sat giant jeeps and other unidentifiable vehicles. The weight of violence confined within the space was overwhelming. The mass of those tanks, the raw lines of their frames, the solidity . . . He'd seen a lifetime's worth of burning metal wreckage and he knew that nothing was invincible, but by God those awful things did look close to it.

The Aussies were all right, but he found himself more comfortable with the company of marines who'd been detached from the 82nd and temporarily assigned to Halabi's task force for the raid on

Singapore. They weren't marines as he knew them. There were even a couple of women, but when you got over how different they looked, and you sat down and talked to them, it turned out they loved barbecues and the football season, and fishing, and baseball, and beer and the constitution of the United States of America as much as any man or woman he'd ever met.

The giant ship was pitching slowly, making it a little difficult for him to get back to the LAV he was supposed to ride in. It was dark in the hold, but they'd showed him how to use the infrared setting on his goggles. It turned the darkest place into a world coloured red and pink. It was unsettling at first, but a hell of a lot better than barking your shin.

There were very few men – or women – moving around now. He could see some of them here and there: a head popping up out of a turret, the driver sitting in the front of a Humvee, somebody checking the missile racks on a LAV. But most of the six hundred or so who were going ashore were already buttoned up in their vehicles.

A huge noise, like the sound of a speeding train in a tunnel, suddenly filled the hold. Shapcott jumped a little but didn't panic. It was the shore bombardment beginning. Rockets were screaming away to destroy the Japs' gun batteries and command centres at the beachhead they were supposed to assault. The captain hurried a little faster – he didn't want to get left behind. And he had the impression that once those big gated doors opened in the bow, there'd be no stopping these guys. They'd just roll right over the top of you if you got in the way.

He reached the LAV just as another racket joined the roar of the barrage.

'What's that?' he asked without raising his voice. He'd learned not to do that. A microphone in his helmet meant he didn't have to.

'Choppers going in,' explained Second Lieutenant Biff Hannon as he reached a gloved hand out to Shapcott to haul him inside. The captain barely had time to strap himself in before the vehicle lurched into motion.

Shapcott felt their departure from the assault ship as a dizzying drop down the ramp, a sickening crunch as the front tyres dug into the sand of Besar Beach, and a moment of floating ambivalence while the LAV swam through the breakers and up onto the sand.

Twelve movie screens glowed in the body of the LAV. Lieutenant Hannon seemed capable of following the action on all of them at once. To Shapcott the world outside was a confused inferno of burning vehicles, secondary explosions, mammoth, rumbling tanks firing at Christ-knew-what and satanic-looking flying machines that pirouetted through the sky like giant mechanical dragonflies, spitting fire and thunder at distant, unseen enemies. Even inside the LAV, with his ears protected by the 'smart gel' lining of his bulky helmet, the sound of battle was still painfully loud.

He was strapped into a large, admittedly very comfortable chair. But the violent stop-and-go motion of the armoured vehicle still threw him around unnervingly. They seemed to speed everywhere, swerving and stopping frequently. At one point the automatic cannon on their own turret fired for a few seconds. Shapcott noticed the movie screens light up as something detonated somewhere.

'Nice shooting, Maryanne,' said Hannon.

But Shapcott never figured out what they had just shot.

After fifteen minutes the bedlam and madness of the beachhead subsided. They bounced over one last rough section of ground and then swung onto a smooth surface.

Hannon spoke into the tiny, wire-thin microphone that emerged from his helmet. 'All units, all units, this is the Biffmeister. We're on the road. Let's roll, chickadees.'

'*Go go go!*' Hannon yelled.

The armoured doors of the LAV sprang open and the six-man crew leaped out into the night. Captain Tom Shapcott leaped with them. Instantly, Hannon flew back into him, knocking him to his knees.

Shapcott tried to help the fellow to his feet, but right away he recognised the feeling of dead weight. That unnerved him. He'd been assured that the body armour would protect them, and not just by Hannon. He'd spoken to sailors on the *Astoria* who had gone on about the virtual impossibility of killing a man who was protected by the battlesuits these people wore.

But as he scrambled out from under Hannon's inert form, he saw that the lieutenant had died from a shot to the face. His jaw and half his nose were gone, and a gluey mess of shattered bone and brain tissue was oozing out of the massive wound.

'Up you get, Captain.'

The voice in his ears was quiet but he heard it without any trouble, even as the battle raged around him. Hundreds of troops in black body armour ran forward towards the smoking breach in the prison wall. Choppers flew over them, rockets and machine-guns pouring out a solid river of destruction. There was still some resistance here and there – a lone Japanese sentry or a machine-gun operator who had escaped the initial rocket swarm. But the marines charged forward as though nothing affected them, not rifle or machine-gun fire, not grenades or mortar rounds. Shapcott did see one or two go down, though. Killed or wounded by stray shrapnel or bullets that found flesh and bone instead of armour padding.

Shapcott started forward even as the most primitive parts of his brain screamed at him to get down, to dig the deepest hole he possibly could and stay there.

He'd turned off the schematics in his goggles. They were just too confusing. But he left the infrared on, moving through a hellish twilight. Three Japs appeared to his right, screaming incoherently.

He fired on them and they burst into a shower of entrails and bloody fog.

Jesus Christ.

'*Come on, come on!*' a voice yelled in his ear, almost uncomfortably loud.

Something hit him. He spun under the impact, and staggered but did not fall. It felt like he'd been punched by a prize-fighter.

Bullets snapped and cracked everywhere, their passage clear to him by the heat trails that showed vividly in the infrared. Enormous volumes of fire saturated the faintest sign of enemy resistance.

He found himself panting at the breach in the prison wall. A tank had muscled through and was demolishing a stone building a hundred yards away with its main gun. Bright red streaks of light shot out of the rubble, but not many of them. The tank's gun boomed again twice. Shapcott felt the pressure wave in his chest and guts, and the wreckage of the blockhouse jumped under the impact of high explosives. No more shots came from there.

Hannon's troops moved with practised certainty through the slaughter and turmoil. They jumped and ran and fired without seeming ever to halt. It was as though they knew the terrain better than the Japs. He had to admit, it was beyond him. He slowed the pace of his advance to a walk, giving himself time to properly examine the surroundings for the first time.

He seemed to be in a large courtyard. The walls of the prison soared above him. Fires burned all around and Japanese bodies lay everywhere. They were all hideously disfigured, as though they had been torn apart by wild beasts not gunfire.

He became conscious of his thirst. It seemed as though he'd had no water in days. His mouth was dry and his tongue felt swollen and numb. He fumbled at his unfamiliar webbing and managed to unclip a water bottle. As he tipped the sweet, cool liquid down his parched throat he saw movement out of the corner of his eye. Someone waving.

Shapcott turned and saw a woman. She was thin, and filthy, and unkempt. He suddenly realised she was also in a cage. In his tunnel vision he hadn't noticed her before. There were others in there with her, all of them waving him over now. He held the muzzle of his gun towards the ground as he approached, but he didn't safe the weapon.

'Over here!'

'We need help.'

'We need a doctor.'

He stepped up the pace. The sounds of battle seemed to be falling away. He wondered whether it was over for the moment.

'Who are you?' the woman cried. 'Have you come to rescue us?'

They shrank back as he drew close. Some of them looked quite fearful of him. When he thought about it, he realised he *would* look pretty intimidating in the armour, and they would have seen the others sweep through, killing everyone who opposed them. He carefully unhooked the strap that held his helmet in place and took it off. He pushed the goggles back up on his forehead and was surprised to discover he could see quite well by moonlight.

'Captain Thomas Shapcott, ma'am,' he said. 'United States Marine Corps.'

41

Off Luzon, USS Hillary Clinton, *8613 hours, 21 June 1942*

Dan Black couldn't believe what he was seeing.

He was standing at the counter in the carrier's main armoury as his girlfriend – Julia let him call her that now – pulled on an outfit that made her look like some kind of character from a Johnny Weissmuller matinee.

'Got your paperwork all filled out, Ms Duffy?' the chief asked.

'What the hell do you need that for?' Black snapped. 'You don't even have a job here.'

He was tired and irritable. They'd already fought twice over this. Julia gave him a stare that said he was pushing his luck.

'If I get waxed,' she said through thin, pressed lips, 'I've signed a waiver giving them the right to harvest my organs for immediate transplant. If I get shot in the brain and go into a vegetative state, I've signed another waiver allowing them to take me off life support, and *then* to harvest my organs. If I just get stitched up and lose a kidney, or an eyeball or a bit of my spinal cord, they need my certificates to access the stem cell deposit I made when I came on board at Darwin. They can force-breed me some new organs. So you see, *Commander* Black, the man needs my codes.'

She gave CPO Toohey a small grey plastic rectangle. He waved it under a computing machine Black didn't recognise. It must have read the information on the stick somehow, because the screen lit up.

'Whoa! We got us a celebrity!' The chief grinned. He was a tattooed old sea dog who would have fit right in on the *Enterprise*. 'This is a premium piece you got yourself, buddy. Authorised for deployment with main force infantry units. Rated to cover close-quarter combat. And cleared for tactical briefings up to and including the Classified Level Oh-Three.'

'Thank you, Chief,' Duffy cooed, smiling broadly. 'Your check's in the mail.'

That just irritated Black all the more. Julia had been on his back about the way he spoke to the women in the Multinational Force, even though he was a goddamned paragon compared with most of the other guys. And here was this lughead talking about her like she was some kind of bargirl, right in front of her, and she fucking joked right back at him!

But he kept his mouth shut because he didn't trust his boiling temper.

The armoury was a hive of activity. He had no idea what units most of the men and women who were checking out weapons and armour belonged to. Why they even *had* an armoury like this on a carrier was a mystery to him. But even if they had a legitimate reason to tool up, he didn't see that a lady reporter had any call to be down here. No matter how tough she liked to think she was.

As Black fumed, the long lines of troopers moved through. An amazing array of guns and equipment came over the counter. The chief ran his eyes down the text on the screen, nodding and grunting as if he'd found a great buy on a used car.

'Hey, you embedded with the 101st for South Yemen,' he said to Julia during a brief lull. 'My brother was in that. Jeez, what a fucking circus that was.'

'Got shot in the ass by one of the clowns,' said Duffy.

'Ha, you got that right.'

She was doing this on purpose now. Black was certain. And Chief Toohey seemed to be playing along.

'Okay, Ms Duffy. You taking body armour?'

She nodded. 'Brought my own on board, back in Darwin. You should have it in there somewhere. Serial number's on the data stick. It's a Brooks Brothers T9 carbon-titanium weave, size 10.'

'I woulda said size eight.'

'You're too kind, Chief.'

Dan rolled his eyes.

He noticed that one of Julia's fellow reporters had fronted the counter a few spots down. He seemed to want nothing more than a flak jacket and helmet.

'You gonna take a personal weapon, Ms Duffy?'

'Do bears shit in the woods?'

'I've heard rumours to that effect. Okay, I can let you have a cut-down AR-15, but not the grenade launcher.'

'How about a G4?'

'Sorry, ma'am. You're not rated for that.'

Julia chewed her lip. Dan was ready to explode. This was nuts, the whole thing, her going in with the marines, the body armour, the guns. What sort of a reporter was she?

An unemployed one, for starters.

'You got an MP5 back there, Chief Toohey? They don't get in the way when I'm working. But they do have a knack of bringing unpleasant encounters to a quick end.'

'Indeed they do, ma'am.'

Toohey tapped a flexipad with his pen. It beeped once.

'How many mags you lookin' at, Ms Duffy?'

'Four, thanks. Taped in pairs. If I need any more, we're all in trouble. Dumdums would be super, if you got 'em.'

The flexipad beeped as he tapped it again.

'Side-arm?'

'Mac 10.'

Beep.

'Knife?'

'Got my own. But I could use an empty helmet. I'm gonna load up with a Panasonic 2300 mini-cam rig. It snaps right in where one of your tac sets would go.'

Beep.

'Okay then, just gimme a second and I'll grab your gear.'

Toohey disappeared into the storeroom.

'Go on, Dan. I can see you're going to blow steam out of your ears if you don't say something.'

Black controlled his temper with great difficulty.

'I don't see the point, is all,' he said, his jaw tight.

Julia shrugged. 'You wouldn't. It's my job.'

'You don't have a job. You keep saying that yourself, about a thousand goddamn times a day.'

'That's right,' she said, pushing off the scarred counter with a cold fury suddenly lighting her eyes. 'I *don't* have a goddamn job. I have nothing here. Nothing! Except that I know how to move around a firefight without getting my ass blown away.'

People started looking their way.

'I got no fucking job. No fucking life. I'm stuck in the wrong fucking century and my fucking Prozac has run out. I am *far* from *fucking* happy.'

'I don't know why Kolhammer even agreed to let you go,' Black exploded as his exasperation finally got the better of him.

Duffy snorted.

'Because he knows he's going to need a positive spin on this whole fucking disaster.'

Kolhammer, like Halabi, had corralled his guests into the now obsolete satellite warfare section of his CIC. Spruance, Halsey and a couple of other 'temps he didn't recognise had sat themselves down and were taking in the feverish pace while Lieutenant Thieu tried to explain how it all fit together.

They didn't care that the *Clinton* didn't have live satellite links to the Singapore task force or the submarine standing off Hashirajima. To them, co-ordinated strategic strikes hitting three locations at once, and feeding back battlefield images within an hour or two, was the stuff of magic. Every movie screen in the huge, chilly cavern of the CIC held something of interest, so that they didn't know where to focus. Tanks ploughing through lines of Japanese field guns on Singapore. Storm-troopers in bulky 'armour' dropping out of helicopters. Jet planes roaring off the one working catapult on the *Clinton*. Armoured hovercraft on fat-bellied rubber skirts pounding through the waves towards Luzon. Marine Corps 'jump jets' settling down vertically on the deck of the *Kandahar*. Missiles diving into Yamamoto's anchorage at Hashirajima.

Even the fact that most of the Combined Fleet had disappeared didn't seem to bother them.

As impressive as it all was, Kolhammer knew this was lulling them into a false sense of security. It was awesome, true, but it had its limits. He was running through land attack missiles at a ruinous rate as they degraded the Japs' ability to resist on Luzon. He envied Halabi her mission to Singapore. Sure, it was a tight trip through some very sharky waters, but she had all of her targets grouped. He had to fire on half a dozen sites over five hundred square kilometres, and even then, without good intel, he could never be sure he'd covered all the bases.

He approached his guests. Spruance saw him coming and nodded.

'It seems to be going well, Admiral, except for Hashirajima, and even then, I'm not going to quibble, with two carriers sunk.'

'Thank you, Admiral,' said Kolhammer. 'I'll be a lot happier when this next phase is done. Jones is going to have his hands full securing Manila *and* Cabanatuan.'

'Two minutes, sir,' a weapons sysop called out. 'Feeding drone coverage to the main screen.'

The three giant panels that formed the main display had been running recorded footage sent by compressed burst from Halabi and Willet. They winked out to a featureless blue for a fraction of a second before coming back online with three live images transmitted from drones high over Luzon.

The smallest of the three showed a city block in Cabanatuan. Thanks to the late hour, the town was asleep. No traffic moved on its streets. It could have been a still photo, except that trees were swaying in a breeze. A complex tapestry of targeting data suddenly appeared over a large white building as a time hack counted down.

'What is that place?' asked Spruance.

'Regional subcommand centre for two Japanese divisions,' said Kolhammer. 'It's a residential as well as an administrative compound, so the higher command elements should all be there. We've had Marine Recon in-country for a week, scoping it out for us.'

'What about the others?'

'Main garrison. It used to be a Philippine army barracks. Now the Japanese are in there.'

The time hack reached zero.

Something flashed across the screen of the smaller window and the whole city block on which the targeted building had stood erupted in a volcanic blast. Even the drone's sophisticated cameras were unable to cope, and the screen blanked out to white for a few seconds.

Two heavy missiles were assigned to the main Japanese camp, which lay sixteen kilometres from the POW camp. They bore in at the relatively low speed of three hundred knots, just above the tree line.

As Kolhammer and Spruance watched silently, a small pop-up window showed a couple of sentries squeezing off a few random shots into the dark. Alerted by the gunfire, hundreds of figures spilled out of tents and barracks buildings.

The missiles detonated and the army camp, in which fifteen thousand men lay abed, vanished inside a colossal explosion.

'Sweet Jesus,' breathed Admiral Halsey. He had been briefed on the effects of the Wide Area Impact Munitions, but Kolhammer knew that to actually watch such power unleashed – especially for the first time – was a humbling, even frightening experience.

The surveillance drone refocused for a wide-angle shot just before detonation, allowing the audience in the CIC to view the blast from a virtual height of six thousand metres. It was obvious to all that nobody could have survived. Supersonic pressure waves blew out across the landscape from the blast centres, flattening trees and demolishing any structures they met for eight kilometres.

'Is that going to hurt our men?' asked Halsey.

'It'll dissipate before it reaches them,' said Kolhammer.

'This is better than ladies' day at the county fucking fair,' Halsey said to Ray Spruance.

'It's only half the game, Bill.'

'Yeah, but what a great fucking half.'

The whine of the giant hovercraft's turbofans was enormous, easily drowning out the snarl of the Sea Comanche gunships riding shotgun on the assault force. The sea state was benign, making for an effortless rush across the South China Sea towards the mouth of Manila Bay.

Colonel Jones could see clearly from the small cabin of the hovercraft. The fallen island bastion of Corregidor stood foursquare in the centre of the bay's entrance. It was easily distinguished from the black backdrop of the island because it was ablaze. Six subnuclear plasma yield warheads had speared deep into the concrete carapace of the fortress and detonated, atomising vast tonnages of concrete and steel, along with the thousands of human beings living within.

'Damn, I'll bet Krakatoa didn't look half as impressive as that,' yelled the chief petty officer who was driving the boat.

They were still fifteen kilometres out, but the conflagration seemed to fill the sky with a golden guttering light.

'Chief Stavros,' Jones cried out amiably, 'I don't think I'll take that bet.'

A small supernova of fire and light blossomed from deep within the inferno. Jump jets screamed overhead, dashing in towards the coast to attack the half-dozen Japanese ships in the harbour. Jones was dimly aware of the small crew working furiously to keep them on the correct heading without the benefit of continual GPS update. They shouted course headings and detailed corrections at each other a few times every minute. At least the ride was smooth, a long gliding lope across the water.

'Five minutes until we breach the entrance, Chief,' shouted a young sailor.

'Thanks, Dolly. Better get buttoned up, Colonel,' Stavros bellowed over the cacophony. 'Good luck, sir.'

Jones clapped Stavros on the back, thanked him for the lift, and hurried down to the vehicle deck where his command LAV awaited him. There was no respite from the uproar of the turbofans and engines. Although it would appear as an armoured behemoth to anyone who stood in its way, the LCAC itself wasn't a combat vessel. Its task was to drop off two platoons from A Company in a half-squadron of light armoured vehicles.

As Jones hustled down a corridor towards the vehicle deck, he quickly checked the flexipad that was Velcroed to his forearm. The other boats were all still in position, lying astern of his own. He strapped on his powered helmet, fitted the combat goggles and jacked into the battalion tac net. His visual field instantly filled up with cascading streams of data. After thousands of hours of training and years of combat experience, it was a completely natural environment for him. He noted the disposition of his units, their progress towards the beach and the condition of the enemy's defences without conscious thought. Small windows fed vision from the FLIR pods of the Comanche gunships. Others carried top-down footage, relayed from surveillance drones, of the dozen or so targeted sites within Manila. They were already burning fiercely, just like Corregidor. Secondary explosions erupted regularly as fuel and ammunition stocks cooked off.

Jones wondered how many people had already died.

'Colonel, sir?'

Jones pulled up just short of the vehicle deck. 'What's up, Sar'nt Major?'

Cocooned within layers of monobonded filament armour, goggles, helmet and tac set, Aub Harrison would have been unrecognisable to most people. But he and Jones had fought together for many years, and even if he hadn't spoken, Jones would have known him immediately.

'It's the colonel, sir, the observer.'

'Maloney.'

'Yeah. He's not playing well with the other children.'

For about the tenth time Julia Duffy checked the tabs on the ballistic gel pockets in her body armour. Her feet tapped rapidly on the nonslip floor of the LAV and she kept raising her hand to her mouth in a nervous reflex. She wanted to chew her fingernails, but her heavy black gloves got in the way. She swore under her breath again.

'Y'all okay, Ms Duffy?'

The name tag on the giant trooper's body armour identified him as 'Bukowski'. From the shoulder-slung gun rig, she knew he was a heavy-weapons carrier. He certainly was big enough, she mused. Even with his helmet off, he still had to crouch over in the confines of the LAV.

'I tapped out my Prozac,' she said. 'I'm just a little jumpy, that's all.'

'I got some Zoloft gum, if you'd like a stick,' said Bukowski.

'Would I!'

Julia would have leaped out of her seat if it weren't for the webbing which held her in place. Bukowski fished a stick of gum out of a pocket and stretched across the width of the vehicle to pass it to her.

'Thank you, Specialist,' she said with real gratitude.

'Is that gum? Do you think I could have some?'

Julia recognised the voice. It was Captain Svensden, a 'temp – one of two observers travelling in the LAV. He seemed pretty cool, but his boss, Colonel Maloney, was an asshole. Svensden sat two down and across from her, but Maloney was thankfully right at the other end of the cabin with Second Lieutenant Chen, the platoon commander.

Even in the dim red interior light the 'temps both stood out. They wore armour, like everyone else, but neither rested comfortably within it. Svensden fiddled with his straps and Velcro tabs. And among the dozen passengers, Maloney was the only other person besides Bukowski who didn't have a powered helmet strapped on. The graphics gave him motion sickness, he said. A pool of vomit lay at his feet and the air-con was working hard to scrub the smell of it from the cabin.

Bukowski was about to toss a stick of the gum to Svensden when Julia spoke up. She didn't have to shout. She was miked up and plugged into the tac net with the troopers.

'Better not, Captain. It's not Wrigley's spearmint. It's a drug. Probably put you to sleep since you haven't built up any tolerance. These guys are used to it.'

'What's that?'

Duffy cursed at herself. It was Colonel Maloney.

'Is somebody drinking up there? Did I hear right? And is it that woman? Goddamn, that's all we need.' Maloney tried to untangle himself from the restraining web. Chen reached an arm across the man's chest, telling him to sit still.

'Get your grubby little fingers off me, Chinaman!' the colonel shouted.

Everybody in the LAV jumped at that. A few threw their hands up to their ears to deal with the shooting pain. Maloney's throat mike had picked up the yell and amplified it tenfold across the audio net.

'Fucking jerk,' muttered Duffy.

'What did you say? What did that woman call me?' yelled Maloney.

A couple of marines ripped off their helmets. One reached over and unplugged the audio cabling that connected Maloney with the link.

'*Shut the fuck up!*' he said.

Sergeant Major Harrison threw back the hatch. The scene inside the LAV startled Jones. A fierce argument was under way. Almost nobody had their helmets on, as per regulations, and Colonel Maloney was out of his seat, standing in front of that *Times* reporter, jabbing his index finger at her. She appeared to be laughing, when she wasn't blowing bubblegum in his face.

'*What the fuck is going on here?*' Jones shouted, loudly enough to be heard over the ear-splitting drone of the turbofans and the commotion inside the cabin. The LAV was uncomfortably close to the huge Avco Lycoming gas turbine plants and the main propulsion fans. Jones took a deep breath, sucking in trace odours of diesel, gun oil, human sweat and bile from the pile of sick that dripped out of the cabin and onto his boots. He let rip with a blast that would have done his old drill instructor proud.

'Colonel Maloney. Sit your ass down, put your *goddamn* helmet on, and shut the fuck up. You are just here to watch. Nothing else. We transit the beachhead in a few minutes, and people are gonna start dying. Unless you want to give me any more grief, in which case we'll start the dying right here and now, because God help me if you endanger any part of this mission at any point I *will* shoot you in the fucking head and throw you overboard myself!'

Maloney stood with his mouth hanging open, like he'd been caught with his pants down. But Jones meant every word of it and the colonel must have known, because he flashed a quick, sour glare at the civilian woman before returning to his position.

A split-screen display dominated the *Clinton*'s CIC. Real-time footage beamed back from Manila sat next to a computer-generated map of the same area with dozens of targets and mission objectives highlighted by flashing tags, alphanumeric codes, unit designations and small icons. Admiral Spruance had no real idea of what it all meant, but at least he could see the burning hulks of Japanese ships in the harbour, and the dazzling emerald brilliance of more fires spotted throughout the city.

'It's fuckin' amazing, don't you think?' muttered Admiral Halsey, sitting next to him in the old anti-satellite work bay.

'What, the movies themselves, or what they're showing?' asked Spruance.

'The whole fucking thing. I mean, look at the way they hit those Jap positions in Manila. It's like needlepoint or something when you think of what the Nazis did to London with the Blitz.'

'But the Krauts meant to tear up the city,' said Spruance.

'True enough.'

Halsey leaned over from the comfort of his chair. The medication they'd given him had effectively cleared up his shingles, and his mood had improved as rapidly as his butt. But Spruance knew him well, and the look in his eyes gave him away.

'What's up, Bill? You don't look entirely happy. The Japs are dying like flies out there. I thought you'd be in a downright festive mood.'

Halsey glanced around the busy combat centre. As much as you could be left alone in such a crowded, frenetic place, they were, at least for the moment, alone. Kolhammer and Judge were across the room, busy coordinating the simultaneous strikes on Manila and the camps at Cabanatuan. Lieutenant Thieu was away, attending to requests from some of the reporters who'd gone out with the marines. Spruance shook his head at that. He was used to war correspondents making a nuisance of themselves at the front, but he simply couldn't believe how deeply involved – or what did they call it, 'embedded' – these people seemed to be. He doubted if you could tell some of them apart from the units they covered.

'I was just wondering,' Halsey said quietly, 'whether this was the right way to use these guys. I mean, look at what they're doing. They've only got so many of these super-rockets and magic bullets. Do you think a glorified prison break-out was the way to go?'

Spruance mulled over the question as he watched a flight of helicopters fan out over the city – the fat ones, which meant they were troop-carriers. Smaller, faster gunships buzzed around them like angry wasps, swooping down on any resistance and hosing it down with rocket and cannon fire. *They must be going for the railway yards*, he thought.

'I don't know, Bill,' he said. 'You saw what happened to those boys, not to mention the poor women they used as camp whores. I don't know what the right thing was. But I do know that these people have a mania about leaving their own behind. They'll lose fifty men just to get one back. It's like a sickness for them. I doubt we could have stopped them from doing this even if we'd wanted to.'

Lieutenant Thieu returned, threading his way through the banks of computer monitors and battle stations. Spruance watched a screen that showed one of those Super Harriers zipping across the big screen, only to stop in midair, turn around and unleash a stream of rockets on some target at the wharves.

Halsey leaned over before Thieu made it into earshot.

'Yeah, but the thing is, Ray,' he said, 'we ain't their fucking people, are we?'

The industrial jackhammer of the LAV's autocannon abruptly ceased as the hatch swung open and the section poured out onto the street. Julia spat out the wad of medicated gum she'd been chewing and checked her heads-up display to make sure she was recording. She flicked her personal weapon to three-round bursts, laid her thumb on the safety, ready to click it off as soon as she was clear of the vehicle, and nodded quickly to Private Bukowski. She'd already decided to hang her story off what happened to the heavy-weapons specialist over the next few hours. Bukowski was cool with that. He wanted to send his granddad a video of himself in battle. Grandpa Bukowski had won – or would win – a Bronze Star in Korea.

Her combat goggles, a topflight set of Ray-Ban Warpigs, automatically adjusted to changing light conditions as the blast door of the armoured vehicle split open and the frenzied stabbing light of the battle rushed in. She flinched as a line of tracer fire flicked across the opening, and reached out for a grab bar as Bukowski recoiled into her.

'You okay, Specialist?'

'Fine, ma'am. Somebody else got clipped up front.'

The two lines of marines, which had momentarily bunched up, surged down the ramp. Duffy slapped Bukowski on the back as he stepped off. A cramped shuffle brought her to the exit, where she found the body of Colonel Stoker Maloney, half his head torn away by a piece of shrapnel. He'd tumbled off the edge of the incline. One leg had folded up underneath his dead weight, the other had caught on the edge of the ramp and now pointed skywards. He wasn't wearing his helmet.

'Dumbass,' said Duffy.

Bukowski's voice came over the sound channel. 'Say what?'

'Didn't mean you. Meant him.'

'Oh, right. Yeah.'

The specialist suddenly swivelled at the hip and poured a stream of light cannon fire into a window across the street. Duffy was jolted into the moment. They were assaulting across a wide boulevard. Half the section, with Chen in the lead, was storming towards the colonnaded entrance of a grand colonial building, pouring selective fire into the upper-storey windows. Nobody except Bukowski was firing on full auto. Discrete three-round bursts of tungsten penetrators chewed up masonry and wooden shutters, smashing glass and pulverising brickwork.

A line of tracers lashed at them from another building two doors down. Duffy saw a trooper stagger under the impact. He sank to his knees for a few seconds before two other marines appeared and helped him back to his feet and over the exposed cobblestone roadway.

Again Bukowski turned fractionally. The heavy gun rig slung at his hip turned with him. Duffy saw the muzzle elevate fractionally. His wrists flexed and a short snarling volley of twenty-millimetre slugs punched through a sandbagged revetment on the top floor of a neoclassical mansion a hundred yards away. A dazzling spark traced the flight path of the shells. Duffy refocused the lens on her video rig, pulling in tight on the French windows the marine had targeted. Streams poured from ruptured sandbags as smoke rose from within the darkened recesses of the room. A disembodied human hand twitched on top of one bag.

Bullets zipped past her, uncomfortably close. Her C/T-weave armour was the best that money could buy. Better than Marine Corps standard issue, in fact. But you could still get yourself righteously fucked up in a free-fire zone like this. Duffy unsafed the MP5 and quickly panned up and down the road. It was a quick and dirty scan. She'd use an intelligent editing suite to clean it up later before laying down her own commentary.

She knew in broad-brush detail that they were swarming the divisional HQ of the Japanese command, that most of the enemy's theatre strategic assets were already just scrap metal and charred meat. But beyond that, like the men and women around her, she knew only what she could see with her own eyes and imaging rig.

They were still taking sporadic but reasonably intense small-arms fire from the surrounding buildings. It seemed more opportunistic than directed. Marines occasionally shuddered or tumbled as rounds hit them and their armoured padding dispersed the kinetic energy. She knew from personal experience that it still felt like getting whacked by a Louisville Slugger. Sometimes, in the background, she'd hear a scream or gurgle over the platoon comm channel as somebody caught a bullet or a piece of shrapnel in the face or throat.

Gunships ripped overhead, pouring autocannon fire into pillboxes on street corners, popping Hellfire missiles through windows, and raking small concentrations of Japanese troops who periodically attempted desperate charges across open ground. She'd seen worse. Damascus was way tougher than this. That had been like the whole fucking city was out to kill you.

Bukowski had moved ahead, and she had to hustle to catch up. He took the steps at the front of the big white building at a run, leaping over the bloodied form of a prostrate Japanese soldier. Duffy was lining up to jump over the corpse when it unexpectedly rose from the dead, rolled up onto one knee and levelled a ridiculously long rifle at the back of the marine's head.

'Bukowski, look out!' she called out.

The marine began an instinctive dive to the side as the guard fired. Duffy saw the big man's helmet jolt, but he kept on moving.

Her momentum carried her right up to the steps and there was no chance of avoiding a collision. She didn't have time to raise and fire her weapon, so she dipped a shoulder and crashed into the Jap with as much force as she could focus, projecting her energy right through him. He flew forward about two feet and slammed into the top step. She struggled for her balance, lost it, regained it and found herself on top of him, stamped her leading boot on top of his thigh and rammed a knee into his face. His head snapped back and as she sailed right on over his body she pointed the MP5 straight down, squeezing the trigger. She didn't even hear the muted cough of the discharge as three rounds of nine-millimetre hollow point sliced open the guard's torso. Blowback splattered her goggles with gobbets of hot offal that glowed a bright opalescent green in low-light amplification. She felt a dull but massive impact on her hip, from a ricochet she guessed, then the ground came rushing up at her and a much hotter, searing pain exploded in her shoulder as she slammed into concrete and snapped a collarbone.

'*Son of a bitch!*'

'Y'all right, Ms Duffy?' Bukowksi hauled her up by

her good arm. 'Thanks, too, ma'am. Owe you one.'

'We'll call it quits for the gum,' she said. 'How's your head?'

The marine punched the side of his helmet where a bullet had glanced off. Duffy switched to infrared for a second. The track mark stood out in glowing pink.

'My circuits are okay,' said Bukowski. 'How's your shoulder?'

A violent crash of gunfire from upstairs drowned her out. She was about to try to speak again when a long burst of firing and the double crump of two grenades shook the building.

Lieutenant Chen's voice came in over the platoon's dedicated tac net.

'Top floor secured. No prisoners taken.'

The video feed wasn't live, which made it infinitely worse. The signal came through on a fifteen-minute delay, and from the looks of the firestorm running through the streets of Manila, that was long enough for anything to happen. Lieutenant Commander Black wanted to turn away from the screen, to shut off the rush of chaotic savagery that swirled around his woman. He wanted to run from the media centre and hop on a chopper into the city to yank Julia right out of there.

Rosanna had him seated in front of a huge flat screen devoted exclusively to a delayed feed from Julia's squad. She furiously worked a keyboard and touch screen next to him, chopping footage, assigning it to dump bins for editing later, tagging significant sections, adding her own initial comments. Without an organisation of her own to report to, she'd volunteered to stand in as Julia's producer. Black was impressed with the furious intensity she brought to the job. She was every bit as focused as one of Kolhammer's bullet-eyed warriors. But she was also every bit as emotionally removed. He'd tried to talk to her a couple of times when Julia appeared on screen, but she'd cut him off.

'Shut up for now, Dan. Talk later.'

When the squad burst from the LAV and onto the boulevard Dan flinched, and his gut went tight. He clearly saw Colonel Maloney lose half his face. His heart hammered faster than it had at any time during the fight at Midway. He felt wretched, impotent and ashamed of himself for sitting comfortably in safety on board the *Clinton* while Julia charged into the Japanese line of fire. When he saw her charge and shoot the guard, he thought he might lose control of his stomach.

Natoli, excitedly cursing under her breath, hammered the keyboard until she'd isolated a video feed from Private Bukowski in a little pull-down window on the screen.

Dan Black hardly recognised the savage, gore-soaked creature he saw in there. But he knew it was Julia.

He'd been happy with the way he had adapted to

the arrival of Kolhammer's ships. He prided himself on the ease with which he'd accepted the impossible and adjusted to the demands of these strange people. But now he found himself staring, uncomprehendingly, at the snarl of rage and bloodlust that flashed across his lover's face, and at the cold self-possession he found in the eyes of her friend sitting in the chair next to him.

Who the hell were these people?

42

Camp 5, Cabanatuan, 0219 hours, 21 June 1942

'How we doing, Amanda?' asked Flight Lieutenant Harford.

Hayes's voice responded inside his helmet, cutting through the dull thud of the rotors. 'Three hours of fuel, ten minutes till insertion . . . You boys get that? Time to get funky.'

The five Navy SEALs and Major Pavel Ivanov, of the Russian Spetsnaz forces, checked their harnesses and weapons loads.

The stealthed Seahawk flew low over the jungle, well below any local radar – although the chopper was sheathed in carbon-composite tiles, which would shed primitive scanning like a bride's nightgown. But Harford was a belt-and-braces guy. He already felt dangerously exposed on this mission.

'Three minutes,' said Flight Lieutenant Hayes as two gunships accelerated past them. The lead Comanche banked over and began to work a dense clump of bushland with rockets and miniguns. Secondary explosions testified to the presence of some sort of Japanese camp.

'One minute,' warned Hayes, who was keeping

a close eye on the combined feed of the navigation radar and SINS, the chopper's self-enclosed inertial navigation system. Not a patch on the third-generation NAVSTAR GPS system, but it would have to do.

It was cold in the back of the chopper. The SEAL team donned their helmets and night-vision combat goggles. Ivanov leaned forward to peer around CPO Vincente Rogas and into the darkness. He switched from the luminescent lime green of low-light amplification to infrared. Immediately the heat leaking from the chopper's engine cowling shimmered in front of him like a curtain. He adjusted the optimum range and it fell away appreciably. A cluster of buildings, blacked out but still bleeding cherry-pink warmth into the night, appeared to the south. Flight Lieutenant Hayes's voice sounded crisply inside his helmet.

'As we are preparing to land the captain asks that you return your tray tables to the upright position, unfasten your seatbelts and jump out of the helicopter. We'd like to thank you for flying with the US Navy, and hope you will choose to travel with us again in the future.'

'The far fucking future,' added Harford.

'Amen,' said Ivanov.

As the Seahawk swooped down on the compound, a platoon of the marine fire team opened up. They had been lying concealed in the elephant grass outside the barbed wire. Twelve Japanese guards perished instantly, shredded by the concentrated volley of caseless ceramic projectiles. A couple of Hellfire missiles reached through the darkness to obliterate the single guard tower.

In the back of the big chopper Airman Toby La Salle checked the fast rope connections as the men prepared to drop the last twenty metres to the ground. The two parties wished each other good luck and then the small special ops team was gone. Into the black.

The compound housing civilian prisoners underwent what was technically referred to as vertical and horizontal envelopment. In layman's terms, the Japanese defenders were swarmed from all sides and above in one mad minute of psychotically violent but finely controlled gunfire and high-explosive bombardment.

The SEAL team signalled to the marines to cease fire and dropped into the compound. The first squad assaulted the main gates, now protected only by dead men, and the rest of their unit poured through the breach. Ivanov and Rogas were already moving, running towards the first of the flimsy huts housing the prisoners. The chief grunted as a Japanese slug spun him around, but his body armour saved him and he was up again in a second. The sentry was dead before Rogas regained his feet, drilled with a three-round burst fired from the hip by Ivanov.

A Japanese officer wielding a sword charged at them from the side of the hut. But his pants were undone, ruining the effect. The Spetsnaz officer took his head off with another three-round burst.

Rogas kicked in the door of the hut and spun to his left, shooting another Jap who was coming at him from the darkened corner. Women began screaming.

'Americans! We're Americans,' Rogas yelled in English. 'Get down on the floor. Get down now! Anybody left standing gets shot.'

The infrared vision lent a nightmarish atmosphere to a scene that already recalled one of the lower levels of hell. The women were naked, or clothed in scraps at best. They were underweight, covered in bruises, sores and their own filth. Alternately moaning and screaming, they writhed and groped in the dark, unable to see what was happening, unlike Ivanov and Rogas. *They* could see at least eight Japs in the room, some of them naked too.

The SEALs hunted them down one after another, shooting each man in the back of the head as he tried to crawl along the floor. When only three were left, the Japs jumped to their feet with both hands in the air.

'No shoot. No shoot!' one yelled.

Rogas shot him anyway.

Duffy had visited some stinking Third World cesspools in her time, but this place took the prize. She tried hard to keep the disgust from showing on her face. It wouldn't be fair to the prisoners, especially not these ones.

The reporter moved among the women of Camp 5 and let her mini-cam run, but they were in no state to be interviewed. She'd just bummed another stick of Zoloft from Bukowski, when her flexipad signalled a message. She still had the theme from *The Simpsons* as her ringer.

Snatching the pad from her arm, she turned away from the marines and walked a short distance towards the camp gates. The signal was strong, which made sense. She was patched into a military-grade comm net. The caller appeared on the screen.

It was Rosanna, back on the *Clinton*. She'd preferred to not jump into a hot LZ, and Duffy respected the choice.

'How you doing, sweetie?' Natoli asked.

'Fucked my shoulder again, but otherwise I'm fine,' said Duffy, her voice shaking a little. 'This place sucks, by the way.'

'Hot?'

'Not so much. We got pretty busy coming into Manila, but nothing to brag about. The shooting was mostly done within two hours. But I hopped over here to one of the women's camps after the SEALs took it. Jesus, you wouldn't believe this fucking place, Rosanna. It's like a Taliban rape camp for Americans. How's Dan, you seen him? I think I might have been a little harsh with him before I left.'

Rosanna chuckled. 'He's fine. I told him you were premenstrual.'

‘Actually, I am, on top of everything else.’

A dull thudding noise told her a chopper was approaching.

‘Gotta go,’ she said. ‘I really gotta get to work. This’ll be a good story if I can keep it together.’ Duffy signed off as a big Sea Stallion dropped down into the field just outside the camp gates.

A woman in full combat rig pounded down the ramp of the heavy-lift chopper and into the compound. As she went past Duffy she appeared to be trying very, very hard to contain her fury.

Lieutenant Chen tried to talk to her as she stormed up, but she sailed right past the platoon commander. The camp women were being tended to in an emergency aid station the marines had run up next to the former commandant’s hut. He was alive, having dived under his bed when the missile attack on the divisional barracks began. Two marines stood guard over him and four other prisoners by the smoking ruins of the guard tower.

Duffy watched as the female officer spoke to the women. The contrast was striking. The marine was of average height but seemed to tower over the women in her combat fatigues and body armour. They gathered closer around her as the parley continued. A girl of perhaps eight or nine, it was hard to tell, was brought forward.

Julia Duffy walked over to Lieutenant Chen.

‘Who’s that?’ she asked.

‘Captain Francois. Battalion combat surgeon,’ he

said. 'She just came in to supervise the evacuation of the camp.'

'Do you know what she's talking to the women about?'

Chen shrugged.

The dull thud of Apache gunships circling outside the camp made it impossible to pick up any of the conversation between Francois and the women.

'Do you think we should help?' asked Chen.

'We can't help,' said Ivanov, who had wandered over from the Sea Stallion after topping up his ammo. 'This is women's business. Best left to the lady doctor, yes?'

'Maybe,' Chen said. He didn't exactly sound sure of himself.

The three of them saw Francois hug the child. She rubbed the girl's matted, filthy hair and seemed to deliver a short lecture to all of the women. Then she waved over the marines who were guarding the prisoners.

'Uh-oh,' said Chen.

But before he could take off, the Russian laid a firm hand on his shoulder. 'It is for the better, my friend.'

'No fucking way, dude. I think she's gonna cap them.'

'Probably,' agreed Rogas. But he made no move to interfere either.

'I can't let her,' said Chen. 'Sanction is my responsibility.'

'Let it be, Lieutenant,' said Rogas, laying a hand

on the body armour over Chen's heart. 'Just let it be.'

He sounded like a father soothing a distraught child.

Julia watched the marine surgeon as though she were underwater. Everything seemed indistinct and slow.

'Some things are meant to be,' Ivanov said gently.

The little girl didn't say anything, as far as they could tell. She clung to Captain Francois's leg as the Japanese were pushed and kicked into motion. Duffy saw the women cringe as a group when the Japs drew near. The girl burrowed further into the surgeon's fatigues. The marines guarding the Japanese prisoners threw a look at their platoon leader. Chen held still for a few seconds, then nodded once and walked away.

'Ms Duffy,' said Ivanov, 'why don't you turn off your recorder now?'

Julia gave the Russian a flat look. She considered the wretched figures of the comfort women as they cringed in front of their former captors.

She slowly reached up and cut the power to the mini-cam.

The five prisoners were a study in contrasting styles. Two swaggered over. One seemed to have checked out completely. Another had to be kicked every step of the way. The commandant was subdued and shaking. As they stopped in front of Francois, the Japanese registered the fact that she was a woman. The commandant's whole body began to tremble.

Francois rubbed the girl's head. One of the women leaned forward and spat.

'Come on,' said Ivanov.

They walked over until they were close enough that they could hear the conversation.

'What's your name, asshole?' the surgeon asked.

The camp commander didn't appear to understand.

Captain Francois pulled the little girl's head closer into her lap and covered her ear with one hand. With the other she unshipped her side-arm and fired one shot into the face of the prisoner furthest from her. A fountain of blood and brain matter erupted and the body dropped to the dust like a big sack of shit. Duffy's heart skipped.

The women jumped and one began to cry. The child uncurled from her hiding spot and walked over to inspect the corpse. She kicked the twitching body.

'I asked you what your name is, you rapist motherfucker.'

The commandant began to babble incoherently. He shut up only when Francois capped off another two of his men.

The other Japanese man broke and ran. She shot him in the back. The impact lifted him right off his feet. He dropped in a heap a few yards away.

'Excuse me,' said Francois. As she walked over to the man, who was trying to drag himself away, the girl followed close at her heels. Francois put a bullet into the base of the guard's neck and he fell still.

She took the girl's hand and led her back to the main group. The commandant had fallen to his knees and was begging the marines to do something. They shared a smoke and ignored him. Duffy found herself glad that she'd turned off the mini-cam. She wasn't sure why. It was a betrayal of everything she stood for as a journalist. But this was a moment beyond professional considerations.

The women were recovering from their shock and had begun to crowd forward.

'You'll want to keep clear, ladies,' said the marine nearest them. 'Give the doc some room.'

The little girl ran forward and slapped the trembling Japanese commandant in the face. A few of the women shouted encouragement. Captain Francois advanced on him, slipping another clip into her pistol.

'Honey,' she said to the girl, 'stand aside.'

The child did as she was told.

'You know what, I don't really give a fuck what your goddamn name is.'

She snapped the gun up and fired three rounds into his groin. He spun into the ground, screaming and jamming his hands into the bloody ruin between his legs. Francois let him lie there for a while longer before she shot him in the head.

She holstered her weapon and scooped up the girl. As they passed Duffy and Ivanov, Julia heard the surgeon whisper, 'C'mon, precious. Let's get you a hot bath and some chocolate.'

The child spoke for the first time.

'I like chocolate.'

Tears welled up in the surgeon's eyes and she hugged the bony child to her.

'Of course you do, darlin'. Everyone loves chocolate.'

43

USS Hillary Clinton, *1512 hours, 25 June 1942*

When the news came, Kolhammer was in his stateroom and very much looking forward to the moment when the safety of this convoy was no longer his concern. He had nearly thirty-eight thousand liberated prisoners under his care, and despite the best efforts of the medics, they were still dying at the rate of nearly a hundred a day. Captain Francois told him that was better than they could have expected, given the terrible conditions in the camps, but Kolhammer prayed that they wouldn't lose too many more.

He hadn't spoken to the combat surgeon about the incident at Cabanatuan. There were rumours that things had gotten way out of hand in there just after she'd turned up. But Kolhammer had personally spoken to half-a-dozen witnesses and none of them could recall anything untoward happening.

He doubted that, but as long as nobody was complaining he didn't see much point chasing up ghost stories. He had more pressing issues to worry about. They couldn't put off the inevitable. He knew that when they returned to Pearl he was going to get hammered from all sides. He'd been able to push through the rescue mission because nobody yet knew what to do about the Multinational Force. But he understood that with each passing day the novelty and shock of their presence would recede and very soon the politics of the situation would assert themselves. Roosevelt's commanders were already fighting among themselves, trying to gain control over his fleet. The British government was still demanding that their ships – and the Australians', for that matter – be detached from the Multinational Force and placed under London's control. And it seemed that absolutely nobody among the contemporary Allies would consider just leaving the force intact.

They still hadn't located any trace of the British and French ships, *Vanguard* and *Dessaix*. And given the discovery of the *Nuku* on top of that mountain in New Guinea, and the loss of the *Garrett* in the Southern Ocean, he was a lot less sanguine about the prospects of their turning up safely or having been left behind.

Kolhammer rubbed his tired eyes and wished that he could crawl under the covers of his bed and wake up back home next to Marie. He felt her absence like a hole in his heart every minute of the day. For all of the mind-bending complexities of the Transition, it was still the intimate, personal consequences that had the power to undo him. In his worst moments he suspected that if he alone could somehow sneak back to be with her, he might just abandon everything here. Duty, honour, friendship. Everything. Just for the chance to be with his wife. After all, this was not his war.

He had an awful feeling that the blood and horror of the past weeks was going to be matched by a crude ugliness of spirit once it became obvious to the wider world that they were not going back where they came from. The murders of Anderson and Miyazaki seemed to lend credence to that fear.

Francois had been in his ear about the investigation, or the 'so-called' investigation, as she constantly referred to it. Nimitz had been more than helpful and sympathetic, but everything just seemed to jam up in the lower levels. He hadn't met the detective who'd caught the case, but he'd heard all about him from Francois. Buster Cherry was not a figure to inspire confidence. Kolhammer was deeply worried that the killing was only the start of their problems here.

They were trapped without hope of getting home, but he had no idea what to do next. His intercom beeped and Commander Judge appeared on the screen, saving him the trouble of pondering the matter any further.

'Admiral, it's the *Sutanto*,' he said. 'She's turned up and she's in trouble.'

KRI Sutanto, *1515 hours, 25 June 1942*

The Japanese had conferred a new rank on Usama Damiri, in honour of his bravery and sacrifice in the service of the Emperor. He was now Captain Damiri of the Imperial Japanese Navy (Auxiliary Forces). He snickered at the idea as shells exploded harmlessly in the waters around him. The *Sutanto* plunged on through the rain of salt water, her little autocannon firing at her pursuers, which were two thousand metres abeam on both sides of the ship.

Every time the deck gun spoke, it raised small buds of fire on the decks of the Japanese destroyers. Every time they returned fire, they missed. Damiri hoped they wouldn't get lucky – or unlucky, as the case would be.

As amused as he was by the insistence of the infidels that he accept the commission into their service, he couldn't fault the courage of the skeleton crew on those three vessels. They knew they wouldn't survive this mission, and yet they were all volunteers.

'We have the *Clinton* on channel three, my sheik.'

Damiri's mouth was dry. Not with fear, of course, but with excitement and anticipation. They were so close now. If he could plunge a dagger into the heart of the infidel empire now, it might never arise to oppress the Dar al-Islam. He took a deep breath to steady himself before taking up the microphone.

The other two martyrs on the bridge watched him expectantly. He invested his performance with as much ersatz desperation as he could muster.

'*Mayday mayday*, this is the *Sutanto* under Acting Commander Damiri. Come in please, *Clinton*. We are under attack by pirate forces. We have casualties and require immediate assistance.'

Damiri fed a random layer of electronic interference into the signal. It would help if they were scratching their heads at the other end. Typically, a woman's voice answered.

'*Sutanto*, this is *Clinton*. We have you on the arrays. Can you confirm you are under attack by three surface combatants?'

Damiri flicked a series of switches to fire off the only two antiship missiles he'd been allowed to keep. They smoked off the rails and lanced away, homing in on the nearest ship. It was an old *Wakatake*-class destroyer, built in 1922. The contrails of white smoke arced over the waves and touched down on the forecastle of the doomed ship, exploding in a vivid flickering flash.

'Only two now,' he radioed back.

There was a moment's delay.

'Got that one, *Sutanto*, good shooting. Hang on tight. Cavalry's on its way.'

Usama Damiri smiled. He knew now that this would be his last day on earth.

He made sure the radio microphone was dead before turning to his comrades.

'*Allahu akbar!*' he cried.

'God is great,' they shouted in unison.

Commander Konoe coughed quietly into his handkerchief. It came away spotted with dark, glutinous blood. He folded the small square of cotton and dabbed at the sweat that threatened to run into his eyes, all the time staring at the spot where the *Huyo* had sacrificed herself. Nothing remained of the gallant destroyer beyond a patch of burning oil and some floating debris. He couldn't quite believe how quickly she'd gone when the barbarian rockets had slammed into her.

He only hoped that when his time came, he could acquit himself with such bravery.

He leaned into the speaking tube. Every breath was a rasping torture. The sickness was advanced and the exertions of the last days had not helped. Not that it mattered.

'Fire the forward mounts,' he croaked.

The 4.7-inch battery of the *Karukaya* barked and he nodded as the shells exploded harmlessly astern of the *Sutanto*. He couldn't quite believe the Americans would be able to follow the course of this counterfeit duel from so far away. But the Grand Admiral himself had assured Konoe that it was so, and that his contribution to ultimate victory would not go unnoticed in the Imperial Palace.

How proud his parents would be when they received a letter from the Emperor's own assistant private secretary, thanking them for their son's sacrifice.

He swelled with pleasure at the thought. Not just for himself, but for the other men on board. He very much wanted to make one last round of the ship, to speak with each of them before they died, but duty demanded his presence on the bridge. There were so few men to run the ship, to fire her weapons and fabricate the radio traffic that would attend such a dramatic chase. Nothing could be left to fate.

'Fire,' he ordered again.

A young midshipman rushed into the bridge with a note for Konoe, telling him that the American planes had arrived. They were so quick! The young boy was suffused with an almost saintly glow. Konoe experienced a fleeting sense of shame in the face of the boy's piety. The commander had volunteered for this mission because he had less than six months to live anyway. The wasting illness that had taken his older brothers was almost done with him, too. But this youngster had willingly thrown himself into the teeth of the enemy.

'Good work, Sato!'

The midshipman straightened himself up and snapped out a parade-ground salute.

Konoe returned the gesture. Then he died.

'Aircraft inbound, my sheik, bearing two-three-one, thirty-two kilometres out. Raptors, judging from their speed.'

Damiri thanked the young petty officer.

It would not be long now.

Static flared on the radio and a man's voice cracked from the torn fabric of the speaker box.

'*Sutanto, Sutanto*, this is Flight Lieutenant Anna Torres off the USS *Hillary Clinton*. We have you on visual. Commencing payload run.'

'Hurry up *Clinton*, hurry please. We are running low on ammunition,' Damiri babbled, hoping that he wasn't overplaying the act.

'Be cool *Sutanto*. The bad guys are toast.'

Damiri rolled his eyes and smiled at his comrades on the frigate's bridge. They all turned binoculars on the remaining Japanese ships, which were performing beautifully. Their guns fired ceaselessly, raising geysers of water all around the Indonesian vessel.

Damiri felt compelled to wish them all the best in hell.

But he didn't pick up the radio. There would have been no point.

The explosion that tore up the nearest destroyer was so violent that Damiri shivered in the face of it. He'd watched the dark, hypersonic bolt as it skimmed across the waves and speared into the *Karukaya*. But he hadn't been ready for the titanic eruption that followed. Even in bright sunshine the flash of the blast dazzled and partly blinded him. Somebody cried out.

'*Allahu akbar!*'

The other Japanese destroyer perished in identical

fashion, ripped apart about three thousand metres off the port side. A few seconds later Damiri distinctly heard the tinkle and clatter of metal rain on the steel cladding of the *Sutanto*.

He gestured for the others to shut up and composed himself before keying the radio mike.

'Thank you, *Clinton*. Thank you.'

The dark, predatory blur of an F-22 streaked past about six hundred metres away.

'Buy me a beer back in Pearl, *Sutanto*. We've got some tall tales for you.'

The fighter rolled over and accelerated away. Apart from two thick clouds of dark oily smoke, almost nothing remained of the Japanese ships.

The speakers crackled into life again.

'*Sutanto*, this is the *Clinton*. Please advise us of your status.'

Damiri grinned. 'We're alive, *Clinton*! But we don't know what's happened. Our communications are down, our GPS is gone, we can't raise anyone. And these pirates!'

A new voice, masculine, broke in over his chatter.

'*Sutanto*, this is Admiral Kolhammer. Please advise us of casualties at your end.'

Damiri raised his eyebrows. The infidel leader himself. Any anxiety he had felt before was gone now. He gazed contentedly out over the long swell of the western Pacific.

'Admiral Kolhammer, sir. I am Sub-Lieutenant Damiri, Acting Commander of the *Sutanto*. Captain

Djuanda is dead. Many of the officers are dead or injured. We have eighteen killed and twelve badly wounded. Over.'

Kolhammer's voice growled out of the speakers.

'Can you care for your own casualties, Lieutenant? I'm afraid we have a situation here too. There's little point sending medevac out to you. Our own facilities are already swamped. Over.'

Damiri didn't want to press too hard. The last thing he wanted was to have Americans coming aboard now. But he had to play for real too.

'We'll probably lose two or three men in the next few hours, sir. Over.'

'I'm sorry about that, Damiri, but you have to try to hold on. We just don't have the facilities.'

Damiri rolled his eyes. That was so like them.

'Acknowledged,' he said, not needing to fake the hint of bitterness in his voice.

'We'll be with you in five hours, *Sutanto*. And you'll have air cover for all of that time.'

'Thank you, *Clinton*,' said Damiri. It was an effort to squeeze the words out.

Was there a waking hour in the last month when she hadn't been confronted by legions of the doomed? Captain Francois couldn't recall one. From the moment she'd regained consciousness after the Transition she seemed to have been running from one casualty to the next, an endless line of them stretching out to a vanishing point somewhere in her future.

Her fingers twitched as she half considered dialling up another shot of stimulant from her thoracic implants. But she stayed her hand. The ward was full of patients, and most of them were not combat casualties. The liberated prisoners needed treatment for starvation, suppurating jungle ulcers, malaria, fungal infections and a hundred minor after-effects of captivity. But unlike the rocket rush of madness that had blown through this place after Midway, these patients died more slowly and, she supposed, more comfortably. Dozens of medical staffers moved among the beds. They adjusted drips, changed dressings and bedpans, administered medicine and vitamin shots.

She was losing patients every day, seventy-six of them since she'd come on shift eighteen hours ago. But by the dismal maths of her profession, that wasn't bad. She knew that were it not for the facilities available throughout the modern ships of the task force, hundreds more would succumb every day. She examined her heart's feeling and found it to be scabbed over with scar tissue and barely pushing blood through her veins.

She needed some rest.

Francois dragged her flexipad out of a coat pocket with fingers that felt numb except for a small tingling at their tips, and found Lieutenant Commander Wassman on Shipnet.

'I'm taking four hours, Helen,' she said. 'You have the floor.'

Her new deputy nodded brusquely in the small screen. Wassman's locator chip placed her down in the burns unit.

'Got it, ma'am. If I might, Captain? You need more than four hours. I can catch an extra shift. I had a whole half-night's sleep.'

The chief surgeon didn't bother arguing. 'Thanks. I'll take an extra two. Call me if I'm needed.'

As she signed off an alarm sounded in the distance, calling for a crash team. Francois checked her pad: a cardiac arrest in the next ward. She brought the patient's file up. An eighty-five-year-old white female from Cabanatuan.

Not a chance, she thought. The wrinklies seemed as if they just gave up on you as soon as they realised they were safe. It was like they'd had something to prove, getting out of that shithole, and then they checked out.

Her eyes burned as she headed back to the temporary cabin she'd taken. The short walk took her through a corridor so crowded with civilians and refugees and a disorderly mix of military personnel that she could have been in the emergency room of a public hospital. She closed the door of her small quarters with relief.

The girl was on her bunk, playing with a Mars Landing Barbie one of the marines had dug up from somewhere. She hadn't spoken again since the camp, but warm and washed and safely tucked up in bed, she favoured Margie with a genuine smile.

'Hello, darlin',' said Francois.

She knew from talking to other inmates of Camp 5 that the little girl's name was Grace, and that was all. Nobody knew anything about what had happened to her parents.

The child looked much less feral than she had on Luzon. She was still underweight, and she couldn't stand having the lights out, but Francois was pleased with her progress.

'Would you like a drink, Gracie? Some bug juice?' She smiled.

The girl nodded.

Francois poured her a cup of the vile-tasting cordial.

She stroked Gracie's thin blonde hair as she drank. She really needed to sleep, but now that she was back in the cabin and the kid was awake, she didn't think she'd be able to. She didn't like palming her off on anybody else, and truth be known, Grace threw a fit whenever she tried.

As she stroked Grace's forehead, which was still scarred by deep cuts and bruises, the girl suddenly grabbed her hand. Her little voice was no more than a squeak.

'My daddy stayed with General MacArthur to help keep the lights on.'

Francois's heart leaped. She hadn't expected anything like this for weeks, maybe months. It was the best thing she'd heard in days. She positively beamed, until Grace spoke again.

'Mommy and Daddy aren't coming back, are they? They shot my mommy, I think.'

Francois's momentary spasm of joy died. She couldn't find an answer that wouldn't crush the little mite's spirit. Part of the reason she was cruising the edge of exhaustion was all the extra time she'd put into trying to get a line on what might have become of the girl's family. Now, it seemed, she had an inkling of their fate. She arranged her features as neutrally as she could.

'I don't know, honey, but I think maybe they're with God now. Did someone tell you about your mom?'

The girl's lower lip trembled and her eyes filled with tears. She shook her head. Margie, choking up too, rubbed her cheek.

'But the thing is, darling, I know your mom and dad are happy now, because if they're looking down from heaven, they can see you're safe here with us. And all they would ever want in the world is for you to grow up safe.'

Grace gathered her composure by means of three gulping breaths. When she could talk without crying she looked into Margie's eyes. 'When I grow up,' she said, 'I want to be a United States marine, just like you.'

Margie pursed her lips and nodded. She patted down Grace's hair, kissed her forehead and turned away.

'Excuse me for just a second, sweetie,' she said thickly.

She jumped up and hurried out into the corridor.

When the door to her cabin was closed, she sank to the floor and burst into tears.

The fierce heat reminded Kolhammer of the days they'd spent off Timor preparing for deployment. He was a universe away from that now. But home seemed as tangible as the salt in the air. Einstein had told him it really was that close, that his wife and home were closer to him than the shirt on his back. But Kolhammer peered through dark sunglasses at the huge straggling convoy of antique vessels, a scene that appeared nearly medieval to his eyes, and he knew that he would never see Marie again.

He kept one eye on the screen where an icon representing the *Sutanto* ploughed towards them from the east. When they rendezvoused, the Indonesian would have to turn around and cover her tracks, but he couldn't blame them for not wanting to spend another minute out there on their own. They'd had a hell of a time of it, judging by the video the Raptors had brought back. The little tub had been comprehensively shot to hell. He had to admit that he might have been wrong about them, though, because they'd fought through.

'Thinking of home, Admiral?' asked Spruance.

Kolhammer had forgotten he was there, so quiet had Spruance been the last half-hour. Like most of them, with the worst behind them, he seemed content to gaze into the heat shimmer that was obscuring the horizon. Choppers thudded between the modern ships, redistributing casualties, supplies and medical personnel as needed. Combat air patrol roared off the *Clinton* and the *Kandahar* at regular intervals. But the threat bubble was clear. Apart from those tin cans chasing the *Sutanto*, they'd had only two passing contacts with the Japanese – a submarine that had been killed before it knew it was in danger, and a faint return off a large body of iron far away to the north.

Yamamoto was wisely keeping his distance.

Kolhammer didn't reply to Spruance immediately. He was exhausted and half hypnotised by the loping passage of the old cruise liners and troopships that carried most of the liberated POWs.

'Home?' he mused aloud. 'I suppose so.'

'We'll be there soon,' said Spruance.

Kolhammer rubbed at the bristles sprouting on his cheeks. He wondered when he'd have to go back to shaving with a razor instead of just using wipe-away gel.

'You'll be home soon, Admiral,' he said. 'And all of these poor bastards.' He indicated the transports with a wave of the hand. 'But we won't be going home for a long time. If ever.'

The blank sheets of paper annoyed Halabi. She'd been staring at them for half an hour, willing the right words to come. But try as she might she just couldn't come up with the correct words for writing a condolence letter to the great-grandparents of a sailor killed in action decades before he'd been born. There had been well over a thousand men and women on the *Fearless*; it was tempting to give up. But even though it was frustrating and the situation more than a little bizarre, she knew the dead sailor's relatives needed to know what had happened. Nevertheless she was quietly grateful when a knock sounded at the cabin door.

'Enter,' she said, instantly regretting it when the doleful countenance of Rear Admiral Sir Leslie Murray appeared. She composed her features as equably as she could.

'I *am* sorry, Sir Leslie, are you still having trouble getting through to London? I've asked my communications officer to prioritise your messages.'

Murray looked ill. The bags of loose flesh below his eyes seemed even deeper than normal and he carried his shoulders with a pronounced stoop. Halabi assumed it was from having to drag his corpulent frame around a working ship for a change. When he twisted from side to side in a bizarre, unknowing parody of a workout video instructor, she kept a smile from her lips only by force of will.

'Please sit down, sir,' she said, paying him the compliment of his rank. They both knew where the real power lay on board the *Trident*.

'No, no. I shall only be a short time bothering you,' he said. 'Are you busy, then?'

His fat fingers played with the polished buttons of a dress tunic.

'I have some letters to write. To next of kin, if I can find them,' answered Halabi.

'Ah, right, good show then. Not too many, I hope.'

'I happen to regard one as too many, Sir Leslie.'

'Quite right, quite right.'

He remained standing, obviously uncomfortable. Halabi had grown used to his inability to look her in the eye. But he was even more distressed by her company than usual. Determined to wait him out, Halabi slowly tapped her pen on the blank writing paper, but it quickly became unbearable. The man seemed totally conflicted. Just as she was about to mouth some inanity to fill up the dead space between them, he suddenly blurted out an apology.

'Look, I'm terribly sorry,' he said, almost gobbling as he spoke so quickly, 'but I feel I've been somewhat unfair, and well, I just wished to compliment your crew on the work they did in Singapore. It was a top-rate performance in the finest traditions of the Royal Navy.'

Halabi couldn't help it. Her jaw dropped open and she took a little while to snap it closed.

'Well, thank you, Sir Leslie, I shall see to it that your, um, kind words are distributed via Shipnet.'

She could feel another excruciating silence ballooning as soon as she was finished. Murray was still finding it hard to look her in the eye. His gaze flicked around the small room, and she remembered that it was the first time he'd ever been in her cabin. She wondered if he was uncomfortable being in the small space with a woman.

'Is there something else, Sir Leslie? You look like a man trying to cough up a fishbone.'

He coloured deeply and his loose lips flapped once as a retort rose and died, unspoken.

'I . . . I've just received word from one of the transports, the *Princess Beatrix*. My son-in-law is aboard. He was with the Colonial Office in Singapore. He's in a quite terrible state . . .'

The rear admiral took in a ragged breath, his shoulders hitching once, involuntarily. Murray seemed to find something fascinating on the highly polished toes of his shoes. Halabi waited for him to continue, but nothing more came. She was suddenly very uncomfortable sitting down while he stood over her, an unstable tower of grief, only just buttressed against total collapse by years of practice at squeezing his emotions into a tight little ball that might somehow be dry-swallowed with gritted teeth and a small grimace.

She pushed herself up and fetched a bottle of spring water and a drinking glass from a small refrigerator by her bunk.

'And your daughter?' she asked as she cracked open the lid on the Evian bottle.

Murray staggered forward and collapsed into the chair she'd just vacated. For a horrible moment she feared it might slide out from beneath him on its wheels, but his large frame butted up hard against the edge of the desk as he dropped his head into his hands. Spasms racked his whole body as a low moaning sound, more animal than human, emanated from somewhere deep within his chest.

Halabi knew enough of inconsolable loss to dispense with platitudes. She simply laid a hand on the back of his hot neck and measured the violence of the emotional quake ripping through his body against the sparse memories of her own private losses. Her fingers looked extraordinarily dark against the rear admiral's pale pink skin.

The bruise on her thigh was going to be a good couple of months fading completely, which ticked her off. *Yeah, but what are you gonna do*? Julia tied up her sweat pants and contemplated the painful gym session ahead of her. She was carrying a load of minor injuries and disfigurements from the job on Luzon.

They were of trivial significance, though, when measured against the material she'd gathered. This was going to be her first story for the 'old' *Times*.

Word was out.

With the Singapore and Luzon task forces safely reunited and heading for Pearl, the Allied governments had finally released news of the Transition. For someone like Julia who'd grown up in a world of instant global news access, it was unbelievably frustrating. She had no idea what sort of reaction had greeted the news at home.

At home?

Well, she figured she'd best get used to the idea. Grabbing her towel from where it lay at the end of her bunk, she hesitated. She couldn't help herself. A telegram lay in the jumble of clothes and field equipment on top of her unmade bed and she picked it up to read for maybe the tenth time.

MISS DUFFY . . .

She'd stopped snorting at that on the fourth reading.

WELCOME. NYT OFFERS SENIOR STAFF POSITION. NEEDS 3000 WORDS ON 'TRANSITION', 2000 WORDS ON POW RAID ASAP.

She'd said yes, of course, after they'd agreed to take Rosanna on as well. Dan had been right. They were so desperate to sign her up, they'd agree to anything.

Dan.

A sharp pang of regret stabbed at her. She shouldn't have been such a jerk before Luzon. She'd been anxious and hanging out for her chillers and she'd ripped him up for no good reason. He was a good guy, a *great* fucking guy, and she just knew she'd blown it with him.

Rosanna said Dan had watched the vid of her wasting that Jap in Manila over and over and over. It was really spooky, she'd said. In the end Rosanna had been too busy to get pissed and she'd ignored him as he compulsively replayed the footage. She hadn't even noticed when he'd finally drifted away.

Julia folded up the telegram, for once failing to marvel at the way it felt, with its crisp paper crunch. Like something out of a museum. Tightness clenched at her throat and she cursed herself for the weakness. Next fucking thing she'd get all teary and . . .

'Hey.'

Dan!

He stood there in the doorway, looking nervous and tentative. She didn't stop. She didn't think. She just spun around and flew into his arms with such force that they nearly tumbled into the corridor outside.

'I'm sorry, I'm so sorry,' she said, unable to stop repeating herself. A flood of tears and nonsense burst from her as his arms stiffened then relaxed, and he pulled her into his chest.

'So am I,' said Black.

Damiri didn't understand at first. Kolhammer seemed to be leading a convoy of dozens of ships, many more than had been in the force off Timor, but a brief laser-linked message from the carrier explained the presence of so many contemporary vessels. It made no difference to his plans, he decided. He might just kill a few more unbelievers, and there was nothing wrong with that.

Smoke plumes from the older ships filled the sky as they drew closer. The beautiful, lilting prayers of his shipmates drifted up from below as they prepared to enter paradise. The few Japanese on board had been banished below decks and Damiri supposed they were making whatever arrangements their false god-emperor required of them. With so few of his former colleagues volunteering for this mission, the Japanese had been invaluable in keeping the ship running at a very basic level, and in coordinating arrangements with their own departed comrades on the three IJN vessels.

Out of respect for their help, Damiri had asked if any wished to surrender their will to Allah in the last hours of their life, but all had declined. He shrugged. There was no saving some people.

To still the drumbeat of his heart as the fatal moment drew closer, Damiri stepped out of the bridge into the fresh air and took inventory of the 'damage' to the ship. Bullet holes, torn metal, scorch marks, shattered glass, broken masts and one particularly impressive shell burst had scarred the *Sutanto* convincingly. She looked like a veteran warship now – just the sort of thing to impress stupidly sentimental westerners who, of course, could not know that Yamamoto's engineers had meticulously crafted every scratch and dent back at Hashirajima. Before packing the ship to the gunnels with high explosive.

He wondered how closely the Americans were reading the bogus ship's log he'd zapped over to them as soon as they drew into laser-link range. The answer came within a few minutes.

*

'Have you seen this yet?' asked Commander Judge.

The lanky Texan was leafing through a printout of the *Sutanto*'s log on the bridge of the supercarrier.

'Nope, not yet,' Kolhammer said. 'Something up?'

He watched on screen as the *Sutanto* passed the lead ship in the convoy, Halabi's stealth destroyer, HMS *Trident.* True to form, the Brits turned on a full salute. Just as typically, the Indonesians responded in a really half-assed manner, with almost nobody on deck to return the gesture. Although, given how badly shot up the boat looked, he could understand that.

'Ask the *Sutanto* to come around onto our heading,' he said. 'We don't need them threading their way through the convoy. They'll run into someone for certain.'

As an ensign relayed the order, Judge walked over, chewing his lip.

'It says here they only woke up five days ago, Admiral. Damiri has no idea how long they were out, but it couldn't have been that long, could it? They'd have died of starvation or thirst.'

Kolhammer eased himself up out of a slight slouch. The Pacific stretched away forever under a diamond-hard sky. Not a single cloud floated over the dozens of ships beating their way back to Pearl.

'Well, what's the elapsed time on the ship's clock?'

Judge flipped over a couple of pages. He never looked happy dealing with hard copy.

'A hundred and thirty-three hours,' he said. 'Close

enough to six days, which don't work for me, since we've been here for weeks now.'

Admiral Spruance joined them from his perch by the lee helm. 'Is there a problem?'

Kolhammer chewed his lip. 'Ensign, why is the *Sutanto* still coming on? She should have changed her heading by now.'

'Sorry, sir, they have the orders.'

Judge examined the print-out as though he'd been handed a three-dollar note.

'I guess there could have been temporal as well as spatial distortions,' he conceded without much enthusiasm. 'If the *Nuku* ended up on top of that mountain, I guess these guys could have been thrown out of sync, you know, time-wise.'

'You don't sound confident, Commander,' said Spruance. 'Can I suggest we ask them to stop before they get even further inside our lines?'

Kolhammer checked the screen again. The Indonesian ship was much closer than he'd expected.

'Have they *increased* speed?' he asked.

'Goddamn,' spat Judge.

A small, perceptible jolt ran through everyone on the bridge who'd ever had to face a jihadi suicide run.

'What's happening?' asked Spruance, who couldn't help but notice the tension.

'Sound to general quarters,' ordered Commander Judge. 'We have a possible suicide run. All hands brace for impact.'

'Comms,' shouted Kolhammer, 'patch me directly into the *Sutanto* right now!'

Telltale static crackled over the loudspeakers as the *Sutanto*'s obsolete communications net linked to the *Clinton*.

'Damiri, this is Admiral Kolhammer. Come to a full stop right now. Are you reading me? Come to a full stop right now or we will fire on you.'

'Turn it off,' said Damiri. 'All ahead full. *Allahu akbar*!'

As the ship leaped forward he braced himself, imagining the eruption of white water at her stern. He was surprised to find himself a little scared, but he took solace in the confusion and fear that would now be gripping the Americans.

The *Clinton* rushed closer with every second. He smiled at the wallowing buckets of iron around him. They seemed to groan at the seams as they poured on steam to escape.

'Look, my sheik, look!'

A wide, beaming smile spread over Damiri's face as he saw two ships collide about a thousand metres away. The sound of the impact reached him as a terrible grinding of steel against steel and he fancied he could even make out the screams and cries of the infidels as they reeled in fear. He smirked.

Shock and awe, indeed.

A missile roared overhead and he ducked without thinking, even though the gesture was pointless. The nearest ship, some sort of passenger liner, he thought, blew apart with a bone-shaking explosion.

'Allahu akbar. Allahu akbar!'

He heard the ghostly, whispering crack of hypervelocity caseless ammunition as it passed harmlessly through the air above the tip of the ship's broken mast.

'They cannot depress their guns far enough, my brothers. Praise God we shall all be in Paradise soon,' cried Damiri.

Kolhammer's mouth was a thin white line chiselled into the granite face of a cold mountain. Alarms sounded throughout the ship and every sailor in the bridge was bracing for the detonation while trying to perform half-a-dozen emergency drills at the same time. The admiral could feel the deck of the giant ship tilting as she poured on the revolutions and tried to accelerate away from the suicide boat.

He did a quick calculation on just how much explosive material you could pack into a vessel of that size, wondering whether the armour sheath could withstand the blast. Probably not, if Damiri rammed them.

The sea around him was a maelstrom, with dozens of ships heading in all directions. Reports of collisions and near collisions flashed up on screens and sounded through the loudspeakers every few seconds. Judge shouted orders to the bridge crew. Spruance had quietly wandered over to the strip window, his hands clasped behind his back, while the crew called out updates in the strained tones of men and women who had been trained to die at their stations.

'*Trident* coming around, sir. No missile lock yet.'

'*Kandahar* is blocked, Admiral.'

'*Kennebunkport* does not have a clear field of fire.'

'CAP is sixteen kilometres out, no target lock.'

'Comanche lifting off the *Kandahar*.'

A dark shape flashed with a vicious buzz. Kolhammer was about to ask what the hell it was when Spruance called out over the din.

'It's a Wildcat! Off the *Enterprise*.'

The antique fighter roared down the length of the *Clinton*'s flight deck, waggling its wings in a salute. It reached the bow and immediately opened up with all six machine-guns. Kolhammer frantically flicked between a dozen battle-cam views on the nearest screen before he found a top-down view of the old F-4F boring in towards the jihadi boat. White light twinkled along the leading edge of its wings. Long, ropy strands of gun smoke trailed behind. Hundreds of rounds of good old-fashioned fifty cal whipped the midnight-blue sea around the *Sutanto* into a fury of white water. The first shells bit into the metal skin of the ship and the pilot adjusted the angle of his shallow dive to keep the fire pouring into the decks. Shards of red-hot metal erupted from the small superstructure as the *Sutanto* shuddered under the assault.

The gap between the Wildcat and her prey closed rapidly.

Seven hundred metres.

Six hundred.

Five hundred.

Smoke and flames streamed from a dozen breaches in the ship's plating.

Four hundred.

Three hundred.

The Wildcat's guns ran dry and the plane peeled away.

Nothing happened for two seconds, and then the *Sutanto* went up in a stunning eruption which Kolhammer felt in his guts as the pressure wave slammed into the *Clinton*. His ears popped painfully. Vision swam. Grey spots bloomed. Sailors tumbled to the floor, and the great, titanic mass of the supercarrier trembled with the shock. She rose up a little as if riding over a wave, and then plunged down again, intact and safe.

The *Sutanto* was gone, and with her the little aluminium monoplane that had saved them all.

Well, not all, Kolhammer realised as he straightened up.

The blast wave had been strong enough to tear apart two nearby liners and a hospital ship. Another two civilian vessels had collided in their panic to get away and one of them was going down quickly. Secondary explosions tore through the crippled liners. Oily smoke and flames poured from the foredeck of the hospital ship, and the sea for miles around was in turmoil with dozens of ships, modern and contemporary, scattering to the four points.

'Damage?' cried Kolhammer.

Commander Judge scanned a nearby screen, glancing out the blast windows as though he didn't trust the data over the evidence of his own eyes. Video coverage from drones stationed overhead and feeding from mast-mounted cams through the modern ships began to appear on screens all over the bridge.

'Jesus, it went off like a baby nuke.'

Kolhammer couldn't tell who'd said that. One of his people, he supposed, given the reference.

'We came through without major structural damage,' Judge reported. 'But we've lost three surface assets and another two are in danger.'

'Projected casualties?' demanded Kolhammer.

'Heavy. Five to six thousand. Search and rescue are under way. No threats on the board. We're scanning clean to eight hundred kilometres.'

'Okay. Round 'em all up before we're scattered to hell and back.'

Kolhammer became aware that Spruance had made his way over from the window. He looked shaken, but not nearly so much as Kolhammer himself felt.

'What the hell was that?' asked Spruance.

Kolhammer wasn't sure how to explain what had just happened. In the end he could only slump into his chair as the adrenaline backwash sluiced through his system, leaving him shaky and on edge. He threw his hands up, a small gesture of impotence.

'That was the future,' he said.

Epilogue

The meeting of the Japanese war cabinet went on late into the night. It wasn't a happy affair. Some faces were conspicuously absent. Many had perished at Hashirajima, and even though Yamamoto had repeatedly urged the Imperial General Headquarters to clear the anchorage, he knew that in some eyes he was to blame for the disaster there. He didn't care. Some of these fools needed shooting in the ass before they would realise what being at war really meant.

Still, even he had to admit some surprise at the raids on Luzon and Singapore. Not at the scale of destruction that had rained down on the Emperor's forces in those places, but at the strange choice Admiral Kolhammer had made. Yamamoto had half expected him to sail right into the anchorage of the Combined Fleet and sink every single ship there. Moertopo said he was more than capable of doing just that, and Yamamoto didn't doubt it for a moment. As an alternative he had wasted precious resources on strategically insignificant targets. It was curious, but the grand admiral didn't make the mistake of dismissing the action as mere folly. It revealed much about the nature of his new enemy and was thus something to be very carefully thought about.

Why would they do such a thing when they could conceivably shatter their enemies instead? Did it say more about the men they were fighting, or the world they had come from? Was it a weakness he could exploit?

Still, these were questions for another day. At that moment ministers surrounded him, demanding to know how it was possible that the Americans had simply sailed into the heart of the empire and carried away their countrymen.

'Because we could not stop them,' said Yamamoto, somewhat impishly.

The cabinet room exploded at that, but he waited them out and eventually calm returned.

'The Americans have made a terrible mistake,' he said quietly when he had everybody's attention. 'They have expended most of their precious weapons rescuing skeletons and camp whores. This tactical victory has cost them an overwhelming strategic advantage, as they shall soon see. I have fashioned a blade to drive through the heart of their fleet as it returns to Pearl Harbor.'

Prime Minister Tojo spoke into the silence that followed that revelation.

'And that is why the *Sutanto* left Hashirajima, Admiral?'

Yamamoto nodded, explaining himself to everyone in the room.

'It is why most of the fleet has left. They are to cover the withdrawal of our forces from China and the invasion of New Guinea and the Australian mainland. We will deny the Americans their base for a counterattack in the Pacific.'

He did not react to the sharp intake of breath around the table. To this point only he and Tojo had known of the plan.

'And what of Hawaii?' asked the Prime Minister.

'I have plans for them too.'

'Even with these supercarriers and warships there?' barked an army general. The army had never been supporters of the thrust to expand the empire southwards. To Yamamoto's way of thinking they were fixated on Manchuria and the communists. He had to suppress a mischievous smirk at the prospect of dragging them out of China, kicking and screaming.

'The *Sutanto* will destroy the Kolhammer force,' Yamamoto promised, raising his hand against the inevitable objections. 'Yes, she is one small ship, but she will sweep them away like a divine wind, a *kamikaze*.'

'And when will we know?' asked Tojo.

'We still have sources in Hawaii,' Yamamoto explained. 'They will send word.'

He leaned forward and smacked the table with his injured hand, slowly growling out his next words.

'But even if by some chance the *Sutanto* fails and this Kolhammer survives, we will *still* forge on with our new plan, because we have no choice. You have all read the reports I gave you. You know where fate will take us if we do not change our path. We have allowed ourselves to be blinded to the real danger. It does not lie in Russia or China. It lies across the Pacific in the United States, and south in Australia where the Americans will first build up their forces. We must defeat them *there* before they are too strong. We must take their base at Hawaii from them. And on the last day of this war we must stand in the Oval Office and put their crippled president to the sword.

'*Because we have no choice.*'

Complete silence greeted this uncompromising speech. A dozen men stared at him, some in awe, some in shock and some without discernible emotion. The moment stretched uncomfortably until Yamamoto began to worry that one of them might actually laugh at him. Finally, a lone voice spoke up. The army officer who had questioned him before.

'But how?' he asked, genuinely perplexed.

Yamamoto smiled.

Moscow, 2215 hours, 25 June 1942

He didn't think it possible that a place even more fearful than the Gestapo headquarters at Prinz Albrechtstrasse might exist, but perhaps he had found it here in this surprisingly shabby waiting room. He knew that if the next hour didn't go well he would not live to see this room again. It was entirely possible he'd simply be shot dead behind the heavy oak doors that led into the inner sanctum of the Central

Committee. Perhaps there would be a secret trapdoor through which they would spirit him away to the cells. He though that was very much their style. There would doubtless be many cells in this building.

He did his best to appear relaxed in spite of the hard, uncomfortable chair on which he sat. Nobody had offered him even a simple refreshment or shaken his hand. The minor functionaries who staffed this chamber treated him with cold formality, for which he supposed he could not blame them. His country was still exterminating their people like millions of rats. Perhaps by morning that might be behind them. For the sake of the Fatherland he could only hope.

He still did not quite believe the case he would have to argue in there. If it had just been a suggestion from the Japanese alone he would have laughed it off, but the Führer himself was adamant that Yamamoto's plan was worth the risk. Of course it was not the Führer's risk to take. It was his.

It was all madness really. But the whole world was alive with talk of the insanity. The Führer was obsessed with reading translated stories from the Allied press about events in the Pacific. For once it had driven news of the war from the front pages around the globe. And now he was here, at the very centre of the storm, on a mission that would assuredly make an irrelevance of these 'time travellers'. He was here and they were listening to him. That was enough to justify the risk.

The German Foreign Minister, Joachim von

Ribbentrop, brushed a piece of lint from his sleeve as he waited for Joseph Stalin to admit him to the Soviet Politburo, to argue the case for a cease fire and a new alliance with the Axis against the liberal democracies.

Designated Targets

World War 2.2

JOHN BIRMINGHAM

I

Tupelo, Mississippi

Lordy, thought the boy. *It's a miracle for sure.*

He was seven-and-a-half years old – the man of the house, really, what with his daddy being away in Como – and he had never seen anything like the fearful wonder of the newly chiselled monument.

Here lies Jesse Garon Presley.
Deeply beloved of his mother Gladys, father Vernon and brother Elvis.
A soul so pure the Good Lord could not bear to be apart from him.
Born Jan. 8, 1935,
Taken unto God Jan. 8, 1935.

Despite the unseasonable heat of the evening, goose-flesh ran up his thin arms as he read the words again. Whippoorwills and crickets trilled their amazement in the sweet, warm air. With a pounding heart the boy inched forward and muttered hoarsely, 'Jesse, are you here?'

The stone was cut from blindingly white marble that fairly glowed in the setting sun. The inscription had been inlaid with real gold, he was almost certain of that. He ran his fingers over the words and the cold, hard stone, as if afraid to discover that they weren't real.

It must have cost a king's ransom . . .

And an enormous bunch of store-bought flowers had been placed on a patch of freshly broken earth that still lay at the foot of the monument. Hundreds of tiny beads of water covered the petals and caught the last golden rays of daylight.

He dropped down on his knees as if he were in church, and started at the impossible vision for many minutes, heedless of the dirt he was getting on his old dungarees. He remained almost motionless until one hand reached out and his fingers again brushed the surface of the headstone.

'Oh, my,' he whispered.

Then Elvis Aaron Presley leapt to his feet and ran so fast that he raised a trail of dust as he sprinted down the gravel lane, away from the paupers' section of the Priceville Cemetery, a-hollerin' for his mama.

'He'll probably get his ass whupped, the poor little bastard.' Slim Jim Davidson smiled as he said it, peering over the sunglasses he had perched on his nose.

'Why?' asked the woman who was sitting next to him in the rear seat of the gaudy red Cadillac. You didn't see babies like this every day. Slim Jim had seen to the detailing himself. The paint job, the bison leather seats, everything.

'For telling lies,' he said. 'Headstones don't just appear like that, you know. They're gonna think he made it up, and when he won't take it back, there'll be hell to pay.'

The woman seemed to give the statement more thought than it was really due.

'I suppose so,' she said after a few seconds.

Slim Jim could tell she didn't approve. They were all the same, these people. They'd bomb an entire city into rubble without batting an eye, but they looked at you like you were some sort of hoodlum if you even suggested raising your hand against a snotnosed kid. Or a smart-mouth dame, for that matter.

And this O'Brien, she was a helluva smart-mouth dame.

She'd kept her trap shut, though, while they'd been watching the Presley kid. In fact, she seemed to be fascinated by him. They'd been waiting in the Caddy up on Old Saltillo Road for nearly an hour before he showed. Long enough for Slim Jim to wonder if they were pissing their time up against a wall. But the kid did show, just like his cousin had said he would. And he'd heard O'Brien's stifled gasp when the small figure first appeared, walking out of a stand of trees about two hundred yards away.

'It's him all right,' she said. 'Damned if it's not.'

Slim Jim had grabbed the contract papers and made to get out of the car right then and there. He'd had enough of sitting still. His butt had fallen asleep and he was downright bored. But O'Brien shook her head.

'Not here.'

He'd bristled at that. His temper had frayed during the long wait. Long enough even to make him feel some sympathy for the cops who'd had to stake him out, once or twice over the years. But he took her 'advice' because it was always worth taking.

Her advice had cost him a goddamn packet, too, over the course of their relationship. But along the way Slim Jim Davidson had learned that you had to spend money to make it. Problem was that up until recently, he didn't have no money to spend. None of his own, anyway. And spending other people's money had sent him to the road gangs.

Mississippi was a powerful reminder of those days. The air tasted the same as it had in Alabama, thick and sweet and tending towards rotten. The faces they'd driven past in town had brought back some unpleasant memories, too. Hard, lean faces, with deep lines and dark pools for eyes. The sort of uncompromising faces a man might expect to see on Judgment Day. They'd sure looked that way to Slim Jim when they trooped in from the jury room, a few years back.

Well, that felt like a thousand years ago. Now he could buy and sell that fucking jury. And the judge. And his crooked jailers. And the whole goddamn state of Alabama, if he felt like it.

Well, maybe not the whole state, but he was getting there. This Caddy was bigger and more comfortable than some of the flophouses he'd crashed in during the Depression. He had an apartment in an honest-to-god-damned brownstone overlooking Central Park back in New York, and a house designed by some faggot architect overlooking the beach at Santa Monica, out in LA. He had stocks and bonds and a big wad of folding money he liked to carry in his new buffalo-hide wallet – just so's he could pull it out and snap the crisp new bills between his fingers when he needed to remind himself that he wasn't dreaming.

Hell, he was so rich now that when those C-notes lost their snap, he could give them away and get some new ones. Not that he ever did, of course. *Ms* O'Brien would kill him. And she was more than capable of it. No doubt about that.

She'd insisted that he pick up the Santa Monica house as a long-term investment, too, even though he thought it was kind of downmarket, given his newly acquired status. 'You can stay at the Ambassador if you don't like rubbing shoulders with your old cell-mates down on the pier,' she'd said. 'Believe me, Santa Monica will come back, and you need to diversify your asset base. Waterfront property is always a sure bet.'

Yes indeed, and Slim Jim was fond of sure bets. After all, they'd made him richer than God. They'd also delivered him a conga line of horny babes, a small army of his own hired muscle, and the slightly scary Ms O'Brien.

Thinking about the slightly scary Ms O'Brien

sitting next to him there in the Caddy, however, led naturally to thinking about the slightly scary Ms O'Brien sliding her body over his in a king-size hotel bed. But that was a dangerous line of thought, he knew. Because Ms O'Brien wasn't inclined to get anywhere near a bed with Slim Jim Davidson, naked or not.

He'd tried feeling her up once and she had nearly broken his arm for it. She'd snapped an excruciating wrist lock on him without even breaking a sweat, no doubt a party trick picked up back when she was a captain in the 82nd MEU. And she'd kept him locked up, gasping for breath and nearly fainting away, while she explained to him the facts of life.

One: She was his employee, not his girlfriend.

Two: She would only be his employee for as long as she needed to be, and she would *never* be his girlfriend.

Three: She could kick his scrawny ass black and blue without bothering to lace up her boots.

And four: She –

'Mr Davidson?'

Slim Jim jumped, feeling guilty and worried that she might have figured out what he'd been thinking. But no, luckily she was just dragging him out of his slightly bored daze.

'Elvis has left the cemetery,' she announced. She said it in a singsong way, and it seemed to amuse her more than it should have. But Slim Jim had given up trying to figure her out.

'Let's go over it one last time, just to be sure,' she said, pulling out a flexipad.

'Oh please,' he begged. 'Let's not.'

O'Brien ignored him, and his shades suddenly flickered into life. Windows opened up on the lenses and seemed to float in the air in front of him. Some carried photographs of the boy they'd just seen. Others were full of words. Small ones in large type. She'd learned not to burden him with too much text. *Bitch thinks she's so goddamn smart . . .*

Slim Jim sighed, and read through the briefing notes again. Some of his reluctance was for show, though. He never really got tired of the amazing gadgets these guys had brought with them.

'Elvis Aaron Presley, age seven and a half. Mother's name Gladys, father's name Vernon,' he recited. 'Dead brother Jesse. Attends school at East Tupelo Consolidated. Father jailed for fraud. Asshole tried to ink a four-dollar cheque into forty . . .'

O'Brien shot him a warning look, but he hid behind the shades, pretending he couldn't see her.

'Daddy's out now, away in Como, Mississippi, building a POW camp for the government. Mama takes in sewing when she can get it. Local yokels call 'em white trash behind their backs . . .'

Slim Jim laughed out loud, glancing out across the ragged fields of corn and soybean that stretched between the cemetery and the edge of the town. 'Ha! There's a fucking pot calling a kettle black if I ever –'

'The *notes*, Mr Davidson. Just review the notes,' said O'Brien.

Slim Jim returned to the readout for what felt like the hundredth time. He'd heard about some big-time grifters who worked like this. Getting so far inside the heads of their marks that they knew what was going on in there before the chumps realised it themselves. He could sort of see the point.

O'Brien had helped him close some amazing deals these last few months. But *damn* it was hard work. Nevertheless, he ploughed on, reciting most of it from memory even though the words still hung there in front of him.

'Gladys drinks in private. She finds her comfort in the church. Her first love was dance, her second music. But she's kind of a fat bitch now so . . . Sorry! *Sorry* . . . She gets around in bare feet and old socks so her kid can have shoes. Elvis, he's aware of his family's low standing. It eats him up and he wants to rescue them. It always tickles him when his mama says she's proud of him.'

In spite of himself, Slim Jim couldn't help but warm to the little prick. They'd listened to his music all the way down here and you had to admit, the kid had a gift. Or *would have*.

Then again, maybe he wouldn't. If Slim Jim bought him a ticket out of Tupelo now, gave him enough money for a comfortable life, maybe the kid would never sing a song worth a tinker's crap. Not that